Bridget Wood is the daughter of an Irish actor and after a convent education worked in newspapers and the legal profession. She now lives and writes in Staffordshire.

REBEL ANGEL is her third epic fantasy novel and follows her acclaimed debut WOLFKING ('Delicately wrought . . . A long book but worth taking the plunge' *The Times*, 'Perhaps the best fantasy on this Celtic legend that I've ever read' Lester Del Rey) and THE LOST PRINCE ('Vivid and enthralling second novel proves that Wood is indeed a force to be reckoned with' *Northern Echo*).

Also by Bridget Wood

Wolfking
The Lost Prince

Rebel Angel

Bridget Wood

First published in 1993
by HEADLINE BOOK PUBLISHING PLC

First published in paperback in 1993
by HEADLINE BOOK PUBLISHING PLC

A HEADLINE FEATURE paperback

10 9 8 7 6 5 4 3 2 1

ISBN 0 7472 4122 8

Typeset by CBS, Felixstowe, Suffolk

Printed and bound in Great Britain by
HarperCollins Manufacturing, Glasgow

HEADLINE BOOK PUBLISHING PLC
Headline House
79 Great Titchfield Street
London W1P 7FN

ACKNOWLEDGEMENT

I am indebted to my brother, Tony, for his technical
knowledge and insight and for his help
with the Renascian background.

Chapter One

The Renascian Council had discovered that the Star patterns were changing. They were changing so rapidly and so drastically that the Star Maps, the marvellous ancient charts made by their ancestors, the long-ago Earth-people, bore hardly any resemblance to the skies any more. And although the Old Settlement had by now been explored fairly thoroughly, the Renascians had not discovered how the Earth-people would have coped with great jagged holes where stars had once been, or with the strange livid sunsets, or with the gradual leeching of daylight and the lengthening nights.

'Whatever it is, it's been happening for some time,' said Floy, facing the Council along the long, polished oak table and spreading the ancient Charts out for them to see.

'And whatever it is that's disturbing the stars,' he said, 'it's getting closer.' He leaned forward, tracing the patterns on the original Star Maps of their ancestors, and comparing them with the ones they had so carefully drawn themselves, using the machine brought from Earth by the first Settlers that was called a sextant.

Floy looked round at the Council rather challengingly, and Quilp, who had been part of the Council ever since most people could remember, said it was all very interesting, but it surely could not be anything to worry about, that there were much more important matters to discuss in Council Chambers.

'I disagree,' said Floy. 'There's something wrong about it all. Can't you feel that there's something wrong?' And then, looking up at them, 'How do we know that the last days of Earth did not begin like this?' he said, and a rather dreadful silence fell. Everyone knew of the terrible ending

1

of Earth. Earth was still there in the heavens, a dead, dark world that they could just glimpse from the Twilight Mountains, though most people found it eerie and distressing to do so. But they all knew of the holocaust that had sent their ancestors fleeing and destroyed almost all forms of life. The optimists maintained that some of the people had survived and that there would still be life of some kind on Earth, but nobody could be sure about this. They only knew about the few who had managed to escape and reach Renascia.

It had not been so very long ago since it had happened, either, which made the difference in the charts even more puzzling. And since the Council did not seem as if it was intending to explore the matter, Floy had taken the Star Maps back to the house on Renascia's outskirts that had belonged to his and Fenella's parents.

'The stars form a pattern,' he said to her, unrolling the Maps on the table and frowning at them. 'A recognisable structure in the skies. Can you see it? It's like an intricate and very beautiful mesh. A lattice. The Earth-settlers charted them when they came here. I suppose they wanted to see how everything looked from Renascia as opposed to Earth.' He traced the pattern again. 'But now it's as if an immense hole has somehow been punched through the lattice.'

Fenella, looking over his shoulder, saw what he meant. The stars had formed their own cobweb structure against the skies; you could see quite clearly their framework in the first Maps. As Floy said, it was rather beautiful. But when you looked at the new maps you could see the difference. There was a jagged centre, a blankness, a sickening absence of colour and light, so that you found yourself thinking of yawning chasms and bottomless wells.

You almost thought that something had torn through the fabric of the skies, and left only an immense black abyss . . .

Fenella frowned and although she did not know very much about stars or maps, she said, 'Couldn't the stars

2

have changed by themselves?'

'I don't think they could,' said Floy, thoughtfully. 'It isn't so very long since our ancestors came here.' He looked back at the Charts. 'The stars *can't* have changed so much in that short time. Something's disturbing them. It's as if something's *warping* them.'

There was something extremely sinister about the idea of a *something* disrupting the stars and creating great black voids in the skies. There was something implacable and merciless about it. It would have been better to ignore it altogether. But since it was there, and since neither of them had been brought up to pretend that unpleasant things did not exist, it would have to be discussed and an answer to it all would have to be found. Floy would tell the Council that there was something very strange happening and although he might have to fight to make them listen, in the end they would do so, because he was his father's son and Renascia's leader.

It was not very long at all since Floy and Fenella's ancestors, the Earth-people, had fled from their dying world, probably no more than six generations. They had managed to reach the small, friendly planet, which it was thought they had been observing for some time through their marvellous, powerful machines. It was not known what it had been called then, because the great fire that had raged through the Old Settlement in Floy and Fenella's grandparents' time had destroyed nearly all records. Whatever the fleeing Earth-people had managed to bring with them had been lost. Fragments and remnants of the Earth-people's ways of life were uncovered in the Settlement from time to time and studied carefully by the two brothers, Snizort and Snodgrass, who were Renascia's chroniclers, and who ran the Mnemosyne. But what there was was pitiably little.

There was the great shell of the Earth-people's craft, which had been carefully preserved in the exact place it had come to rest, constructed of some strange substance nobody had ever been able to fathom. But it did not really tell the Renascians very much about Earth. Quilp and the

Council thought it was very important to give proper reverence to this craft, which Quilp said the Earth-people would have called an *Ark*. They had the annual Earth Feast, when tables were set up in the *Ark*'s shadow and people dressed as they thought Earth-people had dressed. Snizort and his people from the Mnemosyne enacted scenes from Earth-life and Snodgrass served them all with a supper of Earth-food. It was all very interesting and something to plan for all year.

But for the rest of the year, to most people, the *Ark* was simply a rather ugly shape that spoiled the view across to the Twilight Mountains.

The story of Earth's last days was interesting, because you did not mind hearing about immense disasters and holocausts when they had happened three or four hundred years ago, and you had not known the people or the world they had happened to. It was only a pity that there was not more information about those last terrible days, or about whether there had been any kind of warning and, if so, what it had been.

There were a few legends, of course; frail, frayed threads that had come down to them after the fire in the Settlement, and which told a little about Earth and about how people had lived. These carefully preserved accounts of Earth's last days told, in tantalisingly sparse detail, of immense walls of flame and of huge, onrushing sheets of fire that had consumed Earth and destroyed civilisation. Some of the stories told of prancing fire-beasts deep within the flames, but this was only embellishment, of course. You had to discount the prancing beasts, said people, but you could not discount the fire itself.

There was another story as well, which told of a great plague that had swept the cities and the towns towards the end, and which had been so virulent and so dreadfully contagious that hardly anyone had escaped, so that, finally, the handful of survivors had known that to preserve the race, Earth must be abandoned.

The origin of this tale was not known, and it was not so widely believed, although the Renascians were not

4

unacquainted with plague. It was not very many years since they had suffered a very virulent one which had killed a great many people and forced a great many more to leave the Centre and go up into the mountains for a time to escape infection. The seeds were still in Renascia's core, said the gloomier members of the community, although nobody paid this much heed, because nobody really believed it, any more than they believed in the fire-beasts, but it gave the sober-minded ones something to be gloomy about.

Floy and Fenella's parents had died in the Plague, which was why Floy was governing now, and trying to rule the Council and for ever fighting Quilp to get laws altered. It was a hereditary thing, to govern Renascia, just as it seemed to have been on Earth. You grew up knowing you would one day step into your father's shoes. As Floy had done.

'He's too young,' said Quilp, who had sat on the Council of Nine ever since anyone could remember and who did not approve of reckless young men who tumbled Renascian laws upside-down and tried to allow ladies in to Council Meetings. 'Too young and too flippant. There's riots and dissension, if not civil war ahead,' said Quilp, and did not know what things were coming to.

Fenella, who shared Floy's ideas and ideals, and was trying to get together a small band of Renascian ladies to storm the Council Chamber and change the only-men-to-govern rule, thought that Quilp was secretly jealous of Floy and concerned for his, Quilp's, position on the Council. This was entirely understandable, but did not help Floy who was attempting to get voted in some very good new laws, partly based on what he and Fenella thought their ancestors had done, but partly based on Floy's own ideas.

Floy had so far been patient with Quilp and the Council, all of whom were much older than he was, because this was only polite, but it was possible that he would not be patient for much longer. He was exactly how Fenella remembered their father being and he might very easily tip up the long oak Council table in angry disgust one day so that all the papers would fall in disarray on to the floor, and then sweep grandly out of the room. Their father had done this more than once, usually because of Quilp. Floy would end up doing the same before long, especially if they could not get Quilp to give proper attention to what was happening to Renascia's star patterns and the creeping up on them of longer nights.

'None of it means anything at all,' said Quilp, glaring at Floy when he faced the Council of Nine at their next gathering.

'I think it means something very serious,' said Floy, who had brought back the Star Maps and had spread them out on the long table, so that everyone could see them. He looked round. 'I think we are facing exactly what our Earth-ancestors faced before their world ended. I think Renascia is moving into perpetual night.'

Perpetual night. It was an eerily descriptive expression. Quilp and the rest of the Council denied it, of course, but then everyone on Renascia knew that Quilp had long since peopled the Council with his cronies, and that they were only interested in thinking up new taxes and finding better ways of making money for themselves. A great many people had rather welcomed the succession of Floy as the Council's head, because it was high time that somebody opposed Quilp's laws, properly and strongly.

Perpetual night. To Floy's annoyance, his words were quickly repeated outside of Council and people began to look worried.

'But they have to know,' said Fenella. 'If something's happening, the people have to know.'

'Not until we can tell them what's behind it,' said Floy, who was furious with Quilp for repeating his words. 'You don't give people half a tale if it's a sinister tale. We need to know more before we start telling people to worry,' said Floy. 'There might not be anything for them to worry about in the end.'

Fenella saw the sense of this and told her little band of

Council-storming ladies that, whatever was happening to Renascia, it was not necessarily threatening but, on the contrary, rather interesting.

And heard herself voicing the words and wished she could stop thinking about the gaping abyss and the yawning tear where the stars had once been . . .

'I'm afraid it's too late to give people platitudes,' she said to Floy. 'The fiery sunsets were rather fun. But now —'

'But now,' finished Floy, 'it isn't just fiery sunsets.'

'No.' Fenella looked at him and, after a moment, Floy said, 'The days are eroding.'

'Yes.' Fenella heard the words with sick fear.

The days are eroding . . .

Little groups of people were already beginning to forgather in the Wine Shop on Renascia's outskirts every evening and measure the decreasing daylight and the days' lengths. Floy had asked Snizort and Snodgrass to do this officially, and they were doing it properly and sensibly, using clocks and using the sextants left by the Settlers, which they were finding very interesting machines. Snizort was keeping a full record of everything in his diaries. They would not disclose their findings yet, they said, because it was important to be sure what was happening, or even if anything was happening at all. There was no sense in worrying people unnecessarily. Floy was quite right about that.

But it did not need Snizort's complex diagrams, or Snodgrass's involved timetables to measure it any more. All that it needed was the growing group of Renascians seated at the Wine Shop's scrubbed tables and a keen eye.

At the end of the following ten days, there was no question about any of it.

The days were shrinking at an alarming rate, and the light was somehow being leeched from Renascia.

It was at this point that Snizort and Snodgrass discovered the Casket in the Old Settlement.

* * *

They had been exploring a new section at the time; Snizort said, earnestly, that they had thought they might find something previously overlooked that might tell them about Earth's last days, and whether the Earth-people had experienced the draining of the light and the rather sinister sunsets.

They were always discovering buried pots and books and utensils, or bits of machinery, they said; it was all very useful, because quite often it was possible to work out what the machines had done, and re-construct them.

The Casket had been beneath one of the buildings to the north of the Old Settlement. It was the farthest north they had ever explored, they said seriously. Previously, they had confined their expeditions to the ruins of the smaller buildings, which would have been the Settlers' homes. You found out far more about a community by looking at its homes, they said. Cooking pots and machines and sometimes even writings. Books and diaries. They had not found many books, but there had been a few. It had given them a remarkable picture of Earth-life. Snizort had formed the History of the Earth Society, which met in their tiny, cluttered sitting room, and which was composed of earnest bespectacled people who talked about Earth and read scholarly papers and essays, and drank Snodgrass's elderberry wine in alarming quantities.

The shell of the large white building had not, to begin with, seemed to hold anything of any great interest. They thought it had been a meeting place, which had been a great tradition on Earth, they explained solemnly.

The Earth-people had built large, sometimes ornate houses, in which they gathered to discuss the governing of the land and the imposing of laws. Snizort said there were a number of names for these buildings: they were Parliaments or Senates or Synods or simply Councils. That was where they had got the name for their own governing body.

The large white building had been at the centre of the Old Settlement and they had taken a party of their best students along with them to explore it.

8

'We might never have found it, otherwise,' said Snodgrass, as they led Floy and Fenella to the spot.

'They're all very enthusiastic,' agreed Snizort. 'And they're very useful for the actual digging, you know, because, of course, Snodgrass and I can't do the *bending* we used to.'

Snodgrass had a very old Earth-recipe, called a *simple*, which contained some remarkable ingredients, not all of them obtainable on Renascia, which you rubbed into your joints when you found them a bit creaky and unwilling. He had had great hopes and had given the recipe in the Renascian Journal, but the simple had not done very much good. His joints were still a bit creaky, but it could not be helped.

Fenella, who was, in fact, getting a bit out of breath keeping up with them, asked about the discovery.

'Very serious,' said Snizort, at once assuming the solemn expression he wore when he was asking the Council for more money to run the Mnemosyne, or when he was presiding over a meeting of the Earth History Society. He re-settled his spectacles firmly on the bridge of his nose. 'That's why we came straight to Floy.'

Snodgrass said he did not know where else they would go with the information, other than to Floy and Fenella.

They rounded the curve in the road and came to the edge of the grasslands, which bordered the old part of Renascia. Fenella felt the familiar shiver of apprehension as they neared the Old Settlement, which many people said was haunted by the ghosts of their ancestors. Fenella did not think it was haunted, although it was impossible not to feel the desolation and the sharp loneliness and the engulfing despair. Probably it was only because the Old Settlement was still blackened and charred from the fire. There was bound to be something a bit desolate and a bit eerie about a place where people had lived and worked, and which now lay in rubble.

But Fenella always had the feeling that it was a bit more than that. She always had the feeling that once, long, long ago, somebody had stood here and stared out over a dark and barren landscape. And felt only an emptiness, and such a complete sense of loss and helplessness, that it had hardly been possible to bear it.

They picked their way over the remains of some small houses, which had piles of bricks tumbled all anyhow, and parts of walls and sections of floor, and beams and joists exposed. It was sad to see these ruined houses, but it was rather interesting to note that their own builders still used what had, presumably, been an Earth-pattern; four-square houses with doors at the front and square or oblong apertures for light, with divisions inside for different rooms and a pointy roof which was supported by thick wooden frames.

Floy was moving ahead of them, his eyes shining, the dark hair falling over his brow. He would be eager to see whatever Snodgrass and Snizort had uncovered, and he would already be thinking of how they could make use of the discovery.

The once-white building was on the outskirts of the Old Settlement. It was larger than either Fenella or Floy had expected, although Floy knew that the population of Renascia, small to begin with and decimated even further by the plague, would have been minuscule compared with Earth before its last days. Even so, he thought, staring at the centre of the great, ruined structure, it must have been possible for several hundred people to be seated in here, an inordinately large number.

There were ornate carvings which might originally have been over the main door and lying close to a raised area at the far end was a massive stone pillar, inset with strips of more of the cool, smooth stone. Floy recognised it as the parti-coloured stone which was to be found at the foothills of the Twilight Mountains, and which could be hewn out and polished to a glasslike surface. They had used it for building and it made marvellous floors and ceilings, cool and attractive and easily cleaned – until Quilp had managed to put a tax on it, so that not many people could afford to use it. This was only one of the many greedy laws that Quilp had sneaked into their

10

Charter during the chaos of the plague months, that Floy was now fighting to get repealed.

The Earth-building had floors of the mottled stone, and walls with panels of it as well. They walked cautiously across the rubble and the heaps of fallen bricks, their steps echoing sadly in the quiet. Through the gaps in the walls, Fenella could see the towering Twilight Mountains, with the pouring colours of the sunset already behind them. There was a flurrying wind out here that she had never before noticed, with an odd coppery scent in it. This was so unusual as to be worth calling attention to, and Fenella had turned round and drawn breath to speak, when Snizort said, 'It's over here.'

The Casket was lying at the far end of the ruined house, beneath the raised area, half covered by debris and dirt and stones. It looked dark and rather forbidding, and extremely old.

Snodgrass said, 'We think it must have been left by the first Settlers,' and Floy, his eyes shining, his dark hair tumbled about his brow, said, 'No it wasn't. Look at it more closely.'

The Casket bore none of the imprints of Renascian workmanship. The tools and the implements of the first Renascians had, perforce, been plain and unadorned and austere. There was no time for embellishments, had said the Settlers, hewing a new world out of the strange, bare planet; there was no time and there was no need. Things must be serviceable and, where possible, adaptable, and that was all. There was no room for ornamentation.

And, although the need for austerity had long since passed, embellishments and ornamentations had developed in the Renascians' own ways. 'Because,' said the artisans and the craftsmen and the journeymen, 'because we make things which are of our world, of Renascia, and not of Earth. We have developed our own patterns and our own designs. They are no better and no worse than those of our Earth-ancestors; it is just that they are different. But they are our own.'

11

But the Casket that sat squarely on the floor now was certainly not of their own Renascian design. When Floy said, 'It wasn't left by the first Settlers,' the others understood at once.

The Casket was of Earth-design.

It had been brought from the dying world of their ancestors.

Chapter Two

As they lifted the Casket from its half-buried place, it seemed as if the livid colours of the sunset were already trickling away and the black and purple fingers of night were stealing silently across the Twilight Mountains and shrouding the ruined Settlement. The wind that had snatched at Fenella's loose hair earlier moaned all about them, scurrying into their faces, breathing dry, sour air. Fenella tasted the coppery taint again and flinched.

Floy glanced at the darkening Mountains and said, 'I think we should go back, while there is still sufficient light.' He moved as he spoke, prising the Casket out of its hole, directing the others to each take a corner.

The light was draining faster now and there was a movement somewhere inside it, as if something they could not quite see might be moving or breathing. Fenella received the sudden, startling image of a great, black creature circling round and round where it crouched, making itself a nest, watching from beyond the skies, licking its lips . . .

She took a deep breath and wished she had not remembered all the stories about the Old Settlement being haunted by the ghosts of the Earth-people. Perhaps this was how they had started, out here at dusk, with the odd, foul-smelling wind blowing down from the Mountains. It was sufficiently nasty to make anybody think about ghosts and strange sinister mountain creatures.

And yawning caverns in the skies that were not there for our ancestors, but are there for us, and that appear in our Star Maps exactly like the slavering maws of monsters . . .

I won't think about it, said Fenella silently. I'll concentrate on helping to bring out the Casket, and I won't look towards the mountains, and I definitely won't look up at the skies. And if there was anything inside the Casket, it would be extremely interesting. Snizort and Snodgrass would be sure to ask her to help them in the sorting of whatever they found, and deciding if anything could be displayed in the Mnemosyne. Perhaps there would be an article to be written for the Renascian News, telling about the Casket's discovery.

She took a corner of the Casket and helped the others to half carry, half drag it out of the decayed house and put it on a cart to carry it down to the pitted and narrow track that would take them back to their own part of Renascia. It was very dark up here now, and it would be nice, it would be *comforting* to be amidst lights and warmth and people and ordinary things like fireplaces and books and furniture and food.

They took the Casket straight to Snizort and Snodgrass's little house which was nearer than their own, and hauled it down the narrow garden path. The Casket was not very big, but it was heavy, and a bit awkward.

'The study, I think,' Snizort said, helping them through the old-fashioned garden and into the warm, firelit study. 'We'll just put it down on the floor for the moment.'

The light had drained completely as they set the Casket down, and Snizort turned to light a fire in the hearth. Warmth and light burned up, driving back the creeping shadows.

The Casket seemed smaller than it had done earlier, and suddenly rather sad. Fenella thought it was somewhere around four feet in length and about two feet in depth. Not so very big at all. But it was made of something none of them recognised; something that was pale and cool and very strong indeed.

Floy, touching the corners warily, said, 'There's no sign of tarnishing or corrosion,' and then, with sudden excitement, 'it's made of the same stuff as their *Ark*.'

And Snodgrass said, 'Bless my soul, so it is.'

'It's seamless,' said Fenella, kneeling down on the floor to get a better look, tracing the edges with one finger. 'Except for the lid, it isn't joined anywhere.'

14

'Nor it is.'

The Casket's corners were rounded and there were thick bands of a darker coloured iron surrounding it. And although Floy was right and there was no trace of blackening or tarnishing, here and there it was pitted as if some strong, burning substance had been spilled on it. The immense hinges were intact and the clasp at the front looked as if it was made of something that might be virtually indestructible.

Fenella caught the tail-end of a thought from Floy.

This is something our ancestors did not intend us to lose . . . This is something they wanted to make sure would reach us . . .

Fenella found that she was remembering a phrase, a myth, an old, old legend about a magic box that had belonged to somebody with a strange name. Pandora, was it? Yes, Pandora. Pandora had possessed a box, and it had contained the most remarkable assortment of things. Some of them had been good and beautiful and helpful, and some had been ugly and sinister and dangerous. I believe, thought Fenella, safe and warm in Snizort and Snodgrass's warm cluttered safe-feeling house, I believe that in that iron or steel-bound box is something ugly and sinister and dangerous, and I really do wish it had stayed buried in the Old Settlement.

Snodgrass thought they ought to take a bite of supper before they got down to opening the Casket and Floy at once said, 'Thank you, yes. We should enjoy that.' Snodgrass looked pleased and took himself off to the kitchen which was hung with bunches of herbs and lined with gleaming copper pots. This was where he wrote articles for the Renascian News about how to cook peculiar foods that nobody had heard of, the ingredients for which could not be procured on Renascia anyway.

Fenella liked this house, where there were always huge fires burning, and deep comfortable armchairs, and desks piled high with books, which you had to be careful not to sit on by mistake. It was in the busiest part of Renascia, with all the groceries and bakeries, and places that sold cooked pies and made up remedies for illnesses. Fenella and Floy lived in their family's house, which was large and stood in the centre of Renascia, and had been built by their ancestors shortly after the fire at the Old Settlement. It was quite grand, but Fenella did not think it possessed the same tumbled charm or the same warmth and feeling of safety that this one did.

The supper was something called Steak and Kidney Pudding, which Snizort said had once been a great favourite of their Earth-ancestors, although Snodgrass said you could not get absolutely all the ingredients on Renascia.

'And so we don't think it's a *true* steak and kidney pudding,' he explained, giving everyone huge helpings. 'It needs something called *suet*, and we haven't been able to fathom what that is.'

In fact, the pudding was wholly delicious, and Fenella had two platefuls. There was rich elderberry wine, sweet and strong, and Snodgrass had three glasses, and unbent to tell them all manner of scandalous stories about the Council of Nine in Fenella and Floy's father's day, and about how Quilp was not averse to an occasional bit of ponderous dalliance with the very young ladies who were employed in the Wine Shop, and Snizort beamed and rubbed his hands together, because he loved gossip and would incorporate it into his Diaries.

And then, without the least warning, they all stopped talking, and looked at one another and Fenella felt her heart give a sudden jolt before it resumed its normal beating. The time had come and they were going to open the Casket and discover what was inside. Pandora's Box. Oh please, no, she thought.

But you cannot unmake an event, said Fenella silently, staring at the Casket. Even if we took it back to the ruined Settlement and covered it over with debris and rubble, we would still know about it. We would still have found it, it would still be there. We would wonder what it was, and why it had been constructed so strongly and so carefully. We would always wonder whether it had contained *something* that we needed to know about.

And, in any case, it might tell us something about what is happening on Renascia now, thought Fenella, firmly.

Floy was not thinking on precisely the same lines as Fenella, but he was not very far off. He was tremendously curious about the discovery; the Casket was more strongly made than anything they had ever found of the first Settlers, and he found this odd and intriguing.

He knelt down and unfastened the plain strong clasp. There was a click, unexpectedly loud in the quiet room, and Fenella felt her heart begin to beat loudly and painfully.

The hinges were clogged with the accretion of several centuries' dust and dirt and Floy and Snodgrass scraped diligently at them until they were free. The dust had a strange smell to it; it did not smell of ordinary dust, the sort you brushed up from the floor, or found behind a cupboard you had not moved for a while. Fenella, curled into the deep soft chair at the side of the fire, felt her fingers curl into her palms in sudden apprehension because, just for a second, she had thought it was going to be the horrid, harsh sourness of the flurrying wind they had encountered in the Settlement.

And then Floy scraped some more of the accretion away, and she knew it was something quite different; it was the bitter-sweet scent of extreme age; of lost worlds and dead civilisations and forgotten empires. Tears pricked her eyes, and she felt the ache of loss for that long-ago world, for the kingdoms that must have risen and then fallen, for the learning and the wisdom and the legend and lore that they would never know about.

For the misty turquoise and blue Earth, the dead world of their ancestors, that still lay in the skies far beyond their reach . . .

Slowly, warily, Floy prised the Casket open and pushed back the lid.

No one spoke and there was no sound in the room now except the steady ticking of the clock over the fireplace.

When a log fell apart in the hearth, Fenella jumped and when Floy spoke, he did so in a whisper.

'Earth craftsmanship,' he said, and there was something near to reverence in his voice now. 'See?' He touched the inner surface of the Casket gently. 'And made from exactly the same substance as the *Ark*. It's something we've never been able to reproduce.'

'Pale and hard and cold,' said Fenella.

'Some kind of metal they had which we do not?' hazarded Snodgrass.

'Truly, I have no idea. Perhaps they were somehow able to blend metal. Perhaps this is a mixture of several metals,' said Floy. 'That would be interesting.' He touched the Casket's inner sides again. 'But it must be something they would believe to be indestructible.'

Indestructible. That word again.

The inside of the Casket was as seamless as the outside. It was almost as if the unknown stuff had been melted and poured in and then allowed to set. It was cool to Floy's touch and had a dully gleaming surface. At the Casket's centre were hinged layers of the same pale, cold substance, not thick, but fitting so tightly that Floy had to borrow Snizort's paper knife to prise them up. There was a teeth-wincing, metal-against-slate sound, and then the hinged sections lifted up and folded back.

'It's very precisely made,' said Snizort, who was seated at his desk, his spectacles firmly on his nose, scribbling notes.

'Yes.' Floy was kneeling over it again, reaching inside. Inside again—

Floy reached into the Casket very gently and Fenella knew he was thinking, as she was thinking, as they were all thinking, that they were about to uncover something brought from Earth, something so ancient that they could barely comprehend it, but something from those long-ago ancestors who had built a marvellous world and then had to leave it to die.

We have only the sketchiest information about that world, thought Fenella, watching Floy. We do not know about its ending. But now, perhaps, we are going to learn more.

Using both hands, Floy lifted out several objects that Fenella had been unconsciously expecting to be papers. And then Floy said, very softly, 'Not papers,' and Fenella knew they had both been expecting the same thing.

Floy said, 'Gold. Look. Isn't it? Thin sheets of gold.' He bent over the sheets, his black hair tumbled, his eyes intent, and then looked up at them, his eyes brilliant, fingers of colour painted across his cheekbones. 'Engraved with writing,' he said. 'Earth writing.'

'Truly?' said Snizort.

'I don't think it can be anything else,' said Floy. 'Can it?' He handed the top sheet to Snizort, who pored over it for a moment. Fenella held her breath.

Snizort said at last, 'Dear me, Floy, I believe you are right. There is the same way of forming letters that we found in the original houses in the Settlement, and the same way of setting out words.' He traced the sheet of gold with a fingertip.

Floy's eyes were shining. 'Then this is a letter to us from the people of the dying Earth,' he said. 'A message from a lost world.'

To begin with, Fenella and the two brothers did not altogether take in the flow of words. The Earth-people wrote in a curious blend of informality and something that was very nearly instruction. Fenella thought that whoever had written these words – perhaps quite a number of people – had wanted to convey information, but in a friendly fashion. And although they did not use a different language, although they used familiar words and familiar phrases, they did not use them in quite the way the Renascians did. Perhaps they had been unused to writing like this at all. Perhaps they had had machines that did all their writing for them. Perhaps it was simply that ways of speech change . . .

Fenella felt a thrill of mingled fear and excitement. She did not move from the fireside chair she had curled herself

19

into, but she thought she was more alert and more aware than she had ever been before in her whole life.

'*To those of you who will eventually read this message, we say Greetings and Hello.*'

Neither a word familiar to any of them, but clearly both meaning some kind of salutation. Floy frowned, and then continued.

'*We believe we may be the last of a dying world and, certainly, there is little time left to us. Already the light is draining from the World, and therefore we must be brief...*'

The light is draining... The four Renascians looked at one another for a moment and shared a thought: so Earth experienced it as well! The light draining from the days, eroding the hours of daylight ... Something cold and implacable and ancient crept into the firelit study.

Fenella, watching Floy's expression, received a fleeting, vivid image of those last Earth-dwellers, huddled together in a cave or the ruins of a destroyed building, summoning their final resources and their strengths, fighting for a place in one of the machines that had brought the survivors to Renascia. And the world burning and dying all about them ... hungry and thirsty and exhausted ... '*The light is draining from the World...*'

Floy's voice said again, '*The light is draining from the World, and therefore we must be brief and we must hand on to our descendants – if descendants we are to have – the story of how we destroyed the world... We must do so while there are still the resources for us to do so ...*

'*For we were the men and women of science and of knowledge, and that is why we, out of Earth's survivors, have the means to leave our world... That is why we have been chosen.*' A pause.

Fenella thought: '*The men and women of knowledge... The ones chosen to go...*' There was a sudden, unwelcome, impression of pride and complacency and arrogance. There was certainly the suggestion of a hierarchy of some kind, a society that was too-strictly layered, that gave privileges to a tiny sprinkling of its people while the

20

rest must take their chance.

It had been only the Chosen Ones who had left Earth, while the rest had been condemned to remain. Was that what the last Earth-dwellers had been like? Haughty and uncaring and self-seeking? Oh, please no, thought Fenella, leaning forward, clasping her hands tightly together. Please don't let them have been any of those things.

And then Floy's voice said, '*Despite all our knowledge and all our science, we have lost our world and we believe that only a few of us can now survive, and try to save Mankind*' and Fenella knew that it was all right; the Earth-people had not been arrogant or complacent; they had been trying to make the best use of what was left to them.

Floy said, '*There are other worlds, and there are other ages, and it is to those worlds and to those ages, we now speak.*

'*We cannot show you what we made of our world, and what we are about to lose.*' Again there was the break in Floy's voice and Fenella knew that he, also, was seeing, albeit briefly, the terrible loneliness and feeling the dreadful desolation of the dying world. Because, of course, he would sympathise and, of course, he would be feeling the pain they had felt all those centuries ago. He has a skin short, my brother . . .

Floy said, '*We were proud of what we had created, and we should have liked to show you the power we had and the beauty and the strength. We should have liked to be able to record the learning and the history and the science and the —*' Floy stopped and said , 'I think the next word is technology and I think it would mean their degree of learning.' He glanced up and Snizort nodded, because it was a word he had come across.

'It is a little like that other word they used, *science*,' he said and Floy nodded, understanding.

'*But it is all lost to us. It is gone beyond recall and our world is dying. It is dying and burning all about us and there is little time left. We know that Earth must be abandoned and, within our group, there are people who have studied the stars and others who have the knowledge of —*' Floy stopped and frowned.

21

'They say *space travel*,' he said. 'I cannot understand that.'

'Their means of reaching us, would it be?' said Fenella.

'I think it must be,' said Floy. 'For they must have possessed that knowledge. Yes, of course they must. We know they came here in the *Ark*, and there must have been some means of sending it here.'

Snodgrass said, 'And they say that there are people within their group of survivors with the knowledge.'

'Yes.' Floy looked back at the thin golden tablet.

'It rather sounds,' said Snizort, thoughtfully, 'as if they had managed to gather together people who had studied these things for many years, and who would therefore be of practical use. I could believe in that very easily, you know.'

'Yes, it would be a sensible thing to do,' said Floy.

Fenella said, carefully, 'I could almost believe that the people with the knowledge had been gathered together first. Before the catastrophe hit them.' She looked at the others. 'In that way, they would know that at least their – what was the word? – their *science* men and women were safe and could perhaps use their knowledge to fight or re-build the world, or somehow rescue the dying.'

Floy said, mischievously, 'Fenella is liking the fact that they refer to men *and* women of learning and knowledge.'

'Yes,' said Fenella firmly. 'Yes, I am.'

'Well, why not?' said Floy, and smiled at her.

'What comes next?' said Snizort from the desk, and Floy reached for the next tablet.

'*We have set our sights on the stars, and on the worlds we have for so long observed . . . And although we know that to be truly safe we should travel farther than Man has ever travelled before, we no longer have the resources or the power.* I think,' said Floy, 'that by power they mean some form of machinery.' He looked up, and the others nodded.

'*It has been decided that we have sufficient power to reach the friendly little planet that we shall name Renascia, which is to say renewal, and we will take to it all that we have salvaged of our civilization and our culture.*'

He stopped, and Snizort made a note.

'*There is very little that we can take with us, for all about us now is the terrible devastation and the stench of decay . . . There is hardly any time left to us, and our choices are limited. And there is nowhere else for us to go —*'

Again there was the sadness, the aching longing. Fenella saw Floy's expression and knew that Floy was now a vessel, an instrument through which the agony and the despair of their ancestors was being poured. For the moment, their pain was his; it was like scalding water flooding through a pipe. Yes, he has a skin short, my brother . . .

Floy returned to the gold tablets. '*Earth's ending was the greatest irony in the history of Mankind,*' he said. '*It was the gods' final and darkest joke.*

'*You will know of comets; you will surely have seen such things from time to time, for they are there for all to see.*' He looked at the others and everyone nodded. It was interesting to hear that Earth had suffered meteors, just as Renascia sometimes did.

'*When the comet we called the Angry Sun made its first appearance in our eastern skies, our —*' Floy frowned over another unfamiliar word, and then said, '*Our astronomers and our cosmologists were excited; it was something that had not been seen in our skies for many hundreds of years. They studied it and charted its paths in the Maps and there was a growing belief that it was the very body that had presaged the birth of Christ.* Who would that be, Snizort?'

'I *think*,' said Snizort cautiously, 'that he was some kind of teacher they had. A widely followed cult. A very *good* cult,' he said, earnestly. 'But that would be a great many centuries ago. Perhaps several thousand years.'

'*It was something of moderate interest to us,*' went on Floy. '*To our people who studied these things, it was of immense importance, but they formed only a tiny proportion and, for most of us, there was only brief interest.*

'*But the comet had changed course since its last appearance. It had altered its journey and, although we believed that it had passed close to Earth several times in our history, it had never*

23

been sufficiently close to cause concern. It had been no more than a blaze in our firmament, a brilliant mass of light, something to bewitch and dazzle earlier primitive peoples; something about which earlier Ages wove many legends and many beliefs.

'This time was different . . .

'This time it would come so close that it would graze the Earth's surface. It would scorch the Earth's crust and there would be great fires in our forests and deserts. There would be immense floods, great tidal waves which would sweep our lowlands. A great many lives would be lost and a great many of our already-dwindling resources would be destroyed if it touched us.'

He paused again and Fenella moved closer to the fire because she was shivering. How would it have been to have known, quite definitely, that a great mass of fire and white-hot rain was hurtling down towards you . . .?

'We ought to have been able to defeat it,' said Floy's voice. *'We set out to defeat it, to turn it from its path and send it spinning into infinity, harmlessly and silently. We had machines and we had weapons, and it did not occur to us that we could not halt it. It was simply an exercise, a rather intriguing project. We had never challenged the stars in quite this way before; we explored them, but we had never attacked them. We were, perhaps, arrogant. We thought, as we had for so long thought, that Mankind had become invincible . . . And for that reason alone, perhaps, we needed to be given a lesson. But if so, it was a harsh and a cruel lesson . . .*

'For our machines and our power betrayed us. We had believed that we were invincible and that Earth was indestructible. We were wrong . . .

'When the comet came, when it was seen in the skies, when the sunsets began to burn with the colour of blood and fire and the wind began to be tainted with the terrible scent of Infinity, Earth changed.

'People who had been cultured and urbane became so no longer. They began to fight, to threaten. They became greedy and violent.

'Worst of all, little sects all over the land began to recall the ancient religions and the long-ago portents . . . the Four

Horsemen of the Apocalypse who would ride into the world in its last days . . . The fire-beasts of the sun-god who would pour down out of the white-hot flames and devour Mankind . . . We had believed ourselves to be a practical, free-thinking world; now we saw that it had been a veneer, a thin outer covering only . . .

'*For at the end, when the comet was in our skies, the frail coating of civilisation was stripped and our people were little better than primitive savages again, believing in pagan gods, calling upon names we had thought long since vanished from our language, praying to deities who had no place in our tongue, reviving cults, sacrifices . . .*

'*We reacted violently and arrogantly. We sent up our weapons and our immense and powerful machines. We flung them into the glowing sky, straight at the comet so that it would be destroyed, or turned off its course. And it did not occur to us that we should fail . . .*'

Floy stopped, and frowned, and Fenella said, in a whisper, 'They failed . . .'

Floy, his eyes scanning the page, said, 'No. No, they did not fail. It was not that.

'*We succeeded in our aim; for although we did not destroy the Angry Sun, called in one language the Feargach Grian, we managed to change its direction. We sent it spinning away from Earth, off into the heavens, to wreak its havoc elsewhere, and we thought ourselves safe.*

'*But we were not safe. The immense forces we had used to save our world from the comet, to avoid the small amount of damage it would have inflicted on us, turned upon us.*'

Floy said slowly, 'I do not fully understand this, but—' he stopped, and Snodgrass said, 'But you have a glimmering of understanding, perhaps?'

Floy said, softly, 'I believe I can almost see them. I believe I can picture them, hurling their powerful weapons and their machines into the skies. The weapons would collide with the comet, just as they had intended, they would knock it from its tracks, and then —' He stopped and looked straight at Fenella.

'And then the weapons would rebound,' said Fenella,

staring at him, her eyes huge and dark. 'They would recoil, they would – what's the word I want? – *ricochet*. They would ricochet and they would go plunging and plummeting back to earth—'

'There would perhaps have been some kind of gravitational force involved as well,' said Snodgrass.

'And when they hit Earth, it would cause the great Final Catastrophe, the historic Devastation that has come echoing down to us,' finished Floy, and then, looking back to the thin golden sheets, 'yes,' he said softly. 'Yes, that is what happened. Listen.'

'*Our own weapons destroyed us. The forces we had thought would protect us, finally betrayed us . . .*'

The achingly sad words lay on the air clearly and terribly.

The forces that should have protected them had burned their world.

'*And so,*' said Floy, reading again, '*and so, the destruction of Earth was, at the last, our own doing, exactly as all the portents and the harbingers had said it would be. Apocalypse had come at last, Armageddon was upon us, and the skies were torn apart with the fire and the terrible heat and the vicious, disease-laden rain that poured down upon the Earth . . .*

'*We burned the world and perhaps we destroyed Mankind, but we did it unwittingly . . . We meant to save the world, not murder it . . .*'

Fenella closed her eyes briefly and felt the sharp pain, yet again. How would it feel to know you had slaughtered the world . . .?

Snizort said, very softly, 'How truly terrible for them.'

'Go on, Floy,' said Snodgrass.

'*Little groups of us escaped. We scuttled underground, into cellars and basements, deep beneath the ruins of our great cities. We avoided the fires that still burned and the charred, smoking wastes that had once been towns and meadows and forests and highways. At length, some of us who had devoted much of our lives to studying and understanding power and travel managed to reach the—*' Floy stopped again, and then said, '*managed to reach the laboratories and the powerhouses*. Power,' said

Floy. 'That word again. Clearly, it was their greatest source of strength and of force.'

'*Laboratory* would perhaps mean some kind of workshop,' offered Fenella.

'Yes. Yes, for they go on to talk of working,' said Floy.

'*We worked in the most horrific of conditions to salvage what we could, and at length we were able to power our craft, which we named the Ark of Ages . . .* Quilp always insisted they had called it an *Ark*,' said Floy.

'*And now we have gathered together as many people as we can. We would like to believe that we could take every remaining creature on Earth, but such a belief would be foolish. There must still be men and women here, sheltering in caves and mountains, eking out a terrible existence in the cellars of devastated buildings . . . We cannot save them all . . . Even if we could reach them, there would not be sufficient room . . .*'

'But they would have liked to do so,' whispered Fenella, hugging her knees. 'They wanted to save everyone.'

'*Perhaps the ones we have been unable to save will somehow live on. Perhaps they will be the new Earth people and perhaps, at some time in a future we cannot see, they will re-build Earth and bring her back to greatness. It is impossible to know, but we will hope for that . . .*

'*For ourselves, we believe we shall be safe on Renascia. We believe that we can reach it and find sanctuary.*'

And then, finally, and devastatingly, like great stones dropping into a quiet pool, '*There is only one cause for concern about Renascia and, although it is a serious one, still we must set our sights for there for we have not the power to go farther and we know of no other planet where life, as we know it, could survive.*

'*Our astronomers tell us that Renascia is on the rim of a vortex, that it is on the very edge of one of the yawning Black Chasms with which Space is studded . . .*

'*We know only a very little about these Black Chasms, but we know them to be places of infinite and incomprehensible density . . . If we are unfortunate enough to pass within the pull of the Chasm that borders Renascia, then we shall almost certainly be torn apart by the strong tidal forces that it will*

27

generate. It may even be that we would cross boundaries that no men have ever crossed before, for it is believed by some that once within a Black Chasm, Time, as we know it, ceases to exist . . .' Floy hesitated.

Time as we know it ceases to exist . . . The words dropped into the quiet room like stones into a pool.

'We have always regarded these Chasms as Dark Lodestars, malign black lures which suck in unwary travellers, and as cannibalistic suns, angry and voracious . . . They are the underside of our bright, luminous suns; perhaps they are necessary, for without true darkness, how could there be true light . . . ? But there are many theories to explain and accredit and account for the things we do not understand, and there is not time to set them down. We have come to believe, however, that all worlds must have their dark undersides . . .

'We shall trust our craft to bring us to safety, for we know that we have not the power to go farther afield than Renascia, and we know of no other planets where life, as we know it, could survive.

'Renascia it is to be, and we shall put our faith in the gods and pray that we are travelling towards sanctuary and towards the salvation of Mankind.

'And that we shall be able to steer clear of the Dark Lodestar that lies in Renascia's horizons . . .'

Floy laid down the tablets and looked at them. For a long time, nobody spoke. At length, Floy said, very softly, 'They did reach Renascia. We know they did. They reached the sanctuary they had sought and they saved Mankind. Their quest succeeded.'

Fenella said, in a whisper, 'The Dark Lodestar,' and Floy met her eyes.

'Yes.'

'Where Time, as we know it, might cease to exist.'

'Yes.' He moved to sit beside her, his face serious and intent. 'I am afraid that it is that – that Chasm that is warping the patterns of the stars,' he said, very gently.

'And eroding the daylight,' said Snizort.

Floy said, in an expressionless voice, 'Yes. That is the

answer. That is what is happening to us. Perhaps, in some way, the Chasm has begun to expand.' He frowned. 'A black density,' he said. 'Perhaps – something to do with a star or a sun dying.'

'Something to do with meteors being swallowed?' hazarded Fenella.

'Truly, we cannot know. But it must be expanding. It is the only answer to the vanishing of the days and the strange livid sunsets.'

'Renascia is on the rim of a vortex. A black density,' said Fenella. 'A Lodestar beckoning us to its centre.'

'And at its centre, Time could turn upside down,' said Snizort, thoughtfully.

Chapter Three

Floy was not yet entirely accustomed to entering the Council Meeting Room and taking the high-backed chair which had been his father's, and seeing the faces turn towards him with a mixture of alertness and respect, here and there blended with wariness. It amused him, this spurious reverence that Quilp and the rest donned with such alacrity; he thought it was a very thin crust indeed, and he thought he would not trust one of them. But he had tried to repay this reverence with deference; even while he had been oversetting the old and tried methods and introducing his own ideas and ideals, he had borne it in mind that these men had been on Renascia's Council for many years and that they had, perforce, far more experience than he had in governing and administering. He thought he had, so far, treated them with the courtesy due to their years, but he thought, as well, that they had never before had to face such a grim situation. It might be that the time for courtesy and deference was passed ...

He was not aware that, as he walked into the Meeting Room, a mantle of unmistakable authority had fallen upon him; his mind was on the contents of the Casket and the golden tablets and he was already framing in his mind the proposals he would be putting before the Council. But, as he took his seat, the Council exchanged meaningful glances and Quilp, looking up, was at once aware of the new light in Floy's eyes. Something has happened, thought Quilp. This will either be very interesting or very awkward.

Quilp knew himself for a reasonable man, and he thought that he was being very reasonable now. He had attended this Special Meeting of the Council which Floy had called, promptly and unquestioningly, and had even cancelled a promising little supper with the pretty young thing who served turnip grog in the Wine Shop. But it would not do to allow Floy to gain the upper hand in the Council. Quilp had not allowed Floy's father – charming, a little feckless, slightly weak – to do so, and he would not allow the son to do so either. He studied Floy covertly and saw, afresh, the charm and a little of the fecklessness, but he did not see any of the weakness. Oh dear, thought Quilp.

They all listened, without interrupting, as Floy recounted the story of the Casket and studied the careful transcripts that Fenella and Snizort had made of the message on the golden tablets.

When, at length, Floy finished speaking, the Council looked towards Quilp who had been making small, neat notes. Quilp did not speak. He finished his notes in unhurried and completely silent fashion (a trick he had perfected years ago and which nearly always discomfited people), laid down his pen, and regarded Floy steadily.

'This is all extremely unexpected,' said Quilp, raising his brows a little. He was annoyed to see that, so far from being thrown into confusion by such steady regard, Floy merely met his look and said, quite coolly, that unexpected was one word for it, certainly.

'For myself, I would have called it alarming,' he said. 'But whatever we call it, we have to decide what we are going to do about it.'

'I think we can accept the story of the comet,' said Quilp, as if the overall direction of the Meeting had passed to him. He glanced round, as if for agreement. 'And perhaps we can just about accept the – what did you call it? oh yes, the *vortex*. We have to allow that there are secrets in the stars which we do not understand,' said Quilp, managing to sound extremely reasonable and open-minded.

He leaned forward, picking up his pen again, turning it back and forth in his hands. 'But this tale about a yawning Black Chasm —' He smiled at Floy, rather sadly. 'My dear boy, I think that perhaps you may have

31

misunderstood the wording a little there.' He thought to himself that this sounded really very courteous and was pleased, because discourtesy was not something he would ever stoop to. But it was necessary to be firm with Floy. He was always telling the rest of the Council that Floy was a good leader so long as people were firm with him.

Floy had felt his temper rising at this rather obvious ploy to make him appear as a supplicant who had been granted audience by the Council.

But he said, quite mildly, 'It is a believable story, Quilp. And the contents of the Casket appear to be perfectly genuine. You may all see them for yourselves. Snizort has them under lock and key in the Mnemosyne. And you must admit that strange things are beginning to happen.'

Quilp said that he was a fair-minded man and would readily admit that strange things were happening. There was something a little out of kilter. Probably it would be no more than an approaching meteor storm and they could deal with it perfectly well if that was so. It might even be that the information Floy had brought to them had a smidgen of truth in it. You had to have a flexible mind, of course, and Quilp would be the first to admit that they did not know all the secrets of the stars. He asked what Floy proposed be done.

'Whatever we do will be a huge gamble,' said Floy and grinned suddenly, because he was not averse to a gamble, and surely this would be gambling against the most fantastical odds of all time? 'It will be a gamble,' he said, 'against an unknown opponent, and against the most overwhelming odds ever known.' His eyes glinted with sudden recklessness. 'We may lose, gentlemen. We may be soundly beaten – and if that is so, then we shall lose our lives, and Renascia will be lost for all time.' He leaned forward, his hair tumbling over his brow. 'But if we win, gentlemen . . . if we win, then we shall have done something tremendous; something that has never been done before.

'We shall have done what our ancestors could not.'

There was a silence round the table. Floy thought: I believe I have them. I believe they are with me.

He said, 'We have not the resources our ancestors had although, at the end, they were not of much help. And so we must keep our battle plan simple.' He glanced round the table and thought: I believe they rather like 'battle plan'.

'I believe we should construct a shelter,' said Floy. 'What the Earth-people called a *dug-out*. We must dig deeply into the ground and make a refuge there. That way, we have a fighting chance.' He leaned across the table, his eyes glowing with fervour. 'We must build a haven for our people, a sanctuary, a refuge to which we can go when the disturbances become severe. And we shall have to live underground for a while.'

'Rather ambitious,' said Quilp. And then, frowning, 'And rather *extreme*, I would have thought.'

Floy brought his clenched fist down on the table angrily. 'We need to be ambitious!' he said. 'We need to be extreme! We have to find a way of protecting our people! If the Golden Tablets are right, then Renascia is in far worse danger than ever Earth was! It is not simply in danger of being blown up, gentlemen, it is in danger of being sucked into a gaping black infinity from which it can never emerge!'

'I fear,' said Quilp slowly, 'that the building of these *shelters* will be a costly exercise.' And thought to himself that, provided it was not his money that was at risk, it did not much matter. In fact, he could quite see that it would look rather bad – well, it would look very bad indeed – if the Council were discovered to be doing nothing at all about the threat to Renascia. The building of a shelter of some kind would at least let the people know the Council were anxious for their welfare. They might even be led to think it was all Quilp's idea, if Quilp could arrange it that way.

Perhaps they ought to go along with Floy's plans. The Council would agree to do so, because Quilp would tell them to. Most of them would not have been on the

Council if they were not Quilp's staunch supporters anyway: Quilp had actually heard them called toadies and yes-men, but this was nonsense.

But Floy did not need to know about any of the profitable little deals which Quilp had been able to set up for the people who gave him their support; it was not something that anyone needed to know about, other than the people concerned. It was not dishonest dealing, either, merely a question of practicalities. But it meant that when Quilp wanted something doing, or perhaps *not* doing, they all agreed with him.

Floy was explaining his plans now; he was sketching plans on a sheet of paper, talking not about several small shelters, but one – or perhaps two – immense ones. Properly built and properly strengthened. Equipped with food and water.

'Sanctuaries,' said Floy, eagerly. 'Our only hope for survival.'

One of the Council asked what kind of disturbances they might have to endure and Floy said, 'I have no idea. But logic suggests that there could be immense tearing winds, violent storms, perhaps volcanic action from the mountains. And certainly the seas would be displaced, so that there would be great tidal waves washing inland.' He stopped and looked at Borage the Builder.

'You can help most of all here,' said Floy. 'We should be entirely in your hands over the building,' and Borage, rather pleased at being deferred to in this way, managed not to catch Quilp's eye and said indeed he could help. For a start, there was that piece of sloping ground on the town's eastern outskirts, just behind the Wine Shop. It was just the place to dig out exactly such a thing as Floy was talking about. They could tunnel into the hillside and the fold of the hill itself would afford natural extra protection. It would not be difficult to dig quite far down. Thirty feet, perhaps, what did Floy think? And they could shore up the underside with good oak struts and maybe give them a coat or two of bitumen. There was nothing like bitumen for sealing, said Borage frowning delightedly over the severity of it all, sketching out one or two plans on his note-pad.

Quilp, leaning forward, said, 'Our good Borage is certainly eloquent on the subject. I imagine we shall not expect him to put his men to work for *nothing*, Floy?'

Floy frowned and said, 'I hadn't actually thought about that side of it. I was more concerned about creating a place of safety for everyone.' He thought, but did not say, that even if they survived the dangers ahead, they would probably emerge to a world so ravaged and depleted that coinage and monetary matters, as they knew them, would have ceased to matter. But since the Council had not yet seen this, he would not stress it to them. He simply said, 'Borage must be paid from Council Funds,' and Quilp nodded, well pleased. A proper transferral of money from the Funds would be made, he said, and various people around the table nodded solemnly. Quilp would arrange the transferral, because Quilp always arranged these things. It was better that way. Nobody ever precisely admitted that certain things were recorded in the Council's dossiers, while other things were not, but everybody, with the exception of Floy of course, knew the plump little deals that went through the Council's hands, and which resulted in various people being given nice little sums of money or, on occasions, pieces of land for Borage to build on, or sometimes even fully built houses.

In fact, it might be extremely awkward if Floy ever asked to see the Records in their entirety. His father had never done so, of course, and probably Floy would not either. There was not really any cause for the Council to worry.

Floy said, now, 'I imagine we would be using public money for the shelters would we? That would be the proper source, I think. Marplot, that is your province.'

Marplot said, genially, that a proper orderly arrangement could be made, Floy need not worry over that side of it.

'Good. Do we need to declare a State of Emergency in order to take the money?'

Quilp, speaking as if he might be selecting his words

35

with great care, said, 'Could I suggest—most respectfully, of course—that a State of Emergency might cause—ah—panic to everyone. Do we really want that?' He looked round the table and people shook their heads, and said indeed they did not.

'No,' said Floy, thoughtfully, 'I believe you are right. And yet we have to give some reason for the work that Borage will be carrying out and also for sending the people into the shelters when the time comes.' He frowned, and then said, 'Supposing we tell them that there's to be a meteor shower? Something rather more severe than usual?' He looked round the table. 'Would you agree to that?'

'Your sister knows the truth,' said Quilp.

'Yes, but she won't say anything.'

Quilp shook his head and gave a rather sad smile. 'My dear boy, I fear you have a way to go in your understanding of the ladies,' he said, and the Council smiled with him.

'Rubbish,' said Floy. 'Fenella will see why the thing must be—'

'Suppressed?'

'Diluted . . .' said Floy. 'Borage, how quickly could you begin work, do you think?'

Borage, feeling rather as if he was being swept along by a whirlwind, found himself in an awkward situation. He was caught, so to speak, between the gentleman who had been instrumental in providing him with a fat bank balance, and the one who was, when all was said and done, Renascia's hereditary leader. He floundered and looked first at Quilp, who smiled and shrugged and sat back with his arms folded as if to disassociate himself from the entire proceedings, and then back at Floy.

'Hadn't you better start tomorrow?' said Floy, impatient with this vacillating, and Borage made a show of consulting a small diary, and said, well they *could* do that, only it would mean abandoning the renovations of the Round House in which they sat that very minute, and whose roof was presently having to be re-tiled on the western side, on account of these strong winds they had been having.

'The winds are merely a small dose of what will come

later,' said Floy, dismissively.

'I was brought up never to leave a job unfinished,' put in one of the Council members, whose name was Prunum.

But Floy was scooping his notes into order, and standing up. 'I think we are all agreed,' he said. 'Borage had better commence work at once, hadn't he?' He nodded briefly to the rest, said, 'Thank you for your time, gentlemen,' and took his leave.

There was another of the difficult silences, and then Quilp said, in a pained voice, 'Dear me, he is not in the least like his father.' And then, with one of the crab-like sideways approaches to the problem, for which he was known, said, 'I do fear that if we do not handle this correctly, we may find that our people are succumbing to panic.' He lifted his eyes from the paper he had been studying and looked at them all very directly. 'And I believe we should avoid a State of Emergency at all costs. Marplot, a word from you, perhaps?'

'I never heard of vortexes and Chasms,' said Marplot, a gentleman of scant imagination. 'Floy's getting carried away.' He leaned forward. 'But I do know,' he said, 'that States of Emergencies lead to the – ah – *scrutinising* of certain Moneyhouse procedures.'

'Really?' said Quilp, who had known this all along.

'Very unwise,' said Marplot, shaking his head. 'Very unwelcome.'

Several other people, to whom the scrutinising of the Moneyhouse's dealing was equally unwelcome, thought that Floy was getting carried away as well. Borage said, rather apologetically, that he would at least have to make a start on the shelters and, anyway, you never knew what mightn't be going to happen. They were all aware of the strange darkening of the days, he said, and of the sudden sour winds that were sweeping down from the mountains, though doubtless it would turn out to be nothing worse than a meteor storm, and they all knew about those!

'So long as Floy doesn't see the ledgers,' said Marplot, and everyone nodded in agreement.

* * *

The people of Renascia thought they might not know a great deal about governing and democracy and decision-making (although they knew in a blink when Quilp and his coterie were up to something). They might not be precisely clever about money and investments and business, they said, solemnly. But when it came to building and digging and the construction of a grand big shelter against a meteor storm, they knew what was needed! A good large dug-out and plenty of stout Renascian timber to support the roof, with maybe a splash or so of bitumen just to seal it. Bitumen was the thing, they said, rolling up their sleeves mentally and literally, preparing to set to under Borage the Builder's direction. And there'd need to be strong doors against any bit of a storm that might get up as a result of the meteors. You couldn't be too careful when it came to such things. Good strong doors would be needed, and no question but that they'd need to be iron.

Survival, that was the thing. They might not be facing a disaster on the scale of their Earth-ancestors, they said, beaming at Floy and Fenella, who came to help; they might not be threatened with the ending of their world and the destruction of the entire Human Race. But it was astonishing how much damage a serious fall of meteors could inflict. It was a very good idea to build these shelters and take refuge in them.

They set to with a will, accepting the plans drawn out by Borage and taking themselves off to the site that had been so carefully chosen. There wasn't any too much time either, they said, importantly. The meteors couldn't be very far off now. If you listened carefully, you could hear them, nasty spiteful things; you could hear them whistling and moaning somewhere beyond the Twilight Mountains. If you were of an imaginative turn of mind, you could very nearly think that there was some huge creature up there somewhere, something black and hungry, howling for your blood. They glanced over their shoulders uneasily as they said this because, just for a moment, it had seemed rather dreadfully real, that unseen beast. It had been very easy to picture it, inhuman and merciless, ravening for prey, stalking the little planet of Renascia through the heavens . . .

There was a nasty-smelling wind whistling down from the skies now; you had to wrap up very warmly indeed against it, and there had been one or two outbreaks of sickness. People took to wearing carefully contrived mufflers for face masks, because you did not have to be in the teeth of the wind for more than an hour now before you were feeling queasy to your stomach.

All the same, they found themselves working with a good heart and a cheerful mien. There was an unexpected feeling of kinship with the Earth-people as well, a feeling of closeness to be working like this, in the shadow of the *Ark* which had come from Earth all those years ago. One or two people (Quilp among them, of course) had questioned Borage's decision to make the dug-outs just here, but Borage, who did not mind standing up to Quilp when it came to a question of a building or a foundation, had said firmly that here was the place; soft, chalky soil to dig into with ease, and a bit of a fold in the land just above them to give extra protection. They'd burrow directly into the hillside itself, he said.

Snizort, who spent a good deal of time on the Plain, supposedly making notes, thought the hillside was a very good site indeed. He got in rather a lot of people's way and provoked a few sharp words from people who said that the writing of diaries was all very well, but there were more important things to be doing just now and so would Snizort please move out of the way, because there was a new consignment of oak timbers coming up. They were lining the floors with planks of oak, and it was important to get the lengths exactly right. You could not be doing with diarists and museum-keepers under your feet at such a solemn time.

And while everybody had started off by regarding it all as solemn and grave, after a time the people who were made sick by the sulphurous winds simply took to their beds and stayed there, and the people who were not affected began to get used to the howling, keening sound

39

that raged across the Twilight Mountains. They wore the face masks and donned their warmest clothes for the work, and almost became accustomed to the feeling of a huge, black beast just out of sight and just beyond consciousness, somewhere in the night skies, circling and watching and waiting . . .

'Sheer bravado,' said Snizort, scurrying about everywhere, and listening to the comments which he reported to Fenella and Floy.

'No, I think they really have come to accept it all,' said Floy.

'It's because it's becoming an everyday thing,' said Fenella. 'You can get used to almost anything if you have to deal with it every day.'

'They're beginning to think of it as a holiday,' said Floy. 'Snizort, I hope I've done right in keeping the truth from them.'

Chapter Four

The danger was getting closer with every hour. Daylight had almost ceased, except for an occasional sickly streak in the east, and Renascia was living in a perpetual night.

Fenella thought it would have been easier if it had been an ordinary night, the kind of night with velvety blackness stealing in from the Mountains, and the night stocks and the sweet-scented jasmines brought from Earth unfolding and laying their gentle touch on the air.

But the night was dull and angry and swollen, the air stale and thick. If you stayed out in the wind, it was sometimes difficult to breathe, so that you felt as if your lungs were being compressed by iron bands, and your head throbbed. The darkness was tinged with livid crimson, as though the skies were torn and bleeding, and the wind had already torn out saplings and dislodged small sheds. Boats on the lakes had been ripped from their moorings and smashed against the Mountains on the far side.

Fenella, feeling sick from the sour, tainted air, but continuing to help with the work, thought it was as if a vast, ancient tomb was slowly being opened, and great gusts of stale dead air were hurtling out at them. It was, she thought, the stench of dead worlds and forgotten civilisations, of rotting universes. How many worlds had it swallowed, that gaping Black Chasm?

But it was important not to let the Renascians think that there was anything more serious than a meteor bombardment ahead of them, and so Fenella, visiting the dug-outs with Snizort, talked about the history of meteors, even managed to find one or two papers in the Mnemosyne that told about their construction, and how they could spiral through the heavens for centuries before touching a planet. That would be the reason for the strange winds and the sickly stench, she said. And everyone nodded and said, a bit too loudly, that that would be the reason, no question about it. And if people were beginning to look far more worried than a severe meteor bombardment warranted, nobody actually spoke out.

They were all working in what somebody said were called *shifts* now, relays of them, turn and turn about, five hours digging and constructing, then resting while another batch took over. They worked by the light of flaring torches, burning chunks of oak thrust into the ground. It was becoming quite difficult to keep the torches alight, but Snizort and Snodgrass had fashioned lanterns out of square boxes made of thin, almost-transparent material, into which the torches could be inserted and be free from the winds.

'Box lanterns,' explained Snizort. 'A *very* old idea.'

The inside of the shelter was almost completed, and it was becoming clearer with every hour that, as soon as the doors were in place and the mechanisms for locking them home were screwed on, they would all go below and stay there.

It was larger and much better equipped than people had visualised when they started it. Quilp had been made to rescind the tax on the parti-coloured stone, and they had lined the shelter with it. It would be extremely strong, said Floy, looking to Borage for confirmation. It would protect them against any splits in the hillside.

'Could that happen?' asked one of the Council.

'Anything could happen,' said Floy.

The strange, slightly feverish mood of the previous days had vanished now; people not on dug-out duty took to huddling together in their houses, little groups of them gathering together for warmth and comfort, tending the fires which would not burn properly because of the wind shrieking down the chimneys and fastening the shutters firmly so that the horrid light would not seep through the cracks.

Seeing the two shelters take shape, helping where he

could, Floy had the strong impression that something ancient and powerful, something steeped in legend, was being re-born.

For Mankind has been here before, it has sheltered from Flood and Deluge before . . . cedar and cypress wood were used then, and the whole was smeared within with pitch . . . Two animals of each sort were taken aboard, and a raven and a dove, so that messengers could be sent out to test the waters when they had receded . . .

Floy shook his head, but for a moment the strange image persisted, so that he had the strongest impression of Time spread out before him like a huge, glistening tapestry, interwoven with crimson and gold and silver, the entire history of every world ever lived and ever lost and ever died for . . .

And Time is running down, he thought, looking up at the darkling skies, seeing the massing clouds piling into pinnacles and peaks and huge, improbable impenetrable castles. Time is running out and running down, and I do not think we have very long left to us . . .

But standing in the shrieking night that was closing down on Renascia, with the Twilight Mountains black rearing silhouettes behind him, he looked down on the little houses and the shops and the grassed areas that people had so carefully tended, and thought: *We have faced catastrophes and deluges and fires and floods and famines before . . . We have somehow survived . . .*

We have been here before, thought Floy.

But shall we escape this time?

'It's all going quite well,' said Snizort, in the warm, safe-feeling house, when Floy and Fenella came to supper to eat Snodgrass's delicious baked ham with potted mushrooms, and blackcurrant pudding to follow.

'I suppose we'll all go in the shelter, will we?' asked Snodgrass, setting out glasses for the carrot wine which was his newest experiment.

'Well, there's certainly room for everyone,' said Snizort, taking a second helping of blackcurrant pudding and adding custard. 'I suppose if there wasn't we might have to draw lots for places. My word, now *that's* an old custom, the drawing of lots. It was the Second Elizabethans who used to do that, or would it have been even earlier . . .? Let me think. I'm bound to have a note of it somewhere . . . Of course, if it was left to me, I'd say we ought to take some of the animals as well. One – or perhaps two? – of every living species on Renascia. Yes, two would be better —'

'It's what the first Settlers did,' said Snodgrass in a down-to-earth manner.

'Is it really?' said Floy. 'I don't believe I ever knew that.'

'Oh yes, my word, yes certainly.' Snodgrass peered at Floy over his spectacles. 'Of course, they couldn't bring two of *everything*,' he said earnestly.

'There wouldn't have been the room,' put in Snizort.

'But they brought – let me see – chickens and ducks for sure.'

'Eggs,' said Snizort knowledgeably.

'And I *think* that lambs and sheep were Earth things as well.'

'I think we ought to take down some seedlings,' said Snizort. 'You ought to prepare for every eventuality. Is anyone having that last helping of pudding?'

Walking back to their house, their collars turned up against the cold, Fenella wearing her fur-trimmed cloak with the hood, Floy said, 'Snizort and Snodgrass think of it almost as a game,' and Fenella jumped, because she had been thinking the same thing and Floy sometimes had the way of echoing your thoughts which could be disconcerting.

She slipped her hand through his arm, and said, 'It's oddly comforting, though, isn't it? And I think that, beneath it all, they are very serious indeed. It is just that they so enjoy their pieces of history and their discoveries.'

'Could you wish they had not made this particular discovery?'

'I don't know.' Fenella considered. 'Would it have been better not to know?'

'I'd rather know,' said Floy, standing still and staring

44

out towards the Twilight Mountains, his eyes narrowed. 'If there's something out there that's sucking us into its black core, I'd rather know about it.' He grinned down at her. 'That way we can at least put up some kind of a fight.'

Some kind of a fight . . .

'Floy, what will happen?' asked Fenella, who had been trying not to ask this ever since they had found the Casket.

'Truly, I have no idea.' He frowned. 'The idea – the whole concept of what our ancestors called a *vortex* is difficult to grasp.' He narrowed his eyes thoughtfully. 'I imagine it as a great, deep, chasm – perhaps a black tunnel, where there is nothing at all, not even Time.'

Nothing, not even Time . . .

Fenella shivered, and said, 'I don't think of it like that. I think of it as a creature, a beast, something up there that is settling down into its lair, circling round as it does so. I know we shall fight,' said Fenella, seriously. And then, 'Why have the days gone?'

'Because Time is slowing down,' said Floy in an expressionless voice. 'Haven't you felt that?'

'Yes.'

He smiled at her. 'Would you prefer me to protect you, as all the other ladies are being protected?' he said. 'To pat you on the head and say, "Now, my dear, there is nothing for you to worry about, and we shall simply live in a shelter for a few hours, and then come out again to our homes and lives"? And tell you to run away and help with the soup-making?'

'No,' said Fenella. 'Oh no.'

Quilp was living in chaos, which was not the sort of thing he cared for. It was not the sort of thing they had ever permitted on Renascia. Chaos could lead to confusion, and confusion could lead to downright anarchy, and they all knew what *that* meant!

It was Floy's fault, of course. Floy was turning the whole of Renascia upside-down and inside-out; he was sweeping aside all of Quilp's carefully thought out taxes

45

and rules, and once a tax or a law had been rescinded, it was extremely difficult to get it restored. It was very nearly impossible. When Quilp thought of how he had worked and planned and – yes, all right, plotted! – to get taxes on the multi-coloured stone, and on people's earnings, and on the houses and the highways, and of how he had been making himself and his fellow Council members a very nice little profit out of it all, black fury entered his heart. He dared say the next thing that would happen would be that Floy would start delving into Marplot's ledgers, which was the very last thing they could permit.

Something would have to be done. Could they somehow get rid of Floy? He considered the idea, and the more he considered it, the better he liked it. He liked even better the thought that with Floy out of the way, he, Quilp, would be the obvious choice for Leader. Leader of the Council of Nine. It sounded well. Ruler of Renascia sounded even better. It would all have to be carefully handled and the Council would have to be subtly manipulated, but Quilp could do it.

And although it was not in his creed to be secretive or furtive, he called a very secretive and extremely furtive assembly of his fellow Councillors, with the sole exception of Floy. He hesitated over the inclusion of Borage the Builder, who was so pleased with having been appointed to oversee the construction of the shelters that he might turn out to have divided loyalties. But if there was one thing Quilp had always been, it was democratic. It would have been undemocratic not to have included Borage. In any case, what about all those houses Borage had built, actually using the cheapest possible materials, but recording that extremely expensive materials had been purchased? Borage had quite as much to lose as any of them. Anyway, somebody might have told him about it behind Quilp's back.

None of them dared risk Floy delving into the Council's financial affairs. There had once been a saying about there being a tide in the affairs of men which, if taken, could lead anywhere at all. Quilp thought there was a tide in the affairs of Renascia's Council now, and if they did not take advantage of it, there might never be another opportunity. It went against Quilp's nature to plot and scheme and intrigue, but there was too much at stake.

They met in Prunum's Wine Shop. Quilp had specified the hour but, even as he battled his way down the street to the Wine Shop's jutting bow windows, it occurred to him that it had taken a very long time for the hour to arrive. His own clock seemed to have run down somehow, and so he had sat in the window of his house, watching the huge Tompion piece in the square outside. That had never been known to give an incorrect time, and so Quilp knew he could trust it. Even so, it seemed to take a remarkably long time to reach the appointed hour. He found himself hoping that he would not be late for this very important meeting.

But when he reached the Wine Shop, the others were only just arriving, so it was all right. Probably this rather nasty perpetual darkness sent people's ideas of time a bit out of kilter. And so he nodded to the pretty young thing who served the wine and the various brews. He noticed that she was looking particularly toothsome, took a minute to suggest that they might sup together very soon, then made his way to the back of the shop.

Prunum had set aside his back room for the meeting and was serving them some of his wortleberry wine, which Quilp did not care for, but which it would have been discourteous and unpolitic to have refused. He seated himself at the scrubbed table which Prunum had provided and eyed them all solemnly.

'Gentlemen,' he said, 'we have on our hands a situation so grave and so fraught with danger that I believe we should ask ourselves questions we have not, until now, needed to ask.' A silence. No one spoke. Quilp sipped the wortleberry wine at his elbow and went on.

'Our dear Renascia is being threatened and menaced,' he said, and several voices murmured, 'the Black Chasm,' and several heads nodded.

'Not only by that,' said Quilp who, in fact, found the

whole thing so outlandish that he could not even bring himself to pronounce the words. 'Not only by that, gentlemen.' He raised a clenched fist. 'It is threatened from within,' he said and looked at them and waited.

'Floy,' said Marplot, who had seen, as clearly as Quilp, that Floy would soon be asking for details about the various monetary transactions that surrounded the shelter-construction. He had taken the precaution of locking away the Moneyhouse's ledgers and had even gone so far as to enter a sum from his own funds against a certain amount he had borrowed for himself without the encumbrance of interest or even repayment. 'Floy,' he said, very grimly indeed.

'Floy,' said Quilp, nodding. He looked round at the Council, and said, very sadly, 'My dear good friends, I fear we can reach only one conclusion about him.' And then, with a nice sense of timing, said in a doom-laden voice, 'Floy will have to be got rid of.'

Prunum said hesitantly, 'Is it absolutely necessary to do that?'

'I fear it is,' said Quilp, sorrowfully.

'Well I say he goes,' put in Prismus who liked to say he had not the squeamishness of the rest. 'And the sooner the better,' he added for good measure.

Borage entered a caveat. Floy was working so hard to save them from the Chasm, he said, worried. Only look how he had thought of the shelters, and how he and his sister were to be found at the dug-outs for several hours at a stretch. 'I speak as I find,' he said, firmly.

'It's a pity you find so little, then,' said Marplot.

'But,' said Prunum, 'it isn't just a matter of Floy asking – ah – *difficult* questions about money matters, of course. It's a much greater matter than that.'

He glanced at Quilp, and Quilp, pleased to find such an ally, said, 'Precisely, my dear Prunum. I am glad to see you have such a *complete* understanding of the situation.' Prunum beamed and thought that the private arrangement between himself and Quilp and the pretty young thing who served wine in the public rooms and provided quite another entertainment in the private rooms, had not done him so badly.

Quilp said, 'As our good Prunum says, it is a much larger matter than Floy's unexpected involvement with the finances of the Council. Floy is making changes. He is already sweeping aside our rules and our laws. He's a reformist,' said Quilp. 'I've seen it from the very beginning. He's a progressivist. He'll change everything, and not for the better, mark my words. Hasn't he already begun?' demanded Quilp, bringing his clenched fist down on the table. 'Hasn't he already swept aside our laws and rescinded the taxes? He *says* it's simply until after the danger is past,' said Quilp. 'He *says* it's until it's known what kind of life we can lead. But is it just until the danger to Renascia is past? Is it just for the duration of this threat?'

He leaned forward. 'We have to ask ourselves that question, gentlemen. And if the answer to it is "no, it is not just for the duration, it is for good", then we have to ask ourselves whether Floy can be allowed to continue as Renascia's leader.' He sat back and folded his arms. 'It becomes a much larger question, a much more *basic* question than Floy simply noticing a few minor discrepancies in our books,' said Quilp, and everyone nodded in agreement, because it was one thing to remove a leader simply because he might catch you out in a smidgen of sharp practice. It was another altogether to remove that leader because he was a danger to the well-being of the people. Those of the Council who had felt a bit troubled about Quilp's suggestion, began to feel very much better.

Marplot said he had always thought that Floy and his sister were exaggerating the threat.

'Of course they're exaggerating it,' said Quilp pouncing on this as a useful point, 'of course they are. They see it as a means to bring in their own method of governing.' He leaned back in his seat, and reached for the wine glass again. 'Before we know it, they'll be transferring our leading concerns into public ownership.'

'What would that mean?' said Prunum.

'Probably that institutions such as the Moneyhouse would not be run by an individual, but by a Council composed of the people of Renascia,' said Quilp, and there was a touch of malice in his tone. 'Which would mean, my dear Marplot, that not just Floy, but every soul on Renascia would be privy to accounts and ledgers and balance sheets.'

Marplot said, 'Dear me,' and took a gulp of wortleberry wine.

'Would Floy really do that?' asked Prunum, who was making a very nice thing out of his private supper room and the young ladies who were not overly particular about whom they entertained there and how they did it. 'Would he really?'

'I happen to know that he would certainly do it,' said Quilp, who did not know any such thing, but was not going to lose any opportunity of turning the Council against Floy.

'I don't think we could allow that, you know,' said Marplot, worriedly. 'I think we would have to do something about that. It wouldn't be anything to do with Floy and the—'

'Minor discrepancies,' said Borage.

'Precisely,' said Marplot.

'Floy must be got rid of,' said Prismus. And then, 'But how could we do it?'

Quilp said, 'Floy and his sister have turned this absurd idea of the *vortex* to their advantage. Well, let us now turn it to ours.'

Marplot said, 'Excuse me, Quilp, but do you *believe* in the vortex?'

'I am prepared to admit that there may, after all, be something in the information on the Golden Tablets,' said Quilp in a dignified voice that indicated that he was of sufficiently strong character to be able to admit when he had made a misjudgment. 'And I think that we may have to endure a few hours of unpleasantness.' He made an airy gesture. 'Some strong winds, perhaps violent storms. Even one or two localised fires on the higher parts of Renascia. It will be a little disruptive, but there are the shelters,' said Quilp, and thought that he was almost managing to make it sound as if the shelters had been his sole idea. 'After a few hours – at the very most a day – we shall emerge and return to our homes.'

The others nodded, as if they, too, thought this.

'And that is my idea,' said Quilp, and looked at them all very steadily. 'Supposing, gentlemen, just supposing that Floy was not with us when we came out of the shelters?'

'How could that happen?'

'Supposing,' said Quilp, 'that Floy and his troublesome sister did not come into the shelters with us in the first place?

'Supposing we *accidentally* shut them outside.

'Just as Renascia tips towards the Black Chasm . . .'

Chapter Five

The shelters were very nearly finished. All that remained
was for the door mechanisms to be put into place so that,
when they were all safely inside, the great, solid doors that
Borage and his workmen had so precisely hewn from the
parti-coloured stone could be closed tight and sealed. An
exact fit, Borage had said, pleased. They could not afford
to have any cracks or crevices through which water might
seep. The doors would fit exactly and precisely. There
were the grilles as well; Borage had been extremely pleased
with these. They were strong, iron, shutter-like structures,
carefully angled so that when the shutters were removed,
they would give a clear view directly on to Renascia's
plains. There was a small chamber directly behind each
grille, sealed off from the main shelter, and one or two of
the men would climb into these small chambers in order
to unseal the grilles and peer out to see if all the danger had
passed.

'There's not really very much danger,' said Quilp to
everyone. 'There's hardly any more danger than when a
single meteor passes over us.' He hurried about his various
Council duties, consulting almost hourly with the other
Council members, his cloak billowing out and his hat
blown out of shape by the relentless wind, so that he took
on the appearance of a huge black crow.

'But he doesn't go out after dusk,' said Fenella,
watching from the window of Snizort's study one evening.

'Well, we don't *have* dusk any longer.'

There was no dusk, and there was scarcely any light left,
now. The whole of Renascia was becoming sucked into
the evil black and crimson night and the howling winds
were tearing across the planet almost without ceasing.

People were beginning to move slowly and to wear a

faintly puzzled air, as if they found it difficult to comprehend what was happening. They began to forget things, to lose things, to find it hard to remember names.

'It's frightening,' said Fenella, curled up in the jutting bow window, looking up at the sky, while Snizort worked anxiously at his desk, trying to record everything that was happening, because they would all like a proper chronicle of events after it was over. 'Not just the physical danger, but the things that seem to be happening inside people's minds. There's a – a slowing down.'

'Time running out and running down,' said Floy, softly.

'Everything seems to last much longer,' said Fenella.

'Quilp's lasting much longer,' said Snodgrass, crossly. 'Everywhere you look, he's there. He gets in people's way.'

He was everywhere, it seemed, and so it was no surprise when he came knocking on the door of Snizort and Snodgrass's house in company with Marplot and Prunum, later that day.

A small Council matter, he said, on being bidden to enter. Really, it was wrong of them to trouble Floy in this way, and also his sister and Snizort and Snodgrass, he said, smiling rather unctuously at Fenella, waving away Snodgrass's offer of some refreshment.

It was just that they – he and the Council – had thought that some small ceremony ought to attend the sealing of the shelters, said Quilp, smiling at Floy in a way that Floy did not altogether trust.

'An historic moment for us all,' said Quilp. 'We thought it ought to be attended by some solemnity.' And smiled again and waited.

Floy said, rather baldly, 'What had you in mind?' and thought it was exactly like Quilp, pompous old idiot, to be thinking of ceremonies and speeches when they ought to have been checking that the shelters were as water-tight as they needed to be or looking over the provisions and making sure that everyone in Renascia knew to go into the shelter later that day, which was what had been decided early that morning. We cannot leave it any longer, thought Floy, glancing through the window.

Because Time is running down, it is slipping away through a tear in the skies, like sand trickling through a man's hands, and we cannot have very much of it left now . . .

'What had you in mind, Quilp?' he said, turning back, trying not to show impatience, because whatever Quilp and the others wanted would probably not take very long and, if it pleased them all, it could not matter.

Quilp said, 'Oh, very little, really. We thought that, perhaps, we would go into the shelter in procession, you know.'

'It will enable us to keep an exact count of everyone as well,' put in Marplot.

'So it will. And if you and your sister—' Again the careful bow in Fenella's direction, 'would perhaps walk at the procession's rear, it would make it quite *ceremonious*,' said Quilp.

'And then you could be the one to actually seal the doors behind us,' added Prunum.

Floy said, 'The old Earth-tradition of the Captain being the last to leave the sinking ship?' And laughed, and said, 'I don't suppose it could hurt.'

'I think it would go down rather well with the people,' said Quilp.

'Very well.' And then, suddenly, 'But Fenella must take her place in the shelter earlier with the other ladies,' said Floy.

'Certainly not,' said Fenella at once.

'It would be rather nice,' said Quilp, 'if she walked at your side. And it would only be a few minutes behind the rest of us, of course.' He made it sound rather trivial, as if he thought Floy was making a fuss, and Floy thought: I suppose it is all right. After all, we shall all be going into the shelters together. And at least he would have Fenella with him. If she went down earlier, perhaps with the other ladies, they might become separated.

And so he said, 'Yes, very well,' and Quilp and his friends smiled all over again, and declined a second offer of refreshments, and said they would all meet up shortly.

'For the last walk through Renascia's streets,' said Quilp.

The last walk . . . It was rather frightening to be dressing for the brief journey to the shelters, but Fenella tried to think that it was a little bit exciting as well. It was difficult to believe that Renascia might be completely destroyed, that it might cease to exist, and Fenella would *not* believe it.

She pulled on dark trousers which could be tucked into the tops of boots and folded a couple of cambric shirts and some underthings into a small bag. Toothpowder? Yes, of course. And hairbrush and comb. Quilp and the Council had told people to bring just a small bag each, not to clutter the shelters with unnecessary belongings. They would frown on the boots, and they would certainly frown on the trousers, which were an old pair of Floy's, altered to fit, and which ladies did not usually wear. But trousers would be warm and sensible and Fenella was more concerned about being practical for what might be ahead of them rather than about satisfying Quilp's sartorial requirements. She would take her cloak as well, which she could put over her shoulders. There was a fur-lined hood with large deep pockets which might come in handy.

The last walk . . . It was strange and rather eerie to walk like this with Floy, down the deserted streets, with the wind buffeting wildly into their faces. Fenella thought that already the streets had an abandoned air, as if no one would ever walk along them again, as if no one would ever live in the houses . . . Stop it! she said silently. I won't think like that!

They walked through the darkness, both aware of the changing quality of the wind and aware, as well, of an immense pressure from somewhere in the skies.

Fenella said, softly, 'It is very close to us now.'

'Yes.' Floy stopped and looked into the massing blackness over their heads, his face pale in the heavy light, his eyes shadowed.

He took her arm more firmly, because the wind was

raging all about them and there was a feeling of tremendous oppressiveness. Here and there the skies were becoming streaked with crimson, great jagged streaks, as if they were wounded and bleeding. But, despite the tearing wind, the black clouds were moving slowly, as if they might be trying to resist the strong pull of something hidden over the far horizon . . .

This is quite terrible, thought Fenella, bending her head against the wind. This is the most terrible thing that could ever happen. And then, with sudden fear: And I believe we are alone in the darkness for ever . . .

With the framing of the thought, came another, not from within her mind, but from somewhere outside of it.

Yes, Mortal, you are outside now. You are outside in the howling confusion and in the raging winds and the endless night that is bearing down upon you . . .

Fenella blinked and looked round because, just for a moment, the words had seemed real and solid, as if someone, quite close by, had actually said them. But there was nothing but the night and the storm and there was no one but themselves.

It was Floy who said, 'Shouldn't we be seeing the others soon?'

'Should we?' Fenella tried to gauge how late it was. They had been careful to leave in plenty of time and Quilp had suggested that they meet in the square in front of the Round House. But it had seemed to take a very long time for the appointed hour to come round; there had been a slowness and a weary dragging out of the afternoon, so that they had both thought several times that the timepieces must have stopped, or perhaps that they had fallen asleep.

To sleep, never to wake . . . thought Fenella. Where have I heard or read or remembered that?

The Round House was in front of them now and it was deserted. There was an abandoned look about it. Could they have missed the others? Had they mistaken the time?

Floy took her arm, and said, 'I think we had better go straight to the shelters.' He had to shout, because the wind was so strong that it snatched the words away.

Fenella nodded and they began to move along the wind-ravaged street. It was difficult to walk very fast and it was disconcerting how different the houses looked now.

The light is draining from the world . . . I could wish I had never heard those words, thought Fenella, struggling to keep up with Floy, feeling the wind snatching at her cloak and trying to wrap it more tightly round her.

The light is draining, and Time is slipping through your hands, Mortals . . .

The horrid coppery taint was all round them, in their nostrils and in their mouths; it was like tasting blood, thought Fenella, feeling sick. And, from somewhere over their heads, was a rushing rhythmic sound, as if they were nearing a huge, gobbling whirlpool. It was becoming difficult to stay on their feet and, several times, Fenella would have fallen if Floy had not kept tight hold of her.

They stopped to draw breath at the intersection of two streets and stood for a moment, looking round.

'Can you see anyone?' asked Fenella, raising her voice above the buffeting wind.

'No one,' said Floy and Fenella caught an undercurrent of anger in his voice. Could Quilp somehow have tricked them? And if he had . . .

And then Floy turned, smiling, and Fenella felt a rush of relief because, of course, Quilp would not have done such a thing and, of course, it was only that they had somehow missed the procession. Perhaps, despite their care, they had simply been late.

She looked eagerly along the street, expecting to see the line of people, and then said, puzzled, 'But it's only two people. It's – oh, it's Snizort and Snodgrass!'

And although they were becoming extremely concerned at the emptiness of the streets, it was remarkably comforting to see the two brothers coming towards them down the street, puffing a bit, hung about with baskets and provisions and scarves and mufflers.

Snizort and Snodgrass were delighted to find they were not as late as they had feared. Snodgrass had been so busy in the kitchen that he had forgotten to keep an eye on the hour and Snizort had lost his turnip-faced watch anyway.

They had brought along everything they thought they might need, probably more than they needed. Snizort had packed a huge bag which looked as if it was made out of sections of carpet and which he said was called a portmanteau. He had brought paper and charcoal sticks which would be more practical than pen and ink, so that everything could be recorded as it happened, and he had added a spare pair of spectacles as well, because you never knew. Snodgrass had packed some of his ham pasties and honey bread and a tin of scones and two flagons each of Elderberry Wine and Damson Mead. It had been quite difficult to know whether this would be sufficient.

'Sufficient for a city under siege,' said Floy. 'Do hurry, both of you.' He took Fenella's arm and began to move down the street again, Snizort and Snodgrass close behind, the four of them bent almost double against the shrieking wind. Fenella's hair whipped into her face, obscuring her vision. The wind was stinging her skin and it was becoming more and more difficult to breathe.

'We must hurry!' cried Floy, and Fenella managed to nod, because they must hurry. They could see that the skies were forming a pattern above them; they were circling round and round, making a whirlpool, a maelstrom, a *vortex*.

Fenella vaguely thought that there were voices in the wind again, singing, crying voices that lived at the wind's heart and would call and beckon to you, and whisper in your ear that the world was ending, it was dying, not with a bang but with a whimper, and they were out here in the howling night and the raging confusion, and if they wanted to escape, they must listen to the voices . . .

Yes, yes, listen to us, Fenella, walk into the wind and the light, and you will surely see us . . .

Fenella stopped and looked round, puzzled, but they had stopped in the temporary shelter of a building and there was a check in the wind's force, and there was no light anywhere. Imagination, nothing more, said Fenella silently, and turned her mind to the more immediate question of where everyone was.

But it was Snodgrass, ever practical, who said, 'Floy, what has happened? Where are the rest?' and Floy frowned, the dark brows making a bar of anger. Fenella felt something cold and vicious clutch her heart.

Snizort said, almost to himself, 'I always said I wouldn't trust that Quilp from here to the end of the street,' and Snodgrass shook his head dolefully.

Floy made an abrupt gesture which took in the empty streets and the shuttered buildings and Fenella realised that he was so angry he could not speak.

'Even so,' said Snodgrass, 'even so, I think we should get on to the shelters.'

'Yes. Yes, of course we must.' Floy straightened up, and took Fenella's hand again. 'We're nearly there, in any case.'

They were nearly there, but still it seemed a long time before they reached the outskirts of Renascia and saw the sloping hillside where they had worked so hard. They could see the small, narrow entrance and the steps that wound down to them.

Fenella, standing still, fighting the wind, said, 'But – the doors are closed.'

'And sealed,' said Snodgrass, peering through the driving rain.

'Both of them?'

'Yes,' said Floy in an expressionless voice. 'Yes, both of them.' And turned to look at his three companions.

They were shut out of the shelters . . .

It was a terrible moment. Fenella stared at the others and tried to form her thoughts into order, knowing that this was the worst thing that had ever happened to any of them.

They managed to stagger back to the lee of the streets again, where the tall buildings afforded some protection from the frantic wind, but they had to fight every inch and Fenella thought the wind was increasing. The red glow was certainly stronger. How long could they stay out here?

Snodgrass said, 'Some plot of Quilp's, do you think, Floy?' and Floy said grimly, 'I do indeed.'

'But—wouldn't the others override him?' asked Fenella, unable to believe that the Renascians would have agreed to something so monstrous.

'There are two shelters,' said Floy. 'The occupants of one could have been told that we are in the other.'

'And the occupants of the other would be told we are in the first. Yes, of course.'

'Clever,' said Snizort, shaking his head. 'My word, he's clever, that Quilp.'

Fenella asked, 'Do you truly mean that he *planned* it?' And heard her voice saying the words, and did not believe she was hearing them.

'Yes. Yes, he has planned it,' said Floy, turning to stare at the blind closed doors of the shelters. 'Perhaps he planned it all along.'

'Why?'

'Well,' said Floy, 'I can't be sure, but it would be a very easy way for him to be rid of us. It would ensure that he would be the unchallenged Council head.' He looked at Fenella. 'Forgive me,' he said. 'Perhaps I was impatient and rebellious with the Council. Perhaps I tried to change too many things too quickly and this is the outcome.'

'Nonsense,' said Snodgrass at once. 'Quilp is out simply to snatch power for himself.'

'And, perhaps, to protect his furtive little money-making schemes,' said Snizort. 'You were a threat, Floy, but not in quite the way you're thinking. I never trusted him. Snodgrass, didn't I always say I never trusted him?'

'Even so,' said Floy, immensely heartened by this, 'I should have seen through his ridiculous little ploy. I should have been more wary.'

Fenella made an impatient gesture, because this was not something that mattered. What was important now was for them to find some kind of refuge until Renascia was out of danger. She did not think: if it ever is out of danger, because this was something else that must not be put into words.

'I suppose,' said Snodgrass, 'that if we shouted and banged on the doors we would not be heard?'

'No,' said Floy, at once. 'No, because one of the things we ensured was absolute sealing of both shelters.'

'Could we shout through the grilles?' asked Fenella.

'We'll certainly try,' said Floy and was moving towards the shelters at once, his face set, his eyes blazing with fury.

Fenella thought: I would not like to be Quilp when Floy finally meets up with him. *If* Floy meets up with him. But this was another thought that was dangerous, and so she concentrated on keeping up with Floy, walking between Snizort and Snodgrass, both of them trying to avoid the pouring rain that was sheeting down on them now, and the howling wind, all of them uneasily aware of the sinister dark mass over their heads.

'And there is a rushing sound now,' shouted Snizort in Fenella's ear. 'Can you hear it?'

'Yes, I've been hearing it for a while now,' rejoined Fenella. 'Isn't it just the wind?'

'I think it's more than that,' said Snizort.

The Black Chasm reaching out its greedy fingers towards them . . . The hungering monster of the skies bearing down on mankind once more, hungering for new victims . . .

I won't think that and I won't look up! thought Fenella. I won't look towards the Twilight Mountains and I won't hear. It'll just be the wind. And, in any case, Floy will make them hear us. They'll unbolt the doors and let us in and we'll be safe. It's just Quilp being malicious for a time.

Floy was ahead of them. He had reached the nearer of the shelters and he was already kneeling down to the grille. Fenella could see it quite plainly; a shuttered square, just large enough for somebody very small or very agile to slither through. Could they be heard?

Floy said, 'Shout together. All of us. As loudly as ever you can. When I signal. Ready?'

He brought his hand down and they shouted and Floy hammered on the grille with a piece of rock.

But there is no sound from inside, thought Fenella. If they hear the wind, then that is all they hear.

'Again!' cried Floy. 'They *must* hear!'

But the shelters remained locked and impassive and, at length, Floy straightened up and turned to face them, his hair whipped into a tangle about his head, his face bitter and angry.

'There is only one thing we can do,' he said and took Fenella's hands as he looked straight at the other two. 'We *have* to find shelter of some kind. We can't be far away from the Chasm now. I can *hear* it,' cried Floy.

'The houses—' began Fenella and, at once, 'No, of course not the houses.'

And then Floy looked at them suddenly, a new light in his eyes. 'Of course!' he cried, taking Fenella's arm. 'Quickly, all of us! It protected our ancestors on their journey here, and it may now protect us!

'We must go to the *Ark*!'

Chapter Six

To begin with, Fenella thought, they would never do it. The wind was relentless now, tearing down on them from every side, so that whichever way they faced they were fighting it. There was the tainted, ancient stench deep within it and, although they had all wound scarves about their faces and Fenella had drawn the strings of her hood as tight as they would go, still the stench seemed to soak into their skins, so that they thought they would never be free of it.

As they moved away from the familiar houses and streets and the two shelters where the Renascians sheltered in safety and warmth, they began to feel as if they were walking towards the heart of some giant panting monster, black and evil and menacing.

Fenella, between Snizort and Snodgrass, thought that if you half closed your eyes you could very nearly see it. Rearing and snarling, with a thick scaly hide, and a hungering black maw, ready to devour the world . . .

Floy was concentrating on reaching the *Ark* and he was forcing every ounce of his will to get Fenella and the two brothers inside it. He did not know whether it would protect them as well as the dug-outs would have protected them, but he could not think what else they could do. Perhaps they might have found shelter in the depths of the Twilight Mountains; Floy cast a glance towards the silhouettes of the Mountains directly ahead of them, limned in sharp relief against the livid skies, great towering shapes. People shunned the Mountains and whispered tales about them, but Floy knew that people had explored them at times; little parties had gone deep into the honeycomb tunnels, taking food and light.

And sometimes did not emerge, said his mind . . .

Sometimes were never seen again . . .

There was no time to consider any of it. They were at the centre of a shrieking, whirling tornado, and the entire world was being turned slowly upside down. There was no time to think, there was only time to try to reach the *Ark* that had brought their ancestors out of danger centuries earlier.

Yes, yes, mortals, out of the land of bondage and into the freedom of Infinity . . .

To their left they could see the lake churning and spiralling, great walls of foaming water rising at its centre.

'Faster!' shouted Floy, half dragging Fenella across the scree. 'The lake is rising! All of us! Quickly!'

They half ran, half fell, over the rough ground below the *Ark*, stumbling and missing their footing, helping one another as they ran. Once Fenella slipped and fell headlong but there was thick springy bracken and she was only winded.

'Not hurt,' she gasped, as they helped her up. 'Not – looking – where – I – was – going —— Hurry—'

It was like being chased by some huge, ravening beast now. The sound and the wind and the steady rhythmic pulsating of the skies was engulfing them and, within the wind, was a great roaring sound.

And the Black Chasm, the monster of infinity is almost upon us, it is rushing down on us, ravening and slavering for prey . . . A predator, a giant snare, a trap opening its jaws ready to bring its teeth slashing down on Mankind . . .

Ahead of them was the sleek shape of the *Ark*, the strange, carefully preserved craft that had come from Earth, that had somehow been sent through the skies, thousands of miles, until it had come to rest on Renascia. It should be safe, thought Fenella, her heart pounding, her lungs ready to burst. It *must* be safe.

She summoned her last reserves and together they ran across the last stretch of ground. Snizort and Snodgrass were still with them; Snizort was puffing and Snodgrass was perspiring and they had certainly fallen back.

But they are with us, thought Fenella, with sudden

gladness. Somehow they have kept up and they are with us.

As if Floy had caught her thought, he stopped, his arm still about her, and they waited for the two brothers, who came trotting and gasping up to them.

Snizort said, 'Bless my boots, I'm getting a bit old for this sort of thing.'

Snodgrass had managed to keep the supplies slung about his shoulder, which had pleased them both.

'Inside,' said Floy, with a worried look at the sky. 'Quickly!'

Time is slowing, and when the last grains have trickled out, it will turn back on itself, and what then, mortals, what then . . .?

Floy was standing at Fenella's side, tugging at the fastening to the small door that was set into the *Ark*'s side. There was a moment, heart-stopping, breathtaking, when they feared it would not open, and Fenella felt a spiral of panic. And then Floy's hands pushed again and the door fell open and they were entering the strange empty craft that had come from the dying world, Earth. It was larger inside than they had expected and there was a strange, cold, sharp scent.

'It's like the cabin of a ship,' said Floy, looking about him.

'There's plenty of room for us all,' said Snodgrass, putting down his haversack. 'Bless my soul, this is a remarkable thing.'

The inside of the long-ago Earth-settlers' *Ark* was lined with the pale, hard substance that the Renascians had never been able to reproduce or, indeed, identify. It was narrower than they had thought from outside, but it was long, and there were several odd-looking seats, curved to fit the body. To the left of the small door were rows upon rows of bewildering squares, all containing numbers and charts and patterns of various colours.

At the centre was a column, the thickness of a man's waist, with more of the enclosed charts and what seemed to be dozens of switches and handles. To their right was a further small door, partly open, through which they could see more of the same seats and what looked a bit like storage units or cupboards of some kind.

But they were inside, and the raging storm was outside and, for the moment, there was stability and some kind of shelter.

They reached the seats and fell into them thankfully. Straps protruded from the sides, a little like belts, but made of some pale, pliable substance.

Floy at once reached for the fastenings and the others did the same.

'Not rusty in the least,' muttered Snizort. 'My word, they knew how to make things, our ancestors.'

The straps were not rusty, but they were cold to the touch, and they were difficult to clip into place. They stretched across the front of the chairs, holding the wearer firmly in place, and Fenella could not decide if this was worrying or comforting. Had the people who built this craft expected it to be so buffeted and so flung about that they knew they must be tied down to escape injury? It was something else not to explore too deeply, and Fenella thought they should just be glad to have such security. And it was quite a safe feeling to be anchored like this. If the *Ark* was turned upside down and thrown backwards and forwards by whatever was ahead of them, at least they would not be dashed against its cold, unyielding sides.

The *Ark* had tiny circular windows, not made of glass as they were used to, but of something very slightly soft and immensely thick. Fenella peered through and thought that they gave a distorted view of what was outside. Then she wondered if it was not the glasslike substance that was distorted, but the outside itself.

It was just possible to make out the dark, swirling clouds and the livid crimson streaks across the sky, and the rather terrible *structuring* of the skies, as if they were massing together for some grisly purpose.

'But we can no longer hear any of it,' said Fenella, staring out. 'We can no longer hear it and we can no longer feel it, either.' Fenella felt her spirits rising. Of course they

would come through, and of course Renascia would not
be destroyed.

*But it is coming nearer, Mortal, it is coming nearer
with every second . . .*

There was the sudden feeling that whatever was over
their heads was swooping down on them and the feeling
of being poised on the edge of a precipice. Floy and
Snodgrass moved to seats and, as they did so, they felt the
Ark shudder with the force of the buffeting winds.

Fenella thought, It is moving. I believe the *Ark* is
moving. And waited, torn between fear and excitement,
because this, surely, was the most immense thing that had
ever happened and, surely, like this they must be safe.

And we shall *see*! she thought suddenly. Whatever is
happening, we shall be able to see it!

And then, without the least warning, the storm ceased,
and there was the sudden, silent feeling of a dark, thick
cloak falling, and the sensation of weightlessness. Fenella
thought the *Ark* moved again, and then was not sure.

It's so quiet, thought Fenella, staring at the others. I
never imagined such quiet and such peace.

Floy, seated close to Fenella, felt the peace and the
sudden immense stillness at the same moment, and cold
dread closed about his heart for he guessed the sudden,
overpowering silence to be the silence of airlessness, and
he thought: Renascia has been plucked from its carapace
of air and sent spinning and tumbling through the skies.
Somehow it has fallen out of its safe cocoon. We can no
longer feel it, but we are hurtling towards something
tremendous, something that will very probably shatter us
for ever. Down into the depths of the Black Chasm? Yes,
probably.

Floy glanced quickly round the *Ark*'s interior and
knew a brief comfort, because the Earth-people must
surely have known about the airlessness of the skies and
they would certainly have somehow rendered the *Ark* safe
against such a danger. But we can't exist without air
for very long, thought Floy, his eyes raking the incomprehensible oblongs of maps and figures and handles

to their left. There will be air in here for a time, but it will soon become stale and unbreathable. He thought there must be machinery in here to combat the airlessness, but it would long since have fallen into disuse and, in any case, they had no way of knowing how to use it. I cannot think what we can do! he cried in silent agonised frustration. I believe the means to help us to be here in this strange craft, but I have not the knowledge!

And then the velvety blackness was split by blinding white light, veined with glittering orange and red fire. Great dust storms whirled before their eyes, dancing and beckoning, grotesque fantastical shapes that reared up and became grinning, threatening monsters, holding out impossible elongated hands, beckoning, reaching for them . . .

Floy, staring, unsure whether his eyes were playing tricks, thought: I believe there must be air again! Those dust storms could not have been raised without air of some kind! Perhaps they had fallen into a pocket of air. I don't know if I believe in strange, within-the-shadows creatures, he thought, but I do believe in dust and in storms. I do believe in swirling clouds and winds.

There was a rushing sound as well, now, and Floy experienced a quick, deep thankfulness, for where there is sound there must certainly be air. But even as the thoughts were forming in his mind, there was a violent wrenching movement and they felt the *Ark* turn completely upside-down and hurtle down and down, twisting and spiralling as it went, faster than anything they had ever known, so that they were gasping and clutching the sides of their seats for safety. Light split the darkness once more, racing past them, blinding, dazzling, white-hot and streaked with fire like blood against a pale skin . . .

Fenella saw a rushing, swirling curtain of gold and brilliance, a maelstrom of fire and light, with glittering shapes deep within it and they felt the swirl of the fire billow out and engulf the *Ark*. There was the sensation of being torn out of the ground and scooped up into the skies and the blackness was somehow behind them, as if they were shaking it from them like liquid. Rivulets of colour and light came rushing out to surround them and they felt the *Ark* lifted bodily, not harshly but gently and firmly, and carried forward.

The light changed. It became tinged with pure, molten gold and there were eyes in the fire now, strange wise ancient eyes, as if there might be beasts who lived in the fire and who were not Human, who might well be dangerous, but who were certainly taking them forward, out of the black tunnel, on and on through the golden river of fire . . .

Floy shouted, 'Keep tight hold, all of you! Is everyone all right?'

'Yes!' cried Fenella. 'What's happening?'

'I haven't the least idea!' cried Floy, and the others caught the wild delight in his voice as he turned to look at them.

'We're moving again!' cried Snizort. 'Aren't we?'

'Yes! Hold tight!'

They were moving, swiftly and smoothly now, going down and down and round and round . . . Into the depths of the whirlpool, thought Fenella, torn between terror and excitement. Into the heart of the Black Chasm and probably, certainly, we shall never come out again . . .

But there are eyes in the fire, thought Fenella, staring through the tiny windows, unable to look away. There are slanting golden eyes, neither Human nor animal, and just beyond the light I can make out strange, silken creatures composed of the fire and the light, eerily beautiful, but somehow friendly.

The *Ark* was gathering momentum. They were going faster and faster and, at any minute, they would surely plunge straight to the Chasm's core where they would be dashed to their deaths against its black heart . . .

But it was possible to see more clearly through the tiny windows, now; it was possible to see that they were travelling along some kind of wide, high, rock tunnel, inside a surging golden River.

Fenella thought: A golden pouring River, tumbling down and down inside a tunnel . . . I think we may be about to die, she thought, fearful and entranced. But I think this is the most exciting thing yet.

And then there was a jolt and a tumbling sensation and a burst of light and the *Ark* came to rest, quite gently, in a vast cave, filled with the soft pouring light.

They sat very still, not daring to move, hardly daring to speak, each of them thinking: are we safe? Has it stopped?

Floy, peering through the windows, saw that the strange golden river was still flowing past them, but shallowly now, so that the *Ark* was only several inches deep in it. It was rather as if they had come to rest on the shores of some kind of sea or the banks of a deep, wide river. Thin light cascaded over the walls and ran along the sides of the cave, spilling over the edges of some kind of cliff. The whole cavern was soaked in soft, prismatic light that rippled gently, like water-light in an under-sea cave, but stronger, more glowing, streaked with flame and gold. Here and there, they could see clusters of hard brilliance embedded into the cave walls and, at intervals, were deep alcoves, niches cut into the rock, each one bearing a strangely wrought flambeau, from which glowed spiralling flames.

The light was pouring from the *Ark*'s sides, as if it was rainwater running off it, and Fenella could see the tiny glinting droplets on the windows.

It was Floy who moved first, unclipping the stout fastenings that had held them safely in the curved seats. He stood up, flexing his cramped muscles, and eyed them all.

'Well, my friends? Nothing broken? Nothing damaged?'

'I don't think so,' said Fenella, cautiously, and looked at Snizort and Snodgrass, both of whom beamed and said they were *quite* all right, aside from being a bit jolted. Snodgrass thought the contents of the portmanteau might be a bit tumbled, but other than that they were unhurt.

'And I do think,' said Snizort, 'that we ought to explore outside.'

Floy said, 'Of course we are going to explore outside. Aren't we?'

'I don't think,' said Fenella, moving warily from the seat and finding that, apart from a bruise or two, she was perfectly all right, 'I don't think, you know, that this is anywhere on Renascia.'

'No,' said Floy, and they could hear the rising excitement in his voice. 'No, it isn't Renascia.' He looked at them again with the glinting delight and Fenella caught his mood and knew that, although they might be in the most dreadful danger, this was the most exciting thing any of them had ever known. It suddenly seemed entirely and completely right to be here like this, with Floy and the brothers, somewhere in this strange place that might be anywhere at all, and which was certainly not like anything they had ever seen before.

And then Floy moved to the small door in the *Ark*'s side and reached for the bolts and the wheels that had sealed it closed.

'Ready?' he said, and spun the wheels.

They were standing quite close to the edge of the cliff and the golden flames were still pouring down the rocks and into the deep chasm. From where they stood they could just see that, far below them, was indeed a river, a great, surging fast-flowing torrent, sweeping its mighty way through the deep chasm.

But it is a river of pure fire, thought Fenella in delight. A River of Fire and Light . . .

It was a surging, pouring mass of licking, rearing flames, of hissing, molten gold that glinted and rippled and sent out a sweet, warm scent. Floy, who was nearest to the edge, stared down into the fiery depths and knew a brief, rather terrible, compulsion to plunge into the great fast-flowing fire. What it would be like to bathe in the flames, to feel them caress your skin and engulf your body . . .? Would it be marvellous or would it be

71

unbearable? Would you die instantly or become immortal?

Fenella, who was as much fascinated by the thin light cascading over the cavern walls as by the great river, was thinking that standing here was rather like being inside a fiery waterfall, and then that it was like standing beneath a gentle torrent of warm, soft rain, only that neither of these seemed quite right. Perhaps it was more like standing near a thin curtain that was made not from silk or cotton, or even beads, but of pure rippling flames that would not burn you but that might, perhaps, do other things to you . . .

And then a voice, quite close by, said, 'The Eternal Fire will not burn you, but you should certainly not go into it without the proper preparation.'

They turned at once, sharply and swiftly, and saw, quite clearly, the figure of a slender, fire-washed young man seated on a rock, his eyes upon them.

It was another of those heart-stopping, breath-squeezing moments. For a moment no one spoke and then Fenella found herself moving forward.

'The Fire will not burn you,' said the young man again, and there was a sudden glint of gentle irony. 'But to bathe there unwisely may cause you to lose your souls and render them ineligible for entry to whatever Heaven you may believe in.' He regarded them thoughtfully with glowing narrow eyes, set slantwise in delicately boned features. He was slender and silky and the light fell all about him, so that he seemed to be not altogether flesh and blood, but somehow composed of the fire and the light and the fast-moving river.

And his hair is not hair, but molten gold, thought Fenella, fascinated and entranced, and just a bit frightened as well.

Floy said, cautiously, 'Will you tell us where we are?' and the figure appeared to consider this carefully.

'In general, you are in the Fire Country that is my domain,' he said. 'I may allow you to penetrate to the inner halls of my country and, then again, I may not. It remains to be seen. Below us is the Fire River, which flows nine times round my country, and which is thought by many to bestow the gift of immortality on those who are brave enough to venture into it.'

'Does it?' said Floy.

'I have no idea,' said the young man, unfolding himself from the rocky ledge. 'Since I am not mortal, it does not have any effect on me.' He regarded them thoughtfully. 'Tell me,' he said, apparently studying them with interest, 'tell me, Humans, did you lose your way?'

There was a rather disconcerted silence, because nobody quite knew how to answer this.

Floy said, 'We thought to escape—' and stopped.

But again, the young man divined their thoughts. 'From the Angry Sun?' he said, and smiled, and Fenella caught her breath, because it was a smile of such brilliance and such pure and undiluted mischief that it seemed to reach out and embrace them.

Floy said, 'It wasn't a Sun at all—' And stopped, and again the young man seemed to understand.

'The Dark Lodestar,' he said, softly. 'But it *is* a Sun, Mortals. For all its boiling darkness, and for all its black allure, it was once a Sun, and will be so again. And there are many worlds who see its other side, who glimpse its glowing inner self blazing in their skies. In that incarnation it is often regarded as a portent for good. But for you it showed its dark other self and perhaps it sucked your world into its core.' He looked at them, his head on one side, and appeared to wait for them to speak.

Fenella said, '*Have* we escaped it?'

'It is possible,' said the young man, thoughtfully. 'Yes, it is quite possible. I have sometimes met other travellers who have fled from the Angry Sun and tumbled into the Time Corridor and lost their way. For within the vortex of the Black Lodestar, Time ceases to exist and worlds may converge. But I do not make a habit of rescuing people who have become lost, you understand.' He said this as if it was the most natural thing in the world, and Floy, staring, said, 'Well, of course not.'

'However, occasionally it is necessary.' He inspected them. 'To blunder about in the Time Corridor is dangerous and unwise. But perhaps your Chariot lost its way?' He did not say any of this as if he was being reproachful, or even as if he was questioning their right to be in his domain, or even as if he thought them inefficient to be lost at all. He simply said it as one interested in a perfectly possible occurrence.

'We didn't actually intend to travel anywhere at all,' said Floy.

'We were sheltering,' said Fenella, and the young man regarded her with amusement.

'I see,' he said, and moved towards them, walking rather fastidiously like a cat. They saw that his skin was the colour of pale amber and his eyes were like topazes. He was rather slight and certainly slender, but the four travellers would not have dreamed, even for a second, of believing him weak or fragile.

'I am neither,' he said, at once, sounding amused. 'If you spring an attack on me, I shall fell you in an instant. If you try to cheat me, I shall know and treat you suitably. And if,' he said, his eyes suddenly glowing and dangerous, 'if you lie to me, you will regret it through many lives.'

Snizort, who had been at the back, said, 'I think we ought to introduce ourselves, don't you? It's only polite. And we *are* trespassing, after all. It's his country. He said so.'

'We're from Renascia,' began Snodgrass firmly, as if this explained everything, and the young man inclined his head gravely, as if, thought Fenella, he knew all about Renascia.

That, and many things besides, Human . . .

Floy put out a hand to draw Fenella forward. He introduced her and then Snodgrass and Snizort, with himself last.

The slender young man listened gravely and repeated their names politely. He nodded with complete courtesy. 'You are well come,' he said, and waited for more.

'Well,' said Floy, 'we should perhaps explain why we

74

are here—' And stopped, because they were not really sure why they were here, or how they had got here, or even where 'here' was.

But the young man was smiling, as if he understood them perfectly easily.

'You are not the first Humans to become lost in this way,' he said. 'There have been others before you and there will certainly be others after you. There will be many of your race who will be brought to me, for the salamanders are ever watchful for those who fall into the Angry Sun's depths. Perhaps you encountered them?'

'Golden-eyed beings in the Fire?' asked Fenella, hopefully, and the young man smiled at her again, as if he rather liked her.

But he only said, 'The salamanders are, in sort, guardians of the Time Corridor. And they carry with them their own fire.'

'You said we had come through a Time Corridor,' said Floy, not quite sure of his ground.

'Certainly you have, just as many of your ancestors, the Earth-people did.' He smiled. 'And since Time is now so old, the fabric has become a little frayed here and there. There are tears in Time, mortals, just as there are tears in silk or hide.' He regarded him with his head on one side.

'Yes. I see,' said Floy, carefully, and the young man laughed.

'It is the truth, Mortal. And many of your ancestors have known of it. Many of them have tried to penetrate the Time Corridor and journey through the Curtain. A few have succeeded, but most have not. Most were taken and devoured and their souls held captive in the River of the Dead. That is why the salamanders patrol the Corridor, to help the lost ones.

'There are greedy beings abroad, Humans. Life is not all like your pleasant, untroubled existence on your small friendly Renascia. There are creatures who prowl the worlds searching for prey. There are Lords of the Dark Realm who would seek out your soul and devour it.'

He studied them again, as if, thought Fenella, he was

learning them. And because she wanted to hear him speak again, she said, 'Would you tell us who you are, please?'

There was a pause, as if he was considering this. Then, 'I am Fael-Inis,' he said. 'And in this world I am known as the rider of the salamanders, the being who can cross time, who can call up the Time Fire.' He smiled and again it was the tip-tilted mischievous smile. 'They will tell you – those ones who believe they understand such things – that I am the rebel of the seraphic hierarchy,' said Fael-Inis.

Snizort drew in his breath and said, in what was not quite a whisper, 'Fael-Inis, the Rebel Angel. Dear me, that's a *very* old legend.'

'I am not quite on the side of either heaven or hell, you know,' said Fael-Inis, and the golden eyes were thoughtful. 'That was never proven. So you should beware of me.' And then, 'But I think these are unfamiliar concepts to you?'

'Well, yes,' said Floy.

'Early Earth myths,' said Snizort knowledgeably.

'Myths, are they?' said Fael-Inis, moving so close that they could see the light that seemed constantly to irradiate from him. 'Are you so sure?' he said softly, and Fenella shivered because, just for a moment, the idea of heaven and hell, strange beyond-the-skies dwellings where you might go after you were dead, and where you might fare extremely well, or rather dreadfully, seemed strongly and sinisterly close.

'But,' said Fael-Inis, with one of his sudden switches of mood, 'you are guests to this world and let us say I am your host.' He held out his hands to them. 'Come with me,' he said. 'I am not really safe to know, but I can be extremely well mannered if I choose. And for the moment, I do choose it.' He grinned. 'And to those who trust me, I can be a strong friend. For now, you will be tired and hungry after your journey and, although my manners are strange,' he said, 'my hospitality is not.'

Snodgrass, who enjoyed his food, remarked in an aside to Snizort that, whatever else you might say, you had to admit that they were not faring so badly thus far. 'We'd be grateful for a bite of food, sir,' he said.

Fael-Inis studied them again and smiled. 'Then come with me to my Palace of Wildfire,' he said, softly. 'Where the Time Fires warm every chamber and where the River of Time flows nine times nine about the walls.' He sent them the sudden, mischievous grin. 'In any case,' he said, 'it is certain that when the salamanders rescued you, their light was seen in the skies. It is possible, even, that the dazzling underside of the Black Lodestar was seen, also. Already, there may be hunting parties out scavenging for you.'

'Hunting?' said Snodgrass, suspiciously.

'Scavenging?' said Floy, and Fael-Inis turned to regard them.

'Certainly,' he said, and now there was amusement in his voice. 'Have you never heard of creatures who hunt Men for sport . . .? You have travelled through the Time Curtain and you were rescued by the salamanders. To do so, they would have sent their brilliance and their fire blazing across the skies. Your arrival will already be known. It is certain you will meet the creatures who hunt Men.' And then, turning away, 'Come with me, Mortals,' he said.

Chapter Seven

The Giants of Gruagach had been very interested indeed in the news that the brilliant fire of the Angry Sun had been seen again in the skies.

As Inchbad, who was the Gruagach King, said, the Angry Sun nearly always meant Humans, and Humans were something the Gruagach Giants were very interested in indeed.

The appearance of the Angry Sun was not something that happened very often. Inchbad thought it had not happened for at least a century, but Goibniu, who was Inchbad's Chancellor, said, 'Oh no, Your Majesty, it was *far* longer than that.'

It did not really matter how long it had been since the Sun, which some people in Ireland called the *Feargach Grian*, had been seen; the Giants would send out search parties instantly, so that any stray Humans could be captured and brought back and roasted in the *Fidchell*. They had not celebrated the *Fidchell* for many a long night, said Goibniu, pleased.

And who was to know but that the *Feargach Grian* might not be here to mark the arrival of the new Golden Age for Ireland, said Goibniu, in his usual unctuous fashion. The legends all told how it frequently heralded the birth of great and talented leaders, or the rising of brilliant rulers. And since they had left Gruagach and driven out the High King of Tara and taken up residence in the great Palace of Tara, Ireland had been ruled better and more strongly, said Goibniu. Certainly it had been ruled in accordance with the Gruagach's ways.

He did not, naturally, refer to the fact that the Gruagach had actually been more or less driven out of their city by the terrible Frost Giants, because this would have been very tactless, and might have suggested to some of the younger giants that the Gruagach could not defend their own city. He merely reminded everyone of how the Gruagach (under Goibniu's direction, of course) had stormed Ireland and driven out the High King and taken up residence in the legendary Bright Palace with no more ado than the squashing of a recalcitrant Human.

This was the sort of thing that Inchbad liked to hear, because when the idea of storming Tara and taking over the Ireland of the Humans had first been put to him by Goibniu and some of the others, he had been doubtful. He remembered that he had questioned whether they really wanted a Human stronghold and a Human land to rule; they all of them knew how sly and subtle and cunning Humans could be, he had said; had they all forgotten the dozens of stories, well hundreds really, of how their ancestors had been outwitted by Humans? Beanstalks and seven league boots, said Inchbad darkly, and had to be talked to for a very long time before he had agreed to it. But of course, something had had to be done, because Gruagach was in the hands of the terrible Frost Giants and their leader, the evil and dread *Geimhreadh* was already building herself a Court in Inchbad's own state rooms and spinning her wicked, cold magic. It was extremely humiliating to be defeated by a giantess, never mind how old and how powerful she might be and how long she might have led the Frost Giants. Inchbad was not going to let people think he had been bested by a giantess, not if he had to turn Ireland upside-down and topple any number of High Kings.

They had put about really a rather good story. Gruagach in ruins, they had said, solemnly and sadly. The entire City crumbling into the most dreadful disrepair; Inchbad's own castle actually with a leaking roof, and you could not get the drains cleaned out for an emperor's ransom. It had worked very nicely. Inchbad had to admit that it had worked well, because here they were, safely inside Tara, which they were all finding very comfortable indeed, and the High King and his sons hardly more than a memory.

Inchbad began to think that, after all, it had all been worthwhile. And of course, in the end, it had been much easier than any of them had thought. That had been Goibniu's doing – Inchbad would admit that freely. Goibniu had fallen into discussion with a very clever Human (well, part Human) called the Robemaker, who seemed to know all about the Frost Giants and the *Geimhreadh*, and who had been the greatest help imaginable. Inchbad suspected the Robemaker of actually being a sorcerer, if not a necromancer, and he had been a bit dubious, because they all knew where trafficking with necromancers led. But Goibniu had said no, the Robemaker was simply a nice old gentleman who had dabbled a little in the old pure magic of Ireland and been able to weave the good and gentle enchantment which had rendered the entire Gruagach party invisible and inaudible until they were inside Tara.

Inchbad had said, 'Oh, I see,' and thought that, after all, perhaps it had been all right. And, after all, here they all were, inside Tara, inside the Bright Palace of legend, the glittering Shining City where every High King of Ireland had dwelled, and the Angry Sun had already appeared in the skies which people would see as a sign, and the Gruagach were ruling Ireland, and so far no Humans had even challenged them, never mind outwitted them. Probably no Humans would even dare approach the Western Gate.

It was over the Western Gate that the *Feargach Grian* had been seen. The doorkeeper had seen lights in the sky, over to the east just before supper, and come running to tell everyone about it. A sign, he said solemnly, his huge stupid face awed; surely a sign that something very momentous indeed was about to happen. Wouldn't they all come along to see?

They went along that very minute, or at least quite soon afterwards, because you could not always just stop what you were doing, and several people had been in the stool room, because the kitchens had served onion broth for noon-day dinner, and it had been a bit strong. But they

80

all went along to the topmost turret because, as Inchbad pointed out, you should not miss seeing things which might herald the arrival of a few Humans, never mind it being probably historic and very likely portentous as well. He was rather pleased to be able to use a word like portentous, which was not the sort of word he would normally have known about, only that Goibniu had explained it to him.

And off they all went with a lot of shouting and pounding along the halls (which made the crystal windows rattle something terrible) and cries of 'Last one up the stairs is a cod's head', and 'What about a game of Catch the Mutton Bone on the battlements', and 'While we're about it, let's de-bag the doorkeeper'.

The doorkeeper paid this no heed, because he was used to the ways of Inchbad's Court. He unlocked all the doors and took them up to the northern turret, which made one or two of them glance over their shoulders, because of it having once been the favourite haunt of the previous High Kings. Inchbad had once seen (or thought he had seen) the ghost of the long-ago Cormac of the Wolves who, some people said, had been the greatest King Ireland had ever known. But since Inchbad was apt to be short-sighted and had, as well, drunk rather a lot of mulled wine at supper that night, nobody had ever given much credence to the story, except for Inchbad himself, who still repeated it at intervals.

But although they looked very hard and stood on the turret for quite a long time, nobody actually saw the Angry Sun. Goibniu said he thought he could just see a faint glimmer of light to the east – 'A new bright star in the firmament, sire,' he said, and Inchbad was pleased, because it would be a very good thing if people remembered him as the King during whose reign a new bright star appeared. It would probably stop them spreading wicked stories about giants, and telling one another how they all supped on Manpies and fattened up innocent children for the ritual of the *Fidchell*.

Inchbad would admit to having had just a taste of

Manpie now and again, and he would admit, as well, that this was usually after they had celebrated the *Fidchell*, which was all quite in accordance with Gruagach custom. Frizzle his Boots, said Inchbad crossly, what else were Humans for!

Anyway, although he had not himself seen the Angry Sun, it was quite likely that it was only that he had arrived at the tower too late. Goibniu had certainly seen it, and the doorkeeper had seen it as well, and this would suffice.

He said they would have to hold a feast to celebrate the new star that had appeared, and thought to himself that probably there was some kind of ritual that ought to be observed. Goibniu would know what to do. Probably there could be a huger than usual supper, with more than normal mulled wine. Caspar, who was the Court pimp, would be told to get up a search party to go out after the trail of the *Feargach Grian* and capture any Humans who might have been about. Perhaps he might supply a few village maidens as well, for a bit of a side-celebration, because he did not seem to do very much else these days and it was time he earned his keep. They might call in the Gnomes of Gallan to perform a few dances, as well. Say what you liked, there was no one the length and breadth of Ireland who could dance a jig as well as the Gnomes. On one or two occasions, Inchbad had allowed the Court sorcerers to call up a handful of demons, but demons were unruly and extremely vulgar as well, and their idea of a jig was not Inchbad's. The Gnomes would be much better – and besides, Inchbad had a commission for them.

Inchbad was quite light-hearted at supper and listened to Goibniu telling about how the new star heralded a new Golden Reign for Ireland, and how it would all be attributed to the Gruagach in general and Inchbad in particular, and how they might even create a new tax to mark the occasion. Several of the younger giants looked rather mutinous at this and Inchbad's heart sank, because a mutiny in the ranks was something they could not really afford to have. Also, he knew very well that Goibniu always sent traitors and mutineers to the Robemaker. Inchbad pretended not to know what use the Robemaker made of the offerings sent to him by Goibniu, but of course he did know, because everyone in Ireland knew, and it was not a very nice fate, even for a traitor.

But then somebody began to sing a ballad all about how the brightness of the star reflected the brightness of the Gruagach King, and the younger giants nodded and told one another that, after all, the Irish were not the only ones who could write a merry tune. Inchbad was relieved and prepared to sit down to the huger than usual supper and the more generous than normal mulled wine. He pretended not to notice that Goibniu, who had a taste for Humans, and whose appetites were nearly always aroused by mulled wine, had already sent one of the footmen out for Caspar, who was the Court pimp.

Acting as pimp to the Gruagach was no picnic. It was, in fact, a particularly thankless sort of job. Caspar sat in his bed-chamber, and pretended not to hear the feasting and the shouting and felt glum and wished he had never heard of the Gruagach. He wished he had never seen Tara, and wished that Inchbad had never been thrown out of Gruagach by the *Geimhreadh* and her creatures, and wished he had never heard of the *Geimhreadh* either. His bed-chamber was splendid, like everything else inside Tara, but if you wanted the honest truth, Caspar would have been happier in a crofter's cottage with a sod floor and a dinner of herbs. He would have been happier as a tinker with a donkey and cart. If it came down to it, he would probably have been happier as the donkey.

Nobody had expected the Gruagach to attack Tara, because it was not the sort of thing that the Gruagach had ever done. People said, darkly, that they had been egged on to it (the Robemaker was a strong suspect for this), and that they were being used as pawns and puppets and straw leaders.

None of this made the Gruagach any easier to put up with. Caspar did not like giants, even when they had a dash of Human blood for leaven, and he was not going to change the opinion of a lifetime just because the Gruagach were housing him and feeding him and being jolly to him. He was, of course, very pleased to be housed in luxury inside Tara (a south-facing bed-chamber it was, which caught the evening sun nicely), and it had to be said that the food that came to the massive carved banqueting table every evening and every noon was extremely good, not to say plentiful (giants were nearly always greedy). The jollity was sometimes a bit exhausting, because the Gruagach's notion of what was funny was not always Caspar's. This was something that had to be endured, however, if you liked south-facing bed-chambers and laden supper tables.

But say what you liked about all creatures being the same under the skin, giants were *different*. They were not Human, and all the pretending, and all the dressing up in Human clothes and pretending to follow Human ways did not make them Human. Facts had to be faced – and the fact was that the Gruagach were giants.

And it was all very well for the ordinary Human people down in the village to smile slyly and nudge one another, and say that, to be sure, hadn't Caspar the fine old job of work up at the Shining Citadel, never mind that it was the giants he served, and wouldn't it do your heart good to know that your only task was to go off out hunting for comely girls to bring up to the castle?

It was not a fine job of work at all, and it did Caspar's heart not the least bit of good. In fact, it frequently gave him indigestion and if anyone thought it was an easy life, all Caspar could say was they were all welcome to it.

It all came of the Gruagach being giants. Caspar had coped quite easily with the ordinary, everyday Court which had been sensible and normal and what they were all used to. He had quite enjoyed being a part of all that, seeking out young girls for whoever commissioned his services, occasionally sampling the wares for himself on the side, because it was a sorry old world if you could not take a perquisite for yourself now and then. Caspar was not over and above partial to that sort of thing really, but you had to conform.

The Gruagach were trying to conform now. That was mostly the trouble. They thought they ought to be bawdy and rollicking, and they thought they ought to bed everything that was beddable – which meant a great deal of extra work for Caspar because, as everyone knew, giants were lazy and would not be going off out to look for suitable bed partners for themselves. And if anyone thought it was easy to find females who were willing to go to bed with a giant who were pretty enough to satisfy the Gruagach as well, then all Caspar could say was just let them try it.

Human females were apt to be extremely apprehensive about getting into bed with a giant and, when you thought about it, you couldn't blame them. Caspar was always careful to explain to likely candidates that, in fact, giants were possessed of unusually small penises and that they were very quickly satisfied (in fact the King nearly always nodded off halfway through), but Caspar was not always believed. It made life very difficult.

He was not especially pleased when the summons came for him to go down to the Sun Chamber, because he knew that this meant that the giants were bored, or perhaps they had decided to celebrate something or other, and they would want Caspar to be bringing up a prisoner or two, and they would probably want him to help them devise some kind of entertainment for the evening. It was a sorry old life at Tara these days and, as Caspar donned a fur-trimmed robe (because the Sun Chamber was apt to be a bit cold at times), and combed his hair into neatness, he thought it was to be hoped that the giants were not planning on celebrating the *Fidchell*. Caspar was no more and no less squeamish than the next man, but the *Fidchell* was the grisliest ritual he had ever come across.

In the great Sun Chamber, Goibniu was setting out the floor for the celebrating of the *Fidchell* and the others were cheering and beginning to lay bets, because it was quite

85

some time since the *Fidchell* had been celebrated. They had celebrated it quite often at Gruagach of course, where there was never any interference and where there would usually be a few Human travellers who had lost their way or were on an adventure, or a quest.

It had all been easy and friendly, because everyone who had approached Gruagach and requested a night's shelter could be assumed to know the dangers. Humans who walked up to a giants' Castle and demanded admittance could be regarded as fair game, said Goibniu, and they had all agreed. But here, at Tara, they were in the Humans' own land and they had to be a bit cautious. Also, you could not go rampaging down into the villages and the towns and just pluck up as many Humans as you felt like, because you would soon find yourselves without any Humans left.

They could all see this quite well, but for tonight, with the Angry Sun rampaging about the skies and surely carrying Humans with it, they could permit themselves a little indulgence. As Goibniu said, with one of his belly-shaking laughs, it was a very long time indeed since they had made the Humans jump and scurry and it was even longer since they had sampled Manpie afterwards. If Caspar had a few Humans in readiness, they might as well have a bit of a taster, said Goibniu.

'What has he in the cages at present?' asked Inchbad, and the younger giants looked about them greedily, because everyone knew that Caspar was under orders to keep a nice little supply of Humans in the dungeons. You never knew when you might be wanting a Human for a bit of entertainment. Some of the very young giants hoped they would be allowed to stay up late, because they had never actually seen the *Fidchell* performed and they had certainly not tasted Manpie.

'An elegant taste,' said Goibniu, who believed in keeping to the old ways. And then, 'Although of course, it depends on the particular Human. They *will* gorge themselves on roast boar and too much poteen, and it makes them *fat*.' He looked round, and said, rather more sternly, 'And *where* is Caspar?'

But Caspar had arrived by now and was crossing the floor, looking rather small and insignificant compared with the Gruagach. He furrowed his brow on being questioned and said he thought they had a couple of poachers and maybe a tinker or two in the dungeons, and if their honours would allow him a few minutes – well, perhaps quarter of an hour, he would have them all up inside the Sun Chamber ready for the *Fidchell*.

'But,' said Goibniu, leaning down and thrusting his large brutish face closer to Caspar than Caspar cared for, 'but, Master Procurer, there is to be *no* escape for the prisoners, contrived or otherwise. Or we shall make you squeal in the *Fidchell* yourself.'

'Let them escape? My word, I should think not indeed,' said Caspar, shocked to his toes at the very idea. 'Bless us all, what would things be coming to if we allowed Humans to escape when your honours were wanting a play at the *Fidchell*.'

'That's better,' said Goibniu, straightening up, and smiling in a way Caspar did not like. 'And after you have *supplied* us, Master Procurer, you had better be off to find the *Feargach Grian*.' He grinned again, because wasn't there something especially comical about sending a Human to trap one of its own kind.

Caspar muttered an assent and took himself off to the dungeons, where the Gruagach had set up cages and where, despite their protestations and their ridiculous attempts at wearing nearly human clothing and pretending that they shaved and could grow beards if they wanted to, they were still sufficiently giantish to want a supply of captured Humans for the cat-and-mouse game of the *Fidchell*. They liked to think of the dungeons as their larder and, in fact, Goibniu was not above coming down here himself, just to see what prisoners there were. Which made it extremely difficult to release people furtively, which was what Caspar tried to do whenever he could. He would have to think of another way of releasing the prisoners, because no Human who was forced into the grisly *Fidchell* ever escaped.

Caspar wondered, not for the first time, whether the game was worth the candle.

Chapter Eight

Fael-Inis was leading the way out of the cavern with the chasm and the rushing Fire River, and down a wide rocky tunnel with the firelight pouring over the walls. Tunnels and passages led off at unexpected intervals. 'Like a honeycomb,' said Snodgrass, who had once attempted to keep bees. Fael-Inis turned at that and said, 'That is astute of you, Human. In the legends of this world, this is known as the Road of the Honeycombs.'

'You say "this world",' said Floy.

'Yes. It is a world in between worlds. A Corridor. Presently you must pass out of it.'

'How?'

'I will take you.'

'Oh. Yes. Of course,' said Floy, and Fael-Inis laughed.

'It is strange and bewildering, but it is not so very strange as all that. You are in a Corridor of Time. There are no doorways into Time, you see. The Time Curtain that was drawn down at the very beginning was intended to prevent worlds overlapping. Any such overlaps would have created problems of a magnitude that Mankind could probably not have survived. You have – I think you would say you have been forced through a tear in the fabric.'

'By falling into the vortex?'

'Yes.'

'Is this your world?' asked Fenella.

'No.'

'What is your world?'

'Perhaps there is no such place. Perhaps I am condemned to search all the worlds until I find my place,' said their host, and sent them one of his strange, slanting looks. 'But for the moment I dwell here. And, for the moment, it is my task to rescue creatures who lose their way.'

'"Task"?' queried Floy, and again there was the sideways look.

'You would prefer me to say "punishment"?' said Fael-Inis lifting his brows and giving Floy one of his remote looks.

'Is it a punishment?' asked Floy, returning the stare.

'It depends how you regard punishment,' said Fael-Inis, unruffled as a cat. 'There are Manmade laws which decree that the sin prescribes the punishment.'

'That is a rather good arrangement,' said Floy, thoughtfully.

'It is the only one I would bow to,' said Fael-Inis, unexpectedly. And then, before anyone could say anything else, 'We have to go along here,' he said. 'And the roof is rather low.'

The roof was very low indeed and they all had to bend over to avoid it, except Fenella who was smaller than the rest. The tunnel floor was somehow soft, and Fenella saw that their feet were sinking, just a little, into its surface, as if they were walking on thick, springy grass. Only it was not grass, it was fire, but it was silky and only faintly warm.

'I control the fires,' said Fael-Inis, apparently picking this up easily. 'If I did not keep them banked down, the poor creatures in the townships surrounding the Fire Country would freeze.'

'The fires would suck all the heat from them,' said Fenella, and Fael-Inis turned to regard her appreciatively.

'Yes,' he said. 'I see you understand better than most, Mortal,' and Fenella felt quite absurdly pleased.

'Also,' said Fael-Inis, apparently considering that more information was needed, 'also, to drain the heat from any one place is to render it vulnerable.'

'To – cold?' asked Floy.

'To the *Geimhreadh* and her terrible armies,' said Fael-Inis. And then, as Floy looked up questioningly, 'The *Geimhreadh* leads the dread race of the Frost Giants,' he said. 'She is a necromancer of the highest order and she will hold Court anywhere that is sufficiently cold and sufficiently bleak and desolate.' He sent them a mischievous glance. 'You are in unknown worlds, now, Mortals. Have I not told you you will encounter creatures who will hunt you for sport, and creatures who will stalk you for your souls, and perhaps even creatures who will stalk you for your bodies?' The golden eyes were impersonal, although Fenella detected a glint of amusement again.

'But if you are to sojourn in this world,' said Fael-Inis, 'you should know something of its dangers.' He grinned. 'I am heedless and uncaring of the laws of all the worlds, but I give you a warning, you see. Perhaps you will have had dangers and enemies in your own world?'

'Yes, but not quite in the same way,' said Floy, remembering Quilp.

'But you can understand. You will understand that there are creatures to be wary of. You should be wary of the Gruagach,' he said, suddenly, his expression serious.

'What are they?'

'They have in them giantish blood, and they hunt Humans for their supper tables,' said Fael-Inis, and Fenella shuddered, and Snodgrass said, rather faintly, 'Dear me.'

'They are stupid and brutish and, if you are clever, you may outwit them.'

'And the *Geimhreadh*?' said Floy.

'Oh, you must be very wary of the *Geimhreadh*,' he said, and then, with another of his mischievous looks at Floy. 'She is endlessly eager for the bodies of beautiful young men.' He regarded Floy and appeared to derive faint amusement from Floy's start of surprise. 'You do not have such beings in your world?'

'Well, we do,' said Floy, 'only that they are not so—'

'Blatant?'

Floy said carefully, 'It was not considered – acceptable – to admit to the appetites of the flesh in our world, you see.'

'But it didn't really make people any different,' said Fenella, who thought they ought to defend Renascia a bit and who did not want to make it sound too meek.

Snizort, rather unexpectedly, said that he had recorded a few quite amazing things in his Diaries about the Renascians in general and Quilp's Council in particular. 'He wasn't all he seemed, that Quilp,' he added darkly. 'My word, I could have told a few tales, my word I could.'

'Double-sided,' nodded Snodgrass. 'That's why we were so pleased when Floy looked like overthrowing him.'

'By waging a war on him?' asked Fael-Inis with interest.

'No,' said Floy, a bit regretfully, the others thought. 'No, that was not our way. It would have been done by plots and intrigues,' he said, and Fenella suddenly realised that Floy would have secretly enjoyed a war in the ancient traditions of the Earth-people.

'It is one way of living,' said Fael-Inis, who appeared to be interested. He glanced at Fenella, and said, 'He was a rebel, your brother.'

'Oh yes.'

'I think you were also something of a rebel, Mortal.'

'Well, I think I might have been,' said Fenella, grinning and remembering the secret meetings in the Mnemosyne and the plans to storm the Council Chamber.

Fael-Inis returned the grin, as if he understood all about secret meetings and subversive plottings. But he only said, 'Life is not always easy for rebels.'

'That shouldn't stop people rebelling.'

'I do believe you are a lady after my own heart,' said Fael-Inis. 'Through here, now. We are almost at our destination.'

Snodgrass muttered to Snizort that he hoped they weren't walking into something very nasty. 'I don't know that I'd altogether trust this one,' he said. 'Wild. Look at his eyes.'

Snizort said he wished they knew where they were being taken.

'We'll soon find out,' said Snodgrass sepulchrally.

They walked along the fire-drenched tunnels, seeing, here and there, curious etchings and symbols carved into the tunnel walls.

'Battles,' said Fael-Inis. 'From before the beginning of Time.'

'Who carved them?' asked Snizort.

'I did,' said Fael-Inis, suddenly remote and unapproachable again.

The tunnel widened unexpectedly into a vast, cavernous structure. The fire was stronger here; it poured down over the walls, and there was a strong, sweet perfume. Floy, who was a little ahead of the others, thought he could hear, quite distantly, the slow, steady breathing of huge, unseen animals. So vivid was the impression that he stopped and tilted his head, trying to make this out.

'You are hearing the salamanders,' said Fael-Inis.

'Yes?'

'But then, you have already met them briefly.'

'We did not see them very clearly,' said Fenella.

'You will see them shortly,' said Fael-Inis. 'They are steeds of fire and light and speed. They draw the Time Chariot for they are able to travel faster than Time, and they are able to pass unscathed through the white-hot fires of Time.'

'Were they once called Fire beasts?' asked Fenella, who had been wanting to ask this for some time.

'There have been worlds who called them so,' said Fael-Inis, in a matter-of-fact tone.

Directly ahead of them were immense, glistening gates. Beyond the gates they could see soft, rippling light, so pure they could look straight into it. Fenella received the impression of glittering pinnacles and fire-tipped spires and of golden turrets.

The gates were lit by hundreds upon hundreds of tiny glowing creatures who darted and swooped, leaving the imprint of brilliant swathes of colour where they flew, so that in front of the eyes of the four travellers were ever-changing patterns and kaleidoscopes of blurring shifting light.

'Fireflies,' said Fael-Inis. 'In some worlds they are called will o' the wisps, or, in the ancient language of the Cruithin, *Tine Ghealain*. There is a belief that they can lead Men to their hearts' desires.'

'Can they?' asked Floy.

'I have never followed them to find out,' said Fael-Inis with perfect courtesy.

The will o' the wisps were tiny winged creatures with delicate, beautiful bodies, not quite transparent, but not quite solid either. They darted about the travellers, and Fenella thought they beckoned.

'They *will* beckon,' said their host, studying the *Tine Ghealain*. 'They are mischievous and entirely unreliable.' He said this as would an indulgent parent regarding wayward but charming children. 'If you try to follow them, they will lead you on an endless, exhausting journey. You might find your heart's desire at the end of it,' he said thoughtfully, 'but I do not believe that anyone has ever managed to reach the journey's end.' He sent them another of his brilliant enigmatic smiles. 'But I am remiss as a host,' he said. 'The gates of the Palace of Wildfire are before us. Let us enter.'

He led them forward, through the gold-tipped gates, and they saw, properly now, that beyond the gates was a glittering, fire-washed palace, bathed in incandescent light, every window lit by flames, and with spires of glowing colour spiralling upwards.

At the front of the palace the drawbridge had been lowered.

Fael-Inis stopped and looked at them and the smile that was not Human slanted his eyes.

Fenella and Floy shared a thought: can we trust him?

But we have no other choice, thought Floy, and took Fenella's hand.

'Come inside, Mortals,' said Fael-Inis, his eyes glittering, and, as they moved forward, the gates swung silently to, shutting them in.

Inside the Palace of Wildfire it was quiet and warm and there was the feeling of moving deeper and closer to the heart of something more alive and more aware than anything they had ever known.

Fael-Inis walked ahead of them, catlike, his head tilted as if he might be listening for something. The four travellers, silent and wary, followed.

To Snodgrass and Snizort, and particularly to Snizort, who had studied the fragments of the Earth-people's civilisations, the Palace of Wildfire was very slightly Eastern in structure. There were pointed arches through which their host led them, and there were more of the niches and alcoves with copper flambeaux and small bright torches of flame. Here and there, silk hangings masked rooms, and, in several of the rooms, weird and fearsome creatures were etched into the floors and the walls. Snizort paused to examine a great rearing beast carved into the wall of an octagonal chamber, and Fael-Inis turned to look at him.

Snizort said, 'What—' and Fael-Inis said, in a voice that had no expression at all, 'That is the One whom your ancestors termed the Light Bringer,' and appeared to wait for a response.

Snizort said, 'The Light Bringer . . .' and then, 'Lucifer?' he said, cautiously.

'That is how I saw him before he was cast from Heaven,' said Fael-Inis. 'But he can assume many guises, for he is a shape-changer like most truly evil creatures.' A brief smile touched his lips. 'He thought he would overthrow Heaven,' he said. 'He was arrogant and beautiful and proud, and he marshalled an immense force and led his armies fearlessly – and he was so nearly successful.'

'But he failed, and was cast out,' said Snizort, thoughtfully. 'Isn't that the legend?'

'Yes. Perhaps, if I had declared for him, there might have been another outcome . . .'

Fenella, who was not entirely following this, but who was intrigued, said, 'You declared for – for Heaven?'

'No. I walked away from the battle. I did not declare for either side. That is why I was called the rebel angel. I had no allegiance then, and I have none now.' The golden eyes darkened briefly, and then he appeared to lose interest and, as Snizort said in an aside to Snodgrass, you did not

95

really feel that you could question him any further.

'Although I'd like to know more,' he said wistfully.

Snodgrass said hadn't they enough to contend with as it was, without Snizort wanting to find out about ancient battles and strange beings.

Floy was finding the inside of the Palace exotic and fascinating, but he thought they ought to be asking where they were, and where they might be going. He thought that he would question their host about this, and then he glanced at the remote profile of Fael-Inis and thought perhaps he would not.

Fenella, walking between Floy and Snizort, was quiet and withdrawn. She thought she was deeply happy and she was certainly completely enthralled. I do not really believe that this is happening, she thought. I think I am inside a dream, mine or somebody else's. But perhaps, thought Fenella, if I do not speak, and if I do not do anything to upset things, I shall not wake up. The thought of waking up and being on Renascia again, where Quilp and the Council had plotted and at the end shut them out to leave them alone with the vortex, was almost unbearable.

And then Fael-Inis was ushering them into an oval-shaped room, the scents were stronger here, and before them was a table set for five.

'Food and wine,' said their host. And then, unexpectedly, 'Do sit down,' he said. 'And eat and drink whatever you wish. I don't know about you,' said the rebel angel, suddenly and rather disarmingly human, 'but I am quite extraordinarily hungry.'

The table was much lower than they had been used to on Renascia, and it seemed to be expected that they should sit on the floor, on the heaped silk and brocade cushions. This was, in fact, more comfortable than it looked, although Snodgrass had to repress a gasp as a twinge of rheumatism caught his knees.

There were dishes of food, strange spiced sauces and platters of fruit unlike any fruit they had on Renascia. The elaborately carved flagons held warm, fragrant liquid.

'Wine?' said Snodgrass, hopefully.

'Silkmead,' said Fael-Inis, pouring them each a chaliceful. 'And also Tawnyfire and Flamewine.' He handed them each a chalice.

Fenella wondered who had prepared the food, but Snizort was busy trying the Silkmead, and Snodgrass was investigating the dishes of food, and it did not seem the right moment to ask. And also, thought Fenella, curled up on a scarlet silk cushion, also I'm not at all sure that I want to have this explained, or not yet anyway. I can be logical and practical later, and I can start to wonder where the light comes from, or what's behind the walls, or through that archway, later.

But, just for a little while, I think I'll just enjoy everything. I'll even believe that there might be shadow beings that come and go here, and lay tables and pour wine and cook food. She looked up to find Fael-Inis's eyes on her.

'Perhaps there are,' he said gravely, and Fenella began to think that this understanding of people's thoughts was not entirely comfortable.

Snodgrass and Snizort were interested in the manner in which the meal was served.

'Eastern,' said Snizort, nodding. 'They always sat on the floor to eat, you know. On cushions. I've read about it. My word, this is all very interesting.'

'I embrace all the cultures,' said Fael-Inis, who was eating a portion of some strange, honey-flavoured dish with industrious pleasure. 'I am glad you find it interesting.' He helped them to portions of the fruit and handed them each a goblet of wine.

Floy said, 'Would you tell us more about how we got here?'

Fael-Inis regarded him thoughtfully. 'Would you believe that you came into my domain by chance?' he said, and then smiled and said, 'No, of course you would not. I have told you that you were brought to me by the salamanders.'

'On purpose?'

'They are guardians,' said Fael-Inis. 'They swim in the Fire River and they are the sentinels of the Time Corridors.' He looked at them, and Floy remembered how, as they neared the brink of the Dark Lodestar, he had felt Time slowing down and running out and how he had seen it as a great gold-and-crimson-veined tapestry, unrolling and stretching out before them.

'A good analogy,' said Fael-Inis, studying Floy. 'Time *is* a tapestry, after all. It is stretched out on a giant loom, and the history of all the worlds is spun and woven into it.' He sipped his wine, the golden glow casting shadows on his face. 'The Dark Lodestars that exist are warps in the fabric, you see. So that when your own world was poised on the rim of one of those Lodestars, when it began to spiral downwards into the vortex, Time began to spin more slowly until, finally, it ceased to exist. That was when the salamanders found you.'

He looked at them and appeared to wait, and Floy said, slowly, 'You are making it sound almost as if the salamanders were looking for us.' And fixed their host with a straight stare.

'Perhaps they were,' said Fael-Inis lightly, as if it was not very important.

'Why?'

'You have an enquiring mind, Mortal,' said Fael-Inis. 'It is something you should strive never to lose.' He sat back, cross-legged, the wine goblet held loosely between his fingers, wholly at ease. 'It is possible that the salamanders *were* looking for you,' he said. 'For there have been times when people of your race – that is, Humans – have saved other worlds from immense evils.' He regarded them. 'Perhaps you are needed to rout an evil,' he said lightly, and Snodgrass murmured to Snizort that it was impossible to tell if he was serious or not.

Floy said, 'But what of our own world?'

'What of it?'

'What will have happened to it?'

'Worlds must sometimes die,' said Fael-Inis gently. 'You could not have saved it. It had played its part, it had been woven into the tapestry, and its time to die had come.'

'That is hard,' said Floy.

'Who told you life was intended to be easy?' He sipped the wine in his chalice consideringly. 'When I brought the salamanders out into the world with me, it was so that they should stand guard at the endless echoing Time Corridors, and that they should steer lost travellers to safety. Sometimes they bring the travellers to me, as they brought you.' He smiled mischievously. 'You should be grateful for that, Mortals. If the salamanders had not found you, you might have been travelling the worlds for ever, and that is not an enviable fate. You might have fallen or been dragged into the River of Souls. Or you might,' he said suddenly, 'have been caught by the Robemaker, and fed to one of the Soul Eaters.'

There was an unexpected wariness in his voice, and Fenella, who had been enjoying the unfamiliar food and the soft, sweet Silkmead, and who could have listened to Fael-Inis's soft beautiful voice for hours without tiring, felt a chill. If she had not been afraid so far, she was afraid now.

'But,' said Fael-Inis, appearing to give himself a shake, 'the Robemaker is rarely seen out in the world. Also, he does not take Humans so very often.' He sipped his wine again, watching them over the rim of the goblet.

'Can we go out from this world?' asked Snodgrass. 'To other worlds?'

'Yes. You must do so, for you cannot stay here. I could lead you out.'

'Will you?' asked Floy.

Fael-Inis leaned forward, the long slender fingers curling about the stem of his wine chalice. 'I can do whatever I wish,' he said. 'I am the creature of fire and light, and I can go in and out and through Time.'

'The rebel angel seeking his salvation,' murmured Snizort, and Fael-Inis at once said, 'Yes. But I shall not find it until the world ends, Mortal.'

'Which world?'

'Who knows?' He sat back on his cushions, watching them. 'So they still tell that story of me, do they?' he said. 'Even in your strange distant world, they tell of me.'

'The creature who witnessed the splitting of the heavens, and who would not fight on either side,' said Snizort, with wholly unexpected poetry. 'I have read of the legend.'

'I am the legend,' said Fael-Inis and grinned. And was suddenly neither the strange, fire-washed creature of the Honeycomb Roads, nor the eerily beautiful half-Human who had witnessed the world's birthing, but a young and rather amusing companion. Fenella smiled and relaxed and felt extremely safe, and Floy found himself thinking that here was one who would be a very useful person to have on your side.

'I am on no one's side,' said Fael-Inis instantly. 'But for the moment, you are my guests, and you are supping in my Palace of Wildfire, and I believe I shall guide you out of here.'

'Where to?' said Floy.

'You have fallen into a strange land, Mortals,' said Fael-Inis. 'There are many worlds into which you might have fallen, but there has always been a nexus between your world and the world you are about to enter.' He paused. 'You are on the borderlands of a world that is peopled by beings who are not quite Human, but not quite beast either.' He leaned forward again, his eyes hard and gleaming.

'You are in what is, to you, the Ancient past,' said Fael-Inis.

'Are we – on Earth?' said Fenella, who had not dared to ask this until now.

'Oh yes,' said Fael-Inis, softly. 'Oh yes, Mortal, you are on Earth.

'You are in Ancient Ireland in the Deep Past. This is the Ireland of Tara, the Bright Palace of legend, the Shining Citadel which was raised from the rock by the sorcerers at the beginning of Ireland's history. It is a land peopled by creatures with the blood of the beasts in their veins. The Ireland of the Twelve Royal Houses, each one of them part beast, every one of them noble and imperious and just very slightly dangerous.' He stood up and held out his hands to them.

'You are in the Ireland of the Wolfkings,' said Fael-Inis.

The Ireland of the Wolfkings.

A host of images tumbled through Fenella's mind; vivid pictures and visions, some learnt and some remembered, and some simply inherited by some queer streak of race-memory or atavism.

The Deep Past . . . the long-ago Ireland of the Wolf-kings . . .

Fael-Inis said, very softly, 'Oh yes, my dear, you are right. You are right to believe. Your people know only a fragment of your history, but there are legends and myths, and palaces and sorcerers and strange half-Human creatures, and Royal Houses. They existed in your mythology long before your ancestors burned their world. They are a part of your heritage.

'And now you are to meet them.'

He rose, indicating to them to follow him, and, as they moved, he led them out of the oval room with the silk cushions heaped before the table and the fragrant warm scents of the wine.

'There is only one way for you to go deeper into this world,' he said. 'You must ride astride the salamanders, for only they can take you through the Honeycombs safely, and only they can ford the River of Souls.'

'Do *you* ford the River?' asked Fenella, and he smiled at her.

'I can go through and beyond and before Time at will,' he said. 'I can harness up the salamanders to the Time Chariot which is made of fire and light and that will come for me if I summon it.

'But for Humans to travel in the Chariot would be dangerous beyond comprehension. You would lose your minds and your souls would burn.' He eyed them. 'To ride the salamanders is unsafe,' he said, 'but it is safer by far than to enter the Time Chariot.'

'Where are we going?' asked Floy as their host led them down a wide curving stair and into a great, square courtyard where glistening trees were heavy with strange, warm fruit, and where gentle fountains played.

'To the salamanders,' said Fael-Inis, and again the smile slid out.

'To the Stables of the Fire Stallions.'

Chapter Nine

The stables of the Fire Stallions. The halls of the silky slender wise-eyed creatures who were composed of fire and light, who could be harnessed to the Time Chariot and who could pull it beyond Time. The strange, molten beasts who had swum through the fiery tunnels with the *Ark* and towed it to the Honeycomb Caverns outside the Palace of Wildfire. The heart and the soul and the core of every enchantment ever spun and every legend ever recounted, and every myth ever written.

The magical creatures who lived at the heart of the Time Fire . . . *Pegasus and Bellerophon and the perfumed fields of Elysium and the gold-streaked skies of Aegia* . . .

The stables were not like anything the travellers had ever known.

'Although,' Snizort was to say, 'the salamanders were not like anything we had ever known either.'

'And we did not really know what to expect,' said Snodgrass.

'Had you no such creatures in your world?' asked Fael-Inis, watching their fascination with amusement. 'No horses, no Barbary steeds, no dolphins or fire-dragons or gryphons or centaurs? For the salamanders are a little like each of these, although, in reality, they are only like themselves.'

'No.' Fenella eyed him and wondered how much he knew about Renascia. 'We did have animals, of course,' she said. 'But only the – I suppose you could say the descendants of the ones who came from Earth. And there was not so very much room in the *Ark*.'

Snodgrass asked about the word *salamander*. 'Because,' he said, frowning, 'to our people, I think it once meant a rather slow creature with a scaly hide.'

'But the creatures we saw weren't in the least like that,' said Fenella.

Fael-Inis said, 'You are speaking of the creatures who were the many-times descendants of the true salamanders,' and sent another of his winged smiles at Fenella, as if to say: you see, Mortal? It happens in all the worlds, this process of evolution.

'The true salamanders, the *living* salamanders are Elemental Spirits of the Fire,' he said. 'They are temporal – that is to say they are flesh and blood and bone – but also they have a little of the spiritual about them.' The golden eyes gleamed suddenly. 'In their veins is the thin, magical trickle of the Eternal Fire,' he said, and the four travellers stared at him and each shared a thought: He, also, possesses the Eternal Fire.

Descending to the stables of the salamanders was like going down and down to the earth's core. Floy thought: I suppose we *are* in the hands of a friend. I suppose that beneath it all, Fael-Inis is not evil and greedy, and a – what did he call it? – a soul eater? He glanced at Fenella, and saw a look of the utmost delight in his sister's eyes as she watched Fael-Inis. For some inexplicable reason he felt suddenly safer, because Fenella, for all her gentleness, could nearly always see the real person behind the covering. He wondered, briefly, whether Fenella might not simply be dazzled by Fael-Inis, because certainly none of them had ever come across anything like him before, but he thought he could trust Fenella's instincts. She had seen behind Quilp and events showed she had been right to mistrust him. But she is seeing Fael-Inis as a friend, thought Floy, and at once was aware of a ripple of amusement from their host.

Do not trust me too far, Floy, for I can be an inconstant friend and a fickle ally . . .

But with the thought came also a warm breath of comfort, as if Fael-Inis understood and sympathised.

I think it is all right, thought Floy, treading carefully where their host led them. I think we are in the hands of someone we can trust. I think it is all right.

They were walking cautiously through more of the wide rock tunnels and there were steps worn into the floors, so that the descent was easier than might have been expected.

'Are the steps natural formations?' asked Snodgrass. 'Or were they cut?'

'They are natural,' said Fael-Inis. 'They have been hollowed by the footsteps of countless ages.'

'Who by?' asked Fenella.

'By me,' said Fael-Inis. 'I have worn these steps away, Mortals. Since the beginning of this world . . . If you do not look where you are going, you will be knocked senseless, Floy. Along here, and be wary of overhanging rock.'

And then they were in a great echoing cave and ahead of them were two forks and between the forks . . .

'Oh!' said Fenella, clasping her hands together in pure delight.

Between the forks were rearing rock formations, veined with gold threads, and within the formations . . .

'Oh!' cried Fenella, clasping her hands.

The Stables of the Fire Stallions . . .

The Stables seemed to stretch back endlessly – to the Earth's core, thought Floy – and, within them, the four travellers could see fire-washed halls, huge, beautiful, high-ceilinged rock chambers, lit by tongues of flame, layer upon layer of fire, orange and red and tawny and deep, deep bronze. There was a sense of beckoning, of allure, so that they were each of them conscious of a strong wish to know more, to want to explore these remarkable fiery halls, but there was a feeling of fear as well, because surely such a place could not be safe . . .

Massive arched openings led into the Fire Stables, great curved doorways, and across each of these were spiralling columns of fire, endlessly coiling and twining upwards, partly obscuring the interior of the Stables from their view.

'Curtains of Flame,' murmured Floy and, as he spoke, they saw, deep within the glowing fires, the slanting eyes of the fire stallions watching.

'Will they come out?' asked Fenella.

'Yes, for they know that I am summoning them,' said
Fael-Inis. 'They do not obey many, but they will obey
me.' As he said this, the flames seemed almost to be
brushed aside, and the salamanders were suddenly there,
strong and sleek and not quite solid, and not quite fluid,
but somewhere between the two, so that the four travellers
could never afterwards describe their shapes. To begin
with, the salamanders seemed to be like the engravings
they had seen of Earth-horses; or, at the very least,
centaurs, half Human, half horse. Or unicorns, thought
Fenella, who had seen pictures in Snizort's carefully
preserved books. But, after a moment, the salamanders
were nothing like this at all. They were high-nosed and
arched-necked and arrogant and imperious-looking, but
you felt as well that they might be friendly and mischievous
and rather fun. And they were strong and sleek and their
skin was glossy and it looked as if it had been polished, or
as if warm sweet honey had been poured over it. They
made you think of things like copper when it was being
melted down to re-shape, and of glowing furnaces and
white-hot metals, and firebrands.

The salamanders were strange and frightening and
intriguing. They moved to stand before Fael-Inis and,
although they bowed their beautiful heads, the gesture
held not the least trace of subservience.

Even so, thought Fenella, staring, I believe they *do*
render him obeisance. I believe they will do whatever he
asks of them.

She thought she would never dare to ride astride one
of these remarkable creatures and, in the same moment,
thought she would regret it always if she did not make that
attempt. I wonder if I ought to be feeling nervous, she
thought, remembering how, on Renascia, ladies had been
expected to be meek and hesitant, and how she had never
been either of these things. How boring! thought Fenella,
her eyes shining, not feeling the least bit nervous. And
then: and how fortunate I am that Floy will certainly not

try to keep me safely in the background of everything!

At her side, Floy was staring at the salamanders, visualising them bridled and harnessed, streaming through Time, pulling Fael-Inis's Chariot. Above and before and below and beyond Time . . . Shall we dare approach them? he thought, and knew at once that they would certainly approach them, and that they would certainly ride astride them. He glanced at Fenella, and knew a swift delight. She is enjoying this with every ounce of feeling she has, he thought. She is certainly apprehensive about what is going to happen to us but, even so, she is still enjoying everything. He knew he would certainly try to protect Fenella against whatever might be ahead of them, but he knew, as well, that he would have to do so covertly, because Fenella would not expect to be protected and she would not want to be protected, either. She would want to be at the centre of everything.

The nearest salamander was regarding them from its dark glowing eyes. 'Human travellers,' it said and appeared to nod to the other three, and the four Renascians jumped because they had not expected the salamanders to speak. But the salamander's voice was warm and deeply interested, and it was inspecting them. The other three, too, were regarding them with friendly curiosity, as if they might be a species that the salamanders only encountered very occasionally.

Fael-Inis had moved closer and laid his hand on the rippling manes of the two leading salamanders. 'Chiron and Charybdis,' he said gently, and Fenella saw that there was a tremendous closeness between Fael-Inis and the salamanders, as if they might have shared many things, perhaps encountered many dangers together. 'They will take you safely out of this place and into a world that will be a little more like your own,' said Fael-Inis. The grin slid out, briefly. 'But not entirely like it,' he said, 'for no one world is ever entirely like any other. But you will perhaps find creatures near to Human.'

'Are they to traverse the River of the Dead, Master?' said the first salamander, Chiron, and Fael-Inis seemed to hesitate. Then – 'If you cannot avoid it,' he said, and the salamanders tossed their heads in acknowledgement, so that sparks cascaded across the rocky cavern.

As they moved towards the archways, Fenella said, 'Shall we meet you again?' and he smiled at her, a genuine smile, as if he liked her.

'I am to be found in many places,' he said. 'Only you sometimes have to look hard to discover me.'

He stood watching as the salamanders turned about, and they saw that he was still smiling and that the gentle radiance was all about him.

And then the first of the salamanders said, 'This way, Mortals,' and they were through the archway and out into a wide tunnel.

Ahead of them were the Honeycomb Tunnels and, beyond those, they could see the golden River.

Riding on the salamanders was a little bit like flying in the *Ark*, and a little bit like walking, and a little bit like reclining in a very comfortable chair close to a glowing fire. There was a strong, sweet wind blowing in their faces as they moved, and all about them they were aware of the rushing rock tunnels. Fenella thought they were not actually travelling very fast, because they could quite easily make out the figures and the symbols carved into the sides of the Honeycomb Tunnels.

Snodgrass and Snizort were extremely interested in these carvings. Snodgrass, who was at the rear, managed to make out several of them, and said he thought they were something called Christian, but Snizort, who had managed to don his spectacles and was peering intently at the etched symbols and figures, said they were much earlier than that.

'My Master *did* know the One called Christ,' said Chiron in his soft warm voice. 'But my Master is older by far than that One.'

'He knew others, also,' said Charybdis. 'Some of whom you may know, and others you may not. Noah and his people were here when Flood threatened another world.

Also Ut-napishtim the Babylonian . . . And Berosus, the Egyptian priest . . . People, races, whole worlds have been threatened by the Angry Sun.'

'Are there truly other worlds?' said Floy, who was finding the salamanders unexpectedly easy to talk to.

'There are many,' said the salamander, tossing its mane and bounding forward. 'You are not the first of your race to have fallen into the Time Corridor and passed through the Curtain. Many of your people have attempted to cross Time. Some have succeeded, but others have been taken and devoured by the Soul Eaters.'

'Others?' said Snizort, who did not very much like the word 'devoured', and who liked, even less, the sound of the Soul Eaters. The creature turned its burning eyes on him.

'There have been others who have believed they have fathomed the secret of Time,' it said, 'but they have failed, and they have become lost.'

Lost for ever in the echoing endless Corridors of Time . . .

'There have only been a few occurrences of the Chosen Few escaping into the Past or the Future,' said Snizort's salamander.

Fenella was thinking how remarkable it was to be one of the Chosen Few, and trying to decide whether she thought she was worthy of it, when Floy said, 'What are Soul Eaters?' and for the first time the salamanders seemed to shiver, as if with fear.

'They are creatures of the Dark Ireland,' said Charybdis. 'They serve the Lords of the Dark Domain that is the dread mirror image of the true Ireland, and where evil rules and where the necromancers spin their strong and fearsome magic.'

'The Soul Eaters do not walk in the world of Men,' said Charybdis. 'They inhabit the Cave of Cruachan, which is one of the Doorways into the Dark Realm,' and Floy felt the tremor go through her again.

'But they have Servants,' said Snodgrass's salamander. 'Beings they hold in thrall, or whom they have chained by a bewitchment, and who must serve them and bring to them the souls of Humans.'

'Servants?'

'They say the Robemaker is one of their Servants,' said Chiron, and Fenella and Floy both felt the wariness they had felt from Fael-Inis earlier. 'And also, the necromancer CuRoi, who rules from his Fortress of Illusions deep within the Dark Realm. Those two it was who used the Giants of Gruagach to storm Tara and oust the rightful High King.'

'The Gruagach are their pawns,' said Charybdis, tossing her mane rather contemptuously. 'You will almost certainly meet with them, but they are stupid and slow-minded, and you will be able to outwit them.'

Floy thought to himself: I hope we *shall*! because he was rather disliking the idea of giants.

Charybdis laughed, as if she had heard the thought. 'You should not worry overmuch about the Gruagach,' she said. 'Only about the Ones who use them as pawns.'

'The Soul Eaters . . .' said Floy.

'Yes. Every night, the Soul Eaters hold court,' said Charybdis. 'And they feast on the souls brought to them by their servants. Few Humans have seen the Soul Eaters,' she said, 'but it is known that they were old when the world was still young.'

'Have you seen them?' asked Floy, and Charybdis tossed her mane again.

'We have seen most things in the world, Mortal,' she said. 'For we were brought into the world by our Master, whom you know as Fael-Inis, when the world of Humans was still cooling.'

'You will have met the creatures who were forged from our blood during that cooling,' said Chiron, with a sudden warm chuckle of amusement. 'For they are woven into the legends and the lore of Men.' He glanced back at Floy, mischievously.

Snizort, who had been listening, said, very warily, 'We know of creatures who were called *dragons*.'

'And unicorns?' said Chiron.

'Yes.'

'And gryphons and minotaurs and wyverns?' said Charybdis.

'I – believe so.'

'And sirens and phoenix and chimera?'

'Well—'

'We are a little of all those things,' said Chiron, and the salamanders exchanged glances as if sharing some brief, faintly amusing secret. And then, suddenly serious, Chiron said, 'But we spoke of the Soul Eaters. You should pray to whatever gods you worship that you never find yourselves at the Court of the Soul Eaters in the Cave of Cruachan.'

It was then that Snodgrass, who had been looking about him very searchingly, said, 'What's that up ahead?' and the other salamander said, quite calmly, 'It is the River of the Dead. The River of Souls.' And then, in a soft voice, 'We shall have to ford it very carefully.'

The banks of the River of Souls. The four travellers slipped carefully from the salamanders' backs and stood for a moment looking out across the vast expanse of dark water.

The River flowed silently and steadily and there was a faint, shimmering phosphorescence on its surface. Floy reached for Fenella's hand, because there was something awe-inspiring and out-of-the-world about the River. Fenella would not show if she was afraid – she had not shown any fear at all so far; she had eaten supper in Fael-Inis's Palace calmly and listened to him with interest, and retained a sense of humour, and behaved as if this sort of thing was very nearly everyday.

Fenella was not thinking about being courageous or calm, or even about pretending not to be afraid or keeping a sense of humour. She was grateful for Floy's presence, and she was comforted by the feel of his hand pressing hers.

But she was staring at the dark-flowing River of Souls and, for the moment, there was nothing else in the world for her.

'Where does it end?' asked Floy in a low voice. 'Does it

111

have a – a source? A place where it ends?'

Chiron, who was watching the dark, glistening water thoughtfully, said, 'It is believed that its end is in the Lair of the Frost Giantess, the *Geimhreadh*. It is said that in its beginning is its end and that she presides over its source.' He turned to look at them, his brilliant eyes unreadable. 'It may be only a myth,' he said, and the travellers each had the feeling that he was holding the belief out for their consideration, as if he might be saying: you may believe whatever you wish; it is up to you.

Snizort and Snodgrass had not said very much, but they were standing silently, watching. The salamanders had fallen back a little, but they were close by, a constant warm presence. If we really needed to, thought Fenella, we could be astride them again and off into the tunnels; we could be pouring like a cascade of molten gold deep into the Honeycomb Caverns again. We could run away from the things that are held captive beneath the water's surface.

The things that are held captive . . .

At first, Fenella thought they were simply tiny winking lights, pinpoints of red that danced and glittered and caught the soft phosphorescence from the cave's ceiling. But then, as they drew nearer, she saw that they were not reflections at all, but hundreds of eyes that peered and moved, and came and went beneath the dark slow-moving River.

The soul-less victims of the terrible Soul Eaters of the Cruachan Cavern . . .

Chiron had moved ahead to where wide, shallow, nearly flat crafts were moored and Snodgrass's salamander was helping him to unfasten the rafts and nose them into place before the four travellers.

'Fortuitous?' wondered Snodgrass, who believed in keeping a firm sight of reality, but Charybdis said in her soft voice, 'No. For those who wish to cross the River, a means is always at hand.'

Chiron pushed the rafts into place, and Charybdis stood back and waited for Floy to take the first step.

'As your people's leader,' she said, 'you must go first.'

Chiron turned to Fenella and, in the dark, rippling water-light, his face was solemn and his eyes serious and filled with wisdom.

'This will be a difficult journey for you, Mortal,' he said. 'For you will see, beneath the waters of the River, the soul-less ones, the victims of the Soul Eaters. They are hideous pitiful things, for the River that imprisons them is wreaking a terrible mutation on them. But we cannot help them. You must remember that we cannot help them.'

'Yes,' said Fenella, staring back at the beautiful slanting eyes. 'Yes. I understand.' Chiron studied her for a moment, and then nodded slightly, his mane swirling like smoke as he did so, and Fenella stepped cautiously onto the waiting raft.

There was a brief turbulence beneath the River as the salamanders pushed the rafts away from the banks and out into the centre of the River, and Fenella and Floy both saw darting fishlike movements in the water, as if there were creatures down there – beings not quite fish but not quite human, moving back and forth in the cloudy depths. The gentle radiance from the salamanders' glossy flanks spilled into the dark tunnel and, as the light touched the water, hundreds of watchful eyes glinted redly below the surface.

'And yet there is a stench of bad fish,' thought Fenella, who did not much like fish or anything to do with fish.

Chiron was guiding the raft and they were nearly at the centre of the River now. The salamanders stood at the prow of the frail shallow crafts, one to each, looking intently ahead, their eyes serious and absorbed. They might have been statues, graven gold figures, had it not been for the continual rippling of their manes and the faint liquidity of their shapes. Against the dark River tunnel, Chiron's outline was slightly blurred, as if at any minute he might melt and dissolve and re-form into something quite different. As Fenella felt the thought take substance in her mind, Chiron turned his head slightly and sent her a winged smile, as if to say: *all is well,*

Mortal, and Fenella felt better.

The punting of the rafts made a rather cold, slightly muffled sound in the enclosed tunnel and, mingling with it, was the steady lapping of the River. Fenella thought it might have been better if there had been some sound from somewhere, and then thought that perhaps it might have been worse.

It seemed a very long time before Floy said, very quietly, 'I can see the far bank,' and his words echoed rather eerily and Fenella knew he was trying not to make too much noise in case the owners of the glinting eyes were alerted.

The salamanders had not spoken, although Fenella thought that they had looked at each other, as if they were sharing their thoughts. Once Charybdis tossed her head, and once Chiron seemed to look up as if something had caught his attention. But there was nothing, and the rafts moved cautiously forward.

They were a little over half-way across the River now and they could all see quite clearly the malevolent eyes glaring at them from the green turgid depths. Floy made out pale man-sized fish creatures darting to and fro in the water, and barely Human things skulking fathoms below the rafts. He knelt down to see better and realised with disgusted pity that the creatures' eternal captivity in the River of the Dead had turned them into repulsive soul-less water creatures: their bodies had changed and adapted to their surroundings; their necks were disappearing and their heads were becoming rounded and hairless. Most of them already had bulging lidless eyes and flat wide, slashlike mouths, and although some of them were still partly possessed of bony and spined human skeletons, others were quite plainly already spineless and virtually boneless and could only squirm towards the rafts.

But the soul-less creatures were purblind from the green murky light of the River; they could sense the intruders, but they could not see them. Fenella thought: we are safe. They cannot attack us. And was instantly ashamed at being so concerned with her own safety when she remembered these doomed creatures' endless captivity.

As they neared the far banks, Fenella and Floy felt their thoughts raked by the creatures' pitiful pleadings. Their cries for help rose up out of the River and lay on the air in a thick dark miasma of suffering.

Whoever you are, take us away from here on your boats, and up into the world again . . .

Help us to escape from the endless waters of the River . . . Help us to return to the world we once knew . . . Help us recapture our souls . . .

Fenella made an involuntary movement and, at once, Chiron said, sharply, 'Remember, Mortals, that you cannot help them.'

'Are they condemned to this for ever?' whispered Fenella, staring into the River's depths in horror. And Charybdis said, softly and pityingly, 'They cannot be killed, for with their souls' loss they are condemned to immortality. But it is a terrible immortality. They are truly the damned ones of the world, for they are doomed to always dwell beneath the River's surface, until their world ends for all time. Then perhaps there will be release for them.'

'I see,' said Fenella, who only partly saw, but thought it would be impolite to admit to this, and Chiron turned his head to regard her.

'You feel pity for them, and that is admirable,' he said. 'But you must remember that if you had tried to rescue them, they would almost certainly have dragged you beneath the waters to share their terrible fate. You would have become one of the thousands of lost creatures doomed to dwell in the half-light until the world's end.'

'How terrible,' said Fenella, softly.

'You should know these things, Mortals, since if you are to sojourn in this world, you may encounter the soulless ones again.' And then, the golden eyes suddenly brilliant, 'But ahead of us now is the far bank,' Chiron said. 'And beyond that is the world to which my Master is sending you.'

'The world he is sending us to?' said Floy looking up sharply, and Chiron smiled.

'The Ireland of the Wolfkings,' he said.

The Ireland of the Wolfkings . . .

As they stepped off the rafts and walked cautiously along the last stretch of tunnel, the River safely behind them, Fenella and Floy saw that the light was beginning to change.

'Purple-tinged,' said Floy.

'Turquoise,' said Fenella. And then, 'Dark blue.'

'It is what was once called the Purple Hour,' said Chiron, who was still leading them. 'That is, the hour when it is neither quite day any longer, but nor is it yet night.' He looked at them. 'I think you have not seen such a thing before?'

'We have something we call twilight,' said Floy. 'But it is not so laden with scents and sounds and feelings.'

'But this is a world where magic is abroad,' said Charybdis, her voice perfectly serious. 'And in this world, twilight, the Purple Hour, is thought to be the time when spells walk and enchantments lie on the air.'

'But,' said Fenella, wanting to believe this, but not quite daring to, 'but surely that is all just an ancient superstition?'

'Is it?' said Chiron softly.

'Wait and see, Mortals,' said Charybdis.

The light was pouring in to the tunnel now, dusky blue and turquoise, dust motes dancing in and out of it, with stirrings and rustlings deep within it and faint, far-off scents of sweet night air and ancient trees and dry, crunchy bracken.

'Twilight,' said Chiron, standing still and listening. 'Hear it, Mortals. *Feel* it. There are spells abroad tonight.'

Floy started to say something and then stopped, because they could all feel it now, the strange, heavy drowsiness, the sense that just beyond vision and just outside of consciousness, there were creatures from other worlds, and there were powers and forces and things which had certainly been unknown on Renascia.

And then the tunnel widened unexpectedly and they

116

were walking out into a forest clearing and the dusk was all about them. The trees were lacing their branches overhead and beyond them they could see the deep velvet blue of a night sky spattered with stars. The salamanders had stopped and were standing watching them.

Fenella turned and started to say, 'But you cannot leave us—' and saw Chiron shake his beautiful head, so that the silken strands of his mane flew about his face.

'We shall meet again, Mortal,' he said. 'For my Master is ever abroad in the world of Men.'

Floy had started to speak, but the salamanders had moved back into the tunnel, only it was difficult to see if it was a tunnel, or only a bracken-covered cave now, because the purple-tinged twilight seemed to be falling all about them like a curtain. The fiery golden light was dimming, until there were only threads of it on the air, and then it was gone completely, and they were alone in the darkling forest.

Chapter Ten

The Halls of Tara were ringing with noise and the discordant laughter of the Gruagach and the even more discordant music of the Gruagach's musicians. Caspar, who liked to think he had a bit of an ear for good music, sighed, and hoped they would not start up the really dreadful *Fidchell Dance*, which had quite the grisliest undertones to any music Caspar had ever heard. It made you think of captured people (Humans?) being stalked and pounced on, and it made you remember that the *Fidchell* squares were being set out upstairs, and that the spikes would certainly be already in place, and the selected portions of the floor would be having the white-hot heat raised in them by the Gruagach's kitchens, where the *Fidchell* was considered the best entertainment ever devised.

It had not been possible to let the three Humans held in the dungeons go, simply because Goibniu, sly old fox that he was, had insisted on accompanying Caspar to the dungeons. 'In case,' he had said, grinning from ear to ear, 'you need any *assistance*, Master Procurer.'

Caspar did not need any assistance at all, but it had been quite obvious that Goibniu did not trust him to deliver the Humans up to the Sun Chamber. But he had managed to look grateful for the offer, because it was actually very generous of Goibniu, who was the King's High Chancellor, to stoop to such a mundane task, never mind that it was only that he did not want the Humans to be let to escape.

Three Humans were not really enough for a proper *Fidchell*. Caspar had heard the most dreadful tales of how, before the giants had come to Tara, they had played the *Fidchell* in the City of Gruagach, using Human travellers who had lost their way in the northern wastes of Gruagach;

saving them up until there were at least a dozen; every one of them impaled on spikes held aloft by the footmen, each of them knowing that with the turn of the dice, they might be moved onto the white-hot squares, where they would slowly roast, until a throw of the dice sent them to another square.

'A little cooking in advance,' was what the Gruagach said, but Caspar thought it would be far worse to be partly cooked, and then taken down to the sculleries to be finished off, than to be thrown into a cauldron of boiling gravy and have done.

It was rather unsettling to descend to the dungeons like this, in company with Goibniu. Goibniu kept looking down at Caspar, as if he might be considering using Caspar in the *Fidchell*. As they were crossing the great echoing landing, where the very nearly legendary Chair of Erin had been put, Caspar was quite certain he licked his lips.

Inchbad was enjoying his evening. He had not expected to, because he did not altogether approve of the *Fidchell*, but it was remarkable how you could discover entertainment where you had not previously thought entertainment to exist. He had raised a doubt as to whether they ought to be celebrating the *Fidchell* at all but Goibniu had said, in a surprised voice, 'But it is traditional when the *Feargach Grian* is seen, sire,' and Inchbad had said, 'Oh well, if it's traditional—' and Goibniu had gone off somewhere to see about something and the scullions and the spit-boys had come running in to the Sun Chamber to set up the *Fidchell* squares. The Court musicians had begun tuning up for the good old Gruagach music, which was always played at such a time, and some of the younger giants had asked some of the giantesses to dance.

Inchbad nodded and tapped his feet in time to the music, and remembered about the *Feargach Grian* heralding the beginning of a Golden Age, and felt that everything was turning out very well for them in Tara.

119

Really, you could almost begin to think that the Frost Giants and the *Geimhreadh* had done them all a favour in taking over Gruagach. You could almost believe that Goibniu had been right when he had held those rather lengthy discussions with the Robemaker, most of which Inchbad had not really followed. In fact, he had nodded off before they were finished. Not that Goibniu would have entered into any unwise arrangement with the Robemaker or anyone else, of course. The Gruagach did not do things like that. They might have ousted the High King and sent him and his sons into exile, but they did not allow themselves to be made use of. By the beards of their fathers, they did not! Inchbad would like to see the creature, Human or otherwise, who tried to use the Gruagach as pawns and puppets!

It was at times like this, with a bit of a celebration going on, that Inchbad ought to have a Queen, a Consort. It was something that Goibniu was seeing to, because the King of the Gruagach could not be allowed to marry with just anybody and they wanted to make a proper diplomatic alliance. There had been a suggestion of making an approach to the *Geimhreadh* herself, but Inchbad had squashed this idea before it could take a hold of anybody's fancy. He had heard all the stories about the *Geimhreadh*, and he did not especially favour the idea of having all his manhood juices sucked out of him drop by drop, which was what most people seemed to think she did. He would be perfectly satisfied with a plain ordinary princess of some kind, said Inchbad, and he would not baulk at a drain of nice Human blood, either. You could get some very pretty Humans. Well, you could get some extremely beautiful ones, actually. He began to rather like the idea of a pretty little Human for his Queen.

Goibniu, in his usual helpful way, had suggested several likely candidates, but most of them seemed to be in some way related to the necromancers of the Dark Ireland, and Inchbad, who could be firm if he had to, had said, quite severely, that if they were to take on any of *that* lot, he might as well have surrendered his manhood to the

Frost Giantess and have done.

You did not really know when you could trust a necromancer, said Inchbad; they were apt to be out for all they could get, and none too scrupulous about the means they employed to get it. They did not want any of the *nasty* magic coming in to Ireland. Inchbad harboured one or two lingering suspicions about Goibniu's discussions with the Robemaker, and was now wishing he had stayed awake a bit more.

They would just have a nice ordinary princess at Tara, he said, and Goibniu had said 'As Your Majesty wishes,' and Inchbad had said, 'I do wish,' and then had relented, and asked were there not any pretty young daughters of quite ordinary sorcerers they might approach. Goibniu had said, thoughtfully, 'Well, there *is* Reflection's daughter, sire. But they say her father was Fael-Inis, and he's a *very* tricky one. You might not quite care for that sort of blood in a Consort, Sire?'

'It might be worth asking,' Inchbad had said, because he did not really mind what sort of blood his Consort had so long as she was sufficiently pretty and rich, and he was, in fact, rather pleased at the way in which he had worked the discussion round to where he wanted it. Goibniu had gone away to consider whether they could send envoys of some kind to Reflection to see if she would sell Flame to Inchbad.

Inchbad thought if he had to marry anybody, he would quite like it to be somebody like Flame, who was reputed to be quite outrageously beautiful, and would probably be inheriting Reflection's money as well. There were rumours that Reflection was over her ears in debt, but Inchbad did not believe this, because he had never yet met a sorcerer or a sorceress who was not extremely rich.

The younger ones were dancing quite strenuously now, and the musicians were beginning to look flushed and shiny-faced. It might be better if they took a rest, because Caspar and Goibniu would be bringing up the caged Humans at any minute. The scullions had already dragged in the great iron squares, half black and half red, and were arranging them at the centre of the Sun Chamber.

The point of the game was to heat only some of the squares, and thus prolong the outcome, and Inchbad had made his selection earlier, frowning over which squares to order heated. It was an important matter, and it would not do to get it wrong. While the squares were being set out, one of the musicians asked permission to sing a song he had written about the *Feargach Grian*, and two of Inchbad's most loyal Courtiers said what a remarkable sight it had been to see it.

'A marvellous sight indeed, Your Majesty,' said one whose name was Fiachra Broadcrown.

'It swept the skies,' said the other, who was called Arca Dubh, and Inchbad had to pretend all over again that he had seen the *Feargach Grian* as plainly as the others seemed to have done.

The three Humans brought up by Caspar and Goibniu were standing huddled together in a corner of the Sun Chamber, and the musicians, seeing them, at once went into the ancient *Fidchell March*, which was a slow, pouncing, cat-after-mouse sort of tune, and which was greeted with shouts of delight.

'And,' said Goibniu, striding into the centre of the Sun Chamber, his meaty hands hooked into his belt, eyeing everyone with great joviality, 'you all of you know the rules.'

'*No* cheating,' cried the giants, delightedly, forming a circle about the squares.

'*No* prodding of the players with heated rods,' said Fiachra Broadcrown.

'*No* secretly heating extra squares,' added Arca Dubh.

'*No* letting the Humans over-cook!' cried someone else.

'And *no* trading of forfeits!' shouted everyone delightedly, and the giants nudged one another and said wasn't the trading of forfeits, one for another, part of the fun, and didn't they all of them know it for one of the best parts of the game.

'Then,' said Goibniu, nodding and beaming and

eyeing the Humans with greedy eyes, 'let the *Fidchell* commence!' He began the grand old *Fidchell Chant* in his great rumbling voice, and at once everyone joined in.

Dance, dance, for the sizzling of the flesh,
We are the Lords of the *Fidchell*.
Squirm and squeal for the roasting of the meat,
Wriggle and shout for the cooking of your feet,
If a throw of the dice brings the sizzling of the heat,
That is the way of the *Fidchell*.

Fee and fie and foe and humdum,
Peg and pig and pug and rumkchin.
With a dree and a drum and a dray and a thumbkin,
Into the ovens you'll go, my dears,
Into the ovens you'll go.

'Heat up the squares!' cried Goibniu, his face shiny with anticipation. 'Bring in the dice!'

Caspar thought that, as ordeals went, it could not have been very much worse. He managed to squeeze himself fairly inconspicuously into a corner of the Sun Chamber – he would have liked to leave the Chamber altogether, but one of the giants would be sure to notice, and fetch him back. And so he stayed where he was and he tried very hard to shut out the sounds of the sizzling gridirons, and he tried even harder not to look to where the three prisoners were waiting, held in chains, staring at the squares of black and red as if they could not believe what was about to happen. Caspar remembered that stories were whispered about the *Fidchell* in the villages surrounding Tara, but that they were generally believed to be no more than a legend. He sighed and wished they could be a legend, and he wished that he himself could be somewhere a very long way away.

The giants were shouting delightedly, dragging the squares into place, here and there yelping as they touched a heated one by mistake, blistering their fingers. Every time this happened, a rather horrid scent of roasting giant wafted to where Caspar was standing, so that he remembered the old legend about giantblood being different to Human. Coarser. Thicker. *Smellier*.

The squares were nearly all in place now, great shining wedges of black and red, laid to form one enormous square, nearly the size of the Sun Chamber, and set alternately, so that it was a bit like an old game which Caspar thought the Wolfkings had enjoyed, called chess. The Gruagach would not have had the brains for chess, because, according to most accounts, it had been quite intricate and extremely subtle. The Gruagach were many things, but subtle was not one of them.

One of the younger giants had brought in the dice; great pale glistening cubes of ivory and bone, which had been made from the compressed bones of their ancestors' victims, together with a few teeth for good measure. Caspar had not believed this to be true, until someone (he thought it had been Fiachra Broadcrown) had taken him down to the sculleries and shown him the huge metal machine with the square mould, which was used to squash the bones into shape.

There were two dice, each one four feet square, and both painted with various symbols all of which meant that various things had to happen on the squares. A red dragon-creature with an erect two-pronged phallus meant that the victim had to move to the right. A squat, repulsive female with six breasts meant a move to the left.

The Gruagach had come up with several other symbols which they thought very funny: there was one of a wolflike beast lifting its leg and pissing on Tara's Western Gate, and there was another of a Human with a wolf's head, staring helplessly at a long thin member which he was apparently trying to raise for the writhing wolfwoman at his feet. The Gruagach considered this extremely comical and there was always great competition to turn up this side of the dice, which gave you two moves to the fore, and nearly always landed your victim on a sizzling square of the board.

The squares were heating now, giving off tremendous waves of heat, and the giants were pointing and laughing, slapping their thighs with delight, telling each other that the Humans would soon be roasting, and there'd be Manpie for supper later.

Goibniu, who was still directing the proceedings, said in his loud rumbling voice, 'But, friends, we have to ensure that the heated squares are sufficiently hot! Hey?' And a great roar of delight, that made Caspar's ears ring unpleasantly, went up, because everyone knew what came next.

'Well?' cried Goibniu, grinning from ear to ear. 'How do we test the heated squares, my friends?'

'By spraying water on to them!' shouted the giants, poking each other and slapping their thighs again. The giantesses, bunched together at one corner of the *Fidchell* board, shrieked with glee, and clutched one another with helpless mirth.

'And,' bellowed Goibniu, standing with his legs apart, thumbs hooked into his belt, 'how shall we do that, friends?'

'By piddling on them!' shouted the giants, delightedly, and at once there was a scuffle and a jostling for places at the edges of the squares.

'Ready?' said Goibniu, and the giantesses shrieked with mirth again and dug one another in the ribs, and told each other not to look, and weren't they all awful, and then said would they just look at that Fiachra Broadcrown, aiming before Goibniu had even given the word, shameless as anything.

'Aim!' warned Goibniu who had produced a stopwatch the size of a large turnip and was making a great play of consulting it.

Caspar shuddered and fervently wished himself somewhere else, as the dozen or so giants unfastened their breeches and stood holding their minuscule organs ready, looking down at themselves with concentrated expressions on their faces.

'Go!' cried Goibniu, and the giants stood straddle-

125

legged, directing streams of thick yellow giant-piss into the centre of the floor.

There were shouts of encouragement, and cries of, 'Pooh! Fiachra Broadcrown's been at the onion wine again,' which was an old joke, and 'Arca Dubh couldn't put out a candle flame with that,' which was another old joke, and in one case, 'Goll the Gorm's splashing everyone's boots.'

As the sour-smelling urine sprayed onto the heated squares, from all edges of the board, there was a furious sizzling, and steam rose at once, sending out a stench of rancid giant and too-strong excrement and old stale sweat. Caspar saw the three humans shudder and he thought that one retched, and he searched his mind for some way to stop the grisly ritual, and let the captives go.

Goibniu was chuckling heartily and nodding and Inchbad, who had not, of course, taken any part in any of this, smiled and nodded to the musicians to strike up again, because the *Fidchell* was far better played to a bit of music and, anyway, it would mask the cries of the Humans.

At last, they all finished and buttoned their breeches again, and Goibniu pronounced Goll the Gorm winner of the pre-ritual, said that the heat was sufficient and turned to eye the waiting prisoners with his pig-like eyes. He gestured to the footmen to put the spikes in place.

'Because,' he said, the smile splitting his coarse red face like an over-ripe melon now, 'we should not wish you to get away before the real fun begins.'

The footmen stepped forward, and lifted the three prisoners over the spikes.

Fiachra Broadcrown and Arca Dubh had started the chant again, and the giants were clapping their hands in unison.

'The spikes, the spikes, spit the prisoners . . .'

There were three footmen to each prisoner now and, as the clapping increased in intensity, they raised the prisoners shoulder-high, and positioned each of them above one of the gleaming needle-sharp points.

The prisoners were screaming now and struggling; Caspar thought one of them had fainted and remembered, grimly, that once the impaling began, he would immediately revive, and when his spike was moved by the footmen to one of the heated squares, he would begin to sizzle and roast. He felt sick and wished himself somewhere else all over again.

The musicians had started up again, and now it was the creeping, stealthy notes of the *Fidchell March*, that terrible slow inexorable music that built up and up, and continued to build up and up, until the prisoners were simultaneously impaled, when it erupted in a discordant clashing of drums and tin sheets and screeching horns.

The three victims were being hoisted aloft, one footman holding each foot, and spreading their legs over the massive waiting skewers.

Goibniu shouted out, 'Avoid the backbone, footmen!' and there was a general cry of agreement, because if you split the backbone too soon, the meat never roasted as juicily.

'And don't puncture their bums!' cried Fiachra Broadcrown and everyone laughed very heartily at this, because everyone remembered the very unpleasant time in Gruagach, when two *Fidchell* players had suffered exactly that fate, and, as Goibniu had said, it had taken four footmen to clean up the mess, and the King's favourite banqueting hall had smelt of Human dung for days, which was not something anyone wanted to remember.

The victims were in place now, and they were squirming and writhing, and trying to escape, but the footmen knew that to let go of a Human at this point was crucial, and they had a good firm hold of the creatures' ankles. Extraordinarily frail ankles Humans had, but probably they looked all right to one another.

The three *Fidchell* players did not look all right now. Two of them were shouting and struggling; one of them was barely conscious, which was a pity, because it took some of the heart out of the game when that happened.

Of course, some Humans had no sense of fight, everyone knew that.

And then Goibniu raised his left hand in the signal, and the musicians began a terrific rolling of the skins of the drums, and one of them began beating the great deep-throated *Fidchell* drum steadily and rhythmically, and everyone started the clapping again, and the giantesses clutched one another in high excitement.

Goibniu brought his hand down, and the three Humans were impaled on the waiting skewers.

It was a very good banquet indeed. Everyone agreed that it was one of the best ever. The Manpies were particularly good this time; one or two people said they had splinters of backbone in their meat, and the footmen ought to have been more careful, but if there was one thing you could be sure of, it was that somebody would always complain about a backbone splinter at a *Fidchell* banquet. It was as much a part of the ritual as Arca Dubh not peeing as much as anyone else on the squares, or Goll the Gorm losing his place in the steps of the *Fidchell Dance*, which always followed the game.

And although three Humans did not make precisely a feast, the sculleries had eked the meat out carefully, and there was a good deal of nice rich gravy and huge dishes of vegetables, and everyone had a taste of Human, which was what it was all about anyway.

Goibniu made a speech and everyone cheered, and somebody else told them to lift their glasses to the *Feargach Grian*, because this was why they had celebrated the *Fidchell*, and somebody else again sang a song all about the Golden Age of the Gruagach, and everyone shouted that they were called Fomoire now, and there was a great deal of laughter and noise and banging of tables, and coarse jokes, which was exactly the sort of feast the giants liked.

Caspar managed to creep away just before the Manpies were served, because it would have been certain death to have been sick all over the table, which was what would have happened if he had stayed.

He sat in his bed-chamber with the south-facing view and the comfortable appointments and stared into the night sky. He wondered if anyone had really seen the *Feargach Grian* and, if so, how soon the Gruagach would send out a hunting party.

He wondered if the *Feargach Grian* really did herald the arrival of strange people from other worlds and, if so, where those people might now be.

Chapter Eleven

The four Renascians stood in the twilight, feeling the heavy heady scents of the Purple Hour close about them.

Fenella thought it was like nothing any of them had ever experienced, this sensing and scenting of a world that was laden with enchantments and filled with magic.

Magic . . . the word rippled across her thoughts, faintly disturbing, but also alluring and beckoning. We are in a world where magic is abroad. Probably we shall never return to Renascia. Probably there isn't any Renascia to return to any more. Fenella examined the thought and wondered whether she minded any longer. Not while there is all of this to find out about, she thought. Perhaps, later, I shall mind very much. And perhaps, later, it will hurt very much, but for the moment there is too much here and it is exciting and a little bit dangerous.

Floy was looking about him, and Fenella saw the same delight, tinged with apprehension, in his eyes, and knew that, for Floy, this was becoming something marvellous and challenging; this was a world to be explored and discovered.

'It's not at all what I expected,' remarked Snizort, staring about him.

'What did you expect?'

'Buildings,' said Snizort, rather vaguely. 'And people. Quite a lot of people. This is a forest.'

'We're on the edge of it, though,' said Fenella. 'If we walked in that direction, we'd come out of the trees.' But she found herself not wanting to leave the trees and the deep blue shadows of the forest. They did not know what kind of creatures might be awaiting them beyond the safety of the dark trees and, although the forest felt strange, it had an unexpectedly safe feeling about it. What had Fael-Inis said? *You will meet creatures who hunt Humans for sport . . .*

'There's something over there,' said Floy, pointing. 'Through the trees and on the other side of the valley. Some kind of palace, perhaps.' But his tone was hesitant, because none of them had ever seen a palace and no one was quite sure if one would look like this.

'It's beautiful,' said Fenella, following the direction of his hand. 'It's easily the size of our entire main square with all the buildings together. And it's bathed in light. Everywhere you look at it, it's shining and brilliant.'

'I suppose,' said Snodgrass, studying the distant building, 'I suppose that this *is* the – what did Fael-Inis call it? The Ancient Ireland of the Wolfkings?'

'I don't know that I like the sound of that, you know,' said Snizort, looking worriedly over the top of his spectacles. 'In all of the Earth's history, wolves weren't what you might call trustworthy. I think we ought to be careful.'

'Wolves were a legend,' said Snodgrass firmly. 'They never existed. They were myths. And I think we ought to find out what the building is.'

'It might be anywhere at all,' said Snizort hopefully.

'It's quite a long way off,' said Floy, who had been narrowing his eyes and trying to gauge the distance. 'It's certainly on the other side of that valley. But if we're going to go anywhere, I think we ought to go by night.'

'Because it would be safer . . .?' said Fenella, in a half-whisper.

'Well, wouldn't it? We'd be less conspicuous,' said Floy. 'And we can't stay here. We'll have to find people. And we can study the countryside as we go. That might tell us a bit more about this place.'

'This place,' said Fenella. 'Shall we ever get back to Renascia, do you think?'

'Shall we ever want to?' said Floy, softly, and Fenella heard the sudden delight in his voice. 'It's Earth, Fenella. This is Earth. The lost world of our ancestors.'

Fenella said, 'I was never entirely sure that it existed, you know.' She looked about her. 'I know we could see it

131

from Renascia, or we could see something we believed was Earth, and something we were told was Earth. But I was never sure that it was anything more than just a—'

'Myth?' said Snizort.

'Legend?' said Snodgrass.

'A myth and a legend, and a – a romantic daydream.'

Snizort said, very softly, 'Utopia and Erewhon and Avalon and the Isles of the Blessed.'

'Yes,' said Fenella. 'All of those. I hoped that, if it did exist, then it might be like this; blue and green and misty and with huge dark forests and shining palaces.' She made a quick gesture with one hand, encompassing the dark wood behind them and the strange landscape before them, blurred with dusk, purple fingers of twilight stealing towards the glowing castle across the valley.

Floy said, very gently, 'You don't expect daydreams to materialise so very exactly,' and Fenella turned to him gratefully, because, of course, Floy would have understood.

'And yet,' said Floy, his eyes still scanning the valley and the strange wild beauty of it all, 'and yet, here it is. The Ireland of the Wolfkings.'

'I don't believe in wolves,' said Snodgrass again, and a cool, rather amused voice from behind them said, 'Do you not indeed?' and they turned at once to see a slender, dark-haired young man, leaning against a tree, watching them.

It is not a comfortable thing to suddenly discover you have been watched and overheard for longer than you have realised, and it is very uncomfortable indeed to discover this when you're at the edge of an ancient wood with night falling, and the air heavily laden with something that might well be magic.

The four travellers eyed the young man cautiously, and then Floy moved forward and said, 'Good day to you, sir,' which was quite an old greeting, but one which Snizort had always maintained the Earth-people had frequently made use of.

The young man appeared amused. He said, 'Good day to *you*,' but the others thought he said it more as one trying out something new and intriguing, than as if it was something he was accustomed to. And, although he used the same words and they could understand him perfectly easily, his voice had a different, softer timbre. But it's rather attractive, thought Fenella, staring, fascinated.

Floy said, 'May we know where we are?'

'Are you lost?'

The young man moved closer, and the slanting blue-green dusk fell across his face, emphasising the curious bone structure. Fenella drew in her breath sharply, and the stranger glanced at her and grinned, but it was not a grin that was like anything she had ever seen on anyone's face before.

Floy said, 'We think we may have missed our way, a little,' and stood still and waited.

'You are in what we call the Wolfwood,' said the young man, and made a rather mocking gesture with one hand, embracing the ancient sprawling forest, as if to say: and it is all yours, my friends.

'Ireland?' asked Floy, trying out the word.

'Where else?'

'Where else indeed?' murmured Floy. 'And – may we ask your name?'

There was a pause, as if the stranger was thinking it over. Floy was suddenly reminded of how Fael-Inis had possessed the same slightly disconcerting manner. As if the creatures of this world might have to adapt to the four intruders' way of speaking and thinking in order to be understood. Floy could not decide whether it was disturbing or very slightly flattering to be studied and learned in this way.

At length, 'I am Nuadu Airgetlam,' said the young man. 'That is, Nuadu of the Silver Arm.' He lifted his left arm in an abrupt gesture, so that the long full sleeve fell back, and they saw that while the shoulder was flesh and blood and bone, the rest was pure, soft silver. 'I lost it in a battle,' said Nuadu, rather off-handedly. 'The Court sorcerer is trying to find a spell to make it whole again, but since he is not a very good sorcerer, I am still waiting.'

Again there was the characteristic tilt of his head and Fenella was reminded of a listening animal. He is listening to us at some unseen level and on some unguessed-at stratum of awareness. A bit like a dog, thought Fenella. Or a fox. Or a wolf . . .?

Floy was introducing them carefully and Nuadu listened attentively and repeated their names as if they were strange pronunciations to him. He took their hands, one by one, which was an unfamiliar, but not unpleasing gesture. Fenella found herself staring at him and saw that his eyes were dark and oddly angled, and that his hair grew close to his skull like an animal's pelt. And I believe that if I look, thought Fenella, in fascinated terror, I shall find that his ears are pointed . . . Only perhaps I had better not look.

Floy said, 'Would you tell us what is that place there?' and indicated the glowing palace across the valley. For the first time, Nuadu Airgetlam seemed to hesitate. Then, 'That is Tara,' he said and, behind them, Snizort drew in a sharp gasp and said, 'Of *course*.'

'You know it?'

'Not in the least, sir,' said Snizort, beaming. 'But it is in the legends, you know. My word, yes. Wasn't it cursed at one time?' he added, and Snodgrass looked doubtful, because this was not the sort of thing you ought to be saying.

But Nuadu only looked intently at Snizort, and then said, 'Yes. Oh yes, it has been cursed. It was cursed at the very beginning, only the sorcerers wove enchantments to keep it safe, and the *sidh* bound it about with their own cold magic. But then,' he said, 'the *sidh* have always been loyal to the Wolfkings.' And smiled rather maliciously at them, as if he might be saying: well? It is your turn now.

Floy, who was by turns fascinated and thrown off balance by their companion, was trying to decide if they ought to divulge where they had come from. At length, he merely said, 'We find it – unexpected to hear stories of wolves,' and the others knew he had been going to say 'hard to believe'.

134

'There are such creatures,' said Nuadu, who had resumed his negligent attitude and was leaning against the tree again, his arms crossed. 'They are rarely seen in Ireland now, but my ancestors lay with them.' He did not say this as if he was boasting or as if he was ashamed, or even as if he was trying to shock them. He merely said it as one imparting information. 'That is why I possess the mystical wolfblood of Ireland's Royal House,' he said. 'Only those who are not entirely Human can rule from Tara.' He regarded them. 'That is the immutable law. I did not make it and I do not necessarily agree with it, but there it is.' There was the glint of amusement again. 'And the Wolfkings ruled Ireland for a very long time.'

'Ruled?' asked Floy, and Nuadu regarded him closely.

'That is astute of you,' he said. 'They do not rule now, for they have been driven out by the Dark Ireland, by the powerful necromancers who made use of the giantish race of Gruagach.'

'How do you know all this?' said Fenella, who thought that although this was probably the least of all the things they wanted to know, they had to start somewhere.

'Because,' said Nuadu, 'I am a bastard son of the Wolfking.' He smiled and unfolded himself from his position by the tree. 'And if you are really lost,' said the Wolfprince, 'then I had better take you to the exiled Court.'

'If you were to ask anyone in Ireland today about the Wolfkings,' said Nuadu, leading them through the darkening forest, his every step light and graceful but also stealthy, as if he was wary of someone or something watching them, 'you would find that every single person would glance uneasily over his shoulder, and deny all knowledge. Everyone you asked would certainly say, as you said, Lady, "Oh, but there are no Wolves of any kind left in Ireland today." It is dangerous to believe such a thing now, you understand.'

He looked at Fenella, and again there was the smile that was not quite human and not quite wolfish. 'You are

135

very perceptive,' he said. 'Of course there are Wolves. It is just that some are a little more – Human than others. But to say that Wolves still exist here, might be to be overheard by the Gruagach and they are afraid of the Wolfkings. They were given Tara for killing my father, the Gruagach, although they will tell you they won it by their own strength. Even so, they have it, and they will not give it up easily.'

'Tara?' said Floy, and Fenella half turned to look again at the shining palace across the valley from them.

'Ireland's great and wonderful Court,' said Nuadu, and there was bitterness in his voice now. 'The Court of Tara, which is sometimes called the Court of Demons, although the only demons there now are those which the Gruagach cause the sorcerers to summon for their amusement. Demons *can* be amusing of course. If you can control them.'

'Yes,' said Fenella and Floy both together.

'Of course you will have seen Tara, and possibly it even guided you, for it is the lodestar that guides all travellers. Over there, to the east,' he said, pointing carelessly with the hand that was ordinary flesh and muscle. 'It sends out its beacon of light to all.'

Floy said, carefully, 'We have heard of the Gruagach.'

'They are rather stupid creatures, as are all with giantish blood in their veins,' said Nuadu. 'They believe they rule Ireland, but of course they do not. The necromancers did not put them into Tara to rule.' He studied the four travellers in the fading light. 'But the Gruagach will have heard of your coming by now,' he said. 'It is their boast that they can smell Humans from seven miles away.' And then, on a different, sharper note, 'You *are* Humans, aren't you?'

'Yes,' said Floy, returning the steady regard, and putting his chin up a little. He started to say, 'What else?' and then thought better of it, and merely said, 'Why?'

Nuadu smiled again, and the dusk-light fell across the upper part of his face, hiding his eyes. 'Humans are highly prized here,' he said, and it seemed to Fenella that he moved more quickly, leading them deeper into the forest. 'The Gruagach will almost certainly be planning to hunt you down. You should be wary.'

'Hunt us?' said Floy sharply.

'For the *Fidchell*,' said Nuadu. 'One of their grislier games. They are over-sized children.' He turned to look at Floy again. 'Do you not have such things where you come from?'

'We do not have creatures who hunt people for sport,' said Floy, an edge to his voice, but Nuadu only said, 'Do you not?' and moved ahead of them.

Snizort, who was trotting happily after the others, sniffing at the air, and occasionally turning round to admire the view of Tara, asked about Fael-Inis.

'Oh, the Gruagach believe Fael-Inis to be some kind of god,' said Nuadu. 'They will not admit to fear of him, but they do fear him. And I do not know,' said the Wolfprince thoughtfully, 'that I disagree with them there. He is unpredictable and possessed of strange powers, that one. I do not think I have ever known anyone to cross him.' He glanced at them. 'He is said to have saved Tara in the past, and there are creatures in Ireland now who believe he will do so again.'

Floy said carefully, 'It is very beautiful, Tara.'

'Oh yes, it is the most beautiful place in the entire western world,' said Nuadu, sounding bored, and rather as if he was reciting something once learned by rote. 'And once upon a time they said that nothing that was not perfectly beautiful or beautifully perfect could ever be allowed to enter inside its doors.'

Fenella, who was walking between Nuadu and Floy, said, '"Once upon a time . . ."'

'The words invoke a meaning for you?'

'No,' said Fenella, slowly. 'Not really. But I have the feeling that they ought to.'

Nuadu sent her a sudden smile. 'As for Tara, Lady,' he said, 'I go only by hearsay, for I have never been allowed inside.'

'Why not?'

'I am neither beautiful nor perfect,' he said, regarding them. 'As you have seen. Also bastard stock is never welcome anywhere and it is especially unwelcome in the home of its ancestors. I might try to lay claim to the Ebony Throne you see.' He smiled again, and now there was no doubt about the bitterness. 'That would be extremely awkward for everyone.'

'But your family?' said Fenella, unaccustomed to creatures who apparently possessed no father or mother, and Nuadu regarded her, his expression unreadable.

'I have no family,' he said at last. 'My mother was a member of one of Ireland's Noble Houses, she was a princess in her own right, and she was also the consort of the High King. But she transgressed the Sacred law and lay with a Wolf.'

Nuadu sent her the sideways glance.

'They will tell you, in Ireland, that Wolves have not been seen since the reign of the High King Erin and perhaps they have not. But my mother travelled widely and trod strange paths.' A sudden mischievous glint lit his eyes. 'She was a reckless wild lady, my mother,' he said. 'But it is sure that my father was a Wolf, and although I am noble, I am also a bastard. Because of it, I was put out at birth to survive or die as the gods chose. The King would have welcomed his own bastard at Court, but he would never have welcomed his Queen's. And so I grew up in the Wolfwood, where I am regarded as neither quite royal, nor quite of the people. It is a strange position to hold.'

Floy said, choosing the unfamiliar expressions cautiously, 'But surely, if you were the Queen's son—?'

'My mother is dead,' said Nuadu in an expressionless tone. 'She died at my birth. As for the King, he was slain by the necromancer, CuRoi. Tara no longer has a Wolfking.'

'Had you no brothers?' asked Floy, trying to remember what the procedure for inheritance had been and how these things had worked on earth. 'Had the – the King no sons of his own?'

138

'I had a half-brother. He was taken.'

'Where is he now? Is he dead?'

Nuadu turned to look at Fenella, and his eyes glinted redly. 'He is deep within the Dark Realm, Lady,' he said, very softly. 'He is held captive at its black heart by the necromancers CuRoi and the Robemaker, both of whom covet Ireland. He will never return to Tara; that has been ensured. For no one,' said the Wolfprince, half to himself, 'no one has ever been known to escape from the Dark Realm.'

As they went deeper into the forest, Fenella's emotions alternated between fear and excitement. To read about giants and half-Humans and ancient enchanted forests in the safety of Snodgrass and Snizort's house was one thing; to walk through a dark, old wood in company with a man who claimed to be half-Wolf and learn that such creatures did, after all, exist, and moreover were close by, was another thing altogether. I suppose I am not imagining this, she thought, sending a covert look at Nuadu. I suppose it is all happening. And then, darker and more dangerous still: I suppose he really *is* part Wolf?

Almost as if he had sensed this, Nuadu glanced towards her and, in the soft green light, something that was certainly not Human looked out from his eyes. As if, thought Fenella, the Wolf was waking a little more strongly with the deepening of the twilight. Hadn't all the ancient tales warned against trusting Wolves? And, in those tales, wasn't it always the half-brother, the illegitimate son, who was the most villainous of them all?

Surely, oh surely, you did not, if you had any intelligence, go walking into the depths of an ancient twilit wood with a young man whose eyes were dark and occasionally glinted redly in the twilight, and who moved with swift, lean grace through the undergrowth, and who had a way of tilting his head to listen to you that was definitely and disturbingly not Human . . .?

The forest was quiet and brooding, but Fenella had the feeling that, just beneath the surface, creatures were stirring and waking and watching. Were they? Was it only her imagination, or was she really glimpsing three-cornered faces here and there, peering out from the trees . . .?

Who are these creatures? Are they of interest to us? Are they Human? Can we use them?

Nuadu said, 'This way, Lady,' and stood back to allow them to walk forward to where the forest path widened.

'Where is this?' said Fenella.

'*Croi Crua Adhmaid,*' said Nuadu, very softly, 'the Place of Ancient Enchantments. The Forest Court of the Six exiled Royal Houses of Ireland.'

Greenish light poured in from overhead, purple-tinged and shadowy, and the trees fringing the clearing were ancient and so immense that their branches interlaced high above them and the light that poured in was dappled, and smoky. On the far side of the clearing were caves, nearly but not quite obscured, vanishing into the deep blue shadows.

The Homes of the Exiled Royal Houses. The Forest Court of the Six Noble Lords . . .

At the centre of the clearing was an immense carved table; Fenella thought it was oak, although she could not be sure. But it was long and ornate, with six high-backed carved chairs drawn up to it, and the remains of some kind of meal still set. There were great silver dishes, and engraved plates, and chalices. Snizort's eyes lit up at the sight and Fenella knew he was remembering how the medieval Courts of Earth had feasted exactly like this; in state and splendour, with elaborate cups and goblets, with flagons of wine and mead, and with great platters of roasted meats: beef and pork and venison and boar.

The clearing was bounded by twelve immense and ancient trees, and half set into the trunk of each one was a kind of rough, half-formed seat.

And then Nuadu said smoothly, 'Allow me to present you to the Six Royal Houses of Ireland,' and Fenella saw that six of the roughly hewn thrones were occupied.

Chapter Twelve

Fenella was not precisely afraid, but she discovered that she was extremely glad to have Floy at her side as they moved forward to the centre of the clearing. There was not really anything to be afraid of, of course. Probably these people would be very friendly and interesting. Nothing nasty had happened to them yet, in any case.

She found herself looking round for Nuadu Airgetlam who had at least been reasonably friendly. Or had he? Had he, after all, led them into a trap? Fenella caught herself remembering how he had looked slantwise at them in the Wolfwood, and said, 'You *are* Human, aren't you?' and had to suppress a shiver.

But there did not seem to be anything else to do but go forward, and Fenella held up her chin, because even if you did not feel brave, you could at least pretend to be brave. It would not be quite as good as the real thing, but it would be better than nothing. Also, they were certainly not going to be intimidated by anyone, and they were definitely not going to be intimidated by a group of exiled half-Humans from out of the Ancient Past.

The Six exiled Royal Houses of Ireland, seen by twilight, seen in the deepening dusk of an ancient, spell-ridden forest, were cruel and beautiful and faintly sinister. Once you had looked at them, you could not help but go on looking, and once you had been looking for a very short while, you could not help seeing, without any question at all, that they were only partly Human. Both Fenella and Floy found themselves wondering about this, but for the moment, there was not time to wonder, there was only time to allow Nuadu to lead them forward and search their minds for suitable greetings.

Nuadu was looking remote and rather bored, as if he

found all this inexpressibly wearying. But he said, quite courteously, 'Allow me to present you to the Six Royal Houses of Ireland.' And paused and added, 'Once there were Twelve, but in the battles against the Gruagach, many were killed and others captured.' His eyes were perfectly steady as he said this, but Fenella caught, without warning, a sudden strong emotion, and looked up, startled.

But he only said, 'I shall, of course, present them to you in order of precedence.'

'How else?' said Floy blandly, and Nuadu shot him a sudden look of surprise, as if he had not expected irony returned.

'They are all Royal, although they would argue that some are more Royal than others. And certainly some of them are of very ancient lineage indeed.' And then, as if the subject had ceased to be of interest to him, Nuadu turned away and led them to the first of the tree-thrones.

'Tealtaoich of the Wild Panthers,' said Nuadu smoothly. 'Cousin to the Wolfprince, may he be preserved, and therefore a prince of Ireland.'

'And therefore standing in direct line to the Throne of Tara,' said Tealtaoich, in a soft, purring sort of voice.

'If,' said Nuadu, his eyes glinting suddenly, 'the imprisoned Prince, my brother, is found to be beyond our recall.'

'Of course,' said Tealtaoich, widening his brilliant green eyes at Nuadu. 'Dear me, what else should I mean?'

'I cannot imagine.'

'Nuadu suspects me of being involved in the most *sinister* plots and intrigues,' confided Tealtaoich, who was dark and slender with glossy black hair and a short, curving upper lip like a cat's. 'When really, I am the most *guileless* of creatures.'

'And the Prince's most loyal subject?' said Nuadu.

'And the Prince's most loyal subject,' agreed Tealtaoich blandly. 'I cannot imagine how anyone could believe otherwise of me. Of course, people are the most *shocking* liars! You would not give credence to the stories that have been told of me. When we have completed our plans for regaining Tara, be assured that I shall ride at the head of our armies,' he said. He fixed the travellers with an unblinking green stare. 'In the meantime, whoever you are and wherever you are from, you are very well come,' he said with sudden courtesy, and eyed Fenella rather fixedly, so that Fenella had the feeling he might be thinking: and *you* my dear are especially well come. This was very nearly sinister, but it would not do to appear at all disconcerted and, in any case, Tealtaoich was apparently a cousin to the captured Wolfprince and, therefore, a person of some importance.

Next to Tealtaoich was a huge, shaggy, earnest but rather friendly-looking creature, with massive square shoulders and a thick brown beard. A bear of a man, thought Fenella, and then remembered how Nuadu had seemed to pick up her thought earlier with such ease and thought she had better be extremely careful about what she was thinking.

'Clumhach of the Bears,' said Nuadu. 'One of the Prince's most *useful* supporters.' He stood back and watched as Clumhach thrust out a friendly paw – Fenella thought you could not call it a hand – and bade them welcome. 'Clumhach supports the Prince,' said Nuadu, 'and was one of the sponsors at his birth.'

'He was a very *lusty* baby,' said Clumhach earnestly, 'and everyone thought he'd make a good king when the time came.' He leaned forward, conspiratorially. 'Between you and me,' he said, 'I never thought he had sufficient of the wolfblood in him to rule. It has to be very strong, as we all know.'

'Well, yes,' said the four Renascians, who did not know at all, but saw it was not the time to be asking questions.

'I didn't say anything then, because it wouldn't have done,' went on Clumhach, 'and anyway, I don't really understand these things.' He sent a worried look round the clearing. 'I daresay it doesn't matter to say it now, what with the poor fellow in the hands of CuRoi and the Robemaker. Dear me, it doesn't bear thinking about.'

Nuadu said, silkily, 'Clumhach and I are, naturally, enemies, since he swore at the Prince's birth to aid him at all times, and I, of course, am secretly plotting to keep the Prince out so that I can take the Throne for myself.'

'Not true, old friend,' said Clumhach in a deep, rumbly voice that made you think he might suddenly break into a ho-ho-ho kind of laugh and clap you chokingly on the back. 'Nuadu likes to pretend he's a wicked sort of fellow,' said Clumhach, 'when we all of us know that he has a heart of gold beneath it all.'

'Even if it is a fair way down before you get there,' observed Tealtaoich, who had seated himself on the edge of his chair and was trimming his nails thoughtfully.

Nuadu smiled rather maliciously and led them on down the line of tree-thrones, not in the least discomposed.

'Dian Cecht of the White Swans,' he said. 'One of the Family of Lyr, and so we are, of course, greatly privileged that she has joined us. I daresay she will tell you that herself.'

Dian Cecht was, thought Fenella, rather beautiful. She was a slender, white-skinned, pointed-faced female, with long narrow dark eyes, and pale cap-like hair. She smiled at Fenella who tried to overlook the fact that the smile was somewhat chilly, accorded Snizort and Snodgrass a remote nod, and then looked with rather more interest at Floy. Fenella saw Floy tilt his head consideringly and hoped they were not heading for a difficult situation.

'The House of Lyr,' said Nuadu in his mocking voice, 'is, of course, one of Ireland's *oldest* families. Therefore, it was unthinkable that Dian Cecht and her son should not be a part of the Forest Court, even though they have to face *considerable* hardships out here.'

Clumhach said, 'But the House of the White Swans have *never* been other than extremely loyal to the Wolfline, Nuadu. I am sure it never occurred to Dian Cecht to do other than be with us all.' He beamed at everyone as he said this, as if he could not imagine anyone anywhere committing any kind of mean or disloyal, or even misguided act.

'Also,' put in Tealtaoich, 'there was really nowhere else for her to go.'

Dian Cecht said, in a distant voice, 'I care little for my own comfort. I am a simple and easily pleased soul.' Without looking, she held out a beckoning hand, and said, 'My son, Miach.'

'The Court Sorcerer,' said Nuadu Airgetlam, as one who says 'the Court Fool'.

Clumhach, who was leaning forward anxiously, as if he was finding this part of the conversation a bit difficult to follow, said firmly, 'He's doing very well. Very well indeed.'

'Oh, certainly,' said Nuadu, and Fenella and Floy shared the thought that Nuadu's tone was so laced with sarcasm that even the plodding Clumhach must have heard it.

But Clumhach beamed; he said they all found Miach's experiments of the *greatest* interest. 'I don't know a great deal about these things,' he explained confidingly to Snizort, who happened to be nearest. 'I leave all that kind of thing to the sorcerers. But it's a very long training, you know.'

'Yes, I'm sure it must be.'

Fenella and Floy both smiled at Miach, who was pale and thin and – and spotty thought Fenella, in horror, because it was hardly to be believed that the imperious and icily beautiful Dian Cecht could have given birth to a son who was spotty.

'But her son he assuredly is,' murmured Nuadu, picking this up without any difficulty at all. 'A mesalliance, or so I believe, with a pure-bred Human. Miach,' said Nuadu in an expressionless voice, 'is the result.' He leaned back against the nearest tree, arms folded, and eyed the unfortunate Miach thoughtfully. 'I daresay that, as a result, the White Swans and, therefore, the House of Lyr, will now become extinct,' said Nuadu.

'*Really?*' said Tealtaoich, sitting up hopefully.

'Nuadu has a bitter tongue at times,' said Dian Cecht, and Fenella thought that her voice was cold and remote. '*My* family have never bred bastards, I am glad to say.'

'Only nonentities,' retorted Nuadu.

'My family,' said Dian Cecht, ignoring this, 'is a tragic one. We are one of the great tragic Houses of Ireland. It is in all of the ballads and in all of the tales of Ireland.'

'How sad,' said Fenella, and hoped that she had managed to infuse her tone with the right blend of interest and sympathy.

'The Children of Lyr,' said Dian Cecht solemnly, leaning forward a little, and nodding. 'You will know of them, naturally.'

'I don't think—'

'The terrible enchantment spun by the sorceress Reflection,' said Dian Cecht. 'An imagined slight dealt her by my family. There was an affair of the heart involved, you understand. Modesty forbids me to disclose what it was.'

'Dian Cecht and Reflection both once wanted the same lover,' said Tealtaoich, by way of explanation. 'And Dian Cecht lost.'

'A wicked and immoral creature, Reflection,' said Dian Cecht, and shuddered delicately, pressing one curving hand to her breast. 'But I would not stoop to her methods, I have that consolation, at least.'

Floy said, as one treading on very thin ice, 'This would be the sorceress Reflection who presides over the Fire Court?'

Dian Cecht at once said, 'I see you know of her. But then who does not? Yes, she rules over her absurd and *vulgar* Court, which she has actually had the temerity to model on Tara. And she is sought, actually sought out by people.' She shook her head in a brooding manner.

'She was once sought by the rebel angel himself,' murmured Tealtaoich. 'And rumour has it that you, also, were – ah – *covetous* in that direction, my dear.'

'Fael-Inis! That charlatan!' said Dian Cecht, and although she did not quite say 'pshaw', the general effect was much the same as if she had. 'I would not soil my *feet* with Fael-Inis,' said Dian Cecht with superbly regal disdain.

'That's not what I heard,' said Nuadu Airgetlam, apparently to nobody at all.

'Nuadu mocks, but he would not do so if his family had suffered as mine has,' said Dian Cecht. 'Ah, Reflection's vengeance towards me for daring to challenge her was a terrible one. Both my poor dear sisters chained for ever to the Rock of Dairbhreach, and constrained to lure sailors to a watery grave until Reflection chooses to release them.' And then, stretching out a hand to Miach, 'My son is my greatest comfort.'

Miach looked uncomfortable, and said, 'Oh, Mother.'

Floy took Dian Cecht's hand and bowed over it, and said, 'But we are glad to know you, at any rate, madam,' and Fenella thought: I have never heard him call anyone 'madam' in his life! and then remembered about the thought-hearing and tried to quench this and waited to see what came next.

What came next was the presenting of the remaining three Royal Houses.

'And they were all extremely friendly and nice,' said Fenella firmly.

'Of course,' said Snizort, shocked. 'True Royalty always is. There's a very good story about Queen Elizabeth I – or was it Elizabeth IV? If I had my notes, I could tell you – you'd be very interested—'

The golden hawklike creature called Eogan of the Eagles came next; his skin was not quite skin and not quite feathers. Fenella found him regal and rather remote and a bit alarming, but he spoke quite graciously, and asked where they had come from. 'Which,' said Floy later, 'was really rather a difficult question to answer when you think about it.'

'What did you say?' asked Snizort.

'That we had come from the Future,' said Floy.

'Goodness me. What did they say?'

'That it was very interesting.'

The other two Bloodline Lords were Feradach of the Foxes, who was slant-eyed and had a silky golden beard, and Oisin of the Wild Deer, who was dark-eyed and rather scholarly-looking.

Fenella thought it was difficult to know what to say to each of these people. 'It always is,' said Miach, who had tagged on to the procession. 'How do you think I manage?'

'But you're a sorcerer,' said Fenella, who rather liked this word, even though she was not yet quite sure what a sorcerer did.

'Only an apprentice.'

'What does that mean?'

'I sometimes get it wrong,' said Miach, and Fenella and Floy both thought that probably Miach nearly always got it wrong, but that it would not do to say this.

'Also,' said Floy, 'you are one of these people. You are a – you are of the White Swan family.' And hoped he had got this right.

'Well,' said Miach, 'yes I am, but unfortunately my mother mated with a Human at the wrong time.' And then, as Floy looked inquiringly at him, he said, rather pettishly, 'Oh, it's that absurd enchantment the sorcerers spun at the very beginning. So that the Royal Houses of Ireland possess what's called beastblood.'

'How?' said Fenella, rather bewildered and trying to remember what Nuadu had said earlier and Miach hunched a shoulder crossly.

'Well, by mating with the beasts under the ancient Enchantment of the Bloodline, of course,' he said, in a where-on-earth-have-you-come-from voice.

'Do they? I mean,' said Fenella, 'do they *have* to?'

'Yes, of course. For the Humans to possess Tara would mean the fall of Ireland for ever,' said Miach. 'Tara would crumble. It's a very old curse indeed. Don't you know *anything*? The whole point of the Enchantment is to keep pure-bred Humans off the Throne.'

'We are but lately arrived here,' said Floy, gravely.

'If you want to know what I think,' said Miach, 'I think

it's all a bit sordid, that enchantment. It's all very well for people like Nuadu, who probably actually *enjoys* doing things like that with Wolves and whose mother the Queen was *very* wild, or for somebody like Tealtaoich, who most people agree has the *oddest* appetites. And Clumhach is so stupid he wouldn't understand. But Mother's different. Well, you only have to look at her! She would *never* subject herself to— Well, anyway, I think it's an outdated convention, that's what I think.'

'One we do not have in our world,' murmured Floy.

'Oh, really? Oh, well, anyway, the Panel of Judges decreed that it was time for the White Swan line to be strengthened – they actually had the nerve to say the blood was getting thin. *Thin!* I ask you! And they ordered the Ritual of Mating, and everybody started to recite the enchantment and they prepared one of their stupid banquets, and everybody thought they were in for a high old time. And then, when it came to it, Mother refused to play her part. She was quite polite about it, but she simply declined to go through with the Ritual. And why shouldn't she, I'd like to know?'

'No reason in the world. She – mated with a Human instead?' said Floy, once more aware that he was picking his words with care.

'Yes,' said Miach, rather baldly. 'Yes, she did. In *private*. And so I inherited only Human blood and nothing at all of the Swans. That isn't to say there's anything *wrong* with being a pure-bred Human,' he said hastily, 'only it will probably mean that the White Swan House will die out now. Also,' he added, 'it's a shame to lose your inheritance.'

'Well yes.'

'It'd have been nice to have had the enchanted blood,' said Miach, suddenly wistfully. 'And been in line for the Throne. That's if the Prince is dead, of course.'

'Naturally.'

'If he's inside the Dark Ireland he might just as well be dead. Anyone knows that.'

'Of course,' said Fenella and Floy together.

149

'Anyway, I view it with the gravest misgiving, I do really,' said Miach, gloomily. 'It's a hard life, you know, being a sorcerer's apprentice. It's even harder when you've been dragged away half-way through your training. There's an awful lot I still don't know.'

'I'm sure it must be very difficult for you,' said Floy, and Fenella, feeling that intelligent sympathy was required, nodded slowly.

'Of course, we left a bit hastily,' said Miach. 'I had to leave all my notes and all the books on sorcery behind. And if they've fallen into the Gruagach's hands, well, I just don't like to think what will happen, that's all. I just don't like to think.'

'Couldn't you have – lived somewhere else?' asked Fenella.

Miach glanced over his shoulder, and drew closer. 'There *was* a suggestion that some of us should go to the Fire Court,' he said, very furtively indeed. 'But it was only a suggestion and, of course, after what Reflection did to Mother—'

'Of course.'

'I wouldn't have gone for anything,' said Miach. 'Even if they had offered me half of Ireland, I wouldn't have gone.' He appeared to consider this and to come to some agreement with himself. 'No, I wouldn't,' he said. 'Mother was perfectly right to decide to come into the Wolfwood and into *Croi Crua Adhmaid*. She *always* knows what's best. I always do what she says. She's marvellous, don't you think?'

'Fascinating.'

'She was the one who arranged for me to go into the Academy of Sorcerers, you know,' he added. '"Miach," she said, "it will be the very thing for you. I shall see to it at once," she said. And so she did. I shouldn't have known how to go about that, but Mother knew. And, of course,' said the sorcerer's apprentice, 'of course, there's not a great deal you can do, practically speaking, not if you're a—'

'Mongrel?'

'I was going to say half-breed,' said Miach, rather hurt.

'A much better word,' said Floy. 'I intended no discourtesy.'

'And so I took up sorcery, you see. Mother said I should and so I did. I'm going to restore Nuadu's arm.'

'Really?'

'Yes, I am. I've been studying what to do and I shall do it. You'll all see.'

Floy said, 'Are you really all going to – wage war on the Gruagach?'

'Well, it isn't so much the Gruagach as the ones behind them,' said Miach, and then glanced over his shoulder as if fearful of somebody listening. 'It's the Robemaker, really, and CuRoi. They're the ones who sent the Gruagach to take Tara. The Gruagach would never have thought of it for themselves. Everybody knows that.'

Nuadu, who had padded silently across the clearing, and was standing listening, said, 'Little Miach has it all worked out.'

'I'm doing more than you are!' said Miach, stung. 'I've written some very good spells already! All you've done is lead us out here and set up a Court!'

'True.' Nuadu arranged himself on the ground at their feet and Fenella thought: everything he does is graceful yet I believe it is wholly natural.

'All I have done,' said Nuadu, 'is to bring the Six Royal Houses safely out of reach of the Gruagach, and into the Wolfwood and *Croi Crua Adhmaid*.'

'I didn't mean—'

'It is little enough,' said Nuadu. '*Croi Crua Adhmaid* is not, after all, invincible.' He glanced behind them into the shadowy depths of the now-dark forest. 'We shall only remain here for as long as it takes to lay our plans and marshal our forces. And doubtless we are already surrounded by the Robemaker's creatures.' He regarded Miach. 'But what are you going to do, my child?' he said. 'Tell us of your plan to beat the Dark Ireland.' And he leaned back and waited.

Chapter Thirteen

'I'm going to wake the Trees.'

Miach sat back and beamed at Floy and Floy stared and thought: how the devil am I supposed to answer that one? He had drawn breath to make some kind of response, although he was later to wonder what he would have said.

Nuadu stared at Miach and said, 'In that case, may all the gods preserve us.'

'It's a very good idea!' said Miach, stung.

'It's a remarkable idea,' said Nuadu, and turned as Clumhach came beaming over to them.

'Food and wine for our guests,' he said. 'Come along everyone, everything is set out for you.'

'We may live like gypsies, but we have retained a veneer of culture, you see,' observed Nuadu, unfolding from his curled-up position and holding out a rather absent hand to Fenella.

'Some of us have retained more culture than others, of course,' said Tealtaoich.

'Some of us brought a positive *army* of servants, with which to do so,' said Dian Cecht.

'That's because some of us have *loyal* servants, my dear,' said Tealtaoich. 'I should not have *dreamt* of leaving my people behind to the mercies of the Gruagach.'

'If you felt like that, you should have put up a better fight against them,' said Feradach of the Foxes, and Tealtaoich turned a look of utter astonishment on him.

'Do you mean *go into battle*?' he said. 'Oh, I could not *contemplate* such an *extreme* measure. I leave that kind of thing to people like Clumhach.'

'I fought,' said Clumhach, pleased to be able to join in this. 'I fought very hard indeed. We all did.'

'We lost,' said Oisin.

'Yes, but it wasn't for the want of trying. In fact, we were going to call up the Beasts,' remembered Clumhach. 'It would have been the first time it had been done for – well, for a very long time, but we were going to try.'

'The ancient art of the Mindsong,' explained Nuadu to the four travellers. 'What was once called the Samhailt. Each of us has the power over our own kind. In times of trouble we can call them to our aid.'

'We didn't have a chance to call them,' said Oisin. 'The Mindsong requires complete silence and utter concentration and we were all of us much too busy trying to fight the Gruagach. Because,' he added, 'despite what Tealtaoich will try to have you believe, he fought more wildly than any of us.' He smiled at Tealtaoich in rather a mischievous way.

'Oh, tooth and claw,' said Tealtaoich, urbanely.

'We all fought,' said Clumhach. 'I think it's very important to remember that we all fought very hard.'

'It's quite important to remember that we also lost,' said Tealtaoich, and there was a sudden anger in his voice, so that the four Renascians realised for the first time that these strange creatures, for all their rather brittle jibes, cared very deeply indeed about Tara, the Shining Palace which had been taken from them.

'They care,' murmured Nuadu, who had seated himself next to Fenella, 'because they each of them want the Throne.'

Fenella said, rather sharply, 'Do you always listen to people's thoughts like that?'

'If they will be of interest,' said Nuadu urbanely. He reached for the wine flagon and filled her chalice. 'Do you not have that power in your world?'

'No.'

'How dull and boring.'

'It makes for privacy,' said Fenella a bit sharply, because they might be these creatures' guests, but it would not do to allow themselves to be patronised at all. Nuadu smiled gently and appeared not the least bit discomposed. Fenella, rather hesitantly, said, 'When the

– the Gruagach drove the King out, were you there?'

'Yes, Lady.'

Fenella said, 'If the others were going to – call up the Bears and the Panthers and all the rest, could you have called up your – that is—'

'Could I have summoned the Wolves?' said Nuadu, sitting back in his chair, and regarding her over the rim of his wine glass. 'Oh, no, Human Child, Fair Lady, I have not that power.'

'Why not?'

'Because I am tainted stock,' said the bastard prince and smiled the smile that was dangerous and sinister and exciting, but which did not seem to care for anything at all. 'They would not have answered me. And also—' He stopped. A tiny frown touched his brow and then he said, as if it was unimportant, 'Also, the Royal Wolves have long since gone from Ireland in any case.' He sent her the slanting look. 'That is what everyone will tell you.'

'But – it is not true?'

'The Wolves of Ireland have not been seen since the days of the High King Erin,' said Nuadu smoothly.

'But your . . . the Queen—'

'My mother the Queen was a very remarkable lady,' said Nuadu. 'She travelled to Ireland's wild and remote parts.' He looked at Fenella. 'It is twenty-two years ago,' he said. 'Perhaps the Wolves still roamed in the off-shore islands and in the great northern forests then. They do not do so now.' And then, as if shaking off a tiresome mood, he said, 'But it is sure that when it is judged time for the Wolfkings to strengthen the line, by lying with the she-wolves, my family will end. The Wolves will no longer be there. And then, according to an old old prophecy, Tara will fall and Ireland will be forever damned.'

'I beg your pardon,' said Fenella, staring at him, 'but don't you *care*?'

'I care for nothing and no one,' said Nuadu at once. 'Why should I? Tara is nothing to me. And Ireland is already in the grip of the Dark Realm. If you go out from here, if you go out into the villages and the towns and the

154

hill farms, you will see that people are already being forced to make sacrifice to the Robemaker.'

'Sacrifice?' said Fenella, who knew the word, but had never actually said it.

'Their sons,' said Nuadu in an expressionless voice, 'sometimes their daughters.' He regarded her and Fenella frowned, because this was a totally unfamiliar concept.

'They have to give them up for – to work for the Robemaker?'

'Yes, some of them are chained in the Robemaker's Workshops and forced to work there. But some are simply killed and their souls offered to the Soul Eaters,' said Nuadu.

Again the mention of souls and their loss . . .

Nuadu said, 'The idea of sacrifice is unknown to you?'

'Well,' said Fenella, 'yes, it is, rather.'

'It is something that Ireland is very used to,' said Nuadu, his eyes unfathomable. 'Throughout our history, sacrifices have been demanded and taken. Sometimes they are called by other names, but the end is always the same. The loss of lives, and the stealing of souls.'

Again the mention of souls and their loss . . .

'But all creatures have souls,' said Nuadu, looking back at her.

'I think,' said Fenella carefully, 'that perhaps our – perhaps my people lost sight of it a bit. I think we have forgotten about souls. Our ancestors' world was destroyed, you see, and so much was lost to us. So many beliefs and faiths and teachings.'

'That saddens you.'

'Yes,' said Fenella. 'Yes, it does.' She looked at him. 'We were cheated,' she said. 'Out of our history.'

'To lose a thing, or even to forget about it, does not mean that it ceases to exist,' said Nuadu. 'Your history existed, nonetheless.'

'Yes.' Fenella was thinking that this question of souls and losing or keeping them was rather intriguing, but also that it might take some sorting out in her mind. But she only said, 'What of the Gruagach. You fought them?'

'Only to relieve the tedium of everything. In any case, we lost the battle. Allow me to serve you with some of this wild sorrel, Lady.'

The food was unfamiliar but delicious, and the wine was strong and fragrant and bore no resemblance at all to any of Snodgrass's brews.

'But it was very good wine,' said Snodgrass later.

'I drank four chalice fulls,' said Snizort.

'I asked them for the recipe,' said Snodgrass.

'How rude.'

'Not as rude as drinking four chalice fulls.'

'Did they give you the recipe?'

'Well, no.'

'There you are then.'

We are very nearly at home here, thought Fenella, listening to them, noticing how Floy had fallen into an absorbed discussion with Eogan and Feradach about the battle against the Gruagach, and how Snizort was making notes – 'I asked if they would mind,' he explained earnestly afterwards. 'I wouldn't have done it without asking, of course. But do you know, they were rather flattered.

'They had what they called *ollam* at the Court; I think that means Chroniclers, but, of course, the *ollam* didn't come with them into the Wolfwood. Oisin said they would be very glad to have some proper accounts of what was happening. He said all this was Ireland's history in the making and it ought to be written down. Very sensible,' said Snizort, happily arranging his papers and pens and the ink-pot. 'I shall make a very careful record of it all for them.'

Snodgrass was discussing the precise ingredients of the hare stew with Clumhach and offering to cook them all his own blackberry pudding for tomorrow night's supper.

'I thought it would be only polite,' he said. 'And my word, the forest's full of them! Blackberry pudding with apple.'

We are very nearly at home out here in this dark ancient forest, with these strange half-Human creatures . . .

Fenella found the thought surprising, but somehow not so surprising as it might have been. Oughtn't they to be wary and suspicious and out of place? And oughtn't they to be finding it difficult and awkward to talk with these creatures? But it isn't in the least difficult. It isn't difficult or awkward and none of it seems strange. Because we passed through so many remarkable experiences before we arrived here? Perhaps. Although I think it is more than that, she thought, curled into her chair at the table, enjoying the fragrant wine and the way the firelight made a pool of safety and warmth. I think it is simply that we were always meant to be here.

'Perhaps you were, Lady,' said Nuadu softly at her side.

'Is that possible?' Fenella would not turn her head to look at him, because that way he might see even more deeply into her thoughts. But she was strongly aware of him watching her and she knew, without looking at him, that his eyes would hold the disturbing glint and his face would be shadowed and secretive in the firelight. But, 'Is it possible?' she said again, her eyes on the others.

'Time is not always reliable,' said Nuadu. 'It is occasionally flawed or damaged and sometimes things – people – whole worlds perhaps – are misplaced.' He waited, and Fenella at once understood that he meant Time as a great glowing tapestry. 'People are not always born into the place and into the age they were intended for,' said Nuadu, very softly. 'Perhaps that is why you are here now, Fenella.' He smiled the wolfsmile, and his voice lingered over the syllables of her name, so that Fenella stared at him and felt a sudden dark stirring, a strong, sensual pull . . . How would it be to be held against him, to feel the cool silver arm imprisoning her so that she could not pull away . . .? I think I had better not wonder about that, she thought firmly, and turned to talk to Oisin and Snizort.

Towards the end of the meal, which Fenella supposed they ought to call supper, there was a whisper of sound from deep within the forest behind them and the sensation of dozens of wings beating on the air and the feeling of dozens of eyes peering from the darkness. Perhaps it would be as well not to look too closely. There was no knowing what strange and sinister beings might lie in wait out there in the dusk, and there was no telling what might happen to them if they inadvertently looked on one.

Floy, sitting with Feradach and Eogan, felt, in the same minute, the stirring and the soft awareness but, unlike Fenella, looked behind him at once to the clustering trees, and caught – or thought he caught – a smudge of blue-green, wisps and curls of something that was not quite smoke and not quite water. There was a shimmer of iridescent wings, the sense of long, narrow eyes watching, of round, hard, seal-like heads.

From across the table, Tealtaoich said in a matter-of-fact voice, 'Are you glimpsing the *sidh*, Floy?' and Floy turned round in his chair, and stared at Tealtaoich, who smiled the catsmile, and said in a purring voice, '*Do* remember, my dear, that to look on the *sidh* properly, to see them in their chill and unearthly reality, is probable death and certain madness.

'Dear me, how *poetic* that sounds,' he said with lazy mischief. His eyes flickered over Floy for an instant and something that was neither lazy nor mischievous gleamed there. 'Do not,' said Tealtaoich suddenly and rather seriously, 'even listen to their music for longer than absolutely necessary.'

'What are the *sidh*?' asked Floy, his eyes still on the drifting blue and green shapes within the Wolfwood.

'They are the most purely magical creatures in all Ireland,' said Tealtaoich. 'They are believed to have served the first sorcerers of all and to have accepted the guardianship of every Wolfprince and princess ever born in Ireland. But although they nearly always serve the Wolfkings in times of war, they are greedy and merciless for the souls and the seed of Men. They live beneath the ocean in the water caves and they will try to lure you to the cold silver Court of their own King, the Elven Aillen mac Midha.' Tealtaoich regarded Floy with faintly malicious amusement. 'To try to follow the *sidh*'s music, or to try to see the *sidh* fully and clearly, is certain death,' said Tealtaoich. 'Remember that, Floy.'

'I shall not forget,' said Floy, but he glanced back to the shimmer of turquoise beyond the trees.

Dian Cecht, who had been eating the food with regal disdain, said, 'It may not be the *sidh* that Floy is seeing,' and turned on Floy her sombre dark eyes.

'No?'

'Perhaps Miach has already summoned the Tree Spirits,' said Dian Cecht.

'I devoutly hope he has *not*,' said Tealtaoich with a shudder. 'I cannot imagine anything *nastier* than seeing the entire Wolfwood wake and surge in upon us.'

'Tealtaoich would tell you that the Tree Spirits are dangerous,' said Dian Cecht, composedly to Floy, and Tealtaoich at once said, 'I most certainly *should*.'

'But of course, Miach will know how to control them,' said Dian Cecht.

'After he has summoned them, that is.'

'Naturally.' Dian Cecht regarded Tealtaoich with surprise. 'Miach is perfectly capable of calling up a few dryads and hamadryads. They will be extremely helpful to us in the battle.'

'Battle?' said Floy suspiciously. 'What battle?'

'Nuadu Airgetlam is going to rally us all to mount an attack on Tara,' said Dian Cecht, as if this had all been discussed and agreed, and as if Floy ought to know all about it.

'In fact,' said Oisin, 'the battle plan is almost ready. Isn't it, Nuadu? All that remains is for us to summon our creatures.'

But Nuadu only said, as if his mind was somewhere else, 'I have been thinking that there are other ways of fighting the Gruagach than riding full pelt down the hillsides.'

'Really? What had you in mind?' asked Oisin, leaning forward eagerly.

'Oh, perhaps the sending in of a little decoy,' murmured

Nuadu, 'something to distract the giants.' And as Oisin looked at him rather sharply, 'I believe the giants are very partial to Humans,' said Nuadu thoughtfully, and smiled the wolfsmile.

Oisin started to say something, but was interrupted by Dian Cecht who was still talking about the Tree Ritual. 'Miach thought it would be useful, you see. He has half completed the Ritual already.'

'I don't trust the Trees,' said Tealtaoich and, farther down the table, Clumhach looked up and said 'Trees? What Trees? Is somebody going to call up the Trees? My word, there's a weighty undertaking. My word, I *don't* like the sound of that.'

'You see?' said Tealtaoich softly.

'Trees?' said somebody a bit farther along – Floy thought it was Feradach. 'Did I hear somebody say something about the Tree Awakening Ritual? Dear me, it must be centuries since anybody tried that? Does it still work?'

'Rituals don't lose their efficacy just because they haven't been used for a few centuries,' said Miach, rather huffily, and Feradach said well of course not.

'I suppose we know what we're doing, do we?' put in Eogan.

'Yes . . . does Nuadu Airgetlam know we're going to summon the Trees?' said Clumhach, and looked to Nuadu as he said this, and Floy received the strong impression that for all Nuadu's brusque manner, and for all his gentle malice, these people still regarded him as their leader. Because he possessed the ancient wolfblood they seemed to set so much store by? Yes, perhaps.

'My children,' said Nuadu Airgetlam fondly, 'I know all about little Miach's games and I know all about the Tree Awakening Ritual. I derive immense enjoyment from it. Miach is welcome to call up the Trees,' he said.

Somebody else said they would be safer with the *sidh* than the Trees, and somebody else said that you could no more trust a dryad than you could trust one of the Gruagach, which was saying quite a lot.

'But they'll be on our side,' put in Miach. 'Nuadu, tell them that the Trees will be on our side.'

'You tell them, my child,' said Nuadu, who was listening to the interchange with a malicious grin. '*I* was not born at the time of the famous Battle of the Trees. I have not the remotest idea of how the Trees behave in times of war, or even which side they give allegiance to. Dian Cecht may be able to tell you more, of course.'

'She may even remember the Battle of the Trees,' remarked Tealtaoich, and Nuadu said at once, 'Precisely my idea, cousin.'

'I am not your cousin,' said Tealtaoich in what was very nearly a growl.

'Ah, the Battle of the Trees,' said Dian Cecht. 'Ah me, one of my family's *cherished* memories for, of course, my ancestors fought at it.'

'I suppose,' said Eogan, 'that we *do* want the Trees with us, do we?' He looked rather stern as he said this and everyone turned to listen respectfully to him, which Fenella and Floy had both noticed they all did with Eogan.

'I wouldn't trust a Tree,' said Clumhach firmly. 'Nothing but trouble, Trees. My great-uncle Beariul – the one that married into the Jackal line—'

'*Odd* ancestors you have, Clumhach—'

'I'm not ashamed,' said Clumhach, staunchly.

'I would be.'

'Everyone knows that the Jackals fight for the Dark Ireland,' put in Oisin. 'They're very high up in the Armies of the Soul Eaters. Captains and Lieutenants and all manner of things.'

'Along with the Rodent People,' agreed Feradach, and both Fenella and Floy noticed that a shiver had gone round the table at the mention of the Soul Eaters and their Armies. Fenella thought it was probably only her imagination that the forest seemed to grow momentarily darker.

'I'd almost rather adopt Nuadu's original plan,' said Tealtaoich. 'The one we were drawing up earlier. Simply

161

muster an army and march on Tara.' He looked at Nuadu, who smiled and said, silkily, 'But since then I have been formulating a much more subtle plan, Tealtaoich.' And looked to where Fenella and Floy were sitting. Tealtaoich lifted his eyebrows questioningly, but Nuadu merely smiled and poured himself another chalice full of wine.

'If we could once regain Tara, we would be in a much stronger position,' said Oisin.

'It would be more comfortable, as well,' put in Clumhach.

'But could we *rely* on the Trees?' asked Eogan. 'And could we trust them? Wasn't there a time when they served the Dark Ireland?'

'Was there? Then we ought to tell Miach to be extremely careful —'

'Miach knows what he is doing.'

Eogan, who had been looking out into the forest, suddenly said, 'If the Trees do wake —'

'Of course they will wake,' said Miach indignantly.

'If they do wake,' said Eogan, 'then I think we ought to approach them fairly and openly and ask if they will join with us.' He looked at Nuadu as he said this and Fenella noticed that, at the same moment, the others looked at Nuadu as well. They will not take any action unless he gives the word, she thought. How remarkable. And: I believe he dislikes it very much when they turn to him in this way, she thought.

Nuadu gave no indication of what he might be feeling. He said, in a disinterested voice, 'By all means ask them. And then what do you propose to do?'

Tealtaoich said, 'March on Tara. As we agreed.'

'Admirable, cousin.'

'I do wish,' said Tealtaoich, in an irritated voice, 'that you would not call me cousin.'

'Do you object to being cousin to a bastard?' said Nuadu. 'Well, be assured, Tealtaoich, that the relationship disturbs me quite as much as it disturbs you.' He studied the forest thoughtfully and a tiny frown touched his brow.

'Eogan is quite right, of course. We must certainly try to enlist the Trees' help.'

'And regain Tara for the Wolfkings again?' asked Tealtaoich, silkily.

'Oh, Tara's Throne is available to whomsoever is foolish enough to take it,' said Nuadu, off-handedly. 'But I do believe, my children, that before we attack Tara, a little stealth is called for.' He looked at them and, just for a moment, something that was neither disinterested nor bored showed in his eyes.

'What did you have in mind?' asked Eogan.

'The employing of spies,' said Nuadu, gently. 'Sending in someone – or maybe more than one someone – who can discover a little about the Gruagach's movements and the extent of their sentries and their guards.' He paused and looked at them, apparently waiting for some response.

'But,' said Tealtaoich, slowly, 'the Gruagach would suspect anyone who approached Tara.'

'Would they?' said Nuadu, silkily.

'They're usurpers,' said Tealtaoich, frowning. 'They will be continually on the watch for any attempt to infiltrate Tara.'

'And they certainly wouldn't extend a warm welcome to any creature who simply requested admittance,' put in Oisin.

'*Wouldn't* they?' said Nuadu, even more gently.

Eogan said, 'The only creatures welcome at Tara these days are—' And stopped.

'Well?' said Nuadu. 'Do go on.'

'Humans,' said Oisin, staring at Nuadu. 'Humans are welcome at Tara.'

'Precisely,' said Nuadu, and smiled.

There was a moment of complete silence and Floy and Nuadu regarded one another steadily.

Then, keeping his voice expressionless, Floy said, 'You are suggesting that we go up to Tara and request admittance?'

'Yes.'

'In order to find out the number of guards and the times of sentry changes?' said Floy.

'Exactly.'

'And there is no danger?' said Floy. 'Have I understood you correctly?'

'Admirably,' said Nuadu.

Floy was looking at Nuadu, his eyes narrowed thoughtfully. 'I suppose,' he said, at length, 'I suppose we can be sure that you are on the side of right, can we?' And smiled with perfect courtesy as he said it.

There was a rather shocked silence.

'You see,' went on Floy, speaking as if he was almost thinking out loud, 'you see, we know nothing of your quarrels and your wars.' He regarded Nuadu, his head on one side. 'It's all extremely interesting,' said Floy. 'It's very stirring and intriguing and you have been eloquent, every one of you. We have no reason to disbelieve anything you have told us and I think we should rather like to see Tara.

'But,' said Floy, 'how do we know that *you* are not the enemy? How do we know you are not planning to usurp the Throne of Ireland and depose the rightful King? How do we know who the rightful King is? Convince us,' said Floy, and sat back and folded his arms.

Chapter Fourteen

'There is only one way to convince you,' said Nuadu. 'And that is for us to exchange bonds.' And then, as the four Renascians looked at him, 'If you agree to go into Tara, we shall send one of our number with you and you, in turn, will leave one of your party behind. As bond.'

'To be held captive?' said Floy.

'As a pledge,' said Nuadu. 'You will have with you one of our people, we shall have one of yours.' He lifted his brows as if saying: how *dare* you question me?

But Floy merely said, 'Your ways are different to ours. Perhaps you will allow us a brief time to consider the matter,' and drew the others a little apart.

'I think we should do it,' said Fenella, frowning. 'I think we have to do it, because we have to become a part of this world now, no matter how strange it is.'

'Fenella's right,' said Snizort.

'Yes,' said Floy. 'Yes, I think she is. This has to become our home. Renascia is lost to us, and we have to make this our home.'

Renascia is lost . . . Fenella felt a sudden sharp twist of loss.

'And if we are truly to become part of it,' said Floy, determinedly, 'then we have to embrace its quarrels and its wars, as well.'

'Take sides,' said Fenella, trying the words out.

'It seems as if it would be difficult to remain neutral,' said Floy. 'Snizort, Snodgrass, what do you think?'

'I say we go along with them, but *warily*,' said Snodgrass. 'Very warily indeed. I don't like the sound of the giants much.'

'Half giants,' said Fenella absently. 'And so long as we avoid the *Fidchell*—'

'I don't much like the sound of that, either,' said Snodgrass.

'We've only got their word about any of it,' put in Floy. 'I wish we knew if what they've told us is true. About the King – the rightful King that is – being killed, and the Gruagach being usurpers.'

'I do think it might be true,' said Snizort, thoughtfully. 'I *know* it all sounds far-fetched – exiled monarchs and sorcerers and lost Thrones.' He adjusted his spectacles and regarded them solemnly. 'But it is only far-fetched because we've never until now encountered it,' he said.

'Earth did have its share of usurpers and outlawed Kings,' offered Snodgrass.

'So it did.'

'And since we aren't likely to get back to Renascia, this will be our home,' said Fenella. 'If there's a war going on, we have to throw in our lot with one side or the other. We have to take sides. And if it's a choice between giants and the creatures of this forest, and given the little we know of giants, I'd much prefer the creatures and the forest,' she said firmly.

Floy said, 'So would I. But one of us has to stay behind. A pledge. It's their suggestion, and it's reasonable enough.'

'Well, we can't leave Fenella on her own,' said Snodgrass at once.

'Certainly not,' said Floy, and Fenella had just drawn breath to ask why not, when Snizort said, 'I'll stay. I don't want to, because I'd rather come with you, and we ought to stick together really. But if one of us has to stay, I think I'm the best choice. They won't harm me because one of their number will be with you and the giants. Especially if it's the prince,' he added, and Fenella looked up, because it had not occurred to her that it might be Nuadu who would accompany them. 'Also,' said Snizort, 'I could listen to what's going on and find out a bit more. That might be useful. I could listen quite openly.'

'You've already established yourself as a chronicler,' said Floy, thoughtfully. 'And although it's not an arrangement we've ever come across, it's clear they have, and they believe it to be—'

'Honourable?' said Snodgrass.

'Honourable, yes,' said Floy. 'Thank you, Snodgrass.'

'It used to happen on Earth sometimes,' said Snizort. 'I've read about it. They called it holding *hostages*. Countries would swop what they called *political* prisoners. I never fully understood it, but now I see the reasoning.'

'If you stay,' said Fenella, who was secretly horrified at the idea of leaving anybody behind, but who saw the inevitability of it, 'if you stay, Snizort, you won't be pretending about wanting to make notes and record the battles. You really will want to know about the war and the Gruagach and the Wolfkings. They'll see that. And I think,' said Fenella, 'that in spite of their bickering and their odd ways, they are very sharp, these people.'

'They would see at once if we tried to deceive them,' said Floy, nodding. 'Snizort won't need to pretend to be other than he is.'

'Well, I *would* like to know a bit more about how the giants were driven out of Gruagach,' admitted Snizort. 'And the – what do they call her? – the Frost Giantess who now holds Court at Gruagach. And I daresay, if I worded it tactfully, Oisin would explain to me the exact nature of this enchantment of the Beastline they all seem to hold in such high respect. It'd be a useful thing to know, that,' he said, wistfully.

Floy said, 'Then we agree? We'll do what they want, and try to get into Tara?' And, as they nodded, he grinned suddenly and a reckless light shone in his eyes. 'I have to confess,' he said, 'that I should very much like to see inside Tara.'

'Then it's settled,' said Snizort briskly. 'But you won't forget about being very wary, will you? Because I *don't* like the sound of those giants.'

Floy said, 'Let's find out who their pledge is to be.'

The Court seemed to regard the pledge idea as perfectly natural and ordinary and appeared pleased, but not especially surprised, to learn that the Renascians would undertake the task of spying out the land at Tara.

'And,' said Floy to Fenella, 'the very fact that they assumed we would believe their cause to be the right cause, adds weight to their case.'

'They cannot believe that anyone would see it other than as the right side,' said Fenella, thoughtfully.

'Exactly. I think we're all right,' said Floy, his eyes brilliant. 'I think this is the side of—'

'Victory?'

'I was going to say justice,' said Floy, grinning. 'But we'll hope that it's victory as well.'

The Court were discussing which of them would go to Tara with Floy and Fenella and Snodgrass.

'How far is Tara?' asked Floy, as he and Fenella took their seats at the oak table again. 'Because although we can see the lights, it's difficult to gauge how far it actually is. Whoever accompanies us ought to know the distance and be able to lead the way without worrying about taking the wrong path.'

'Oh, that's not a problem,' said Clumhach. 'It's quite near, anyway.'

'How near is quite near?'

'Well, it won't take long to get there.'

'If I go with them, I could lead the way very easily,' said Eogan.

'No, you could not,' said several voices at once.

'You'd be seen and recognised,' said Tealtaoich. 'If anyone's going with them, it ought to be me. I've been to Tara more times than I can count.'

'That's why you'd give the game away,' said Feradach. 'You'd be recognised. Now if *I* went, I could slip through the forest and spy out the land for them first.'

'I thought whoever went was going as pledge,' said Dian Cecht. 'If that is so, it doesn't matter about spying out the land or being recognised by the Gruagach. I submit that whoever goes, ought to be the *nearest* to the Throne.' Several people looked up sharply at this and Dian Cecht said, 'I merely make the point. I do not expect anyone to listen to me, because I quite see that I am of little account to anyone.'

'I'm nearest,' said Tealtaoich, ignoring the latter part of this speech.

'No, you're not.'

'If I went,' said Oisin, 'I should be quicker than the rest of you.'

'Yes, but we don't want quickness, particularly.'

'Why not?'

'We want stealth.'

'Then let Feradach go. He's pretty stealthy when he likes to be.'

'I had a third cousin who was so stealthy you wouldn't even know he was in the room with you—'

'It isn't a matter of stealth, Clumhach, it's simply that we have to send somebody who isn't known at Tara—' said Tealtaoich, and then stopped, frowning.

Nuadu smiled the wolfsmile, and said, 'Precisely, cousin.' And then, turning to Floy and the others, 'It seems that I am to be your companion into the giants' lair,' said the Wolfprince. 'Shall we prepare for the journey?'

Nuadu padded ahead of them through the dark blue Wolfwood, occasionally pausing to tilt his head and listen, rather as if, thought Fenella, he could hear things the rest of them could not.

As if he had picked this up, he turned to look at her.

'I *can* hear the creatures of the forest, Human Child,' he said softly, and fell into step beside her. Fenella felt something unfamiliar and faintly disturbing twist the base of her stomach. 'If you listen properly, *fully*, you might hear them as well,' said Nuadu.

Fenella said, 'I don't think—' And stopped abruptly as Nuadu reached out to her and placed his hand lightly across her eyes. There was a sudden shiver of awareness and the impression of distant but strong thrumming, as if somewhere, a long way off, gentle fingers were being drawn across a huge stringed musical instrument, or as

169

if someone was tapping lightly on a tightly stretched skin . . .

And beyond that, again, was the awareness of Nuadu's closeness, the light touch of his hand on her face; his fingers soft but with a steely strength under the softness; the sharp, masculine scent of warmth and power and clean hair and, under that again, the impression of a prowling, snarling strength that might be harnessed at the moment, but that would not always be harnessed, and that would certainly not always be entirely safe . . .

Fenella gasped and blinked. Nuadu withdrew his hand and Fenella felt her mind become her own again and managed to say, with creditable calmness, 'What was it?'

'It is what was once called the *Samhailt*,' said Nuadu, walking softly on again down the bracken-carpeted forest path. 'That is, the art of hearing and feeling the thoughts of others. It has almost died out now, for people no longer trust it, and perhaps they no longer dare admit to it either.' He sent her one of his sideways glances. 'Once it was the sole prerogative of the Royal Houses of Ireland,' said the Wolfprince, softly. 'But now that it is dangerous to possess the enchanted Royal blood, it is also dangerous to possess other things. And so the *Samhailt* has been almost stamped out.'

'But not quite?' said Fenella.

'It comes with the Royal blood,' said Nuadu. 'That is why I was able to lend it to you, a very little, just for a brief time.' And then, unexpectedly, 'It is not always an easy thing to possess,' he said.

He was leading them farther away from the safe-feeling Forest Court now; into the twisted shadows cast by the ancient Trees and down narrow, overgrown paths. It was an eerie, none-too comfortable journey now. Each of them was aware of the night rustlings and of the tiny invisible forest creatures close by. Each of them felt the tiny wind that scurried into their faces and stirred the Trees high above them, making the leaves rustle and murmur.

'I believe,' said Snodgrass, in an awed whisper, 'that they *are* waking.'

'That was the idea,' said Nuadu, hearing this. 'Miach woke them because he thought they would aid us.'

'Will they?'

'I have no idea.'

'I believe you think we shall aid you more,' said Floy.

'I believe you will be of immense help to our cause,' said Nuadu, politely. 'That is, if we can persuade you that ours is the side of – what did you call it? the side of *right*.'

'And providing we can outwit the giants?'

'Providing you can avoid the *Fidchell* board,' said Nuadu caustically.

'Are we really risking our lives?' said Floy.

'I have no idea,' rejoined Nuadu, lightly. 'But I don't think it's very likely. You are sufficiently intelligent to outwit the Gruagach and, although I am only a bastard Wolfprince, still I can summon a thread of magic and I can certainly call the *sidh* if I have to.'

'Can you?' said Floy, and Nuadu smiled.

'I can. The *sidh* are bound by a very ancient bewitchment to answer the enchantment known as the *Draoicht Tarrthail*, which is the Enchantment of Peril. I have never pronounced it, but I know the words, and the *sidh* would never dare disobey the *Draoicht Tarrthail*.' He regarded Floy blandly. 'Despite my birth there are still some things that have come down to me from the Wolves of Tara,' he said. 'Will you believe that we shall not go into the giants' lair entirely unprotected?'

'I am glad to hear it,' said Floy.

As they neared the edges of the Trees, the Wolfwood became quieter and more strongly tinged with the strange dark blue light that Fenella and Floy had found so eerily beautiful.

'Twilight,' said Nuadu, leading them between the Trees, and nearer to the glow of light that was Tara. 'The hour once known as the Purple Hour.' He sent them a sideways look. 'The hour when magic is at its strongest,' he said.

'Should we be afraid?' asked Fenella and Nuadu hesitated.

'You should be wary,' he said at length. 'There are many layers of magic. Some of it is good and some of it is evil and some of it is ancient. But between the good and the evil and the ancient, there are shades and half-shades, and there are degrees and half-degrees, and nothing is ever quite good or quite evil, Human Child.' He regarded her with the characteristic tilt of his head.

'Have the Gruagach any magic?' asked Floy. And thought it remarkable that he was able to ask this question quite normally and quite calmly, as if it was the most everyday thing in the world to be discussing giants and their possible involvement in magic.

'No,' said Nuadu. 'Giants have never had the – I think you would say the *sensitivity* – to harness anything magical or enchanted,' he said, and Fenella started to breathe a sigh of relief, because if you had to be dealing with giants, it would be better if they did not have any magical powers. And then Nuadu said, 'But they are able to command the services of those who *do* have powers,' and Fenella remembered that it was always as well not to be lulled into a false sense of security. Even when it came to giants. Especially when it came to giants.

They were strongly aware of the presence of the Trees now; 'There is a kind of whispering,' said Floy, standing still on the edge of the forest and staring into its depths. But Fenella thought it was more that the Trees were listening and watching them. Were they? Was it only her imagination that made her catch a glimpse of eyes peering from the gnarled trunks of the largest Trees, and was it only her eyes playing tricks that made her see the slender twining branches as long arms with branchy fingers at the ends, or long flowing tresses of hair that was not hair at all, but leaves and twigs and fronds?

I won't look too closely, said Fenella silently. I'll remember that we are leaving the Wolfwood behind us, and that Miach will certainly be able to keep the Tree Spirits confined within the forest. At least, thought Fenella, turning to follow the others through the forest fringe, at least, I hope he will.

If the Wolfwood had been dark and rather sinister, and full of secret whisperings and laden with unseen enchantments it had, in some unfathomable way, also been safe. Both Floy and Fenella thought there had been a sense of security there; a feeling that at least you were protected by a *something*. Fenella thought she would not examine too closely what the *something* might be. But they had been safe. They had very nearly been cosy in the Forest Court.

The road that led to Tara was not cosy at all. It was open and bare and, although the Trees still fringed the road, there was something extremely disturbing about it. Several times, Floy turned round suddenly, as if expecting to see something (what?) creeping along behind them, and once Snodgrass stopped dead in the middle of the path and looked very intently at the high thick-thorn hedge that fringed the road.

Nuadu appeared unconcerned. He led them on down the road, guiding them when the path forked; apparently perfectly sure about which route to take.

Floy said, 'You know the way well?'

'Yes.'

'But you told us you had never been to Tara,' said Floy, and Fenella looked up because Floy's voice held an edge to it.

Nuadu did not appear particularly perturbed. He simply eyed Floy with faint amusement and said, 'You're not altogether trusting yet, are you, Floy?'

'Not altogether,' said Floy.

'Maybe you are right not to,' said Nuadu softly and, as he spoke, the gathering twilight lay across his face and his eyes were dark and unreadable. Fenella shivered, because just for a moment, it had seemed as if something alien and cruel and inHuman was looking out through his eyes. 'I have not been inside Tara.' And then, his eyes still in shadow, 'But perhaps I have been there in my mind. Perhaps I have traversed its halls in my mind and perhaps I have wandered in its marble galleries and perhaps I know it as well as if I had spent my every waking hour there.' He looked back at Floy. 'I have never been inside Tara,' he said, again. 'Even though it is the home of my ancestors, for my mother was of the ancient Royal House, and my father—' He stopped, and the slanting wolfsmile touched his face again. But he only said, 'Tara is the shining castle, the bright palace of all the Wolfkings. I possess the ancient royal blood, but I am tainted stock and if I had tried to gain entrance, I should have been turned from the doors.'

'And yet,' said Fenella gently, 'yet now you come with us.'

'Yes.' The slanting eyes were on her. 'You see how much I am prepared to risk, Human Child,' he said, mockingly. 'Or perhaps it is only on account of your bright eyes.'

'Will the Gruagach know you?' asked Floy.

'It is possible.' There was the familiar tilt of his head. 'I have the wolfmark on me.' He shrugged. 'If they recognise me, they will turn me from their doors and they will deal with you as they deal with all spies.'

Fenella and Floy stared at him. 'Is that any different to how they deal with other Humans?' said Floy at length.

'Not in the slightest,' said Nuadu. 'But they'll call it by a different name.'

'But supposing—' began Floy, and then stopped and half turned. In the same moment, Nuadu whipped about and Fenella saw his right hand curl in a sudden predatory movement and his eyes narrow.

Snodgrass, who had been a little ahead, stopped, and said, 'What is it?'

'Into cover quickly,' said Nuadu, pulling Fenella with him. 'There's something following us.'

Something following us . . . They all heard it in the same moment and, in that moment, knew that it had been with them for some time. There was a swirling of the shadows, a clotting malevolent coalescing of the night. Something evil, thought Fenella. Whatever it is, it is evil. It is something ancient and evil and faceless and it is creeping along the moonlit road towards us.

As they crouched in the rather sparse cover of the thin trees at the side of the road, the three Renascians tried to think that the *something* might be just another traveller, an ordinary, innocent-intentioned wayfarer, on his way to the nearest village, or the next township. But with the thought, came another: innocent travellers do not remain just out of sight and just beyond hearing, and just over the borders of vision. And even though Renascia was small enough to make travel an easy matter, the three Renascians understood the universal code for travellers; the almost obligatory courtesy that lone travellers, or parties of two or three, meeting on a journey, banded together, shared food, companionship, the protection of numbers against danger.

Solitary travellers did not prowl furtively down deserted roads without making their presence known.

Floy, lying in the bracken between Fenella and Snodgrass, hearing the sounds coming closer, realised that they had been hearing them for some time and glanced to Nuadu, remembering how Nuadu had seemed able to hear the night creatures of the forest so easily. Why, then, had he not heard this creeping slithering sound earlier and led them to safety? Is it a trap? thought Floy wildly. Is he about to give us up to some evil being? Nuadu was lying flat, his flesh and blood arm thrown half casually, half protectively about Fenella. His eyes were narrowed almost to slits, and he was so still that he had become part of the shadows.

Footsteps . . . Rather hollow-sounding. Fenella did not pause to examine why this should be so very frightening. Footsteps and a soft silken swishing sound. Silken skirts brushing the road. Or perhaps a long dark robe trailing the ground. A robe. And mingled in with all of it, was the feeling of a darkness so complete and so all-embracing, that you thought the light might at any minute be blotted out for ever. Fenella remembered, and wished not to remember, words like necromancy and sorcery and remembered, as well, that when the world was very young, there had been old and evil enchantments . . . *And this is the world where those enchantments walked and where they might still walk.*

What kind of creature prowled stealthily through the night, wearing a dark whispering Robe, and carrying with it the aura of an ageless dark evil . . .

Fenella remained very still and felt Floy's arm about her protectively and was immeasurably reassured. And then realised that it was not Floy, because Floy was several feet away.

I am lying on the outskirts of an old dark forest, and something ancient and powerful and probably immensely evil is creeping along the road towards us, but his arm is around me . . . I am in the embrace of a wolf creature, a prince of an old Royal House, and I feel as if I was never alive until this moment . . .

The fear was thudding in her heart, but the delight was still pouring over her, and she felt, in the same breath-space, Nuadu's arm tighten briefly about her. Protecting her? Or something else?

As if in answer, the fingers of his hand closed about her waist and there was a flare of understanding and of deep, primeval closeness, sudden and wrenching and – surely in these circumstances? – shocking. Fenella, briefly suspended between fear of what was coming towards them and purest delight at Nuadu's touch, felt the misty forest blur and then right itself again.

She turned her head, and saw that Nuadu was scanning the shadowy road and that his features had somehow sharpened, so that there could be no doubt at all about his strange ancestry.

The sounds were nearer now, only just beyond the curve in the road; there was a slithering silk-against-bone sound, as if something cold and bloodless was clothed in slippery, oily satin, and, in another minute, in just another few seconds, the creature that was inside the silken robe would appear . . .

Nuadu said in a low, urgent voice, 'Stay completely quiet. Do not move,' and Fenella felt him tense to meet the danger.

176

Lying flat in the briar hedge, between Nuadu and Floy, with Snodgrass to the left, Fenella was chokingly aware of a thick, fetid staleness drifting over them and the sense that, as the creature drew closer, the very air was becoming fouled with something leprous and diseased.

The sound was identifiable now; a whispering slimy softness that concealed something foul and dripping and terrible . . . something that was tainting the air with its ancient, noisome aura, something that came prowling towards them, thinly clad in whispering softness to conceal its true self . . .

A monstrous, elongated shadow fell across the roadway directly in front of them, and Fenella thrust one hand into her mouth to stop from gasping, because the shadow could surely not belong to anything Human, or even partly Human, because it was so sinister, so eerie, so entirely soul-less that it was not to be borne.

At her side, Nuadu said very softly, 'Dagda preserve us. *The Robemaker.*' And, without warning, he murmured a string of words in an unfamiliar tongue.

There was a blurring and a humming on the night air and the shimmer of blue-green, iridescent wings, distant and unearthly and eerily beautiful. There was the faint, far-off sound of singing, of music so inHuman and so coldly seductive, that the three Renascians forgot for a moment about the dark, prowling evil, and the terrible shadow and the giantish castle that they must soon enter and surrendered, briefly, to the singing.

And then the shadow was upon them and they were in its darkness. The light from the night sky was blotted out and there was a heaviness on the air, the feeling of huge wings beating somewhere overhead.

Round the curve in the road, there came the hooded and cloaked figure of a thin, tall shape, its eyes and face hidden by the deep hood, a long, carved staff held in one of its gloved hands.

The blue-green iridescence deepened and the singing was momentarily stronger. Fenella thought that long, narrow, turquoise eyes gleamed from within the

Wolfwood. The dusk thickened and, without warning, a thin mist-curtain of dark blue and indigo and sea-green, threaded with glistening silver veins, seemed to shroud the four travellers, so that they were obscured from view.

The dark hooded figure of the Robemaker passed by and went on down the road towards Tara.

Snodgrass made and lit a small fire and they sat round it, chilled and shaken, dusty from the tumble into the briar hedge. Snodgrass had even fallen into a bed of nettles. They sipped gratefully at the tiny but fiercely potent portions of some thick, sweet liquid which Nuadu had produced. 'For strength,' he said, and Snodgrass and Floy had drunk appreciatively.

The fire burned brightly, sending the creeping shadows slithering back into the Wolfwood and there was a sharp scent of burning within the smoke.

'Peat,' said Nuadu, regarding the fire critically. 'In all Ireland you wouldn't find anything to make a better fire.' He grinned suddenly and, in the flickering light of the peat fire, he seemed very much younger and very much more ordinary and, for the first time, without bitterness.

'You pronounced the – what did you call it? – the enchantment to summon the *sidh*,' said Fenella.

'I did.' The grin deepened. 'The *Draoicht Tarrthail*.' He leaned back against the bole of a tree and looked at them, his fingers curled about the wine chalice. 'The Enchantment of Peril,' he said. 'Once pronounced, by a member of the Royal Wolfline of Ireland, the *sidh* are compelled to come to that person's aid and to that of his companions.' The smile lifted his lips again. 'They would not have liked doing it, because they would not recognise me as truly Royal,' he said, 'but for all that, it is powerful, the *Draoicht Tarrthail*, and they could not ignore it. It is the oldest of all the enchantments, that, and it was spun by the first sorcerers who came out of the North and built Tara, the Bright Palace, for Ireland's first High Queen.'

He sat back, watching them, the glow from the fire making red lights gleam in his eyes. 'I grew up in the forest,' said Nuadu softly. 'And I know little of my ancestors, other than what is known to all Ireland. But I am glad that I knew enough to call the *sidh* to render us momentarily invisible to the Robemaker. And I am glad that I have sufficient of the ancient magical wolfblood to summon the *sidh*.'

Floy said, carefully, 'How *did* you know the words of the spell?'

'Spells and enchantments do not necessarily have to be learned,' said Nuadu, looking at Floy across the firelight. 'It is not a question of sitting down with a parchment or a manuscript, and learning by rote. It is – I think you would call it a race memory. I was born knowing the words of the *Draoicht Tarrthail*.'

'What is the Robemaker?' asked Fenella, who had been wanting to know this ever since the dark silk-clad evil had passed on and vanished round the curve of the road.

'He is a necromancer of the highest order,' said Nuadu, seriously. 'I do not know the details of the bargain the Gruagach struck with the Robemaker, I do not think anyone knows it. But the Robemaker is ever greedy for souls and that is why he comes out of the Dark Ireland. That is why he would have trafficked with Goibniu. The Gruagach certainly have not sufficient wit or sufficient – I think you would say – *enterprise* to vanquish and kill the King and then take and hold Tara. It simply would not have occurred to them,' said the Wolfprince, and poured himself another glass of wine.

Floy said, 'It is difficult for us to understand this question of souls,' and Nuadu said, quite lightly, 'If you have not the understanding, then it is something you will have to come to in your own way. It is difficult for me to explain it properly, because it is something I was born to. But believe me when I tell you that every sentient creature possesses a soul and that there are evil, hungering powers who would take those souls for their own dread purposes.'

'Yes, I see that,' said Floy. 'But the Dark Ireland . . .' He looked questioningly at Nuadu.

'It is the mirror image of this Ireland,' said Nuadu.

179

'The black and leprous underside of the world, which most people never see, but which is nevertheless there. All worlds have a dark underside,' he said seriously. 'Did not your own?'

'I don't think—' began Floy, and then stopped.

'What of the Dark Lodestar?' said Nuadu. 'The Black Abyss that sucked in your world?'

'Was that our Dark World?' said Floy. And then, looking at Nuadu, 'Is that possible?'

'If you encountered a Dark Sun, then for sure it will have been the evil, hungry underside of a true fair world,' said Nuadu. 'Our philosophers and our learned men and our druids could no doubt explain it fully to you. It is an interesting thing, this question of light and darkness and of every thing having its direct opposite. It would be that Dark Sun that forced you through the Time Curtain into this world,' he said.

'You seem to accept it very easily.'

'It is not unknown here, the existence of other worlds.' He looked at Floy. 'For you, Floy, I think the very idea holds out great allure.'

'I should like to understand more of it,' said Floy, slowly.

'You should not try to understand too much,' said Nuadu. 'For it is told that the Dark Realms are more beautiful and more sensuous than we can imagine. It is dangerously easy to fall under the thrall of the Dark Ireland. We have ballads that sing of the Dark Fields of Enchantment and tell of how, once you have supped at the tables of the necromancers and swum in their Crimson Lakes of Ancient Magic, you are for ever enslaved. You would never wish to return to the world, even if you could do so.'

For a moment, something dark and devilish glowed in his eyes and something so strongly and irresistibly alluring showed in his face that Fenella felt a sudden unwelcome suspicion unfold: Supposing, after all, this is a being from that Dark Realm, and supposing he is drawing us deeper and deeper into its embrace, and closer and closer to its terrible powers . . . ? She shivered suddenly, remembering how that other Darkness had called to them on Renascia and how they had slowly and terribly become aware of it, crouching in the skies, holding out its hungering arms . . .

And then Nuadu moved and smiled, and a log fell apart in the depths of the fire, sending out brightness and the warm, safe-feeling peat scent. The shadows receded and the impression of something dark and menacing vanished at once.

'My brother is inside the Dark Ireland,' said Nuadu and his eyes were in shadow again. 'He is held prisoner in the Fortress of Illusions, the citadel of the greatest necromancer of them all, CuRoi.'

'Can he not be rescued?' asked Snodgrass, and Nuadu frowned.

'No creature has ever been known to escape from the Dark Ireland, and certainly no creature has ever been able to come out of the Castle of Illusions, for it is sealed by strong magic every evening at sunset and there are no doors and no windows.' He paused. 'Perhaps the offering of a soul in return, for it is an age-old law, that, the taking of a soul in return for a soul.' He stopped again, and his eyes glinted redly in the fireglow. 'It would depend on the soul,' he said. 'For my brother is Tara's heir and, therefore, a great prize. I do not think that CuRoi would easily let him go. The necromancers of the Dark Realm have always coveted Ireland and they have always been greedy for Tara,' he said. 'That is why they have taken the prince. They know of the ancient curse that was placed on Tara which warns against a pure-bred Human ever occupying Tara's Throne. That is why the Beastline Enchantment was spun, so that Tara should be ruled by creatures not entirely Human. That is how the curse has been held at bay for so many centuries.'

'But what is the Robemaker?' said Floy. 'What does he do?'

'He is a very powerful sorcerer,' said Nuadu, his eyes gleaming in the firelight. 'Also, he is a necromancer – that

181

is, one who deals in the dark magic and in the forbidden power over the dead.'

'Why is he called the Robemaker?' asked Fenella, and Nuadu smiled again.

'He has dark underground Workshops where he keeps the Silver Looms that weave the enchantments,' he said. 'Have you such things where you come from? Enchantments and spells? No? Well then, you will not know that when a spell is created, it must be woven, like cloth, on a Silver Loom. All who study sorcery can do it, although some can do it better than others.'

'Miach?' said Fenella hesitantly, and Nuadu laughed.

'Miach is a child,' he said. 'He could not control a Silver Loom to save his life. But the Robemaker has in his Workshops the Black Looms of Necromancy, and it is there he weaves robes of spells for the greedy and evil people who seek him out.'

'Do you mean,' said Fenella slowly, absorbing this, 'that it is possible to – actually to commission a spell?'

'Yes,' said Nuadu.

'Oh!'

'But the Looms must be kept weaving constantly; they must never be still for an instant for, if they were, the power they draw down would be lost. The Robemaker knows this and he is constantly searching for poor defenceless creatures to work for him. If he had seen us,' said Nuadu, 'he would certainly have chained us by magic and thrown us into the Workshops.' He looked at them very straightly. 'To be captured by the Robemaker and sent to the Workshop of the Looms is one of the most terrible fates that can befall any living creature,' he said. 'The Robemaker is a merciless master; his slaves must work at weaving the robes of enchantment without ceasing. For them there is no night and no day and there is only the endless sound of the Looms.'

'Do they never try to escape?'

'No one has ever escaped from the Robemaker,' said Nuadu.

'But there must be a way—'

'Floy, there is no escape. The enchantments the Robemaker casts to keep them prisoners are too strong. And once their bodies cease to be of use,' said Nuadu, 'he takes their souls and offers them to the Soul Eaters of Cruachan.' He turned to look at them, his eyes brilliant in the firelight. 'The *sidh* protected us from him this time,' said the Wolfprince, 'but I think it was with extreme reluctance and only because they were constrained to do so. And it is written that no one may call on the *Draoicht Tarrthail* more than a very few times in a single lifetime.

'You should pray to whatever gods you have in your world that if we meet the Robemaker again, some other power comes to our rescue.'

Chapter Fifteen

The fire burned lower and there was the gentle scent of peat smoke on the air. Floy and Snodgrass seemed to have fallen into a discussion about the engravings in the Honeycomb Tunnels of Fael-Inis's Palace, and Fenella thought that Snodgrass was suggesting that perhaps they could somehow persuade the salamanders to aid Nuadu and the others in the fight to regain Tara.

'Always supposing,' said Snodgrass, glancing at Nuadu a bit uneasily, 'always supposing, that they *are* on the side of right, so to speak.'

In the flickering firelight, Fenella saw Nuadu smile as if this rather amused him. But he only said, softly, 'Your friend is still very wary of me, I think. And your brother does not yet entirely trust me.'

'Well,' said Fenella, determined to be fair, 'you can't blame either of them. We *don't* know very much about any of this, you know.' She stopped, because she found herself wanting to say: and however much *I* trust you, Floy and Snodgrass don't feel the same.

He heard that, of course; he leaned forward and took her hand, as he had done earlier and Fenella felt the delight wash over her again and frowned, because it was not to be thought of that she should fall quite so heavily under the dark romance of an unknown creature such as this. A piece of wood fell apart in the heart of the fire, and the light shifted, and a bar of shadow fell across the upper half of Nuadu's face, so that she could not see his eyes. When he spoke, his words were like a caress brushing her skin. 'You may trust me, Human Child,' said the Wolfprince. And then, in the old, mocking tone, 'But you already know that,' he said, and Fenella, who did know it, but who was not yet prepared to admit it, said, 'You don't exactly behave as if we can trust you.'

'No.' He leaned forward. 'Would you have me plead with you to help the exiled Court?' he said. 'Shall I beg you to give us your allegiance?'

'Of course not,' said Fenella sharply, and Nuadu smiled again.

'I thought not,' he said. 'You do not admire weakness in any form, I think.'

'You would never be weak,' said Fenella involuntarily. 'Floy is not weak.'

'No. He will question things, however. He will certainly challenge you at every stage of this mission,' said Fenella, mischievously pleased.

'He is doing so already,' said Nuadu. 'I should not have wanted any of you for allies if you had come blindly and unthinkingly to our aid.'

'Are we aiding you?' said Fenella.

'Oh, yes.' His eyes were on her, and there was the sharpening awareness of him again. 'Oh, yes, Fenella, you are aiding us. There is a long-held belief at Tara—' he stopped, and frowned.

'Go on.'

'There is a long-held belief that only a pure-bred Human can help an exiled Wolfking back to the Throne,' said Nuadu, and Fenella caught her breath, and said, 'Your brother—'

'He may be beyond our reach.'

'But you think he is not.'

He lifted the warm, fragrant wine to his lips again, watching her over the rim of the cup, and when he spoke, the caress was back in his voice.

'Would you come with me into the Dark Realm, Fenella?' he said, softly. 'Travel with me in the Fields of Necromancy and across the Crimson Lakes of Sorcery?'

'I'm – not sure,' said Fenella, staring at him, and he smiled.

'It would be a perilous, darkly beautiful journey,' he said. 'And perhaps we would find our journey's end, and perhaps we would not.'

Journey's end . . .

'And perhaps we would emerge unscathed, and perhaps we would not,' said Nuadu, gently.

Fenella started to say something, although she was never, afterwards, quite sure what it would have been, when there was a stirring, a rustling of movement behind them in the Wolfwood.

'The Trees—' said Fenella, turning to look. 'Nuadu— are the Trees really waking?'

If he had recognised that this was her first use of his name, he did not react, nor did he betray any impatience that the thin, gently seductive spell he had been sending out to her had been splintered. He merely turned his head to look into the heart of the forest and narrowed his eyes. 'Yes, they are waking. They are not fully awake; I think they have not been so for many centuries. But they are waking.'

'It's remarkable,' said Fenella, who knew, quite well, that she had cut into his soft, alluring words, and was torn between wanting him to go on and wanting to feel safe again.

Nuadu said, with a suddenly more *aware* edge to his voice, 'Come and see them.' And stood up and held out his hand to her.

Floy and Snodgrass barely looked round as Fenella and Nuadu Airgetlam moved towards the forest fringe. But Floy said, 'Do not stray too far, sibling,' and sent her one of his grins. Fenella smiled, because *sibling* was a word that Floy did not very often use, only when he was being particularly protective and close, and she knew that Floy was wanting to tell her, without actually saying the words, that he was close by if she needed him. She did not need Floy, or anyone, to protect her, but all the same, it was a good feeling to have.

It was secret and exciting to walk like this, Nuadu's hand holding hers, into the outskirts of the forest. Fenella had hesitated before following him. Curled up in front of the peat fire, discussing plans and strategies, she had seen,

186

quite suddenly and very clearly, that two paths had opened up for her; the safe, familiar path which was with Floy and the firelight and the discussion about what they were going to do next. And the other path, the dark beckoning groves of Nuadu's gentle seduction . . .

Because, said Fenella to herself, of course that is what he has in mind. I do know that. And stopped and looked very clearly at the two paths she could take. And saw that the familiar path with Floy and Snodgrass was not, after all, so safe, because nothing in this strange blue and green world was safe. And if I go with Nuadu now, that will not be safe either, thought Fenella. Only it will be unsafe in a different way entirely. It will be thrillingly unsafe, temptingly unsafe. And I think I want to find out what it is like to tread such an unsafe path. I suppose I could always turn back, anyway . . .

The dusky blue light poured in from overhead as they walked into the Wolfwood and Fenella could hear, much more definitely now, the soft susurration of the Trees. She found herself concentrating on this, because it would stop her from thinking about being here alone with Nuadu and how his hand felt, lying in hers, and whether he would move closer to her as they drew away from Floy and Snodgrass, and what she would do about it if he did.

There was a pattern in the forest sounds now, as if the Trees might be whispering to one another. As they walked, the branches were brushing neighbouring Trees, as if for strength and help. Here and there, the ground felt soft almost as if the Trees' roots were beginning to move somewhere deep in the earth. Would the Trees truly move and wake and come surging out to them?

'I don't know,' said Nuadu, looking about him. 'Certainly their spirits will come out; naiads and dryads and hamadryads. The stories tell how they are beautiful and wild and filled with strange woodland magic.'

'Are they,' Fenella paused, searching for the right words. 'Are they on the side of the Wolfkings?' she said, and was pleased to hear that this sounded to be a perfectly natural and normal question.

187

Nuadu smiled. 'They have always been so,' he said. 'Tealtaoich is right to be wary of them, but he is wrong to mistrust their allegiance.' He stopped by a massive old oak Tree and leaned against it, looking at her. Fenella stayed where she was, but the blood was beginning to race in her veins and something seemed to be happening to her breathing. If she had to speak now, she was not at all sure she would be able to. She thought: this is the moment when he is going to reach for me, and this is the moment when I have to decide which of those two paths I shall take. I am not quite on that path yet, thought Fenella. I think I have set foot on it, but I think that is all.

And then Nuadu said, very softly, 'Come here, Human Child,' and Fenella knew that the moment was upon her and that she had still not chosen.

Nuadu smiled. 'I shall not hurt you, Fenella,' he said. 'But come here and see and feel the stirring of the Tree Spirit.' His eyes were gleaming and there was a mocking amusement in his expression. He was talking to her on two levels, of course, but it did not seem to matter, because they both knew that he was talking on two levels.

If he touches me I shan't be able to go back, Fenella thought wildly.

And then Nuadu did touch her, reaching for her with the arm that was flesh and blood and bone; he pulled her closer, until she was standing before him, closer than she had been to him yet, and she could feel the warmth and the masculine strength and, so far from being worried now, the remembered delight was washing over her skin and nothing had felt so right and nothing had felt so natural ever before.

I believe, thought Fenella, I do believe that if he asked me now, I would go with him into the place they call the Dark Ireland. *Into the Dark Fields of Necromancy and into the Crimson Lakes of Sorcery . . .*

In the same velvet-on-iron tone he had used when he drew her into the forest, Nuadu said, 'Were you thinking I brought you here to make love to you, Fenella?'

'No,' said Fenella, who knew he would not believe this

any more than she believed it herself.

'Were you not?' said Nuadu, pulling her closer, holding her with the arm that was flesh and blood and bone, and Fenella found that she could no more resist than she could have flown.

'The Gruagach will play games with you, Human Child,' said Nuadu, his lips close to her ear, his breath warm and sweet and sending shivers of purest delight all over her skin. 'They will know you for a maiden, Fenella, and that will delight them and excite them.' He regarded her, his head on one side.

Fenella said, in a voice that was barely a whisper, 'Should I be afraid?'

'Of the Gruagach?'

'Of you.'

He smiled down at her and, in the mist-shrouded, twilit forest, there was a sudden recklessness about him, and Fenella, staring at him, thought there was a slant to his eyes that had not been there before. The twisting shadows from the Trees fell across the lower part of his face so that, for a heart-stopping moment, it was not a slender, dark-haired young man who stood there, but a creature that would have high pricked ears and lean, silky flanks, and soft sable fur, and that might walk not upright like a Human, but on all fours . . .

'In your world, Fenella,' said Nuadu, 'are there not tales that warn about maidens who walk in the woods with Wolves?' And regarded her, his eyes glowing.

Fenella thought: he is doing this deliberately. I *know* he is doing it deliberately, because I can feel that he is. He is quite calculatingly letting the Wolf wake, because he believes it will lure me. And of course he is right, she thought. Even though I know he is doing it, it does not make any difference. Because the Wolf *is* there.

'We do not have Wolves in our world,' said Fenella.

'But you know of them?'

'Only in legends,' said Fenella and hoped she had struck the right note; the one that said: and that will put you in your place!

But he sent her the three-cornered smile, as if he had heard her thoughts very precisely indeed, and when he spoke she was sure of it.

'*Are* you afraid, Human Child?'

'No.'

He took her face between his hands and began to kiss her, running his unharmed hand down over her body, the arm that was not flesh and bone holding her imprisoned against him, so that now she could feel the strong sweet arousal between his legs pushing against her.

'You know what I am, Fenella?' said Nuadu softly.

'A Wolf.'

'Does that frighten you?'

'No,' said Fenella, although she was not entirely sure about this yet and he smiled again and drew her down on to the forest floor.

I do not believe that this is happening, thought Fenella. I believe that this is some kind of dream. I am not here and he is not here and there is no forest and no purple-tinted twilight and all of this is a dream. She thought she ought to protest; she certainly thought she ought to push him away – only I cannot, thought Fenella, the blood singing frantically in her veins now, her heart slowing to a soft, sweet pulsing. She felt his hand unfasten the cambric shirt she had donned in Renascia – in another world and surely in another life! – and she felt the two hands then, one warm living skin and the other cold, silky, silver, caressing her naked breasts and then her thighs.

Delight was exploding all over her body now and there was the feel of his hand on her breasts, skin against skin – how lovely! – and deep, strong intimacy, the sudden closeness, because the soaring feeling of joy was something they were both sharing, it was like being one half of a whole, it was like completing something that until now had been only a fragment. I am moving along that path now, I have not quite reached the point where it will be impossible to turn back, but I am approaching it . . .

But just another few steps, she thought. Just a very little farther down the path . . .

190

There was a moment when the wolfmask lay across his face again, making it sharper, leaner . . . Crueller? thought Fenella, tumbling between fear and steadily rising delight.

Never that, Lady, not to you . . .

Fenella whispered, not wanting to break the delight, 'You are hearing my thoughts again.'

'Yes.' He bent his head and there was the caress of his dark hair against her naked breasts and surely there had never been anything so immensely intimate as this feeling of another's hair, silky, warm, against your skin . . .

He moved away then and there was a quick sharp pang, a coldness. But he simply discarded his own clothes, quickly and easily and without the least trace of embarrassment and, for a fleeting instant, Fenella saw him stand over her, the woodland shadows twisting all about him again, so that there could no longer be any doubt about his ancestry.

Half Wolf, thought Fenella, helpless now in purest fascination. Half Wolf and half Human, and I am no longer sure which half is in the ascendant, or whether it is deliberate, or even whether I care any more . . .

The Wolf was strongly in his eyes; they were slanting and brilliant. He is no longer Human, thought Fenella, but she could not have looked away from that shining stare if worlds had depended on her doing so.

His body was lean and hard and beautiful and as he lowered himself on to the thick pine needles of the forest floor, to lie alongside her, there again was the curious, abrupt grace that was not the least bit Human.

He parted her legs gently and easily and his arms were about her and she felt his weight, strong and warm and insistent.

There was a brief moment, the span of a heartbeat, when he stopped and looked at her, as if trying to hear her thoughts again, and then she felt the thrust of strong hard masculinity and there was the sensation of falling into a whirling, rainbow-coloured well, more exciting than anything she had ever imagined, stronger and wilder than anything she ever believed could exist . . . Nuadu was holding her tighter and his face was no longer wolfish but suddenly vulnerable and his eyes were filled with an unexpected longing, as if he might need her desperately and as if, beneath everything, he might be very easily hurt.

Fenella felt her own heart lurch and felt a great melting and a warmth, so that she wanted to wrap her arms tight about him and shut out the pain he had suffered and the bitterness and the deep, aching loneliness . . .

He was moving strongly against her, but there was a gentleness she had not expected and a helpless need . . . Something unfamiliar and painful closed about her, because she had expected the strength and the – yes, the passion! – but she had not expected the gentleness or the need.

And then there was the sensation that they were blending into one being now, sharing a single, thudding heart beating deep within one of them . . . She could hear him breathing faster and there was an urgency now, incredibly laced with fear, as if he was afraid she might suddenly reject him. Fierce protectiveness arose within her, because she could not bear to think how he had been shut out and cast off and how he had lived as an exile, a bastard prince of the royal house . . .

Nuadu made a sudden convulsive movement and cried out softly and Fenella felt the delight explode and then a gentle, sinking sensation as if they were falling into a huge deep soft bed of feathers . . .

Nuadu lay watching her, the narrow wolflook still pronounced, but Fenella saw at once that the slightly cynical, slightly bitter mask was back in place, and that there were to be no more glimpses of the loneliness and the vulnerability.

But we shared it, that brief moment of oneness, we shared it, and I saw beyond the mask to the real person, thought Fenella. Does that mean anything, I wonder? Ought I to refer to it? And sat back and waited to see what he would say and what he would do.

'Well, Human Child,' said the Wolfprince softly, and

Fenella saw that he was smiling at her and that something very gentle had touched his eyes.

She thought: *I have known the creature who exists behind the arrogant and cynical prince of the Royal House.*

Nuadu was looking at her with his head tilted and there was a sweet and secret smile in his eyes, as if he might be saying: we are centuries and worlds apart, you and I, and perhaps our languages are far apart as well. But still we have met on a level that does not count centuries and we have shared a world where there is no need of language.

There is no need of language . . .

'Of course there is not,' said Nuadu, and Fenella thought: I think he is telling me that what has happened between us is private and special. I'll have to be very careful about this, she thought, because I daresay that it is not an out-of-the-way thing to happen here. I'll have to pretend, just a very little, that I'm not in the least awed or dazzled, or even a bit bewitched. I *am* all of those things, I suppose, but I hadn't better let him know. Not yet.

The difficulty was that she had no idea what kind of behaviour was normal here, or whether people did this casually. It had seemed natural and right to be made love to in the twilit Wolfwood, but it did not mean that it *was* natural and right. It would not have been natural or right on Renascia, or at least, so far as Fenella knew, it would not have been.

The fire had burned considerably lower and Snodgrass was jotting down a few notes which Snizort would be glad to have when they got back to the Forest Court. Floy, who had been sitting with his back against a Tree trunk, holding the stem of a wine chalice loosely between his fingers, looked round as Fenella and Nuadu walked back into the firelight. Fenella thought he looked at her rather searchingly. But he only said, 'We are ready to go on up to Tara now, if you agree?'

Nuadu at once said, 'Certainly, for the Gruagach will have finished their supper and be at a loss for entertainment.

I daresay we shall provide them with some form of interest.' He regarded Floy tranquilly. 'Also,' he said, thoughtfully, 'I believe we – that is the three of us – are now sufficiently in accord for us to protect Fenella if we have to.'

'Yes?' said Floy, and Fenella caught the sharpness in his voice.

'Yes,' said Nuadu softly, and held Floy's eyes steadily.

Floy said, slowly and deliberately, 'I should not like to think that any of us would go unthinkingly into danger, or into anything where there might be hurt,' and Nuadu smiled the sudden, glinting smile.

'No one will be hurt,' he said. 'That has never been my intention.' And then, as Floy continued to regard him, 'You have my word on it, Floy,' said Nuadu, and Fenella thought that Floy relaxed just a very little and was aware that something had been exchanged between them both; that some kind of question had been asked by Floy and answered, more or less satisfactorily, by Nuadu.

But as they walked warily on down the road, the provisions they had brought carefully packed and distributed between them, Floy hesitated and glanced at her.

'All right, sibling?'

'Yes,' said Fenella. 'Isn't it?'

'I hope so,' said Floy, and Fenella understood that Floy had guessed what had happened between her and Nuadu and was concerned for her, was concerned about her, and had only been partly reassured by the odd, two-levelled conversation. She started to say something – some kind of reassurance – when Nuadu turned round sharply, and Snodgrass said, 'What's that?'

Nuadu said, 'Footsteps again,' and tensed, ready to spring.

Before any of them could move, the long, sinister shadow of the Robemaker fell across the forest road, and the necromancer himself was before them.

There was a terrible moment when no one moved and no

one spoke. Then Fenella felt Floy tense to spring, exactly as Nuadu had done moments earlier and, in the same instant, heard Nuadu begin to intone the words of the spell that would summon the *sidh* and knew that Nuadu's action was the right one, because this dreadful being would never be vanquished by ordinary flesh and blood, daylight strengths.

The Robemaker, if he could be defeated, would not be defeated by physical attack.

But to Floy, still unused to spells and enchantments, physical attack was the only means to hand. The figure before them was repulsive and evil; he could feel the ancient malevolence that emanated from it. The stench of corruption was in his nostrils and in his mouth, strong and sickening, as if the door to a vast charnel house had been pushed ajar. Nausea twisted his stomach, but he tensed his muscles to spring, knowing at one level that this was a necromancer, one of the fearsome Dark Lords, but aware, on another level, that the creature must somehow be vanquished.

He leapt forward on to the hooded shape and, at the same moment, heard Nuadu pronounce the *Draoicht Tarrthail*.

The Robemaker flung out a hand and a spear of crimson light shot from his fingertips, sending Floy spinning across the ground. Fenella and Snodgrass, standing together helplessly, saw the gleam of white bone within the deep hood, and the malevolent red stare of inward slanting eyes without flesh or skin around them . . .

The Robemaker lifted his long arm again and the crimson light spat and curled like a whip about Nuadu. Fenella, unbelieving, saw the words of the *Draoicht Tarrthail* take shape on the air, silvery and delicate, and then melt and blur and run into nothing.

A still-born spell . . .

The crimson rope of light had snaked about Nuadu's waist and the Robemaker made a quick, practised movement. At once the rope tightened and started to draw Nuadu nearer to the waiting figure, closer and closer. Nuadu was struggling and snarling and Fenella started to run forward, Snodgrass at her side. Floy, still a little way off, barely conscious from the first bolt of light, had risen to his knees; he was sick and dizzy and he was only vaguely aware of Nuadu's captivity. There had been a moment when he had been sufficiently close to the Robemaker to catch a glimpse of a terrible, ravaged face, partly eaten away, of ulcerated bone, a gaping cavity where the nose should have been.

As his senses steadied, he saw that the words of the *Draoicht Tarrthail* were falling and fading and he realised that, in some way, the Robemaker was deflecting the enchantment. Nuadu was held captive, fighting the tangling rope-lights, but they held fast, bit into his skin. Floy saw Fenella tearing at the crimson ropes uselessly and he saw blood well on her hands.

Nuadu said, 'There is nothing you can do, Lady—' And even at such a moment, Floy registered Nuadu's use of the ancient, courteous title. He calls her 'Lady' thought Floy. And then: Later. I'll think on that later.

He saw at once that Nuadu could do nothing, for the rope-lights were binding him strongly and cruelly and, although he had certainly never seen anything like the Robemaker before, he thought that if they could somehow disable him, they might be able to escape.

He looked about him for a weapon of some kind and snatched up a sharp stone, judging the distance between himself and the Robemaker. Nuadu was pronouncing the *Draoicht Tarrthail* again, and again the words formed on the night air quite clearly and then, just as clearly, died as the Robemaker dissolved them effortlessly.

And then the Robemaker chuckled and Floy felt a sick dread, because it was the most evil and the most sinister sound he had ever heard. It rang through the dark forest and Fenella thought, and then was sure, that the Trees that had been unfolding and reaching out ever since Miach's spell, flinched, and drew in their leaves and that their branches dipped suddenly and fearfully.

For that is the terrible sound of the Robemaker, the One who dwells in the Dark Ireland, and who serves the Soul Eaters in the Cavern of Cruachan . . .

Nuadu was fighting the Robemaker every inch of the way, but slowly, inexorably, step by step, he was being drawn closer to the towering cloaked figure who was standing watching, arms folded, his face still in deep shadow. Floy, his earlier suspicions of Nuadu vanished completely now, drew back his hand to hurl the boulder. As he did so, the Robemaker turned his head towards him, as if to say: *do not waste your energy, my poor Human victim, I am a creature of the Dark Ireland, and I dwell in the High Towers of that realm, and I can anticipate your every move with ease . . .*

There was something so repulsive about having your thoughts overlooked by a creature such as this that Floy flinched and then was furious with himself. It did not matter that the Robemaker could hear his thoughts, it did not matter that he would be aware of their revulsion and fear. He flung the sharp-edged stone straight at the hooded face and saw the Robemaker throw up a long bony hand to shield himself. So he is not entirely invincible! thought Floy in triumph and leapt to his feet, ready to spring forward and knock the Robemaker to the ground.

And then the stone struck the gauntletted hand and there was a sickening pulpy sound, as if the hand beneath the black glove was not bone and flesh and muscle at all, but something rotten and soft, like overripe fruit, like diseased meat . . . The gloved fingers caught and closed about the stone and flung it contemptuously away. There was the evil glitter of eyes from deep within the hood again.

'Puny Human,' hissed the Robemaker. 'Absurd, ineffectual creature to imagine you could so easily overcome me.'

Floy barely heard. He had gathered his strength again and, as the Robemaker hissed his contempt, leapt straight for the creature's heart. At once, the crimson lights spat and whirled and Floy was momentarily blinded by the brilliance and the dark forest was lit to weird, unnatural life. There was a strong burning sensation; the feeling of white-hot wires penetrating his skin and, for a moment, he thought there was the pungent scent of skin and flesh scorching.

The crimson lights sizzled again and Floy was thrown back several feet. The sky and the Trees and the forest spun wildly all about him.

Fenella had still been trying to free Nuadu but, as Floy was felled, she ran forward at once, helping him to his feet, and the Robemaker laughed again, arms folded, his face still in deep shadow.

'Ridiculous creatures,' he said. 'For although I may don the cloak of flesh and blood and bone when I walk here, in reality I am a Lord of the Dark Realm, and your blows and your stones cannot touch me. I shall not waste my powers on such weaklings.' The crimson lights faded, and the Robemaker turned back to where Nuadu was still standing helplessly before him, unable to move. But his head was tilted in the characteristic arrogance and his eyes were brilliant with fury. He looked as if he could easily leap at the Robemaker's throat and tear it out and fling it to the ground.

'Yes,' said the Robemaker, watching him, his horrid whispery voice clotted with amusement. 'Yes, you would like to rip me open and throw my entrails to the jackals, princeling.'

'I would,' said Nuadu. 'And one day I shall do so, filth. Be very sure that one day I shall do so.'

The Robemaker laughed again. 'The threats of futility, Wolfprince,' he said and paused, the hidden eyes inspecting Nuadu very thoroughly. 'So,' said the Robemaker, a lick of sinister pleasure in his voice, 'so, I have caught a prize tonight.' He paused again. 'One of the greatest prizes I have caught so far,' he said, and Fenella thought his voice sounded exactly as someone's voice might sound if there were no muscle surrounding the lips, and no skin over the jaw and probably no lips either . . .

'At least allow the Humans to go free,' said Nuadu.

'The Humans do not interest me,' said the Robemaker, still studying Nuadu as if he found him of immense interest. 'I have very little use for Humans.' He said the word contemptuously. 'And you have seen how easily I dealt with them.' There was a movement inside the dark cloak and a second shaft of crimson light split the twilight and snaked about Nuadu's features, fashioning itself into a thin cruel crimson mask that completely concealed the lower part of his face.

'A precaution,' said the Robemaker. 'For although I can continue to dissolve the puny enchantment that would bring the *sidh* to your aid, I find it tedious to do so. You will wear the Mask of Silence until I choose to remove it, Wolfprince.'

Floy, who was standing with his arm about Fenella now, said, angrily, 'Where are you taking him?' and the Robemaker turned to look at Floy with a faint air of surprise.

'He will be chained in my Workshops, Human, where he will work the treadmills with the others and see to it that the Silver Looms of Enchantment weave without ceasing.' He studied Floy for a moment. 'And if you oppose me again, you will be chained with him.'

'I should kill you first,' said Floy, his fists curling. 'I should *like* to kill you,' and the Robemaker let out his hissing mirth again.

'Impossible. You could not get near me. You could not reach me.'

'Do not be so sure,' said Floy, and Fenella looked at him, startled, because even though there could surely be nothing that Floy could do, still his words held remarkable confidence.

'I am sure,' said the Robemaker. He reached out a black-covered hand and touched Nuadu's upper face.

Nuadu, unable to speak, hardly able to move for the thin, glittering bonds, jerked his head back from the terrible caress and, in the uncertain light, his eyes above the harsh dark red mask glittered with undiluted hatred.

Fenella was standing with Floy's arm about her. Seeing

199

Nuadu like this was the worst thing that had happened yet. Even so, she thought, her eyes meeting his, even so, he is not cowed or humbled, and he is not the least bit subservient and, instantly, the thought came back at her:

Many things, but never those, my Lady . . .

Never that. There had even been a thread of affectionate amusement in the thought, as if he might be saying: of course he will not cow me and of course he will not subdue me.

Of course he will not, thought Fenella, torn between fierce pride and dread at what was ahead. Because wherever the Robemaker took Nuadu, wherever his terrible Dark Workshops were, they would surely be guarded, and there would be little hope of a rescue.

As if in response, the Robemaker turned the deep concealing hood to where Fenella stood, and said, 'Your paramour will be out of your reach, Human,' so that Fenella felt, as Floy had felt earlier, revulsion at the knowledge that the Robemaker could see with such ease into her mind.

'He will be kept safe and he will be kept close,' said the Robemaker, in the same fleshless, lipless whisper. 'He will be my creature and he will work for me in the Workshops until he is bent and aged and until his back is breaking with the constant weaving of the Silver Looms. He will work until his legs are bowed and useless and the soles of his feet are flayed and raw from the treadmills that turn the Looms . . .' Once again the dreadful, bubbling chuckle rang out. 'And when *that* has happened, Human,' said the Robemaker, 'when *that* has all happened – and it will not be so very long, for the creatures in my Workshops do not see the years accumulate into old age – then I shall take his soul and give it to the Soul Eaters, and his body will be flung to the River of the Dead.

'And the baseborn son of the Wolves will never be seen or heard of again.'

Chapter Sixteen

The Robemaker had taken Nuadu, melting into the shadows, keeping them at bay with a glittering mesh of crimson lights, rendering them powerless.

And then the crimson lights had disappeared and, although the night air had smelt sweeter and fresher and lighter, they were alone on the dark road and Nuadu was gone.

Snodgrass thought there had been a mist that had come down to blur their vision. 'So that he could get away with Nuadu,' he said wisely. But Floy had thought it was simply that the Robemaker had gone, as he had come, in a swirl of darkness, in some terrible vortex of blackness, taking Nuadu with him.

Floy wanted to put his arms about Fenella and say that he understood that she was hurting and that he would bear it with her. If there was anything they could do, they would do it. He did not do this, because Fenella could sometimes be unexpectedly withdrawn; a shuttered look would come into her eyes and, although she would be entirely polite and even friendly, Floy would feel that a small, private part of her had been closed off.

Floy had not entirely understood Nuadu and he had been very wary indeed of trusting him, although he thought, trying hard to be honest, that this had partly been because of Fenella. I believe I may have been jealous, he thought, appalled. Am I, then, so possessive of Fenella?

He did not know. He had been proud of his sister; he had enjoyed her quick intelligence and her instinctive understanding, and he had encouraged and been interested in her schemes and her plans. It was rather dreadful to think he might have been jealous of Nuadu, who had called Fenella 'My Lady', and who had exchanged that look of sudden intimacy with her at the last. Well, he'll have to be found, thought Floy. That's all there is to it. Somehow we shall have to find him and rescue him.

Snodgrass was discussing the Robemaker with Fenella. 'You saw how the spell – what did Nuadu call it? – the enchantment to call up the *sidh* was quenched before he even finished it.' And then, taking her hand, and looked at her earnestly over his spectacles, 'We shall try to rescue him, of course.'

'We shall try and we shall succeed,' said Floy, and Fenella looked at them both with immense gratitude. 'And I believe,' he said, looking across to the brilliance of Tara, 'I do believe that we should continue with the original plan.'

'Go up to Tara?' said Fenella.

'Yes. Inside Tara, we may learn where the Robemaker's Workshops lie,' said Floy and Fenella remembered that they had no idea where the Workshops were and that they had not even been able to tell in which direction the Robemaker had gone. They would have to try to find this out.

And so she said, 'Yes, of course.'

'We have to do something,' said Floy, frowning. 'And anyway, Nuadu and the others were so definite about the giants being stupid and easy to outwit. Now we have to outwit them on two counts instead of just one.'

'Obtain the information about their guards for the Court,' said Snodgrass.

'And find out where the Robemaker's Workshops are,' finished Fenella.

'Yes,' said Floy, and the reckless light shone briefly in his eyes. 'It'll be easy,' he said. 'If we can't fool a few giants, we aren't worth much.'

Even so, they approached Tara with extreme caution.

'Although,' said Snodgrass in a practical manner, 'there's no call to let them know we're afraid.'

'We are afraid,' said Fenella, staring up at the great bulk of the Castle and remembering that, no matter how

202

dull-witted the giants might be, still they had managed to drive out the Wolfkings.

'They didn't do it by themselves,' said Floy. 'Don't we know that already? They were simply the Robemaker's pawns.'

'And that other one – what did Nuadu call him? – CuRoi,' put in Snodgrass. 'But at least it means that they'll know about the Robemaker, Fenella.'

'And you can't be afraid of pawns,' said Floy.

'I'm not afraid,' said Fenella. And then, 'Well, not *very* afraid.'

'You don't look at all afraid,' said Snodgrass.

'No, I'm believing that I'm brave. If I believe hard enough it might turn out to be true.'

As they drew nearer to the great Western Gate, where the soft radiance seemed to spill into the night until it surrounded them, Fenella found herself remembering that this was the place of Nuadu's ancestors. He had never been inside it and now perhaps he never would. Was that why he had come with them? But that might mean that he had only been using them. And I refuse to believe that, thought Fenella. She would remember how he had called her 'Lady' and how he had been gentle and exciting, and how they were going to rescue him. They would be very subtle and clever with the giants, because giants were not really people to be afraid of. They were stupid and slow-witted, giants, and they were simply the puppets of the Robemaker and CuRoi. Once inside Tara, it would probably be quite easy to find out about the Robemaker and the terrible Workshops and the Silver Looms. They would not forget the quest for the creatures of the Forest Court though, because that was important, but they would make sure to find out the whereabouts of the Workshops.

But, said a tiny, whispery voice inside her head, *but Nuadu should have been here. He should have been here with us, demanding admittance to the home of his ancestors . . . the Wolfprince returning . . .* Only, of course, he was not really the Wolfprince, the rightful prince was somewhere deep in the heart of the Dark Realm.

The Palace of Tara, the legendary Shining Citadel, the Bright Castle of every tale ever told, was larger and more brilliant than anything they had ever seen.

Snodgrass was very impressed. 'I'm very impressed indeed,' he told them. 'It isn't at all what I expected. Is this the Western Gate? The one that Nuadu told us we would enter by? My word, it's a massive affair, isn't it? Was it originally built for giants, I wonder?'

'I think it was just built to be awe-inspiring,' said Floy, standing beneath the great soaring arches of brick, and looking all about him.

Snodgrass said that it succeeded, my word it did. 'I ought to be taking notes,' he said worriedly. 'Snizort will be expecting a detailed account of all this, you know.'

'Let's get inside first,' said Fenella, who was still reminding herself that she was not frightened.

They approached the huge iron-studded oak door which was pointed at the top and had great brass hinges and a round, carved knocker with a wolfhead carved into it. *The place of Nuadu's ancestors* . . . What had he said: *I am bastard stock, but my mother was a Princess of the Royal House in her own right* . . . So this is truly the place of his forebears, thought Fenella, and discovered an unexpected comfort in this. Was it because within these walls, she would always feel he was not so very far away? Perhaps. And any sort of courage is better than none at all, thought Fenella.

Seen close to, Tara was smooth and elegant and still bathed in the strong, vibrant light. Floy, who liked to know what made things work and what lay behind things, thought it was some kind of inner radiance. He thought it was not artificially produced, in the way that the early Earth-dwellers had apparently been able to produce bright lights, which was interesting. And then he remembered that the creatures who inhabited Tara were years and centuries and worlds before the Earth-people who had known how to make light and heat water and shine vivid lights that meant you could see as clearly by night as you could by day.

They could see Tara very clearly indeed.

'Massive,' said Snodgrass. 'My word, it must stretch for miles.'

'It's awe-inspiring,' said Floy. 'And it's beautiful. Fenella, isn't it beautiful?'

Fenella was standing with the other two, staring about her, her eyes huge. She said, softly, 'I think it is the most beautiful thing I ever saw in my life.'

Set in the saucer-shaped valley, bastioned in light and bathed in its own iridescence, Tara was a fairy-tale palace, a shimmering castle, a walled city of beauty and colour and brilliance.

And it was inhabited by the usurping Giants of Gruagach. If there was to be any point at all to this strange quest, and certainly if they were to help the captured Nuadu Airgetlam, they must knock boldly on the great oak door and request admittance.

It was Floy who did it in the end. 'Of course it was,' said Snodgrass. '*I* was mortally afraid. I don't care who knows it.'

'It wasn't easy,' said Fenella.

'You were the least afraid of us all.'

'I was very afraid indeed,' said Fenella.

'No one would have known.'

But by now, Fenella was not as afraid as she had expected to be. Was it possible that Nuadu was still touching her mind and that he was imbuing her with his own yearning for Tara?

I don't understand it, thought Fenella. I am not even sure if the thoughts are my own thoughts any longer. But I don't think I shall question it.

Floy had walked under the brick arch, which was not built of the ordinary red-brown warm bricks they knew on Renascia, but of some kind of pale, smooth, faintly luminous substance. He stood squarely in the centre of the courtyard, his hands on his hips, his feet planted firmly on the cobblestones.

He was not particularly afraid, although, like the others, he knew that they would have to be very wary indeed. But he was fascinated by the remarkably beautiful place called Tara, and he was intrigued by the tales of its history. They would not forget Renascia or its people, but it was difficult to think about Renascia, lost beyond recall to them. He wanted to know more about these people and their world, and he certainly wanted to know more about Tara. Beautiful, thought Floy, staring up at it. And then: I wonder what kind of creatures we are about to meet?

There was a grille with a bell rope and Floy reached up and pulled it. A vast, rather hollow-sounding clanging sounded somewhere inside the castle and then there were footsteps coming down some kind of vast corridor. The three travellers moved together almost without realising it. For warmth? wondered Fenella, and realised, in the same moment, that it was not for warmth at all, but for security. They would have to keep very close together throughout whatever might be ahead of them.

The grille opened with a rather horrid grating sound. 'Needs oiling,' muttered Snodgrass, 'Dear me, they don't keep house very well, these giants,' and was told to hush by Floy who was trying to gauge the size of the owner of the footsteps.

'Giants vary,' he said.

'Will he be *very* large?' said Fenella, who had been thinking about the height of things like old apple trees, or three-storeyed houses, or even the masts of ships; there were not very many ships on Renascia, because there was not very much sea, but there had been pictures of ships in the Mnemosyne, because some of the Earth-people had been a sea-faring race.

Floy started to say that he thought the owner of the footsteps did not sound alarmingly large, when there was the sound of bolts being drawn back and keys turned in locks. The iron-studded door swung to and they were confronted with their first giant.

* * *

Inchbad's first thought, when the gatekeeper brought up the news about the Humans requesting admittance, was that it had something to do with the appearance of the Angry Sun. You could not always be telling quite how these things would work and it was quite likely – well, it was very likely really – that the Humans had in some way come from the Angry Sun. There was no accounting for the ways of Humans, any more than there was any accounting for Beastline creatures, although, of the two, Inchbad would far rather deal with Humans. Beastline creatures were neither quite one thing nor the other, when you looked at it plainly. Inchbad did not like dealing with the Beastline, and he very particularly did not like dealing with the Wolfline, who made him nervous and unsure of himself, which was not something a King ought to be made to feel.

He turned his attention rather frowningly towards the gatekeeper – quarter-witted, poor soul, but you could not have everything these days – and listened to the story about the Humans, two men and a girl, asking could they be given food and shelter for the night.

'Has the Star fallen to Earth?' he asked, very cunningly, because the Gruagach could be very cunning indeed if they had to. It was not in Inchbad's nature to be cunning, but he could do it if it was necessary. And so – 'Has the Star fallen?' he asked, and the gatekeeper, who was called Balor, and who was in fact not nearly as quarter-witted as he let the Gruagach King believe, said, 'I wouldn't be knowing, Sire,' but said there were two Men-Humans and a Girl-Human, and looked more wooden-brained than usual, so that Inchbad recalled the tale about the boy's grandsire breeding from a Human, and remembered that what was in the meat came out in the gravy and thought you could always tell.

Inchbad looked to Goibniu for direction about the Humans, because Goibniu always knew what ought to be done. He was always a great help to Inchbad. He looked, as well, at Caspar, because there was a Girl-Human with the travellers and Inchbad was quite partial to a young toothsome Girl in his bed now and then. Humans were very pretty; they were much prettier than giantesses, if a bit on the small side. Inchbad would be very interested in the Girl, and perhaps something could be arranged for later. Caspar would see to that, of course.

'Bring the Humans in,' said Goibniu, in his rather rumbling voice and Balor took himself back to his cubbyhole by the Great Western Gate, thinking that, to be sure, didn't His Majesty appear addle-brained at times and bethought himself of the old gossip that told how the King's granddam had mated with one of the Ogres of Olc Acha than whom you could not get more stupid. These things often had the way of skipping a generation, but say what you liked, you could always tell the tree by looking at the fruit.

Goibniu had been rather pleased at this unexpected piece of good fortune. It was not often you got Humans actually asking to be let in. They would make the most of this.

He stood before the fire that they all liked to have lit in the evenings and hooked his thumbs into his belt and prepared to be affable. Inchbad, who was looking forward to seeing the Humans, and who was especially looking forward to the Girl, thought that Goibniu was becoming a bit obese these days. He was fond of his supper of course. Well, so were they all fond of their suppers. But Goibniu took the thing a bit too far. Inchbad had heard the younger ones sniggering about the village wenches that Caspar brought up for Goibniu and about how Goibniu had squashed three of them one night because he had rolled over in bed before they were ready for him.

Inchbad had thought this extremely vulgar of Goibniu and it had caused great trouble from the villagers who would not be letting their daughters (pretty little things) come up to the Castle to be squashed and rolled on by thoughtless giants. You might as well be baked and served up in a Manpie, said the villagers angrily, and they had actually marched on Tara by night, carrying flaring torches and brandishing pitchforks, and shouting things like 'Death to the Giants!' and 'Tara for the Irish!' and 'No more Manpies for Goibniu the Greediguts!' Some of them had even had the temerity to get up a Petition, which they had presented at the Western Gate, which had said they were sick of the Robemaker scouring the land for victims for his horrid Workshops and they were tired of hiding their strongest young men whenever he walked abroad and they were going to ride on the Workshops and slay the Robemaker.

This was extremely worrying, because the Gruagach did not dare to offend the Robemaker, particularly not when they were settling into Tara so very nicely and particularly when Goibniu was in the very process of arranging the weighty matter of Inchbad's marriage. And although Inchbad had not been altogether happy about the plan to invade the south and wrest Tara from the Wolfkings, he was beginning to agree with Goibniu that matters were turning out very nicely.

To begin with, Fenella thought it was not so very bad. She thought she could cope with it. She thought she could certainly manage not to be afraid, or at least not very much.

The gatekeeper had been quite affable. He was probably not so very large as giants went although, as Floy was to say, it depended on your previous experience, of which they had none whatsoever.

Balor the Gatekeeper was somewhere around twelve feet high and dressed in a leather jerkin and moleskin breeches with the ends tucked into leather boots which had the tops rolled over. He had surveyed them with his thumbs hooked into his belt (they discovered later that this was a characteristic pose for most of the Gruagach), and he had a thatch of straw-coloured hair and rather small eyes, with a wide grinning mouth below.

'Oho,' he had said. 'Bless us and save us and may we all grow to be two hundred and ten! What have we here?' He bent over a little, the better to see. 'Humans,' he said, nodding delightedly. 'By the hairs of my beard, Humans!

Come along in, do. The King *will* be pleased. Come inside.' He flung the door wide and beckoned with one hand and Fenella and Floy and Snodgrass stepped inside.

Once inside, it was not nearly so alarming. The room where Balor had been sitting was very nearly normal. The three travellers, still keeping close together, thought it was furnished just as you would expect a gatekeeper's abode to be furnished. To be sure, there were giant-sized tables and chairs and the cups and plates were giant-sized as well. But there were also ordinary, human-sized things; a rather nice oak table with carved chairs and what Snodgrass thought was called a dresser, where you would arrange your best china, or perhaps pewter or copper mugs. Fenella thought there was the feeling that the human-sized things had been pushed to one side to make room for the Gruagach's and this was suddenly extremely reassuring, because it gave the Gruagach's occupancy an unexpected air of impermanency. They would not be here so very long, after all, these giants.

Balor was pouring them each a thimbleful of mead, 'For,' he said, in his rumbling voice, 'I daresay you'll be chilled to the marrow and that's a nasty thing, to get a chill in your marrow, by the great toe of the god Dagda, it is.' He reached down and gave them each a cup of mead, and the cups were, after all, proper cups, and not thimbles, which was what they had looked like in Balor's huge hands.

'Drink it up, Humans, while I go along and see if the King will receive you,' he said, and chuckled suddenly, as if enjoying some private joke.

Fenella and Floy sipped cautiously at the mead in case it might have something peculiar added to it, but Snodgrass, who was interested in food and wine, drank it all and smacked his lips and said it was very good indeed, and quite probably made from *pure* honey, which was extremely important when you made mead.

When Balor came back, which was quite soon, he was beaming all over his coarse red face. The King would be delighted to receive them, it appeared. Balor had strict instructions to take them straight up to the Sun Chamber which was a very great honour. And so, if they had all finished their mead and had had a bit of a warm at his fire – 'best beechwood, and burn my bristles if there weren't four beech naiads roasted in the process and the smell of it enough to turn your stomach!' – he'd take them along that very instant.

There was no help for it. And anyway, thought Fenella, this was what they had come for. They had come to beard the giants in their lair. She wished she had not used the word *lair* because it conjured up rather unpleasant visions. But then she remembered that this was Tara, the beautiful shining palace, the home of Nuadu's ancestors, the Wolfkings and that, surely, oh surely, nothing inside Tara could ever be truly evil.

Balor led them along corridors and galleries; through halls and chambers where the ceilings were painted with unearthly beings and the floors were etched with unreal symbols.

'Minor sorceries,' he explained, huffing a bit as they ascended a great, curving stairway with carved gilt balustrades. 'They're all over the place here. I don't like 'em a bit, but His Majesty likes to dabble a bit now and then. And Goibniu calls up the demons from time to time. Wicked sly things, demons, for all the sorcerers tell you they're easily controlled! But the sorcerers say one thing and Goibniu says another and between them His Majesty ends up with demons dancing when they play the *Fidchell*.' He sent them what Fenella and Floy both thought of as a sudden sly look. 'I daresay they won't have the *Fidchell* where you've come from,' said Balor.

'I am afraid not,' said Floy tranquilly.

They had reached the top of the curved gilt stair now and there was a huge echoing, galleried landing, with double doors directly ahead of them, with wolfheads carved into the panelling. More of the strange symbols writhed about the architraves and Balor stopped and said, 'Here it is. The ancient Sun Chamber of the exiled Wolfkings. The place they called *Medchuarta*, although

I'll lay you the fire demons of Reflection that it won't be called that much longer.' He threw open the great double doors and the three travellers stepped into the Court of the Giants.

Chapter Seventeen

To begin with, Floy and Fenella and Snodgrass were dazzled by the light and the noise and the heat which seemed to billow out in an immense, solid wave.

There were rather unpleasant smells in the heat; rancid sweat and stale, onion-tainted breath. Unwashed bodies, thought Fenella with a brief twist of nausea. This is going to be rather nasty. And then she looked directly ahead of her and knew that it was all going to be very nasty indeed.

The Gruagach were all waiting, standing in a half-circle about the King who was seated on a great carved Throne, on a raised area at the far end of the Sun Chamber. Fifteen feet tall at least, every one of them. With great heavy bodies and ugly brutish faces and thick, ungainly hands like blunt clubs. In the main, they wore leather boots, with the tops rolled down, and leather jerkins and breeches made of some kind of skin. Over this, most of them had put on fur-trimmed robes, in dark reds and purples and plum colours, and the females had twisted garish jewellery about their necks and threaded pearls and circlets studded with brilliants into their hair.

They were as ugly as they were huge. Their faces were coarse and red and small-eyed. They had straw-coloured thatches of hair and thick repulsive necks and wide stupid mouths that just now were grinning and showing rotting teeth. The females had powdered their faces with thick white powder which had caked into the folds of skin, but, beneath the powder, they were still red-faced. Fenella, staring, could not decide if this was better or worse. Here and there, their great clumsy hands were curved into predators' talons. Floy, moving closer to Fenella, noticed that one of them, who wore some kind of chain of office over a purple robe with a very short pleated skirt that left most of his crimson-hosed legs bare, was eyeing Fenella with dreadful grinning lechery and his hands were curving and flexing.

As the three travellers crossed the floor and drew nearer to the waiting giants, the giants grinned rather slyly at one another, and bent down – The better to see us, thought Floy – and the King, who had not moved, but who was resting his chin on one hand and watching, beckoned to the travellers to come nearer. His hand was fat and podgy and the nails were curved and thick and looked as if they might be made of horn.

'We shall not hurt you, Humans,' said the one with the chain of office and the giant who occupied the Throne, who had elaborately curled hair that made him look stupider than the rest, said at once, 'We do not hurt Humans, you know,' and a rather sinister laugh went round the watching circle.

Floy felt Fenella shiver, and he stepped forward, and said, 'We bid you welcome, Your Majesty,' and eyed the giants very directly, and supposed that this would be an acceptable form of greeting. Slow, thought Floy, studying them covertly. Brutish. Yes, I do believe that if they show themselves hostile, we could outwit them. The King looks mild enough and as if he might be persuaded one way or the other. But I don't trust that one with the purple robe and the heavy gold chain, thought Floy, glancing sideways to where Goibniu stood at Inchbad's side. I believe he'd have us all in the dungeons or into the sculleries before we could turn round.

Goibniu had come forward to meet the travellers, smiling with his wide, flat mouth. He bent down to take Floy's hand in his own, the golden chain of his office swinging and clanking about his neck.

'You are *very* welcome at Tara,' he said and straightened up and eyed Fenella with his small hot eyes. 'Dear me, it's a *very* long time since we could welcome Human travellers to our supper table, is it not, Sire?'

At once the King said eagerly, 'My word, it is.' And,

leaning forward, said, rather anxiously, 'I wonder, are you anything to do with the *Feargach Grian*?'

Floy felt the waiting silence descend on the Sun Chamber and guessed at once that the Gruagach *had* seen the Angry Sun and that they had woven stories about it, as Fael-Inis had said they would. He drew in a deep breath, because surely this was something they could turn to their advantage.

'We have travelled with the Sun,' he said at last and saw at once that they drew back a little. Good! thought Floy. He felt an unexpected surge of confidence and felt, in the same moment, the identical emotion from Fenella and with it a shared thought: *We can beat these great stupid giants with ease!*

'At times,' said Floy, his mind vividly alive, searching deep into his memory for help, 'at times, we have followed the flaming fire that in our world is called the Angry Sun and at other times, it has followed us.' He looked at them and thought: well, that's shaken them a bit at any rate! I believe they won't quite know what standing to accord us now! And stood his ground and waited to see what they would do next.

Inchbad was rather impressed by Floy. Indeed he was very impressed by three Human travellers who might have come from anywhere at all but who had, apparently, come, in some inexplicable manner, from the *Feargach Grian* itself. He thought that this might very well turn out to be quite a solemn occasion, because it was not often you met Humans (were they truly Humans?) who had travelled from another world in the *Feargach Grian*.

Inchbad looked to Goibniu, because Goibniu usually knew what to say on these occasions, but Goibniu was staring at the Girl, pretty creature she was as well, and clearly the only thing that Goibniu was thinking about just now was sending Caspar to bring the Girl to his bed-chamber later on. Inchbad hoped that Goibniu would not roll on this one before they had had a chance to find out a bit more about the *Feargach Grian* and the world that the Humans might come from. It was quite important

215

to keep your mind open and learn about other worlds. And so he leaned closer to the Humans and said, very cunningly, 'And what is it like inside the *Feargach Grian*?' and sat back, pleased with himself, and pleased to note that the Court was looking at him with respect and nodding at one another. Arca Dubh had dug Goll the Gorm in the ribs and looked as if he might be saying hadn't the King the way of cutting straight to the heart of the matter.

Floy said, clearly and loudly, 'To journey inside the Angry Sun, the legendary and eternal *Feargach Grian*, is the most remarkable thing you would ever know, Your Majesty,' and grinned. Then he turned to wink, in the most casual way imaginable, at one of the giantesses, who looked taken aback and then simpered and twisted the rope of pearls she wore about her fingers and hunched a shoulder, coyly.

Floy said, 'You are an unusual race, Your Majesty,' as if he was considering the Gruagach rather in the manner of one who might collect weird specimens. And then, to strengthen this impression, he turned to Fenella and Snodgrass. 'I do not think we have met a more unusual?' he said.

'Well, no,' said Snodgrass, gamely joining in.

'There were the Star People,' said Fenella, plundering her mind for any snippet and tag-end of legend that might help them and that might intrigue the giants further. 'But of course, they were filled with the – the Magic of the Far Skies. You can't really count them,' said Fenella firmly.

'Nor you can,' said Floy, and sent Fenella one of his grins, so that Fenella knew that Floy believed that to fascinate and dazzle these fearsome creatures might very well be their salvation.

'And there were the people of the Fire Court,' said Fenella, remembering that this had been discussed in the Wolfwood.

At once, a murmur of interest went round, because wasn't the King actually negotiating for an alliance with the daughter of Reflection who presided over the Fire Court.

Goibniu said, 'You have visited the Fire Court?' and the tiny pig-eyes were shrewd.

'We were honoured guests of Reflection,' said Floy, unblushingly.

'But,' put in Fenella, who was finding it remarkably easy to maintain this pretence, 'we are, of course, pledged to secrecy about its people.'

'You will know why,' said Floy, in the sort of confidential tone that is hardly ever questioned. He grinned at the simpering giantess again, who giggled and nudged her neighbours.

'Yes,' said Inchbad, staring at Floy. 'Yes, to be sure we will.' And hoped that this sounded convincing, because of course it would not do for them to let these rather unexpected Humans suspect that they did not know very much about the Fire Court. Well, if the truth were to be told, they knew nothing at all.

Goibniu did not like Humans (except for use in the *Fidchell* of course), but he was finding Floy and Fenella a bit out of the usual run. He stroked his chin and thought that, although they would certainly put these three to the heated squares, if they did indeed know the Fire Court they might be very useful in an unexpected manner.

Goibniu had intended to send a deputation to the Fire Court, with what was really a very generous offer of a marriage settlement for Reflection's daughter Flame. The King had been very pleased with it, although one or two of the younger ones (Goll the Gorm had been particularly obstructive) had questioned whether they really needed to give away quite so much and whether they really needed to commission the Gnomes of Gallan to fashion a complete set of Royal raiments for Flame. Goibniu had squashed such rebelliousness at once, of course, and the Gnomes had been given the commission. If these three had, in truth, been guests of Reflection, and if they really did know the Fire Court, it was something they might very well make use of.

So Goibniu smiled kindly at Floy and Fenella and the odd-looking person who was with them and said they'd be bound to be cold and tired after their journey; he'd heard that the *Feargach Grian* could be a wearisome thing to deal with. They would be most welcome to a bed for the night. And pretended not to hear the chuckles that went round because, as a general rule, when Goibniu offered a bed for the night to Humans, he meant a bed in the dungeons for the Men and a share of his own bed for the Girls. The giants rubbed their hands with delight and nodded to one another, because nobody had expected to have such a catch of Humans so quickly after the last celebrating of the *Fidchell*. One or two of the younger ones thought it was a pity they had not saved the first batch, because with these three added to it, it would have made for a much better game and certainly more strongly flavoured Manpies, but the older ones said no, wasn't it better by far to be able to celebrate two *Fidchells* within days of each other.

Caspar was summoned from wherever he had been to take the guests to two of the bed-chambers.

'And then,' said Goibniu, who was beginning to suspect Caspar of not being as zealous as he might be in his duties, 'and then, good Caspar, perhaps it is time that you arranged that *other* little matter we spoke of?'

'Oh, very well,' said Caspar, who knew perfectly well that the other little matter was the searching out of more Humans who might have been in the Angry Sun, but who had been hoping to avoid this.

'But before that, you must of course, settle our guests into the *nicest* of our rooms,' said Goibniu, reaching down again, unable to resist just pinching Fenella's cheek. Fenella gasped and just managed not to flinch, because Goibniu's finger felt bristly and scratchy and leathery like the hide of a very old pig and altogether horrid. But clearly it was important not to show any discourtesy to these people and so Fenella smiled up at him.

'You are very kind,' said Floy, who had seen the pinch and felt Fenella's repressed distaste. He would have liked to leap at the gross ugly creature and drive a sword into him, but since this was impossible, he merely said, 'We should be glad of a night's rest.'

'And after that,' said Goibniu, with a glance at the King, 'I think we may have a *task* for you.' And beamed again.

'*I* think you'd better be careful,' said Caspar, leading them through a bewildering array of rooms and galleries and halls.

'They seem friendly enough,' said Floy cautiously, in case Caspar might be in league with the giants.

'They're giving us a bed for the night anyway,' said Snodgrass, and Caspar looked at them.

'Don't you know, don't any of you know that when giants give a *task* to anyone, and when giants – any giants – show friendliness to Humans it is very dangerous. In fact, it's *extremely* dangerous,' said Caspar, scurrying along through the brightly lit halls where once Nuadu Airgetlam's ancestors had held court and where once the entire western world had flocked.

Snodgrass wanted to know why.

'Well,' said Caspar, with a warning glance to Fenella, 'they're partial to Humans in rather sinister ways, if you take my meaning.'

'What sort of ways?'

Caspar said 'Oh, *really*!' in an exasperated voice. 'Where *have* you come from?' he said, and then at once, 'And *don't* say the *Feargach Grian*, because don't we all of us know that nobody really comes from that. At least, those of us with any wits know it. Giants,' said Caspar knowledgeably, 'aren't particularly clever, you see.'

'No?' said Snodgrass, who was saving this all up to tell Snizort later on.

'They're very stupid indeed,' said Caspar, hurrying across a huge, galleried landing with a marble floor and queerly shaped wall sconces. 'That's why most Humans can outwit them. Dear me,' he said, stopping outside two carved doors, 'dear me, how do you suppose I've been coping with them since they came to Tara?'

'I beg your pardon,' said Fenella, 'but *what* are you exactly? I mean, what is your position here?'

'I'm a pimp,' said Caspar, tucking his chins into his neck solemnly. 'I'm not especially proud of it, but there it is.' And then, seeing Fenella's lack of comprehension, 'I procure girls for them,' he said.

'Oh!'

'It's nothing to be ashamed of,' said Caspar, a bit more loudly than he intended. 'I did it for the Court – I mean the proper Court and I might say that pimping for the High King – the *true* High King that is – has always been considered rather an honourable profession. Not that the Wolfkings ever needed much assistance in that direction, of course, because there's a saying that they had only to lift a finger and half the females in Ireland would lie down and— But I'm forgetting my company,' said Caspar, with a belated look at Fenella. 'It's all this living so close to Inchbad's people. It coarsens you.

'Anyway,' he went on, opening elaborate, carved doors with the wolf emblem engraved on them and brass wolfhead handles, 'anyway, the Gruagach inherited me.'

'Yes.'

'And you needn't think it's an easy task,' said Caspar, crossly, who had been saying this to people at regular intervals ever since the Gruagach came storming down out of the North and took everyone by surprise. 'You needn't think it's all poteen and parties.'

'Of course not,' said Floy and Snodgrass politely.

'I dislike it very much,' said Caspar, glaring at them. 'And if anyone can tell me how I can get out of it, I'd be very glad to know.'

'Couldn't you simply walk out?' asked Floy and Caspar, who had been unlatching the door of the first bed-chamber, turned round to stare at him.

'Where would I go?' he said. 'Wherever I went, they'd catch up with me. Ever since CuRoi and the Robemaker put the Gruagach into Tara, every single house for miles around – probably all of Ireland really – is visited on a regular basis.'

'Why?' said Floy, because they had to learn as much as they could. 'Why is that?'

'So that the Robemaker can be sure he's being given all the finest young men to work his Looms, of course,' said Caspar, shaking his head in sorrow at people who did not know something so basic. 'He's taken a great many as it is but, of course, nobody lasts long inside the workshops. Also,' said Caspar, warming to his theme, 'also, have you ever tried to walk away from a giant?'

'Well, no.'

'I thought not. They'd catch up with me inside of ten minutes. Even now, when they're sending me out down into the valley to see if there's any Humans they've missed from the Angry Sun, even then, they'll post sentries to be sure I don't stay away too long.'

'How terrible,' said Fenella, sympathetically, wondering whether this might be the time to ask about sentries and guards.

'They'd simply stride down to the village and pluck me out of hiding if I tried to get away,' said Caspar. 'And then, of course, we all know what they'd do with me.'

'What?' said Fenella and Snodgrass together.

'They'd eat me,' said Caspar, and Fenella turned so pale that Floy reached out for her in case she fainted.

'Or,' said Caspar with relish, 'they'd give me to the Robemaker for his Workshop. And, on balance, I don't know but what I wouldn't prefer to be eaten, really.'

Snodgrass said, 'Dear me,' and peered over his spectacles.

'As it is,' said Caspar, 'I'm of some use to them. They think I'm better at catching Humans for the *Fidchell* than they are. Which is perfectly true. I *am* better.' He glanced over his shoulder, and then drew nearer. 'I manage to let most of them go,' he said in a conspiratorial whisper. 'Only the Gruagach don't know that. If they did, I'd be Manpie for certain.'

'But,' said Floy slowly, 'didn't you say that giants could usually be outwitted? Can't you think of a way to escape them?'

'Can you think of one?' asked Caspar. 'No, and no more can I. And I have to eat, you know,' he said, crossly. 'People forget that people have to eat.'

'Especially giants,' murmured Floy and Caspar looked at him sharply in case this was meant to be derisive. But Floy smiled back guilelessly and Caspar hunched one shoulder and turned his back, because it was not worth worrying about.

'Here's your rooms,' he said, throwing open the second door. 'I'll leave you to sort yourselves out. I'm off into the valley, now. They'll expect me to be back before dawn with any captives. I suppose there *weren't* any others with you, were there? No, I didn't think there were. And, even if there were, you'd be as well not to tell me. I do try to spare people where I can, well, I told you that. But I have to go through the motions.'

'You have to eat,' said Floy and Caspar shot him a suspicious look.

'If I were you,' he said, 'I'd try to find a way out and see if you can't be off into hiding somewhere. Couldn't you just get back into the *Feargach Grian* and be off? It'd be far better for you. Because otherwise,' said the giants' procurer, 'otherwise, they'll have the *Fidchell* board out again, and there'll be Manpies on the supper table tomorrow night.' With which he took himself off, because if he had stayed, he might have fallen into conversation with these three travellers and, if he had done that, he might have found himself rather liking them. And say what you wished, it was entirely pointless to make friends of any Humans who landed themselves in the Gruagach's hands.

The rooms were very comfortable indeed. There was a connecting door between them: 'Safer,' said Snodgrass nodding. 'Floy and I can have this room and Fenella will be just through there.'

'They're very lavish,' said Fenella, fingering the bed hangings and the thick, fluffy towels that someone had wrapped about huge copper ewers of hot water. Both rooms had jutting bay windows with tiny panes of glass in them and comfortable, velvet-padded seats directly below. There were thick, brightly patterned carpets on the floors and things which Snodgrass thought were brass warming pans and carved chairs and silk cushions.

'Beautiful,' said Fenella, in an abstracted voice. The three travellers stood still and looked at one another.

'We're inside,' said Floy at last.

'And we seem to have thrown dust in the giants' eyes so far,' added Snodgrass. 'Bless us and save us all, that all went down well, you two. My word, I couldn't have kept *that* up for the life of me.' He nodded at them both. 'Star People and the Fire Court,' he said. '*Very* astute.'

'I think they believed it all,' said Fenella. And then, in a worried tone, 'But we have to get out of here.'

'Did you believe that person?' asked Snodgrass, who was inspecting the furniture and peering into cupboards.

'Yes,' said Fenella. And then, 'Didn't we?'

'I don't think we ought to trust anyone inside Tara,' said Floy.

'Caspar was a Human,' said Fenella.

'Was he?'

'He *looked* like a Human.'

'I don't think that necessarily means very much here,' said Floy. 'Let's not trust any of them.'

'Nuadu would have known who to trust and who not to,' said Snodgrass.

'Yes, he would,' said Floy. 'But we'll have to rely on our wits.' He looked at them both. 'And we mustn't lose any opportunity to find out about the Robemaker,' he said very seriously. 'We mustn't miss any chance at all.'

'Caspar knows about the Robemaker,' said Fenella.

'Yes, but we have to remember that Caspar might be in the Robemaker's service,' said Floy. 'He might be working far more subtly than it seems.'

'He didn't seem subtle,' said Fenella, thoughtfully. And then, half to herself, 'But of course, somebody who was really subtle wouldn't. It's difficult, isn't it, trying to remember that people mightn't be what they seem.'

Floy was inspecting the two bed-chambers. 'Comfortable, at least,' he said, grinning at them.

'The beds are enormous,' said Fenella. 'Although they aren't *giants'* beds. I think I'd have hated to sleep in a bed that a giant might have slept in last night. They're large, but they're *Human*-sized beds.'

At each of the four corners was a post, elaborately carved. Rich hangings were draped from the posts so that you could pull them across and be quite private once you were in bed.

'Fourposters,' said Snodgrass. 'Bless my boots, Snizort will be sorry not to see this.'

'Snizort will be very glad indeed to have missed out on this,' said Floy, who was kneeling on the deep window seat and looking out over the darkened countryside. He turned back into the room and looked at them both, his eyes bright. 'For the moment, we seem to be honoured guests of these creatures,' he said. 'But I suspect that we shall have to sing for our supper.' He looked at Fenella. 'Well, sibling? Can we sing? How many stories can we come up with about Star People and the Fire Court, and the dozens of other worlds we have visited in the *Feargach Grian*?'

'I expect we could keep them quiet for a few nights anyway,' said Fenella, and Snodgrass muttered something that sounded like 'Scheherezade' which, as Floy pointed out, was not very helpful.

And then Fenella, who had been exploring both rooms a bit further, said suddenly, 'Floy. The doors are locked.' The doors were not only locked, but bolted from the outside as well.

'So much for being honoured guests,' said Floy, trying the doors and pulling hard at the door handles. 'They meant to lock us in all the time.'

'And so much for Caspar's friendship,' said Snodgrass.

'He told us to try to escape,' said Floy, thoughtfully. 'I wonder what he'd have done if we had tried.'

'We don't know for sure that it was Caspar who locked us in,' put in Fenella, who had found Caspar friendly.

'I wouldn't mind laying a bet that it was,' said Floy and sat down on the nearest of the beds, looking at them. 'If it had been one of the Gruagach, we'd have heard.'

Fenella, who was beginning to feel frightened in earnest now, said, 'It's not an adventure any longer is it? It's not something interesting and unusual and just a little bit dangerous. It's real,' she said, white-faced.

She tried to think that of course they would get out, there would be a way out and they would find it. But all Floy's resourcefulness and integrity and shrewdness, and all Snodgrass's scholarship and intelligence could surely not get them out through solid oak doors which were probably about two feet thick, or out of windows that were certainly a hundred feet from the ground with a sheer drop directly below. The combined strengths and wits of all of them would certainly not prevail against the strange enchantments and the dark powers that were abroad in this unknown land. Fenella found herself remembering that even Nuadu, with his magical wolfblood and his inherited knowledge of the old enchantments, had not been able to save himself from the Robemaker.

'The floors are of stone,' said Floy, who had been prowling the room. 'I can't see how we can get out of here until they let us out.'

'Isn't there anything we can think of?' asked Snodgrass worriedly and then, in case they thought he was being a touch unhelpful, 'I haven't really got an *adventurous* mind, you know. I just don't know very much about escapes and plots.'

'That doesn't really—'

'There were a good few escapes in the Earth-people's history, of course.'

'Yes, but that won't help us now.'

'There was the chap who was shut away and made to wear a mask because he looked a bit too much like the

King – oh, dear me, now *that* was tactless. Fenella, my dear, I didn't intend—'

'Of course you didn't,' said Fenella at once.

'And there was that fortress, somewhere in what they called World War Two, where they put people captured by the enemy,' went on Snodgrass, trying to re-direct the conversation, because he would not have hurt Fenella for all the worlds put together. 'I forget its name,' he said, 'but it was supposed to be absolutely escape-proof, only people did manage to escape.'

'This isn't escape-proof,' said Floy, pacing the floor and frowning. 'I won't believe that it's escape-proof. We'll get out of Tara somehow.'

'Colditz, that's the name,' said Snodgrass, triumphantly. 'Or was it Zenda? No, that's something else. Dear me, my memory isn't what it used to be.'

Fenella started to say that perhaps if they waited until morning, probably somebody would bring them some breakfast, and there might be a means of getting out then, when Floy, who had been standing by the door, his ear pressed to it, raised a hand and said, 'Hush!'

'What is it?'

'Footsteps,' said Floy.

'Caspar coming back?' asked Fenella hopefully.

'No.' Floy stayed where he was, his expression intent, his eyes serious. 'It's too heavy for Caspar.' He put his head closer to the door and, as he did so, Fenella and Snodgrass heard it as well.

Footsteps. And as Floy had said, they were far too heavy for Caspar.

Giants' footsteps.

It had been Goibniu's idea for them all to meet quietly, to discuss how far they had progressed with the marriage negotiations for Inchbad and Flame, and also to consider how best they could make use of the three Humans who claimed to have come from the *Feargach Grian*. Inchbad had thought it a fine idea and had said they would use the place the Wolfkings had called the Star of the Poets, which seemed to have been some kind of special Council Chamber. It was thought that the Wolfkings had considered it to be a rather tasteful place, but Inchbad and the others thought it pale and insipid. And blue and silver was a poor sort of arrangement of colours when you were having a bit of a think about State matters. Goibniu had ordered up some nice dark red paint and had promised that there could be purple hangings at the windows (the windows were huge and made out of crystal with silver and pearl tracery, so they were something you would want to cover up as much as possible).

And they were all pleased to think that the pale, gold-etched floor would soon be covered by several of the grand new floor coverings from the East. It gave you a shivering grue just to sit here and have to look at the ceiling, with the spattering of silver stars and the maps charting the journey through the skies to Dagda's country and the strange symbols that were probably the Wolfkings' ancient spells. None of the giants wanted to look at the journey to Dagda's country and none of them, certainly, wanted to see the spells of the Wolfkings. The chairs were comfortable enough, because Goibniu had decreed that the Gruagach's own chairs should be brought in, along with a decent-sized table. You could not be sitting on Human-sized chairs, said Goibniu firmly, especially when they were made of what appeared to be solid silver. You could get all manner of nasty illnesses from sitting on cold silver for hours on end, said Goibniu, and several of the older giants, who suffered from unsociable ailments which meant they had to spend longer than most people in the Stool Room and had to be given large helpings of prunes and figs three times a week, supported this view.

Inchbad donned his maroon robes, since this would be a proper Council, and remembered his crown, which he sometimes forgot, and was pleased to see that Balor had been told to bring up a few firkins of best onion wine. Arca Dubh and Fiachra Broadcrown would probably drink too much, and become quarrelsome and hurl the silver chairs at one another and Goll the Gorm would certainly fall asleep and snore loudly, but this could not be helped. If one of the silver chairs happened to go through the crystal window during an argument and shatter the ugly, ivory tracery, Inchbad would not waste any tears.

Goibniu opened the Council by reading out a list of the Settlements that had been offered to the sorceress Reflection for her daughter's hand in marriage.

'Impressive,' said Fiachra Broadcrown.

'Generous,' added Arca Dubh.

'Not sufficient for Madame Reflection, however,' said Goibniu, shaking his head.

Inchbad, who was hoping that they could agree to Reflection's demands, asked what else they would be offering.

'The Gnomes of Gallan are forging an entire new set of Crown raiments, Sire,' said Goibniu. 'And when they are ready, we are sending them to the Fire Court, in earnest of our good intentions.'

'I see,' said Inchbad, nodding ponderously, feeling his crown slip a bit.

'In fact,' said Goibniu, 'even as we speak, Sire, the Gnomes will be journeying to Tara from Gallan.'

'If they can find the way,' said Arca Dubh with a guffaw, and everybody nodded and laughed, because this was a traditional joke. Everyone knew how the Gnomes frequently lost themselves and were never where they were supposed to be. They nearly always had to be looked for and found and brought to wherever they were supposed to be going.

Fiachra Broadcrown wanted to know, rather belligerently, who would be going to the Fire Court. The giants looked at one another rather doubtfully, because didn't everyone know that the journey to the Fire Court was beset with all manner of dangers. You had to pass very close to the City of Gruagach to get there, they said, and wasn't the Frost Giantess still in possession of the City? Not that they were in the least bit afraid, they said, banging the table firmly to show their courage; it was just that once you had encountered the Frost Giantess, leave aside the Storm Wraiths who served her, you thought twice – well, you thought more than twice, about risking another encounter.

Goll the Gorm said they could cope with Storm Wraiths and with any other nasty things that Reflection and the *Geimhreadh* might have set about the countryside to guard their domains. 'As for sentries and guards,' he said licking his lips, 'I say fry 'em.'

'But what about the fire demons?' asked Arca Dubh. 'Wasn't Reflection always thought to be hand in glove with them?'

Goll the Gorm said that fire demons were a different pair of boots altogether, which did not seem to help the discussion much.

'But,' said Inchbad, '*somebody* has to go with the new proposals and the Crown Jewels.'

'Well, it won't be *me*,' said Goll and loosened his belt and belched comfortably and reached for the onion wine.

'It occurs to me,' said Goibniu, as if he had only just thought of this, 'that our guests have some acquaintance with Madame Reflection's Court. We all heard them say so.' He sat back in his chair, revolving his thumbs and nodding, and Inchbad looked at him and waited.

'Why not,' said Goibniu slowly, 'allow one of the Humans to act as our emissary?'

'Let a Human go!' cried Arca Dubh, who was particularly partial to Manpie and who did not think he had had his fair share after the last *Fidchell*. 'I never thought to hear you say that, Goibniu!' He looked at Goibniu in horror.

'I say skewer them tomorrow!' agreed Fiachra Broadcrown.

'Fry 'em,' muttered Goll. 'You can't beat fried Human. My old grandmother always said it made your beard grow, fried Human—'

Goibniu banged the table and the crystal window rattled and the firkins of wine jumped and slopped onto the table.

'Would I let Humans go?' said Goibniu, very

meaningfully, and the giants looked a bit sheepish. 'Well?' said Goibniu. 'Have you ever known me to let a Human slip through my fingers? Didn't I order Caspar, under pain of being spitted on a skewer and roasted slowly, to lock them into their rooms?'

'He obeyed as well,' muttered Arca Dubh. 'I was standing in the gallery and I saw him do it.'

'Exactly,' said Goibniu, leaning back in his chair. 'I can always smell out Humans,' said Goibniu, grinning now. 'And I shall smell out these three if they try to get away.' He rearranged the Marriage Settlement and stroked his chin. 'The Gnomes should soon be here with the Crown raiments for Flame,' he said. 'We'll send to the Fire Court and we'll send the Man-Human – what's his name? Floy?'

'Yes?' said Inchbad, as Goibniu paused.

'But because we want Floy to return,' said Goibniu, 'we'll keep the Girl-Human here. As pledge.'

'Yes?' said Inchbad again, and Arca Dubh poured another measure of onion wine. 'Ought we to trust him to come back, though?' said Inchbad, frowning.

'Of course we shan't trust him!' said Goibniu, shocked to think that anyone would believe him so stupid as to trust a Human. 'We'll send somebody with him,' he said and the giants all looked at one another worriedly, because the journey to the Fire Court was long and arduous, and brought you close to all manner of nasty things. It was all very well to be brave and fierce when you were in your own Castle (Tara or Gruagach, it did not make very much difference), but being brave and fierce in the depths of the forest on your own was another thing altogether. Goll the Gorm reminded everyone that the road to the Fire Court passed dangerously close to the Robemaker's workshops and a shudder went through the giants.

'I'm not going,' said Fiachra Broadcrown firmly. 'Risk being taken by the Robemaker and put to the treadmills? Not for a dozen Marriage Settlements! Your Majesty,' he added, belatedly.

'Well, nobody need expect me to go,' said Goll the Gorm. 'Fiachra's perfectly right. The Robemaker's servants haunt that road; nasty skulking things. Everyone knows that.'

'Yes but see here—' began Inchbad and was shouted down by the assembled giants, all of whom feared the Robemaker, none of whom was prepared to risk passing so closely by his workshop.

'Send Goibniu,' said Goll, with a sudden grin.

But Inchbad knew they did not dare send Goibniu on his own with two Humans. They would never see the Humans again. He said, a bit hastily, that Goibniu was needed at Tara to deal with important matters of State.

'So are we all needed at Tara to deal with important matters of State,' said Fiachra Broadcrown, and a general murmur of agreement went up.

Goibniu said, thoughtfully, 'We might send Balor,' and the giants all turned round to stare.

'He's quarter-witted,' said Goll.

'He'd never find the way there, never mind find it back,' added Fiachra.

Goibniu looked towards Inchbad. 'Sire?' It's your decision, said his tone, you're the King after all.

And Inchbad, who was getting really rather annoyed with people who tried to tell him what to do and who thought he could not make proper decisions, spoke.

'We'll send Balor. He's quite capable of finding the way if we give him a map.'

'Of course he is,' said Goibniu. 'And as well as that,' he added, 'if we keep the girl-Human with us, it will be a little extra inducement to Floy to secure Reflection's consent to the marriage, and to return. I think we can trust Floy to find the way there and back.'

He grinned, and drained another goblet of the onion wine. 'If Floy doesn't return from the Fire Court, inside of a week, with Madame Reflection's assent to the marriage, then the Girl can be thrown onto the *Fidchell* board.' He smiled round at them all. 'And in the meantime,' he said, 'she can tell us some tales of their travels each evening at supper. It will keep us amused.'

'And after supper?' said Fiachra Broadcrown, beginning

to grin hugely. 'What shall we do with her after supper each night?'

Goibniu smiled even more widely. 'I daresay I can think of something,' he said.

Chapter Eighteen

Caspar had gone rather irritably out of Tara, through the Western Gate, and was making for the first sprinkling of cottages on the edges of the Wolfwood. He had a friend or two there, who would be sure to ask him in and maybe offer him a drop of poteen, or even a bite of supper. He had eaten one supper already tonight, but eating in the presence of Goibniu and the rest could be a rather unpleasant experience and frequently took away any appetite you might have brought to the table with you. A bite of supper, taken with proper, ordinary people who did not spray soup over the table, or hold competitions to see how far they could spit out kipper bones, or search through the gravy with their fingers to find onion pieces, would go down very nicely.

Caspar had not decided whether or not he believed in the Angry Sun, even though Goibniu and the others had asserted that it had been a fine old sight. In any case, even if the Sun did exist, there was no more reason to think it had Humans in it than there was of believing that Tara would return to the Wolfkings. Caspar did not think he believed in the Sun, but he did think it was a sorry thing when you had to go hunting your own kind, simply to please great brutish lumps of giants. It had been enough being ordered to lock Floy and Fenella and Snodgrass into their rooms and then to be positively stood over by Arca Dubh to make sure he carried the order out. Arca Dubh had thought he had been very furtive about hiding at the far end of the gallery but, of course, everyone had known he was there.

It had felt deceitful and sly to sneak furtively along the gallery and turn the locks and slide the bolts across on Floy and Fenella and Snodgrass and Caspar had disliked himself very much. It was traitorous and treacherous and he was feeling very bad indeed about it.

He was still feeling bad about it now, prowling down the hillside, keeping a weather eye open for any stray Humans who might be taken up to Tara on some pretext or other and thrown into the dungeons to await the next celebration of the *Fidchell*. It was a terrible thing to have to do.

He had decided to try to get Floy and the rest out of Tara and away from the giants' greedy clutches. It would be quite hard and it would probably be extremely risky, but if Caspar could just come up with a plan, a really good watertight plan that would fool the giants, he would put it to Floy and they could be off out of Tara and Caspar would be off with them as well! People had their limits and he had reached his.

He was skirting the fringes of the forest now and he was just starting to look out for the first of the cottages where he might be given a welcome and thinking it would be O'Dulihan's and his daughter's cottage and very nice too, when the sound of singing, coming through the trees, assailed his ears.

> Gobble gobble gow; it's off to Tara we go.
> Gobble gobble gach, off to the Gruagach.
> Shall we escape the King?
> Yes, if we run fast.
> Shall we escape the tables?
> Yes, if we are able.

Since this was not the sort of thing Caspar had expected to hear when he was supposed to be hunting Humans, he stayed where he was and waited. Presently, along the forest path and out on to the road, came a band of the strangest creatures that he had ever seen in his life. He recognised them for gnomes at once, although he did not recall ever having actually met a gnome before.

There were at least eight of them; Caspar thought there might easily have been nine or ten. They were marching

quite jauntily along the forest path, plainly bound for
Tara's shining citadel, and not a one of them was above
three feet in height. They had quite elderly, quite wizened
faces, with jutting chins and rather happy expressions,
and they nodded and bobbed amiably, one to another as
they marched. They were colourfully dressed, some of
them in scarlet jerkins and bright green breeches; one
wore a yellow neckerchief with blue spots on it and
another was topped by a wide, mushroom-shaped hat
with a pleated brim and a feather in it and they all carried
bundles tied to sticks on their shoulders. Several appeared
to have shovels, and the yellow-neckerchiefed one sported
an enormous spade, which appeared to be giving him
considerable trouble.

They sang as they marched.

> Off to Inchbad's Court,
> For the dancing of the *Fidchell*.
> Oh there'll be fun and games, my boys,
> And there'll be skips and hops, my boys,
> If the giants bake you for pies, my b-o-y-s —
> If the giants bake you for pies.
> There'll be no more digging for you.
> There'll be no more dancing for you.
> If the giants bake you for pies, my b-o-y-s —
> There'll be no more digging for you.

A wave of amiable chuckling wafted across to where
Caspar stood and then the leader of the little creatures
(the one with the mushroom-shaped hat) stopped short
and said, 'Oho, there's a traveller waiting to meet us, lads.'

'A traveller, to be sure. Isn't that a traveller and him
knowing it in the twinkling of a gnat's whisker?' cried his
comrades. 'A traveller it is, and very likely come out to
show us the way to Tara.'

They beamed at Caspar and several waved their hats
and several more said, to be sure, wasn't it a remarkable
thing that just as you thought you'd missed your way,
didn't someone come along to direct you? The one who

seemed to be the leader, whose name turned out to be Bith of the Bog-Hat, took a firmer grip on his shovel and trod purposefully across the remaining stretch of forest path and said, quite politely, 'We bid you a good evening, sir!'

'Isn't that the way of it?' cried the others. 'A good evening it is, and him knowing it straightaways!'

'Good evening to you,' said Caspar, torn between annoyance at having his journey interrupted, and amusement at being addressed by creatures quite half his height and easily three times his age.

'Would you be from Tara, by any chance?' said Bith of the Bog-Hat, his head on one side, his eyes rather twinkly and definitely curious.

'From Tara, that's where he'll be from!' put in the others, and three of them sat down cross-legged and beamed at Caspar, while four dug their shovels into the ground, handle end up, and used them to sit on.

Caspar said, 'Indeed I am from Tara. Would you, by any chance, be from Gallan?'

The gnomes said they were, to be sure they were, and on their way to Tara, only that they'd just missed their way a bit, which was a thing that might happen to any man, or even any gnome.

'Is Gallan very far?' asked Caspar. 'How long a journey have you had?'

The gnomes were vague on this point. It was several days' march from Gallan, they said, although it might very well be a week or two. It depended on how fast you travelled, of course, and on how many times you missed your way. But you started out keeping the sun in the west, of course, although it was a remarkable thing how often you lost it on the way and ended up with it on the other side altogether.

The gnome with the yellow neckerchief started to tell about how the sun sank in the west and rose in the east and an animated debate arose over this, because not all his colleagues went along with this view.

But be that as it might, they said, they'd finally got

here, and hadn't they a fine old commission to be undertaking for Inchbad, the finest commission for many a long year and as welcome as a Wolfking returning. They looked a bit worried at saying this and glanced over their shoulders, to see if anyone might have overheard, and Bith of the Bog-Hat frowned at them and told Caspar that wasn't it difficult to guard against the old sayings sometimes and he hoped that Caspar would not be repeating such a slip of the tongue in quarters where it might be misunderstood.

'Of course not,' said Caspar.

The gnome with the yellow neckerchief, who appeared to be something of a nonconformist, said if you had to watch every word you said it was a terrible old world and you might as well be inside the Robemaker's Workshops and have done.

To which his companions said, very hurriedly, that Culdub Oakapple had no sense of self-preservation to give tongue to such a remark and it the Purple Hour, with everything fine about them, and a gentleman traveller from Tara come to show them the way, which they'd unaccountably missed.

To which Culdub Oakapple said, be bothered and be blowed to self-preservation, because couldn't a person with half a wit spread in his head see that it was a Human they were talking with, and had they any of them ever heard of Humans consorting with giants? 'And no more have I,' said Culdub Oakapple and the gnomes nodded solemnly and said you never heard of Humans and giants together, no more you did, and the Oakapple knew what was what, with him having the wits of three people put together.

'At least,' said Bith, turning round rather suddenly, so that the brim of his hat flapped wildly and nearly fell off, 'at least, I suppose you *are* a Human are you?'

'Yes, of course,' said Caspar, rather crossly. 'Can't you *see* that I'm a Human?'

The gnomes said they could, couldn't anyone with half an eye see it, and one or two got up from their spades and slapped their thighs in agreement and clapped one another on the back and Culdub Oakapple was knocked off his spade-seat and had to be helped up and Bith lost his hat altogether.

'And,' said one of them after Culdub had been dusted down and Bith of the Bog-Hat's hat had been squashed back into shape, 'and, we haven't yet introduced ourselves, sir, no more we have.'

His colleagues said no more they had and wasn't that the rudest thing you'd come across in a ten-month?

Caspar started to say he thought he knew who they were already, but the gnomes had decided on proper introductions and would not be put off.

'We're the Gnomes of Gallan,' said Bith, proudly, 'and the finest goldsmiths in the whole of Ireland!'

'You'd travel far and far worse before you found finer,' added another and Bith said, even more proudly, that they were Court goldsmiths as well and wouldn't that make you feel as great as great could be, just to know that you were responsible for forging the Royal Crowns in the Mountain Fires of Gallan. Then he turned to frown at Culdub Oakapple, who was polishing the toes of his boots by rubbing first one and then the other on the backs of his breeches, which was the height of discourtesy when you were making an introduction.

'Well, now we're here,' said Culdub loudly. 'We're here because of the commission.'

Bith said, with great solemnity, that it was a fine old thing to be given a commission and it the low season, when the most that people would ask you to fashion was a silver ring, or at best an armlet.

'You can't live on that,' he said seriously to Caspar. 'Not when there's taxes and Partholon's Pence to be paid, never mind the stoking of the forges. So we accepted the commission.'

'What is the commission?' said Caspar, who thought that if he was going to think up a plot to free the Humans, it might be useful to find out as much as he could about what Inchbad and the rest were up to.

Bith scratched his head and said frizzle him for a flying fish if he hadn't for the moment forgotten. 'But it'll come back to me,' he said firmly. 'It'll be all that travelling, never mind missing the way a time or two, sir, because that's a powerful fine thing for driving thoughts out of a person's head. I wouldn't have thought I'd forget something so important, but that's just what I have done!'

Several of the other gnomes said they had forgotten it as well, and wouldn't it make you fit to worry into a nothingness to know it.

Culdub said, crossly, 'It's a commission for an entire new set of Crown Raiments for Inchbad,' and Bith at once said that was the very thing and hadn't it been on the edge of his tongue all the while.

'Inchbad,' Bith said confidingly to Caspar, 'is going to take a wife. Well, you'd call it a Queen, wouldn't you, him being a King? Not that he'll ever be a true King of Ireland, of course, long live the Wolfkings.'

'Inchbad wants to marry the daughter of the sorceress, Reflection,' said Culdub, morosely. 'He thinks that by sending her a casket of jewels—'

Bith turned round at this and said that this was the first he had heard of any *caskets* being involved and did Inchbad suppose them to be vulgar box-makers? 'We're goldsmiths and silversmiths,' he said, hurt. 'Craftsmen. It's a tradition in Ireland. Why, sir, if you were to say to anyone, anyone in the entire world: Where would you buy the finest-wrought gold and silver, bless my soul if the answer wouldn't be: From the Gnomes of Gallan!'

Culdub, who was looking extremely gloomy, said, 'We didn't want the commission, of course. Well, I put it to you, sir, who *would* want to be working for the Gruagach. But we took it on and we'll make a fine old job of it. I've got several ideas already,' he said, and his companions beamed at him and said you could always rely on the Oakapple to have an idea.

'If,' said Culdub, 'Inchbad marries Reflection's daughter, it's very likely that people will point to the new

Crown Jewels, and say: my word, there's a fine set of jewels. My word, we ought to be thinking of consulting whoever it was who wrought those. You never know,' said Culdub. 'So I've got some very good ideas for a crown, and maybe a nice diadem or two and a gold torque. You can charge a very good price for a gold torque,' said Culdub seriously. 'And what with Partholon's Pence—'

'That's been increased again,' said Bith.

'So it has. And what with the new taxes, never mind the stoking of the forges — Well,' said Culdub, unexpectedly finding the drift of his sentence again, 'well, we thought we'd better accept. We thought we'd get the very best prices we could.'

'The Gruagach will be getting the very best workmanship, of course,' put in one whose name was Flaherty.

'So they will, isn't that the way of it?' chorused the others.

'And so,' said Bith, who appeared to be taking part in the conversation again, 'and so, we're off to Tara, to consult with the Court about the designs.'

'I wore my best boots,' said one of the younger gnomes.

Several of the other gnomes said they had worn their best boots as well, and one of them had bought a new neckerchief.

'And if,' said Bith, 'if you were minded to just show us the road, sir—'

'Or better still, walk along with us,' put in Culdub hopefully,

'—we'd get there a sight faster,' finished Bith, and everyone nodded and looked at Caspar hopefully.

Caspar hesitated. He was supposed to be out looking for Humans from the Angry Sun, or from anywhere else if it came to that, and it would not go down very well if he returned empty-handed.

But, on the other hand, he was not going to roam the countryside in the dark for giants or anyone else and, anyway, Goibniu would be so pleased to see the gnomes that nobody would be asking questions. Also, he was still turning over in his mind various plans about getting Floy and Fenella and Snodgrass out.

So he said, quite amiably, that he would walk along to Tara with the gnomes and be pleased to. At which the gnomes beamed and said there was nothing like a walk, to be sure there was not, and all of them well used to an hour or two's march.

'For,' said Bith, 'why were we given feet, if not to march with?'

'Feet, to be sure, ah, there's the thing, feet,' cried his companions, delightedly, and slapped their boots admiringly and said there was nothing like a foot, unless it might be two feet, because you didn't get very far with only one foot. They looked pleased at this display of wit and remembered that they had donned their best boots and said, didn't it go to show that you never knew.

'It's no more than a half hour's walk,' said Caspar and the gnomes beamed and said half an hour, wasn't that the thing, even if you got lost a couple of times there was nothing like half an hour, and would they be singing a bit of a song to help them on their way?

'So long as we're there in time for breakfast,' said Culdub Oakapple, picking up his spade with an air of determination.

Chapter Nineteen

Floy and Fenella and Snodgrass had passed an almost totally sleepless night. Floy had spent several hours in deep discussion with Snodgrass and, between them, they had made an attempt to sketch out the layout of Tara, so that they could see if there were any weak areas they might make use of.

'But I think it is a pointless exercise,' said Floy, somewhere towards morning, a thin, cold light filtering in through the windows to where he sat at a great desk, his black hair tumbled, hollows in his cheeks, his face white with fatigue. 'For one thing we've hardly seen Tara and, for another, we don't know what kind of spells and enchantments they might have strewn about.'

Snodgrass, who had studied more sketches and impressions of the lost castles and palaces of Earth than he could remember, said he thought that nothing like Tara had ever existed anywhere in any world.

'Didn't someone in the Wolfwood say it was partly raised by sorcerers?' he said. 'That'll be it, mark my words. You're almost sure to be right about the spells and enchantments. Difficult. It'll be the kind of place you might walk out of as brisk and easy as a knife cutting butter, or you might very well wander about for days, well, weeks even, without finding a proper door. It's always the same with enchanted castles,' said Snodgrass, as if, thought Fenella, only vaguely listening, enchantments were the sort of thing you met up with every day.

Fenella had not heard all of the discussion. She had curled up in the deep old window seat, the velvet coverlet from the bed wrapped about her for warmth, and had drifted in and out of an uneasy sleep. Of course they would escape and of course they would outwit the Gruagach, thought Fenella, her mind tumbling with images, fighting to stay awake in case she could help Floy and Snodgrass. Of course they would escape and they would rescue Nuadu. It was important not to remember how Nuadu had looked in those last moments, defiant and unafraid, his head thrown back as the Robemaker had dragged him forward by the vicious crimson rope-lights. I won't remember it, thought Fenella, leaning her flushed cheek against the cold window. I'll remember how he looked at me just before the Robemaker took him and how he called me 'Lady'. And I'll remember, as well, those strange fragments of memory I had when we arrived, because they certainly weren't anything from my memory.

But it was probably better not to think about Nuadu at all. Fenella pulled the velvet folds of the cover about her and tried to sleep and not to think about what would happen and whether they would be let out of these rooms and what stories she might have to tell the Gruagach about Star People and the Fire Court and the other fictional places they were supposed to have travelled to. Her mind swam in and out of sleep and the fire burned lower.

And then, quite suddenly, it was full morning and the sun was slanting across the floor of the rooms. Floy was sleeping where he sat, his head resting on his folded arms, a look of such exhaustion on his face, that Fenella almost wished to be back on Renascia fighting Quilp and the Council and trying to plan to outwit the Dark Lodestar.

But it is morning, thought Fenella, washing her hands and face in the water from the brass ewers, liking the thick, fluffy towels left for them. It is morning and it is sunny and there is a world to be explored. And surely, oh surely, we shall be able to go after Nuadu, and surely the giants are friendly and last night was only a bad dream. And, said Fenella, very firmly indeed, I will *not* believe that any of us are in danger.

They were taken to breakfast by Caspar, who unlocked the doors, and regarded them rather shamefacedly.

'Good morning,' said Floy, as if nothing had happened

and Caspar, who looked uneasily over his shoulder, then said, in an urgent whisper, 'I didn't like locking you in, you know, but I didn't have any choice.'

'I don't think we expected anything else,' said Floy, with complete courtesy and Caspar hunched his shoulders crossly and said, 'There might be a plan. Could you be ready and keep your wits about you, do you think?'

'Of course.' Floy did not say: even though we do not really trust you, but Fenella and Snodgrass both felt him think it. Fenella thought that it was a pity that Caspar was so scared of the giants, because he knew so much about Tara that he might have been of considerable help. He certainly knew the whereabouts of the Robemaker's Workshops. But he had locked them in last night and he had done so on orders from the Gruagach so they did not dare rely on him. They would do much better to rely just on their three selves.

'I'm quite hungry for some breakfast,' said Snodgrass, as they followed Caspar along the galleries and down the staircases and through huge, high-ceilinged chambers.

'It's always *very* plentiful,' said Caspar seriously. 'And His Majesty has particularly requested your presence.'

'How very good of him,' said Floy, blandly. Caspar shot him a suspicious look.

'I suppose you don't trust me after I locked you in,' he said.

'Quite right. We don't.'

'I suppose I can't blame you,' said Caspar, morosely. 'I wouldn't trust me, either. But you'll see. I shall come up with something. I'm supposed to be guarding you, but I shan't. Only we'll have to make it look as if I am. In here. If you could try to look as if you're being guarded, it would go a long way. But don't worry too much about it, because they won't notice very much. They're not *morning* people, the Gruagach.'

Breakfast was served in a long, low-ceilinged room, with a deep fireplace, on which were roasting several animals which Snodgrass said, in an awed whisper to Fenella, were oxen. There were barrelsful of butter and platters of fruit and great sides of bacon and ham and sizzling sausages. The giants washed their breakfasts down with immense tankards of mead and ale and grunted and were inclined to be morose, which seemed to bear out Caspar's remarks about them not being morning people.

The Gnomes of Gallan sat together at the far end of the table. They were presented to Floy and Fenella and Snodgrass by Caspar and they had all swept bows (Bith's hat had fallen off) and been charmed to meet travellers like this. But then, wasn't Tara the place for travellers, they said. Hadn't it always been known as the centre of the Western World? They were rather pleased with themselves for saying this, because it was something the Gruagach would find quite flattering and, also, it had not referred to the Wolfkings, which would have been extremely discourteous, not to say disastrous. They sat together, in the small-sized chairs brought up by Balor, and ate their breakfasts and told one another wasn't this the finest meal ever and would they all look at the roasting oxen, because it was a long time, well it was years, really, since any of them had seen such a sight. Bith took off his hat, which was a polite thing to be doing, and Culdub Oakapple tucked his yellow neckerchief into his collar by way of table napkin.

Fenella, who rather liked the look of the Gnomes, thought they were a bit like careful children, diligently remembering their manners, sprinkling their conversation with 'please' and 'thank you', and with things like, 'I'll trouble you for the jam pot, your honour', or 'after you with the tomato chutney, your worship'. They polished off most of the sausages, which they seemed greatly to enjoy, and Bith of the Bog-Hat and Flaherty shared a firkin of the giants' ale, which Balor had brought up from the cellars.

But after they had finished eating (which seemed to the travellers to take for ever), Goibniu sent the other giants out of the room, because he had important business to discuss.

245

'You'll be told in good time,' he said and would not listen when Goll the Gorm said, crossly, as they trooped out, that it was always the same; they were not told what was going on and it was a disgrace and a scandal and there'd be a revolution at Tara before much longer, if there wouldn't be an outright war.

'Now,' said Goibniu, resting his elbows on the table rather vulgarly and eyeing Fenella greedily, 'now, my guests, we have a little *proposition* to put to you.'

Floy, who had been cutting himself a slice of ham, looked up, because there was a lick of anticipatory pleasure in Goibniu's tone. He exchanged a look with Fenella and saw that she was watching Goibniu quite politely, but that there was a wariness in her eyes.

But Goibniu was smooth and courteous; he was very nearly urbane. He paid a brief homage to the Gnomes, who had journeyed all the way from the Gallan Mountains to bring their ideas for the new Queen's Crown Jewels and did not refer to the fact that they were four days late on account of getting lost on the way. He said they would all be wanting to study the designs the minute Balor had cleared away breakfast and Bith at once reached for the knapsacks, and said he hoped Flaherty had not spilled jam on the drawing of the four-pronged diadem and Flaherty, injured, said indeed he had not and it the best damson jam he had ever tasted.

'And if there's a bite more, I won't refuse, your prominence.'

Goibniu remembered that Gnomes were reportedly extremely greedy, but said they would take a look at the designs now, if the Gnomes were quite ready, thus galvanising the Gnomes into anxious industry, resulting in much unpacking of knapsacks and unrolling of parchments and remarks such as, 'Who's got the plan of the turquoise bracelet?' and 'Why did we bring along *four* sketches for the everyday silver tiara?' and 'Flaherty's sitting on the Coronation sceptre!'

But, at length, the drawings and sketches were laid out and the plans for Flaherty's new steam-powered melting pot which had unaccountably been packed by mistake put away again. Weights were placed at all the corners of the sketches to stop them springing back into tight rolls.

'And there it is, your throneships,' said Bith, beaming, because when all was said and done, hadn't they produced the finest old sketches ever heard of and wasn't there good reason for them to feel proud?

Goibniu was pleased with the designs. The Gnomes had gone to considerable trouble; Culdub and Bith had sat up long hours and consulted books and chronicles and there had been much burning of late candles and worried scurryings to and fro between the Gnomes' houses in the little mountain village. Flaherty and MacKnobb had produced thin gold and silver and emerald paint with which they had coloured the fine charcoal designs and the end result was really rather good. The Gnomes sat together at the end of the breakfast table and waited anxiously for the verdict. They thought that Goibniu was looking happy (although it was always difficult to tell with giants) and thought, wasn't it a fine old thing to see how well the designs were being received and wasn't it great, altogether, to see how well received the Oakapple's sketches were, because hadn't he been the guiding light behind most of the work?

Goibniu studied the parchments for some time, seeing that there was an elaborate circlet of gold for Flame if she became Inchbad's Queen, studded with firestones which would be mined from Fael-Inis's Fire Mountains. There was a corresponding Crown for Inchbad, of course, and the Gnomes had cleverly managed to make these subtly similar. There were ornate neck circles with chippings of moonstones and slender, silver anklets engraved with the tree symbols of fertility and great chunks of raw gold somehow veined with amber which would be used as Coronation accessories. And there were silver amulets studded with turquoise, bearing the insignia of the Gruagach and also the insignia of Flame's ancestry. This had been quite difficult and the Gnomes had scratched their heads a good deal, because, although people did not openly refer to it, everyone knew that Flame's father was Fael-Inis and it had meant a lot of worrisome discussions as to whether this fact ought to be openly acknowledged, or whether it might be discourteous to draw attention to it.

Goibniu thought it all looked very nice. He did not refer to anything so vulgar as payment, of course, because the Gnomes would not expect it. But he said they would present the designs to Reflection, these very sketches, and there would be a great deal of acclaim given to the Gnomes as a result.

Culdub Oakapple opened his mouth to say that acclaim was all very well in its way, but they had been hoping for something a bit more *financial* than that, but the two Gnomes on each side of him trod on his foot to stop him, because you could not always trust the Oakapple to be tactful. They could not be offending the Gruagach, and they especially could not be offending Goibniu the Greediguzzler. Bith remembered a nearly forgotten, seldom-told belief that, although Gnome was an acquired taste amongst giants, they would occasionally serve it at very special occasions. If Inchbad married Flame, it would be a very special occasion indeed; it might be just the occasion when they would want a dish or two of roast Gnome and, more to the point, it would get the Gruagach out of paying for the new Crown Jewels.

Fenella and Floy and Snodgrass had sat quietly at the other side of the table, not eating very much, listening carefully to everything that was said. Floy had been interested in the Gnomes' sketches; like Fenella, he found the Gnomes rather attractive, friendly people and he thought their designs were clever and subtle and beautifully drawn. Snodgrass embarked on a story about a very famous jewel called the Koh-i-noor, which he thought had once adorned a great King's State Crown and explained how it had been so rare and so heavy that it had had to be kept locked away behind bars and guards, so that nobody could steal it.

The Gnomes were very interested in this; as Flaherty

said, you could not know too much about these things, although it was a pig's pity that such a jewel couldn't be worn by the King of the day when he went about his reigning, because wasn't that the purpose of crowns and jewels anyway?

'But,' said Flaherty, 'it's all for your exaltednesses to say.'

'We thought,' put in Bith, who was feeling a bit bolder now that Goibniu had approved their ideas, 'we thought that the lady – that is Reflection's daughter – might like to see the designs before we put them to the forge, your honour.' He looked wise and solemn when he said this, because he knew that ladies – even sorceress's daughters – had their own ideas about what they ought to wear and it was not to be supposed that Flame would be any different. 'Colours,' said Bith rather vaguely. 'It'd be nice for her to be given the chance to make a suggestion or two.'

Flaherty asked who was to take the sketches to the Fire Court and the Gnomes at once looked alarmed, because hadn't they already travelled all the way from Gallan and it a terrible long journey, never mind getting lost twice, as well as the Robemaker's Workshops and the Cruachan Cavern being on the route.

'But of course,' said Bith firmly, 'if your honourships were wanting it, then we'd go and be pleased to.'

And the Gnomes looked at Goibniu worriedly and waited.

Goibniu was still studying the drawings and thinking that Reflection, greedy creature, would surely not be able to resist them and that it mightn't be a bad idea to revive the ancient traditional dish of roast Gnome for the wedding feast, which would save them having to pay the Gnomes anything. But he smiled rather overpoweringly at the Gnomes, and said that: no, they would not dream of asking them to make such a journey, so hard on the heels of their march in from Gallan.

'We are hoping that our two new friends will assist us by acting as emissaries to the Court,' said Goibniu and, turning his head, smiled at Floy.

'It wasn't,' said Floy, in the privacy of their bed-chamber, 'a request.'

'An order,' said Fenella, nodding.

'Carry out this task, while we keep your lady hostage,' said Snodgrass. 'They've locked us in again, you know.'

'I do know,' said Floy, his eyes glinting angrily. 'It was politely done—'

'That one they call Goll the Gorm,' nodded Snodgrass. 'I don't call him polite; in a pig's ear I don't.' He frowned and said, 'You know, dear boy, I think we may have to do what they want.'

'Go to this place – what do they call it? the Fire Court – and take the proposals for the marriage of Inchbad,' said Floy.

'Yes. But that,' said Snodgrass, worried, 'would mean leaving Fenella here.'

'We can't do that,' said Floy, staring at his sister. She was listening intently and her eyes were thoughtful, as if she might be toying with some idea of her own. It was unthinkable that they should leave Fenella here at the mercy of the giants. 'We'll have to find a way of taking Fenella with us,' he said.

Fenella, leaning forward eagerly, said, 'But listen, the journey to the Fire Court takes you past the Robemaker's Workshops. We heard them all say so. It's the very thing we've been waiting to hear.'

'Yes,' said Floy. 'But it's too high a price.'

'It sounds rather fearsome,' said Fenella, slowly, 'to be left here with the giants. But I truly think we can't miss the chance of getting there.'

'Not if it means us going off without you,' said Snodgrass. 'We can't possibly do that.'

'I don't think we're going to be given any choice in the matter,' said Floy, rather grimly. 'Goibniu said they'd send the gatekeeper – what's his name? Balor – along with us.' He looked at them. 'That wasn't simply to show us the way,' he said. 'They could give us maps and we could find the way perfectly easily. It was to make sure we didn't run away. Balor's coming as a guard.'

'To bring us back,' nodded Snodgrass.

'But of course we'd come back for Fenella,' said Floy. 'Don't they think we would?'

'They can't know. It's this question of different beliefs and different loyalties,' said Snodgrass. 'If it wasn't all so dangerous, I'd almost be finding it interesting, you know.'

'Goibniu suggested that I could mark the evenings by telling them tales of our travels,' Fenella said, remembering. 'One tale each night. I don't know how long I can keep that up,' said Fenella. 'But I think I could keep it going for quite a while. I could tell them about Renascia to begin with.' She glanced at the other two. 'Doesn't it seem an awfully long way away, now?'

'Worlds and aeons,' said Floy, softly.

'Shall we miss it when we have time?' said Fenella, a bit wistfully. 'I do think I'd like to miss it. It seems so – so callous not to be thinking about it and wondering what happened to it.'

'We'll mourn for it when we have time,' said Floy, touching her hand, and Fenella looked at him gratefully, because that was exactly what she had been feeling. Of course they would mourn for Renascia and remember all of the good things about it, only just now they had other things to concentrate on.

'I'll spin the Gruagach some tales,' she said now, frowning. 'Renascia and as much as I can remember of Earth legends and perhaps something about the Dark Lodestar as well.'

'Scheherezade,' nodded Snodgrass. 'The lady – well, she wasn't a lady at all, really, but she saved her life by telling exotic tales to her captors. She spun it out for years.'

'There you are, then,' said Fenella. 'It's been done before and it can be done again.'

'But look here,' said Floy, 'you won't have to do it, because we'll find a way of taking you with us.'

'As if we'd leave you here on your own,' said Snodgrass,

clicking his tongue at the very idea.

'I think you'll have to,' said Fenella, who found the idea completely appalling, but who was trying to be practical and sensible and make it sound safe for them to go so that they could get Nuadu. 'Also—' She stopped and looked up, and Snodgrass said, 'Someone's coming.'

'The Gruagach?'

'I don't think so.'

It was not the Gruagach, but Caspar, who had come quietly along to their rooms when the giants were taking their midday snooze.

'They always do,' he explained, unlocking the door and coming in cautiously. 'It's the one time when Tara becomes almost quiet. Could I sit down? I've thought of a plan.'

The three travellers looked at one another and then Floy said, 'Sit down.'

'It isn't brilliant,' said Caspar, 'I'd have to say it isn't brilliant or clever or even very subtle. But it might work.'

He looked at them, his head on one side, and Floy said, 'Do go on.'

Caspar said impatiently, 'Oh, for *goodness*' sake, Floy! Do I *look* like the sort of person who consorts with giants!' He leaned forward. 'I don't know where you're from,' he said, 'and I don't *want* to know. I've got enough to worry about without wondering if you're from the Ancient Past or the Distant Future, or somewhere quite different altogether. It's your business,' said Caspar firmly. 'But I do know that the Gruagach have only one use for Humans and *if* you stay here long enough you'll find out what that is. Into the dungeons and then onto the *Fidchell* board,' said Caspar, tucking his chins into his neck and looking solemn. 'And it's a nasty end, that one.'

'Quite,' said Floy.

'Well, I've had enough of it,' said Caspar, looking plumply mutinous. 'I've had enough of hunting down Humans for them to play their grisly games with! It's—it's little short of traitorous,' he said. 'And I'm not going to do it any more. I'm going to do what you said; walk out of Tara and hide.'

'Well?' said Floy, sending a warning glance to the other two.

'You'll have to go to the Fire Court with Balor,' said Caspar, earnestly. 'You do know that, don't you? If you don't they'll certainly have you all for supper.'

'What about Fenella?'

'Fenella can follow you in a day's time.'

'How?'

'I'll bring her,' said Caspar, and sat back and regarded them with the plump pleasure of a person who has reached a final decision.

It took longer than he had expected to persuade Floy to agree. Floy was suspicious and Caspar did not really blame him for that.

'I don't blame you one little bit,' he said, earnestly trying to win them over. 'But you can't stay here, that's for sure.'

Floy said, slowly, 'If Snodgrass and I were to agree to it—' He stopped and Caspar said, 'Yes?'

'How long would the journey take? And what sort of things might we have to encounter on the road?'

As to that, Caspar had no definite information. He thought it would certainly be a couple of days' journey to the Fire Court – the giants would be sure to know, he said, because they had already sent emissaries with the marriage proposal. But he thought it could not be more than a couple of days.

'Fenella and I would set out a day later,' he said, looking at Fenella and thinking that she was rather a nice sort of companion to be having on a journey. Probably she would have a good few stories to tell about the world they had come from. Caspar would quite enjoy hearing about that.

Floy said, very carefully, 'Could you show us the route?' and Fenella looked up, as if, thought Caspar, she had heard something in Floy's voice that the rest of them had not heard. But he thought it a reasonable request to ask for a route and he took himself away to Tara's great map room to procure maps for them. He did this quite openly, because if anybody asked where he was going, he would say he was finding out the route to the Fire Court for Floy and Snodgrass's journey. It was nice to be able to tell the complete truth for once.

But the only person he met was Balor, on his daily forage to the wine store during the Gruagach's afternoon snooze, to replenish his secret stock of ale and mead, which had been sadly depleted with all these unexpected visitors to Tara. Balor did not grudge offering guests a mite of good wine, because it was only polite, but there was no denying it made inroads on your hoard. And if he had to set out on this nonsensical journey to the Fire Court with the Humans, it would be as well to just stock up a bit for his return.

They spread the maps on the floor of the larger of the two bed-chambers and Caspar pointed with a podgy finger to the Fire Country where Reflection had set up her Court.

'It's on the edges of Fael-Inis's country,' he said, 'and we all know why.'

'Why?'

'Because,' said Caspar patiently, but wondering where these three had *come* from, for goodness' sake, 'because Reflection once had a bit of a – well, more than a bit really . . . And they do say that Flame is *very* like him.' He eyed the three travellers a bit hesitantly.

Floy said, 'Do you mean that Reflection and Fael-Inis were once lovers?' and Caspar, hugely relieved, said, 'Well, so they *say*.' He glanced over his shoulder and Snodgrass, who loved gossip, glanced over his as well, because you never knew who might be listening in an enchanted castle.

'They do say,' said Caspar thrillingly, 'that she pursued him for positively *centuries*, until he gave in, purely to get her out of his way. He's elusive, you see,' explained Caspar earnestly. 'You never know quite when you've got him.

Well, that's always supposing you can get him in the first place, because the number of people who have actually *seen* him, you can count on one hand.' He paused for breath and regarded them expectantly.

But Floy said, in an expressionless tone, 'Do go on,' and Caspar looked at Floy doubtfully, because he was not altogether sure of Floy yet and he had the feeling that Floy might very well be thinking and assessing and generally not revealing all his feelings. And so Caspar, who thought he could be as reserved as the next man, merely said, 'Oh, he's a strange one, Fael-Inis. A bit of a fly-by-night.' And returned to charting the journey to the Fire Court.

Fenella, who had never seen a map quite like this one, had curled up on the floor to listen. The road to the Fire Court looked quite straightforward really; it seemed as if you had to go past a large lake and on down a narrow, windy mountain road with houses dotted on each side. Floy had asked about dangers and what they might expect to encounter, but Fenella did not think it looked especially dangerous.

'Well, it isn't dangerous precisely,' said Caspar. He hesitated and tapped the map with his finger. 'Or, at least it isn't so long as we avoid *that* bit of road.'

'Why?'

'Well, they do say,' said Caspar, and stopped and looked at them again. 'They do say that it's there that the Robemaker has his Workshops.

'And the Robemaker's Workshops,' said Caspar, shuddering, 'are the worst place in the world.'

Chapter Twenty

The Purple Hour was descending as the Robemaker thrust Nuadu Airgetlam before him down the final stretch of road that led to the grisly Workshops.

Nuadu, aching in every bone, the lower part of his face constrained within the harsh red mask fashioned from the Robemaker's ropes of light, had not made a sound. He thought that the Robemaker was waiting for him to do so; perhaps somehow to indicate that he would ask for mercy, but he had done nothing. He could not speak and he would not make any gesture that would show weakness. He would, somehow, behave as the true Wolfprinces would have behaved in such a situation. He would behave as his mother's people would have behaved. And so he walked quite calmly and very nearly leisurely before his captor. And although the Robemaker lashed out at him from time to time with the thin, cruel rope-lights, he managed not to flinch.

He had some idea of what was ahead of him, for he knew the terrible tales about the Robemaker's Workshops. He knew it was unlikely that he would ever see the true Ireland again because he was being taken to the place that many people believed to be one of the Gateways to the Dark Ireland. Certainly, now, he would never see inside Tara. He could think, with a brief twist of the old cynicism, that he had never seen inside Tara anyway and that he could not miss what he had never had.

But he did miss it; he thought he had been born homesick; he certainly thought he had spent most of his life waiting and longing and aching for the Bright Palace where his mother's people had quarrelled and laughed and made love and war, and where the charming ruthless Wolfkings had woven Ireland's history. But he had never seen Tara; he had been abandoned at birth, he had been flung out by the King, who would have none of his Queen's bastard wolfson at his Court.

Finally, Nuadu had found his way to the strange twilight community of the Wolfwood; the place that gave shelter to the half-breeds: the bastard sons of Royal Houses, the creatures who were not possessed of sufficient Beastblood to be acknowledged at Tara, but yet were not entirely Human. Creatures welcome in neither world, he had thought, bitterly. We were all of us outcasts; we were all of us flung out by the Lords of Tara, who were jealous of their lineage and protective of their inheritance.

These half-breed mongrel creatures had acknowledged Nuadu as an aristocrat; a bastard but still a Wolf-prince, royal through his mother's noble blood. They had made him their leader and Nuadu, cynical and bitter against his own kind, had thought that for all he was a base-born prince, still he had a Court of a kind and subjects of a sort.

When the Gruagach had come storming down from the Northern Wastes and attacked Tara and stolen away the Wolfking's son, Tara's heir, the people of the half-world of the forest had vanished, afraid and timid. They had wanted no part of the terror and the bloodshed, and they had hidden in the mountains and the caves and the remote Northern Isles. Perhaps, when the battles were over and Ireland was whole once more, they would return, but perhaps they would simply remain in the hill-farms and the distant mountains, forging their own cultures, making their own legends, weaving their strange secret stories into the fabric of Ireland's history.

But Nuadu had ridden out for the King and for the captured half-brother he had never known. He had ridden out for his mother's people as well, and finally, he had joined with the people of the Court, 'For,' he had thought, 'it is my people, my half-brother the Gruagach seek to drive out.' He had thought he had not cared what became of him in the battle and he had thought that, when it was over, he would return to the Wolfwood and that the creatures amongst whom he had lived would return, also.

But the Wolfking had been killed and the prince imprisoned inside the Dark Realm. The giants had taken Tara for their own and when Tealtaoich and the others had fled to the Forest Court, Nuadu had gone with them, neither quite one of them nor quite not one of them, but feeling a cautious kinship with them and discovering, with cynical amusement, that they were looking to him to lead them back.

'After all,' Tealtaoich had said silkily, 'you may be a bastard, my friend, but you are a High Queen's bastard and you were sired by a Wolf. You have the blood of the Wolves of Tara and there is no question but that it makes you a Wolfprince.' The green eyes had been steady. 'You have a claim on Tara,' said Tealtaoich. 'You are the heir presumptive.'

'If we are honest, you have far more right to Tara than any of us,' put in Oisin.

'Even though we shall not necessarily admit it,' said Feradach and Nuadu had seen that they would serve even a bastard scion of the Wolfline before any other creature.

And for all that, I have fallen into the hands of the Robemaker, he thought angrily. I am as much a captive as my half-brother. Nuadu knew that the Robemaker would put him to the treadmills; that he would be forced to work at powering the Silver Looms to weave the Robemaker's enchantments. He would have said that he was as courageous as most, but he knew that no one ever escaped from the Workshops. People lived and died there; they did not grow old there, because no one could live for very long in the Robemaker's hands. And once their physical usefulness was at an end, the Robemaker tore out the souls of his slaves and carried them to the Soul Eaters in the Cruachan Cavern, which some believed were the Gates of Hell. Well, at least, he thought, with a glimmer of the old wry humour, at least I shall witness things the legitimate Wolfprinces did not.

They were nearing the Workshops now and Nuadu could see, in a saucer-shaped dip, the dull red glow rising into the night sky.

'The furnaces,' said the Robemaker, in his dreadful, diseased voice. 'My creatures stoke them and work the treadmills, and so the Silver Looms are never allowed to be still.'

'My creatures . . .' And now I am one of them, Nuadu thought. The crimson rope-lights still held him, so that he was forced to go on down the slope until they stood before the terrible dwelling place of the necromancer.

Nuadu stopped and the Robemaker stopped with him, as if he might be saying: well, Wolfprince? Savour this last moment out in the world. Look your fill on my domain for, once inside, you will never come out.

'Not until you are useless and flayed and bent,' said the Robemaker softly and Nuadu knew that his thoughts had been heard with ease. 'Not until the skin is hanging from your back and your thighs in strips and your flesh is withered from the heat and your sight is dimmed from the dry fire of the furnaces.'

The Workshops were a huddle of black, rather low structures; made of some kind of harsh, dark stone. Here and there were archways in the stone and through the archways, low doors. The windows were narrow and mean-looking, but from each one glowed the dull red fire from the terrible furnaces.

And everywhere, at every corner, within every stone and door and roof was the immense, thrumming power of the Silver Looms.

It poured out into the still night and Nuadu shivered, because he knew it for the evil magic of the Dark Ireland; the ancient, malevolent enchantment of the necromancers. Within the Wolfwood he had known and experienced the strong pure magic of his people; the music of the *sidh* and, later, the beautiful wild bewitchment of the stirring Tree Spirits. He had inherited, as well, a thin vein of sorcery of his own; a little from his mother, but a great deal from his father the Wolf. He would have said that he had as

259

reasonable an acquaintance with sorcery as anyone in Ireland.

But now, here, in the hands of the most purely evil being ever known to Ireland, on the very threshold of the Dark Realm of the Necromancers, Nuadu felt, as if it was a solid wall, the evil strength and the merciless dark magic emanating from the Workshops.

Behind the Workshops was flat, barren wasteland, with stunted trees, and twisted roots. Nuadu glanced at this and saw that there might once have been verdant greenery, perhaps even a small forest. But the heat and the darkness and the twisted magic had long since drained the heart from the land; the dark sorcery had sucked out the goodness and turned it into a stunted, abandoned place.

Black fury rose in him against this creature, this monstrous being who was turning Ireland into black barrenness; above the mask his eyes glinted and he wanted to spring on the Robemaker and tear his throat from his body. But he could not move and, even if he had been able to, he knew that the Robemaker could fell him in a breath-space by sorcery.

As they moved nearer, Nuadu felt the heat belch out. The dull red glow was all about them now and the baleful light fell across the Robemaker's cloaked figure so that, although his face remained hidden, Nuadu caught the glitter of his eyes, red and inverted and, despite the belching heat, he felt ice close about his heart.

I shall never escape from this place. I shall die here and then this creature will tear out my soul and carry it to the Court of the Soul Eaters. And then I shall be flung for ever into the River of the Dead . . .

And then they were inside, and the doors had closed to.

The sound of the door to the Robemaker's Workshops closing, was one of the worst sounds Nuadu had ever heard. For a moment, he did not move and, at his side, the Robemaker waited, the slanting eyes watching from deep within the hood.

And then, 'Well, Wolfprince?' he said in his hissing,

bubbling whisper, making Nuadu think of lipless jaws and clotting wounds. He wondered what hideous deformity might lie beneath the silken cloak and the deep dark hood.

'Well, Wolfprince?' said the Robemaker. 'Where are your supporters now? Where are the creatures who swore to you their allegiance if you would regain the Bright Palace for them?' He leaned nearer and Nuadu stood his ground. 'They are cowering in the Wolfwood, Nuadu Airgetlam. They are trembling and hiding,' he said, the slimy lick of pleasure overlaying his voice. 'They are protecting their miserable skins while Ireland falls further into my grasp.' He paused and then said, in a soft, menacing tone, 'And Tara, Nuadu of the Silver Arm? What of Tara? Who now walks its silver halls and dwells in its marble galleries?' One hand was flung outwards in a clutching gesture. 'In the hands of *my* creatures, Wolfprince, just as you, now, are in my hands.' He indicated the seething red-lit Workshops. '*Here* is the True Ireland,' said the Robemaker. 'Here is *my* Ireland, Wolfprince. Here is the powerhouse of necromancy.' And stood back and folded his arms as Nuadu looked about him.

The Workshops of the Looms were far larger than he had expected. They seemed to stretch back for a very long way and Nuadu, narrowing his eyes, trying to find his bearings, thought that they must go back and back into the hillside behind the road and deep within the earth. The ceiling was low and there was a thick, suffocating feel to the air and a stale, old stench. Despite the heat, Nuadu felt again the chill about his heart.

On each side of the room where they stood were massive iron furnaces; great, glowing stoves that belched out waves of heat so that the air was heavy and fetid. Huge pipes of what looked like iron protruded from the furnaces and ran along the sides of the workshops, disappearing into the ceiling in places and, in other places, into the walls. Steam rose here and there, not in puffy, damp, friendly clouds as if a kettle was boiling, but in hissing, angry spurts, as if some unseen being was venting its spleen.

Before the furnaces were some of the Robemaker's captured slaves; Humans, once-strong sons of Ireland's farmers and woodcutters and blacksmiths and builders and woolmen. The ordinary, honest, good-humoured people who had lived under the protection of the Wolfkings and rendered them allegiance. Will it never cease, thought Nuadu, this endless hungry *taking* of our people by the Black Ireland?

He stood very still, staring about him, his eyes adjusting to the glowing heat. He thought that here and there in the slaves he could detect traces of an old lineage. There was the dark-eyed, slant-featured look of the ancient lost Royal Houses of Ireland in several of them, the glossy hair that might easily have been fur in others. But he knew it to be a frequently found trait, for most of the Noble Lords of Tara had long since dispersed and the enchanted Beastblood, once guarded so jealously, had nearly died out. If these young men possessed traces of the Beastblood, it was from so far back that it could not be measured, and it was so slight that it could no longer hold the power to call upon the beasts for aid. Black fury rose in him against the evil creature who was leeching Ireland of her youth, but Nuadu quenched it, lest the Robemaker turn it to his use.

As his eyes adjusted to the scorching dry heat, he saw that the slaves were all lightly clad; in the main, they wore ragged breeches, with the upper halves of their bodies and their feet bare. The exposed skin was flushed and glowing; here and there it resembled tanned leather and, in some cases, it looked as if it had split and healed, and split again. The slaves' hands were blistered and flayed and oozing, covered with angry weals that were burns from direct contact with the white heat of the furnace doors. They moved slowly, shamblingly, and there was a terrible hopelessness about them.

Several of the furnace doors were open, and threw out merciless, scorching fire. The creatures who were working had shovel-shaped implements with which to throw in an endless supply of wood and Nuadu, scarcely able to believe this, thought: but they are felling the Trees! They are murdering the Trees! And blinked and looked again, for the felling of living Trees, the cutting and slicing and mutilating of Trees which had not died and dried and seasoned naturally, was one of the oldest and most strictly forbidden practices in Ireland. As he stood there, a massive double door at the far end was kicked open and several more of the Robemaker's creatures came shuffling in, dragging a wheeled cart, with a newly cut-down beech Tree lying on it. The Robemaker lifted a hand in their direction and the creatures at the cart took up massive double-edged axes and began to hack the Tree into small sections.

As the first axe cut into the Tree, a great wailing cry of agony rent the thick stifling heat of the Workshop and Nuadu knew at once that the Tree had been taken down while it lived and while the naiad still dwelled within it.

From where he stood, Nuadu saw the slender, copper-haired Beech Naiad emerge from the murdered Tree, her arms chopped to ribbons, her body maimed in a dozen places, the red-gold blood of the beech spurting from her. She hovered for a brief time over the trunk of the Tree, tears streaming from her eyes, shuddering as the axes continued to cut into the wood, shaking her head from side to side. Nuadu could see that her fingers were gone now, and that she was trying to pull herself back into the heartwood, which would have been her dwelling and the place from which she drew sustenance and vitality, but the Robemaker made another of his sudden curt gestures and the slaves fell to their work again, sweat streaming from their half-clad bodies and Nuadu saw the heartwood splinter and fall apart. The Beech Naiad let out a last cry of desolation, and fell to the floor. There was the sudden achingly sweet scent of burning logs on an autumn night and then the drift of thick, crisp, beech leaves in the depths of a forest and the Beech Naiad seemed to melt and shiver and dissolve into nothing.

The furnaces were blazing up more strongly now, and the slaves began flinging the freshly chopped beech-wood into the molten depths. There was the cold ring of iron, as they levered the great doors shut and the rhythmic clanking of machinery as the steam from the furnaces was forced along the great pipes. Through the doors at the far end, Nuadu caught the whirring sound of the Looms. The slaves continued their stoking, shuffling to and from the cart, heaving the beech logs into the next furnace.

The Robemaker moved forward, prodding Nuadu onwards and, as they moved down the centre of the Workshop, the blazing furnaces roaring on each side of them, Nuadu felt his skin already shrivelling from the heat. How must it be to work here day after day, month after month, knowing there was no end to it? He glanced at the working slaves, and saw that their skin ran with fluid from fresh blisters and their eyes were bloodshot, the eyebrows and lashes singed to nothing; many of them walked awkwardly, as if they had become deformed.

The Robemaker said, emotionlessly, 'The soles of their feet are skinless from the heat of the floors. There are trays of salt for them to walk across when that happens, so that the raw flesh can be hardened.' From within the deep dark hood, Nuadu caught the sudden glint of white bone and heard the guttural laugh. 'And, of course, I hear your thoughts, Wolfprince,' said the Robemaker. 'You have surely not forgotten the ancient necromantic art of the *Stroicim Inchinn?*'

Nuadu did not move, but the icy fear closed about him again. The *Stroicim Inchinn*, the ancient forbidden art, sorcery of the strongest and most dangerous kind: the power of one mind over another. It was an enchantment expressly forbidden by the Ancient Academy of Sorcerers, and Nuadu had thought that even the Lords of the Dark Ireland hesitated over it. In the realms where it was studied, it was recognised as the ability to tear and claw into the mind of another. It was the terrible and forbidden dark side of the pure and honourable *Samhailt* and, although Nuadu had heard of it, he had thought it extinct.

The Robemaker was watching the slaves. 'It would not be practical for their feet to be ruined,' he said. 'And if they flinch at the sight of the salt, there are *persuasions* I can use.' The crimson rope-light snaked out and Nuadu saw the nearest slaves cower and put up their hands to shield their faces. One, who did not appear to be as badly scorched as the others, stood his ground, and eyed the Robemaker rather challengingly. Nuadu wanted to cry out to him not to be so defiant, for the Robemaker could certainly not be vanquished in such a way.

'Dear me, a reckless one,' said the Robemaker, sounding amused. 'A small lesson for you, Human slave. And the Wolfprince shall see it.'

The crimson rope-lights whipped forward effortlessly and the boy who had glared angrily at the Robemaker was forced back against the nearest furnace. Nuadu could see that his eyes were distended with fright now, but he stared back at his captor, unflinchingly.

'You,' said the Robemaker, gesturing impatiently to the nearest slaves. 'Take up the axes. *Do it!*' He folded his arms and power streamed from his eyes, so that the two slaves were caught in the white glare. Slowly, blindly, they raised the axes to shoulder height.

Nuadu knew the young man was already lost. The Robemaker had only to exert his will; he had already clawed his way into the minds of the two slaves with the axes; it would be nothing to him now to whip their minds to his will. And his will was that the slave, the young man who was scarcely more than a boy, should somehow die for his brief moment of rebellion.

The two slaves moved jerkily, as if they were at the ends of strings. Puppets, thought Nuadu, unable to look away. He is using them like puppets.

The boy was backed against the wall between two furnaces, and Nuadu saw his face twist with pain. He guessed that the wall would be excruciatingly hot and that the boy's skin would be blistering and shrivelling.

265

The Robemaker said softly, 'Slice by slice – and *slowly*,' and the slaves moved mechanically forward.

Slice by slice . . . The slaves swung the axes low, with one accord, and the boy's feet were cut from his legs, so that he fell suddenly on to bleeding stumps of leg. The colour drained from his face and he would certainly have fallen, had not two crimson rope-lights shot out and pinioned his arms to the wall, so that he was forced to stand, vertically, half hanging by his hands, half supported by his mutilated legs. Blood and splinters of bone spattered the floor, and Nuadu saw that the thin rivulet of blood nearest to the furnace actually bubbled from the heat of the floor.

And when the soles of their feet are skinless, there are trays of salt for them to walk across to harden the skin . . .

'Again!' said the Robemaker, his voice liquid and clotted now, and the two slaves swung again, a little higher this time, so that the hard, straight shin bones were sliced across, and the boy's legs were shortened a little more.

'Fuel for the furnaces,' said the Robemaker. 'You! Into the fire with the dead meat!' And at once, two more leapt forward and scooped up the bleeding lumps of flesh and bone and flung them into the open furnaces. There was a roar of heat and, briefly and nauseatingly, the sudden sharp scent of cooking. Nuadu felt his stomach twist and clenched his teeth against it.

The boy was screaming and begging for mercy now, his lips bitten through.

'Again!' cried the Robemaker and now his voice had ridden to a high excited whine and Nuadu, glancing covertly at him, saw that he was roused to a devilish excitement.

The boy was barely conscious now; his face was the colour of tallow candles and his body sagged, held only in position by the crimson lights. The two slaves were hacking at his thighs now, and two more came forward, moving jerkily, so that Nuadu knew that the Robemaker was using the *Stroicim Inchinn* on them also.

'The thighs!' cried the Robemaker, 'the thighs and the hips! Take them before I hurl you, also, into the furnaces!' He stood for a moment, a towering dark figure and watched as the blood – sluggish now – seeped from the boy's mangled body.

'Human weakling!' said the Robemaker, contemptuously. And then, in a different, gloating voice, 'But his soul I shall take.' He moved and the slaves cowered back, as if, thought Nuadu, they had witnessed the next part before and feared it even more than the mutilating of the boy. The two who had used the double-sided axes seemed to become more aware and Nuadu thought that the Robemaker had probably withdrawn the piercing spikes and the pinchers of the *Stroicim Inchinn* from their minds. They looked about them a bit hazily and then at the bleeding half-thing that had been the young boy and scuttled into a corner.

The Robemaker stood over the remains of the boy and lifted his arms wide, so that the cloak fluttered and his arms resembled great black wings. He pronounced a string of words in an unfamiliar tongue and, as he did so, the light changed abruptly and became dark and malevolent, tinged with purple. Black-edged shadows fell across the glowing floor.

There was a beating of wings overhead and a leathery, rustling sound and the slaves cringed and covered their faces. Nuadu stood his ground, his eyes raking the shadows. *For I believe I am about to witness a thing few people see and live to tell of*, he thought.

Into the magenta light of the spell-ridden Workshop there appeared a monstrous creature, composed of great leathery wings and claw feet and a hideous, horny head, with great dark, gaping eye sockets and a bony, sloping jaw. The face of the creature was pointed, animal-like, goat-like, and there were cruel curving talons protruding from its front paws and curling toes with gristly joints and sharp nails at the back. There was a dry, rustling sound, as if old dry bones were being rubbed together and the sound of fleshless lips chuckling.

Nuadu stayed where he was, but his mind was tumbling with horror and revulsion. There was a dreadful, fetid stench on the air and the creature swooped across the Workshops, the wingspan of its great jagged wings immense.

Nuadu knew that the Robemaker must have summoned one of the creatures from the Cruachan Cavern to take his victim's soul and, as he watched, the winged creature fell on the remains of the young boy, and settled on his chest, nibbling and clawing its way into his face. Sickness rose in Nuadu, but he fought it and forced himself to watch.

The boy's eyes had been drawn out by the Soul Eater and it gave a dry, evil chuckle of triumph. Its talons whipped out and embedded themselves into the boy's skull, using the emptied eye sockets as a means of entry and Nuadu, narrowing his eyes against the dimness, saw that the talons were in fact hollow tubes, thin transparent bones.

The Soul Eater crouched for a few moments and Nuadu saw that a thin silvery fluid was beginning to course along its hollow talons. It gave a low moan and Nuadu felt the nausea lift his stomach again, because there had been a very nearly sexual quality in the sound.

The Robemaker was standing very still, his hooded face turned in the direction of the Soul Eater and its victim.

The slaves were huddled together in a corner, their faces turned away, as if afraid that the Soul Eater's attention might suddenly turn to one of them.

For from the power of a Soul Eater from the Cruachan Cavern, there is no escape, ever . . .

The winged creature had finished with the boy now and Nuadu thought it had taken its fill of the strange silvery liquid. But it remained still for a moment and there was the shimmer of silver about the boy's head.

For the soul does not easily yield to those who will steal it for the purposes of evil . . .

And then the Soul Eater spread its wings again, and the pointed skull-like head turned to the Robemaker.

'*Another soul against your debt, Robemaker,*' said the

creature in a dry, whispery voice. '*The scales will have tipped a little farther over. But we ask far more of you before your bondage is at an end. There must be more souls for us, Robemaker.*'

'There will be more, Master,' said the Robemaker.

'*You know the pronouncement,*' said the creature. '*You must live with your curse until we have eaten our fill.*' And then, turning its head to look round the Workshops, it said, '*We do not ask of you that you give us your slaves, Robemaker, for it is vital that the Looms are kept weaving. It is vital that you continue to suck from Ireland her heart and her being and her puny strengths.*'

'I continue to do so, Master,' said the Robemaker and, although there was not the smallest trace of subservience in his voice, Nuadu, listening intently, received the impression that the Robemaker was choosing his words with care, as if he was in some kind of thrall to this being.

The Soul Eater said, '*We shall meet again, Robemaker. In the Cavern of Cruachan, at the Court of my people.*' It spread its wings again, and the heavy dark beating of them filled the air. '*There are many centuries before the debt is paid and the curse we placed on you lifted. There are many more nights when you will attend the Court of the Soul Eaters and render us homage.*' There was a deepening of the shadows and a swirling of something heavy and turgid and foul, and then the creature was gone and the Workshops were once again lit to crimson and the slaves turned back to their tasks.

Chapter Twenty-one

Snizort thought he was getting on rather well. He had spent most of the day talking to the people of the exiled Court and had made copious notes. He had rather enjoyed it and it had helped him to keep his mind off what might be happening to Snodgrass and to Floy and Fenella. He had asked a great many questions of the exiled Court and he hoped, he said earnestly to Oisin, that they would not think him inquisitive. It was only that none of this was quite what he had been used to.

Oisin said, very courteously, 'Since our own Chroniclers and our Poets and Story Tellers were unable to follow us into exile, it is we who should be grateful to you for creating an account of what is happening.'

This was extremely polite of Oisin and Snizort had been heartened. He would make a very careful and very thorough account of it all, he said. He had already made some notes about the battle, and about the Gruagach besieging Tara—

'On the orders of the Robemaker and CuRoi,' said Eogan sharply.

'Yes, the Gruagach would never have done such a thing if it hadn't been suggested to them,' put in Feradach.

'Or even if they hadn't been well paid,' added Tealtaoich. 'I hear that Goibniu, the Gruagach High Chancellor, is quite the most *venal* giant you could ever meet.'

'Giants are all venal,' said Feradach.

They were seated round the long oak table, with the remains of supper still spread out. Behind them, the Wolfwood was shrouded in the blue and violet shadows of the Purple Hour and Snizort could hear the night rustlings and scurryings and patterings of tiny woodland creatures. But within the clearing it was warm and safe-feeling; Clumhach had lit their usual fire, which was burning up brightly, and somebody had placed a cauldron of spiced wine to simmer over it. Snizort thought that this was probably the time of day that the Beastline enjoyed best; supping at the long oak table, making plans to regain Tara, drinking spiced wine or mead.

At his side, Oisin said gently, 'It is how we lived at Tara.'

'Yes?' said Snizort, who had forgotten this business of having your thoughts overheard.

'The days were spent in – oh, many things,' said Oisin, his dark, velvety eyes far away. 'Hunting, perhaps, or travelling. Chasing the white stag through the forests – never catching it, of course, for it is a – a creature of legend, the white stag.'

'Yes. Do go on,' said Snizort, reaching for a newly sharpened charcoal stick.

'Perhaps there would be guests to be welcomed – travellers, or merchants from the East who would display their wares of silk or gold or ivory,' said Oisin. 'Perhaps there would be studying for some of us, discourse with the druids or the sorcerers. For those who held Office under the King – that is, Chancellorships or Council positions – there might be meetings in the Star of the Poets.' He looked at Snizort to make sure that Snizort understood and Snizort at once said, 'Yes, we had our own governing people in Renascia. A Council of Nine we called it.'

'Nine is interesting,' said Oisin, thoughtfully. 'It is a very mystical and very powerful number, although twelve is more frequently found. Although there are only six of us here now, once there were Twelve Royal Houses.' He indicated the twelve carved thrones at the edges of the clearing, set into the immense Trees. 'I do not know when those were carved,' he said. 'Our legends say that it was at the same time as the great Ebony Throne of Ireland.'

'That is inside Tara?'

'No. No, the Ebony Throne is lost to us, as so much else is lost to us,' said Oisin.

'I understand,' said Snizort, who had lived in a world

271

where entire civilisations had been lost and who had spent his life searching for fragments of them.

'It happened not all at once, you understand,' said Oisin. 'Not as it happened to your people, in one immense disaster. It happened naturally, over many years, and always sadly. Our people were killed in battles such as the great CuChulainn of the Chariot Horses at the Battle against the Erl-King in the High King Cormac's time. Sometimes they embarked on quests and did not return. Sometimes they were taken by the Dark Lords and imprisoned for ever in the Black Ireland. There were many causes and many reasons and nothing lasts for ever. And so now there are only six Royal Houses.'

'That is very sad,' said Snizort.

'But twelve has always been a number of great meaning to us,' said Oisin. 'You will find it repeatedly. We have the Twelve Sacred Couches of Conchobar in the Hall of Light within Tara. And there were the twelve evil Lords who served the necromancer Medoc. And twelve stone idols surrounding the ancient monster-god, Crom Croich.'

Snizort, on his own account, offered the Twelve Knights who had sat at a round table so that no one of them should be at its head and no one at its foot.

'That's something I've never come across,' said Oisin, his expression absorbed and interested.

'And there were the Twelve Companions of Odysseus and the Twelve faithful Apostles,' said Snizort. 'And we know that our ancestors kept twelve days of revelry for some feast or other. We tried to keep those as well, in memory of them, although we did not know which part of the year they had their twelve days.'

'Perhaps,' said Oisin, 'our worlds are not so very far apart.'

'Go on about Tara,' said Snizort.

'Oh, Tara,' said Oisin and the sudden, slightly mischievous grin lifted his face. 'It was said to be the most brilliant Court in the western world. And although the days would be taken up with working and hunting and discussions, every evening we would gather in the Sun

Chamber and every evening there would be a banquet of some kind. We would eat and drink and there would be entertainments and music and dancing and stories. Travellers and pilgrims and men of unknown cultures and religions would be there, for no one was ever turned away, and every creature was welcomed and given food and shelter and his story listened to. You and your friends would have been accorded places of honour,' said Oisin, 'for certainly you have one of the strangest stories ever told.'

Oisin had managed to bring a number of books and chronicles out of Tara and Snizort had studied these during the afternoons. Eogan had told Snizort about the ritual mating between Humans and beasts, which could only be done under the strict control of the Court Sorcerers and the Panel of Judges, and Snizort had been entranced.

'It's fascinating,' he said, scribbling away busily. 'Now, have I got it quite right? I don't want to make any mistakes. Every fourth or possibly fifth generation, the youngest son or daughter of each house has to appear before the Panel of Judges—'

'Sometimes it's longer than four or five generations,' said Feradach.

'It depends on the *strength* of the blood, of course,' said Dian Cecht.

'*My* family could go for seven generations,' said Clumhach. 'In fact, I once had a third cousin – or was it a great-aunt . . .?'

'If the Bloodline is judged to have weakened, then the Ritual is ordered,' said Eogan.

'The – dear me – the actual mating with a fox or a—'

'Yes,' said Oisin, and smiled. 'Contrary to what you would think, it is rather a solemn occasion.'

'I think it's unnatural,' said Miach, rather defiantly, from the other end of the table and Dian Cecht shuddered.

'*So* unpleasant,' she murmured. 'And to one who has been *delicately* reared—'

'Of course,' said Feradach loudly, 'you do get the

occasional bastard outside the Enchantment. They're frequently mutants, because of the mating being done without the protection of the Enchantment. But sometimes it works.'

'Like Nuadu,' said Dian Cecht urbanely.

'Well yes.'

Oisin had drawn breath to respond to this, when Eogan, who had been looking towards the forest, suddenly said, 'What's that?'

'What?'

'There's something moving in the Forest!'

'I expect it's the *sidh*, isn't it?'

'The *sidh* are out there,' said Feradach, looking searchingly into the trees. 'But Eogan's right. There's something else out there as well. Something that isn't the *sidh*. Can't you hear it?'

'Yes,' said Oisin, after a moment. 'There's something moving in the shadows. Something huge . . .'

They were all scanning the forest's depths now and Snizort saw that a sudden stillness and an intense wariness had stolen over them, as if whatever was moving out there in the Forest was strange and alien and menacing.

Feradach and Eogan had both been right. Deep within the shadows of the Wolfwood, there were unmistakable movements; not ordinary movements as if somebody was walking quite normally and openly through the Trees, or even furtive movements as if somebody was creeping along, dodging between the Trees, hoping not to be seen. It might have been very nearly normal if the movements had been like that. Snizort thought you might very nearly expect creatures, beings, anything at all, to steal through a darkling forest and lie watching the strange group of people eating supper and drinking wine in the glow from the fire.

The movements were fumbling and searching and somehow groping. It was as if there was something out there – or perhaps several somethings – struggling to break free of a force that had held them for a very long time. Things that had been yoked, harnessed, held down and held back by a power that was dissolving.

Things that had for centuries slept without stirring, but that were now stirring and waking and might, at any moment, come prowling through the forest . . .

Here and there they could see long, reaching arms, struggling dark shapes, the occasional ripple of something that was touched with silver by the moonlight, but that might be green-tinted and golden by day . . .

It was the most remarkable thing any of them had ever witnessed. It was strong and deeply magical and filled with power and enchantment and with the twilit scents and the dusk-laden sounds that were part of the ancient Wolfwood. From somewhere quite close by they could all hear the faint, unearthly singing of the *sidh* and Snizort caught glimpses of blue-green iridescence and of shimmering wings beating on the air.

'Yes, the *sidh* are close to us,' said Tealtaoich softly, when Snizort touched his arm and nodded towards the sounds. 'They are singing the Tree Spirits back into the world.'

'Is that something they always do?'

'Oh yes,' said Tealtaoich, his eyes on the shadowy forest and the struggling Tree Spirits. 'Oh yes, they would pour out their music for something so magical as this.'

The Tree Spirits were discernible now; it was as if they had broken through a thick veil, through a smothering black curtain, and they were recognisable as distinct forms, moving slowly in and out of the forest. The Purple Hour had come and gone and it was full night now, so that moonlight lay across the forest, gleaming coldly, silvering the outlines of the Trees and the silhouettes of the awakening naiads and dryads.

There were more of them now. Oisin, who knew a little of the theory of sorcery – 'Although I have never aspired to its practice,' he would have said modestly – knew that with the emerging of the first, the others would have gained strength and confidence. He knew, as well, that Tree Spirits cling tenaciously to their homes until those homes become untenable because of the Tree dying and drying and he thought that Miach's spell must have been stronger than any of them had thought for it to draw the Spirits so fully and so firmly into the open.

The Tree Naiads and Dryads were a curious blending of flesh and skin and muscle and bark and tree and leaf. You could not be quite sure where the Tree part ended and the Human part began, although nobody was sure if Tree Spirits possessed any Human blood. Most people thought they did not. In the main, the Spirits were Oaks; solid, not young forms, with rather benevolent and scholarly expressions. Their arms were half arms and half branches and their faces were part of the trunk part of the Tree. They did not have hair, but trailing fronds of leaves and bracken.

The Elms, who seemed to stand next in line, were plain and sturdy, with pale-ish bark for skin and a good deal of greenery. They stayed close to the Oaks, as if they considered it their duty, and they looked as if they might find life a serious business.

In between the Oaks and the Elms darted the Silver Birches, slender and frivolous-looking, with wild, shining white hair that streamed out behind them and mischievous features and trailing garments that might have been some kind of cloth, but might as easily have been simply their pale leaves. The watchers thought that the Silver Birches would certainly be a bit wild and probably without any moral sense at all and Clumhach thought he must remember to tell everyone about his great uncle who had succumbed to a Silver Birch one scandalous afternoon. It would not do to forget something so interesting.

The Copper Beech Naiads were the most beautiful creatures any of them had ever seen. They were exquisite, rather fearless-looking creatures with manes of flowing red gold hair and skin the colour of an autumn sunset, long narrow eyes and slender, graceful arms and feet.

As Snizort and the Court sat, barely moving, the Trees seemed to become aware of the watchers and, one by one, ceased to move and turned to regard them. A great hush fell over the entire Wolfwood, as if, thought Snizort, every

276

living creature knew or heard or sensed what had happened and was waiting to see what the Trees would do.

And I believe the Trees are judging us, thought Snizort. They've broken free and they're turning to see what kind of creatures called them out of their enchanted sleep. They're inspecting us and they're considering what we are and whether we're all right.

Tealtaoich said, very softly, 'You know, one of us must approach them.'

'Yes,' said several voices, rather doubtfully.

'Had it better be me?'

'Well, you're next after Nuadu,' said Feradach.

'Yes, but he didn't actually say—'

'He wouldn't,' said Eogan, his eyes still on the Trees. 'He never accepted the leadership of us all, not officially. He wouldn't appoint anyone to lead in his absence.'

'Because he didn't care?' asked Clumhach anxiously.

'No. Because he cared too much. And Tealtaoich is nearer to the Wolfkings than any of us. He's the King's cousin.'

'I should not *dream* of putting myself forward in any way at all,' said Dian Cecht. 'But I do think that someone of *authority* should go into the forest and approach the Tree Spirits.'

'All right,' said Tealtaoich, suddenly. 'I'll do it.'

He stood up and moved stealthily and warily forward and Snizort saw, for the first time, the sleek, feline grace. Tealtaoich was not exactly padding into the forest and he was not precisely slinking into it either. But the impression of dark, catlike prowling was there; the image of fur-covered paws and of sheathed claws and lashing tail. Snizort glanced at the others and saw in each of them, now, faintly but definitely the unmistakable traces of their lineage. As if something within them had sharpened to awareness, or perhaps as if the darkling forest had wakened their strange ancestry and quenched the Human side of them.

I suppose it *is* all right, he thought. I suppose we are right to throw in our lot with them. But there was no time to give this disturbing idea attention; Tealtaoich was nearly at the Trees and the Trees were grouped together watching him and waiting for him in complete silence and it was important not to miss a single instant of any of it.

Tealtaoich had moved with a soft, measured tread towards the flowing, twining shapes, not once hesitating.

'And,' said Oisin softly, 'it's actually quite brave of him. We none of us know if the Trees are safe or not.'

'Tealtaoich is far braver than he'd like you to think,' said Feradach.

Tealtaoich had passed through the twisting shadows and was standing facing the Trees now, a slender, solitary figure, silhouetted darkly against the massive solidity of the Oaks and the flowing silver-tipped hair of the Birches and the cascading russet leaf-hair of the Copper Beeches. The Tree Spirits were a great deal taller than Tealtaoich and, from out of the blending, shifting, gold and green and russet, their eyes were ancient and wise and beautiful.

'And watchful,' thought Snizort. 'Bless my soul, they are certainly not to be lightly regarded, these creatures.'

Behind the Spirits they could see the shapes of the Trees themselves, stark and empty-looking, rather dark and brooding, like abandoned houses whose windows stare blindly and blankly.

The Oak Naiads were at the centre of the group, with the Elms in attendance. They're Elders, thought Snizort. The Oaks are the Elders of the Forest and the others are aware of it. They'll all have opinions and ideas and suggestions, but it'll be the Oaks who decide and the rest will bow to their decision.

The Silver Birches looked rather fun. They seemed to giggle and shrug and eye Tealtaoich mischievously and be unable to decide where they would like to sit. They darted about on the front of the group, their silver-leaf hair rustling like raw silk. On the edges of the Trees, the Copper Beech Naiads had simply sunk to the ground, their hair falling about their bodies in rich cascades of colour, making pools of glowing russet and brown all about them. They fixed their huge unreadable golden eyes on Tealtaoich.

The Trees seemed to be waiting for Tealtaoich to make the first move and the largest of the Oaks had inclined their heads quite courteously. 'But,' said Clumhach in one of his huge whispers, 'you get the feeling that you could easily be made to feel a fool by them, don't you?'

'Speak for yourself,' said Oisin, to whom this remark happened to have been directed.

'Those Silver Birches don't look very reliable. Still, I'd rather have them with us than against us,' added Feradach.

Tealtaoich stood quite still, regarding the waiting Trees and seeing that they were listening and apparently politely prepared to hear anything he had to say.

'You are well come,' he said at last, and the Trees inclined their heads again.

'They'll like that,' murmured Oisin to Snizort. 'It's the ancient welcoming Ritual and, in all of the stories, the Tree Spirits set very great store by rituals. And they'll like the fact that it's a Prince of Ireland who has been sent to talk to them.'

Tealtaoich, facing the Tree Spirits, was remembering this as well. Then, hoping he could remember enough of the ancient language of chivalry and selecting his words with extreme care, he said, 'Good Trees, we ask your assistance,' and saw the Elms nod to one another meaningfully, as if they had been expecting all along to be asked to do something for the Humans.

'Tara is in the hands of the Dark Powers,' said Tealtaoich, hoping that this was the correct thing to say, because nobody had seemed quite sure which side the Trees would be on. 'It is in thrall to a Necromancer of the highest order and the Wolfking is dead.' There was a rustle of emotion at this. The Beeches drooped their beautiful heads and their copper leaf-hair rippled across the forest floor. The Elms looked at them rather disapprovingly and then turned back to Tealtaoich.

Tealtaoich said, 'You have always been on the side of justice, Trees; come with us and fight with us and for us, as you have done in the past.' He lifted his voice slightly. 'Come with us and help us to beat back the Dark Ireland once again.' A pause. 'Once before,' said Tealtaoich, reaching into his memory, 'once before, you answered the Wolfkings' cry for help. It is a part of our history, that, and a part which we revere greatly. Once before, you rose up from the great forests of Ireland and came to the aid of our greatest King of all, Cormac of the Wolves. You turned the tide of a battle then, centuries ago.

'We have kept that memory with us ever since and we have always believed that the Trees would ever be on the side of the Wolfkings and the Beastline and the One True Ireland.' He paused for breath. 'Will you fight with us and for us again?' said Tealtaoich. 'Will you come with us to Tara and help us sweep to victory? Will you fight for the descendants of the great Cormac and his daughter Dierdriu and the descendants of Grainne the Gentle and of Erin and of Niall of the Nine Hostages? And of all the Wolfkings and Queens who have made Ireland great?'

Tealtaoich paused again and stood waiting and a murmur of approval went through the others. Feradach whispered to Oisin that you had to give credit where it was due; Tealtaoich really did this sort of thing extremely well.

'Yes, but I don't know if he's reaching them,' said Oisin, his eyes on Tealtaoich's slight form. 'They're rather overpowering, aren't they?'

The Trees seemed to be thinking Tealtaoich's words over and Tealtaoich, still standing before them, received the impression that they might be somehow conferring with one another in some silent fashion of their own. The Oaks bent their branchy heads closer and the Silver Birches rippled and chattered. And then the largest of the Oaks moved forward and Tealtaoich saw that he had the high, domed forehead of a scholar and a thinker and that his ancient eyes held wisdom and knowledge.

'Son of the Wild Panthers,' said the Oak, in a warm, woodsy sort of voice, 'son of one of Ireland's most ancient

Bloodlines, is it solely to ask our help that you have woken us?'

Tealtaoich thought, rather grimly, that this was a nasty one. They *had* woken the Trees only so that they could ask for their help, of course. As he hesitated, searching for the proper words, the Oak spoke again.

'We have slept the enchanted slumber, the *Draoicht Suan*, for many centuries,' it said. 'You will know of our history and you will know that we were sent into that slumber many hundreds of years ago, by the Dark Lords who held sway in the reign of the High King Cormac.'

'I do know,' said Tealtaoich, and thought there was a note of reproof in the Oak's tone, as if the Tree Spirits were angry at being summoned like this. They are not going to help us, he thought, and knew a rush of complete despair.

The Oak said, 'But we *have* lent our aid to the Royal Houses of the Beastline in times of extreme danger and we have also fought to regain Tara for the rightful heir.'

The rightful heir . . . Taken and imprisoned and held fast in the black depths of the Dark Ireland. I wonder if they know about that, thought Tealtaoich. But he only said, 'Will you join with us?' and looked at the Oak very straightly.

There was a pause, and the Oak seemed to study him afresh with solemn, scholarly eyes.

'Ireland is threatened by a terrible force,' it said, and the listening Court held their breath. 'It is menaced by the evil CuRoi and by the Robemaker.' At the mention of the Robemaker, a shiver went through the Trees. 'We know it and we feel it,' said the Oak.

'We do not promise to help you, Son of the Panthers. But we will attend a Council of War and hear your plans. If we believe that Ireland can be purged of the Dark Lords and the Wolfline reinstated, then we will join with you.'

The Oak regarded Tealtaoich severely. 'For,' it said, 'unless the Wolfline is reinstated, Ireland is surely doomed for generations to come.'

Chapter Twenty-two

Floy and Snodgrass, with Balor accompanying them, set out from Tara at noon the next day.

'Carrying,' said Goibniu, 'the new marriage proposal, and the designs for Flame's jewels.'

The new proposals contained a revised list of the territories the Gruagach were prepared to cede to Reflection in exchange for her daughter but Caspar, who had managed to get a look at these, had told Floy that the Gruagach were only ceding some barren bits of wasteland surrounding the Robemaker's Workshops, the Lake of Dhairbhreach – which nobody in their right minds would want – and a mountain or two. 'It looks quite good on paper,' he said. 'In fact, it looks very generous. But it's nothing more than a double-cross, really. Goibniu will never give away anything that is worth a button.'

The Gnomes had rolled the designs for the new Crown Jewels into cylinders and packed them carefully into long, hollow tubes, which they had brought with them for the purpose.

'Best copper on gold,' said Bith of the Bog-Hat.

'Engraved with tongues of flame,' said Flaherty, who had thought up this himself and did not want it overlooked.

'I did the engraving,' said Culdub Oakapple. 'What you do is, you heat up an iron spike—'

'Don't let Floy forget the chart of colours.'

'—until it's so hot it's white—'

'And there's the pearl diadem we made, just as a bit of a gift—'

'—I blistered my thumbs on it—'

Floy said, 'I shall not forget anything and I feel sure that Reflection and Flame will be greatly impressed by your sketches.'

The Gnomes broke into wide grins at this and said wasn't impressing the thing and Floy in the right of it, and impress was what they'd set out to do and hadn't Floy the way with words?

'And if,' said Bith of the Bog-Hat, 'your impress-ship should ever be wanting an armlet or two, or maybe a plain everyday crown circlet, we'd be happy to oblige.'

The Gnomes chimed in, saying to be sure they would, obliging was what they were, and it the best thing of all to be, leave aside impressing, which was just as important.

'And so,' said Floy, looking at Fenella, wondering how all this might have been received on Renascia, 'and so, we will set off.'

Fenella looked at Floy and remembered about the Robemaker and the way he had captured Nuadu and rendered them all helpless, and about the exiled Court and the *sidh* and the Tree Spirits that Miach had almost awoken, and which might turn out not to be friends, but enemies. And thought: and Floy is going off into the midst of all these and it is perfectly possible that I shall never see him again.

But it would not do to show any emotion before the giants, who had all gathered to see Floy and Snodgrass off, or before Balor, who was waiting in high good humour at the unexpected excitement of a journey to the Fire Court. And so Fenella said, 'I wish you a safe journey,' and was pleased that her voice came out firm and perfectly calm, as if she was quite accustomed to seeing her brother off on a journey to the Court of a Sorceress, which would take him past all manner of weird and darkly enchanted places.

'And a speedy return,' said Caspar, winking plumply on the side that the giants could not see. 'That's important. A speedy return.'

They were to depart from the Western Gate. 'Which,' said Caspar, 'is where all important journeys start from.'

'It will be our first real sight of Ireland,' said Floy to Caspar, as if there was nothing more on his mind other than surveying the land they were about to travel through.

He stood for a moment, framed in the great gateway, and Fenella saw how the early morning light touched his dark hair and brought out red glints in it and saw, as well, that his eyes were shining, as if he was already looking ahead to the dangers and the adventures. Yes, perhaps it will be all right. Of *course* it will be all right.

Snodgrass was discussing with the Gnomes the best route to take and Caspar was making sure that they had packed the maps and Inchbad and Goll the Gorm and Arca Dubh were nodding and smiling and, of course, there was nothing sinister in their smiles – and there was certainly nothing in the least sinister in the way that Goibniu was looking at Fenella, thumbs hooked in his belt, his wide greedy mouth curving into a satisfied grin . . .

Balor was going to let down the drawbridge so that they could ride across it. 'Seeing that it's a special occasion,' he said, and Goibniu had procured two horses for Floy and Snodgrass to ride. Balor would walk, because giants did not ride.

'There aren't horses that would carry them,' muttered Caspar. 'And on horseback you'll get a better chance of losing him.'

The provision of horses was unexpected, but curiously cheering, because it seemed to show that the giants were sending Floy and Snodgrass off in reasonable style, as if they expected them to return.

'Of course you will return,' said Goibniu. 'The lady will be here, waiting for you.' There was another of the smiling glances at Fenella. 'She will entertain us every evening after supper,' said Goibniu and Floy nearly abandoned the entire thing there and then, because there had been something so meaningful in the way that Goibniu had said *entertain* that he wondered how they could ever have considered leaving her here alone.

'I suppose,' said Floy, thoughtfully, fixing Caspar with an equally meaningful stare, 'that we can trust you, can we?' and Caspar said, 'Oh, for the—Floy, I've been trying to get away from these creatures ever since they took Tara!

We'll meet you on the road leading to Lake Dhairbhreach as we arranged.'

'Yes,' said Floy. 'All right.'

Neither Floy nor Snodgrass had ever actually seen a horse, let alone ridden one. 'But it is not really so very difficult,' said Snodgrass, after he was hoisted into the saddle and discovered how to take up the reins.

Floy stood where he was for a moment, looking up at the great, shining edifice that was Tara, Ireland's Bright Palace, the great legendary Citadel of Light, the home of the Wolfkings . . . *Shall I ever see this again?* And then, with a pang of real anguish: *shall I ever see Fenella again?* he thought. But there was nothing to be done; Goibniu had made it a request that Floy and Snodgrass travel to the Fire Court leaving Fenella alone. It had been courteously framed, but Goibniu had arranged for Balor to go with them and Floy had known – and everyone had known – that it had not really been a request but a command.

There was a quick, rather fierce embrace. 'Go safely, Floy,' whispered Fenella, who thought it safer not to say more, and then one of the stable hands brought the second horse forward and Floy found, as Snodgrass had, that it was actually quite easy to spring into the saddle and it was rather a safe feeling to be seated astride a horse like this.

And then the drawbridge was falling, with a clanking and a whirring of machinery and the light was pouring into the courtyard and the Gnomes were cheering and the giants were nodding to one another, and there was nothing for it but to ride away with Snodgrass, with Balor loping along at their side, with Fenella behind in the hands of the Gruagach.

It was a rather dreadful feeling to know you were alone inside a castle of giants. Fenella, tidying her hair for supper, thought she had never felt quite so alone in her life. Probably everything would be all right and probably there was nothing to be afraid of. Probably Inchbad and the others would be extremely friendly and entirely courteous. Also, the Gnomes would still be there. Fenella, who had almost forgotten about this, was cheered, because it was impossible to be afraid (well, almost impossible) with Bith and Culdub and Flaherty and the rest of them.

Caspar came to collect her before supper. 'In case you miss your way,' he said, but Fenella had heard the key turn in the lock earlier and knew she was still being treated as a prisoner.

Supper was rather an odd meal. Fenella was seated next to Inchbad, who patted her hand and said she was a pretty little thing, but seemed preoccupied. Goll the Gorm sat on her left and devoted all his attention to the food and Goibniu was two seats down. The Gnomes sat at the far table, eating and drinking happily, whiling away an amiable half hour by telling anyone who would listen the entire history of the Crown Jewels and the history of the Gallan forges. Flaherty took a drop more of the giants' mulled wine than was good for him and very nearly disgraced his fellows by reciting an extremely improper poem, describing the exploits of a fair maiden who had fallen foul of a wicked and lustfully intentioned knight, but who had then escaped by invoking a demon who withered the knight's passion. The Gnomes thought this very funny and Caspar laughed loudly but Inchbad and the giants missed the point.

'Stupid,' mouthed Caspar at Fenella, under cover of the serving of half a dozen roast boars. 'I told you. We ought to be able to creep out easily when they're all asleep,' he added and Fenella frowned at him, because they could not risk the giants guessing what they intended to do.

They were three quarters of the way through the meal when Caspar, who did not miss anything any of the giants said and who had, in fact, long since perfected the art of listening to three different conversations at once, suddenly went rather white and made frantic gestures to Fenella.

'What's the matter?' said Fenella as Caspar trotted round to her chair, under cover of bringing round a Human-sized bowl of fruit. 'And do, for heavens' sake, be watchful or they'll suspect us of collusion.'

'What's that?' said Caspar. And then, 'No, don't tell me, we haven't got time.' He took a deep breath and glanced round at the giants. 'They're going to celebrate the *Fidchell* again,' he said.

'Yes?'

'Yes. With you and the gnomes. They're not overly partial to gnomes, but they think it's too good an opportunity to miss.'

'But they were going to wait for Floy to get back! I was going to tell them about Renascia and the Angry Sun and—' Fenella trailed into silence, staring at Caspar.

'They aren't going to wait for Floy to come back,' said Caspar. 'In fact, from what Goibniu said, I rather think they don't expect him to get back at all.'

'Oh,' said Fenella, suddenly feeling rather sick. 'But that means—' And stopped.

'It means,' said Caspar, 'that you and the Gnomes are going to be impaled on spikes and partly roasted on the *Fidchell* board. And then you'll be finished off in the sculleries.

'And then they'll eat you,' said Caspar, and Fenella stared at him in horror.

It was difficult to make the Gnomes understand. Caspar and Fenella had to explain it four times, and a fifth for Flaherty, who was still recovering from his overindulgence in the matter of the mulled wine.

To begin with, the Gnomes thought it a fine idea to be part of the traditional *Fidchell* and Bith of the Bog-Hat told how the Wolfkings had played it during the Winter Solstice with solid gold figures studded with ivory and pearl, which the Gnomes always had the supplying of. Flaherty said to be sure this was true, although he misremembered the last time they'd been called on to supply them, it being all of two years since the Wolfkings had been driven out by the Gruagach.

It was all very difficult.

'And dangerous,' said Caspar, with a backwards glance

to where Goibniu was standing before the fire in the characteristic pose, thumbs in belt, surrounded by half a dozen or so of the others. He got down to the serious matter of explaining to the gnomes that the intricate, almost scholarly, *Fidchell* that the Wolfkings had enjoyed, bore no resemblance to the horrid gruesome version that the Gruagach played.

Fenella was watching the giants, feeling cold inside at the way in which they all kept glancing slyly in her direction. There had to be something they could do.

'Couldn't the gnomes do something?' she said. 'Bith, Culdub, can't you think of something we can do? You know more about this kind of thing than I do. What *do* people do when they're threatened by giants?'

'If we don't do something extremely soon,' said Caspar, who was watching the giants furtively, 'they'll be heating up the squares any minute.'

One of the older Gnomes, who had a face like a wrinkled nutcracker and bright twinkly eyes, asked would a bit of magic be of any use anywhere, because wasn't magic a powerful thing when you had a difficulty, and the other Gnomes said to be sure it was.

Caspar said crossly, 'Well, of *course* it would be of use, only we haven't got any.'

The Gnome, whose name was Pumlumon said, 'But of course we have,' and the Gnomes all shook their heads sadly, and did not know what things were coming to when Humans did not remember about Gnomes having any magic.

Fenella, trying to keep her voice low, so that Goibniu and the others would not hear it, said, 'But what sort of magic, Pumlumon?' and Pumlumon beamed and said weren't there all kinds.

'But if it's the giants you're wanting to fool, then it'd be the grand old *Draoicht Suan*,' said Pumlumon, and the Gnomes nodded sagely and said that would be it, the *Draoicht Suan* it would be, the spell that had kept the Trees fast asleep for so many years now, and wasn't it a powerful strong spell and Pumlumon the fellow to be spinning it for them all?

'Well, what does it do?' asked Fenella, who was by no means sure about trusting an enchantment and who did not like the way Goibniu and Fiachra Broadcrown were flipping coins and chuckling sinisterly over the results.

Pumlumon said in a voice of utmost astonishment, 'But has your honour never heard of the *Draoicht Suan*?' and was instantly hushed by Bith of the Bog-Hat, who had by now sensed that something was wrong, being a gnome of more percipience than his fellows and who liked, no more than Fenella, the manner in which Goibniu was eyeing them all. He told the others they must not forget about roast Gnome being a traditional dish for the Gruagach's grander festivals. Such as a wedding feast, said Bith severely.

'It's the Enchantment of Slumber,' said Pumlumon. 'It sends your enemies into the deepest of sleeps. My word, I'm surprised that your worshipfulness has never come across it. At one time, you couldn't travel more than a half day across Ireland without coming across the *Draoicht Suan* in one form or another. Well, that's what keeps the Trees from waking,' said Pumlumon, looking solemn. 'And if we're to outwit these giants, there's nothing for it but for me to call up the *Draoicht Suan*. We'll send the giants into the enchanted slumber and be off back to Gallan in the whisk of a glowworm's tail.' He beamed at them again and Caspar was beginning to relax, because it seemed as if they might escape after all and Fenella was remembering about magic being very nearly everyday here, when Pumlumon said, 'Of course, that's so long as I can remember the words.'

He thought he probably would. He said there was not much of it to remember, really. Wasn't it one of the simplest magics there was and his grandfather, to say nothing of his great-grandfather (who had lived long and fared well) passing it down to him. Why, said Pumlumon, hadn't there been a time, not so very long ago either, when he could rattle off the words that set the *Draoicht Suan* working with no more ado than you might make in the squashing of a flea, always supposing you wanted to do something so pointless, which Pumlumon himself never had.

'But you *can* remember it all?' said Fenella, anxiously, and Pumlumon pushed his hat well back and scratched his head and said once he got it going, it would follow as the night the day, or maybe it was the other way round.

'The thing is getting it going,' he said. 'If I could have a few minutes – let's say half an hour – to think it over and make some notes, I daresay we'll be as right as a snail's whisker.'

'But we haven't *got* half an hour,' said Fenella. 'They'll be bringing up the squares at any minute. You'll have to pronounce it at once.'

'Yes, but we want to get it the right way about,' said Pumlumon. 'It won't do to be saying it backwards, or inside out, or to be missing a bit out that's important, or adding a piece from another enchantment. Bless my best boots, that would never do at all. I'll just recite it through quietly to be sure I can remember it first, shall I?'

'We'll have to distract the giants, then,' said Fenella practically. 'Supposing I offer to tell them about the *Feargach Grian*?'

The Gnomes thought this a fine old idea. In fact, Flaherty thought it was a better idea than invoking the *Draoicht Suan* until it was explained to him that unless Pumlumon did invoke it, they would all of them be roasting on spits in the Gruagach's sculleries before the night was out, to which he said that giants had always been partial to roast Gnome and he had always thought it was a mistake to come to Tara in the first place.

'Give me a few moments,' said Pumlumon, setting his features in a frown of concentration and Fenella looked at Caspar with a have-we-any-choice expression and then, taking a deep breath, walked across to the group of giants by the fire.

Inchbad was pleased to see Fenella, pretty little thing, approach them. Of course, it was probably quite an ordeal for Humans to sup with giants, although Inchbad was pleased to think that they had all treated Fenella and the other two with courtesy. The Gruagach were strong on courtesy; Inchbad had always been very firm about this, even to the extent of feeding prisoners before the *Fidchell* which Goibniu had always said was a waste of good food and wine.

But it paid off in the end; here was the pretty little Girl-Human walking over to talk to them, smiling up at them – Inchbad always noticed the fair, smooth skins of Humans, whereas giantesses were apt to be a bit coarse and occasionally had incipient beards. You could not really beat a Human's skin. Inchbad found himself thinking he would rather like to stroke Fenella. Perhaps they should reserve tonight's *Fidchell* solely for the Gnomes. Nobody wanted to stroke a Gnome, except perhaps another Gnome. He thought he might just have a word with Caspar to see if Fenella could be brought along to his, Inchbad's, bed that very night. Goibniu would have had his eye on her, but that was just too bad. Goibniu would have to wait his turn. There was really no reason why the Girl-Human could not be brought to all their bed-chambers, one after the other, before she was used in the *Fidchell*. This was an eminently reasonable arrangement and nobody could possibly object.

The Girl-Human had seated herself before the fire; Inchbad could see how the firelight fell across her face and brought out red lights in her hair. He bent to hear what she was saying, because she had a rather soft voice. Soothing you might call it. The sort of voice you could just nod off to. Yes, he would very much like to stroke her. Face, neck, breasts . . . Giantesses tended to have loose thick-grained breasts. Inchbad was rather partial to a soft, tender Human breast. He shifted in his seat a bit. Yes, certainly Caspar would be told to make ready the royal bed-chamber tonight.

The Girl was explaining how she thought perhaps she ought to make some kind of thanks to them for their hospitality. (Goibniu and Fiachra Broadcrown sniggered at this, but nobody took any notice.) The Girl said that they had been so kind and welcoming; food all served to them and very good, too, and such comfortable bed-chambers for their use. And they had expressed such interest in the *Feargach Grian* she was saying; as people of culture and learning, naturally they would be interested in it, she quite understood this.

This was appealing to everyone's better instincts and most of the giants looked alert and nodded at one another, because, of course, the Gruagach were known the length and breadth of Ireland for their culture and learning. It had been really quite sharp of the pretty little Human to see that.

Perhaps a tale or two from other lands? the Girl was saying, smiling up at them. In her own country, there had been a saying: 'Singing for your Supper'. She could not sing, she said, not really, but she could tell some stories for her supper. Would that do? And she smiled so nicely at Inchbad and Goibniu that everyone smiled back and thought it would be really very interesting to hear about some of the strange lands and the faraway worlds the Humans had visited from the great *Feargach Grian*, and also that it was always a shame to eat Humans when they were pretty and young and friendly. And while nobody wanted precisely to abandon the *Fidchell* which everybody enjoyed so much, there was really no reason why they could not play it with the Gnomes tonight and save Fenella for tomorrow, or even the day after.

And so Inchbad sat down and beamed at Fenella and said they would be interested to hear her stories and, at the same time, nodded to the waiting Fiachra Broadcrown to get the *Fidchell* squares ready for the Gnomes.

Fenella took a deep breath and, leaning forward, clasped her hands about her knees. It was warm over here by the fire and there was an unpleasant stench of stale giant and the surreptitious breaking of wind from Goll the Gorm who had eaten too much onion broth again, but these things would have to be overlooked. From the corner of her eye, she could see Pumlumon frowning and tapping his forehead for inspiration and the others standing in a worried circle about him.

Fenella began to speak at exactly the same moment that Pumlumon began to intone the *Draoicht Suan*.

To begin with, it did not seem as if anything was going to happen. Caspar, who distrusted most magic on principle, thought that probably nothing would happen at all and the evening would end as so many evenings were ending lately; with the heating of the squares and the terrible screaming of the victims.

But Fenella seemed to have caught the Gruagach's interest fairly and squarely; Caspar, only partly listening, heard her telling them about another life, another world, where people had fled in panic from the *Feargach Grian* many centuries earlier and how the *Feargach Grian* had, on that occasion, appeared in one of its truly terrible aspects.

'The Angry Sun in truth,' said Fenella, her expression absorbed, her eyes fixed on Goibniu and the others.

Caspar saw Inchbad nodding and Goll the Gorm was utterly rapt. Pumlumon seemed to have got himself quite well into the enchantment now; he was looking much less worried than he had looked ten minutes earlier. ('For doesn't it always come back?' demanded Bith. 'Isn't he the grand feller, chanting away, as if it was only yesterday he called up a spell or two?')

Pumlumon set his hat more squarely on his head and continued. Caspar, sending a worried glance to the group around the fire, heard Fenella describing something called Renascia; Twilight Mountains and Seasons with different colours. Something about an Iron Casket that had held secrets of the Ancient Past . . . It might have been extremely interesting if Caspar had not been so worried about Pumlumon's knowledge of the spell. Oughtn't it to be working by now?

Fenella, seated by the fire, trying not to flinch from onion-tainted breath and unwashed feet (there was something particularly revolting about the thought of giants' feet and their toenails), thought so as well. Inchbad had moved across to sit beside her and had taken her hand between his finger and thumb and was exclaiming what a pretty little thing she was and it the shame of the world that her brother had had to ride off and leave her all alone.

'But I'll console you, my dear,' he said and Fenella smiled valiantly and tried to quell the nauseous lifting of her stomach.

'That would be nice, but shan't I tell you about the Fire Country of Fael-Inis now?' It might be as well to sound a bit childish, and even slightly simple. 'Or,' said Fenella, hopefully, 'should we save it for tomorrow?'

Goibniu opened his mouth to say something – Fenella wondered what it would have been – when an arrested look came into his small eyes.

Into the great Sun Chamber, the legendary crystal and silver hall, the place the exiled Wolfkings had called *Medchuarta*, stole something so delicate and so strong, and so – so *beckoning* thought Fenella hazily – that it was almost as if a thin, sugar-spun veil was falling over them. There was a faint sticky feeling to it, as if it might trap you if you tried to struggle against it – but no one would want to struggle against this, thought Fenella, bemused with delight.

For a moment, she thought she could see it: fragile silver filaments of enchantment, gentle brittle frost-webs of something that was not quite light, but not quite solid, but somehow composed of both. The Enchantment of Slumber . . . gentle and strong and wrapping itself about you . . . *And within the enchantment are dreams, Mortal, within the enchantment are worlds within worlds within worlds and there are no longer boundaries and there are no longer the finite things that bind you . . .*

Surrender now, Mortal, come into the deep folds of slumber, where your heart's desire awaits you, where all things are possible . . .

Nuadu! thought Fenella, her mind tumbling with delight. *And Floy! And all things are possible . . .*

She gave a deep sigh and felt the silver threads spin

filaments of pure light about her and the soft folds of slumber enveloping her . . . like a soft light veil, like a warm, wine-dark sea, like hazy afternoon sunlight . . . And then felt, with a rude awakening, Caspar's hands shaking.

'You can't give in to it,' he was saying urgently. 'Fenella, you *must* wake up—' Fenella considered this and blinked. And from a great distance, heard Caspar say with irritation, 'Damn and blast, I *knew* we shouldn't have trusted those Gnomes—'

With a huge effort, Fenella said, 'What's wrong with the Gnomes?' And then, remembering a bit more, 'Didn't Pumlumon manage the Enchantment?'

'Very well indeed,' said Caspar grimly. 'Only he forgot to make sure that the gnomes kept out of range.

'They're all fast asleep!'

'How did we manage to escape it?' asked Fenella.

'Pumlumon was directing it straight at the giants,' said Caspar. 'I stood behind him, but you caught the outer edges of it.' And then, curiously, 'Did you *see* it?' he said.

'Well, I saw something,' said Fenella rather uncertainly. 'And I certainly felt something. But I don't think it was as strong as it could have been. I mean, I'm awake, aren't I?'

'You were only on the outskirts of it,' said Caspar. 'But I don't think it was very strong. I think the giants might wake up quite soon. We'll have to be quick. I suppose,' he said, 'that we can't just slip out now. Just the two of us?'

'And leave the Gnomes?' Fenella was shocked.

'No, of course we can't. We'll have to wake them somehow.'

But the Gnomes could not be woken and, eventually, Caspar and Fenella gave up.

'But we can't leave them,' said Fenella worriedly. 'Caspar, we *can't.*'

'We could *put* them somewhere.'

'Could we? Where could we put them?'

'In a locked room?' said Caspar, half to himself, and then, with more assurance, 'Yes, in a locked room.'

'Won't they wake up and be angry?'

But Caspar said this was unlikely; the *Draoicht Suan* would probably keep everyone inside Tara asleep until somebody came along with the counter-spell.

'And,' he added gloomily, 'who's to know when *that* will happen. It might be a hundred years from now for all I know.'

In the end they hauled the Gnomes into a small anteroom across the galleried landing from the Sun Chamber.

'Not ideal,' said Caspar. 'But it gives them a fighting chance. I tell you what we'll do, we'll try to find someone on the way who knows the counter-spell and send him back to wake the Gnomes up.'

'Can we do that?'

'You never know,' said Caspar rather vaguely. 'I've known stranger things happen.' And then, impatiently, 'And now do come on, or we shall never get away.'

Chapter Twenty-three

In the end, it was relatively easy to steal through the darkened halls of Tara and out into the night.

'Although Tara never is really dark,' said Caspar as they stopped to look back at the great shining edifice outlined against the sky. Fenella, who had found Tara a place of breathtaking beauty and who would have very much liked to explore it, saw how it gleamed gently against the night and seemed to have some inner radiance of its own.

'I have seen it brighter,' said Caspar in a rather expressionless voice.

'Yes?'

'When the Wolfkings rule,' he said, and Fenella remembered Nuadu Airgetlam all over again and had to bite down the ache of loss.

They had stopped briefly in the great sculleries to pack up provisions. 'For,' said Caspar, 'we shall need food and clothes.'

Fenella had gone back to the bed-chamber and pulled on her boots and found the warm woollen cloak she had brought from Renascia while Caspar had raided the sculleries and packed the maps.

'Were they all asleep?' Fenella asked as they stole through the quiet Palace.

'Yes. Pumlumon's spell must have been better than we thought.'

'Where are we going?'

'To the stables,' said Caspar, sending her a surprised look. 'You didn't suppose we were going to walk all the way to the Fire Court did you?'

'I did, as a matter of fact,' said Fenella, who had forgotten how Floy and Snodgrass had ridden out earlier. 'I've never actually ridden a horse before. I've never actually *seen* a horse until yesterday.'

Clambering on to the horse's back felt odd and briefly unsafe and then, unexpectedly, exhilarating. Fenella, who on Renascia had walked everywhere, found her breath snatched from her as her mount followed Caspar down the great avenue of beeches that guarded Tara and out on to the Tree-fringed high road. She thought she would have to hold on extremely tightly if they were to go any faster, but she thought it was a thrilling, intoxicating sensation to be borne along like this.

Moonlight was silvering the countryside as they rode slowly along, draining it of colour, and all about them were rustlings and scurryings and the impression of tiny pattering feet and the beating of small, unseen wings.

'Only night creatures,' said Caspar. 'Squirrels and hedgehogs and owls.' But he glanced over his shoulder as he said this, as if he was not entirely sure.

The huge mass of the Wolfwood sprawled darkly to their left, black and rather forbidding, a place of thick impenetrable shadows. As they drew alongside, on the road they had travelled on their way to Tara, Fenella found herself staring into its depths and remembering the ancient Forest Court at its heart . . . *Croi Crua Adhmaid* . . . the Place of Ancient Enchantments . . . the Heartwood of the Forest . . .

But out here, on the high road, it was difficult to recall the purple and blue shadows and the firelight and the long oak table where they had all taken supper. It was very hard indeed to believe she had walked in there with a wolf creature and that he had drawn her down onto the forest floor and made love to her . . . I won't think about it, said Fenella firmly. I'll think instead about meeting up with Floy and Snodgrass and finding the Fire Court. Yes, that was a much better way to think.

But the Wolfwood was not entirely in darkness. As they rode cautiously along, Fenella caught glimpses of movement in between the trees. Several times, there was the brilliant smudgy turquoise streak of the *sidh* and, more than once, the impression of gold and green and amber beings, neither quite human nor quite woodland. Tree Spirits? Oh I do hope so, thought Fenella, peering into the forest depths, trying to make out the shapes more clearly. As they skirted the forest and came out on to a stretch of road fringed by slender copper beeches, Fenella had the feeling of something deep and ancient and strong moving all about them. The Dryads and the Naiads waking? But then the moon slid behind a cloud and the images vanished and Fenella thought that perhaps she had been mistaken.

She turned to say something about this to Caspar and then stopped and listened, because now – yes, surely – there was the faint eerily beautiful singing of the *sidh*.

'Be wary of the *sidh*,' said Caspar as they skirted the Wolfwood. 'And be very wary indeed of their music. They are greedy for Humans, the *sidh*, and if they can once trap you with their music they will carry you down to the caves beneath the sea and steal one of your five senses and tear out your soul.'

But Fenella thought the sounds and the movements were not all the *sidh*. Here and there, they caught sight of a fluid red-gold figure in between the trees and once a huge oak tree seemed to bend forward as if inclining its head to inspect them. Delight rose in her, for surely these were Tree Spirits.

They did not stop to rest, because Caspar thought they should put as much distance as possible between them and the Gruagach.

'They *oughtn't* to wake,' he said, worriedly, 'but you never know. Let's get as far away as we can.'

This was clearly sensible so Fenella did not argue. She had sorted out the reins now and Caspar had explained about just touching the horse's flanks with her heels to spur it to a gallop.

'I won't try that yet,' said Fenella, who was rather enjoying riding the horse, but was not sure how she might get on with whatever was a gallop. 'I'll get a bit more accustomed first.' And then, 'Or if we hear the Gruagach following,' she said. 'I'll gallop then.'

Ahead of them would be the road that would lead to the Fire Court of the sorceress Reflection and her daughter Flame. They had studied the maps very carefully before setting out and Floy had marked out the way that he and Snodgrass would take. It had looked quite straightforward, thought Fenella, who was not very used to maps and was still adjusting to the vastness of this world after small Renascia. Floy had said he and Snodgrass would try their best to leave markers on the road as they went, providing that Balor did not catch them at it.

'We'll leave arrangements of stones,' suggested Floy, and Snodgrass had said that he believed this had been done on Earth.

'But many many centuries before the Devastation,' he said. 'There was something about a Bronze Age, I believe. It's a good idea, Floy.'

Floy had said they would do their best, but Fenella and Caspar ought not to rely on it too much. 'Because although we'll try to outwit Balor, we might have him with us for a goodish while,' he said.

It was strange to Fenella to know that presently the night would begin to die and that the pale grey and pink streaks of the new day would start to lighten the sky as it had done on Renascia before the Star Maps changed and the Dark Lodestar had sent out its hungry beckoning.

She had always rather liked the very early morning, which had been a little like the lifting of a curtain, a thin silver veil, spangled with droplets of moisture. It was one of the things that had disappeared from Renascia towards the end and it gave Fenella an odd, rather out-of-balance feeling to see dawn light again.

As the sky lightened even more and they began to make out their surroundings more clearly, Fenella and Caspar both found themselves looking out for the signs that Floy had hoped to leave.

'Stones arranged in heaps,' said Fenella, frowning, reining her horse in to a slow walk.

'Boulders. What they call cairns in the north,' said Caspar. 'But very tiny ones. And they were going to put them in the shape of an arrowhead. That's if they *could* put them there.'

'Floy would have found a way,' said Fenella firmly. 'He knew we were going to be following him.'

'What about Balor?'

'Oh, he'd have got rid of Balor by now,' said Fenella. And then, 'Wouldn't he?'

'I hope so,' said Caspar, gloomily.

As the road lengthened and the sky began to lighten overhead, they were able to see their surroundings more clearly. Fenella shivered and drew her cloak more tightly about her. There was a dead, barren feeling to the road now; the trees were becoming sparse and most of them were stunted and twisted. The grass was shrivelled and blackened and the leafless branches stood out against the grey morning and seemed to reach skeletal fingers towards them. There were great rocks on the road and thin mist seemed to cling to everywhere. And it was growing very cold. Fenella shivered and drew her cloak more closely about her. There was a dry, raw whiteness to the sky and when, at last, Caspar stopped to consult the maps and discuss with Fenella which road they should take, his breath formed a vapour on the air.

'Because,' he said, 'there aren't any signs from Floy or, if there are, we've missed them.'

'I don't think we've missed them,' said Fenella. 'I think that either Floy couldn't leave them for some reason, or—'

'Yes?'

'Or we're lost,' said Fenella, rather crossly.

'Let's trace our route on the maps,' said Caspar, dismounting and tethering his horse to the low branch of a leafless Tree. 'It ought to be easy enough.'

Fenella slithered down from the horse's back and stood for a moment in the road, feeling the fingers of mist swirl into her face and touch her skin with damp clammy hands. It was rather a horrid mist; you felt as if it might be concealing peering, grinning creatures who were being very careful to stay just out of sight, but who were creeping after you as you rode along, or who were tiptoeing on ahead of you, rubbing their hands together, waiting until you reached them . . . Perhaps the Gruagach had been following them, keeping just out of sight, waiting until they dismounted, ready to reach out and scoop them up and carry them back to Tara and the roasting spits . . . I had better stop this, said Fenella to herself very firmly. I had better remember that there's nothing in the least bit sinister about mists and fogs. And we should most certainly have heard the Gruagach if they had been following us.

She helped Caspar to spread out the map and, together, they traced the road from Tara along the sides of the Wolfwood and down through a couple of tiny villages.

'We've done that,' said Caspar, pointing.

'Yes, there's the villages we rode through,' said Fenella, frowning. 'And that's the fork in the road where you said left and I said right.'

'Which was it?'

'Well, it was right, actually,' said Fenella. 'We consulted the maps to be sure.'

'Oh, yes.'

'We haven't got lost at all,' said Fenella, who had been secretly rather afraid of this. 'We're on the right road.'

'Oh, yes. It's just that it would have been nice to have seen the signs,' said Caspar, rolling the maps up and packing them in his saddle bag. He did not say that he hoped Floy and Snodgrass were all right, because he did not think he had to say it. Fenella would be thinking it without anybody to suggest it to her.

Fenella was thinking it, but she was trying to be sensible and practical. It was important to remember that it was only a few hours since Floy and Snodgrass had left Tara, the Shining Citadel, the Bright Palace, and that there was not very much that could have gone wrong for them in those few hours.

We'll be with them in the Fire Court by nightfall. Or if not tonight, certainly tomorrow. I'll believe that we will, thought Fenella, firmly. I'll believe that we'll catch up with them; probably quite soon. I wish this mist would lift.

Riding on again, down the road which they thought would be the easiest route to the Fire Court, Fenella began to have the feeling that the twisty Tree stumps were not Tree stumps at all, but horrid, stunted living things and that malicious ancient eyes looked out from their depths. So strong was the feeling that several times she thought she caught the tail-end of a movement as they passed by several blackened stumps and she turned sharply, expecting to see something leering evilly at them, but there was nothing.

'And,' said Caspar, 'there is a *heavy* feeling to the air now, can you tell that?'

'Yes,' said Fenella in rather a small voice. 'It's quite difficult to breathe.' And then, because it would not help to show fear, 'What would it be?' she asked and was pleased to hear her voice quite ordinary and sensible.

'It might be a number of things,' said Caspar, who was looking about him. 'But what I *think* it is, is the Robe-maker.'

'Here?' Fenella shivered again, but at the corners of her mind, something said: Nuadu! By finding the Robemaker (or being found by him?) they might somehow rescue Nuadu.

'I think we are nearing the Robemaker's Workshops,' said Caspar. He reined in his horse and made a gesture with one hand that took in the flat dead wasteland and the strangled trees and the black barrenness. 'Necromancy,' he said, lowering his voice. 'Do you know, I never believed in that hoary old tale about necromancy sucking all the goodness and all the warmth from everything, but perhaps I've been wrong. You'd certainly say the heart has gone from the land hereabouts, wouldn't you?'

'Yes,' whispered Fenella, and wished that Caspar had not used the word *sucking*, because it made you think about coldly evil creatures with grisly appetites, who might leap on to you and cling to you and sink teeth and claws and needle-sharp pincers into you and suck out your blood and your marrow and all your life juices . . . 'What ought we to do?' said Fenella, a bit more loudly than she had meant. 'We can't turn back. Can we?' Because if we turn back, said her mind, then you will be going away from Nuadu, you will be losing what might be the only chance of rescuing him from the Robemaker. Caspar had said that no one ever escaped from the Robemaker – but I shall not believe that, thought Fenella. I will not. If she half closed her eyes, she could still see Nuadu, the thin, rather sardonic smile twisting his lips, his eyes narrowed and mocking. And there had been that brief time in the Wolfwood – I *won't* remember it! thought Fenella, but she did remember it. The mockery fled, the Wolfprince suddenly and disarmingly vulnerable . . . Had he loved her at all? Perhaps just a little. I'll believe he loved me just a little at least, thought Fenella, sitting quite still on her horse and looking about her. I'll believe it and I'll believe we can rescue him and then perhaps I shall manage. It was important to believe, and it was important not to give up. The early Earth-people had not given up on anything; they had conquered and explored and invented and they had made a marvellous and memorable world.

Caspar was slowing down, his eyes on a dip towards their left, where the road seemed to fall away into a natural valley.

'What is it?' said Fenella.

Caspar said, in a rather flat voice, 'At least we can be sure of being on the right road.'

'How can you—' Then Fenella stopped as well, because the maps had been very explicit. They had listed all of the places they would have to pass on their way to the Fire Court; they had shown the tiny villages and the Wolfwood and the forks in the road and the long flat road down to Reflection's country and the glittering decadent Fire Court.

They had shown the cluster of dark low-roofed buildings huddled together at the road's side, reaching far back into the hillside.

The Robemaker's dark and evil Workshops.
And they were directly in their path.

To begin with, Nuadu had not found the crimson mask particularly punishing. The rope-lights were tight-fitting, but they were not cruel; he could breathe easily and he could move. He did not waste any energy in trying to break free of the mask, because he knew it to be pointless; the Robemaker's dark enchantments were seldom broken and he knew, as well, that there would be far worse torments ahead.

After the winged Soul Eater had gone from the low-ceilinged Workshops, its leathery wings beating on the night, the soul of the mutilated boy held in a merciless grip between its claws, the slaves had scuttled back to their tasks and the Robemaker had conjured up another of the thin, whiplike lights that had lashed out and thrown Nuadu to the floor.

'Hurry, Wolfprince, for my work does not wait for such as you,' he said in his sibilant whisper, but now Nuadu detected a lick of pleasure in the voice. He moved at once, for he would not lie here on the floor before this ancient evil creature and, although it was awkward and painful to stand up because of the ropes that bound his arms, he did so in a swift fluid movement and stood eyeing the Robemaker.

For a moment, the Robemaker did not speak and then he drew nearer, the dark, silken folds of his cloak brushing the floor with a hissing sound. Nuadu had the sudden impression that, everywhere it touched, the robe left a thick slimy trail; faintly phosphorescent, certainly foul. A snail's trail. A slug's trail. An emission of pure evil. And this is the creature who is draining Ireland's heart away and this is the creature who holds sway over Tara, he thought.

But he stayed where he was and he continued to regard the Robemaker from over the restricting mask and, presently, the Robemaker said, 'Does it not irk you and chafe you to be so confined, Wolfprince?' For the first time, Nuadu caught the briefest hint of discomposure from the necromancer and knew that by remaining calm and apparently indifferent he had succeeded in disconcerting the Robemaker a little.

But the moment passed and the Robemaker had folded his arms, the deep sleeves hanging down. Nuadu saw that his hands were hidden by dark gloves, but that they were thin and hard-looking. Emaciated. What was behind the dark robe and what was within the deep, all-concealing hood?

The Robemaker turned his head and Nuadu felt a sudden white piercing pain deep inside his mind and he knew at once that the Robemaker had made use of the ancient, forbidden *Stroicim Inchinn* again and that he had pierced into his secret thoughts. He felt a sudden unwilling awe for this creature who could with such ease summon and bend to his will the terrible *Stroicim Inchinn*.

'The paths of your mind are mine to walk if I wish it,' said the Robemaker. 'You find that alarming, I think? Yes, for amongst your own puny sorcerers, there is a code of honour.' The words came out on a sneer. 'A code that forbids the *Stroicim Inchinn*.' Again the dark hood moved and Nuadu caught the glint of dark, malevolent eyes. 'I have only contempt and hatred for your sorcerers, Wolfprince,' said the Robemaker, and again Nuadu had the sense that the Robemaker was gauging his reactions. He fixed his eyes on the cloaked figure and waited.

'Your sorcerers cast me out,' said the Robemaker. 'Did you know that, Wolfprince? Did you know that they exiled me – *me*! I was the greatest of the spell weavers and I was the most powerful enchanter they had ever known.' He stopped, breathing harshly, and, within the hood, his head seemed to tilt slyly. 'I was once at Tara, Wolfprince,' said the Robemaker in his soft insinuating voice. 'Does that surprise you? Once I served the High King Erin – oh, long since. Decades and centuries.' He made an abrupt gesture, indicating the enveloping cloak, the deep, hanging sleeves. 'Your ancestors were gracious to their servants, Nuadu of the Silver Arm,' he said, sneeringly. 'They were generous.' He paused, and Nuadu felt the black hatred emanating from him again. 'I brought immense powers to Tara in those days,' said the Robemaker after a moment. 'I sought to increase my powers, for to master the ancient art of sorcery, *truly* to master it, it is necessary to master all else. It is necessary to understand and master every pleasure and every pain, every cruelty and every kindness.' He stopped again, and Nuadu waited. 'I had mastered the pleasures and the kindnesses,' said the Robemaker. 'But it was still necessary to master their counterparts.' The half-hidden eyes gleamed. 'It was necessary to explore, to the utmost, pain and cruelty and the dark secret yearning of men's souls,' he said.

'And so I did what few dare to do, Wolfprince. I went through one of the gateways that exist between this Ireland and the Dark Ireland, that other Realm, that mirror-image which is no mirror-image at all, but a land in its own right. The underside of the Wolfkings' Ireland, Nuadu of the Silver Arm; the place where the necromancers and the dark Fields of Sorcery lie, where the Black Citadels of the powerful enchanters exist deep in the desolate Mountains of Twilight.' He stopped again and Nuadu, trying to guard his thoughts, certainly trying to shield his eyes, thought: and once in the Dark Ireland, you were lured to the side of the necromancers! You were enticed by the dark magicians into their palaces and their dark citadels and you were shown the powers and the sinisterly beautiful rewards of sorcery.

It would not be the first time that a Court sorcerer had been lured away from the strong pure magic of Ireland and sworn allegiance to the Dark Realm. He remembered the ancient and persistent belief that once any living creature has walked in the Black Fields of Sorcery and dined at the tables of the Lords of the Dark Ireland, he is for ever lost to the true Ireland. For a terrible moment, something flared in his heart and he felt an insidious tug at his mind: *how would it be to enter that Realm, and talk with the Dark Lords and learn their secrets . . . ? How would it be to walk in the Dark Fields and journey in the Mountains of Twilight and swim in the underground Crimson Lakes . . .?* And then his mind cleared, and he was looking at the Robemaker and feeling contempt for him again, feeling as well, the dangerous, powerful white spears of the *Stroicim Inchinn* withdraw, so that he knew the Robemaker had again called up the *Stroicim* without giving any outward indication of having done so. Nuadu thought that a glitter of amusement showed from within the folds of the hood. When the Robemaker spoke again in his soft hissing voice, he knew he had been right.

'You see, Nuadu Airgetlam?' said the Robemaker. 'You see how easily I can influence your mind? You see how effortlessly I can conjure up the visions and tempt you into that Realm where I, too, am a Prince?' He turned about abruptly, as if the subject was suddenly painful or an irritation. 'It was the High King Erin who ruled in those days,' he said. 'And he it was who summoned the Court sorcerers to drive me out. It was those clever, smug *Royal* sorcerers, who wove the spell of punishment.' A brief glitter of triumph showed deep within the hood.

'But they were unable to chain me with their own powers,' he said, softly. 'They could not yoke me. And so they had to harness my own power – mine! They had to tap the source of my strength and turn it against me, until it formed a carapace, a cage that held me until they were ready to pronounce punishment.' He turned about, the silken skirts of his robe hissing across the floor's surface.

'I was caged by my own power,' he said in his soft, malevolent voice. 'I was imprisoned and held captive by the very forces I had so long sought to perfect and that I had honed and polished until they were stronger and more glittering than anything ever known at Tara.' He came back to stand directly in front of Nuadu.

'But it was the High King Erin who pronounced the spell,' he said and the cold bitterness was in his voice again. 'He it was who stood in the deepest Sorcery Chamber of Tara and read from the Book of the Academy of Necromancers the incantation. For that,' said the

Robemaker, viciously, 'I am sworn to inflict every curse and every torment I may summon on his House. That is why I joined with the Master CuRoi in his quest to possess Ireland. That is why I *stooped* to traffic with the Man-greedy Frost Giantess, and why I intrigued with her to drive out the Gruagach and why I helped the Gruagach to vanquish the High King and take Tara.'

A rather terrible bubble of mirth broke from him. 'The Gruagach did not suspect,' said the Robemaker. 'Never once, during our association, did they guess that I was using them to further my revenge against the Wolfkings. But the Wolfkings have been exiled and, although the Gruagach are at Tara, it is *I* who truly rule. That was always my intention. It is still my intention.' He paused, and appeared to study Nuadu. 'It is why you are here, Wolfprince. Your half-brother lies deep inside the Dark Realm and, unless he is rescued, you are Tara's heir. You are a bastard, but you possess the Royal blood and also the Wolfblood. If you called to the people, they would follow you because of that.' Deep within the concealing hood, there was a gleam of pure hatred. 'You are the heir presumptive,' hissed the Robemaker, 'and as such you must be quenched and crushed.'

'I shall put you to the treadmills, Nuadu of the Silver Arm, and I shall enjoy seeing you suffer. I shall enjoy seeing you suffer as I have suffered.' With an abrupt gesture, the dark, bony, black-clad hands came up and the hood was thrust back. The flickering light from the furnaces fell across his exposed face.

'You see?' cried the Robemaker harshly. 'You see what it was that the High King Erin pronounced over me! You see the curse I bear, Wolfprince!

'Erin pronounced on me the *Draoicht Tinneas Siorai*.

'The Enchantment of Eternal Disease.'

Nuadu was glad that he was unable to speak, for to have done so, to have uttered any kind of sound, would certainly have been to betray the utter revulsion that engulfed him. He thought he made some kind of strangled gasp; he knew his eyes would have expressed his emotions. He found himself hovering for a dangerous moment between pity and fear and he fought down the pity at once, for it was not to be thought of that he should feel such an emotion for this evil being. But as he stood facing the Robemaker in the low-ceilinged workroom, the humming of the Silver Looms all about them, the dry heat stifling and the air thick with the red glow of the furnaces, he looked fully into the face of his captor and thought: *what did he do to Ireland's Royal House to deserve such punishment?*

Seen without the concealing hood, the Robemaker's face was mutilated and eaten away, so that here and there white bone gleamed. But even the bone itself is eaten away in places, thought Nuadu, sick with horror.

The Robemaker's skin was covered with suppurating sores, great festering, oozing ulcers, leprous growths, cancerous chancres. In places, the bone was exposed and, in the uncertain light, Nuadu could nearly believe that it had been nibbled.

Yes, Wolfprince, nibbled, gnawed, ravaged by the bone-eating curse of Erin's sorcerers . . . The Draoicht Tinneas Siorai . . .

There was a lipless mouth, there were deep eye sockets from which gleamed the small evil, *old* eyes of the necromancer. Nuadu could see that even the pale, jellied part of one eye was partly missing and he had the sudden sickening impression that it had been eaten away from *within.*

At the centre of the face was a concave portion and Nuadu knew that the jutting bone of the nose had gone. There were two cavernous nostrils and Nuadu realised that this was the reason for the hissing whispering voice.

The malevolent smile lifted the terrible mouth again. 'You see?' said the Robemaker. 'You see how the Wolf-kings reward those who dare to go against them?' With a swift, savage gesture, he tore off the dark gloves. 'You see?' he said, thrusting skeletal hands forward and Nuadu

310

flinched, for the hands were as ravaged and as eaten as the Robemaker's face; the nails hung by shreds, and the remaining skin was matted and crusted.

'One of the most malicious and vicious curses of the Amaranth sorcerers of Tara,' said the Robemaker and pulled the hood back into place, so that it was once again the forbidding cloaked being who stood there. 'I have worked for many centuries to lift it, Nuadu, but it is a long hard task, for the punishment was to be eternal.' He stopped, and Nuadu waited. 'At last I bargained with the Soul Eaters,' said the Robemaker softly. 'I bargained with them to regain my body and my powers. I traded with them so that the young girls of the country would no longer shrink from me in revulsion,' he said, and there was a lick of sensuality in the hissing voice now. 'For,' said the Robemaker, softly and slyly, 'if the *Geimhreadh* has the voracious appetites of all her race and seeks to suck dry every man who comes into her power, then I have the carnal appetites of Men.' His eyes gleamed redly again. 'The Gruagach think to buy the daughter of Reflection and Fael-Inis for their King,' he said. 'But it is I who will have that one! I will embrace her and caress her and possess her.' Lust glowed redly in his terrible face, and then faded.

'The Soul Eaters know me well by now,' he said. 'For I have gone many times to the Cavern of Cruachan. I have many times entered into the place that is called, and rightly, the Gateway to Hell.

'I have taken souls to my Masters, Wolfprince, and every one I give them is placed on the Silver Scales of Justice.' He looked up as Nuadu made a quick movement and Nuadu caught again the amusement.

'Yes, Wolfprince,' said the Robemaker in his soft diseased voice. 'Yes, those Scales that the faithful foolish Gnomes of Gallan wrought for Erin and which disappeared towards the end of his reign.' He moved closer to Nuadu and Nuadu caught the stench of diseased flesh. 'The Soul Eaters took them,' said the Robemaker. 'Just as they will take everything of any value in Ireland. The Scales are in the Cruachan Caves, in the Court of the Soul Eaters, and every soul I offer up is placed on the Scales. And every time that happens, the Scales weigh a little more heavily in my favour.' He was standing looking down on Nuadu now, the dark, silken cloak swirling. 'Soon the Scales will tip in my favour,' he said. 'Soon I shall have given enough souls to my Masters. It is then that I shall be restored.' The Robemaker laughed, and the sound made Nuadu's skin prickle with horror, for it was a sickening bone-against-bone sound. Lipless mouth . . . noseless face.

And then: *he has rendered up countless souls to the creatures of the Cruachan Caves,* thought Nuadu. *Why, then, has he not been released?*

The white shafts of the *Stroicim Inchinn* darted again and Nuadu felt the piercing brilliance.

'You are very innocent, Wolfprince,' said the Robemaker. 'There is one soul I must still take and give to my Masters.' And then, as Nuadu tilted his head, waiting, 'The soul of Ireland's High King,' said the Robemaker, and again the fleshless chuckle bubbled from him.

'But you know already that he is held within the Dark Ireland and that he is captive in a deep and subtle enchantment. You have long since suspected what happened to your half-brother after the Gruagach stormed Tara and killed the King.' He leaned even nearer and Nuadu stood his ground and managed to withstand the stench of the suppurating flesh and the rotting bones. 'We fought over him, Nuadu Airgetlam,' said the Robemaker, and there was a slick lascivious tone to his voice now. 'The Dark Lords fought over who should have the chaining of him.' A frown touched his eyes for a moment. 'And because there are those whose powers are yet greater than mine, I lost him,' he said. 'He is held in thrall to the Dark Ireland, but it was not my enchantment that chained him.'

He stared at Nuadu, and Nuadu stared back, and thought: CuRoi! So CuRoi *does* have him!

The Robemaker said, 'I shall reach him, of course. I shall reach him and when I have done that I shall break

312

him.' He studied Nuadu for a moment. 'I shall break him,' he said. 'If it takes me seven centuries, I shall do it.' There was the white gleam of bone as he smiled. 'I shall give him to the *Geimhreadh* to play with for a few nights,' he said. 'Perhaps I shall watch while she drinks her fill of his manhood and sucks him dry of his accursed wolfseed. She and I are long since sworn one to aid the other,' said the Robemaker. 'And there is much pleasure in watching a virile young creature brought to impotency.'

The lipless mouth leered. 'Have you never heard of the *Geimhreadh*'s pincer hands that hold her victim's phallus in place and have you never heard of her darting pronged tongue that licks and pierces into the shaft of her victim's phallus?' said the Robemaker, softly and insinuatingly. 'Then you, also, must be given that pleasure, for I should not care for you to miss an instant of any pain, Wolf-prince.' He leaned closer and Nuadu regarded him unflinchingly. 'I shall break you as well, Nuadu of the Silver Arm' said the Robemaker. 'You may defy me now, but you will not continue to do so. Even though I have chained and muzzled you for the Wolf you are, still your eyes challenge and your mind defies.' The lipless mouth smiled again.

'I shall put you to the treadmills,' said the Robemaker. 'I shall make use of you and you will work alongside my slaves here. You will work until your feet are stripped raw of flesh and until your legs are bowed and your skin is shrivelled. Only then, Wolfprince, only when you are cowed and submissive, only when I have drawn from you every shred of defiance, when I have extracted every sliver of pleasure I can from your predicament, shall I take your soul.

'And when you and your royal half-brother have been sucked dry of every drop of accursed wolfseed by the Frost Giantess; when you have been deprived of every drop that might bear fruit in some unknown womb and create another wolfcreature, I shall give you both to the Soul Eaters.

'With those two souls placed on the Scales of Sorcery

313

and rendered to the Soul Eaters, my debt will have been paid.

'My powers will be restored – and I shall rule Ireland for ever.'

Chapter Twenty-four

Floy and Snodgrass had stopped to rest on the outskirts of the Wolfwood.

Floy thought he would have rather enjoyed this journey if it had not been for the nagging concern about Fenella, left behind in the giants' hands. He would have enjoyed seeing more of this blue and green misty world with the lingering scents of ancient magic everywhere and he would have liked to see some of its people and found out how they lived and what they did and if they were happy.

But the few houses they passed seemed to have their doors locked and bolted and their windows shuttered. Floy looked with interest at the fields and pastures and thought that, although they were much larger than the ones on Renascia and the crops and vegetables were not quite the same, there was not so very much difference, really.

But they were untended. They were deserted and desolated and there was a terrible, bleak air of neglect everywhere. Floy remembered what Nuadu Airgetlam had said about the Robemaker taking sacrifice from the ordinary Irish people and putting the sons to work in the Dark Workshops and guessed that the people had simply lost heart. How must it be to tend your bit of land and sow crops and vegetables and perhaps rear animals, knowing you were building up a comfortable home and an inheritance for your children and then see your children taken and forced into slavery by the Robemaker?

As they rode farther along the road, Floy glimpsed the occasional peering face at a cottage window and guessed that the sounds of their horses on the highroad and perhaps the sight of Balor's huge menacing figure, had sent them all scuttling indoors for safety. This was a truly dreadful way for people to live. Plainly they went in constant fear of the Robemaker and the Dark Realm. Clearly all the heart was going not only from the land, but from the people as well. He began to feel extremely glad that they had agreed to help the exiled Court. He thought they had unquestionably been right to believe Nuadu and Tealtaoich and the others.

With Balor loping along at their side, they could not discuss whether Fenella would be all right, or speculate how soon she and Caspar would catch them up, or even try to spy out a place to stop and wait for them. Several times Floy cast sidelong looks at Balor, trying to decide how percipient he might be, but Balor simply turned his head and grinned the gap-toothed grin and occasionally nodded amiably. Once he hummed a snatch of song, which was something about hunting Humans for the *Fidchell* and about turning them on spits and serving them up as Manpie.

But although he might not be bright, Balor's head was on a level with Floy and Snodgrass as they sat astride the two horses and he was twice the size of either of them. He would very easily subdue them if they attempted to escape. He would certainly notice if they tried to leave signs for Fenella and Caspar to follow.

The Wolfwood was as dark and as secretive as it had been when they journeyed through to the Forest Court with Nuadu, but here and there, deep within the Trees, Floy caught the darting movement of green and gold; the rustling of silver-tipped leaves that looked, for a moment, like the trailing hair of a creature almost Human . . .

He touched Snodgrass's arm and nodded in the direction of the forest and Snodgrass said, very softly, 'The Trees. Miach's spell,' and Floy thought: so, after all, he woke them. He wondered whether they would see the Tree Spirits and then he wondered whether they wanted to see them. They had sounded rather fearsome beings.

'Puny things, Trees,' Balor said. 'Chop 'em down and use 'em for firewood, I say.' He dealt a nearby Tree a rather contemptuous blow with the flat of his hand and Floy saw the Tree trunk quiver under the impact. 'And now a bite to eat,' said Balor, grinning the wide, flat grin of all the Gruagach. 'A bite to eat and then we'll be getting along again.'

There was nothing for it but to do as he suggested. As they dismounted it crossed Floy's mind that the longer they could delay, the better chance Fenella and Caspar had of catching them up. In the same moment, he realised that it would be extremely dangerous for Fenella to join them. Balor would at once know that they had outwitted Inchbad and Goibniu.

They walked a little way into the Trees, where it would be more comfortable to sit on the thick, dry forest floor and eat their food and rest. Dusk was beginning to touch the forest and deep shadows lay across the small clearing where they sat down. Balor leaned back against the nearest Tree and Snodgrass unpacked the food and spread it out.

'A good spread,' said Balor, his small eyes lighting. 'I like a good spread.' He reached for a half loaf of bread with both hands and said, by the six hairs of his grandmother's beard, they were doing very well out of all this.

'And it's a fine day for a journey,' he said.

Floy was still turning over in his mind ideas and schemes for getting rid of Balor. It was extremely difficult to know what to do with a giant who loped along at your side and who could reach out and pluck you from your horse's back with one hand. Floy thought that, even if they broke into a gallop (which he was not at all sure about doing), Balor would simply increase his own pace and catch them very easily.

Floy and Snodgrass ate the food without noticing it very much, but Balor snatched great handfuls from the pack and crammed them into his mouth, spraying crumbs everywhere, letting grease dribble down his chin.

'Pork,' he said, nodding. 'Roast pig. Very nice.' And then, with a sudden cackle, 'But not as nice as roast Human. By the whiskery snout of the gods, it's nowhere near as good. But I see there's blood sausage,' he said, and sent them such a terrible leery grin, that Snodgrass, who

317

had been cutting himself a slice from this, which he had innocently thought was something like the spicy Renascian liver-and-wine-roll, recoiled and snatched his hand back as if he had been burnt.

Balor grinned at Snodgrass and smacked his lips and grabbed the cask of mead and thought that hadn't the Humans strange, mimsing appetites to be sure. There was nothing so fine as a good meaty portion of best blood sausage.

Floy had been surreptitiously trying to gather up stones which they could arrange at the roadside, perhaps in the form of an arrow for Fenella and Caspar. But, even as he did so, he knew that such a small sign would almost certainly be missed. They needed to leave something noticeable, something that could easily be seen and not misunderstood. And anything noticeable by Caspar and Fenella would also be noticed by Balor.

Balor had unbuttoned his jerkin and brushed the crumbs from his front and was preparing to take a snooze. He was rather liking this bit of a jaunt, although he had not been very enthusiastic when Goibniu had ordered him to set out. Accompany a brace of Humans on a journey and not touch hide nor hair nor whisker of either of them! he had said. There was a thing to make a decent Human-eating giant shiver in his boots and think shame! Could he not deliver just one of them, he had asked, looking at Goibniu slyly from the corners of his eyes.

But Goibniu had said no, both the Humans must be taken to the Fire Court and Balor must go along with them and, after they had talked with Reflection, Balor must bring them safely back to Tara.

He dropped into a bit of a snooze, which any giant might be pardoned for wanting after so much walking and a bit of eating, never mind a sup of mead. The Humans were sitting a little way off; Balor would hear them if they tried to get away. He would be up and after them in the blink of an eye.

As Balor's eyelids closed and snores emitted from his mouth, Floy and Snodgrass exchanged looks. Dare they try to steal away now? Floy got up, not furtively, but quite openly and naturally, so that if Balor should open his eyes it would not seem as if Floy had been trying to run away.

It was an eerie feeling to be stealing through the forest like this. Floy began to have the sensation that he was being watched, not by Balor or Snodgrass, but by other creatures, creatures who lived in this huge, dark forest, and crept out only under cover of darkness . . .

He glanced back over his shoulder but Balor was still sleeping. If I can just reach the horses, thought Floy, moving stealthily forwards. If I can just reach the horses and reach up and untether them, I believe we could be off and down the road and the creature would never catch up with us.

He was strongly aware of the Wolfwood all about him as he walked cautiously under the Trees. There was a stirring, a sense that at any minute the branches over his head might dip over him and brush his face, or that the roots that had thrust up out of the earth might wriggle and become alive and twine themselves about his feet. Several times he stopped and listened, thinking that there had been a movement just behind him or just to the side of him, or that something had padded after him on stealthy feet and was standing watching him. But each time there was nothing and Floy thought that perhaps, after all, it was simply the half-light of the Wolfwood and the ordinary scurryings of the night creatures. He remembered that they had forgotten about dusk and about twilight on Renascia and about the strange tricks that the shadows could play. The light was fading perceptibly now; they had set out in the full glare of the midday sun, but they had ridden for several hours and dusk was creeping across the land.

The Purple Hour, thought Floy, fascinated and a bit fearful. What had Nuadu said? *The hour when magic is abroad.* I refused to believe it then, he thought, but I believe it now. Magic, stealing through the ancient forest, lying thickly on the air . . .

The Trees had thinned out now and he could see the

road ahead of him. Could it be this easy? Could they simply creep away from Balor and ride out of his reach?

The stirrings and the rustlings were louder and Floy was suddenly and strongly aware of eyes upon him. He turned sharply, looking back to where the sleeping Balor lay. Snodgrass was nearby, sitting bolt upright, watching Floy anxiously.

There was a movement within the Trees, the sudden shifting of green and gold and russet, so that Floy knew the dusk had not been playing tricks after all. There were beings, creatures, strange inHuman presences everywhere in the forest.

He stood, looking, and there was the movement again; the blurring of shapes and silhouettes that were like nothing Floy had ever imagined; inHuman and ancient and filled with wild woodland enchantment . . .

The Tree Spirits of the ancient Wolfwood were awake and they were creeping through the darkening forest towards them.

Chapter Twenty-five

Balor had never been so rudely awoken from slumber in his life. At one minute it seemed that he had been having a fine old dream about Humans and banquets and the Frost Giantess frying on a spit. The next he had been jerked fully awake and found himself at the centre of a circle of strange, hostile creatures, the like of which he had never seen in his life.

It seemed to his slow, sleep-sodden mind, that there were hundreds of the horrid things and that they were all bearing down on him, a rushing curtain of green and gold and brown, with here and there wild, menacing eyes and reaching, clutching hands that were not hands at all, but nasty, skeletal twigs. He stumbled to his feet and looked frantically about him, because although no self-respecting Gruagach would run from a danger, these creatures were too many and too huge and too *angry*.

He scrabbled into a half run, going deeper into the Wolfwood, not looking where he was going, not caring overmuch. He would outrun the horrid things who had stood leering at him, because there was never a being yet created that could catch a Gruagach once he put his mind to running. By the seven beards of his ancestors, Balor would run, and they'd see who could run faster! It certainly would not be the sinister Treelike beings who had regarded him with such terrible vengeance in their unnatural faces!

Floy and Snodgrass stared at one another and then Floy said, 'We'll have to follow them.'

'Why? Isn't this the exact chance to escape?' said Snodgrass.

'No,' said Floy. 'Because supposing they don't catch him and supposing he does escape—'

'If he came back and found we'd made off by ourselves, he'd go back to Tara and tell them we'd reneged on the bargain,' finished Snodgrass.

'And Fenella would be at the mercy of Goibniu and the rest. Yes. That's why we'll have to see what happens,' said Floy. 'Hurry, and we'll catch up with them!'

They broke into a run, seeing the Tree Spirits directly ahead of them; a pouring, changing, blurring mass of russet and green; a sweep of autumn tapestry, moving and reaching and sweeping through the forest after the giant.

'But he won't get far,' cried Floy, managing to keep the Tree Spirits in sight. 'He won't get far, because this is their territory! They have him in their own country! Come on, Snodgrass! We mustn't lose them!'

They were going deeper into the green and blue heart of the Wolfwood and Floy felt his lungs beginning to ache and his chest pound. At his side, Snodgrass was capering along, occasionally leaping nimbly over a patch of undergrowth, one hand holding his hat on his head, his cloak flying about his ankles, but keeping pace with Floy.

'He's fallen!' cried Floy, and they slowed to a walk, gasping and trying to get their breath. 'But you're fitter than you look,' said Floy, with a sudden grin at Snodgrass.

'A touch dishevelled, of course,' rejoined Snodgrass, who was puffing a bit. He righted his spectacles which had been knocked askew and straightened his cloak.

Ahead of them, Balor was lying on the ground and they saw that the Tree Spirits had grouped themselves about him, rather in the manner of people arranging themselves to watch some entertainment, or hear some kind of cause being pleaded.

'He didn't get so far at that,' said Snodgrass, as they stood rather warily on the outskirts of the group.

Floy glanced over his shoulder, trying to gauge how far they had come and in which direction the road now lay. The light had almost gone from the day now and the forest was becoming bathed in soft, subtle hues of the Purple Hour. Dark blue and turquoise light slanted in through the trees, turning the Wolfwood to a place of dark secret shadows and heavy ancient magic.

Balor had fallen headlong and was lying on the forest floor, one foot caught and held by the root of a huge old ash Tree that protruded from the ground.

The wild golden eyes and the pitiless faces of the naiads and dryads and hamadryads loomed over him, hands that were not hands but branches, reaching for him, pinioning him down.

The Tree Spirits were wild and beautiful, but rather terrible. Closer to them, it was possible to make out individual characteristics; to see that they had trailing leaves instead of hair and huge, reaching branches instead of arms. They looked what they were: creatures, Spirits of Trees, that had emerged from the ancient Wolfwood from a long, long sleep and who were alive and alert and completely without pity towards their enemies . . .

Floy and Snodgrass stayed where they were, standing quietly, watching from the edges of the clearing. Floy thought they probably ought to be afraid themselves, because the Tree Spirits were so inHuman and so wild and so clearly filled with strange woodland magic that once they had finished with Balor they might very well turn to the two Renascians.

'Ought we to try to get away?' whispered Snodgrass, whose mind had been going along similar paths.

'I think it's all right,' responded Floy, warily, but even as he spoke he was wondering whether it *was* all right, and whether they mightn't be better simply to walk back through the forest and on to the road. And then he thought: I suppose we shall find the road again, shall we?

The Trees had surrounded Balor; a towering wall of reaching branches and immense trunks and snaking roots, veined with the golden threads of the Beeches and the glossy green Oaks and with the shimmering, silver rivers of the Birches.

To Floy, they were beautiful and rather frightening and immensely powerful. Their eyes were ancient, filled with the wisdom of their long lives, and their shapes were not quite Tree and not quite Human, but a blend of the two.

If you looked at the Trees' upper halves; at the streaming leaf-hair and the mischievous faces of the Silver Birches and the wise, implacable solemnity of the Oaks and the cool, wanton beauty of the Beeches, you could very nearly see similarities to Human features and Human characteristics.

The Tree Spirits' bodies did not thicken in the way that the Trees, their homes, thickened, except for the Oaks who had sturdy, rather shapeless trunks. They had graceful, slender bodies, tapering into root-like shapes where a Human would have ankles and feet. To Floy, these strange, rootish feet were the most alien feature of all.

'And they are fibrous-looking,' murmured Floy, half to himself. 'They are too graceful for claws, but they are very like claws. They can almost grip the ground as they walk.'

'They're strong, as well. They would break a man's neck easily, those roots,' said Snodgrass.

They would break a man's neck easily, and they would break a giant's back with hardly more effort . . .

Balor was still clumsily trying to scramble to his feet, but the twining roots held him firmly. His brutish, stupid face was blotchy with fear now and his eyes were bolting from his head. He tore at the roots that were pinioning his ankles, breaking his thick horn nails in the process, but the roots held and it seemed to the two watching Renascians, that the Tree Spirits swayed and murmured with amusement. Balor let out a bellow of fear and, in the same moment, the Trees closed in.

They did it singly and purposefully, as if a silent command had been given. They surrounded him so completely that, for a few moments, Floy and Snodgrass could not see him. As they moved, the Trees sent out a wailing, keening cry, splitting the quiet forest.

'It's a war cry,' said Snodgrass. 'Isn't it? They're angry with him.'

'For denigrating that oak where he tethered the horses?'

'Yes. Yes, that, and the way the Gruagach ignored the – what did Nuadu and Caspar call them? – the Tree Laws,' said Snodgrass, his eyes intent on what was happening. 'Don't you remember how, at Tara, they had those huge, roaring fires and how they had baskets and boxes piled high with logs and branches?'

'Yes,' said Floy. 'Yes, of course. They're being revenged on Balor for it.'

The Trees were all about Balor now and the Wolfwood was ringing with the shrieks of their blood lust. Their eyes glittered and their branches reached out. The fearsome, fibrous roots whipped across the ground.

What happened next was rather terrible. Floy and Snodgrass, unable to look away, were sickened and awed.

'It's no more than he deserves,' said Snodgrass. 'It's no more than any of them deserve.'

'Oh no,' said Floy softly, remembering Fenella and the *Fidchell* board and Caspar's descriptions of how the Gruagach used Humans. 'No, they deserve no less.'

Even so, it was terrible. The Trees reached down to Balor with their branches and spread him flat on the ground, unlashing the ground roots that had held him, replacing them with the strong, clutching roots of two of the largest Oaks. Two more Oaks lashed their roots to his wrists and the Trees watched, critically.

Balor was bellowing for help; he was calling down vengeance on the Trees and promising that Inchbad and the Robemaker and the Master CuRoi would certainly punish the Trees for this.

'By the hairs of my ancestors' beards, you'll be cut into collops and burned in the chimneys of Tara!' he cried.

The Trees paid him no heed. They simply continued to secure him, coldly and efficiently, as if this was just something that had to be done and as if there was no particular feeling in doing it.

The largest of the Oaks, who had the high-domed features of a scholar and a thinker, and who had massive powerful shoulders, made a sign and the four Oaks who held Balor captive moved.

'Away from one another,' said Floy, in horror. 'They are all moving in opposite directions.'

'They're tearing him into four,' said Snodgrass. 'Each of the Oaks is pulling on an arm or a leg and pulling *outwards*. This is – I suppose we can't do other than let it happen.'

'I don't see how we can stop them,' said Floy, his eyes on the circling Tree Spirits and on the four Oaks who were now hauling on their claw-like roots, dragging Balor's limbs outwards away from his body.

Balor was braying in anger and pain. As the Trees moved, both his arms and legs were jerked into taut, out-flung positions. The coiled roots bit into his flesh, dragging against the skin, so that blood welled to the surface.

'But the roots will hold firm,' said Floy, unable to look away.

Balor was struggling and writhing, but his limbs were held fast and only his thick, shapeless body could move. It threshed this way and that, as the giant tried, uselessly, to pull free of the Trees' cruel grip.

They moved again, pulling away, but Floy and Snodgrass could see that it was hard work for them. But they are gaining an inch at a time, thought Floy, in horror; they are stretching muscle and flesh. The farthest of the Trees made a sudden jerking, twisting movement and Balor's arm wrenched out of its socket and lay flaccid and limp.

As the Trees bent to their grisly task again, there was a terrible cracking, bone-against-muscle sound and Balor screeched, sweat beading on his face and running down into his thick coarse neck. His eyes bulged from his head, red-veined and ghastly, and his lips were drawn back from his blackened, stump-like teeth, as the full horror of what the Trees were doing impinged on his dull mind.

The watching Trees showed no emotion. They simply stayed where they where, circled about their prisoner, their faces implacable, their eyes cold.

The four Oaks were still hauling on their prisoner and

Floy and Snodgrass could see that Balor's arms and legs were all wrenched from their sockets now, twisted at awkward, unnatural angles. Floy felt a lurch of sympathetic pain, because surely to simply dislocate an arm was purest agony, but to have it then pulled and pulled until the skin began to split and bleed, must be the most exquisite agony ever.

The Elms had moved forward in their stolid fashion and were leaning ponderously over the tortured Balor. As Floy and Snodgrass watched in silence, the Elms stretched out their hard, lichen-crusted branches and brought them down on the prisoner's shoulders and thighs, at the place where the skin had started to tear.

Balor had let out a screech of purest agony, but the Elms bent over him with serious, heavy-featured faces and sawed partly through each of the pinioned limbs. They did not make any hurry about it and Balor writhed and flailed helplessly and blood began to run out on to the ground beneath him.

'They're making it easier for the Oaks,' whispered Floy. 'The Oaks couldn't quite pull off his arms and legs, so they're helping them.'

'It's like something from a medieval torture chamber,' said Snodgrass. 'We had a woodcut of one. Terrible things. They could wrench their prisoners' arms and legs from the sockets. But I don't think even they went this far.'

Balor had stopped struggling, but was moaning and panting shallowly. His face was the colour of tallow and blood and saliva ran down his chin and the two Renascians saw that his lips were bitten to shreds.

'Dreadful,' said Snodgrass, shuddering, but Floy said, 'It is only what the Gruagach have done to the Trees.'

Dark, sluggish blood was running from the wounds made by the Elms and there was the gleam of whitish bone and of raw muscle. As the Oaks moved again, the wounds yawned and slowly, slowly, inch by terrible inch, they gaped wider and skin began to tear and the muscle and bone began to part with a sound that made Floy and

Snodgrass both feel sick. It was the sound of flesh being rent from bone, and the sound of gristle and fat and marrow being torn apart. Floy thought, with sick dread, that it was the exact sound made when you twisted a leg of chicken from the carcase.

Balor gave a last bubbling cry and a sudden ripple of triumph went through the Trees as the farthest of the Oaks pulled free an arm and held it aloft, a bloody stump, a torn-off gobbet of flesh.

'A trophy,' murmured Snodgrass.

'Yes.'

The other three Oaks had redoubled their efforts now and, one by one, the rest of the giant's limbs were torn from their moorings and held aloft, wet, bleeding rags of flesh. The bloodied torso of what had been Balor lay twitching on the ground, moving clumsily, trying to pull itself along the ground, like a monstrous beetle which has been turned on its shelly back and cannot right itself. Thick, sluggish blood seeped from the great jagged holes where his arms and legs had been and, with them, a watery pus. A thick, too-sweet stench lay on the air.

As the Trees moved back, silently watching their victim, Balor's bitten lips emitted a bubbling moan and saliva and blood dribbled out again. There was a choking rattle and his eyes turned upwards, so that only the whites showed, red-veined and protruding slightly.

'Dead,' said Floy softly, and then looked at the Trees.

The Oak, who had seemed earlier on to be the leader, said, 'Yes, Human creature, he is dead. It is no more than he has done to our people.'

'Yes. I see.'

'We shall bury him,' said the Oak, and Floy saw that already the Tree Spirits were scrabbling at the earth, their roots scraping and shovelling, so that, quite soon, a deep trench was opened.

'Into the earth with the remains,' said the Oak, turning to watch. 'Let his rotting carcase mingle with the forest.'

It was rather dreadful to see Balor's remains flung unceremoniously into the trench, first the mutilated torso and then the arms and legs.

'Meat for our roots,' said the Oak, and a rather grim smile touched its features.

'Yes.' But Floy was still sickened; he remembered how on Renascia they had tried to follow what they had known of the Earth-people's death rituals and how they had had the large, austere Firehouse with the ornate bronze lamps which were always kept burning in memory of those who had died. The dead were consumed by cleansing fire at a ceremony which every Renascian was bound to attend and there would usually be a carefully arranged display of the dead person's life and a small booklet telling about his life and his work, nearly always written by Snizort and Snodgrass in gentle and tactful collaboration with the bereaved family.

'We shall eat the giant as its people ate our people,' said the Oak and regarded Floy and Snodgrass steadily. 'And as its people eat your people,' it said. 'That must not be forgotten. It is a fitting punishment, although it may seem harsh to you Humans.'

'It is not what we have been used to,' said Floy. 'But I understand.'

'The only basis for punishment,' said the Oak, rather severely, 'is to fit the punishment exactly to the transgression. It is a practice which has been followed in Ireland, since the High King Erin introduced it. He was strong and wise and believed in exact and precise forms of justice.'

'I see,' said Floy, who did not completely see, but who understood the premise.

'And now,' said the Oak, 'you will wish to continue your journey, Human creatures.' Its wise eyes were kindly and interested. 'We shall wish you Good Speed and Safe Arrival.'

It sounded like some kind of ritual in the way the Oak said it and the other Trees bowed their heads in acknowledgement.

Floy said, 'We thank you all,' and hoped that this had the correct formality.

'And we shall hope to meet you again,' said Snodgrass and the Trees suddenly looked pleased and unexpectedly Human. The Silver Birches giggled in a skittish fashion and the Copper Beeches shook out their rippling manes of glowing leaf-hair and regarded the two Renascians through the red-gold curtains.

'Perhaps you would do well to rest for the night and journey on by daybreak,' said the Oak. 'If you will accept the hospitality of the Wolfwood, we shall assure you of safety and warmth.'

'Well – thank you very much,' said Floy. 'But I believe we must go on. It is a question of – of meeting up with our people, you see.'

'Then,' said the Oak, bowing its wise solemn head, 'we shall not detain you.'

There was a murmur of assent and the wise, strange heads were dipped in the gesture of acknowledgement they had used earlier and the Tree Spirits moved away, not quite fading into the gloom of the forest, but somehow becoming one with it.

The moon was high above them as they walked cautiously through the dark forest and the pale, eerie light lay across the woodland path, cold and unfriendly. Over their heads, the trees interlaced their branches so that only tiny patches of the velvet night sky were visible.

'And the Tree Spirits have retreated,' said Floy, softly.

'Yes. Interesting creatures, those Trees,' said Snodgrass, trotting along beside Floy.

'We should perhaps have asked the Trees the best path to take,' said Floy, presently.

'It's only that this is such a vast place,' said Snodgrass, firmly. 'That's all it is. Renascia was so small that you hadn't to plan journeys at all. You could go from one end of Renascia in two days and from side to side in three. We aren't used to such – such hugeness. The Wolfwood's immense.'

Floy said, 'If we could find the path to the Forest Court we could be sure of help.'

'And food,' said Snodgrass, rather sepulchrally. 'We left the food with the horses, in those packs.'

'Well, we can't be far from either the road or the Forest Court,' said Floy. 'I won't believe that we're lost. And look, if we—'

'What?'

'I was going to say if we carve notches on the Trees, at least we shan't go round in circles,' said Floy, grinning. 'I don't think we'd better do that, however.'

'Bless my soul, no,' said Snodgrass, shocked.

'We could make a – a circle of stones, though,' said Floy. 'At the foot of the Trees. That's more or less what we were going to do for Fenella and Caspar. Yes, look, we'll do that, and then at least we shan't go round in circles.'

They walked on, scanning the shadows, leaving markers at the foot of the Trees, trying to gauge their direction by the stars.

'But the trouble is that we don't know the pattern of the stars here,' said Snodgrass, who had sent himself quite dizzy by standing perfectly still and craning his neck as far back as he could in order to see the night sky. 'We could have done it on Renascia, because we knew where the stars where and what their names were. But here there's so much of everything. Stars and forests and paths.'

Floy was becoming uneasily aware of the looming bulk of the Trees and of the scurryings and the rustlings and the patterings of unseen creatures all about them. Night was all about them and the Wolfwood was a strange, none-too-safe place. It was very easy to imagine eyes peering from the gloom, or strange beings creeping along the path behind them.

And there is magic abroad here . . . I wish Nuadu had not said that, he thought.

Snodgrass said, 'Do you know, I believe the Trees are thinning. Over there.'

'Where? Oh, there. Yes, I can see,' said Floy, with a rush of thankfulness. 'Yes, you're right.' And quickened his steps because, of course, they had not been lost at all

331

and, of course, it had been ridiculous to think they had been. They had simply come a little deeper into the forest than they had realised. At any minute they would see the two horses and they would mount them and ride on down the road and all would be well. It might even be rather pleasant to ride through this strange, beautiful world with the silver moonlight. Floy had begun to get the hang of riding after a while. It was a question of balance and of bumping when the horse bumped. And on horseback they would feel so much safer. They would be able to gallop hard away from anything that might spring out at them. It was remarkable how unsafe it had felt walking through the forest like this.

They made their way through the thinning trees, the moonlight touching the grass with silver, seeing the shadows changing as they neared the forest's edge, becoming thinner, less mysterious, more like ordinary shadows that lay across ordinary roads at night.

Ordinary roads . . .

The road ahead of them was narrow and winding, silvery and black in the moonlight. The forest sprawled behind them and ahead of them and, beyond the Trees, they could see the remote, beautiful outlines of mountains.

'Mountains,' said Snodgrass, frowning. 'But there weren't any mountains when we came along the road earlier.'

'There wasn't forest on both sides of the road either,' said Floy.

'Then – it's a different road.'

'It must be,' said Floy, staring about him. 'I've no idea where we are.'

They unrolled the map which had been tucked in Snodgrass's cloak and spread it out carefully on the ground. It was important to find out exactly where they were, so that they could get back to where they wanted to be. It was even more important to do this quickly, because they had no food and they had lost the horses. Wherever they went, they would have to go on foot, which might take a long time.

'I think we're here,' said Floy, after a moment, indicating a spot on the map. 'D'you see the mountains and the Wolfwood? And this must be the road.' He pointed, and Snodgrass nodded. 'We've simply walked across the Wolfwood and come out where another road runs through it,' said Floy.

'Well, at least we aren't *lost*,' said Snodgrass, bracingly.

'No, of course not.' Floy frowned at the map. 'We can go back through the Wolfwood and hope that we reach our original road again,' he said. 'Although that might take some time, of course.' He glanced at the sky. Was it already streaked with the first faint grey fingers of dawn? Perhaps not.

'If we continued down this road *here*, we'd still reach the Fire Court,' said Snodgrass, who was quite good at maps and found them interesting. 'We'd approach it from the south instead of the east, that would be all. But it looks much quicker than re-tracing our steps.' He glanced uneasily in the direction of the Wolfwood and then said, 'What about Fenella?'

But Floy had already faced this one. 'We have almost certainly missed Fenella by now,' he said. 'If they set out from Tara at the hour they intended, they will have gone down the forest road hours earlier.'

'While we were trying to find our way in the Wolfwood,' said Snodgrass. 'Perhaps while the Trees were setting about Balor. Dear me, yes.'

'Fenella will go on to the Fire Court, of course,' said Floy, who had very nearly managed to convince himself of this. 'Caspar will be with her and he knows the roads.' He did not listen too closely to the small, cold voice that had persistently asked how far they could trust Caspar. He thought they could be almost sure about Caspar. I'll have to believe we can trust him, he thought. And Caspar helped us to escape. It's important to remember that Caspar helped us to escape. I won't believe that he was in a plot against us.

He looked back at the map. 'I think you're right, Snodgrass,' he said. 'This road we're on looks to be the shorter way now. Let's continue on it, shall we?'

Snodgrass thought this would be best. 'We might lose our way in the forest again if we go back into it,' he said. 'We might wander about for hours and waste a great deal of time. That's a mountain road ahead,' he said, pointing to the map. 'That means going a little way into the mountains and I don't see how you could get lost on a mountain road. You'd have mountains on each side of you and there'd only be one way to go.'

Floy was tracing the road on the map. 'We shall have to be careful there,' he said, pointing. 'The other side of that mountain road.'

'Why? What's there?' said Snodgrass, adjusting his spectacles the better to see.

'Just over the peak of the mountain,' said Floy. 'It's the City of Gruagach. The City of the Giants.'

They looked at it in silence. The giantish city, the immense northern township where the Gruagach Giants had lived and lured Humans to their doom.

'They're no longer there, though,' began Snodgrass. 'They're all at Tara,' and then stopped.

'No,' said Floy. 'The Gruagach are no longer there. But something else is. Something that we must avoid at all costs.'

He looked at Snodgrass. 'Don't you remember?' he said. 'When the Gruagach came storming down from their city to take Tara, Gruagach was taken by the *Geimreadh*.'

The *Geimreadh* . . . The terrible Human-hungry creature that Fael-Inis had warned them against . . .

Snodgrass said, 'But can't we avoid Gruagach?'

'No,' said Floy, and traced the route again on the map. 'If we are to reach the Fire Court, we must pass close to the City of Gruagach.

'We shall be inside the territory of the Frost Giantess.'

334

Chapter Twenty-six

Fenella stood very still and stared at the dark, hunched buildings at the side of the road.

The Workshops of the Robemaker . . . Dark and imbued with the evil of the necromancer and forbidding beyond anything she had ever seen.

And Nuadu is in there . . .

She had not expected anything quite so twisted and stunted-looking. A miasma of despair rose from the cluster of black Workshops and Fenella felt it billow out and engulf them in its sick, cold desolation.

'And there is a sour sad scent on the air,' said Caspar unexpectedly, his eyes on the Workshops. 'The scent of despair.'

They were standing on the side of the road, with the forest behind them and the Robemaker's Workshops directly ahead. It was not quite night, but it was very nearly night. The Purple Hour . . . Fenella shivered, because surely if there were any creeping darknesses abroad here, they would be abroad now, with the twilight stealing through the Wolfwood behind them . . .

But it was important not to think about things like shadows and creeping, unseen things. It would be better to concentrate on finding a way into the Workshops and getting to Nuadu and bringing him out. And I suppose, thought Fenella, with a sidelong glance at her companion, that I shall have to find a suitable way, an *acceptable* way, of explaining about Nuadu to Caspar.

In the uncertain light, they could see the dull glow that emanated from the Workshops and they could hear the steady thrumming of the Looms.

'They never cease,' said Caspar at her side. 'They must never cease, otherwise the Power they draw down will be broken.' He frowned. 'All sorcerers know that,' he said, 'but only the Black Sorcerers use Humans to turn the treadmills.'

'How else can they be turned?' asked Fenella, partly from interest, but partly because it would be a good idea to know as much as possible about the Workshops.

'They use water quite often,' said Caspar. 'Like mills.' And looked at her questioningly. But Fenella knew about mills and mill wheels.

'Or they use minor sorceries,' said Caspar. 'The best sorcerers do that. They create another source of power, a secondary source, to turn the Looms.' And Fenella remembered the thin, frayed legend of how the Earth-people, at one time in their history, had created a race of machines and how they had then created machines to run the machines and how it had all got out of hand. So, after all, there was nothing so very new in the world . . .

'Will the Robemaker be in there, do you suppose?' Fenella was trying to decide how to explain to Caspar about the captured Nuadu. 'Or might he be out looking for other slaves to turn the Looms?' Nuadu had said that the Robemaker and CuRoi took sacrifices from the ordinary people of Ireland; strong young sons to work at the Looms, although presumably they would not actually do this work themselves. Had they servants to do it? Or was it done by necromancy?

'They say that, for some of the time, the Robemaker dwells in the heart of the Dark Realm,' said Caspar and glanced over his shoulder uneasily. 'But he might as easily be here. We can't be sure. That's why we'd better move on without any delay.'

But Fenella, who had twice now seen the terrible hooded and cloaked shape creep up on her, thought that the Robemaker was not here. There had been a heaviness in the air on the Robemaker's approach those other times; a cold, greasy feel, as if thick, oily fog had swirled out into the clean air.

'I'm going to look inside,' she said at length, and Caspar turned to stare at her.

'You can stay here or go on without me,' said Fenella, returning the stare very straightly. 'I don't much mind, although I'd *prefer* you stay. But whatever you do, I'm going to look inside.'

Caspar, genuinely appalled, said, 'But don't you know that it's almost the most dangerous place in the whole of Ireland?' And looked at her and said, 'You *don't* know, do you? But it truly is, Fenella. If the Robemaker is there, or even if one of his horrid spells – what they call Sentry Spells – is lurking, we'd be taken up and captured before you could say Gruagach. I'd be put to work on the Looms and you'd be — Well,' said Caspar, who, despite his work for the Court and later the Gruagach, had retained a vestige of delicacy, 'well, I'd rather not say what might happen to you. Let's go on to the Fire Court. We can't be so very far from it now.'

Fenella was trying to be very patient, because it was not in the least unreasonable of Caspar to want to go on and leave the Dark Workshops as far behind them as possible. She weighed the advantages of telling him about Nuadu and the terrible crimson mask against the matter of his allegiance. Was there a middle course she could take? Something to account for her needing to get into the Workshops, but something that did not give away the Beastline people's plans to attack Tara? Yes, of course there was.

'Caspar,' said Fenella, looking at him very intently. 'We didn't tell you the entire truth, Floy and I.'

'Didn't you?' said Caspar, suspiciously.

'When we arrived here,' said Fenella, and spared a thought for the absurdity of these words, because the manner of their arriving had been something so remarkable as to defy explanation or description. 'When we arrived here,' she said, firmly, 'we lost one of our – our party.'

'Well?' said Caspar.

'He – the Robemaker took him,' said Fenella. 'And we vowed to try to rescue him.' She looked back at the huddle of low-roofed buildings. 'He's in there,' she said, and something so sad and so wistful entered her voice that

Caspar, who was by no means insensitive, looked at her more intently.

'We must get him out,' said Fenella, abandoning all pretence. 'Please, won't you help me?'

Caspar hesitated. As well as not being insensitive, he was by no means impervious to the sudden plea for help from a young and attractive lady. He had never met anyone quite like Fenella and he found her rather intriguing. He supposed he was more or less honour bound to help her. But his eyes went back to the Workshops and he frowned and sought for the right thing to say.

'If you won't,' said Fenella, 'I shall quite understand. But I shall have to go in by myself, that's all there is to it.' She studied the Workshops, frowning, and Caspar, who was becoming alarmed by this time, saw that this was no ruse to secure his assistance; Fenella intended to get into the Robemaker's Workshops and rescue whoever it was who was in there. And whether he went with her or not, she would do it. This was not something that could be allowed, not by anybody's standards. So he said that they could perhaps take a look round to see were there any secluded windows anywhere or any openings where they might just squeeze through. And heard his voice saying these things with appalled horror.

'That,' said Fenella warmly, 'is a very good idea. You should always inspect the terrain before going into battle.' And then, 'I read that somewhere,' grinned Fenella. 'Shall we try this side first?' and was off before Caspar had time to collect his thoughts.

He managed to detain her long enough for them to tether the horses, because there would be no sense in coming out of the Workshops (with, or without the prisoner) and finding that the horses had turned their heads for Tara and that they had to walk the rest of the way to the Fire Court. He thought, privately, that they might be very glad of the horses, because they might find that they came out of the Workshops much faster than they went in, but he did not say this.

'Ready?' said Fenella, having helped with the tethering and fastening her cloak more tightly about her shoulders.

'No,' said Caspar gloomily. 'No, I'm not ready and I wish I hadn't come, if you really want to know. In fact, if you want the truth, I wish I was back at Tara with the Gruagach.'

'That's not at all the way to think,' said Fenella severely. 'We'll get inside somehow and we'll find the – the person who was captured and be out again before you know it!'

She sent him the sudden grin again and Caspar said, 'Oh dear me, *what* optimism,' but he said it quietly.

Fenella moved down the narrow, steep slope with the stunted trees and the blackened, scarred ground and felt, as she neared the Workshops, a thick, clotted malevolence belching out towards them. It was rather like going down into a horrid, dark, earthy hole, where dull crimson fires burned and where grinning creatures might be peering at you from the shadows.

But I don't believe there are, thought Fenella firmly. I truly don't believe there are. The Robemaker isn't here – I *know* he isn't here – and we shall find a way to get inside and Nuadu will be there and we shall bring him out.

Caspar walked rather ploddingly along at Fenella's side, but Fenella thought that at least he was at her side and found this unexpectedly comforting. There had been one or two Earth stories of how warriors going into battle had gone shoulder to shoulder, which had always seemed a rather odd expression, but which suddenly made sense. Caspar was not the ideal person to be shoulder to shoulder with, because he would probably melt away altogether if there was a real threat. But at least he is here, she thought, and wondered if she would really have tried to get into the Workshops by herself if she had had to. Would I? Oh yes, if it meant rescuing Nuadu.

As they neared the Workshops, Fenella heard the continuous thrumming of the Looms and saw the pulsating red glow of the furnaces. She thought that the sound and the scent would surely hammer your mind into a state of numbness, eventually. What must it be like to be imprisoned here, day after day, month after month? I wonder, does he keep them chained and manacled, thought Fenella, or does he use sorcery? And, so utterly immersed was she in this strange blue and green land that was not feeling strange any more, that she did not even notice that she was weighing sorcery against steel chains and seriously considering the likely outcome.

Closer to, the Workshops were much larger than either of them had realised. They seemed to stretch back into the hillside as if they might, at some stage, cease to become manmade buildings of stone and wood and brick and become ancient caves; tunnels that would penetrate deep into the earth's core.

The walls were built of dark, rough stone, almost black, pitted here and there by the heat of the furnaces. There were narrow high windows, far above them; Fenella thought they would open on to rooms at a higher level than the ground. The windows had a sly, mean look, and Fenella had the sudden impression that the Workshops were not workshops at all, but a single crouching monster, black and hard-backed and scaly on the outside, but possessed of roaring, flaming innards, so that every breath it took belched out hissing steam and curls and wisps of flame.

The windows are its eyes, she thought, staring upwards. They are the eyes of the monster, red and evil and calculating, and they are watching us, those eyes, and thinking: oh yes, here are two *very* useful morsels of Humanity . . . And I had better not think like that, said Fenella silently, or I shall be too afraid to go any nearer. I'll concentrate on getting inside, getting to Nuadu.

'The Looms generate immense heat,' said Caspar, as they drew nearer and Fenella flinched from the dry, gusty warmth. 'It'll probably be quite uncomfortable.'

'Very uncomfortable, I expect,' said Fenella and went on studying the black stone buildings to see if there was a small, partly hidden door that they might use to get inside.

As they skirted the western side of the Workshops, they both saw how the grass here was blackened, the walls charred in places, the great smokestacks thickly crusted with cinders. Fenella, moving ahead, saw, as Nuadu had not been able to see, that there were tiny cracks in the walls, from which the glowing heat threw out threads of fiery light and through which little angry hisses of steam continually escaped.

Caspar was peering along the darkened west wall, when Fenella said in a whisper, 'Caspar! See over there? An open window. Exactly what we want.'

'Yes. Yes, it is. And,' said Caspar, 'there doesn't seem to be any heat coming from it. There certainly isn't any light to speak of in the windows. Does that mean there are no furnaces in there, I wonder?'

'Might it be a storeroom? Set a bit apart?' The open-windowed room looked as if it was quite far away from the main body of the Workshops. And surely there must be fuel of some kind to feed the great furnaces, and surely there would have to be a store-place. 'It could be a fuelhouse,' said Fenella. 'Which would make it a good place to try to get in.'

'They say the Robemaker uses human fuel,' said Caspar, half to himself, and then, 'Fenella, do you really think we ought to be doing this? Wouldn't it be better to raise help of some kind?'

'What kind of help?' said Fenella. And then, 'Caspar, have you ever actually *seen* the Robemaker? Really seen him?'

'Well, no.'

'I have,' said Fenella and repressed a shiver. 'And he's evil and merciless and terrible. He'd fell you with an enchantment in an instant. And he'd *never* be defeated just by strength. If you sent a great army against him, he'd simply cut it down with his sorcery. It's stealth and trickery that's needed to outwit him.'

The place that Fenella thought might be a fuelhouse

was a small, added-on section, jutting out from the main body of the Workshops. Fenella remembered the houses on Renascia and how they had nearly always had sculleries and washing houses jutting out from the main rooms. This had the same kind of look to it. It was a part of the main building, but it was not a central part. Probably it was not used very much and probably they could climb through the window and be inside without anyone even realising.

'I suppose you want me to go first,' said Caspar as they stood looking up at the open window, which was grimy and smeary, but much lower than the other windows.

'I'd go first,' said Fenella, who would do so unhesitatingly. 'I'm perfectly capable of climbing through a window. But I can't reach the window by myself. You go up first and then help me.'

'Let's not be hasty,' said Caspar, moving to the window. 'Let's just take a look first and wait till we see what's inside.' He grasped the narrow sill and hauled himself up so that he hung, partly suspended by his hands, his chin level with the lower sill.

'Can you see?' Fenella was standing on tiptoe alongside him, but the window was too high and she could not see. 'What can you see?' said Fenella. And then, as Caspar drew in a shocked gasp, 'Caspar, what's in there?'

Caspar let go of the sill and slid rapidly to the ground with a bump, looking a bit sick.

'Oh, dear me,' he said, standing back from the window and dusting himself down, wiping his face with a handkerchief. 'Dear, dear me! I never thought to see such nastiness, not even serving the Gruagach, I didn't. Well, it's no sight for a lady, that I *do* know. I think we'd better forget the whole idea.' He eyed Fenella uncertainly and Fenella, who was becoming impatient, said, 'Well, for heaven's sake—' which was an expression she had picked up from Snizort and Snodgrass and which was as meaningless as most of their expressions, but descriptive of strong emotion.

'Do come away,' said Caspar, taking her arm. 'I

promise you we'd be much better to go quietly back on to the road and make our way to the Fire Court.'

'You can go to any number of Fire Courts,' said Fenella, crossly. 'But I'm going in there whether you come with me or whether you run away. I don't much care which,' said Fenella, who did not really want Caspar to ride off and leave her alone out here, but who was not going to get so close to Nuadu and then ride away and leave him. 'And first of all, I'm going to climb through the window,' she said and reached for a stack of sacking which had been thrown down near the wall and which, piled carefully, might enable her to reach the sill.

'I wish you wouldn't,' said Caspar, but Fenella took a deep breath and clambered on to the sacks and grasped the window ledge, rubbing a bit of the window pane clear. And looked in.

The storeroom (yes, she had been right about that after all) was not very big and not very well lit. There seemed to be a door cut into the wall that was farthest away from the window; Fenella, trying to get her bearings, thought it would lead more deeply into the Workshops, perhaps even back and back into the cave part. Odd pieces of broken and split machinery were strewn about or propped against the walls.

The room looked to be what they had thought; a store or perhaps a fuelhouse which might be left unattended for most of the time. The sort of deserted outbuilding that might easily be forgotten, until a fresh supply of fuel was needed. The twisted machinery pieces cast shadows on the floor, weird and grotesque, so that, for a heart-stopping moment, Fenella thought that strange beast-things were crouching in the corners and remembered that Caspar had said something about Sentry Spells; minor enchantments that the Robemaker might have left on guard in his absence.

But light was spilling in through the seams of the door at the far end of the room; crimson, glowing light from whatever lay on the other side. After a moment Fenella's eyes grew used to the dimness and she could see quite plainly into the room. She could see what had made Caspar turn pale and sick.

A great pile of felled Trees. Trees which had been hacked and chopped and mutilated, which had had branches torn away so that they could be roughly stacked against the wall. Fuel for the Robemaker's roaring furnaces that must never be allowed to cool . . .

But the Trees were not just Trees. They were people, beings, half-formed creatures who might have been strange and beautiful and filled with wild, woodland magic. Beings who were now dead or dying, and who were lying in tangled, dreadfully mutilated heaps.

Fenella, clutching the narrow ledge, standing precariously on the piled sacks, thought, in horror: *Miach's spell*. The emerging of the Tree Spirits. What had Miach called them? Naiads and Dryads and Hamadryads. Nymphs and oreads and nereids. Beautiful, half-human forms, partly emerged from the ancient beeches and oaks and elms and birches and ash Trees, taking shape under the summoning of Miach's magic.

But here were hacked limbs and truncated bodies. Strange, greenish-gold fluid staining their skin which was not quite skin and not quite leaf. Tree-blood flowing down, mingling with the rippling bronze hair of the copper beeches and the pale, frond-like arms of the ash Trees and the poor, split, high-arched feet of the silver birches. There was a deep, thick blood from the old oaks, still trickling slowly out here and there, as if the Trees might not have been cut down so very long since, or – and this was much worse – as if there were still vestiges of life in them. Branches and limbs and hair and eyes all jumbled and mixed, so that you could not tell where the Tree part ended and the naiad part began.

The ancient Tree Spirits, awakened by magic after their centuries-old sleep, captured and taken by the Robemaker. Bound and held by his terrible evil magic, thought Fenella, sickened. Held, perhaps, by the crimson rope-lights, as Nuadu was held, and then butchered and slain and thrown into a dark woodshed, to await burning in the heart of a necromancer's fiery furnace . . .

'I'm going to climb in,' said Fenella, at last, and pointed to a thick chunk of dried-out wood. 'We can drag that underneath the window and then I'll be able to get through the window.'

'Best oak,' said Caspar, looking at the log and shaking his head. 'The Robemaker must have been taking the Trees for years.'

'Well, we mustn't think about it now,' said Fenella in a practical voice. 'It can't hurt the Oak now if I stand on it to get in, can it? No, I didn't think it could. Would you help me up?'

But Caspar, belatedly gallant, said that it was for him to lead the way. 'I'll go in first and then pull you up.'

'It would be much easier if I went in first and then you could push me up,' said Fenella.

'It doesn't seem right,' said Caspar, half to himself. 'It doesn't seem *polite* if you know what I mean.'

'We can't worry about manners. Do hurry,' said Fenella impatiently.

Fenella clambered cautiously on to the oak log and grasped the ledge. If the Robemaker had left any Sentry Spells, then surely this was the moment for them to come rearing out to challenge the intruders. She sat for a moment on the narrow window ledge, scanning the shadows in case shapes, creatures, sentinels should materialise. But nothing happened and Fenella felt a small, frail spiral of confidence and thought that the very suggestion that the Robemaker needed sentries at all indicated that he was not as all-powerful as they had feared. And if he has left any to catch us, then they aren't very good, she thought. We're partway in already.

'Hurry *up*!' said Caspar urgently, from outside. He hauled himself after her and Fenella gasped and half fell, half pulled herself over into the Robemaker's wood-store, to be followed, a minute later, by a rather out-of-breath Caspar.

They stood silently together in the dim, rather narrow room, with the sharp scent of the butchered trees all about them and, underneath it, a soft, sad scent that Fenella thought must be the spilled Tree-blood. In the red-lit dimness it was possible to see the mutilated Tree Spirits more plainly now and Fenella thought there had never been anything quite so dreadful.

They were not all quite dead. Fenella and Caspar could see this clearly; they could see that some of the Tree Spirits were still breathing, shallowly and painfully, their strange, wise faces shuttered and suffering, their branches torn from their bodies and great, gaping wounds still bleeding.

'Terrible,' said Caspar, rather pale.

'Can't we do anything for them?'

'I don't think so,' said Caspar. 'I think they are too – too cruelly hurt.'

'We'd better try to find the prisoners,' said Fenella at last, although she did not really want to leave the comparative safety of the wood-store. 'Through there, do you think?'

'As well there as anywhere,' said Caspar.

The door that Fenella had indicated was the one with ill-fitting seams that permitted the red glow to seep through. It was wider than it had looked and Fenella thought she had been right to think it led away from the road, deeper into the hillside.

'Can you hear anything?' she said as they stood looking round.

'I can hear the Looms,' said Caspar. 'But then, they never stop.' He listened for a moment. 'I can't hear anything,' he said. 'Ready?'

'Ready,' said Fenella.

'We'll leave this door propped open,' said Caspar. 'In case we need to—'

'Escape quickly.'

'Yes.'

And then, because there did not seem to be any reason to wait, they moved cautiously to the door at the far end of the wood-store and inched it open.

The noise and the dull angry light of the furnaces poured in.

Chapter Twenty-seven

Caspar and Fenella stood in the Workshops, with the wood-store behind them, their skin shrivelling and flinching and every sense assaulted by what was before them.

The room they were in stretched back and back – Into the hillside, thought Fenella – and far above them. In the evil, glowing red light they could see that the walls were not of brick or timber or of anything that walls were normally made of. They were earth; dark, hard-packed earth, here and there cracking with the endless dry heat. There was the feeling of being in a dark, hot cave and there was the sudden swift impression of ancient malevolent creatures that dwelled here and slept for decades, or sometimes centuries, until they were disturbed . . .

There are things in here that are sometimes asleep and sometimes not asleep, thought Fenella. Sentry spells? Yes, perhaps. I can feel them, thought Fenella, standing very still just inside the huge, high-ceilinged, firelit room. I can feel that there are forces in here that could very easily be woken and, if they are woken, they would come crawling and slithering out from their lair and we would not have very much chance against them . . .

At the far end, huge double doors opened on to the furnace room. The doors were partly open, showing the great iron stoves and the furnaces and the immense black pipes that disappeared into the floor. Billowing gusts of heat came from the furnaces and they could see the immense iron hods of wood, waiting to be fed to the furnaces. I hope their spirits are dead, she thought. I hope they are not like the ones we found in the store, still a bit alive.

Directly in front of them were the treadmills; huge,

fearsome, steel and mesh wheel-cages, stretching far above them, at least twelve or fifteen feet high, great roaring, relentless, nightmare machines which rotated on and on. Fenella, horrified, her mind tumbling, saw that the treadmills were like huge fly-wheels, like the sides of giant spinning tops. They gyrated endlessly round and round . . . Immense grinding, grating, pounding things . . . On and on, and up and up . . . And then down again to begin the circle over again. To watch the ceaseless spinning for too long made you feel sick and dizzy and a bit out of step with everything else.

The noise was dreadful. It was a continual clanking, rotating sound, a whirring rhythmic, steel-against-steel sound that made your teeth wince. Fenella and Caspar staring, saw that huge spindles and cogs and pinions protruded from the dark-packed earth of the ceiling and that the motion of the great wheels caused these to turn and rotate and drive one another into rather horrid, grinding, gobbling motion. The red glow from the furnaces fell across the treadmills, turning the steel mesh to angry crimson, bathing the creatures inside them to eerie, unnatural life, blending and merging them with the machinery, until it was very nearly impossible to tell where the treadmills ended and the human creatures began . . .

The human creatures . . .

Within each treadmill were two workers; chained and manacled. Affixed horizontally to the inside of the treadmill were stout iron bars for the prisoned workers to grasp. Fenella, who understood in a vague way about mill wheels and how they had to rotate continually to provide power, saw with horror that the slaves inside the steel mesh cages were forced by the motion of the wheels to tread endlessly forward to keep the treadmills revolving. Each of them must tread on and on, a ceaseless, bone-grinding trudge, if they did not want to be taken up and up by the gyrating treadmill into the clanking, turning cogs in the roof and ground to dust between the pinions. They must tread ever forward, regardless of discomfort, heedless of exhaustion.

Sweat poured from their bodies and they wore only the thinnest of breeches. Their feet were bare and, even from where she stood, Fenella could see the knotting of the leg muscles from the agonising cramp which they must surely suffer almost continuously. In every case, dried blood caked the mesh cages and the thick iron bars which they used for the momentum of walking. A look of hopeless desolation, of almost animal acceptance was in their faces; they had long since passed beyond defiance and hope; their life was bounded by the ceaseless rotating of the treadmills which served the Robemaker's Looms. Their life had become a never-ending trudge to keep the Looms of the necromancer weaving dreadful enchantments.

Sparks flew from the mesh cages and Fenella saw that great black iron pipes ran from beneath each wheel, along the wooden floor and out through a massive, carved silver door at the other end of the Workshop. She glanced at Caspar and saw that he was staring at the silver door. Somewhere through that door must be the Chamber of the Looms, the powerhouse of the Workshops, the force field of the necromancer.

The clanking of the machines was almost deafening, and Fenella wanted to clap her hands to her ears and try to shut it out. But she stayed where she was, her eyes raking the red lit chamber. Presently, she grew a little more adjusted to the noise and she began to make out the details a little more plainly; she could see that the captives were all young men, some of them not much more than boys, but certainly strong and lithe. She thought that not one of them could be more than eighteen or twenty, and she remembered how it had been said that the Robemaker scoured Ireland, taking the sons of the ordinary Irish families to work here.

And then Caspar, who had been narrowing his eyes and taking stock of everything and everyone, suddenly gripped Fenella's arm and said, in a voice from which most of the breath had been driven, 'Fenella – over there.'

'What—'

'The Prince,' said Caspar, softly.

Fenella looked to where he indicated, to the farthest of the treadmills and saw the single creature held captive there, and her heart jumped and missed several beats, and then went on again erratically.

Nuadu Airgetlam. The Wolfprince.

To begin with, they thought that the Robemaker had injured him in some unimaginable way, for the crimson mask still had him in its grip and in the flickering light, it looked for a moment as if the lower part of his face was covered in blood. Fenella gasped and then thrust her clenched fist into her mouth, because she would not, she emphatically would *not* give way to foolish emotion. But she moved at once and stood below the pounding clanking mesh wheel, looking up. She saw him look down at her and saw that his skin was raw and flayed in places; the arm of flesh and blood was scraped and scorched and the silver arm on the other side was reflecting the tremendous heat, so that it was copper coloured and glinting and must be causing him immense pain. But his eyes still held the old mockery and the remembered cynicism.

So you have sought me out, Human Child . . .

Fenella, hardly daring to speak, but knowing she must raise her voice above the treadmills, said, 'Where is—' And saw his eyes smile, as if to say: he is not here for the moment. For the moment, you are safe. And then there was a warning flare and Nuadu's eyes moved in the direction of the shadowed corners.

Fenella followed his eyes and at once said, 'Sentry Spells,' and there was a gleam of acknowledgement above the glinting mask.

'Yes,' said Fenella, looking up at Nuadu. 'Yes, I understand. And we will be wary.' And wondered, in the same moment, how they could possibly hope to cheat the Sentry Spells.

Caspar had crossed the room to stand at her side and he said, 'Sire—' And stopped in some confusion, because he had known Nuadu at once – he thought every person

351

in Ireland would recognise him, for the wolfblood was unmistakable, and everyone knew the story of the Queen's bastard wolfson and the fierce quarrels that had taken place between her and the King when Nuadu was born. He understood, as well, why Fenella had been so chary of telling the entire truth. Because I suppose I must have appeared a bit untrustworthy, thought Caspar, what with working for the Gruagach and everything. I suppose I can't blame her or Floy for being wary, he thought, rather sadly.

But he was a bit flummoxed at the reality of Nuadu, because nobody had ever told him how to address a bastard of the Ireland's Royal House. However, it would be better to err on the side of too much courtesy, and so, 'Sire,' he said firmly, 'if there is a way to get you out, we will find it.'

Nuadu's eyes went to the other captives and Fenella at once said, 'Yes, of course, all of you. If only there is a way—' And stopped, because Nuadu's eyes had gone to the silver door.

'In there? Do you mean—' Fenella stopped, trying to read the meaning in the dark eyes above the dreadful mask. 'Do you mean there is a – is there a *spell* we could use? Oh, but—' And stopped and felt, with remembered delight, the shower of golden needle lights as his thoughts poured into her mind.

It is the only way, Human Child . . . *The only thing that will release us is the thing that imprisoned us. Magic, Fenella. And in there is the Robemaker's cache of enchantments* . . .

The stockroom of spells . . . The necromancer's treasure-house.

But beware the Melanisms, Fenella. They are the Robemaker's sentinels, the effluence of necromancy, and you must be very very wary indeed of them.

The Melanisms . . . Fenella stayed where she was for a moment, still staring up at the imprisoned Nuadu. The Melanisms . . . With the words had come the fleeting impression of dark, sinuous creatures who could slither out of the shadows and wind their cold, serpentine fingers about you, so that you were trapped, who could twine about your entire body, so that you were smothered and suffocating from the cold embrace . . .

'But there isn't really any choice,' said Fenella, firmly, and turned to the ornate silver door at the far end of the room.

Fenella had expected the silver door to feel cool and silvery and solid and was surprised when it actually felt extremely hot.

'Yes, that'll be the Looms,' said Caspar. 'This will be an ante-chamber, mark my words. It'll be very hot because of being so near to the Looms themselves. We wouldn't get near to the Looms, of course. Well, very likely we won't get near to the store house, either. We'll very likely be burned to a crisp the minute we get in there. Still, it's all one to me. As well be fried and roasted on that side of the door, as turned to something very nasty by the Robemaker and fed into the furnaces. *I* don't care,' said Caspar.

There would not be very much time. They both knew this. Fenella could feel the shadows stirring already; she could feel a dark, slimy *something* uncoiling somewhere close by. The Melanisms, the Robemaker's Sentry Spells, torpid and stagnant for most of the time . . .? Sleeping in the darkness until some creature, some reckless, heedless Human should try to penetrate the ancient secrets of their Master . . .?

They are waking, thought Fenella, struggling with the elaborate handle of the silver door, then standing back to give way to Caspar who seemed to understand the mechanism.

The shadows moved; they seemed to darken and to creep nearer, and long, groping fingers of blackness stretched across the floor.

As they began to turn the silver handle with the strange, serpent-like beasts engraved deeply into it, Fenella felt the Melanisms creep nearer. They are only shadows, she said firmly to herself. Not solid things at all. Effluence.

But the Melanisms did not feel like only shadows. They

did not move like shadows; they did not shift and blur. They crept, developing rudimentary arms with nasty, elongated fingers as they went, groping across the floor towards the two intruders, as if they might not be able to see, but might be able to feel or smell their way to Caspar and Fenella. They were blind, seeking things, reaching out, feeling their way closer with every minute. It was unspeakably horrid to know that a great, slithering, inchoate mass of effluence was crawling and creeping and *smelling* its way towards you.

Fenella said, a bit impatiently, 'Oh, do hurry up, Caspar! Shan't we be able to open it? Isn't it just an ordinary door?'

'Of course it isn't,' said Caspar, crossly. 'It's a silver door, guarding something that's strongly magical. I've seen the same kind of thing in the Sorcery Chambers at Tara. You have to keep turning until there's a kind of silken click.'

Fenella was standing with her back to the silver door, watching the Melanisms. They were oozing closer, no doubt about it. I suppose, thought Fenella, that I was rather innocent to think that we could get in so easily, or that the Robemaker would not in some way guard his secrets.

'Almost there,' gasped Caspar. 'I think we're—' He broke off abruptly as Fenella let out a cry of purest revulsion and looked down to see the Melanisms at their feet, surging thickly upwards.

Fenella had managed to not quite scream. She had thought she had been keeping watch on the creeping grey-streaked matter, but it had moved suddenly, the embryonic fingers clutching the ground, pulling the oozing, mucousy river forward until it was bubbling over her feet.

She would not scream and she would not panic. She tried to back away and, at once, the Melanisms seemed to wriggle and chuckle, to slop forward with a dreadful, glutinous, squelching sound. Fenella, clinging to self-control, thought that it was a gobbling, lip-smacking sound, as if the soupy fluid was savouring her, as if it was going to enjoy bubbling upwards until it had engulfed her entire body . . .

She sent a frantic look to where Caspar was now standing and saw that the Melanisms had reached him as well now; his legs and knees were already covered.

This is dreadful, thought Fenella, struggling against the thick, cold viscosity. This is certainly the worst thing that has happened to me ever. Am I going to be able to get out? Am I going to be able to pull free?

As if in answer, the Melanisms tightened their hold, sucking and gobbling, the half-formed arms twining themselves about her thighs, tendrils of grey-streaked black curling upwards to her waist. The heaving fluid was not cold, as it had looked, but slightly warm, as if somewhere at the centre there might be a heart, and veins, and lungs to breathe with . . .

To reach down and try to free her legs would be disastrous. The minute she sunk her hands into the glutinous fluid, her hands would be trapped as well. She had the dreadful thought that once her hands plunged into the foul greasiness, she would feel reaching, grasping hands under the surface, clutching at her, pulling her down until she was drowning.

Drowning in the effluence of necromancy . . . Suffocating and smothering in the gelatinous mucous . . .

Fenella was using every ounce of her strength to climb free, but the Melanisms were tenacious and strong. They held on, tightening their grip, and Fenella felt herself being sucked in. She thought: but I *can't* simply stand here and be drowned by this horrid stuff! I can't just do nothing! And looked up at Nuadu, encased in the terrible cage of the treadmill, and saw black, bitter fury in his eyes. Because she was being slowly smothered by the Melanisms? Or simply because they had come so close to rescuing him? I won't think about that yet, said Fenella, silently.

Caspar was shouting to her not to struggle, because it would only mean she would sink quicker, but Fenella was struggling fiercely, because she could not just give in. She was feeling rather sick at the thought of drowning in the creeping, sucking mess. It was exactly like standing in a cauldron of lukewarm soup and feeling it inch its way up your body. There were nameless jellylike things within the Melanisms now; eel-like creatures that brushed against her skin and which felt boneless and yet gristly.

She managed to make a half turn so that she could see the silver door, because perhaps she could reach out and reach over and grasp the elaborate handle and somehow pull herself out. As she did so, Caspar turned with her, and Fenella knew he had had the same idea. They were both straining to reach, leaning forward as far as they could, agonisingly aware that the door and its ring handle that might have given them some leverage were out of their reach, when another sound fell on their ears.

They both turned back instantly, scanning the shadows, and Fenella saw Nuadu look up, sudden hope in his eyes.

From the other side of the room, from the shadows of the wood-store where they had entered, something was dragging itself across the floor towards them . . .

There was nothing any of them could do. Whatever was creeping towards them through the half-open door would have them completely at its mercy. Fenella and Caspar were both held fast by the wet gumminess of the Melanisms and Nuadu and the Robemaker's slaves were chained and manacled inside the treadmills.

The sounds came nearer; dragging, crawling sounds, as if not one but several creatures were struggling across the floor. Fenella, her heart thudding frantically, kept her eyes fixed on the door and a fearful hope began to unfurl.

Through the half-open door, into the dry, shrivelling heat of the great, evil-smelling room, there appeared branchlike shapes and then a fall of blood-stained, leaflike hair.

Caspar said, very softly, 'The Trees. Fenella, the Trees.'

The wounded Tree Spirits that the Robemaker had hacked and mutilated were coming to the aid of the two Humans who would free the Wolfprince.

356

Fenella felt ridiculous tears sting her eyes and brushed them away impatiently because this was no time to be emotional.

The Trees were moving slowly and painfully and it was terrible and marvellous to see them. But will they reach us before this horrid stuff covers us? thought Fenella, frantically. *Can* they reach us?

There looked to be three or perhaps four of the Tree Spirits. They were twisted and butchered and maimed and it was difficult to see if they had been Oaks or Beeches or Elms or what. But there was a glint of green and gold still in them, and their eyes were pain-filled, but determined.

The Tree Spirits were clinging to the black iron pipes that ran along the sides of the floor, using them as levers and pulleys to help them across the floor.

At Fenella's side, Caspar said softly, 'They are unable to stand, poor things,' and Fenella felt the pity of it hit hard at the base of her throat.

The Trees had crossed half of the floor now and the nearest one – Fenella could see now that it had been a Larch, elegant and slender – was already inching its way across the slimy black pool of the Melanisms, creating a kind of bridge. As it did so, the other two Tree Spirits did the same, the branches of the Larch reaching forward, until Fenella could lean over and grasp them.

She thought she gasped, 'Oh, thank you!' and she felt the Larch incline its head in acknowledgement. And then she was holding on to the branches, feeling where the Robemaker had hacked and sawn at them, knowing she must be hurting the Larch even more, and trying to be as gentle as possible.

The surface of the Melanisms heaved and panted, and Fenella felt the suction about her waist increase. The Robemaker's sentries were not letting go easily . . .

'Pull harder!' cried Caspar. 'Fenella, you must break free!'

'Yes,' gasped Fenella. 'Yes, of course.'

And then the Larch moved back, and Fenella clung to

its poor torn branches and the sticky evil effluence melted back, and there was a horrid oozing clutching feeling, and then she was pulled across the floor, and she was free.

The fact that they were both half covered with the slimy grey Melanism-fluid did not have to matter. Fenella and Caspar both knelt down, taking a gentle hold of the Tree Spirits' maimed branches, searching for the right words to convey their gratitude.

At length, Fenella said, in very nearly a whisper, 'Thank you, Trees,' and there was a ripple of awareness from the Trees and a soft rustling of the trailing leaf-hair.

'Is there nothing we can do to – to save you?' said Fenella, and saw the wise ancient eyes regarding her.

'Nothing, Human Creatures,' said the Larch at last, in a warm, timbery sort of voice. 'We shall die in the Robemaker's fires.'

'Can't you simply – escape from your – your Tree homes?' asked Fenella, unsure whether she understood the principle of all this, but hoping she had conveyed her meaning.

'We are bound to our heartwood Trees in death,' said the Larch. 'We are the Robemaker's victims.' Its head bowed over.

'But you must enter the Robemaker's Storeroom of Spells, and free the Prince,' said one of the others – Fenella thought it was a cypress. 'He will lead your armies against the Dark Lords.'

'If you can do that, then perhaps others will not be sacrificed and tortured and become soul-less,' said a third.

'Yes,' said Fenella, who had not really been thinking in terms of armies and battles quite so definitely as this. But she said, very firmly, 'Yes, we will do it.'

She eyed Caspar: 'All right?'

'Yes,' said Caspar, who was not really all right, but who was not going to admit to it. 'A bit muddied and splattered,' he said.

'Yes. But we'll attend to that later,' said Fenella, who was also muddied and streaked with the oozing matter.

She looked round. The Melanisms seemed to have retreated into their dark corners again, but Fenella had the feeling that they were simply mustering their strength again; they had been baulked of their prey and they had retired. But they would slither out again, and they would probably do so quite quickly. They had not very much time.

'We'd better be quick,' said Fenella to Caspar, taking his arm. 'Hurry up – did we manage to get the silver door open?'

As they moved cautiously towards it, Fenella saw that it had opened for them just the smallest sliver and that beyond it were shards of light.

They pushed the silver door open warily and Fenella stepped forward. The door swung to behind them, shutting out some of the noise of the treadmills, but it did not quite close. 'And we'd better make sure that it doesn't,' said Caspar, moving back to prop the door open with a stone. 'We don't want to find ourselves locked in *here*, that would be extremely nasty. You'd be forever wondering what might come at you from the shadows. I suppose the Melanisms have gone, have they? They aren't slithering around in here?'

'I don't think so. But we'd better hurry up.'

They both glanced behind them and then moved into the coloured shadows of the necromancer's storeroom.

Chapter Twenty-eight

They were in a rather long, quite narrow chamber, lined with shelves and with long racks with poles. And suspended from each pole . . .

'Oh!' said Fenella and stood still and clasped her hands together, and for a moment forgot entirely about being in danger in the house of an ancient and evil sorcerer.

Because from each pole there hung a robe, and each robe was of a different hue, and every robe was of a different consistency.

'The Robes of Enchantment,' said Caspar in an awed voice. 'The necromancer's wardrobe of spells.'

The Robes shimmered and gleamed and reflected the dim light. Each one glowed with its own prismatic brilliance and each one was soaked in pure, living colour, in rainbow light, in fluid iridescence. Fenella's first thought was that the Robes were the most beautiful things she had ever seen. Her second was that although they might be beautiful, they were not all good. There was a darkness, a sinister menace clinging to some of them, as if simply to touch them might call up dreadful visions and evil forces.

Caspar was explaining in a hushed voice that they were looking at the Robemaker's stocks of enchantments. 'The Robes of Spells,' he said. 'People consult him. And they say he will fashion any spell so long as someone will pay him enough.'

'Pay?'

'Living bodies. Living souls,' said Caspar rather hurriedly, as if he thought it might be dangerous to say things like this aloud. 'Bodies for fuel, souls for offering to the Soul Eaters. They say he has traded with the Soul Eaters for centuries, although I don't know why. Nasty!

Let's not think about it. Fenella, we should try to find something—'

'Yes.' But Fenella still stood, drinking in the wild, glorious kaleidoscope of colours, seeing the marvellous chequerwork of form and shape. Surely, oh surely, there would be something here that would rescue Nuadu and the other poor creatures . . . 'Only,' she said aloud, 'only, we do not really know what we are looking for.'

Caspar was moving forward, frowning, inspecting the robes as he passed them, occasionally reaching out a hand to touch a fold of colour. Fenella saw, with a thrill of horror, that as his hand went through the colours, the robes shivered as if they were not made of plain cloth, but of some living, breathing substance.

Music and colour and the secrets of Men; the innermost desires of the heart and sunlight and twilight and hopes and dreams . . . All here, thought Fenella, walking cautiously in Caspar's wake. Yes, all here. I can *feel* them all, thought Fenella. Music and colours and dreams and hopes . . . Oh yes. And she thought: but evil longings and greedy desires and black sour emotions, as well. She put out a wary hand and felt her fingers sink into the softness of a robe made of albescent whiteness, pouring ivory and soft, glinting pearl. Something good. Something pure and hopeful and silken. Perhaps a love potion? But the one next to it was veined with crimson and dull purple and, as Fenella touched it, she was instantly aware of a stinging pain, a boiling of hot sourness. She took her hand away at once.

Caspar was studying falls and swathes of crimson and gold. 'Something nasty these, I should think,' he said. 'Can you feel it?' And Fenella, coming to stand beside him, did feel it. She touched it warily and again there was the hot, dark heat, the feeling of suffocation closing about her, the surging upwards of bitter scalding liquid, as if she had drunk something that was too hot which was laced with a bitter and evil drug.

The heavy darkness seemed to hover above the deep magentas and purples and damson-hued gowns and, as they moved on again, to where the paler, gentler robes

361

were hanging, the feeling passed.

'We can differentiate the evil from the good,' said Fenella, frowning. 'But we don't know what any of them mean!' she said. 'Oh Caspar, this is going to be impossible.'

'Well, we'll think,' said Caspar. 'See now, if the crimsons and the purples are evil—'

'Yes, very evil,' put in Fenella.

'Then the *paler* ones must be good.'

'Does it follow?' said Fenella. 'And also, can we be sure that the Robemaker would ever weave a good enchantment at all?'

She regarded Caspar and Caspar, to whom this had not occurred, looked more worried than ever. But he said, thoughtfully, that he believed the Robemaker would weave anything so long as he was paid sufficiently highly.

'All right. And,' said Fenella, studying the robes and frowning, 'would it matter if we used a – an evil spell to rescue Nuadu and the others? Would it hurt anyone?'

But Caspar, who had only the sketchiest knowledge of these matters, did not know.

'Well, could we try one or two?' said Fenella. 'Could we simply take an armful out to the treadmills and put them on and see what happened? Would the Melanisms leave us alone for long enough, I wonder, or would the Robes themselves keep the Melanisms at bay? This is much more difficult than I thought it would be. But we can't get so close to freeing Nuadu and fail now.' She reached out for a pale, beautiful robe that seemed to be a continual pour of colour, like a mountain river with the sun shining on it and, as she did so, there was a whisper of sound behind them. Fenella whipped round and saw a long and terrible shadow fall across the floor.

The Robemaker was in the room with them.

Fenella had been standing towards the back of the Robe-room, half hidden by the racks of shimmering robes, but Caspar had been in the centre of the room, midway between two of the racks. As the Robemaker's shadow fell blackly across the floor, Fenella ducked behind the nearest rack, but Caspar, caught without hope of concealment, simply turned and made the briefest of bows.

'Good morning to you, Sir Enchanter,' he said, and Fenella, crouched behind folds upon folds of living colour, half suffocated, heard at once, that he had put on a slightly simple voice. Hope sprang up in her, because if Caspar could make the Robemaker believe that he was merely foolish and not an intruder, they might have a chance. It was rather a good device and one which Fenella admitted to herself she would not thought that Caspar was capable of thinking up so quickly.

'Good day,' said the Robemaker and Fenella suppressed a shudder, because it was the hissing, whispering voice she remembered from the forest road earlier.

'I have sought you for many a long day,' said Caspar, cheerfully, pursuing the rather frail ploy he had thought up earlier in case of precisely this eventuality. 'Yes, I have sought you,' he said, nodding, half to himself, 'for they tell me you are quite the best there is.' He regarded the Robemaker and Fenella, peeping out cautiously, saw him smile a bit vacantly at the hooded figure. 'And,' went on Caspar, 'I do need the best. That is *very* important.'

'Who are you?' The Robemaker had not closed the door, but he had pushed it to a little. The red light from the treadmill chamber spilled across the floor. 'And how did you get in?'

'Well,' said Caspar, and then glanced over his shoulder as if to make sure no one was listening, 'well, the truth of it is, that I work for the Gruagach. As a procurer,' he said, and tucked his chins into his neck solemnly and put on an expression that said: and that is a reasonable thing for a man to do, of course.

'I am not in the way of trafficking with Humans, but I know of the Gruagach,' said the Robemaker, standing very still. 'You do not answer my other question, Human.'

'Oh, about getting in,' said Caspar, and chuckled to himself. 'Well, to tell you the truth, Sir Enchanter, I met one of your nasty, wriggling creatures on the way in.'

'Yes?' said the Robemaker, and Fenella held her breath, because this, surely, was a trap.

'It inspected me,' said Caspar, sounding as if he had found this amusing. 'It took a look at me and then melted away into the shadows. I daresay,' he added, in a confidential tone, 'that it could see I was no enemy.'

'Go on,' said the Robemaker, and Fenella dared to hope again.

'The Gruagach sent me here,' began Caspar, and stopped, and then went on with more assurance, 'they sent me along to see if you can provide a – well, I don't know what you'd call it really. A spell of some kind for the King. Is that possible? Dear me, do you know, Sir, I had no idea this would be so difficult.' He frowned and chewed his lower lip quite naturally and Fenella, hardly daring to breathe, saw that the Robemaker appeared to be listening.

'The King,' said Caspar, having apparently thought matters over, 'is *wishful* to marry Flame. I daresay you'll know of her, will you?'

'Daughter of the sorceress Reflection and the creature Fael-Inis,' said the Robemaker, and a sneer had crept into his voice. 'I know of the Gruagach King's plans and I know of the charlatan Fael-Inis.'

'Is he a charlatan?' asked Caspar, apparently interested in this. 'Well, of course you'd know about that, far more than I would.'

'He is an illusionist, no more. As for Reflection—' The cloaked figure made a quick movement. 'A dilettante. A dabbler in magic. A greedy, grasping, lascivious creature.'

'Still,' said Caspar, 'Inchbad is quite wishful to secure her daughter's hand in marriage. The blending of two territories, so they tell me. I don't understand, really. Well, I don't *need* to understand.' He eyed the Robemaker with wide, ingenuous eyes, and beamed. 'But the thing is, Reflection is being rather – well, *very* greedy about the Marriage Settlement,' went on Caspar, feeling that he was doing really rather well with this random blending of truth and fiction. 'And she has locked Flame up until an agreement is reached.'

'Daughters need to be whipped into line anyway,' said the Robemaker rather dismissively. 'And Reflection was ever over-reaching.'

'Yes, but you see,' said Caspar, feeling his way cautiously now, 'you see, Inchbad would like to talk to Flame himself. And he – that is, he and Goibniu, thought that if we asked you – well, consulted you – you might provide a spell to get her free,' said Caspar. And stood very still and waited – and prayed to every god he had ever heard of that the Robemaker would not utilise the dread *Stroicim Inchinn* and read into his mind. He thought the tale was reasonably plausible. Well, it was the best he had been able to come up with and, if it was not sufficient, he could not think what else he could do. Had the mention of the Melanisms lulled the Robemaker's suspicions? Surely a person who had not been caught and killed by the Melanisms could be considered to have been inspected and found harmless.

The Robemaker was standing with his head bowed, sunk in thought. At length, he said, 'And the fee? The price your masters will pay?' Caspar managed not to breathe a huge sigh of relief, because this sounded very promising indeed.

He grinned rather slyly, and said, 'We all know your fee, Sir. And the Gruagach will pay very well.' He managed to achieve what was nearly a knowing wink. 'The dungeons at Tara are always filled with Humans. That,' said Caspar, managing to inject a note of pride into his voice, 'that is *my* responsibility, you know.'

'I do know,' said the Robemaker. 'I have heard of you, Master Procurer, and I know every one of your duties.'

'Good,' said Caspar, meaning it, and Fenella, still curled into her uncomfortable corner, crossed her fingers and tried not to disturb the shining folds of the Robes all about her.

'It can be done,' said the Robemaker. 'But I should

require – we will say six Humans.' He did not say this as if he was asking Caspar as if six Humans might be possible or even negotiable. He simply said it. My fee. Take it or leave it.

Caspar at once said, 'Certainly.' And beamed again.

'You will bring them here to me at the fall of the Purple Hour.' Again, it was a flat statement.

'I don't – yes, I could do that,' said Caspar, who could not do it at all, but could see that there was no other answer to be given.

'And then, in return, you shall be given the Robe of Human Hands.' Malevolent amusement gleamed from the shadowed eyes. 'You will know of the spell, perhaps? The incantation that must be chanted with the wearing of the Robe? *Open, locks, to the Human's hand . . .*' He stopped and Fenella repeated the words in her mind.

'I see. Well, no, I don't know it as it happens,' said Caspar. 'Could you – would you mind just – running over them for me. I don't remember things too well,' he added apologetically. 'And so if you could—'

For answer, the Robemaker lifted his arms out so that the great black cloak fanned out giving him the outline of a massive bat or a creature of prey.

Open, locks, to the Human's hand . . .
Schism, latches, and sever, turnkeys . . .
Fly open, bars, dissolve, untie, unchain, unfetter . . .
Slash and gash and carve and gnaw.
Pluck the splinters of iron, and slice the thews of steel.
Scission and sunder, steal and plunder.

He lowered his arms and folded them, then stood regarding Caspar.

'Thank you,' said Caspar. 'Yes, I think I can remember that.'

The Robemaker inclined his head and turned to open the silver door again, holding out one robed hand to indicate that Caspar should precede him. 'The Purple Hour,' said the Robemaker. 'And six Humans.'

Caspar went out and the Robemaker followed, closing the silver door.

Fenella emerged from her corner only after the footsteps had died away and she was as sure as she could be that there was no danger of the Robemaker returning.

And I am not really sure of it at all, she thought, standing up and looking about her. I daresay he doesn't even need to walk. He can probably simply appear. Materialise where he likes.

She would not think about it. She would try to find the Robe of Human Hands, which sounded rather horrid, but which would surely release Nuadu and the others. She would concentrate on remembering the incantation: *Open, locks, to the Human's hand . . .*

And I won't think, said Fenella, even for an instant, that the Robe might not be here, that the Robemaker might need to return to weave it on the great Silver Looms. How long did it take to weave a spell? It has to be here already, thought Fenella, trying to quiet the frantic thudding of her heart. I'll make a proper search, and I'll listen very hard, so that I can hear if the Robemaker comes back.

She would start nearest to the door and work her way along the jostling, glistening, pouring swathes of colours. She would be quick and quiet and efficient and she would not miss a one.

The Robe of Human Hands . . .

It was not, after all, quite so difficult to allot a vague identity to the Robes. The dark red and damson robes were heavy and stifling and they could not possibly be what she was looking for.

There were clusters of robes that seemed to pulsate and breathe, and there were others that slithered sinuously and rather nastily when she approached. There were rainbow clumps of raw colour which sizzled and suddenly coiled into snakelike forms as she approached and lifted serpentine heads to hiss at her; there were pouring cascades of things that had appeared to be silk or velvet, but which were molten gold when she got nearer and made her remember Fael-Inis and the cascading River and the salamanders. Was there something here that would help them? But when she reached out a hesitant hand, the heat from the liquid was so intense that she could not get any nearer to it. Even if this was the Robe they wanted, they would not be able to touch it!

She hesitated over several, dark, rather unobtrusive garments in one corner, thinking that they looked harmless until two creeping, fog-like hands reached for her and an evil chuckle filled the room, so that she shot back to the room's centre out of their reach.

There were robes where the pouring light suddenly solidified into rather grisly bones that rattled and gibbered and, on the same racks, were robes made of several different kinds of skin. Others were wet and clingy and had pulsing red veins and stringy muscle cords woven into them. It began to seem that the entire storehouse was made up of substances which looked harmless and beautiful on the surface, but which changed and blurred and coalesced as you approached them. Perhaps this was some kind of protection. Perhaps, thought Fenella, the Robemaker had drawn a veil of colour and light over his spells, rather as people covered their favourite gowns or pieces of furniture with dust sheets. And I am disturbing the veils, she thought.

Towards the far end of the chamber there were several robes half hidden by billowing folds of grey clouds, but which seemed to be composed of eyes as she drew nearer. Like a veil lifting... Yes, I was right about that at any rate, thought Fenella. They *are* veiled, and they *are* covered by something thin and light-filled and magical. And as I get nearer, the veil dissolves. This is very remarkable.

There was something rather nasty about the robe of woven-together eyes. Would it be for seeing into people's minds? Perhaps this was part of the *Stroicim Inchinn*. Fenella stood very still and stared at the Robe, seeing that the lids were closed and that here and there the lashes were matted and sticky-looking.

The *Stroicim Inchinn* . . . The thought that this was something that would be more useful than anything else in Ireland formed itself treacherously and slimily in Fenella's mind.

Because with that, we should be able to hear our enemies' thoughts and we should be able to tell what everyone else was planning . . .

The knowledge of how easy it would be to just reach out and take the Robe of Eyes and wear it and be able to see into other people's deepest thoughts flooded her mind, scaldingly. Fenella gasped and felt the sour bitterness of evil magic touching her and remembered that the *Stroicim Inchinn* was the most strongly forbidden enchantment of all, and that whatever else they were going to be doing here, they were not going to be dealing with forbidden spells.

But she looked at the robe again and several of the eyes opened and blinked and swivelled in their sockets, as if they had heard her thoughts and were rather amused by them. There was a rather sickening, glutinous sound as the eyes moved, the sort of sound you hear if someone with sore eyes rubs them too hard and they squelch. I'm having nothing to do with it, said Fenella firmly. It's evil and forbidden and I'm not even thinking about it!

The Robe of Human Hands was probably somewhere here, by the Eyes and the Skins and by the cloak made up of what looked like nail and hair . . . It must be here, thought Fenella, nearly in despair. It must be here, please let it be here, and please let me find it. *Open, locks, to the Human's Hand* . . .

Would Caspar be outside somewhere? Yes, he would certainly not abandon her. There was not really time to think about Caspar and there was not really any energy to spare to think about him, either.

And then she saw it. By itself, half hidden against the far wall, nearly obscured by billowing folds of grey cloud that huffed sweet, damp breath into her face as she approached.

The Robe of Human Hands . . . the enchantment that

369

would release the prisoners . . . Yes. It could not by any stretch of the imagination be anything else.

It was not, as Fenella had supposed, a cloak in the way she knew cloaks. It did not have shoulders or long enveloping folds or a hood. It was rather small and it had been hung, quite casually, on a nail protruding from the wall. It was rather like a large belt; you could probably fasten it about your waist and it would sit snugly over your hips. If you pulled an ordinary conventional cloak over it, nobody would even see it.

The hands were not, as Fenella had feared, frightening. They were rather sad; dead-looking, woven and folded and, in places, plaited together. They were rather submissive-looking hands, as if they might be waiting, quite patiently and happily, until someone might need to make use of them. It was quite difficult to believe that there could be any animation in them. It was very difficult, indeed, to believe that they could snap open the cages of the treadmills and free Nuadu and the others.

Open, locks, to the Human's hand . . . Would it work?

It must, thought Fenella, snatching the spell off the wall and holding it between her hands as she stood at the silver door, waiting for an indication that the Robemaker had gone.

In the end, it was much easier than she had thought to push the silver door open by a few inches and to stand listening, trying to see, trying to hear, trying to *feel* the lingering dark presence. Had he gone? Yes, thought Fenella, drawing in a huge breath of relief. Yes, he has gone. She was not sure how she could be so certain of this except, perhaps, that there had been a miasma of heaviness, a cold, black *diseased* feel to the air which was not there now. Yes, the Robemaker had gone.

She pushed the door wider and slipped through into the treadmill chamber again.

Nuadu's eyes were on her and, as she stood before the giant rotating wheels, she saw amusement in them.

So you have stolen the Robemaker's spells, have you, Fenella?

Well, thought Fenella, it seems that at least I have found the right spell. At least, Nuadu seems to think I have. I have got that far. But what do I do now? She had not the least idea of what she should do next, other than perhaps to fasten the strange garment about her waist. Would that be right?

Yes, yes, Human Child!

His eyes were dark and brilliant above the cruel red mask and Fenella stood looking at him, seeing how the fireglow poured over his half-naked body, seeing how the silver of his left arm gleamed in the flickering light and was clamped about the horizontal iron bar with as much assurance as that other flesh-and-blood and muscle arm. The dark hair clung to his forehead and his body was flushed and glistening and bathed in the dull crimson glow.

He is caged and caught, thought Fenella, staring at him. He is caged and he is muzzled – and *still* he is arrogant and defiant and *still* there is the cynical mockery in his eyes.

Of course there is, Fenella. Would you have me cowed and obedient to Ireland's greatest enemy . . .?

Behind her, the other treadmills still turned and clanked and the captive creatures trudged ever on and on, ever forward. Fenella looked over her shoulder at them and saw that they were looking at her with such blind trust and with such faith that cold anger rose in her at the evil Lord who had forced them to his work. I don't think I shall bear it if this does not work, thought Fenella. I don't know how we shall get them out, because they are exhausted and probably they will find it difficult to walk. But somehow we have to do it. She looked back at Nuadu and knew that it had to work. If I have to tear open the cages with my hands, I shall rescue him. I shall rescue all of them!

He caught that at once and his eyes above the mask glittered.

Well, Fenella? Use the spell. Or are we to stand here all day?

Caged and muzzled, but as arrogant, as imperious, as he always was and always will be . . .

Fenella fastened the garment about her waist, by no means sure that this would be sufficient, expecting it to feel uncomfortable and even grisly. But it was neither of these things. It moulded itself about her waist and it felt warm and rather safe, as if it might be armouring her against the evils in here. She sent a glance to the corners where the shadows still lay, thick and clotted and sinister, but nothing moved.

Fenella turned back to the treadmills and half closed her eyes, the words of the Robemaker still clear in her mind.

Open, locks, to the Human's hand . . .
Schism, latches, and sever, turnkeys . . .

The words seemed almost to repeat themselves on to the air and to lie there for a moment, perfectly visible, perfectly readable.

Open, locks, to the Human's hand . . .
Schism, latches, and sever, turnkeys . . .

The Hands about her waist moved at once, urging her forward, so that she was standing before the treadmill almost before she realised it. What came next? Yes, of course, the part about bars flying open.

Fly open, bars, dissolve, untie, unchain, unfetter . . .
Slash and gash and carve and gnaw.

She stopped, because something was happening to the strong steel mesh of the cages. Were they shivering? Razor-sharp shards of light pierced the shadowy red darkness and began to fasten about the metal cages of the treadmills.

Go on, Fenella. Continue the spell . . . There can not be very much time to us . . . For if the Robemaker does not return, the

372

Melanisms will surely wake again . . .
   'Yes,' said Fenella, gasping.

Pluck the splinters of iron and slice the thews of steel.
Scission and sunder, steal and plunder.

Little curls and wisps of steam were rising as the tough,
thick steel dissolved and, as it did so, there was a terrible
slowing down of the machinery, a grinding grating noise,
as if the cogs were crashing against one another, as if the
great engine above them was labouring.

Through the doors Fenella heard a shout go up and the
red glow dimmed and wavered, as if a giant hand had
doused it.

The great treadmill came to a halting, screeching stop,
and the steel cage fell open.

Fenella dropped the Robe of Hands on the ground and
Nuadu fell through into freedom and bounded forward
and took her in his arms.

It was a hasty, unreal, Council of War they held, a little
way into the forest, still dangerously close to the Workshops.

Caspar, who was extremely anxious about the whole
thing, had wanted to go deeper into the protection of the
Trees, but Fenella had said this was far enough for safety
and, anyway, it was as far as most of the freed slaves could
get. They would only rest for a brief time and they could
keep a sharp lookout for the Robemaker or any of his
creatures. They would see and they would hear and they
would *feel* if anything sinister was approaching.

'Because,' said Fenella firmly, 'although Nuadu is
unscathed, the rest have been imprisoned for much longer
and they cannot walk so very far yet.' She had looked at
Nuadu rather challengingly as she said this, but Nuadu
had only smiled as if it did not matter.

And so they had helped the Robemaker's prisoners as
far into the Wolfwood as they could manage, sufficiently
far to feel safe, and they had bathed their scarred and
blistered feet and hands in a forest stream and sat down

to consider what to do next.

There were about a dozen of the slaves, some of them badly wounded, all of them exhausted. They seemed grateful for Fenella's careful ministrations, but they were bewildered and dazed.

'There will have been many many more of them,' said Caspar in an aside to Fenella. 'Ones we were too late to save.'

'Yes. What happens to the ones who die?'

'Fuel for the furnaces,' said Caspar rather hurriedly.

'Oh! Yes, of course. I left the – the thing behind,' said Fenella, rather hurriedly. 'The spell. Ought I to have—' she stopped, because she had been trying to ask whether she ought to go back for it. 'Ought I to have hung on to it?' she said at last.

'I *think*,' said Caspar, 'that it will be temporarily used up. I don't think it could be used again anyway.' He looked at her and Fenella said, 'Thank you,' because she had been secretly fearing that someone – and probably Nuadu – would say that the spell might be of great help to them and that it would have to be retrieved. I suppose that Nuadu or Caspar would go back, thought Fenella. And looked at Nuadu and thought that she would find it almost more than she could bear to see him go back into the Workshops and have to brave the Melanisms and perhaps encounter the Robemaker. It was difficult to know if Caspar had spoken truthfully, but Fenella thought she would not question what he had said. It was probably a rather cowardly avoidance, but it was what she would do.

The freed slaves sat where they were put, but Fenella and Caspar both saw that their eyes turned involuntarily to Nuadu, as if they regarded him as their leader, as if they might be waiting for him to say what they must do next. Fenella, who was trying not to look too much at Nuadu, understood that the poor, exhausted creatures had been so firmly in the grip of the Robemaker's dreadful tyranny that they no longer had the power to think and reason and plan.

374

They were young men; perhaps Fenella's own age, or perhaps Nuadu's, but they gazed at Nuadu with the trustfulness of small children. Pity for them sliced through her and, with it, a new and different kind of anger against the Robemaker who had not only taken these young men's strength and youth, but who had taken their independence as well. But they sat attentively on the forest floor and several of them turned their heads up as if drinking in the forest air and the night scents, and they listened carefully to everything that was said.

Nuadu appeared not to notice any of this; he was curled with his usual careless grace against a tree, sketching out a map on the ground for Caspar to study.

Nuadu leaned forward, his dark eyes brilliant, and Fenella caught herself thinking: oh yes, *that* was how he looked in the forest! That is what I remember! And then quenched the thoughts at once, in case his strange, disconcerting perception should pick them up.

'You must all go on to the Forest court,' said Nuadu. 'To where the Beastline Lords are raising an army to march on Tara. There you will be looked after and perhaps you can return to your homes.' He eyed them. 'But,' he said, a sudden lifting to his voice, 'but if you should wish to be avenged on the creature who held you in such terrible captivity, and if you choose to fight for the rightful Wolfking against the Gruagach and the Dark Ireland, you should go to my cousin, Tealtaoich of the Wild Panthers, and make yourself one of his army. He it is who is controlling the attack on Tara. Or so he will tell you,' said the bastard Wolfprince with a grin.

For a moment there was silence, as if no one quite knew what to make of Nuadu. And then one of the slaves, who was not so badly wounded as the others and who looked to be a little older than the rest, said, rather hesitantly, 'Sire. That is, Your—' And Fenella saw the first twist of real anger on Nuadu's face.

'I have no right to that title,' he said. 'Remember that.'

'I am sorry,' said the young man at once. He frowned, as though he still found it difficult to marshal his thoughts, or even give tongue to them. 'But, Sir, are you not accompanying us?' He looked at the others, who all murmured, and said, 'Yes, we need you, Sir,' and 'How else should we go?'

'I can not accompany you,' said Nuadu, and now his eyes went to Fenella. 'There is a task I must complete.'

Caspar looked up and Nuadu said, 'There is no reason why you should not know.' In the thin light, Fenella could see little pinpoints of red light dancing in his eyes. 'The Dark Lords hold my half-brother captive deep within the heart of the Dark Ireland,' said Nuadu. 'Until he is rescued, then the High Throne of Tara is vacant.' His eyes glittered with mockery. 'And therefore vulnerable to usurpers and adventurers and bastard lines of the Noble Houses of Ireland.' Utter stillness fell over the freed slaves, as if no one dared even to breathe.

'Therefore,' said Nuadu, 'the Prince must be brought out of the Dark Realm.' He paused and then said, 'I must go in and bring him out.' He looked at Fenella again and appeared to wait.

'How?' said Fenella, staring at him.

'Through one of the Gateways that exist between this world and the Dark Realm. There are a number of them, but I think I must use the most ancient of all.'

Fenella drew breath to ask how this could be done, when Caspar, who had been looking worried, said, 'Fenella, what about Floy and Snodgrass?'

'I'm afraid we've long since missed them.'

'Yes, that's plain,' said Caspar, frowning.

'But,' said Fenella, who had already thought this out, 'they'll have gone on to the Fire Court. We'll just have to continue the journey and meet them there. They'd know we'd do that. It's what any sensible person would do.' And thought that, as long as she did not look directly at Nuadu, she could continue with this really very practical discussion about what everybody was going to be doing and who was going where and who was accompanying whom. I'll concentrate on that, said Fenella to herself.

Caspar said, thoughtfully, that somebody ought to go

along with the freed slaves. 'Somebody's got to get them to safety and to somewhere they can have a bit of a rest and their wounds looked at.'

'Yes,' said Nuadu, eyeing Caspar.

'How would it be if I took them in charge for a while?' said Caspar, who had seen and interpreted the look. 'I could make sure they got to the Forest Court; I daresay you could be giving me directions, because we don't want to be wandering about in the Wolfwood for days. If you could direct me, I'll take them to your cousin and then be off after Floy and Snodgrass. How would that be?' said Caspar, who thought that once you had made up your mind to a thing, it was not so bad as you had feared.

'Excellent,' said Nuadu crisply and Caspar felt pleased, because wasn't it a fine thing to be pleasing a Prince of Ireland, never mind that it was only a base-born one? He said, choosing his words with care, 'About the Dark Ireland, Sir—?'

'Well?' said Nuadu, lifting his brows, so that Fenella thought: arrogance! Something I don't like! And was not sure whether to be pleased that she had discovered something to dislike, or not.

'You mentioned the Gateways,' said Caspar.

'Yes?'

'Yes. Well,' said Caspar, 'I don't wish to be speaking out of place, but you aren't going through a Gateway alone, are you? To fetch the – that is, your half-brother? I don't wish to be discourteous either, but won't it be extremely dangerous? Oughtn't you to have a—' He broke off and glanced at Fenella, as if caught out in deception.

Nuadu said, quite calmly, 'The Spell of Human Hands would not be strong enough to dissolve the powers of the necromancers. We shall not attempt to retrieve it,' and Caspar, relieved, said, 'Ah.' Fenella, watching him, suddenly had the feeling that this was not quite what Caspar had been meaning, and when Caspar spoke again, was sure of it.

'Begging your pardon all over again, Sir,' said Caspar, 'but which of the Gateways did you think of using?

Because there's only one that is anywhere near to us.'

Nuadu said, 'There is only one that would be possible to force open.'

'Yes?'

'The Gateway that lies deep within the Cruachan Caves.'

'Yes, that's the one I thought you meant,' said Caspar. 'And it would mean passing close to the Court of the Soul Eaters, wouldn't it?' he added. Fenella felt a tremor of fear go through the listening slaves.

'It may mean passing through the Court,' said Nuadu. 'I do not see that it need deter me.' He looked at Caspar coldly and Caspar said hurriedly, 'Oh no of course not. But it's only that I was thinking if you're intending to make the journey without any – any *magical* help—' He stopped again and looked unhappily to where Fenella sat listening.

Nuadu said, as if the matter was of small importance, 'To rescue an exiled Prince of Ireland, a Human must take an active part in the rescue. That is what you are thinking, perhaps?'

'The Humans have always been the Kingmakers of Tara,' said Caspar. 'I know it's an old belief, but it's in all the ancient stories. How the Humans must never rule from Tara because of the ancient curse, but how they possess immense strength in the rescuing of exiled Kings. It's actually happened here several times, hasn't it? It happened in Cormac's time and then again in Erin's. I was brought up on those tales.'

'So was I,' said Nuadu politely.

'And I was thinking,' went on Caspar, not looking at anybody now, 'that if you truly mean to go through the Court of the Soul Eaters and into the Dark Ireland to find the Prince, then—'

'Then I should take a pure-bred Human with me?' said Nuadu. And then, turning to look directly at Fenella, he said, very softly, 'But that is precisely what I shall do.'

378

Chapter Twenty-nine

At the centre of the Wolfwood, in the place called *Croi Crua Adhmaid*, the exiled Court was deep in a War Meeting. This was what Snizort, with delighted memories of War Councils and Coalition Governments and Pentagons and Congress and underground War Rooms, had said it was called. He had explained earnestly to Oisin about how the Earth-people had elected small bodies of people to run the land and decide on strategies and laws and how, when there was a war going on, the battle plans had always been kept secret.

'Why?' asked Oisin, who was interested in the ways of these curious people whom Snizort called ancestors, but who, as far as Oisin was concerned, had not yet been born. 'Why did they have to be secret?'

Snizort had not been very sure. 'But I *think*,' he said, 'that it was because of the possibility of information being let out to the other side.'

'Oh,' said Oisin, who found it difficult to visualise a war where you did not have all your armies massing and which would be over in the course of a day, or perhaps a couple of days.

'They fought for years sometimes,' said Snizort proudly. 'With machines.'

'What kind of machines?'

But Snizort was not very clear. 'Only we do know that the machines ended in destroying nearly all the people,' he said sadly. 'I expect your way is much better, really.'

Tealtaoich and the Oak Tree Spirits had ranged themselves round the oval table and Clumhach had helped by clearing away the supper things and going round with a cask of their best mead, which Eogan said ought to have been beneath Clumhach's dignity, but which Clumhach had quite enjoyed.

'Because I'm a homely sort of person,' he explained. 'And I chose the mead very carefully. It's the very *best* mead. I wouldn't offer them anything inferior.'

'The Trees won't drink mead, will they?' said Feradach. 'I don't see why not.'

In fact, the Trees had accepted the mead with grave courtesy and had sipped it with quiet pleasure, although the Silver Birches had become a bit giggly.

Tealtaoich had asked Miach to lay one or two Sentry Spells so that nothing could creep up on them unseen while they unrolled maps and drew up the battle plans and generally explained to the Tree Spirits what had been happening in Ireland and what they proposed to do about it.

This had greatly pleased Miach, because it showed that people were beginning to regard him as a proper sorcerer at last. He had walked around the edges of the clearing, muttering and drawing symbols on the ground and, although he had not been able to call up the strongest of Sentry Spells, he thought he had summoned one or two quite useful Snares and a couple of Traps.

Snizort, who had accompanied Miach on his walk, wanted to know what Snares and Traps looked like.

'Well, they're quite small,' said Miach. 'And they're silver and black and they have jaws, clamplike mouths that will close on the feet of anybody that comes creeping up on us.'

'Supposing it's somebody like Nuadu or Floy coming back?' said Snizort, worried, but Miach said the Snares and the Traps were meant to protect the Forest Court and would not attack friends.

'I hope they don't,' said Snizort, casting a worried glance into the forest depths.

Tealtaoich had unrolled the maps of Tara and the surrounding countryside which they had managed to bring with them and had spread them out on the oak table. The Trees had been deeply interested and had listened in courteous silence when Tealtaoich had explained about the Gruagach taking possession of Tara and killing the King and how his son the prince had disappeared.

'We fear that he is in the Dark Realm, perhaps held prisoner in one of the necromancer's Black Citadels,' said Tealtaoich, and the Tree Spirits had nodded, as if this was entirely possible.

'I fear that we shall not look upon his face again,' said Dian Cecht. 'Ah me, our beloved Prince. He is lost to us for all time.'

'I recall you once called him a spoiled cub and said he needed whipping,' remarked Feradach, and the Tree Spirits appeared not to have heard this, which Snizort said was as fine an example of diplomacy as you could hope to get. 'My word,' he said to Oisin, pleased, 'I never thought to see it quite so strongly alive.'

The Oak who appeared to be the leader, and who was almost always the Trees' spokesman, said, 'Son of the Panthers, we know a little of the ways of the Dark Lords and, if your Prince is indeed in their hands, they will keep him and make some use of him.'

'That's what we fear,' said Eogan.

'And the truth is,' said Tealtaoich, 'that we have no clear idea of whether we should go in search of the Prince, or whether we should rout the giants.' He looked at the Tree Spirits and Snizort, who was seated at the table's foot, busily taking notes, thought that the Beastline creatures were actually a bit lost without Nuadu to tell them what ought to be done.

'I say we rout the giants,' put in Clumhach. 'I can't be doing with the thought of them rampaging about inside Tara.'

'You are right, Brother of the Bears,' said the Oak, and Clumhach, unused to being agreed with, looked startled. 'To defeat an enemy, you must first strike at the enemy's weakest point.'

'The *Gruagach* are weak?' said Tealtaoich.

'They are stupid and brutish,' said the Oak. 'Their appetites are coarse and clumsy.' He inclined his wise

381

head. 'We would join with you in a battle against the Gruagach,' it said, thoughtfully. 'For the Gruagach are no friends to our kind.'

'We would certainly join with you to vanquish the Robemaker,' said one of the Elms, and a shudder of fear seemed to go through the rest of the Tree Spirits.

'Well, thank you,' said Tealtaoich.

Eogan said, 'We had thought to assemble our people by night and take the Bright Palace by surprise.'

The Oak said, 'Battles fought by night, particularly when there will be the forces of dark sorcery on the other side, are seldom victorious. To fight for your people by night would mean that you would be at the mercies of every evil enchantment abroad.'

'Then,' said Tealtaoich, 'if we go openly and honestly by daylight, will you come with us? You have seen our plans; we intend to call up our Beastline creatures and mass a large army.'

Eogan said, 'If you would join with us, it would make our army so much stronger.'

'We will come with you,' said the Oak, and everyone breathed a sigh of relief. As Oisin had said to Snizort, they were not any of them very used to planning a battle and he and the Oaks were carefully charting the journey they would all take back to Tara.

'But,' said the Oak, very seriously, 'you must all call up your Beastline creatures.'

'Yes, we intend to do that.'

The Oak regarded Tealtaoich rather thoughtfully, but only said, 'Then let us study the maps, Son of the Panthers.'

Eogan, who was seated next to Tealtaoich, suggested that, in the old days, armies had frequently sent in a three-pronged attack: 'It confuses the enemy,' he said, and Snizort began to tell them about how, somewhere back in history, armies had done just this and had nearly always been victorious.

'Air, sea and land,' he said. 'That's what they used to do.'

'How did they attack by air?' asked Feradach, looking up at the sky.

'Had they winged people in their armies?' said Eogan.

But this was something else that Snizort did not know. He said, rather vaguely, that it had all been done with machines and they would probably do better with people out here. Tealtaoich began to draw up a list of three different armies.

'Headed,' he said, 'by three different leaders.'

'Which three?' asked Feradach, and a discussion ensued as to whether the Trees should be all together to form one single army, or whether it would be better to divide them and make three detachments, with each detachment composed of Trees and Beastline people and their particular creatures.

Dian Cecht had drifted, in an apparently aimless way, to where the Copper Beeches were grouped and was now seated at their midst. Feradach said it was not by accident that she had chosen to seat herself with the Copper Beech Spirits at her feet – 'As if she was holding Court,' he said crossly – but Eogan said this was unjust. Even Dian Cecht would not try to compete with the Copper Beeches.

'Oh, wouldn't she just,' muttered Feradach, but he said it quietly, because Miach was within earshot and everyone was treating Miach with unwonted respect since the waking of the Trees.

'Because,' said Feradach to Oisin, 'I didn't think he could actually call up the Tree Spirits. I'll admit to it. I didn't think he could do it.'

'He's even managed to lay a few Sentry Spells, did you know that?' said Oisin. 'He took rather a long time about it, but they're out there. If you look carefully you can just see them, glinting in the forest.'

Miach was having a grand time. He had performed what he felt to be a really useful piece of sorcery in waking the Tree Spirits. It was true that he had hit on the right invocation by mistake and that he had actually been trying to pronounce a quite different spell altogether at the time, but this was not anything that anybody needed to know.

And whatever else they might be saying about him, they could none of them deny that he had done something no sorcerer in this Ireland (or the Dark Ireland either) had done for centuries (never mind that it had been by the purest good luck).

The Trees had all thanked him very politely for summoning them, which was what you would expect of Trees who were a whole lot better mannered than most of the Beastline. Miach had listened to what the Trees had to say by way of homage and had acknowledged their thanks in a very dignified fashion, which he had fancied became him rather well. Mother had been pleased with him.

The discussion had gone quite well. The Tree Spirits had been helpful and intelligent. They had discussed the various routes which ought to be taken and had asked Miach, very politely, if he would summon the rest of the Tree Spirits from their slumber.

'Because,' said the Oak, 'you will see that we are still quite a small number.'

'We should like our brothers the Ash Trees and Spruces and our sisters the Trembling Poplars to be with us,' said the Elm.

'Yes,' said Miach, rather uncertainly. 'Yes, of course.'

'And,' said the Oak, turning back to Tealtaoich, 'and now, you should be ready to call up your Beastline Creatures, using the ancient *Samhailt*.'

There was a rather unexpected silence. Snizort, from his place at the foot of the table, saw sudden alarm reflected in every face. He had been intrigued by this idea of summoning the Beasts; Clumhach's bears and Eogan's eagles and Oisin's wild deer and all the others, and he had been looking forward to seeing it happen.

'Our scribes and our story tellers, the *ollam*, write that it is a truly awesome sight,' Oisin had said to him, and Snizort had looked at Oisin rather thoughtfully, realising that this was something that none of them had ever had to do, something they had only read about. He studied

384

the creatures seated round the table now and saw that the Tree Spirits were silent, clearly waiting for an answer. The Oak had looked at Tealtaoich in rather speculative fashion earlier and he was doing so now. Bless my soul, thought Snizort, bless my soul and boots and whiskers, I believe that there is something wrong here! He did not reach for his inkhorn and paper, which would have been extremely rude at such a moment. But he thought that he must certainly not omit to record all of this exactly as it was happening.

Tealtaoich was looking very straightly at the Oak and, although his elegant pose lost none of its grace, there was a tautness in him that had not been there before. Farther down, Clumhach was looking decidedly worried and Snizort thought that even Dian Cecht had lost some of her languor. They're worried, he thought. They've never done it, they've never summoned the Beasts; and they're worried.

The Oak said, quite tranquilly, 'The Purple Hour is almost upon us and that is the hour when all magic is at its strongest.' It stood back a little and the other Tree Spirits moved with it, so that they were grouped together, flowing green and gold and amber, against the darkening forest.

'Our thoughts are with you and about you,' said the Oak, and instantly, as if some kind of ritual had been pronounced, the other Tree Spirits said, 'And ours, also.'

Tealtaoich looked at the others and Snizort had the strong impression of someone who has been edged into doing something that is slightly frightening and certainly alien. He knew, then, that his earlier judgement had been right; these creatures had never before had to invoke this strange-sounding ancient enchantment and they were fearful of failure.

But Tealtaoich stood up and looked quite calmly round the table, so that Snizort felt unexpected respect for him.

'Well?' said Tealtaoich. 'As the Trees have said, it is up to us to add our strengths to the army. As the remaining

385

Royal Houses of Ireland, it is for us to call up our kind and then to ride on Tara.' His eyes flickered, but he said, 'Shall we commence the Ritual? Shall we summon the Beasts?'

The Ritual of the Beastline . . . The ancient, mystical *Samhailt*, the Mindsong, the call of these strange half-Human, half-Beast creatures to their people. I only understand a very little about it, thought Snizort. But I understand enough, I think, to write about it. I believe I understand enough to know that they are all very fearful indeed of it. Had the Oak Naiad guessed this? Yes, of course he had. But he had subtly made it impossible for them actually to refuse; he had simply appeared to assume that the Ritual would be taking place quite soon and had, perfectly reasonably, suggested the Purple Hour for its intoning. Clever, thought Snizort, glancing to where the Tree Spirits had gathered, watching. Clever and subtle and showing – what's the word they would have used on Earth? – statesmanship, yes, that's it.

And although it was a little unfair and certainly ungrateful to have put into definite thoughts the suspicion that Tealtaoich and the rest were perhaps just a little bit weak, Snizort found that he was thinking it. Hadn't the Earth-people found, at some time in their history, that ancient aristocratic lines could eventually become a bit ineffectual? I wonder if that's happened here? thought Snizort. I wonder if there's been just a bit too much reliance on this inter-marrying and in preserving this ancient royal beastblood they seem to set so much store by, and if it's let them down a bit now? But then he remembered Nuadu Airgetlam, who was certainly not weak and clearly not ineffectual. Still, he is bastard stock, thought Snizort. Dear me, this is all completely and utterly absorbing. I hope I can do justice to it. They'll certainly want a proper record of it all.

The Beastline people were standing at the centre of the clearing and Snizort thought them a strange and impressive sight.

The Panthers and White Swans and Bears and Deer

and Foxes and Eagles . . . The Six Royal Houses of Ireland, in the heart of the ancient enchanted Wolfwood, silhouetted against the Tree Spirits, the naiads and dryads and hamadryads, outlined against the darkening forest . . .

Tealtaoich stood a little to the fore, with the others making a half circle just behind him. Snizort and Miach moved quietly to the clearing's edge and stood motionless in the shadows that had crept in from the forest.

'For,' said Miach, very softly, 'I believe it is a very difficult thing to do, this Summoning. They will need every shred of concentration. We dare not distract them in any way.' He looked suddenly very serious and very concerned.

'What will they actually do?' asked Snizort, hoping this was not an impolite question.

'I don't know,' said Miach, his eyes on the Beastline. 'I think it's something that's—'

'Instinctive?'

'I was going to say inbred,' said Miach. 'But instinctive describes it just as well. It's something from within. Perhaps they simply – open their minds and call, or perhaps they just concentrate on the animals. It's the – *un*Human part of them. I've only got the tiniest trickle of Beastblood myself, you see. I wouldn't know.'

He narrowed his eyes as the Beastline fell into silence and Snizort saw that Miach had for the moment forgotten about making a good impression on people and reminding them about being a sorcerer. I believe he cares very much about all this, thought Snizort and discovered that he, also, cared very much.

Light slanted through the Wolfwood, purple and blue, falling about the Beastline like a thin veil. Snizort thought that each of them were becoming subtly more akin to the Beasts now; it was more marked with every minute, difficult to pinpoint precisely, but there, in the feline grace of Tealtaoich and the massive strength of Clumhach, and in the sharp light in Eogan's eyes.

Their ancestors lay with the beasts of the forest to cheat the old, old curse and they have in their veins the blood of those creatures . . .

Their eyes were half closed now and a great stillness had fallen upon them. Within the Wolfwood there was a sudden stirring, a deep and primitive feeling of something incalculably ancient, something that had been old when Man was learning to walk upright; something that had, for countless centuries, lived just below the surface of civilisation, something that was not, itself, civilised in the least . . .

The stirring of the beasts answering an enchantment which had been forged in Ireland's magical dawn by the first sorcerers for the long-ago High Kings and Queens.

The *Samhailt* . . . The strong, light-filled power of one mind over another . . .

Snizort and Miach both felt it at once; a dark, sensuous lure, a throbbing beckoning that you could no more help resisting than you could breathing. Snizort thought: it is working! They are succeeding! At any minute, at any second, we shall surely see the creatures come sweeping through the forest . . . panthers and bears and deer and fox . . . We shall hear the beating of wings on the night sky as the swans and the eagles obey . . . How remarkable and magical, thought Snizort.

And then, without warning, between one heartbeat and the next, the feeling faltered. It hesitated and wavered and, in that instant, the lure weakened its hold.

The light which had started to shine from the Beastline dimmed and the Wolfwood sank into its deep purple night. The watchers were sharply and dreadfully aware that the strange, mystical force which had lifted its head for a moment and listened, had turned back to its dark, deep sleep.

The Enchantment of the Beastline, spun at the beginning of Tara's history, was beyond their reach . . .

Chapter Thirty

Floy was trying to be sensible about Fenella. He was remembering that she was not entirely on her own; she was with Caspar and Caspar would certainly have brought her out of Tara by now. They might already have reached the Fire Court and be there, waiting. This was a heartening thought, and Floy would hold on to it. He would remember that Fenella was brave and sensible and intelligent, that she had never, so far as he could remember, shirked anything. In fact, she was so far from shirking things that she sometimes went out to meet them of her own volition. Floy knew she would not be daunted by anything here. She had been fascinated and intrigued by the Forest Court and by the magic and the ancient enchantments – and she had certainly been fascinated by Nuadu Airgetlam.

Nuadu Airgetlam . . .

If Nuadu hurt Fenella, if he deliberately set to work that subtle, ironic charm and hurt her, Floy would kill him. Fenella was not weak, she was strong and perceptive and intelligent, but she would have no defences against Nuadu's charm, because he was not like anyone she had ever encountered. Floy smiled rather ruefully at this, because Nuadu was not like anyone Floy had ever encountered either. But Floy had seen, as Fenella might not see, that Nuadu's gentle malice was filled with dangerous allure.

The exiled Court had looked to Nuadu as their leader, had unquestioningly accepted him as the one who would regain Tara for the Wolfkings. The dark charm working again, had that been? And also, thought Floy, also, Nuadu is a son of one of the ancient, Royal Houses of Ireland. The words themselves were brimful of a beckoning romance and Fenella, for all her intelligence and perception, had a strong vein of idealism. If Nuadu beckoned, Fenella might well fall into his arms.

Floy was still unsure about Nuadu and he was very unsure indeed whether Nuadu was simply using them all as a means to get Tara's Throne. And, although they were all still grappling with this business of thrones and exiled kings and palaces, Floy had seen enough of Tara to fall a little under its spell himself. Even with the brutish Gruagach inhabiting it, it had been the most beautiful place Floy had ever dreamt could exist. He found he had to quell a traitorous thought that whispered that Nuadu could not be blamed so very much if he was intriguing to get Tara. If Tara had been within Floy's reach, Floy thought he might have been tempted to intrigue a bit himself.

They had both rested while it was dark and, when the first light was streaking the skies over to the east, they found a stream where they drank some water and washed a bit sketchily.

'To freshen us,' said Snodgrass.

There were Trees with apples growing and they had looked at them for a moment. 'But I should think,' said Floy, 'that it's all right to take fruit from the Trees. It's a *natural* thing, isn't it?'

Nothing happened when they reached up to pluck the apples, which turned out to be crisp and ripe and much juicier than the ones they remembered from Renascia. Then Snodgrass discovered a few blackberry bushes and picked some blackberries to go with the apples.

'They'd be better if we could just simmer them over a fire,' he said, rather regretfully. 'With a drop of my blackberry wine.'

'We haven't the means of making a fire and, if we had, there aren't any cooking pots,' Floy pointed out.

Snodgrass said it was to be hoped that the journey would not be a long one, because they were going to get extremely hungry if all they could find to eat were a few apples and a handful of blackberries.

390

'We shan't get hungry,' said Floy. 'We'll be at the Fire Court by noon. And from all accounts it's a pretty hospitable sort of place.' He grinned at Snodgrass. 'They'll wine and dine us royally.'

'Well, I hope so.'

They set off straight away, taking the narrow, winding mountain path, intrigued and interested in the great violet and blue mountains ahead of them.

'But we don't go very far into the mountains,' said Snodgrass, who was consulting the map at intervals. 'It's only a very little way.' He looked up at the glistening peaks with the thin, beautiful morning light pouring over them. 'They're awesome things,' he said, frowning over his spectacles. 'It's as well not to get lost in mountains, you know. You don't know what might be prowling about.'

'We shan't get lost,' said Floy. 'We'll follow the map. And there's only the one road to take and Gruagach isn't so far along.'

'Well, so long as we're careful not to actually go into the City of Gruagach,' said Snodgrass. 'I didn't like the sound of that creature – what did they call it? – the Frost Giantess – did you?'

'We'll be sure to avoid Gruagach,' promised Floy, who had not liked the sound of the Frost Giantess any more than had Snodgrass.

As they walked cautiously along the narrow mountain road, which wound upwards away from the rather friendly, forest-fringed road, the air became colder and the light began to change subtly.

'It's bluer,' said Floy, who thought it was attractive. 'Sharper.'

'It's certainly colder,' said Snodgrass, fastening the flaps of the rather odd-shaped hat he had worn. 'It's not a very friendly feeling, is it?'

They walked steadily on and, as they neared the great ice-blue Mountains of the Morning, Floy began to feel farther from the world he had known than at any time since they had left the doomed Renascia. He thought it was just the desolate road they were travelling, or perhaps it was the persisting worry for Fenella, or maybe it was simply that he had never visualised a world quite like this one. It was beautiful and eerie and sinister and filled with unexpected creatures. I think I'm liking it though, he thought cautiously. I think we can make a home here. After all this is over, I think the four of us can live here and work here and find friends. He paused to wonder what kind of work they might do and then dismissed this, because they could only cope with one thing at a time and the thing to cope with now was delivering Inchbad's proposal to the Fire Court and then finding Fenella and Snizort.

The mountain road, washed with the aqua tints of the morning, was the most desolate place either of them had ever imagined. They walked on, the sun rising somewhere behind them, indicating that they were nearing the middle of the day. But there was no warmth from it up here and the higher they went the colder it became.

Twice they stopped to rest. Snodgrass said that the people of this world would probably have made what was called a *camp*; building a small fire and cooking over it.

'We could eat some of the berries,' said Floy, but he looked at the sparse fruit growing there and was doubtful. They had no way of telling if this fruit was edible and it would be better to go hungry for a few hours than risk poisoning themselves.

They consulted the map at intervals and Snodgrass thought they ought to be nearing the City of Gruagach quite soon.

'We'll only *skirt* it,' he said. 'We don't want to actually go through it. I think we can avoid that. It looks as if there's a road that goes round it instead of through it.' He proffered the map for Floy's inspection. 'And once we've passed Gruagach – because it doesn't look very big – once we're past there, we'll be in sight of the Fire Court.'

The mountain road wound even higher and there were drifting wisps of white cloud almost within their reach now. The ground was hard beneath their feet and there were no longer the sparse bushes, or the occasional, rather beautiful, scarlet-berried trees which they did not recognise. The Mountains of the Morning were harsh and barren and there was a sharp iciness in the wind which scurried in and out of the crevasses. When Floy stopped to point out how the road widened a little way on, his breath formed clouds of vapour.

As the sun began to sink low in the sky, the cold air became tinged with darker blue and they both glanced uneasily at one another. They had been here long enough to understand that twilight, what these people called the Purple Hour, was the time when sinister forces prowled.

'I think,' said Floy, 'that we must go a little faster.' He did not say that they had been walking all day and that they were beginning to be extremely tired as well as hungry, because it would not have served any purpose. He remembered that Snodgrass was no longer a young man and that he had been used to a gentle, rather academic existence, and he knew a swift gratitude to him because he had not once complained, or wanted to rest, or bewailed their lack of food. But he must be extremely weary, thought Floy, who was extremely weary himself. If they could have rested and eaten, or even taken a hot drink of something, it would have put fresh heart into them. But to be up here on this cold, desolate mountain path by night would be a truly dreadful thing. They must go on.

'It isn't so very dark yet,' said Snodgrass, valiantly. 'We can see where we are going perfectly well.'

'Yes. I think we shall reach the Fire Court well before night falls properly,' said Floy, and wondered whether they were both simply encouraging one another, or whether they both believed this. The giants had explained that the journey to the Fire Court would not take an entire day – but that had been when they were using the horses. On foot it would take much longer.

But a little further along, with the mountain path winding suddenly and steeply downwards, Floy stopped and said, 'Look.'

'I can't see anything,' said Snodgrass. 'Is it—' And

stopped as well, because directly ahead of them, beyond the last curve of the mountain road, unmistakable and forbidding, were the outlines of great rearing buildings and huge grim castles and towers and turrets.

Gruagach. The ruined City of the Giants.

Floy said, 'And the road goes straight through it. We can't avoid it.'

They walked cautiously through the outskirts of the ruined City of Gruagach . . .

'I don't *think*,' said Floy wearily, 'that we need to worry. If there's anything here, it probably won't even see us.'

'No.'

'But it would be as well to be very careful.'

It was as well to be very careful indeed. Neither of them cared very much for the bleak, desolate city, with the crumbling walls and the abandoned buildings, and the cold, dry wind that sang in and out of the ruins. Both of them knew, one layer beneath consciousness, that Gruagach was not entirely deserted and both of them had the feeling that they were being watched from the ravaged buildings and from the piles of rubble and the tumbledown houses that lined the streets. Both remembered, although neither mentioned it, that the grim-named Frost Giantess, the creature the giants had referred to as the *Geimhreadh*, would be somewhere close by.

But despite the feeling of lurking danger, despite the strong impression that dozens of eyes were peering out at them, Floy found himself thinking not of Gruagach and the *Geimhreadh*, nor of the dangers that might lie ahead of them, but of Renascia. Renascia, lost now for ever, had looked a little like this towards the end. Cold and barren and deserted. And swept by a terrible, keening wind.

The roads were filled with great craters, and at every corner they came to were great heaps of debris. All about them were half collapsed buildings, gaping windows, doors hanging on rotting hinges. Mould grew on rooftops and the stones were covered in bright green lichen. There were frostings of white everywhere, and everywhere was dust and decay. Weeds had forced their way up through the cobbles of the road and it difficult to walk without stumbling.

'It's so cold,' said Snodgrass, shivering and pulling on his hat with the earflaps. 'I've never been anywhere so cold.'

There was a whiteness to the air. 'Snow,' said Snodgrass. 'My word, now *there's* a thing I never expected to see! Frozen rain, that's all it is, of course. And traditional for quite a lot of Earth feasts, if my memory serves me. We seem to be walking into it rather than out of it. Shouldn't we have left it behind in the Mountains?'

'I suppose we're quite far north,' said Floy. 'That might have something to do with it.' He turned up the collar of his cloak against the biting wind and narrowed his eyes, trying to gauge how large the giants' city was.

They moved warily in between the desolate buildings, here and there having to pick their way amidst the fallen rubble.

'I didn't much care for the giants,' said Snodgrass, who had not cared for them at all, 'but I have to say it must have been rather sad for them to see their city fall like this. What do you think happened, Floy? They were rather chary of saying much, weren't they?'

'I think,' said Floy cautiously, 'that they were made use of.'

'By the Dark Ireland?' Snodgrass had lowered his voice instinctively.

'Yes.'

'I'd have questioned all that,' said Snodgrass, thoughtfully. 'In the ordinary way, I'd have questioned it, you know. Necromancers and enchantments and another Ireland, an Ireland that's the dark reflection of the true one.' He peered up at Floy earnestly.

'But we saw the Robemaker and we saw what he did to Nuadu,' said Floy, understanding.

'Yes.'

'I think the Robemaker and the other one – CuRoi –

ousted the giants from Gruagach and put them into Tara as a – a foothold,' said Floy. 'A stepping stone. I think they mean to take all of Ireland. And, as the first step, they've got rid of the rightful King.'

'Yes. I daresay it's been done like that before,' said Snodgrass, thoughtfully. And then, 'I suppose we're sure that it *was* the rightful King they got rid of, are we?'

'It sounded all right,' said Floy, who had been asking himself this at intervals. 'And it *felt* all right.' He glanced at Snodgrass. 'I think Nuadu and the rest *are* the right side.' He frowned. 'And I don't see how we could have remained neutral.'

'I don't think we wanted to remain neutral,' said Snodgrass. 'If we are to live here – and there doesn't seem to be any alternative – then we have to become involved. You can't live in a country – or in a world – without embracing its causes and its struggles. At least, not unless you intend to live like a hermit.'

'What's a hermit?' asked Floy, momentarily diverted from their surroundings.

'Somebody who goes off to live by himself and never has anything to do with the rest of the world,' said Snodgrass. 'People occasionally did that on Earth. Mind you, when you think about some of the peculiar ages that Earth lived through it isn't surprising. I'd have wanted to do it myself at times.'

'Yes, and—' Floy stopped and turned sharply. From somewhere to their left, from the huddle of empty buildings, white-rimed now with the stinging icy rain, came a light, brittle sound of voices, as fragile as icicles tapping against window panes . . .

Come closer, Human Wayfarers, come farther in to the Icy City where you will find warmth and succour . . .

Floy and Snodgrass stood still, peering into the growing dimness, but there was nothing to be seen.

Floy said, in rather an uncertain voice, 'You did hear it, did you?'

'I heard something,' said Snodgrass. 'But I couldn't say what it was, you know. Not to swear to, that is.'

'Listen,' said Floy, his head tilted to catch the sound, but now there was nothing, other than the stirring of the wind and the flurries of icy rain in their faces.

They moved on, every now and then glancing over their shoulders. Once Floy thought he heard the faint, rather sinister sound of laughter and, at the intersection of two streets, where the cobbles were icy and treacherous, Snodgrass said he had caught the glimpse of a vanishing shape in between the ruins.

'Something thin and whitish,' he said apologetically. 'Beckoning fingers and a sort of swirling mist. I couldn't see any more than that.'

Here and there they caught the frenzied scufflings of rats and several times they saw tiny red eyes peering at them from the dark buildings. Floy, who was still listening for the brittle voices they had heard earlier, thought: I suppose they *are* only rats, and quenched the thought before it could take any stronger form.

'It's very quiet,' said Snodgrass at length. 'Normally you'd think it was deserted, seeing it like this.'

'Only we know it isn't deserted,' said Floy. 'We know that the Frost Giantess is here somewhere.' And thought that, even without the laughter and the strange, half-formed voices, they would have known that Gruagach was not deserted. There was an impression, a sensation, an extra instinct at work that heightened their awareness, so that they felt, at every corner, at every curve in the road, as if eyes watched them and unseen creatures flitted out of sight just as they turned to look.

Snodgrass suggested that they had only imagined the voices earlier on, but he said this in the slightly too emphatic voice of one trying to convince himself.

'Let's just keep walking,' said Floy. 'As if we aren't at all worried by any of it. Do you feel that the wind's growing colder?'

The icy wind was growing colder and it was growing stronger. As they walked on it began to feel as if it was cutting through their clothes to their very bones. 'We can't be so very far from the Fire Court,' said Floy, lifting his voice above the howling wind. 'Can you see it, yet? I'm sure Caspar said it had been modelled on Tara to a large extent and that it shone over the surrounding countryside. There'd be lights and perhaps spires or turrets.'

They both stood still and looked about them in all directions, but there was nothing but the black shapes of the giants' dwellings and the whiteness of the icy rain against the darkening sky.

Floy, who was bitterly cold, said, 'I think we ought to try to find some kind of shelter for a while.' He turned to catch Snodgrass's reply and, as he did so, the evil laughter rang out again.

Shelter, Human Wayfarers, oh yes, there is shelter here for those who wish it . . . There is warmth and food and fires, and there is a welcome for you . . .

'It's only the wind,' said Snodgrass a bit too loudly. 'The wind whipping through that empty house there.'

'It's more than that,' said Floy. 'There's something here – perhaps several somethings. I wish we could see them.' He peered about them, but there were more flurries of whiteness within the wind now and an ice-cold stinging rain was beginning to swirl all around so it was difficult to see anything. The wind tore down, making them gasp for breath, and Snodgrass had to take off his spectacles because it was impossible to see through them any longer.

The snow was driving relentlessly into their faces and the ground underfoot was icy and dangerous. Floy and Snodgrass, neither of whom had ever seen snow, both thought it would have been interesting and rather beautiful if they could have admired it from inside a warm room, with fires burning, and steaming drinks, and perhaps tureens of hot soup . . .

Then come to us, Human Wayfarers, come to us, and see our banqueting hall . . . let us welcome you and succour you and let us warm your poor, icy bodies . . .

Floy said, very loudly, 'What are you?' and at once there was a shriek of tinkling, ice-tapping-on-glass laughter.

We are the Wraiths, Human Wayfarers . . . we are the

Spirits of the Frozen North, and of the Snowbound Ice Mountains. Where warmth is we cannot exist, but once the heat has been drawn from the land, then we live, and then we flourish. We are storm creatures and blizzard spirits . . . we are glaciers and ice caps and we are frozen seas and icy wastes . . .

'But what are you?' cried Floy, standing with his feet planted apart, the wind whipping at his cloak and tumbling his hair. 'Tell us what you are!'

The cold, silvery laughter echoed all about them again, part of the raging wind and yet not quite part of it. It was very nearly impossible to tell if the voices came from within the howling storm, or from outside of it, or even, thought Floy, lifting one hand to shield his face from the biting cold, or even if the voices were there at all.

Oh yes we are, Human Wayfarers, oh yes we are . . .

'Then tell us who you are!' cried Floy with sudden impatience. 'Or are you so ill favoured that you must hide away like monsters!'

There was a sudden lull in the blizzard and Floy and Snodgrass both thought it was dying. They both peered into the blinding whiteness of the storm, trying to make out the road, trying to gauge how far into the city they were.

Without warning, the storm raged again, whipping their cloaks, snatching at their hair. Great torrents of icy rain slashed down from the skies, blinding them with its intensity. Snodgrass gasped and fell backwards and, at once, the cold laughter intensified. Floy, his eyes streaming with the fierce cold, his skin feeling as if dozens of razors were slicing at it, saw, deep in the raging blizzard, grinning faces, icicle-nosed features . . . clutching, reaching hands with grasping, bony fingers . . . with frosted eyes and hair that was made of the snow and the ice and the freezing, cutting wind . . .

The voices came again, closer this time, clearer.

We are the Children of the Geimhreadh, Human Wayfarers . . . We serve the Geimhreadh and our names are many . . .

'Tell us your names!' shouted Floy, trying not to flinch

from the driving blizzard, trying to see more clearly into the heart of the storm.

We are many, Human . . . Storm we are and Sough . . . Sigh we are and Wail . . . Tempest and Blizzard and Winter-night . . . moaning wind and keening rain . . .

Icy fingers snaked about Floy's cloak and drew him, struggling, into the heart of the blizzard. Snodgrass moved forward at once, but a dozen pairs of cold, bony fingers came darting from out of the whirling snow and held them both in a tight cruel grip.

We lie in wait for Wayfarers and we lie in wait for HUMANS . . . Those that the Mistress discards, we fall upon . . . We may fall upon YOU, Human Travellers . . .

'Begone!' cried Floy, trying to fight free of the cold, bony hands, feeling them bite deep into his wrists and legs.

Let us stroke your pale Human skin with our icy fingers . . . Let us kiss you with our cold lips and eat away your flesh in the embrace called frost-bite . . . The grinning, white, ice-dripping faces loomed nearer suddenly.

Come with us, Human Wayfarers, to the Castle of the giantish ones . . . Come into the ice-fires of our magic . . .

The cold laughter rang out again and Floy, struggling, half blinded by the fierce wind, his lungs raw from the icy blizzard, found himself drawn forward into its heart by the icy-cold hands of the storm creatures.

He thought that they bound him with wet, cold ropes which seemed to be made of coarse, rough hair that cut cruelly into his wrists and ankles. A grey mist swam before his vision and there was a sudden terrifying silence all about him, so that he thought the creatures had in some way blinded him and rendered him deaf . . .

And then the cold, cruel mirth assaulted his senses again.

We do not cover your eyes, Human One . . . said the voices. *It is only our cloaks of hoar frost that obscure your vision, and it is only the keening of our blizzard songs that stop your hearing . . . Your senses are safe for the moment, Human Traveller . . . Until we embrace you, and THEN, Human*

Traveller, you will feel your flesh shrivel and you will see it decompose before your eyes ... you will hear yourself screaming with the pain of the ice-burn ... You will cry with the agony of the marrow freezing inside your bones ... The blood will congeal in your veins and you will die slowly and you will be forever ours ...

'Where are you taking us?' said Floy, gasping and trying to see through the blinding mist, but able only to make out thin, bony hands and pale, thin faces with frozen icicles on them.

To our Mistress, Human One ... And then, with another eldritch shriek of laughter, *To the centre of Gruagach and the Lair of the Geimhreadh.*

Chapter Thirty-one

The Lair of the *Geimhreadh* . . .

Floy and Snodgrass could see, through the howling snowstorm, the great rearing outline of the castle above them. Ruined and crumbling, thought Floy. And then: or is it? Because lights showed at the narrow slitlike windows; torches burned in wall brackets on each side of the massive, iron-studded doors.

The ice creatures half carried, half dragged their two victims across the immense drawbridge (And who lowered that? wondered Floy) and beneath the great black arch. Ahead of them was a courtyard, with windows overlooking it on all sides. As they passed into the shadow cast by the bulk of the giants' castle, Floy felt cold fear close about his heart.

The storm creatures scuttled and slithered as they went and occasionally took flying leaps through the air, so that they might almost have flown. They chuckled evilly as they went and pinched their prisoners with their cold, dripping wet fingers. Floy saw Snodgrass struggle and try to hit out, but the grey mist things simply laughed and melted out of reach and then formed again.

They passed through empty, echoing galleries and through huge, pointed doorways and down flights of stone steps.

'Where is this?' cried Floy. 'Where are you taking us?'

To our Mistress . . . to the Geimhreadh . . .

The white fingers came out again, prodding, poking, pinching. Floy saw the leering snow-frosted faces grinning and tried to see, in the dimness, if the creatures were male or female.

Neither, Human prisoner, we are both male and female and we can pleasure you in the ways of women with men, or of men

402

with women ... Malevolent mirth trickled from the inward-slanting eyes. Or of men with men, or women with women... It is all one to us, Humans ... Greed licked into the voices. We can freeze your marrow and we can congeal your blood and eat at your flesh with the stinging agony of frostbite ...

The sharp, grinning features thrust forward into the prisoners' faces and clawlike fingers, icy cold, pinched their skin.

Our Mistress will like you, Humans ... she will enfold you with her cold arms and pillow your head on her ice-cold breasts and she will empty you of every drop of Human blood and Human seed and Human marrow ...

'Let her try it!' said Floy. 'We shall kill her if she tries to harm us!'

The Geimhreadh is invincible, Humans ... She is beyond the harm of your puny swords and your ineffectual daggers and your flailing Human strength ...

The ice creatures half carried, half dragged the two prisoners down winding flights of narrow, worn stairs that went down and down until it seemed to Floy and Snodgrass that they were descending into the very bowels of this grim fortress. The steps were surrounded by ancient, crumbling brick; moss-covered here and there from the clammy dampness, in places sprouting horrid fungoid growths. There was a smell of dank wetness and the sound, somewhere close by, of water steadily dripping.

'Where is this!' demanded Floy, and there was a brittle cascade of laughter.

It is where we bring our victims, Human creature ... It is where we crouch in the cold darkness, gnawing at the bones of those whom the Mistress has discarded ... The grinning faces darted closer.

After we have torn away your skin with our claws and eaten away your flesh with the agonies of frost-bite, we shall wind our long, dripping fingers about your thin Human bones ... We shall freeze the bone-juices as they trickle out and then we shall crack open your frail, puny bones, and gnaw on them ...

They stood outside a great, carved door with huge

black hinges and a massive ring handle carved into the shape of a grinning gargoyle face. As Floy and Snodgrass half fell to their knees, the storm creatures darted forward, their hands eager to unlock the catch, their white-rimmed eyes grinning.

An eerie, bluish light emanated from within the room and, as the door swung open at the hands of the storm creatures, they both gasped and reeled from the blast of intensely cold air.

To begin with, Floy and Snodgrass thought the chamber was empty. A cold, bluish light filled it and a thin, evil-smelling vapour hung on the air, so that the shape of the room and the things in it were hazy.

And then, gradually, their eyes became accustomed to the cold light and they saw that it pulsated rather horridly, as if they were at the centre of a giant heart that was beating and pumping thick sluggish blood. Floy found this feeling extremely repellent, but he stood up very straight and managed to ignore the grinning storm creatures who had gathered behind him. And, although his hands were bound tightly behind his back, he made himself stand quite calmly, with what was very nearly a relaxed air. He put up his chin and looked down his nose at the room, as if he found it all faintly boring.

It was lined with the dark stone that they had glimpsed on their journey through the castle; great square blocks of blackness from floor to ceiling. Giants' stones, thought Floy, and put the thought from him at once.

To the left was a great archway and, beyond it, they could see an expanse of dark glistening water, ink-black, its surface frost-rimed. There was a rather slimy look to the water, and a secretive look to it, as if half-fish creatures, cold-blooded webbed-footed beings might lurk beneath its depths, and might come slithering up in the dark and reach out their dripping wet arms. Floy found himself remembering the dark underground River of Souls in Fael-Inis's country, and the dreadful pitiful beings who had lurked in its depths.

The cold mists swirled and moved and, for a moment, the great stone room was partly obscured. And then the mist cleared and they could see.

The *Geimhreadh* . . . the Frost Giantess who battened on her victims and emptied them of seed and blood and marrow . . . The terrible evil ogress who had come out of the Dark Ireland and who must certainly be counted as one of the evil black necromancers.

She is not as massive as the Gruagach giants, but she is far taller than any Human, thought Floy, staring. And then: whatever else she is, he thought, she is certainly not Human.

The *Geimhreadh* was not Human at all. She was seated on a great, glistening throne of ice with a high carved back and long, elaborate arm rests. The chair loomed high above them and the *Geimhreadh*'s terrible head rose above it. Floy and Snodgrass both thought that she must be eleven or twelve feet high and they both stood, transfixed, unable to move, their senses spinning, their skins crawling with horror.

The *Geimhreadh* was the most extraordinary blend of giant and snake and . . . And fish! thought Floy, his skin crawling with horror. For all her towering height, she possessed a narrow saurian body with no neck or shoulders. The head was a continuance of the wormlike body – slightly pointed, snake-shaped, darting . . . it was darker than the rest of the body, with reptilian eyes, hooded and black and unblinking, ancient and cruel. There was a flat, curving mouth, with the permanent, enigmatic smile of all snake creatures. And, as they stood looking, unable to speak, the lips opened slightly and the forked tongue darted and licked the flat scaly lips.

All the better to drain your marrow, my dears . . .

Short, fin-like arms protruded halfway down the narrow body, with rudimentary hands and fingers at the ends and they saw that the creature had some kind of thin pale silk wound about her. For some reason, instead of concealing the serpentine shape, this served to emphasise it. It was rather as if a giant pale-skinned worm had stolen human

405

clothing and dressed up in it and sat on a human chair, waiting for a victim . . .

Swathes of silk hung at her back, but there was a cold, slimy look to the silk and there was the same foul river-weed stench they had been aware of earlier.

The *Geimhreadh* moved, her thin draperies stirring slightly, and they saw that the embryonic hands ended in webbed, star-shaped fingers. Snodgrass, who did not like fish things, shuddered, and Floy put out a warning hand. Whatever they were feeling, whatever they were thinking, they must try not to let this monstrous half-giant, half-snake being see their revulsion. And they certainly must not let it see their fear.

The neckless head poked forward and the hooded eyes examined them.

'You are well come, travellers,' said the *Geimhreadh*, and Floy and Snodgrass heard the throaty, gobbling voice with revulsion. The dark eyes flickered again, as if the creature was inspecting them, assessing them, visualising what it would do to them.

Floy said, 'It seems that we had no choice other than to accept your – hospitality, ma'am,' and the *Geimhreadh* laughed with a dreadful braying sound that made Floy's teeth wince and her monstrous head swayed and darted in a way that made them both remember half-forgotten Earth words like basilisk and serpent and white slug and worm. Worm was particularly nasty. It was a slimy, creeping sort of word, a blind, toothless word . . .

The *Geimhreadh* turned her eyes towards them and said in her soft, bubbling voice, 'I *am* of the worm family, Humans. You read my bloodline correctly. I have many different strains in my blood and I am the result of many strange alliances.' She regarded them unblinkingly and Floy remembered about thoughts being overheard.

The *Geimhreadh*, moving a fin-like hand in the direction of the grinning storm creatures, said, 'My people will tell you that I am descended from a race of fish-creatures and snakes. Of how, many hundreds of years ago, there was an alliance between those houses and that of the giants of the north. I am the daughter of snakes and giants, Human travellers, and the descendant of an ancient and powerful race who dwelled in the wintry wastes of this land long before the Gaels or the Cruithin, and long before the accursed Wolfkings.' The terrible head swayed again. 'Once, Human creatures,' said the *Geimhreadh*, 'this land was sheeted in ice and crusted with snow and once it lived in endless, howling blizzards. It was then that my ancestors reigned here, prowling the petrified forests and crawling on their bellies through the frozen wastes.'

She regarded them, and Floy said, with perfect courtesy, 'That is a strange ancestry.'

The snake-head swivelled. 'Is that discourtesy, Human morsel?'

'Merely a statement of fact, ma'am.' Floy smiled blandly, and the *Geimhreadh* drew her head back and a faint, hissing sound emitted from her jaws.

'Listen, Human morsel,' she said, 'when I made my Lair here, I did so because I knew that deep beneath the Castle of Gruagach ran a branch of the River of Souls.' The lidless eyes flickered to the stone archway, where the dark, sinister River lapped greedily at the banks.

'Deep within the Realm that is sometimes called the Dark Ireland, I have built an ice palace,' said the *Geimhreadh*. 'A place of cold northern winds and dark icy gales, with dark, subterranean rivers where I and my people can live for many years without once seeing light.' She regarded him, the fin-hands quivering, the forked tongue darting. 'But no Humans ventured there,' she said. 'No warm-blooded Human morsels came to my Lair and I became *hungry*.' The worm's head undulated slightly.

'And so, when the one your people call the Robemaker drove out the Gruagach Giants, I made my nest here.' A fin-like hand gestured. 'Here, where the ancient, eternal River of Souls runs deep into the mountains, until it reaches the terrible Prison of Hostages from which no creature ever escapes.' The head swayed again. 'Once I have emptied you of your seed, Human,' said the

Geimhreadh, 'once I have *tasted* your marrow and your blood, I shall throw your dried-out husk of a body to the River.' The flat, scaly lips parted in amusement. 'The Soul Eaters fish the River,' said the *Geimhreadh*. 'It is one of their hunting grounds. Your body is for my pleasure but, afterwards, your soul will be trapped beneath the surface of the River of Souls; it will be caught in the endless ebb and flow of the River, until it is taken by the Soul Eaters.'

'We shall see,' said Floy, and smiled with the same courtesy.

'Are you mocking me, Human?' asked the *Geimhreadh* in a soft voice. 'I do not allow Human creatures to mock me.'

'I do not mock,' said Floy, but his eyes were defiant. 'Will you tell us why we have been brought here?'

'The Storm Wraiths are ever on the watch for victims.' There was a soft, boneless movement from the ice throne and the *Geimhreadh* came towards them. Floy and Snodgrass saw that she had to push herself from the throne with the half-formed webbed hands and that, once upright, she did not walk like a human creature, but half slithered, half dragged herself.

A pale worm, a slithering, crawling, sluglike thing . . . part fish, part snake, part ogress . . . Floy stayed where he was and set a guard over his thoughts, but when she stood directly in front of them, the vermicular head studying them, he could not repress his revulsion. The creature's head was darker than her body but, even through the thin, gauzy wrappings, he could see the pale, writhing body, the thin-ringed skin, here and there covered with the faintly luminous scales that bespoke the fishblood, thick and repulsive.

The *Geimhreadh* laughed, the obsidian head swaying from side to side again. 'You find me ugly, Human,' she said, 'I wonder how you will feel when you are held in my embrace?' A fin-like hand moved and brushed across Floy's thighs and, despite himself, he flinched.

'Strong,' said the *Geimhreadh*, her voice becoming

clotted with pleasure. 'Well fleshed. Well *muscled*.' The hooded eyes narrowed. 'I shall *enjoy* this one.' And then, with a sudden writhing movement, she turned to the waiting storm creatures. 'Tie them down,' said the *Geimhreadh*.

The storm creatures leapt at once and Floy and Snodgrass were both held in an icy vice-like grip.

'The ropes!' cried the *Geimhreadh*. 'Use the ropes!' And then, as Floy felt the ropes binding him again, she said, in a thick, mucus type of voice, 'Made from the pubic hair of my victims, Human. Can you not feel that? Can you not smell the blood and the spent seed?' She writhed nearer again on her squat, waddling feet, the tiny hands flapping. 'And soon you will contribute, Human,' she said. 'Soon you, also, will be drained of seed and blood. What is left will be given to the Storm Wraiths and *then*, Human morsels, then you will be thrown to the River so that the Soul Eaters may take your soul.'

She fixed her slitted lidless eyes on Floy and, the slimy lick of pleasure overlaying her voice again, said, 'Tie this one well, for tonight I feel *hungry* for a Man-Human.'

409

Chapter Thirty-two

Fenella and Nuadu Airgetlam stood on the shores of the dark, lapping lake, with night closing about them, and stared out across the wide expanse of water to the Isle of Cruachan. Mist swirled before them and the black, rearing bulk of the island swam in and out of drifting clouds.

'Cruachan,' said Nuadu softly. 'The Court of the Soul Eaters. Or perhaps it is only the Gate to Hell.' And then, looking down at her, 'Well, my Lady? Are you ready to traverse into Hell and beyond with me? You certainly entered Hell to find me, Fenella. You certainly braved worse than Hell to rescue me.' He was standing very close to her and Fenella could detect, very faintly, the strange, exciting golden wolfscent.

But it would not do to let him see how delight ran all over her when he called her 'my Lady', and how her skin burned at the touch of his hand, so she said, in a rather preoccupied voice, 'How do we get across the lake to the centre?' She saw him smile and make a brief gesture of acceptance, as if he might be saying: well, if you do not wish to discuss what you did for me, then we will not.

He pointed across the lake and Fenella saw that there was a narrow causeway of rock, which would enable them to walk straight across to the black island. 'You see?' he said, and narrowed his eyes for a moment, gauging the distance. In the fading light, his eyes were brilliant and a lock of dark hair had fallen across his brow, making him appear younger, suddenly and disarmingly vulnerable. Cruachan was directly behind him as he looked at Fenella and, for a moment, he was silhouetted against the crimson-streaked sky. He was smiling at her, but there was a reckless light in his eyes. 'Come, Lady,' he said, softly, and took her hand.

The crag was at the exact centre; as they walked cautiously towards it, it reared up before them, a great dark shape against the violent night sky. Fenella stood still and craned her neck to look at it. You had to stand back from it and lean right back to see to the top and, if you did that, you had the feeling that the crag might be toppling forward onto you. It was not difficult to imagine that there were dark worlds within it and that dark, grotesque beings lived inside it, and peered through the chinks and watched them approach, and nodded and said to one another: yes, yes, these two will do very nicely . . . we will snare these two.

Nuadu said, very softly, 'Fenella. Look. Up there.' And pointed with the gleaming silver hand, and Fenella narrowed her eyes, and tried to follow his hand.

And then saw, half-way up the crag, a little to the left, what Nuadu was indicating. A deep fissure, a great wide split in the rock about a third of the way up. A deep, echoing, jagged-edged crack, yawning and gaping . . . There was a narrow-looking ledge just beneath it. Fenella thought it was just about wide enough for someone to stand upright. And it would lead into the rearing crag, and down and down beneath the surface of the lake . . . Into the dark bowels of Cruachan and on to the Gates of Hell.

Nuadu said, 'Ready, Lady?'

'No,' said Fenella, her eyes on the fissure. 'No, not really.'

'But if I lead you will follow?'

'Do I have any choice?'

She saw the sudden whiteness of his teeth as he grinned. 'Of course,' he said. 'You can go back the way we came. You will probably find help somewhere.' He looked at her. 'Well, Fenella?' said the Wolfprince softly and Fenella shivered with pure delight, because his tone held the caress again, the lick of desire, the soft *stroking* note. 'Do you want to turn back, Lady?' said Nuadu, softly.

Fenella returned his look and at last said, 'I don't really think I *can*, do you?' And looked at him, and was delighted all over again, because, of course, they were not simply referring to the Cruachan Caves and it was remarkable and a bit frightening as well to know that, whatever she said, no matter the words she used, he would always hear the meaning behind them.

'There is no going back, Fenella,' said Nuadu, and again the smile slid out. He reached out and traced the outline of her face with the hand that was warm, living flesh. 'There will never be any going back, Lady,' said the Wolfprince softly and turned to begin the climb to the cave entrance.

The ledge was wider than it had looked from the ground. Nuadu reached it with ease pulling Fenella after him. He stood up, looking about him, and there was a look in his eyes now which suggested he was enjoying himself.

Of course I am enjoying it, Lady . . . Wolves prowl in all kinds of dark and dangerous places . . . Or did you not know that?

'Also,' he said, aloud, 'for the first time for – oh, I do not know how long – I am actively serving Ireland.' He turned to look at her and the shadows fell across his face so that the wolf-look was more strongly marked than Fenella had ever seen it. 'I am no longer bored,' said Nuadu. And then, studying her, his head tilted consideringly, 'Have you never experienced boredom, Fenella?' he asked. And Fenella, who had known all about boredom on Renascia, where ladies were not expected to do very much at all, and who had tried to change it, nodded and did not speak. And Nuadu said gently, 'Yes. Of course you have.'

The fissure was directly before them, and as they passed under the overhang of rock into the darkness within, Fenella felt a great smothering heaviness descend. She shivered, and at once Nuadu drew closer, the flesh and blood arm about her, warm and strong and comforting.

Moonlight seeped into the crag, silvering the rock floor

and touching the hard irregular walls. Here and there, alcoves had been cut into the tunnel's side: man-shaped and man-height. Iron stakes were embedded into the alcoves, with thick, black chains. It was impossible not to conjure up vivid image of prisoners caught and held and manacled, left to rot in the dark . . .

From somewhere came a distant sound of water dripping, echoing coldly and rather desolately, and there was the faint, foul stench of ancient evil. It was as if something loathsome had died and lain rotting in a pool of putrescence for a very long time. Fenella hoped she would not be sick.

From time to time darting shadows flickered on the tunnel walls and the rock ceiling, black and sinister, moving and then vanishing. Fenella began to have the impression that they were being watched and followed and that, at each twist in the tunnel, evil peering things waited and watched and then whisked quickly out of sight, to be replaced, further along, by others.

But the shadows never quite materialised and although they could hear the scurrying of clawed feet quite plainly now, and the rather horrid sound of thin, boneless tails slithering across the rock floor, and although several times they whipped round quickly to confront something behind them, they did not actually see anything.

'But,' said Nuadu, very softly, 'we are certainly being watched and certainly reports of some kind are being carried ahead of us.'

'To the Soul Eaters?'

'Probably,' said Nuadu. 'For the Soul Eaters are served by strange peoples.' His arm tightened about her. 'Afraid, Lady?' he said, and, as she sought for the right words, 'Of course you are afraid. But you are refusing to admit it.'

'I'm pretending,' said Fenella in a very low voice. 'I'm pretending that I'm not afraid, because if I pretend hard enough—'

'You may even discover it to be the truth. Of course.' He looked down at her. 'You are the most courageous lady I shall ever know,' he said. Then, without warning, he

413

turned, his head tilted in the listening pose, and said sharply, 'Fenella, is that light ahead?'

Fenella peered into the shadows, which were still thick and clotted and rather horrid. It was very easy to look at them and imagine that grotesque beings were standing behind you, silent and waiting; it was very easy to visualise all manner of creeping, lurking evils.

But she said, firmly, 'Yes, I believe it is light. A bit to the left. Reddish and dull-looking. And there's a stone archway – what would it be?'

'I have no idea,' said Nuadu, and stopped and looked down at her again, his eyes serious and intent. 'I am frequently ironic and nearly always cynical, Lady,' he said. 'But if I can keep you from danger, I vow to you now that I will do so.'

Fenella stared at him, her mind tumbling. In the strange reddish light from beyond the archway, he was smiling the wolfsmile, exciting and mischievous and intimate, and Fenella sought for something to say.

And then the shadows leapt and pranced wildly and into the narrow tunnel came swarming nightmarish beings, lean feral creatures neither quite human nor beast, but a dreadful lumpish blending of rat and weasel and stoat... Scores of them, thought Fenella, shrinking back, appalled and frightened.

At her side, Nuadu said very softly, 'The Rodent Armies of the Dark Realm—' And reached at once for Fenella, pulling her to him. The creatures had surrounded them easily and swiftly, almost before there was time to think; their mean red eyes glinted evilly from the shadowy tunnels and their saliva-drenched teeth grinned in their fur-covered faces. Fenella, knocked back against the tunnel wall by the sudden onslaught, received the tumbled impression of pointed hungry muzzles and thin sinuous fur-covered bodies and sly vicious faces with whiskers and snouts.

The creatures pinioned the two intruders' wrists at once, holding them in tight cruel grips. Fenella gasped and tried to pull away from the grinning slavering faces,

414

but they were all about her, holding her firmly and dragging her forward to the red-lit Cavern. The stench of them closed about her in a smothering, fetid blanket, so that for a few nightmare moments she could barely breathe.

To her left, Nuadu was snarling and lashing out, and for a moment Fenella thought he would overpower their assailants. He was being held by four of the creatures, but he was still fighting, he was resisting their attempts to pull him into the Cavern and in the uncertain light his eyes showed red. For a second, Fenella saw the planes of his face shift and blur, until it was no longer a Human face, it was a wolfmask, lean and hungry and snarling ... He will not give in to them, she thought. Whatever they are, he will fight them every inch of the way. We are here to find the Soul Eaters and to enter the Cruachan Cavern but he will not enter it as a captive.

As if he had caught this, Nuadu sent her a sudden grin, and seemed to shrug, and to say: after all, what does it matter? and allowed the rodent creatures to drag him forward.

Into the Court of the Soul Eaters.

The ancient and terrible Cavern of the Cruachan Soul Eaters was lit to sinister life by flaring wall torches that gave out a thick, menacing glow, and cast dark evil shadows in the corners.

To Fenella's horrified eyes, it seemed at first to be filled with the evil red-eyed creatures who had captured them. They were ranged along the walls, each one bearing a thin cruel spear with a gleaming spike at the top. Fenella caught the warm feral stench of rat and stoat and weasel, and overlying it all, a nauseating, stomach-churning miasma of putrefaction and decay and old rotting flesh.

They were both flung forward onto the hard rock floor and their captors stood over them, spears poised to lunge. Fenella, gasping for breath, caught the whisper of a thought from Nuadu: *at least they have not bound us, Lady ... At least we are unfettered* ... He leapt upwards in a single

415

angry bound and stood challengingly on his feet glaring, as if he might be saying: how *dare* you treat me in this manner!

A great circular table, hewn from the solid rock of the cave, and worn smooth by the usage of centuries, stood at the cavern centre and Fenella, staring at the smooth-as-silk stone, felt all of the old Earth legends ebb and flow in her mind . . . Sacrificial altars and stone tables and tabernacles and oratories . . . There were sinister dark stains on the table's surface – don't think about them, said Fenella silently, and managed to stand alongside Nuadu, looking about her with a fair assumption of bravery.

The legendary Cruachan Cavern was high-ceilinged and vast. Etched into the rock walls were carvings, elaborate cave-pictures, and there was the gleam of silver from the great stone table. Fenella saw that it was set with chalices and platters and remembered that the Soul Eaters were said to hold a nightly banquet and to feast on the Souls brought to them by their dark servants. Behind the table were Thrones, each one on a small, raised platform, and behind each platform was a heavy swathe of black velvet, marked with symbols of some kind. Fenella noticed briefly that each symbol was different, as if each Soul Eater might be descended from a different lineage, although it was difficult to think what lineage such creatures might claim.

And on each of the Thrones sat the Soul Eaters themselves . . .

They were not identical. Fenella and Nuadu saw this at once. There were differences, individual characteristics. Somehow this was the most sinister thing about them, because it suggested that each one would possess its own warped personality, it would have its own peculiar traits and desires and greeds.

Each Soul Eater sat watchfully on its carved throne, its massive wings folded across its breast like a cloak, partly obscuring the rest of its body. Their bodies were not so very large; perhaps no more than man-size, but it was easy to see that their wing-spans would be many times wider than a man's outstretched arms. Nuadu, remembering the single one he had seen in the Robemaker's Workshops, guessed that the wing-spans would be easily fifteen feet in width. The creatures were covered in something that was not quite skin and not quite leathery scale, but something between the two. Something dark and tough, something that made you think of words like crust and hulk and hide.

Their heads were bony, long narrow skulls with slanting, baleful eyes. There was a flat, slashlike mouth and a rather horrid insect-like formation in the way the central bone – in a human it would have been the nose-bone – joined to the mouth. Several of them had horned heads, but in a few the horns were stumplike protuberances high up on the bony skulls.

They were wizened and shrunken and shrivelled and it was possible to see that their legs were gristly and jointed, with reptilian feet, ending in three clawlike toes. They were sapless and juiceless and mummified and Fenella thought she had never seen anything so repulsive.

There were twelve of them. Of course there are twelve, thought Fenella, there are always twelve. And I believe that each one has twelve soldiers, she thought suddenly; each one has a guard of twelve of the rat-creatures who brought us here.

Nuadu, regarding the occupants of the Cavern with his head tilted arrogantly and his eyes glinting dangerously, had known the rat-creatures for what they were at once. He looked at them now, and thought: Rodent People! Vermin! The Rodent Armies of the Dark Lords! The warped greedy mutant creatures bred from rats and weasels and stoats, created by a jealous necromancer during the reign of Niall of the Nine Hostages. He saw, as Fenella had seen, that each of the twelve Soul Eaters had a guard of twelve Rodent creatures.

One hundred and forty-four Rat-creatures here with them in the great torchlit cavern with the merciless Soul-Eaters . . .

They stood as if to attention and, as the flaring torchlight fell across them, Fenella saw that although they

417

were certainly partly Human, they were not Human in the way that the Bloodline People in the Wolfwood had been partly Human. Tealtaoich and Eogan and the others had been half-Beast and half-Human, and it had been a rather attractive blend. There had been Human features with a feline slant, or with aquiline features, and with fur and flesh and tail and paws gently and mischievously mingled.

The Rodent People of the Cruachan Court were a nightmarish mixture of fur-clawed viciousness and sly, creeping Human. They were made up of lithe bodies and harsh, bristly fur. Their features were a dreadful blend of Human and vermin; in several cases they had both ordinary, rather sly, Human eyes and slitted red rodent eyes as well, just beneath. Here and there were fleshy Human lips, but beneath the lips were rows of vicious, pointed teeth. The Weasels were particularly horrid; they had Human features which had been somehow distorted into snoutlike leers and their eyes were heavily lidded and lashed.

Fenella thought that here, for the first time since she had penetrated into the Robemaker's terrible Workshops and seen the treadmills, was the real darkness that threatened Ireland; here was evidence that the spells that were abroad were not all good spells, that the magic which had survived from Ireland's beginning was not all pure woodland magic.

Here was the frontier, the border, the boundary of the Dark Ireland.

Nuadu had moved forward and Fenella saw that his head was still held as imperiously as ever. The Rat People surrounding them did not move, but both Fenella and Nuadu sensed the ripple of watchfulness and felt the tensing of muscles. If they tried to run, they would certainly be caught at once.

Courage, Lady. It came as strongly and as warmly as ever and Fenella felt Nuadu's hand brush her arm lightly and was at once strengthened.

Nuadu walked up to the stone table and placed his hands on it, palms downwards, the silver left arm gleaming redly in the glow from the wall sconces. Fenella, following, saw the flaring light fall more strongly on the Soul Eaters, so that the narrow, bony skulls were more sharply outlined and the dry leathery skin was thrown into horrid relief. She saw, as well, what she had not seen until now: beneath the folded wings, each Soul Eater possessed tiny, clawlike hands, delicately webbed, each finger ending in cruel pointed talons.

Nuadu said, quite politely, 'We crave your pardon for intruding into your domain,' and glanced to the half a dozen or so Rodent creatures who had brought them to the Cavern. A brief flicker of amusement showed on his face. 'But you will allow,' said Nuadu, gently, 'that your invitation was difficult to resist.' He studied their captors and the watching Armies moved warily, their claws scraping on the floor as they did so. Several of the Jackals turned their squat ugly heads and regarded Nuadu unblinkingly while the Stoats growled with a thick clotted sound.

The most ancient-looking of the Soul Eaters, who sat on the Throne at the centre, and who had short, hard, bone-like horns and cruel, curving hands beneath his wings, moved slightly, with a dry, papery, bone-against-skin sound that set Fenella's teeth wincing.

'Son of the Wolf,' he said, and his voice was sapless and harsh, as if the saliva had long since dried out.

'Son of the Wolf, you disturb our nightly revel, and will certainly be brought to our table for us to feast on.' The reptilian eyes studied Nuadu. 'For that reason our servants caught you and brought you here. But, since you are of an ancient house, and since you possess the wolfblood, we do not, for the moment, bind and chain you and we will permit you a brief time to speak.'

The Soul Eater next to him said, 'In your world, your House is regarded as an honourable one and, although we do not recognise such things in our domain, we recognise that you possess royal blood.'

Nuadu said, in a soft ironic voice, 'You will accord a bastard Wolfprince royal standing, will you? You will hear me out before you eat my soul. I am indebted to you,' he said, and the Soul Eater's thin mouth stretched into a smile.

He said, 'Precisely so, Nuadu of the Silver Arm.'

'You will be served to us on a golden platter,' said a third, and several of the Soul Eaters leaned forward, their talons curving.

'Your Lady will accompany you,' said the first.

'We are both in your debt,' said Nuadu with sardonic courtesy.

'You will tell us why you seek us out, wolf-creature, when your world regards this place as one to treat with abhorrence.'

Nuadu appeared entirely at ease. He moved forward to seat himself with careless grace on the edge of the table, and the Soul Eaters rustled their wings uncertainly and eyed him. Fenella stayed where she was and kept her eyes on the serried rows of Rodent Soldiers. Directly above them were the flaring torches. Would it be at all possible to somehow bring down those torches and create a fire? I wish I could remember what frightens rats, thought Fenella. Does fire?

Nuadu had arranged himself comfortably on the stone table. He was sitting on it, one leg stretched out before him, the other bent, resting his flesh and blood arm on the bent knee. He was studying the Soul Eaters and appeared to be finding them interesting.

Then the leading Soul Eater said, 'Your visit here is not, of course, purely from the curiosity of your kind.'

'Of course not,' said Nuadu, his voice tinged with amusement. 'Although, I have always been curious about you.' He regarded them, his head tilted to one side consideringly. 'Your place in the legend and the lore of my people is an assured one,' he said. 'You have formed part of our storytellers' repertoire for countless centuries. But you will know that.'

The Soul Eaters did not move, but Fenella had the sudden impression that they were listening very closely. *Could* it be this easy? Could Nuadu woo them and flatter them and somehow talk them both out of danger and on through the Gateway to the Dark Realm?

Nuadu was leaning forward, the flaring torches casting reddish shadows across his face. Fenella thought she had never seen him look so nearly evil before and repressed a shiver. She tried not to remember all the old stories about wolves and how they could unexpectedly turn on a friend.

Nuadu said, 'I wish to go through into the Realm of that other Ireland which you guard.'

'Yes?' It was a cagey tone now, as if the Soul Eaters could not quite decide what to make of this strange traveller.

'You have the power to open up the Cruachan Gateway,' said Nuadu, and for the first time there was an authority in his tone which cut through the oppressiveness of the cavern like cold steel.

The Soul Eaters remained motionless, but Fenella saw several of the Weasels exchange glances.

At length, the Soul Eater with the horned head said, 'You will tell us why you wish to enter the Dark Domain, son of the Wolves.'

'You will also tell us how you have the arrogance and the insolence to request such a thing,' said another.

Nuadu smiled round at them and rearranged himself on the edge of the stone table. 'My people have always been arrogant,' he said.

'That we know.'

'Why do you wish to journey in the Dark Domain of the Necromancers,' said the first Soul Eater.

'For reasons which need not concern you.'

The first Soul Eater leaned forward, his little eyes glinting. 'But your reasons do concern us,' he said.

'And,' said another, 'you should know that entry into the Dark Realm is never permitted without some form of payment.' There was a lick of nearly sexual pleasure in its voice over the word *payment*, and Fenella shuddered.

Nuadu said, 'I am aware of it. You could be called venal for it.'

'The Wolfkings and Queens have rarely been noted for

their altruism, Nuadu Airgetlam.'

Nuadu smiled gently, but remained silent, waiting.

'If we agreed to open the Cruachan Gateway,' said the first Soul Eater, 'what would you offer us by way of payment?'

Nuadu regarded the Soul Eaters very straightly.

'The soul of Ireland's High King,' he said at last. 'If you will allow me to go through the Cruachan Gateway, I will bring you the soul of the imprisoned Prince, my half-brother. I will serve him to you on a golden platter and you may eat your fill before you fling his drained body into the River of the Dead.

'And then,' he said softly, the wolfmask lying strongly across his face, 'and then, Soul Eaters, Tara will be within my grasp.'

Chapter Thirty-three

Fenella stared straight ahead of her. It was extremely important not to look at any of the Soul Eaters, and it was even more important not to look at Nuadu.

I will bring you the soul of my brother, and then Tara will be within my grasp . . .

Of course it is only a ploy, she thought. Of course it is nothing more than that. She forced her concentration back to what was happening, because it was not to be thought of that she would miss any single shred of this.

Nuadu had leaned forward, his eyes fixed on the Soul Eaters. He said, very softly, 'I understand you, Soul Eaters. I understand your needs. You are not greedy, but you need Human souls to survive.'

'They are our life-blood,' said the Soul Eater, and a murmur of assent went through the others. 'If our kind is to survive, then we must suck dry the souls of—'

'Humans?'

'They do not have to be Humans,' said the Soul Eater, a sudden grating lust in his voice. The opaque eyes inspected Nuadu. 'The soul of Ireland's Crown Prince would be a very great prize.'

'Better,' said another who had not yet spoken, 'than the puny, half-dead things brought to us by the Robemaker, after he has wrung out their sap on his treadmills.'

'Better by far than the shrivelled, ineffectual souls we weigh for him on the Silver Scales of Sorcery,' said yet another.

'He has ten thousand years of his curse yet to endure. That is a great many souls he must bring to us. A great many warm, living souls for us to feed upon.' The Soul Eaters laughed with such malignancy that Fenella thought that if she could, with safety, have turned and run, she would have done so. Nuadu did not appear to move, but Fenella saw the skin on his hand whiten as if he might have clenched his fist. But when he spoke his voice was as silky and as persuasive as before.

'Better by far, sirs,' he said. 'For I am as aware as you that there are different qualities of soul.' He leaned forward again. 'But the soul of Ireland's uncrowned King,' he said, and the soft, caressing note was back in his voice. 'The soul of one who is descended from the first High Queen, Dierdriu the Great, and from the famous Cormac, and Erin the Wise and Grainne the Gentle. From Niall of the Nine Hostages and from every Wolfking and Queen who ever ascended to the Throne of Tara. The hereditary High King. The one who has the right to ascend the ancient Throne of Tara.' He regarded them. 'I have not that right,' he said. 'For although I have royal blood, and although I have wolfblood also, I cannot claim such ancestry.' The thin wolfsmile touched his lips again. 'That is why my half-brother must be removed. Unless and until he is dead, Tara will elude me,' he said. 'And so I would bargain with you. Just as the necromancers bargain with you for extra powers, so will I bargain. If you will allow me, with my companion, to go through the Cruachan Gateway, then I will bring to you the imprisoned Crown Prince and you may take his soul and hold the greatest feast you have ever known.'

He looked at them and, at length, the leading Soul Eater said, 'What of your companion?' and there was a greedy rustling of wings and the hard bony heads turned to Fenella.

'She is a Human,' said Nuadu. 'A *pure-bred* Human. You will assuredly know my people's beliefs that the Humans are Kingmakers. You will doubtless recall the many times in our history when a Human has rescued an exiled or imprisoned High King? Cormac of the Wolves himself owed his freedom to a Human lady from another world,' said Nuadu, smoothly. 'The High King Erin the Just was only able to ascend Tara's Ebony Throne because of another Human brought from the Far Future by his

Court.' He made a brief rather off-hand gesture to where Fenella stood listening. 'If I am to reach my half-brother, I shall need the Human,' he said.

'The necromancers will assuredly fight against you,' said a Soul Eater slightly smaller in stature than the others, but with such ancient, evil knowledge in his eyes that Fenella shuddered.

'They will not wish to let their captive go,' said the leading one, eyeing Nuadu and Fenella intently. 'Whatever prison they have devised for him will be difficult to penetrate.' He paused. 'It may not be a prison of bars and walls.'

'I am aware of that,' said Nuadu levelly.

'It may be a prison of dark enchantment.'

'Yes, I understand that also,' said Nuadu. 'It is one of the reasons why I shall require the Human's assistance to free my half-brother. After we return with him, you may do with her what you will.'

The first Soul Eater said, thoughtfully, 'You know, Wolfprince, that it is CuRoi, the one they call the Master, who is believed to hold your half-brother? CuRoi is the most powerful Dark Sorcerer ever known.'

'I am aware of that.'

The Soul Eater whom Fenella had thought to be the most ancient said, 'You have heard of CuRoi's fortress inside the Dark Realm? And how, no matter where he might be, he may still chaunt a spell to seal his fortress? So that any creature who has been able to breach it by day will be locked in with the darkness once the sun has set?'

'I know,' said Nuadu carefully, 'that CuRoi was once a great chieftain of Ireland, but that he took to wandering in the annals of the darkest sorcery known to the Court. He was banished by Erin at the same time as the one you know as the Robemaker.' He paused. 'He is said to be the greatest illusionist my people have ever known,' he said. And then, eyeing the Soul Eater who had spoken, 'None of that makes him invincible,' said Nuadu. 'I shall enter his fortress and I shall find the Prince and bring him out.'

He smiled. 'And then you shall have his soul.'

There was a silence. Fenella, hardly daring to move, almost not daring to breathe, saw they were thinking it over. They had retreated into their dark, wizened minds and they were thinking over this extraordinary and imperious request. She glanced at Nuadu, and felt the sliver of a thought from him. *Courage, Lady. I believe we have them beaten* . . .

The leading Soul Eater stood up and spread his wings and Fenella flinched, seeing the size and the power of the creature, and wondered how on earth they had dared to oppose such beings and how they were managing to escape unscathed this far.

But the Soul Eater said, 'We will open up the Gateway for you and the Human, son of the Wolf,' and Fenella felt the bolt of relief go through Nuadu.

'We will open up the Gateway and we will permit you to enter the Dark Realm and seek out CuRoi, whose fortress is sealed at sunset every night,' said the Soul Eater. He stopped, and the one next to him took up the pronouncement.

'But we charge you, and we bind you by our own magical powers, to return to us within seven days with the Prince, and to render up his soul for our feasting.' The dark, basilisk stare devoured Nuadu and Fenella for a moment. 'We shall savour your return,' said the Soul Eater.

'We shall so return,' said Nuadu, and the Soul Eater stretched its narrow lips in the travesty of a smile. He moved closer and Nuadu stood his ground.

'If you do not return, son of wolves,' said the Soul Eater, 'then we shall make use of the ancient Summoning of Medoc, created by the greatest necromancer of them all. Medoc could pass in and out of the Dark Realm at will and his necromancy was the strongest in all the Dark Realm. But perhaps you know of him?'

'Oh, yes,' said Nuadu, softly. 'Oh, yes, I know of Medoc and the dark cruel, beautiful sorcery he once spun over all of Ireland.'

'We plundered Medoc's Black Citadel and took his necromantic annals for our own,' said the Soul Eater with sudden relish. 'The corrupt Dark Starred Book of Enchantry and the priceless Codex of Necromancy that was Medoc's own creation, for he was one of the Scholars, Medoc.' It leaned forward, the stench of its ancient withered body gusting towards Fenella and Nuadu. 'If you do not return to us with the prince,' it said, 'we shall weave the dark Summoning of Medoc. Wherever you are, it will reach out its talons towards you and entrap you and bring you to us.

'You will be caught by the beautiful and cruel Beckoning of Medoc which no living creature has yet been able to resist.

'That is how we shall ensure your return.'

As the Soul Eaters moved from their carved thrones, a wave of awareness went through the serried ranks of the Rodent People and, with it, a shudder of fear. To Fenella, this was the most frightening thing yet, because if the Soul Eaters' dreadful armies were afraid of the Gateway into the Dark Ireland, then surely, surely the Dark Ireland must be something so immensely and overwhelmingly evil that she could never hope to survive it. Almost immediately she felt the now-familiar ruffle of amusement from Nuadu: *can you think I should risk the ignominy of failure, Lady? Of course we shall survive . . .*

The Soul Eaters were moving into what appeared to be some kind of formation at the far end of the cave; the leader turned to beckon Nuadu and Fenella to stand with them and instantly the Rodent Armies parted to let them through. Fenella felt the touch of warm furred bodies as they brushed against the creatures and the dry, fetid scent, but she put up her chin and followed Nuadu and then they were through the lines of the army and standing next to the Soul Eater who had held most of the discourse with Nuadu.

Nuadu looked at Fenella. 'Ready, Lady?'

Fenella was staring at the grisly figures of the Soul

Eaters, seeing how the ancient evil gleamed in their eyes, seeing as well, that the nearest two had turned to regard their prisoners with malevolent glee. What are we going into? thought Fenella. What are they sending us into? She glanced at Nuadu, and thought, as well: *and what do I really know of this half-Wolf creature whom I do not think I altogether trust, and who may well make sinister use of me in this dark other-world?*

Aloud, she said, 'Is there a choice?'

'There is always a choice, Lady.' But his eyes were brilliant with anticipation and the wolf-look was more pronounced than it had been earlier on.

'If we draw back now, these – creatures will kill us,' said Fenella, casting a quick look at the Soul Eaters and at the serried ranks of the Rodent Armies.

'Oh yes,' said Nuadu, softly. 'Oh yes, they will kill us – and it will not end there.'

They will eat your soul, Lady, and to be forever soul-less is the worst, blackest, most eternal torment ever . . .

'All right,' said Fenella, staring back at the waiting Soul Eaters. 'Yes, all right,' and felt his hand close about hers.

At the back of the cavern, the Soul Eaters had formed a half circle. The leader was standing with his scale-covered head sunk and his narrow shoulders stooping, leathery wings folded at his side. Fenella and Nuadu both felt at once that he was summoning up some kind of hidden power and Fenella saw the Weasels and Jackals flinch and knew they were feeling the approach of something invisible and malevolent.

The Gateway to the Dark Ireland is forming . . .

They both saw it the minute it started to take shape; at first there was only a thread of colour, the thinly traced outline of an immense door, livid against the dark rock . . . But, as they stood motionless, the thread thickened, became solid and substantial . . . it is becoming *real*, thought Fenella, staring.

It was materialising into a huge soaring Gate, with black-tipped spires and with ebony and jet staves; it was

428

wrought from crimson fire, streaked with scarlet and gold, powerful and ancient.

The Dark Ireland's Gateway forming . . .

The most ancient Soul Eater was still standing in the shadow it cast, his head still sunk on to his chest, his eyes in darkness. As the Gateway stretched out into the darkness of the Cavern's high roof, his eyes flickered open and he turned to face the Gate, rays of baleful light pouring forth from his eyes.

At once, belching black smoke was emitted from the Gate and with it a thick clotted malignancy. There was a faint, far-off chanting, a sinister rise and fall of gloating voices. Slowly the chanting increased, and inch by tortuous inch, so that for a moment Fenella and Nuadu thought their eyes were deceiving them and their ears playing tricks, the Gate into the Dark Realm began to open . . .

There was an enveloping darkness beyond and then Fenella glimpsed the Crimson Lakes and the Dark Fields and the Black Citadels, and knew that this, at last, was the terrible other-world, the fearsome mirror image of the Wolfkings' Ireland, and that they must go into it. Panic seized her and there was a moment when she thought: I can't do it! This is too much!

And then Nuadu was drawing her forward and there was no turning back: the Gateway was directly ahead of them and they could see beyond it more clearly now; they could see the vast black mountains and the glassy lakes and the crimson fields with the waving blood-coloured harvests.

Nuadu's hand tightened about hers and Fenella caught his thought more clearly than anything he had yet poured into her mind.

We have surmounted every danger and every enemy so far, Fenella . . . Why should we not do so again?

She glanced at him and saw his eyes glinting and felt the excitement that was blazing within him and saw the wolfmask lying redly across his features.

I am stepping into the Dark Realm of the necromancers and I am doing so handlocked with a Wolf, thought Fenella, wildly. I suppose this is really happening, is it? And again was the warm flurry of amusement touching her mind.

It is all happening, in truth, Lady, and is it not the greatest adventure yet . . . ?

She understood that Nuadu's strange ancestry was urging him on; that he was thinking that never before had any Wolfprince entered voluntarily into the terrible netherworld of the necromancers, and there was an unexpected response to that. Perhaps it will be exciting, she thought, and perhaps we shall find the one they call CuRoi and defeat him and find the one who is his half-brother and Tara's rightful heir. We defeated the Robemaker, she thought suddenly. Yes! Perhaps it will be all right.

And then a silence fell over the watchers and the Soul Eaters brushed the air with their huge wings, as if they were growing impatient, and there was nothing else to do but to step forward.

Into the Dark Ireland.

Chapter Thirty-four

The Forest Court sat in worried conclave around the oak table with Oisin and Miach in command.

'For once,' said Feradach.

'Well, Miach's the proper person after all,' said Eogan. 'He's the Court Sorcerer.'

Feradach made a derisory noise and Dian Cecht, who was seated next to Miach, looked up.

'Gimlet-eyed,' said Feradach.

'Better than ferret-faced,' said Miach, who was not going to have Mother maligned by anyone.

Snizort had been given a place next to Oisin and he was feeling extremely gratified, because it seemed to be taken for granted that he should play an integral part in these really very important discussions. The Oak naiads were there as well; they were not exactly seated at the table, because they did not seem to sit down anywhere. But they were in attendance. Snizort thought that was the nearest description you could give. 'With us but not quite of us,' said Oisin.

Oisin was looking solemn and concerned. He had spread out the chronicles and the manuscripts he had managed to bring out of Tara and Miach had done the same. Nobody had said very much, other than the somewhat automatic sniping between Feradach and Dian Cecht, because everyone was very worried indeed about the failure to summon the Beastline creatures. When Tealtaoich said they were little better than useless, everyone nodded, and even Feradach, who could usually be trusted to provide a sharp remark, said nothing.

'We failed,' said Tealtaoich, who had curled himself into a chair and was glowering at the mead which Clumhach had poured for them all. 'We failed roundly and soundly and ignominiously.'

'Oh, I don't think it was as bad as all that,' said Clumhach, frowning anxiously.

'Clumhach doesn't know what the word means,' said Feradach to Eogan.

'Yes, I do,' said Clumhach indignantly. 'It's just a bit difficult to explain.'

'It means we are failures and losers. We were unable to call the Beasts and we were unable to invoke the ancient Beastline Enchantment,' said Tealtaoich, as one explaining a simple truth to a very stupid child. 'It means that the noble and mystical blood we thought we all possessed no longer has any power. Well, we might as well hand Ireland over to the Robemaker and CuRoi and have done,' he said with a gesture of dismissal. 'We'll never hope to regain Tara just by ourselves. We need an army.' He scowled at the table and Snizort thought that if he had possessed a tail he would certainly have lashed it.

'Our Houses are at an end,' said Dian Cecht, musingly. 'Tara is forever doomed.'

'Well, that ought to please *you*,' said Feradach. 'Because ever since I can recall, you've done nothing but prophesy death and ruin. I suppose you're quite pleased to see your prophecies come true.'

'She didn't *mean* any of it,' said Miach, firing up at once. 'You ought to know she didn't mean it. She never does.'

Oisin said, in his calm, cool voice, 'We must be very sensible and very clear-sighted about all of this.'

Tealtaoich said, 'But we dare not let the Beastline Enchantment die. To do so would mean the end of Tara.' He looked round the table. 'You all know the words of the original curse,' he said.

If ever a pure-bred Human should ascend Tara's Throne, then the Bright Palace will crumble and die, and Ireland will be forever damned . . .'

'That is why the Beastline Enchantment was spun,' said Tealtaoich. 'So that a Human never would ascend the Throne. So that Tara would always be ruled by a creature

432

with a little of the beasts in its veins.'

'And the Wolfkings have ruled ever since,' said Eogan, very softly. And then, in a stronger, firmer voice, 'I think there is no question but that we must try to re-create the Beastline Enchantment.'

'Yes,' said Oisin, shuffling the chronicles again. 'Yes, it has become a larger matter than driving out the Gruagach and finding the King. It's no longer just a – a brief war which, in the normal way, we'd probably win.

'It's a question of Tara's whole future,' he said very seriously. 'Without the Beastline Enchantment, not only are we without hope of beating the Robemaker and CuRoi, but Ireland's entire history is at risk. We *must* be able to summon the Beasts.'

For a moment, no one spoke, partly because it was unusual to hear the normally quiet and gentle Oisin speak so vehemently, but largely because they were all so appalled at the thing that was happening. Without the Beastline Enchantment, the mystical golden power they had believed themselves to possess, they were helpless. The ancient prophecy that forbade a Human to rule would at last come true and Tara would crumble and fall.

Then Tealtaoich said, 'Miach. This is your territory. May we hear from you, please?'

Miach was torn between gratification at being deferred to by Tealtaoich in this way and panic that he would not be able to do anything about this really terrible disaster. He had studied the few sorcery annals he had brought with him from Tara and he had talked earnestly with Oisin, who was quite knowledgeable, and also with the Oak Naiads who had been interested and concerned and sympathetic. 'Although,' they had said, politely, 'it is for you to find the means to strengthen the Beastline Enchantment.'

'Do you believe that it is lost?' asked Miach, furrowing his brow.

'That is for you to discover,' said the Oaks, which, as Miach had crossly said to Oisin later, was not very much help.

433

But it would not do to appear to be at a loss – Mother would have died of the shame of it – and so Miach shuffled his papers importantly and donned an air of gravity.

'Don't put on airs,' said Feradach at once. 'It doesn't become you and it doesn't fool any of us. Just get on with it.'

If it had not been for matters being so very grave, Miach would have spoken quite sharply to Feradach, who needed putting in his place. He would not do so, however, because of not wanting to upset anyone any further. They were all upset enough as it was. Miach would make allowances.

And so he pretended not to hear Feradach and explained that he had studied the annals and the manuscripts. 'What you might call the *recipes* for sorcery,' he said, which he thought imparted a nice, homely touch to the proceedings.

'Sorcery isn't a homely thing,' said Tealtaoich, who could usually be trusted to hear people's thoughts in the most vulgar way imaginable. 'As Feradach said earlier, get on with it.'

Miach said, 'We do know that the Beastline Enchantment has wavered before.' He looked down at his notes. 'In fact, at one time it was believed to be lost altogether and the High Queen of the day set the sorcerers to weave a completely new one.'

'I heard about that,' put in Feradach. 'It was during the reign of Erin, or perhaps it was just before.'

'But it's very probable,' said Miach, 'that the Enchantment is being smothered by the Robemaker's darkness. As you know, this is the Trees' idea,' he said rather hurriedly, because although it would have been nice to have presented this as his own idea, everyone had heard the Oak Naiad say this, which meant that nobody was going to think it was Miach's own deduction.

'I haven't many of the sorcery annals here,' he said, 'because there wasn't time to bring much from Tara.'

'Oisin managed it,' said Feradach.

'Yes, but Oisin's bedchamber was near to Tara's great

434

library,' put in Eogan. 'It made it easier for him.'

'But Miach ought to have made the sorcery annals his first priority,' said Feradach.

'I *brought* what I could,' said Miach very crossly. 'And if you remember, the Gruagach were actually in the courtyard at the time. They were about to use a battering ram on the main doors. And I must say that if Feradach's going to be *carping*, then I shan't weave any spells to help you, I just shan't.'

'Miach,' said Dian Cecht to the company in general, 'is such a sensitive boy. It is unkind of Feradach to bait him, particularly when Miach has worked so hard for us all.' The great black eyes were turned on Feradach for a moment. 'But then,' said Dian Cecht sadly, 'to suffer such discourtesies and such indignities is what I have become used to.'

'I apologise,' said Feradach, after what was clearly an inner struggle.

'Our good Feradach is as worried as the rest of us,' put in Clumhach, who was not following all of this, but who thought it incumbent on him to smooth a few ruffled tempers. 'He doesn't mean any harm,' he added, beaming. 'And I am sure that Miach will know what has to be done.'

'I hope he will,' said Tealtaoich. 'Miach?'

Miach said, 'It's necessary to strengthen into the original Enchantment so that it can break free of the blanket of darkness that the Robemaker has thrown over everything.'

'Yes?'

Miach cast an unhappy glance at the Oak Naiad. 'There seems to be only one way of doing that,' he said.

'What is it?'

'To invoke the original Beastline Enchantment,' said Miach.

There was a sudden silence, then Tealtaoich said, 'But that means—' and stopped.

'It means,' said Miach, who was very upset about all of this, and was not, in fact, entirely sure of his ground, but had decided to be firm, 'it means that we must recite the

435

Ritual that was written at the beginning of Tara's history and that one of you—'

'Must lie with the beasts,' finished Tealtaoich, staring.

'Exactly so,' said Miach.

'We'll have to do it,' said Tealtaoich, at last. 'I'm quite sure that this isn't the way it should be done – hastily and uncertainly, but if Miach believes it's the only way—'

'Yes, I do,' said Miach, rather truculently.

'Then it had better be done at once,' finished Tealtaoich and frowned. 'Has anyone seen it done, by any chance?'

Nobody had, although Oisin remembered reading an account of the last time the Ritual had been invoked. 'For the Red Foxes,' he said. 'Feradach's people. It sounds rather solemn and serious. Not at all what you'd expect.'

'Sorcery is a solemn and serious business,' said Miach, because it might be a good idea to try to surround himself with a bit of mysticism if he could.

'Do you know the Ritual?' demanded Tealtaoich. 'Have you got the exact words?'

'Yes,' said Miach. 'It's in one of the annals I *did* manage to bring,' he said, with a nasty look at Feradach. 'It's actually a rather simple chant.'

'We ought to do it at the Purple Hour,' said Eogan.

'Yes, we'll need all the help we can get.'

'*Someone* will need all the help he can get,' said Feradach, and there was a sudden and rather nasty silence.

'Oh, I don't think we need worry,' began Clumhach, and then stopped uncertainly.

Tealtaoich said, 'No, Feradach's right. If we've got to do it, then we'd better face it properly and sensibly.' He looked round the table. 'Who's going to be the one to do it?'

'I'm not,' said Clumhach at once. 'I think it ought to be Tealtaoich.'

'Clumhach, if you think we can find one of the Wild Panthers out here—'

'It would mean travelling as far as Gallan—'

'Farther. Panthers haven't been seen in Ireland since –

well, for a very long time,' said Oisin. 'I remember once travelling to the ancient Mountain Palace of Tealtaoich's ancestor – Cait Fian. The mountains overlook Gallan and it's the most beautiful *wild* countryside you'd ever find. But the Palace is a ruin and the surrounding countryside was barren. There were no panthers.'

'Well, that's going to make it *rather* awkward for poor Tealtaoich when the Panel of Judges next decree that his line needs strengthening, isn't it?'

'Yes, and as for catching an eagle—'

'Oh, you'd never do that. Also,' said Eogan looking rather haughty and remote, 'also, my family always said that ours was the most difficult of all the ritual matings.' He looked round the table. 'The eagle has to be held down,' he said.

'I suppose it sometimes pecks,' said Tealaoich, amused.

'There have been cases of injury,' said Eogan, coldly.

'Well, if you want to put it like that,' said Tealtaoich.

'What about Feradach?' asked Dian Cecht with what Snizort could not help feeling was more than a trace of malice. 'There are enough foxes in the forest. Rather a *common* creature, the fox.'

'It has to be a *red* fox,' said Feradach at once. 'Rather *rare*, my dear Dian Cecht.'

'And also, if it was the Red Foxes last time, to repeat it might not be much good,' added Eogan.

It was then that Miach said, a bit unhappily, 'There's something you ought to know . . . a sort of qualifier, a rider.'

'Yes?'

'What?'

'The Ritual can only be chanted over the – the Royal House that has been judged ready to – oh, this is very difficult – ready actually to mate,' said Miach, getting redder in the face with every minute. 'If you invoke it over a House that doesn't need it, it probably won't have any effect. And we do need it to be effective.'

'Well, who was last pronounced as needing the Ritual?'

'The White Swans,' said Miach in an expressionless

voice, and every head turned to look at Dian Cecht.

Rather to Snizort's surprise, Dian Cecht accepted the matter fairly calmly.

'Oh, she'll like being the centre of attention,' said Feradach, who had been despatched, with Eogan, to the *sidh* pool on the Wolfwood's eastern side, to capture two White Swans. 'She'll make a great play of reluctance and false modesty, but she'll do it.'

Snizort said, 'But didn't she refuse the last time to – that is, I understand that she found the Ritual distasteful . . .'

Feradach grinned. 'That was Dian Cecht's way of being different to everyone else,' he said. 'The normal thing, the *traditional* thing, would have been for her simply to submit to the Ritual. We all know it has to be done every fourth or fifth generation or so. It's purely luck – good or ill depending on your point of view – whether it's necessary in your own generation. Dian Cecht only refused in order to make a stir at Court.'

Snizort asked, as delicately as he could, about Miach's sire.

'Dian Cecht had a rather pallid relationship with one of the lesser sorcerers at Tara,' said Feradach. 'That's how she got Miach into the Academy of Sorcery.'

'Pallid?'

'Wouldn't you think it would be pallid?' said Feradach, and Snizort, who had read about these things but had not actually had a great deal of practical experience of them, said, 'Dear me, yes of course. And so, she will go through with it this time, will she?'

'She'll be saving Ireland,' said Feradach with a touch of asperity. 'Of course she'll go through with it.'

'And will there be – dear me, this is very difficult – will there be – ah – *progeny*?' enquired Snizort, who had not quite liked to ask this of Oisin, but who thought that the slightly more robust Feradach would not mind the question.

'Not necessarily,' said Feradach, considering. 'That's

438

usually the object of the Ritual, of course. But this time it's a bit different. We simply want to – well, reinforce the Enchantment I suppose you could call it, strengthen the powers of the Beastline.' His teeth gleamed whitely in a sudden malicious grin. 'But it would almost serve Dian Cecht right if there was a result of the mating,' he said.

Dian Cecht had seated herself a little apart from the remaining Beastline creatures and was gazing soulfully into the depths of the forest. As Snizort approached, she half turned her head.

'I am calming my mind for the ordeal ahead of me,' she said, in a remote tone and Snizort said he was very sorry if he had disturbed her.

'My life has been nothing but a series of troubles and tragedies,' said Dian Cecht, turning her enormous black eyes upon him. 'My House is a *doomed* House, you see. And although the Ritual will be extremely repulsive to one of my *delicate* upbringing, I shall not complain, because it is for the saving of Ireland.' One slender white hand was pressed to her breast. 'Ah, Ireland, my dear *tortured* land,' she said, and Snizort repressed the uncharitable thought that she was overdoing it a bit.

'I have only one fear,' said Dian Cecht.

'Yes?'

'It is that my son should not be *wounded* by my ordeal,' she said, and Snizort thought, but did not say, that since Miach would be the one chanting the actual Ritual, it was going to be a bit difficult for Miach to avoid doing other than witness the Ritual first-hand. He thought it was not up to him to say this, however.

'Miach is so sensitive,' said Dian Cecht, with a sad, small smile. 'Alas, he fatally takes after me.'

Snizort, greatly daring, said, 'His father . . .' and Dian Cecht turned her soulful look onto him.

'For a little time he was blessed,' she said.

'Yes?'

'I loved him.'

'Ah. Yes. Dear me, of course,' said Snizort, and took himself off rather hurriedly.

Miach was running through the Ritual with Oisin and the Oak Naiad. It was, as he had said, a fairly simple matter; he thought he could manage it quite easily. In fact he thought he could manage it without any trouble at all. He was a bit worried about the Swan – and he was very worried indeed about Mother, who ought not to be subjected to this sort of thing. He did not quite say, 'at her age', because that would have been disrespectful as well as uncomplimentary, but he thought it.

Oisin and the Oak Naiad were encouraging. Oisin said that the Ritual was simple, because it had always been intended to be so; the first sorcerers who had woven it on Tara's great Silver Looms had deliberately made it plain and straightforward so that it could always be kept alive. The Oak Naiad said that the finest and purest sorcery was always remarkably simple.

'It is only a question of the power the sorcerer himself draws down,' he said, regarding Miach kindly, which Miach thought was the most alarming thing anyone had said yet. But it did not seem to have occurred to any of the Tree Spirits that Miach might fail in the Ritual, and so Miach thought he had better go along with this point of view. He squared his shoulders and flexed his mental muscles experimentally and, without the least warning, fully felt, for the first time since he had started studying sorcery, the strange, silvery stirring. Excitement gripped him and he thought: the enchanted power! So *that's* what it feels like! Remarkable! I believe I can do it! he thought in delight. I truly believe I can do it. And thought wouldn't it be the most tremendous thing ever heard of if he invoked the ancient and legendary Ritual of the Beastline and enabled the people of the Court to call up the creatures of the forest and ride on Tara and rout the giants.

It was nearly dusk when Feradach and Eogan returned and, as they trod through the trees, Snizort and the others saw the pale flutter of white wings and saw the slender, graceful shape of the two White Swans.

'Why two?' asked Snizort of Oisin.

'Swans mate for life,' said Oisin, watching them approach. 'It would have been dangerous to have brought the cob without the pen.'

'Oh, I see,' said Snizort. And then, 'Won't the pen be dreadfully jealous?'

'Miach's trying to concoct a spell to make her sleep.'

Miach was, by this time, very busy indeed. He had found a version of the Enchantment of Slumber, the *Draoicht Suan* which could safely be recited over the pen, and he had also found the opposing enchantment which would dissolve the *Draoicht Suan* so that they could send the two White Swans back unscathed when it was all over. This was extremely important, because you should not invoke any ritual without being sure you could dissolve it if you had to. Anyone knew that.

He had drawn a circle at the exact centre of the clearing and he had found the ancient symbols of fertility and also the Hazels of Wisdom of the Tree of Amaranth, which was the root from which the oldest Sorcery House of Ireland sprang. He traced these carefully into the ground and glared at Clumhach who inadvertently smudged one by walking across it.

They were not going to leave anything to chance, said Miach, because it was very important that they succeeded. Ireland was at stake, he said very solemnly.

As the Court and Snizort assembled outside the circle, Miach thought that it was a pity he had not been able to don the proper ceremonial robes for the ritual. The sorcerers under whom he had served at Tara had placed immense importance on the proper robes for each spell-weaving. Miach thought he ought to have been wearing something grand and ornate; scarlet and gold, instead of the plain dark breeches which were only made of homespun, and the very ordinary shirt and jerkin he had donned when they had all fled from Tara that night.

Dian Cecht stood at the exact centre of the circle which Miach had drawn. She was wearing a thin, silken, white robe with a narrow girdle of gold and her short, caplike hair shone, emphasising the long, slender lines of her neck

441

and shoulders. She looked remote and austere and as if she might already be wreathed about with the strong gentle magic of the Purple Hour. Snizort, who had elected to sit a little removed from the ceremonies so that he could quietly and respectfully record everything, thought that if it had been possible to reach out and pluck the air it would have thrummed and vibrated like a musical instrument.

An air of solemnity had fallen over the watchers and Snizort, who had not quite known what to expect, saw that their expressions were serious and that there was an air of immense concentration about them. At the culmination of Miach's ritual chant, they would attempt again to summon the beasts.

He thought: and if they fail this time . . . And discovered that the idea of a second failure was something he could hardly bear to contemplate. They would not fail. Of *course* they would not fail.

Miach was standing with the Trees directly behind him and, in the fading light, their leafy heads were touched with the violet and blue of the approaching night. It was possible to make out the Tree Spirits here and there; the fall of a Copper Beech's rippling hair, or the flutter of the Silver Birches' skittish arms but, in the main, the Tree Spirits stood silently, dissolving into a swathe of gold and indigo and purple.

Miach looked young and vulnerable and suddenly extremely earnest. Bless my boots, thought Snizort, writing busily, I believe the boy means to succeed. As Miach frowned and lifted his arms, with the palms held upmost in the age-old gesture of supplication, Snizort knew that Miach was determined to succeed beyond all odds. And I do not believe it is purely for the glory of it, he thought. He cares what happens to Tara. They all care, thought Snizort, looking at the rest. They quarrel and taunt one another, but they care very deeply indeed.

Snizort did not understand Miach's Ritual Chant, but he had not expected to. Oisin had explained that enchantments were written in what was called the Language of Magic, and that it was a tongue so ancient that no one had ever been able to trace its roots, but it was so immensely powerful that understanding was not really necessary.

'Although the really scholarly sorcerers, the ones who have devoted their lives to its study, probably have some understanding,' he had said. 'Miach will not understand it, but it will probably not matter so long as he chants it correctly.'

Oisin and Tealtaoich were carrying the Swan to the circle's centre; their faces were intent and absorbed and it seemed to Snizort that the Swan – lovely graceful thing – was lulled by the chant. Miach had sent the pen into a gentle sleep and she had simply folded her wings and sunk to the ground in a fall of silken paleness. But this was the cob, this was the male, suspicious, defensive, albeit subdued. A cold finger of fear, or was it distaste, touched Snizort's neck.

But Oisin and Tealtaoich seemed to be managing quite well. They moved with a measured tread – everything seemed to be being done rather slowly – and Miach lifted his hands again and raised his voice. Slowly, slowly, so imperceptibly that it was almost impossible to be sure that it was happening, thin filaments of silver light began to twist and shiver all about him. Dusk was stealing in from the depths of the Wolfwood, fingers of dark creeping shadow, but the silver threads spun and hummed and the vagrant light fell across the forest floor like spun glass. Snizort, realising that even the faint scratching of a quill-pen might distract Miach or disturb the magic, put his notes aside and sat very still, absorbing the sights and the sounds and the scents.

Dian Cecht had discarded the white silk robe naturally and easily, and was standing completely naked at the clearing's centre. She was rather thin and her skin was very pale. There was the faintest sheen to it, so that as the silver threads touched her it was easy to imagine that it was not skin, but sleek, smooth down. As Oisin and Tealtaoich approached, she turned towards them.

The White Swan was watching Dian Cecht from its

dark, unblinking eyes, and there was an awareness about it. As Miach lifted his voice again in the ancient chant, the Swan unfurled its wings suddenly and seemed on the point of flight. A stir of fear went through the watchers.

But the Swan did not take flight. It spread its wings a little wider and a whisper of warm, musklike perfume touched the air. Tealtaoich and Oisin moved back and there was the outline of pale, glossy light as the Swan's wings were silhouetted against the dark forest.

The entire forest seemed to wait as if it were suspended and caught on the threads of Miach's enchantment and a tiny night wind caressed the leaves and whispered about the faces of the watchers.

The silver threads whirred and hummed more strongly and then the Swan glided effortlessly downwards and folded the waiting Dian Cecht in its massive wings as if it had wrapped a silken white cloak about her . . .

At once there was a strong dark stirring in the Wolfwood and Snizort saw that the rest of the Beastline had moved to stand quietly together and that they were facing out towards the forest, their hands held out, their eyes narrowed.

They were suddenly and disconcertingly less Human. There was the glint of gold in Eogan's eyes and the sleek ripple of fur on Tealtaoich and Feradach and Oisin. There was an alertness, a sharpening, as if senses and instincts they were not normally aware of had awoken, and as if they could hear things not usually audible and see things not ordinarily visible.

The Swan was still enfolding Dian Cecht in its immense wings and Dian Cecht was deep in its strange embrace.

Deep within the Wolfwood, above the rise and fall of Miach's chanting, there was a stirring, rushing sound; the faint, far-off hum of something singing on the night air, the darting of the blue and green *sidh* in between the Trees, and the movements of the Trees themselves, green and gold and beautiful and wise.

And then they all heard it. Scurrying and padding. The

sound of creatures not Human approaching the clearing. Hope and delight surged across the clearing and, as it did so, the silver enchantment that Miach was weaving so fast now strengthened and glistened.

For a moment, Snizort thought they had been mistaken; that their senses had deceived them into believing what they wanted to hear and see. He frowned and, as he did so, the scuttering and pattering and running came closer.

Fur and hoofs and paws and wings.

Slant-eyed creatures with three-cornered faces and creatures with pointed muzzles and pricked ears, with ancient woodland instincts and ancient woodland ancestries.

There was a beating of wings on the air and, above them, beyond the highest of the Trees, the air was becoming filled with gold and bronze and white.

The creatures of the Forest finally and at last obeying the ancient summoning, the strong, sensuous luring of the *Samhailt* . . .

Chapter Thirty-five

Deep within the ruined City of the Giants, Floy and Snodgrass lay helpless and bound, awaiting the arrival of the *Geimhreadh*.

They were lying on their backs in the terrible inner chamber of the Frost Giantess, in the cold, echoing, blue-lit lair with the dark waters of the River of the Dead lapping against the walls. Cold green waterlight rippled on the walls and there was a dank, slimy stench on the air. Floy, who had occasionally travelled among the famous Twilight Mountains on Renascia to hunt the Rainbow Ikons, recognised the stench for what it was: decaying water vegetation and fetid fish-breath and trailing viscous, mucus-like plants and gelatinous pale river-creatures with long slithery tails and boneless bodies ... Revulsion washed over him and he concentrated his mind on trying to find a way of escape. It was unthinkable that they should endure being thrown into the River, to be at the mercy of the half-fish, half-human things they had seen outside Fael-Inis's Palace of Wildfire.

At the *Geimhreadh*'s nod the storm creatures had carried Floy and Snodgrass from the outer room through to the cold, dank inner chamber, laughing and writhing, taunting their two victims, twining more coarse, sticky ropes about their limbs.

For you shall not escape us now, Humans, you shall not escape the cold, hungry embraces of the Geimhreadh ... You will not loosen the bonds that confine you ... The Mistress told you of the ropes, Humans, of how they are fashioned from the coarsest hair of her victims ... They are the strongest form of bond ever made, Humans.

The Wraiths shrieked out their mirth again. *You are bound by the fibres of sexual bonds, Humans ... do you feel*

446

the spent seed and the clotted blood on them . . . ? Do you smell the stale juices and do you feel the shreds of torn skin, Humans . . . ? Our Mistress has strong appetites, Humans, she is merciless in her desires, and you will be expected to satisfy them all . . .

The cold, eerie laughter echoed all about them and the storm creatures swirled high above Floy and Snodgrass, their icicle-features grinning and pointed, their long, sharp fingers reaching out to stroke and prod their victims' flesh. Their touch was icy and sharp and, although they constantly grinned and darted into the travellers' faces, they never quite materialised; they were cold, smokelike beings, neither quite substance nor shadow, but somewhere between the two.

We are Wraiths, Human morsels. We were born out of the coldness that lives in Men's hearts and out of the greed that lives in their souls, for greed is the coldest of all the emotions and we are COLD, human travellers, we are cold and ice and we are frozen winter night and bleak winter dawn . . .

Floy and Snodgrass struggled and twisted, but the hair ropes held. In each of their minds was the thought that surely the storm creatures would leave before the *Geimhreadh* approached and surely, then, there would be a chance to escape.

Floy and Snodgrass felt icy needles pierce their thoughts.

We can hear you, Humans, cried the Wraiths in delighted triumph. *We can hear you and we can understand you, for the Mistress has bestowed on us the ancient Stroichim Inchinn, the power of knowing the thoughts of others . . .*

Floy, with memories of Nuadu Airgetlam, said, 'But surely that is forbidden—' and the Wraiths shrieked with mirth again.

Nothing is forbidden, Human weakling, nothing is not permitted in the realm of the Frost Giantess . . . You will see, Human morsels, you will see . . . The laughter became fainter, and the cold blue shapes seemed to blur.

Floy, keeping a firm control on his thoughts, said quite calmly, 'May we know what is to happen next?' and the Wraiths laughed again.

*You will be the Mistress's lover for the night, Human . . .
perhaps for more than one night if you please her . . .* There
was a break in the voices and then they went on. *For more
than one night if you please her. If you have the endurance to
withstand the things she will do to you . . .* Floy shuddered
and made a sudden convulsive movement, but the ropes
held.

*And after that, Human morsel, after that, the Mistress will
render you up to the Soul Eaters who feast every night in the
Cruachan Cavern, and they will take your soul, and then fling
your drained body into the River of the Dead . . . And your body
will submit to the constant lapping of the waters, so that in time
you will change, Humans, little by little, into the fish-creatures
you have already seen . . . You will become scaly and cold-
blooded, your fingers will join into webs, your eyes will become
lidless and staring . . .* The laughter rang out again. *You will
CHANGE, Humans, you will change most fearfully and most
repulsively, so that if your people should come in search of you
– perhaps in a hundred decades or so – if more lost travellers
on a freezing winter's night should find their way to the Lair
of the Geimhreadh, they will turn from you in shuddering
disgust . . .*

Snodgrass said in a low voice, 'Floy this is terrible. Can
we not—' And stopped.

'Wait,' said Floy softly. 'There must be a way to
escape.'

*There is no escape, Humans, there never was any esc-
ape . . . no one ever escapes the embraces of our Mistress . . .*

The voices were growing fainter, but they could still
hear the creatures' words, lingering on the air.

*You belong to the Geimhreadh now, you are her chosen
bridegrooms . . . You must pleasure her in every way she wishes,
Humans . . . She is greedy for the bodies of Men-Humans, and
she is insatiable . . . You will see, Humans, you will see . . .*

After what seemed a very long time, but was in fact only
minutes, Floy said, 'I think that if we are to escape, now
is the time.'

'Yes,' said Snodgrass firmly and very definitely, and

Floy wondered if Snodgrass was quite as firm as he was sounding, or if it was just to make them both feel better. All the same, he was grateful for Snodgrass's firmness, because it was something good to have in this sort of situation. Aloud, he said, 'We probably don't have very much time,' and Snodgrass said, 'No, I expect we don't.' Floy managed to half raise himself and look about the cold, dank, stone chamber and take stock of their surroundings.

The horrid lapping River tributary was a little way off, to their left, although they could see the silvery darting shapes just beneath the water's surface and they could feel the miasma of cold despair which rose from the River's depths. Floy repressed a shiver and thought that, surely, despair was the coldest and the loneliest of all the emotions of Man. To know yourself utterly and forever abandoned; to be without hope, without anything in the world ever again . . . To have to think: this is all there will be anywhere, ever.

They were bound by the repulsive ropes to two long, rather high couches. The couches were covered with some soft slippery stuff; Floy thought it might be silk, but whatever it was it was cold and faintly slimy and Floy found himself wondering who had lain here last. Then he glanced to the dark River and wished he had not.

Above them, the stone walls stretched up and up into the distant shadowy roof of the chamber. Within the shadows, they could see thick, pale cobwebs and there were faint stirrings in the cobwebs, as if blind scuttling things might lurk there. Floy received a fleeting impression of whitish, boneless creatures watching them. *Creatures of the Geimhreadh . . . creatures of the Wraiths . . .* But I had better not think that, said Floy silently, and I had certainly better not start imagining things that might not be there. It would be better, it would be far more practical, to assess this situation and try to get out of it. The storm creatures had gone. At least, it was to be hoped they had gone.

To begin with, Floy thought it might just be possible

to pull the hair-ropes off, strand by revolting strand. He levered himself into a half-sitting position, his legs bent to one side, and tried working his thumbs against the ropes. But the coarse hair, the pubic hair of the *Geimhreadh*'s past victims, had been tightly plaited and it held. Over how many years have these ropes been fashioned? thought Floy, sickened, and then pushed the thought from him. No matter how many years, no matter how numerous the victims, the *Geimhreadh*'s ropes held strong and well.

'No good,' said Floy, at length, and cursed softly and angrily.

'Could we reach each other's bonds?' asked Snodgrass. 'And somehow loosen each other's ropes?'

'We could try.'

But the silk-covered couches were several feet apart; and the Wraiths had tied the ropes to the couch legs and arms. Neither of them could move more than an inch or so in any direction. Floy tried to think that the *Geimhreadh*, when she came, would surely have to free them. Wouldn't she? But that depends on what she is expecting me to do to her, thought Floy, grimly.

With the coming of the night, the lapping waters of the River seemed to have grown quieter, as if the creatures that dwelled beneath the surface might be sinking into a torpor. From time to time, there was a brief turbulence, as if the soul-less, half-Humans beneath it still moved, but the River had become more quiescent. It is listening, thought Floy. It is listening and it is waiting, and it is saying: soon we shall reach out and welcome two new brothers to our depths. Floy half turned his head again and caught the white gleam of the River creatures and glimpsed a flash of iridescence. Dozens of pairs of eyes, watching, waiting, expectant.

And then Snodgrass said, 'Floy. There's someone coming.'

And Floy heard it as well.

Slithering footsteps coming closer.

The *Geimhreadh*.

* * *

As the *Geimhreadh* slithered into the room her neckless body reared up and forward, her narrow flat eyes blinking in grisly anticipation. Floy saw the lipless mouth smile and the forked tongue dart in and out and saw, as well, the gleam of sensuous pleasure in the creature's expression. He thought: she is going to enjoy us. She is going to subject us to whatever dark, unnatural desires she possesses. I cannot think of a way out of this, thought Floy, but he held the dark, unblinking stare steadily, because however unthinkable it was that they should succumb to the *Geimhreadh*'s horrid appetites, it was even more unthinkable to Floy that they should show this monster fear.

The *Geimhreadh* was still swathed in the loose pale wrappings she had worn earlier; a fold partly covered her head, lending her the semblance of a Human, but it was still the snake-disguised-as-female they had seen at the first encounter. As she came nearer, the dreadful head poked out, and the swathing cloths loosened a little.

'So you have not tried to evade me, my precious ones,' said the creature, in her gobbling, clotted voice.

'We have no choice, ma'am,' said Floy. 'It seems that we are yours to command.' Incredibly, a smile widened the *Geimhreadh*'s mouth.

'Courtesy under these circumstances, Human. That is something I had not looked for. You have some spirit. That will make this all the more enjoyable.'

And all the better to devour, my dears . . .

She moved closer, towering above them. Eight feet tall? wondered Floy, staring up. More?

'The Wraiths have done well by me this time,' said the *Geimhreadh*, swaying a little on her tiny, stumplike feet and staring down at Floy. Floy had the impression that she was inspecting his body and was liking what she was seeing. 'And you are healthy, I think.'

Floy said, acidly, 'That is for you to discover, ma'am,' and again there was the smile.

'We shall see, Human,' said the Frost Giantess, and

made another of the sudden undulating movements, so that the loose wrappings fell to the floor, and she was naked before them.

As a young man on Renascia, Floy had been considerably sought out by unprincipled ladies, and sometimes by ladies who were quite principled, as well. On occasion he had done the seeking on his own account. But the results had nearly always been the same. Nights in beds that were not his own, afternoons in beds that were not his own, as well: for the long drowsy afternoons on Renascia had always been made languorous and sensual by the slow sinking of the light into the Mountains, and by the heady, heavy golden rainbow light from the chasing Ikons who came out at this time of the day and spread their light everywhere. Afternoons had been times when no one had quite known where anyone else was, very nearly traditional for seduction.

Floy would have said, had he been questioned, that he had loved wisely rather than too well; his heart had never been in danger, although his loins had certainly been led astray a time or two, and there were a number of Renascian ladies whose cheeks were bepainted with a far from maiden blush when his name was mentioned. Certainly he would have admitted that, if the pleasures were offered, he had seldom refused.

There had always been a moment in the love-making, during the slow, sweet seductions, which he had always particularly savoured. He supposed it was quite a trivial part of love-making, but it was a brief moment he always looked for because of the way it seemed to lend an extra strength to the intimacy of the encounter. It was the moment when the lady of his choice (or the lady who had chosen him) slid from her silken gown, or velvet robe, or unfastened her satin nightgarb and let it slide to the floor in a whisper of sensuous movement and the faint drift of feminine perfume.

That was the moment that always touched Floy deeply and fired him to genuine ardour, occasionally even to a fleeting love. That sudden gentle stirring of fragrance. It was that which lent the edge to his appetite, which sharpened his every sense. It had always seemed to him a moment of intense intimacy; the scent, the fragrance, the *essence* of the woman with whom you were about to share an immense closeness.

It was something he had come to look for, to enjoy briefly but lingeringly, spinning it out, rather as a man about to enjoy a five-course banquet will spin out the savouring of what on Earth had once been called an aperitif. An appetite teaser. Floy had viewed that ruffle of fragrance, that flurry of female perfumed skin, as an appetite teaser. An emphasis, a reminder, a precursor of the delight and intimacy to come.

Now, tied down to a cold couch by plaited coarse fibres; the cold greasy lapping of a sinister River in his ears, almost certainly facing not death, but a terrible, endless, soul-less existence, Floy remembered every one of those gentle, feminine flurries of fragrance, every single one subtly different, every one an indivisible part of its fair owner, and felt a shuddering sickness at what was happening now.

Instead of the flurry of scented feminine skin he had always looked for, now there was a sudden breath of ancient stale flesh; of unwashed limbs and of tainted, carious juices, long since bereft of any freshness. Floy felt his stomach lift with revulsion; but when he spoke his voice was light and fearless and very nearly insouciant.

'And are we to spend the night together, you and I, ma'am?' said Floy, and had the satisfaction of seeing brief surprise flare in the dark eyes.

'If you satisfy me, Human, there may be several nights.' She leaned closer and Floy saw again the glistening ringed, wormlike skin. A cold, finlike hand came out to caress him. 'My needs are many, Human, and my appetites are voracious.'

Floy said, rather coldly, 'I fear I shall be unable, ma'am,' and regarded her challengingly.

The *Geimhreadh* laughed and Floy and Snodgrass

shuddered. 'Your body will harden when I wish it to, Human,' she said. 'There are caresses I can give you that your weak Human females would never dream exist.' She bent even closer and Floy tried not to flinch from the stench of fetid breath and unwashed scaly skin. 'And although I have never failed yet to harden the loins of my victims,' said the *Geimhreadh*, in a hissing whisper, 'if that should happen now, morsel, then I have many enchantments at my beck. Not for nothing have I trafficked with the one called the Robemaker.'

She moved away a little and stood watching him, the forked tongue flickering again. 'Shall I begin by licking the tip of your manhood, Human?' said the *Geimhreadh*, and her voice had thickened with anticipation. 'Shall I insert the prongs of my snake-tongue into the shaft of your phallus, Human, and shall I probe deep within it so that I penetrate to the core and lick your juices at their source?' She moved again, and Floy felt the thick, rough snakeskin against his arm.

'And,' said the *Geimhreadh*, close to his ear now, 'shall I caress you in the ways of men with men, so that we can see if your desires lie in that direction, so that we can then summon the Wraiths to pleasure you?' A thick, clotted chuckle broke from her and rang eerily round the stone chamber. 'They have their own appetites, the Wraiths,' said the Frost Giantess and, with a sudden jabbing movement, slid the length of her body alongside Floy's.

It was far worse than Floy had believed possible. It was like being wrapped in the boneless embrace of a giant worm or a flapping, finned fish-creature. The *Geimhreadh*'s breath was cold and fetid in his face, so that his insides churned with nausea. He could feel the thick, flaccid body pressing and writhing against him; she could feel every line of him, making him shudder at the horrid intimacy of it. He could feel the tiny fin-hands sliding between his thighs, probing, touching, exploring . . .

'Harden,' hissed the Frost Giantess, the tiny embryo fingers working against him. 'Harden, Human, or must

I call up the Wraiths to weave their spells and make you!'

Floy looked her in the eye and said, 'You may weave your enchantments and work your filth until fire freezes, ma'am, but you will never take any satisfaction from me.' And saw the dark fury in her eyes and knew himself bound now for the worst the creature could devise.

She reared back, slithering from the couch, and paused, gathering her strength. There was a furious hissing and the *Geimhreadh*'s eyes glinted redly. She towered above Floy, her thick body whirling into a column of pale, mucous matter, spinning higher and higher in the cold stone room, a great pillar of curdled gelatinous matter, neither Human nor snake nor fish, nor any creature of the earth at all now.

There was the piercing whine of icy wind and the Storm Wraiths were there, laughing and shrieking, blue and glacial, their jeering faces hovering above Floy, their long icicle fingers darting at him, tearing at his clothes, ripping his breeches from him, and then caressing him with their freezing fingers.

Floy gasped and flung his head back on the silk couch and felt the icy cold creep over his entire body. He was dimly aware of a filmy silver garment being thrown over him, partially obscuring his vision, and from a great distance he heard the *Geimhreadh*'s voice saying, 'The Cloak of Sensuality, Human – and one of the Robemaker's best achievements.'

Floy set his teeth and curled his hands into clenched fists. The Cloak had descended about him now; he was vaguely aware that it was enveloping him, thin, cool, not quite transparent, but not opaque either, so that he could see the *Geimhreadh* and the Wraiths through a mist. *Aye, Human, through a glass darkly, but yet face to face . . .*

The cold was creeping over his body, now; it was stealing inside his skin, so that he was cold inside as well as out and it was licking his nerve endings now, with tiny, roughened tongues . . . This is not in the least bit sensual, said Floy's mind. I am not responding to any of this in the smallest bit.

455

He was not responding at all, he was shivering with cold, and repulsed by the *Geimhreadh*, who was still rearing up over him, darting her snake-head face at him, reaching out the tiny fin-hands to touch his skin . . .

And I am not responding . . . I do not believe in enchantments, and I do not believe in the Robemaker's Cloak of Sensuality.

Without warning, the blood descended between his thighs and there was a rush not of heat, but of repulsive congealed coldness, a terrible travesty of lust. Repulsive! thought Floy, shuddering and sickened, but, as the thought formed, he heard the Wraiths screech with triumph, and the sound echoed and reverberated round the stone walls, and sent the waters of the River churning and foaming.

He hardens, Mistress, see how he is ready for your embrace . . . see how MANNISH he becomes . . . And then: what easy prey these Mortals are!

Floy's eyes were half-closed, but he could still see, very clearly, the evil, grinning masks of the Wraiths, and he could see the flat snakesmile of the *Geimhreadh*; he could taste the sour stench of her rancid flesh. He knew his body to be hardening, responding, betraying him, making a sick mockery of every sweet moment enjoyed in the rainbow-lit afternoons and of every scented hour stolen or snatched or enjoyed. *I will not respond,* said Floy silently, furiously. This has nothing at all to do with the sweet longing of one creature for another. This is malevolent magic. I won't respond.

But the Wraiths were swarming over him now, tracing icy patterns across his naked skin with their sharp, dripping fingers, and there was a frenetic throbbing between his thighs, a horrid cold coagulation of blood and seed.

'There is no fighting, Human,' said the *Geimhreadh* and slid on to the couch beside him.

The Wraiths shrieked their rasping cries again and swooped all about him, but the *Geimhreadh* had lumbered her great writhing shape on to the couch and she was twining all about his limbs. There was a moment when she coiled her body into a spiral, so that Floy felt the tail somewhere against his feet, thick and crustlike. And then she straightened, the neckless torso pressing against him.

I shall endure it, said Floy silently, setting his teeth. I shall endure it and she will soon have done and then, perhaps, there will be a chance to escape. It cannot last for ever.

The *Geimhreadh* was flicking her forked tongue over his skin, little darting jabs that made his entire body crawl with repulsion. She squirmed her head across his body and darted between his legs. Floy felt the scaly skin brush his thighs and flung his head back, willing himself to endure without murmur.

The forked tongue darted again and the finlike hands curved about his stiff phallus, cupping it in a travesty of a lover's caress . . . I shan't feel any of it, said Floy silently. I shan't know this is happening. I'll remember that it's part of the quest to help Nuadu and the others, that it's part of the fight for them to regain Tara. Tara, the Shining Palace . . . Yes, that was better. That was a good thought, a *clean* thought. I'll think about Tara and I'll think about how Fenella and I might be able to be there properly, openly, how we might be able to enjoy the banquets and the feasts and the entertainments.

The forked tongue darted again, long and flickering, longer than seemed possible . . . it lengthened, curling whiplike from the creature's flat lips and slid down into the shaft of Floy's captured penis.

And down and down, probing deep into his body . . .

It felt like a million slimy cold needles pouring down, penetrating the most vulnerable part of him. It felt like every foul thing and every nightmare, and every slimed creature he had ever imagined, and every one of them was invading his body . . .

The *Geimhreadh* paused for long enough to glance up and to fix him with her basilisk eyes . . . See how I can enjoy you, Human morsel . . . And then returned to her horrid work, writhing and squirming against him, the fin-hands resting on Floy's thighs to support her weight.

She made a really dreadful *settling* movement, as a creature about to hatch eggs will settle on a nest, and Floy felt the tongue again and struggled, for the cold wet was turning to white-hot needles. His loins felt as if they were being pierced, invaded by millions of tiny sizzling pokers . . .

The *Geimhreadh* made a terrible sucking sound and Floy's muscles tensed and tightened. He set his teeth again and clenched his fists, but the creature's tongue was embedded deep in his vitals and the Robemaker's Cloak of Sensuality was all about him and there was no possible escape.

The climax, when it came, bore no resemblance to the soft explosions of pure pleasure he had known on Renascia. There was a deep, wrenching pain, a feeling of smothering, of something being suffocated, aborted, so that muscles which had been about to unfold, cramped, and nerve-endings winced. Floy half lifted his head and saw, with helpless disgust, the neck muscles of the *Geimhreadh* rippling as she swallowed his seed from its source . . .

Then there was a sound from the second couch and a sudden cry. The *Geimhreadh* turned her head just as Snodgrass slid from the second couch and into the River of the Dead.

Snodgrass had not intended to go directly into the dank waters of the River. He had, in fact, been working quietly and doggedly at the hair-ropes that bound him, as he had thought that the *Geimhreadh* and the Storm creatures would be so busy with Floy that they would not notice what he was doing.

He had thought that it ought to be quite easy to slip from the couch and hide somewhere outside the stone chamber until some kind of hue and cry was raised. (He had, in fact, been rather pleased at remembering this archaic expression.) Then he might find some way to rescue Floy.

It ought to have been easy to slip from the couch and hide somewhere. There was nothing to lose by at least trying this. Snodgrass had loosened the ropes carefully and furtively; it had been quite difficult, but he had managed it, strand by horrid strand, and he had actually been free for several minutes before he made his move. This had had to be judged very carefully indeed, because too soon would have attracted attention, too late and it would not have been worth escaping.

So he had judged carefully and he thought he had judged quite well, really. The pity was that he had not allowed for – or perhaps not seen – the cold slipperiness of the stone floor. He had slipped, not much, but enough, and the slip had turned into a skid and he had skidded straight into the River of Souls and found himself clinging to the sides, with the waters lapping about his ankles. There was a dreadful feeling of being *pulled* and a really terrible sensation of grasping hands within the River . . .

Come down into the depths, Human, and make one with us all . . . Snodgrass shuddered and tried to reach a safer footing, but the sides of the River were greasy and it was impossible to gain a hold anywhere. Snodgrass felt himself sliding away, so that the turgid waters of the River of Souls inched higher, and the reaching hands felt a little closer.

When Snodgrass cried out, Floy felt the *Geimhreadh* start back and, as she did so, the Wraiths swooped down about her head. There was a moment when the hooded eyes searched the shadows.

'Where is the other one?' said the *Geimhreadh*, and Floy saw the forked tongue flicker and dart, and then the Wraiths dived again and the Frost Giantess turned to urge them on.

The ropes that bound him had loosened beneath the *Geimhreadh*'s writhings and Floy, working frantically, managed to loosen them a little further. By dint of using his fingernails to saw at the ropes, strand by strand, he felt the coarse ropes part and his wrists spring free. The *Geimhreadh* was swaying to where Snodgrass was clinging to the sides of the River; for the moment she was not paying Floy any attention and Floy slid a furtive hand to the ropes about his ankles. It would be strand by strand again and he would have to work quickly and stealthily. I don't know if I can do it, thought Floy, his eyes never leaving the undulating snake-form of the *Geimhreadh*. I don't know if there will be time . . .

The waterlight was rippling frantically on the stone walls now, as the River was churned into turbulent life by the threshing of the creatures within. Floy, hearing Snodgrass's struggles, knew that the fish-Humans were no longer in their night torpor; they were alive and alert, and they were reaching out for the Human.

Come down down into the River of the Dead and join us, for we are sick for company and we are greedy for new friends . . .

The *Geimhreadh* had approached the River's edge, moving with her ugly, legless gait which was not quite a walk but not quite a slither. The Wraiths swooped and screeched, darting at Snodgrass, prodding him with their long fingers, leering and chuckling and emitting their shrill cold cries.

Floy thought: and I am almost free. Only another few strands, only another minute or two, and I shall be free. And then the strands parted and he *was* free. He leapt from the couch and made for the River's edge. He reached for Snodgrass at exactly the same moment as the *Geimhreadh*.

There was a hissing screech of fury as the monster whipped round, Floy felt his balance miss and he went headlong into the River of Souls, dragging Snodgrass with him . . .

At once, the River swirled into angry turbulence, and white spume appeared everywhere. From the dark turgid depths, there reared up dozens of pale, barely Human things, riding the waters and surrounding the helpless Floy and Snodgrass. The stench of rotting fish gusted into their faces, and there was the touch of scales brushing their skins, the sudden downward sucking of an underground tide.

Help us, Humans, SOULLED Humans . . . We cannot see you, but we can hear you and sense you and smell you, and we know you are free as we are not . . .

The soul-less creatures of the River of the Dead . . . They were all around Floy and Snodgrass, they were reaching for them with their rudimentary arms, riding the River's flow in their blind fumbling compulsion to reach the creatures they could sense were close to them.

Floy, gasping and half-blinded by the churning waters, clutched at Snodgrass lest they should both be submerged. His vision was obscured by the white spumy River, but he could see that the creatures closest to them possessed scaly skins and that here and there the scales had thickened, repulsively, into shell.

Shell-backed creatures, grotesque crustaceans that once were Human . . .

Their eyes were already protruding on thick gristly stalks and the bulbous growths at the ends of the stalks swivelled, seeking the fish-creatures' prey. Floy struck out at the nearest, hating himself for hurting the poor doomed thing, but knowing it was the only chance to break free. He sliced frantically at the nearest creature's eye stalk, severing it from the hideous body and, at once, the thick pale blood oozed over him so that he felt his entire body engulfed in sickened disgust.

But even as the half-blinded, shelled thing fell back, churning the River to boiling turbulence again, Floy and Snodgrass both felt the cold scaly creatures pulling them down beneath the surface. The thick slabby waters of the terrible River flowed into their eyes and their mouths and they tasted slime and weed. Snodgrass choked and fought and, as he did so, the pale bloated faces of the soul-less fish-beings loomed yet closer, and the anguish and the greed of the distorted minds flowed outwards.

Help us, Human ones, help us out of our eternal prison . . .

They were being pulled down and down, gasping and helpless, the green muddy River closing over their heads. Floy could feel Snodgrass's hand on his arm and he grasped it at once, for they could not possibly lose one another.

Human, but covered partly in silvery scale-like growths;

fins that were not quite hands but not yet fins flapped and reached, and in the dimness, they could see the breathing flap-like gills that the creatures had developed in their necks.

To Snodgrass, who did not like fish in any form, this was the most repulsive thing yet, and to Floy, who was feeling his lungs begin to burn and scald with the lack of air, it was sinister in the extreme. *For these creatures, these soul-less victims of the Robemaker and his kind, have managed to survive down here ... they have adapted to a half-life in the River because they have no souls and therefore will never die ...* But we shall die, thought Floy, feeling his vision blur and waver, knowing that in another moment, in a very few seconds, they would both be forced to draw in breath and, when that happened, water would flood their lungs and they would die ...

They struggled frantically to get above the surface again and there was a brief respite as they emerged, gasping and retching, gulping in precious lungfuls of air before the fish-Humans reached for them again, and the dark green waters closed about them once more.

And then, just as Floy thought they must be facing death, Snodgrass clutched Floy's arm and thrust his other hand ahead in a slow pointing gesture and Floy saw, directly ahead of them, light pouring outwards from somewhere, throwing into sharp relief the darting misshapen fish-Humans.

They both surged forward at once – although the light might mean nothing at all, thought Floy – and the fish-Humans surged with them, churning the River into turbulence again, so that the light shivered and blurred.

But it is still there! thought Floy, feeling his lungs nearly bursting, red lights beginning to flash before his vision. The light is there and if only, if only we can reach it ...

And then, without warning, the fish-Humans moved faster, creating a sudden current of water, and then they were in the light, and there were dark walls of some kind of tunnel all about them. Floy summoned up one last shred of resolve, and pulled Snodgrass with him straight at the light.

They emerged, gasping, dripping wet and exhausted, into an underground cave, where the waters of the River of Souls lapped gently and quietly against pale white rock.

Floy thought they were both certainly more alive than dead. They drew in air thankfully and neither of them moved or spoke for a very long time.

And then Floy, pulling himself together, sat up and looked about him and saw that the cave was quite a shallow one; it was possible to see straight ahead, to where the mouth of the cave opened onto a calm, flat, night landscape of fields and trees and star-spattered sky.

There was a cold clearness to the scene and a cleanness about the air.

And then Floy looked to the left and saw rearing, elaborate gates and high city walls. From within the walled city there glowed warmth and light and, occasionally, tongues of flame licked high into the night air. Even at this distance, he could see that the city walls were red-gold and that the elaborately wrought gates were tipped with flame.

The Fire Court of the Sorceress Reflection. There was no doubting it.

Chapter Thirty-six

It was extremely boring to have to go down into Mother's nightly gathering and pretend to be enjoying the revelries and the feastings. Flame thought it was the most boring thing that anyone could ever be expected to do.

She had a new gown, of course; Mother had chosen it, because Mother always did choose her gowns, which was something else that was extremely boring.

It all came of Mother pretending that Flame was actually much younger than she was, so that Mother could sigh and tell everyone how young she was herself, 'Of course, I was the merest *child* when that *creature* Fael-Inis took advantage of my innocence.'

Fael-Inis was Flame's father, and everyone in the Court knew that Mother had not been innocent at all, although everyone fell in with the story because none of them wanted to be flung incontinently from the Court and perhaps find themselves on the Gruagach Road which would mean facing the Frost Giantess and the Wraiths.

Reflection did not trouble her head over the Frost Giantess. 'Oh, I can easily send out a spell or two to deal with *her*,' she said, when people wondered whether the Frost Giantess ever posed any kind of threat to Reflection's territories. 'Of course she is not a threat! The very idea! Everyone knows she never got beyond the most *basic* of spell-weaving – I feel rather sorry for her, if you want the truth. Poor creature, she is not much sought after these days. I have sometimes wondered whether it would be a *kind* gesture to ask her to supper . . . What do you think? Or even,' said Reflection thoughtfully, 'for a few days' stay. But then, of course, she would *devour* all my young men and that would *never* do. Poor things, they are *utterly* loyal to me.' She smiled her catsmile.

'They do say,' said Reflection, growing confidential, 'that she *bites* off their phalluses, before she eats their bodies and *spits* them out into the River of Souls for the fish-Humans to catch. Well,' said Reflection, with one of her superb shrugs, 'such *vulgarity*, leave aside the *waste*. No, I really could not have such a person staying in my beautiful Fire Court. It would lower the tone and people are so *quick* to notice these things. Before we knew it, they would be saying that I had become *common*. And if there is one thing I will not become, it is common. The *Geimhreadh* will have to stay where she is. Although they do say,' said Reflection, thoughtfully, 'they do say, that Gruagach is in positive ruins. Well, it is very sad, but we cannot be worrying about other people's problems when we have so many of our own.'

Mother did not really have any problems, or none that Flame knew about, unless it might be the almost certain arrival of a new set of bailiffs at the Fire Court, which was an occurrence so frequent that nobody remarked it any longer.

'Fling them into the River,' Mother usually said on these occasions. And then, 'Or no, on second thoughts, let me *inspect* them first. Bailiffs can be quite *extraordinarily* attractive now and then. I believe it is the *power* they have over one. You would be almost certain to submit, just a little, to someone who could throw you out of your house if he wanted to. Authoritative,' said Reflection, nodding. 'Yes, *very* attractive.'

They had a total of twenty-seven bailiffs now living at the Fire Court as a result of Mother's finding the species attractive. This was generally thought to be a reasonable proportion when you considered that nearly a hundred had come to the Court over the years.

'Dear souls,' said Reflection. 'And they *do* enjoy one another's company. I believe they have set up some kind of *money-lending* institution, solely for everyone here, and if that is not generous, I do not know what is. I believe, you know, that you could say I had founded a *community*,' said Reflection thoughtfully. '*Services* to the rest of the Court.

465

Very altruistic of me, wouldn't you say?'

Mother liked it thought that she was generous. 'I am the *soul* of generosity,' she said whenever anyone was around whom it might be useful to let hear this. 'Stories of my benevolence precede my coming everywhere.' But, later, she would remind Flame that she had not a bottomless purse. 'And *where* you find these hangers-on, Flame, I do not know. I do not know the quarter of the people who are to dine tonight.'

It was pointless to say that Flame knew none of the people either, because they would nearly all be adventurers or young men seeking their fortune, or poor younger sons on the make. Now and again there would be a few pilgrims, or genuine travellers, which could be quite interesting, but, in the main, the people who came to the Fire Court were ruffians and gamblers and opportunists.

'The raff and skaff of Ireland,' said Reflection, studying a guest list for that evening's banquet and frowning. 'Well, of course, my dear, it is *entirely* your affair who you ask here. I should not *dream* of turning away your friends. I *never* interfere,' said Reflection, to whom interfering was meat and drink. 'And I certainly never gossip,' she said virtuously. 'Your father would tell you that, if he was here to tell you anything, which of course he is not.'

Flame's father had never, to Flame's knowledge, visited the Fire Court – 'Too arrogant,' said Reflection, 'we are *quite* beneath his notice.' – and, although Flame had never met him, she was intrigued by the stories, all of which she listened to. If you had to have a father whom you had never met, it was rather fun to have one who was mysterious and enigmatic and who was supposed to be able to whisk himself in and out of Time. As a child, Flame had listened to the servants' gossip for hours on end, stealing down the narrow, curving steps which led to the sculleries and curling into a chimney corner where she could not be seen. She had crept down to the firerooms as well sometimes, where the immense furnaces that lit the Court were kept, and which had to be stoked and fed and maintained round the clock. This had not been so easy,

466

because the fire-room workers guarded their domain jealously.

But she had heard a great many of the stories about Fael-Inis, the creature of fire and light and speed, and how Mother had somehow seduced him in the Fire Mountains and then quarrelled with him just before Flame was born. She had laid a great many plots for getting out of the Fire City and somehow travelling to the Palace of Wildfire where Fael-Inis lived, but Mother usually found these out (Flame suspected that this was not sorcery but plain old-fashioned spying) and confined Flame to her room for a week with bread and water to eat, and sometimes even summoned up a demon or two to give her nightmares so the game had ceased to be worth the candle. Flame would probably get to meet her father eventually, but not until she was quite old, by which time her father would have lost his famous charm and his intriguing habit of travelling through Time and it was all a very great pity.

It was going to be extremely tedious in the Court tonight.

'I do wish,' said Reflection, sweeping into Flame's bedchamber an hour before the ball was due to start, 'I do wish you would make an effort.' She began to pick disconsolately at the contents of Flame's wardrobe, remembering how this gown had been ordered for the night of the Masquerade Dance, and how this one had been worn on the day Inchbad sent his special envoy with the marriage proposal.

'When I think,' said Reflection, wringing her hands, 'of how I scraped to give you a chance – well, I despair, that is all I can say, and that is a truly terrible thing for a mother to do of a daughter.' She eyed Flame crossly. 'Here you are,' said Reflection, 'approaching the age of – oh no, do *not* tell me your age, for I do not wish to know, so *elderly-making* – and how you are to be properly and honourably joined with Inchbad when all you do is scowl, I have not the remotest idea!'

'Would you marry a giant?' said Flame, and Reflection flung up her hands in despair.

'If you knew the debts I have incurred,' she began, which was quite an old ploy and one which Flame was entirely familiar with. 'I am *famous* for my debts,' said Reflection, who enjoyed her debts enormously and would not have relinquished one of them. 'Do you know how many times I have escaped being flung into a debtors' prison?'

'Six,' said Flame in a mutter.

'Six,' said Reflection dramatically. 'My dear, the *indignity* of it! They would all be very pleased to see it happen, of course,' she added. 'The other sorceresses and the Court hangers-on. I should be the talk of the Sybilline Ladies' Circle for at least a *year*, because they have very little else to occupy them, poor things.' She eyed Flame. 'But really, Flame, there is no help for it other than for you to marry Inchbad. They say he is quite reasonable-looking for a giant. And we should have the most *lavish* celebration.'

Flame said, 'What about the Fire Ritual?' because she had been brought up on the legend that if anyone with a vein of Amaranthine blood wanted to lie with a Human, the Human must first bathe in the Fire Rivers of Fael-Inis's country. 'Or,' said the legend, 'he will be shrivelled up at once.'

And so Flame, espying a possible escape here, said, 'What about the Fire Ritual?' every time Mother became too insistent on the proposed marriage with Inchbad.

'A mere ritual,' said Reflection, at once. 'Hardly necessary, really. And you know perfectly well that the donning of a Fire Robe more or less gets round the problem.'

Mother had a cupboardful of Fire Robes, which the Robemaker supplied at a special price. She boasted that it was one of her hallmarks to coax her Human lovers into donning one of these before she took him off to bed, so that the Amaranthine blood did not harm him. Sometimes she did not bother with the Robe, of course, which meant that the poor young man had to be flung out the next morning, dried and scorched and shrivelled. Sometimes he was flung out anyway, Robe or not.

The Fire Robes were actually rather beautiful; they were made of a particular combination of fire (to match the Amaranth blood) and ice (to prevent the fire from scalding the colder Human blood). The Robemaker wove them with delicate threads of living flames and thin, pale icicles so that they hung to the wearer's feet and down to his wrists, swathes of glittering scarlet and icy blue. They were silken to the touch and had the peculiar quality of feeling first blazingly hot and then exquisitely cool. Flame had seen several of Mother's more favoured young men wearing them and they were extremely becoming. But the thought of Inchbad donning one made her feel ill. There was something quite horridly intimate about getting into bed with somebody who had put on a beautiful silken robe on your account. It ought to have been the sort of thing you only shared with someone with whom you were extremely close.

Flame knew quite well that, in fact, Mother's ancestry was at best questionable. She had even heard whispers that her only claim on the Amaranthine House was that her great-grandmother had once caught the eye of a very famous Amaranthine sorcerer and spent a night with him, as far back as the reign of Cormac of the Wolves. With this ancestry, Mother could therefore claim nothing better than a bastard connection with the Amaranthines. And a tenuous one at that, said Reflection's detractors dismissively, although nobody ever dared to say this to Reflection direct, because no matter how fragile the connection, Reflection could still call up remarkably effective enchantments, never mind the fire demons, with whom she was on very good terms. The servants said that Madame was a rare old one with the fire demons, and it more than a body's life was worth to risk having them set on you.

Reflection smiled vaguely on Flame and departed in search of the sempstress who had left her new gown a half inch too short and would, as a result, be put to the mercies of one of those very demons for an hour or so, because

Reflection did not believe in allowing menials to think they could get away with slipshod, slapdash work.

At the centre of the Fire Court, Reflection's chefs and scullions and spit-boys and scrub-women were hard at work on the banquet that Madame had ordered for the evening's entertainment. It was a fairly small banquet as banquets went; there would probably not be more than a hundred or so sitting down to the feast, although this could not be relied upon, because Madame sometimes had the way of adding upwards of a dozen extra guests at the last minute and it all made for a very difficult time. It made it hard to assess the number of roast swan and stewed peacock to serve and it made it very difficult indeed to know how many oxen to put on the roasting spits, because if the numbers at table were not what you had expected, you were left with a surfeit of roast ox, which was all very well, but could be a nuisance, since nobody wanted to have to eat roast oxen for a week, and Reflection would not entertain the idea of left-overs of any kind in the Aurora Banqueting Hall.

But a banquet had been ordered, and so a banquet would have to appear, never mind that they were all of them scratching their heads to get in the necessary food and wine, let alone clean table linen and crystalware, because if Madame had ever paid a bill in her life, nobody could remember it.

The bedchamber staff turned their energies to the laying of clean silk sheets on all the beds, because everybody knew how Madame's banquets ended, and they were careful not to forget the discreet placement of flagons of aphrodisiacal wine for those whose strengths might flag a bit towards dawn. They were hotly in dispute with the kitchen staff as to which of them was the most overworked; Madame was very particular about her bedchambers, they said, and she was very particular indeed about her own bedchamber. When you considered that you never knew just what you might be finding on the floor of Madame's bedchamber on mornings after a banquet, you might count yourself very fortunate if all you had to do was conjure up a few roast geese and maybe a swan or two to grace the table. Also, hadn't Madame the habit of drawing up a strict rota for her own night's activities. And if the kitchen staff thought it an easy task to have to keep an eye on the clock all night, and send in the young men every hour on the hour, they were welcome to try it.

The kitchen staff refused to be drawn. They said that, when you remembered that Madame had the way of flinging nearly all the unsatisfactory lovers bodily through the window before breakfast, it cut down on the tidying up of a morning, never mind reducing the number of breakfasts to be carried in.

Deep beneath the great Court, the furnace rooms would pour out the leaping firelight and the fire-room slaves would be working throughout the night to keep the furnaces fed. Nobody knew very much about the fire-room slaves, who kept themselves to themselves, (although the kitchen staff said they ate pretty heartily), but it was rumoured that Madame had an arrangement with the Robemaker, who kept her supplied with slaves from his own dark Workshops, and that they were kept happy by Madame taking them to her bed, once a week in strict rotation. Nobody had ever been able to find out the truth of this, but it was the sort of thing you could easily believe. Amongst the kitchen staff (who considered themselves overworked) and the bedchamber staff (who considered themselves under-valued) the fire-room slaves were known as Madame's rough-rides, because work in the furnace rooms was apt to coarsen a person.

And so the great Fire Court hummed and throbbed with preparation and the scents of food and wine mingled with the scents of burning applewood and fruitwood, which Madame caused to be flung into the furnaces in cruel defiance of the laws governing the Trees. The ladies of the Court studied their wardrobes and sighed, because no matter what one wore, one would certainly be outshone by Madame herself, and the gentlemen wondered, a touch uneasily, which of them might be beckoned to

471

Madame's bedchamber and whether they would be able to stay the course if so, or whether they would end in being thrown from the window, which was the sort of fate which could bring eternal shame and disgrace to your descendants.

Reflection herself passed a pleasant hour in trying on a new enchantment which she had ordered from the Robemaker, which would have the happy effect of making every man who saw her fall desperately in love with her, and Flame sat in her bedchamber and thought up four ways of escaping from the Court, and wondered if she would have the courage to try any of them.

The doorkeeper, preparing to take his usual post-prandial snooze, noticed two somewhat bedraggled travellers approaching and sighed, because it was a sad old life when a man could not have a bit of sleep after his dinner. Still, you could not turn away two poor creatures who had fallen foul of the *Geimhreadh*. They would have to be brought inside and warmed and fed, and probably provided with clothing. Also, orders were orders, and Madame's orders were that all travellers were to be taken inside and made welcome, because, Madame said with one of her greedier smiles, you never knew what might turn up on your doorstep.

Flame was not particularly interested in the news that two travellers had come from Inchbad with designs for Crown Jewels, although there were rumours about their escape from the Frost Giantess which sounded as if they might have an interesting tale to tell.

But Inchbad had been sending presents and deputations and concessions to the Fire Court ever since it had occurred to the Gruagach to try to ally themselves with Reflection's daughter. The thing to do was to go on reminding Mother about the Fire Ritual, and the necessity for persuading Fael-Inis to let them into the Palace of Wildfire to accomplish this. Since Mother had spent eighteen years denigrating Fael-Inis, it seemed pretty unlikely that he would open his Palace gates for something so trivial. Flame was rather pleased to have hit on the word trivial, because it seemed to reduce Inchbad and the entire

472

scheme to something that did not matter very much.

But she donned the new gown for the banquet because it would probably be quite rude to just not turn up, and tried not to arrive too early when nobody would be there, but tried not to be too late either, which would have meant making a grand entrance, and which would, moreover, have annoyed Mother, who liked to arrive last, so that the musicians could play a fanfare and everyone could turn to look. Mother enjoyed making sweeping entrances; she made no secret of this and liked to tell people that she had designed the Aurora Banqueting Hall, if not the entire Fire Court, with this in mind.

Flame knew this to be stretching the truth because the Aurora Banqueting Hall had been Mother's attempt to rival Tara's Sun Chamber and the legendary Palace of Wildfire of Fael-Inis. Opinions were divided as to how well she had succeeded. Her detractors were wont to smile sadly and shake their heads and say that *poor* Reflection had done her best, but that *really* there was no comparison, quality would always out and dear Reflection had allowed her Hall to be spoiled by shoddy workmanship and cheap materials. Her followers, loyal to a man, if not sycophantic, were loud in maintaining that the Aurora Hall was *infinitely* superior to the brash Sun Chamber and the austere Palace of Wildfire.

The Palace itself was built of the pale dressed stone which Reflection had managed to discover in the distant quarries of the Western Isles and had brought inland at considerable expense – although Flame did not think it had been at Mother's expense exactly, because the bailiffs said that the stone masons had never been paid, although Madame might have handed out a few discarded spells by way of reimbursement. The cluster of buildings and houses and lodges which had grown up around the Palace, and which housed the servants and their families, was built of the same pale cream stone. Flame, who was rarely permitted to step outside the City Walls, but who sometimes sneaked out at night when everyone was busy, thought that even when you did not have anything to compare it with, it was a beautiful place.

The City Gates had been angled to catch the evening sun and were tipped with raw gold to catch the light of the dying day, so that every evening the entire palace could be bathed in fiery light.

Chapter Thirty-seven

The fiery light from the City Gates was the first thing that Floy and Snodgrass had seen when they emerged from the terrible water caves of the Frost Giantess and the River of Souls, and in their cold and exhausted state, it seemed like a beacon, a bright warm lodestar sending out its allure. They had stood looking at it for a moment, Floy wrapped in Snodgrass's cloak and they had known that their mission for the giants was almost completed.

They had entered warily at the behest of a rather dozy doorkeeper, then they rested and bathed and refreshed, and then had been provided with clean new garments by Reflection's servants; who had appeared to find nothing at all untoward about the appearance of two cold and exhausted travellers who had escaped the *Geimhreadh*'s evil machinations by the skin of their teeth.

They were unsure of what they would find in the Banqueting Hall and they were wary about these people who served a sorceress.

'But,' Floy had said as they prepared to leave the comfortable, silk-hung bedchambers allotted to them, 'we have to explore as fully as possible, because of Fenella.'

'I should think she'd have got here long since,' said Snodgrass, comfortingly.

They stood together looking about them, scanning the assembly for Fenella's dark head and seeing only the sycophantic faces of the panoply of beings who had found their way to the Fire Court; noticing that there was a rather odd, certainly raffish set of people here.

'I can't see Fenella,' hissed Floy.

'Nor can I.'

Snodgrass started to say that in a place the size of this one it would be possible for a hundred people to remain hidden when there was a fanfare of music from the musicians and every head turned to the great, curving stair.

Snodgrass, who was rather short, stood on tiptoe, and wanted to know what was happening.

'I rather think,' said Floy, 'that it's our hostess.'

The musicians had sprung to attention and were playing the fanfare which always announced Reflection's arrival. Everybody prepared to kneel in homage, because wouldn't there be the devil to pay if Madame entered the Aurora Hall music-less and unnoticed? And *nobody* wanted to risk having the fire demons summoned.

Reflection stood framed in the great golden archway at the top of the stairway, smiling and nodding, lifting her left hand in acknowledgement, because, as she told everyone, there was *nothing* like a fanfare to attract people's attention.

Floy, standing with Snodgrass, found himself thinking he had never before heard any music quite so garish or quite so grating, and he had certainly never seen anything to equal the arrival of the lady who was now descending the stair. He thought, as she moved down the stair and along the line of waiting people, that she had the pleased air of a wayward child who has dressed up in grand clothes and is expecting the grown-ups to praise her. See how important I am! she was thinking to herself. See how everyone kneels and renders me obeisance!

Floy thought she was not young by anybody's reckoning, although he thought that to calculate her years by ordinary reckoning probably could not apply. How long did sorceresses live? She was rather tall and slender and her skin was the pure pale colour of buttermilk or of polished ivory. Her hair was dark and, although there were red lights in it, Floy thought these might be the reflection of the fireglow of the Banqueting Hall, rather than natural colours. Her gown of real leaping flames was the most dazzling thing he had ever seen; he thought to begin with that it was frightening, and then he thought it was beautiful, and then he thought it was neither of these, but part of the wilful child out to shock. Look at this outrageous gown I am wearing!

She is probably rather fun, thought Floy, but she is probably perfectly capable of calling up a nasty enchantment or two if somebody displeases her. I wonder what Fenella thought of her, wondered Floy, and looked round for Fenella again, because although he was rather enjoying Reflection and her bizarre Fire Court, he would have enjoyed it all much more if he could have shared it with Fenella.

As Reflection progressed down the stair, the musicians quickened the flourishing music and there was a flurry of instruments that sent banner-like sounds into the waiting Banqueting Hall. The leaping fire-gown swirled and the thin, light wrap which cloaked it swished and the people of the Court fell to their knees.

Floy and Snodgrass, sons of a world where nearly all men were equal, stayed where they were, although Snodgrass inclined his head a little because, after all, this was their hostess, by all accounts a lady it would be better not to offend. Floy remained standing upright and, when Reflection looked across at them, grinned at her. At once, Reflection walked across the floor towards them, as if her attention had been caught, the flame-gown swishing on the polished surface. She held out a hand and Floy, amused at himself, raised it at once to his lips. He saw the fire-gown's sleeve slip back over the dainty wrist and saw the tiny, curling flames rear back a little.

'I am glad, madame,' said Floy, urbanely, 'that you are able to control the more active sections of your gown.'

'Oh,' said Reflection at once, her eyes fixed on Floy, 'oh, this old thing. Oh, I promise you it is the veriest rag and it is only that it was the first thing to hand when I opened my wardrobe this evening.' She stayed where she was and her eyes raked Floy from head to toe. Her smile widened a little and there was no question but that she was thinking: dear me, *here* is an attractive plaything. There was something childlike about the sudden, intense interest and the lack of any attempt to conceal that interest.

'Do tell me,' said Reflection, after a moment, lowering her voice thrillingly, 'do tell me, are you merely travellers, or something more interesting? I am *always* interested in travellers,' said Reflection and widened her eyes a little.

Floy said, 'We are filled with gratitude for your hospitality, Madame,' and Reflection at once said, 'Oh, I am the *soul* of hospitality, everyone will tell you that. No one is ever turned from my doors, you know.' And drawing closer, '*Do* tell me where you are from,' she said.

'We come from Tara, Madam,' said Floy, and Snodgrass bobbed his head in agreement. 'With,' said Floy, documents from Inchbad.' He knew a brief moment of gratitude that the Gnomes' designs and Goibniu and Inchbad's letters had been tucked safely in Snodgrass's cloak and that, although they had been soaked in the River of Souls, they had dried out quite successfully.

'Inchbad,' said Reflection, purring. 'The *dear* creature. You must tell me *all* about Tara.' And then, 'I thought you were not simply chance-met pilgrims. I can always detect—' she paused, and then went on. 'I can always detect *quality*,' said Reflection.

Floy said, 'We have deliberately sought you out, madame. Can you think it otherwise?' He grinned. 'Also, we have braved the clutches of the Frost Giantess to reach you.'

'Oh, that creature,' said Reflection, dismissively. 'Oh, she is the *greatest* nuisance. Nothing but trouble, for if she is not *eating* all the best young men around, she is doing *unspeakable* things to their bodies.' She paused and studied Floy. 'You appear remarkably unscathed, sir.'

'I escaped within inches of my life,' said Floy gravely, and Reflection narrowed her eyes.

'I should like to hear of your adventures,' she said.

'It will be my pleasure. But,' said Floy, 'to begin with, we must discuss matters of business. Also, we were to meet two of our party here?' He stopped, and Reflection furrowed her brow slightly.

'I do not think we have had any other travellers arrive here lately,' she said. 'But they may still be on their way, for it is easy to miss the road.' She drew a little nearer and Floy was conscious of the warm, musky perfume emanating from her skin. 'I have deliberately cut myself off from the normal travel routes,' said Reflection, thrillingly, 'although, of course, people still manage to reach me.' Again, it was the pleased child, proffering a clever deed for praise.

Floy said, 'I see. Yes, that is possible.'

'No one would be turned away,' said Reflection earnestly. 'I do promise you that.'

'Your hospitality is famous, madame,' said Floy, who was finding this rather superficial, rather insubstantial conversation remarkably easy. 'And your legend goes before you.'

Reflection looked pleased.

'And,' said Floy, 'you should know that we have brought from Tara the designs for the new Crown Jewels for your daughter —'

The smallest frown creased the smooth brow again. 'Such an *ageing* word,' said Reflection. '*Daughter*. And, of course, she is the merest child. As for marriage, well, it is quite absurd, but there it is. I am not one to stand in the way of *anyone's* happiness. And child brides are quite the fashion you know.'

'Of course,' murmured Floy.

'I was one myself,' disclosed Reflection.

'Indeed?' said Floy.

'I was a babe, no more, when that *creature* Fael-Inis took advantage of my innocence,' said Reflection. 'I was seduced by an unprincipled stealer of virtue! Oh, I shall have my revenge, make no mistake. But in the meantime,' said Reflection, apparently recalled to a sense of her surroundings, and certainly recalled to a reminder that she had marked Floy out as a possible lover, 'in the meantime, I have sought to hide my disgrace from the world, along with the poor child who was the result of my sin—' She broke off and eyed Floy. 'I promise you it is all true,' said Reflection in a very different voice, and it was the engaging child again, solemnly promising to tell the truth, holding out a secret to be shared.

'I am sure it is. And your – self-imposed enclosure is a very luxurious one,' said Floy.

'I cannot live without beauty about me,' said Reflection firmly. 'And when you have reached *my* level in sorcery, people expect certain things. Feasts and banquets and pageants. And you would not *believe* the amount these things cost! I have removed myself from such sordid subjects,' said Reflection. 'I cannot give of my best to my calling if I am constantly harried. I told them all that. I said, "You may do as you wish, but do not trouble me with your columns of figures and your nasty accounts."

'Also,' said Reflection, 'I was brought up *always* to have the best, and one becomes *accustomed*. And Flame, poor child, had to be given some kind of life.' She drew a little closer and glanced over her shoulder. Floy and Snodgrass, fascinated, did the same. 'It is *most* unfortunate,' said Reflection in a dramatic whisper, 'that the child's *parentage* will not permit of her *joining* with a Human without having first bathed in the Fire Rivers of her father's country. You take my meaning, sirs?'

'Really?'

'She has missed so much,' said Reflection, her huge dark eyes still on Floy. 'It has meant that so many suitors are *quite* ineligible, because the ceremony of bathing in the Fire – oh, it is *ruinously* expensive. Well, I doubt there is anyone in Ireland who could afford it. I could not afford it,' said Reflection firmly. 'I have told Flame so. "My dear," I said, "if you are ever to be joined with anyone, it will have to be with a *very rich person indeed*, for your father will delight in charging us the earth for the Fire River ceremony. I should be a positive *pauper*, if I had to foot the bill, and the mere thought is enough to send me into a shivering wreck," I said. And that,' said Reflection, 'is positively the *only* reason I entertained Inchbad's suit, because he can afford the Fire River ceremony and *still* have a king's ransom left over. But I daresay you will know this if you are from Tara.'

'We are the souls of discretion,' said Floy, gravely, which, as Snodgrass was to remark later, might have meant anything at all.

'Inchbad has made his mind up that he will have Flame,' said Reflection, with one of her shrugs. 'And who am I to stand in the way of such an *advantageous* alliance for the child? Well, we shall discuss it later,' she said, and studied Floy thoughtfully again.

'For the moment, we shall eat and drink and dance. Dear me, it is all so tedious. Really, I do not know a *quarter* of the people here tonight. But it is expected of me and, as I have always said, who am I to disappoint my people?' She smiled benevolently on them and moved across to where a group of hopeful young men were waiting.

'Well,' said Snodgrass. 'What now?'

'No Fenella,' said Floy, dropping the light, frivolous pose he had donned for Reflection. 'I think we can believe Reflection.'

'I don't much care for this place,' said Snodgrass, doubtfully. 'It's got a nasty feeling of decadence to it.'

'Yes.' Floy was still scanning the assembly and, as he did so, a slender girl with Reflection's glossy hair and pale skin entered the Aurora Hall from a door at the far end.

Floy stood very still. He saw the golden eyes and the slightly reckless tilt to the girl's head; the faint impression that she might see things other people could not see, or dance to music that no one else could hear. As she walked through the great Banqueting Hall the impression strengthened. There was an other-worldliness about her, as if she was not altogether real and might vanish at any minute.

Floy thought: she might be made of moonlight and starlight and the golden fire cressets that lit the Palace of Wildfire.

The Palace of Wildfire . . .

Fael-Inis's daughter!

* * *

481

Flame was quite surprised to be sought out by the young, dark-haired traveller. Usually people were so dazzled by Mother that they barely saw Flame at all, which generally pleased Flame who did not much like the people Mother asked to her banquets anyway. In fact, it was the gods' mercy that the Robemaker had not turned up tonight, which happened sometimes, especially since Mother had recently discussed with him the possibility of his taking Flame in marriage.

The traveller was different to the usual guests. He had come straight to where Flame was watching the dancing and had asked her to dance, and then grinned and admitted he might not be very good at dancing because, where he came from, they did not have this kind of dancing. In fact, they did not have dancing at all. Perhaps they might sit and talk?

This was instantly intriguing, because Flame had never heard of a place that did not have dancing and feasts. It might be interesting to hear more about it.

It turned out to be very interesting indeed. Flame took him out into the gardens, away from the dreadful music and the lights, so that he could see the Fire Court blazing against the night sky which was what people often liked to do.

'Astonishing,' he said in a voice that sounded as if he might really have been thinking: Hideous, and Flame glanced up at him hopefully, because she had long since suspected that the Fire Court was extremely ugly, but she could not be sure about this on account of having nothing to compare it with. It would be extremely interesting to talk to someone who might be able to tell her for sure if it was as beautiful as Mother's followers said, or simply downright grotesque.

They sat in one of the remote corners of the gardens which Mother had not yet spoiled and where there were sweet-scented night roses and honeysuckle and Flame asked to be told about Tara, which was where she thought the young man had come from, and heard, instead, about a strange world called Renascia and about a dark and fearsome Lodestar which had swallowed it up, and about how Floy and his sister and their two friends had fallen into some kind of Golden River and passed through Time.

'We were rescued and brought here by Fael-Inis,' said Floy, watching her closely.

Flame said, 'Oh!' in a rather breathless voice, and clapped both hands to her cheeks which had suddenly grown warm. She had pretended for years that she would run away to Fael-Inis who would welcome her, but it was not really possible.

Or was it? Seated here with Floy it seemed, in some inexplicable way, to be more possible than it had ever seemed before. Was it because Floy had escaped from his world into another world? Or was it simply that he was proving that other worlds existed?

There are other worlds, thought Flame, entranced. There are other worlds and people live in them and sometimes move from one world to another. She turned her mind back to Floy, wanting to hear more about Renascia, which was quite different from anything here.

It seemed that Floy had tried to change things; he had been on the governing body of his people – there had been something called a Council of Nine and they had not liked it when Floy had tried to introduce new ways, or replace the old laws with new ones, all of which Flame thought sounded rather sensible and interesting. It was fun to try new ideas. In the end, said Floy, he had fallen out with the Council, because he had challenged too many of its traditions.

'Really challenged them?' said Flame, hopefully, hardly daring to believe that he would turn out to be a genuine rebel.

'I'm afraid so,' said Floy, and grinned again. This time it was the grin which Fenella had always called the buccaneering grin, the pirate who had wanted to turn Renascia upside-down.

'I was a rebellious leader,' he said, and this time Flame heard the amusement and the touch of self-mockery. It was absurd to think: *this is how my father might sound*, but she found that she was thinking it. Because Floy is a nonconformist, a defiant challenger of the shibboleths . . .

Floy is a rebel . . . Flame sat back, savouring this, and staring at Floy in delight.

Floy smiled, enjoying her strange, ethereal quality; seeing how her hair had red lights in it and how, as well, her eyes slanted and shone exactly like her father's. Her skin was a warm golden colour, as if whatever had laid its burnishing fingers on her hair had let the colours run into her skin as well.

Fael-Inis's daughter, born of a long-ago night when he was lured into a sorceress's bed . . . I wonder what the truth of all that really is, thought Floy. I wonder why I am finding her so extraordinarily beautiful, when I did not find her glittering mother in the least bit beautiful?

But he only said, in a conversational tone, 'The Fire Court is a remarkable place,' and waited for her response.

'It is believed to be beautiful,' said Flame, politely, and then, 'I do not have anything to compare it with, of course.'

'No.'

'I think it's loud and vulgar,' she said, defiantly, silently willing him to agree, and Floy saw with delight that her chin tilted in exactly the way her father's had done and that her eyes sparkled with his golden luminosity.

'I would not have said vulgar precisely,' said Floy, and Flame felt the tendrils of disappointment uncurl, because, after all he was going to be just like the rest.

'I would have said garish and pretentious and barbaric,' said Floy, and Flame sent him her sudden blinding smile, because it was all right again.

Flame said, confidingly, 'I sometimes pretend that I'll run away.' It was not something she would normally have disclosed to somebody she had only just met, but it would be all right to say it to Floy who had challenged his people and had been branded a rebel.

'How?' Floy seemed to be listening quite seriously, as

484

if it might be entirely possible, and Flame was encouraged to expand.

'I'd go by night,' she explained. 'Or perhaps early morning when no one was about.' She leaned forward, clasping her hands about her bent knees. 'Then I could be sure of not being missed and brought back. You can have no idea how – how dreadfully boring it is living here, with only Mother's stupid admirers and people who don't dare to oppose her, and nothing but horrid, glittering banquets every night. I'd like to see the other worlds. I'd like to travel to them and see how the people live, and find out about them.'

Fael-Inis's daughter, travelling all the worlds like a will o' the wisp, slipping in and out of Time as effortlessly as her father, the rebel angel, did . . .

Floy said, in a voice carefully devoid of any expression, 'Then why don't you?'

'Run away?'

'It would be easy,' said Floy. 'We could be out into the night and gone.'

'Over the hills and far away,' said Flame, and her voice was soft and her eyes held such delight that Floy knew that the image of those other worlds, and of the will o' the wisp creature that longed for them, had been a true one.

'Into Fael-Inis's country and safe,' he said to test her and, at once, the golden delight leapt to her eyes and he saw that she had meant it about running away, that she was not just being whimsical to attract his attention.

'It is not so very far,' he said.

But the habit of years held. Flame said, 'It isn't possible.' And looked at him and waited for him to say that of course it was possible, that anything in the world was possible.

'Why isn't it possible?' asked Floy, and Flame gazed at him in purest joy. 'It wasn't possible for my sister and me to travel from another world here,' said Floy. 'And yet we are here.'

Flame drew in a deep breath and started to say that it was a difficult, dangerous journey to Fael-Inis's Palace, when a blaze of light erupted on the other side of the garden and people started screaming.

Chapter Thirty-eight

To begin with, nobody in the Aurora Hall had realised that anything was wrong. The banquet had finished; everyone had enjoyed it and they had been getting ready to dance, because the musicians had struck up for a roundel of the grand old Bedchamber Chase. This was greeted with cheers, because everybody liked the Bedchamber Chase, which was performed to extremely sly and saucy-sounding music and which required the participants to dance in and out of every bedchamber in the entire Court, meaning that if you happened to just stay on awhile in a bedchamber other than your own, (or even more than one) nobody noticed. It was all very friendly.

And then, just as the line for the Chase was assembling (the bailiffs had been a bit out of line, which was only to be expected, of course), people had begun to notice that Madame was nowhere to be seen, which was rather odd. Madame might be anywhere at all, of course, and it was nothing to do with her people; but it was unusual to find her not in place to lead them in the Bedchamber Chase and it was very unusual indeed not to see her waiting at the head of the gold staircase, watching everyone assemble.

A number of people thought that perhaps Madame had already taken her twin lovers off to her bedchamber, but then others said, no, *there* were the twins, on the other side of the Aurora Hall, as perplexed as everyone else.

A buzz of consternation started up and then, without warning, Madame was with them, swishing in through the great crystal doors that led out to the gardens, sweeping across the golden floor of the Banqueting Hall with the flames of her gown sizzling, and shafts of light streaming from her eyes.

Everyone dodged out of range, because a shaft of light could inflict quite surprising damage, and it was perfectly plain that Madame was in one of her tantrums.

Reflection stood in the centre of the glittering golden Aurora Hall, directly beneath the great, ruby-studded chandelier, and the musicians faltered into silence and everybody looked at everybody else and most people tried to think who might have incurred Madame's displeasure, but nobody could think who had.

Reflection said, in strident tones, '*Where* is my daughter?' and people looked anxiously around for Flame, who was not to be seen.

'And where,' said Reflection, glaring across at Snodgrass, 'is the *other* traveller to whom I have extended my generous hospitality?' But Snodgrass, who had fallen in with several of the bailiffs, had not noticed that Floy had disappeared. He had been listening to the bailiffs who were telling him about Reflection's numerous and gargantuan debts and he had been so interested that he had not seen Floy and Flame vanish into the gardens.

'I haven't the least idea,' he said, and belatedly added, 'Madame,' which was what the bailiffs had said Reflection liked to be called.

Reflection's people, who knew their mistress very well indeed, guessed what had happened. They might even have breathed a sigh of relief, if Madame's tantrums were not something to be so earnestly avoided. Flame, naughty child, had for once caught the eye of one of Madame's young men and Madame was in a high old rage as a result. Well, there would be no escaping some very nasty fate or other for the young man – and probably there would be something very unpleasant ahead for Flame as well, saucy minx.

'Out into the gardens and find them!' cried Reflection and, as she turned on her heel, she appeared to grow in stature and become a whirling column of fire, so that she towered above the guests and the people of the Court.

The flames of her gown sizzled and spat and the smoky dark cloak billowed. Everyone began to walk stealthily backwards from her, because they all knew what happened when Madame whipped herself into one of her famous fire-rages. They all remembered the last time it had happened, when the fire demons had nearly broken from her restraints and a number of the Court had fallen under their malevolent sorcery and been forced to dance the terrible Fire Frenzy of the Demons to exhaustion point, until Madame had managed to imprison them again.

But they went out at once, rushing into the cold night air, and Madame stood at the centre of the walled rose garden with the silver and crystal fountain and the fire column swirling angrily, and pronounced a stream of apparently meaningless words. Shafts of light streamed from her fingertips and the terrible dark circle that would pen the fire demons appeared. The Court backed away all over again, because didn't they all recognise the immense circle of sorcery which was supposed to hold the demons penned within it, but which did not always do so. But there the circle was, glinting redly, and there, within minutes – the bailiffs said it was within seconds – were the fire demons.

And there, presiding over the demons, was Madame, in the worst temper anyone had ever known.

The walled rose garden with the pouring crystal fountain, once Reflection's pride and delight, and once the favourite place of the Court for summer evening assignations, was at once transformed into a raging ferment of noise and fury and panic and spitting crimson fire.

The demons were leaping and dancing within the dark circle and chuckling and reaching out to the people of the Court, brandishing their horrid white-hot tridents. They seemed to be unable to break out of the circle, but no one was taking any chances about this. And in any case, the demons could still fling their spears a remarkably long distance, and they could still hurl the sizzling firethorns which embedded in people's flesh and skin, and which inflicted agonising burns for days afterwards.

None of the demons was more than two feet in height and they were coal black, with rounded, hairless skulls and huge pointed ears. They had long, twitching tails and their fingers ended in barbed, clawlike hands. Their eyes glowed redly, like living coals, and they had evil, toothless mouths, which grinned and leered as they danced and leapt to and fro, seeking a weak place in Reflection's circle. The Court drew back at once, because you could not altogether trust Madame's circles, and you especially could not trust the ones she created in a tantrum.

Reflection stood with her arms outstretched, the silver fountain directly behind her, her brow dark with blazing fury. The light became flooded with dark red and the demons climbed into the fountainhead and jabbed their fiery talons into the shimmering cascade, so that the water became a pouring crimson mass. Fire sparks flew upwards and outwards and little licking pathways of flame started up all over the garden. Scarlet flames and evil-smelling smoke began to rise into the night.

Flame and Floy, standing in their shadowy corner, watched in horror, and Flame felt sick, because although she had seen the fire demons many times before, she knew that this time Mother had called them up out of sheer jealous rage.

'My fault,' said Flame, staring down into the garden. 'Floy, this is all my fault.'

'Why?' said Floy, not understanding, and Flame, her eyes never leaving the terrible sight, said, 'Because you preferred me to her. She had indicated to you that she would like to have you for a lover. And you ignored her and preferred me. But,' said Flame carefully, 'I am quite glad you did prefer me to her, Floy.'

Floy started to say something and, as he did so, a terrible screech of triumph split the garden. Fire erupted into the night sky and with it the sizzling sound of hundreds upon hundreds of firethorns raining down on the Court.

The demons had broken out of the circle and were swarming over the rose garden.

Reflection was still chanting the spell that would keep the demons imprisoned, the licking flames of her gown swirling and hissing.

'Only it is failing,' whispered Flame. 'It is failing because she is in a great rage.' She glanced up at Floy. 'Sorcery – any kind of sorcery is weakened by anger,' she said. 'The concentration is not total. She will fail to keep them penned.'

'Go after the faithless ones who betrayed me!' cried Reflection, at the fire demons prancing about her skirts. 'Find my errant daughter and the Human who has abused my hospitality!' shouted Reflection, her eyes sending more showers of sparks everywhere. 'And bring them here to me! We all know what can be done with Humans!' she added, and the demons chuckled and ran off, scuttling across the ground at a tremendous speed.

Snodgrass, who was keeping well back, and trying frantically to see where Floy was, saw several of the Court move warily towards their mistress, as if to calm her.

'Get back all of you!' screamed Reflection in a towering fury. 'Stay back! Or do you wish me to send the fire demons to capture you! Is that what you want!' shrieked Reflection, her voice soaring in triumphant spite. 'Shall I let the creatures take you! Shall we see you all dance the Fire Dance of Frenzy!'

As she spoke, the demons let out squeals of delight and ran across the garden, encircling several of the terrified Court. People began to scream, and Courtiers ran this way and that, trying to dodge their captors and escape.

'The girl!' screeched Reflection. 'The girl, you foolish, greedy creatures! Leave my people and seek out the traitorous flesh of my flesh! The seducer's spawn who is betraying me! Seek her out and with her the Human who spurned me!'

But the demons chuckled and began to chant something that sounded, to Floy, so ancient and so incomprehensible, and so utterly and completely evil, that icy hands closed about his heart.

There was a terrible compulsion about the chanting; there was a rhythm, a pulsating that drew you and beckoned you and crept inside your head, and said: *come into the heart of the dancing, Humans*... and made you see a dark, swirling column with hands reaching out from its core that you would have to obey... Floy, his arms about Flame protectively, felt his feet move of their own volition, and at once Flame said, 'Floy! No! You must not listen! You must not hear the demons' Fire Dance!'

The dark chanting was forming on the air, taking substance and shape. As it increased in intensity, Floy saw the dark column forming, a whirling, coiling, smoke-wreathed serpent towering above the gardens, long fingers beckoning from its depths. The imprisoned Court people began to dance, slowly and unwillingly at first, as if they were fighting the dreadful enchantment, but then faster, frenetically, jerking their limbs, leaping higher and higher.

The demons squealed with glee and, as the imprisoned Courtiers whirled and leapt, Reflection strode to the grinning demons, anger in every line of her tall figure, her eyes spitting the streams of fury so that little rivulets of fire sprang up and ran sizzling along the ground and then died away. The sickening stench of burning rose on the air.

'The girl, you fools!' she cried, beating at the demons with her hands, snatching their tridents. 'Go after the girl and bring her to me!'

For answer, the demons chuckled their horrid laugh and dodged out of her reach, hurling their spears at the frenzied victims of the Fire Dance. The spears sizzled through the air, several of them embedding in the victims' flesh. Blood sprang to the surface, but the wounded Courtiers danced with a terrible grim concentration, sobbing now and gasping for breath, some of them pleading with the demons for mercy.

The once-quiet garden was ringing with the sobbing of

the imprisoned Courtiers and, from where they stood, unnoticed, Floy could see that blood was staining their shoes.

He was horrified and appalled. When he spoke, the anguish was in his voice, and Flame, who was as horrified as Floy and who was frightened of what Reflection might do next, shuddered. 'We must do something. This is unbearable—'

'No. Floy, there is nothing . . .' And even like this, thought Flame, even in the midst of panic and fear and chaos, there is such delight in saying his name. 'There is nothing we can do,' she said. 'If Mother has failed to keep the fire demons penned in the circle, then there is nothing you or I can do to stop them.'

'We could try,' said Floy, and started across the garden.

'No!' said Flame, pulling him back. 'Floy, you would be taken and forced into the Frenzy and you would die of exhaustion.' And then, in a quieter tone, 'And it would take you a very long time to die.' She stopped, and felt Floy's arms about her, the first time he had touched her, and at once there was a soaring delight and an overwhelming sensation of sharing. She was conscious of thinking that she had not known it would be like this, that she had not imagined that there could be such deep, pure joy. And then Floy bent his head and, as he did so, his mind seemed to pour outwards to hers, enfolding her. Almost, thought Flame, dizzily, almost as if we are not separate people at all, almost as if we have a single mind. A deep, sweet pain closed about her and she was drowning, helpless in an ocean of sweet, slow rapture . . . There was a moment when she surrendered to it completely, and then another moment when she heard, from out of nothing, the distant roaring of fire, and glimpsed a brief, blinding sheet of flame that would pour down on them at any minute . . . Flame pushed Floy from her at once, and stood rather shakily looking at him, and saw that he had seen the fire and heard the flames and that he understood.

But he smiled, and said, 'Once, lovers slew dragons for their ladies.'

Flame could feel that his mind was still somehow alongside hers, and the delight was still there between them and the sharing, only both of these must be put aside for the moment. But they will be all the sweeter for being saved, thought Flame. They will not fade.

But when Floy said, 'We cannot stay here,' Flame at once said, 'No, for Mother will soon recapture the demons, or perhaps she will summon others and they will be sent to find us and then, Floy, you will be punished and perhaps you will die.'

The demons were dancing and leaping, sending their sinister dark music on to the night. Sweat was pouring from the Courtiers, soaking their hair and darkening their clothes. Blood had spattered the thin silken shoes and their faces were the colour of tallow candles. Several times, one of them would fall, gasping for breath, flailing wildly at the air as if for strength, but each time this happened, the demons shrieked and jerked the weak one to his feet. The dancers were beginning to resemble puppets, inanimate creatures of wood and straw, manipulated from above.

'They will die before dawn,' said Flame. 'Mother will try to cage the fire demons in a circle, but she will not succeed. And once those victims have died, then the Fire Demons will look for other prey.'

Floy said, questioningly, 'The traitorous daughter they were summoned to punish?'

'Yes,' whispered Flame.

'And the Human traveller who preferred the daughter?'

'She will kill you, Floy,' said Flame, her eyes huge as she looked at him. 'She will kill you with no more thought than you would have given to squashing an insect.'

'Then we must escape now, while she is still trying to quell the Fire Demons and while everyone's attention is on the poor creatures in the circle.' He looked at her very straightly and, in the red glow from the rose garden, Flame saw that his face was set and intent. 'It is your only chance,' said Floy, his eyes shining. 'We could be out of the Palace before anyone knew. Into those other worlds.

494

Come away with me now, Flame.'

Flame said, 'Can it be done? Oh, Floy, can it really?'

'I have to escape,' said Floy. 'Because, demons aside, I have to find my sister.'

'Yes, of course.' Flame could understand this.

'Then come with me,' said Floy again.

Flame looked up at him and saw that his eyes were shining with a reckless light and that the dark hair had fallen across his brow, giving him the look of a rebel.

In the pulsating light from the rose garden Flame smiled and said, 'Yes. All right.'

And the years of planning, and the years of pretending, fell suddenly into place and it was seamlessly easy to know what to do.

Floy stayed where he was, his eyes scanning the gardens, marking out gates, escapes, narrow paths down which fleeing lovers could steal.

'But first I must find Snodgrass,' he said, and Flame at once said, 'Yes, of course,' because it was not to be thought of that Floy would simply rush off with her, leaving the other traveller, his friend, to Mother's mercies. Mother was quite likely to fling Snodgrass to the fire demons purely out of anger. Flame said, 'He was talking with the bailiffs earlier on. And that is their tower.' She pointed. 'It is the one place where he would be safe from Mother,' said Flame, and grinned. 'Mother has never quite dared to offend the bailiffs,' she said. 'Your friend may well be there.'

Floy narrowed his eyes and saw the outline of the small tower, set a little apart from the main buildings. It would be easy to slip through the carnage and the tumult and get to it. He looked at Flame. 'Can you put together a few things? A cloak and warm things for travelling?'

'Yes. I can reach my room by a back stair. I don't think I should meet anyone,' said Flame, and then grinned. 'But in any case, I can invoke a Spell of Invisibility.'

Floy stared at her. 'Can you?'

'Certainly,' said the sorceress's daughter, and then,

'Did you think I had lived at this Court without learning anything? It will not be a very strong enchantment,' she said, seriously, 'and it will not last for very long, because I have not Mother's power. But I can do it.' The grin flashed again and it was disconcertingly her father's grin, winged and mischievous.

'Then hurry,' said Floy. 'Come over to the tower as soon as you can.' He stood, watching her melt into the shadows, and then turned back. The imprisoned Courtiers were sobbing and gasping, dancing and jerking horribly, the fire demons hurling tiny, glinting darts at their feet to make them dance faster.

Everyone was running somewhere, and people were on the verge of panic. Nobody will see me, thought Floy. I haven't Flame's Spell of Invisibility, but if I am quick and unobtrusive, nobody will notice me.

As Flame had suggested, Snodgrass was in the bailiffs' tower, his face creased with anxiety for Floy, whom he had lost sight of. He beamed with pleasure at discovering Floy to be not only unscathed, but planning to escape Reflection's wrath.

'But I don't think I can come with you,' he said. 'What about Fenella?'

'We're going to be travelling the road that Fenella should be on,' said Floy, who had already worked this one out. 'We're bound to meet up with her, or get news of her.'

'But you don't know that,' said Snodgrass. 'You might very easily miss her. One of us ought to stay here just in case she manages to reach the Fire Court.'

'I can't let you,' said Floy, appalled.

'Do you know, I believe you could,' said Snodgrass thoughtfully. 'I've become rather interested in what's going on here. They're rather interesting people, these bailiffs. And it's quite private here in this tower, not to say discreet. I've been talking to them about all manner of things; their system of money and how the Court pay their debts, and *all* about Madame's accounts. My word, she's in deep trouble, that one.'

'But would you be safe?' said Floy, still unconvinced.

Snodgrass thought he might be very safe indeed. 'They tell me she's secretly rather afraid of the bailiffs,' he said. 'On account of her owing so much money everywhere. She's bound for what they call a debtors' prison, that one, and not for the first time by all accounts. Also, she's drawn one of those circles they all set so much store by right round the bailiffs' tower, and it seems that nobody can get inside without the bailiffs' permission. That's neither Madame herself, nor those nasty creatures she let loose a while ago.' He regarded Floy with his head on one side and Floy said, slowly, 'It sounds reasonable—'

'As well as that,' said Snodgrass practically, 'I'd be a shocking hindrance to you if you're going to be running away. I wouldn't be able to keep up for one thing. I'd slow you down.'

'That wouldn't matter.'

'I daresay you'll come back for me later on, when it's all over, won't you?' said Snodgrass. 'Yes, I thought you would. I'll have a word with the bailiffs to be sure that they don't mind. You can't simply inflict yourself on people,' said Snodgrass sternly. 'It wouldn't be polite. So I'll ask them, to see if there'd be any difficulty.'

There was no difficulty at all. He met Floy and Flame at the foot of the bailiffs' tower and said it was all arranged.

'I shall be quite safe,' he said. 'I've had a word with the bailiffs – nice people. We've been getting on rather well. They're going to give me a bed and we're going to look into the accounts of Inchbad's people. Madame's requested it,' said Snodgrass, suddenly looking serious. 'It's all quite official. She seems to think that the Gruagach haven't always been – dear me, how should I put it? – haven't always been quite *straight* in their dealings. Well, not to put it too bluntly,' said Snodgrass, 'the bailiffs think they've been fiddling the books from here to the other side of Ireland, not that that's something I'd like repeated, you understand.'

'Of course not,' said Flame, who did not wholly

understand, but gathered that Snodgrass thought Inchbad's people were guilty of something vaguely dishonest. 'Are you sure you will be comfortable here?' she asked, and Snodgrass beamed and said he would be very comfortable indeed, thank you kindly, and thought it was a very nice thing indeed to see Floy so taken with this rather unusual young lady, although it was certainly a pity that she had to be Reflection's daughter, and you had to remember the old saying about what was in the meat came out in the gravy.

The bailiffs, who appeared to be quite agreeable to everything, shook Floy's hand and wished him well on his journey. One of them, who was about Floy's build, produced a couple of shirts and a woollen cloak, because you could not be letting a fellow Human go off into the night without a change of shirt.

'Snodgrass'll be all right,' said Floy, as he and Flame stole round the eastern wall of the Palace. 'All the same—'

'All the same, he is a good friend and he shared danger with you and you are unhappy about leaving him to strangers.'

'Yes. That's very perceptive of you.'

'If we go down here,' said Flame practically, 'we can reach the side gate and be out into the world without anyone seeing us.'

'Here?' Floy led the way along a narrow pathway and saw the small, latched door directly ahead.

'Yes.' Flame watched as he lifted the latch and saw, through the doorway, the dark wastes of Ireland. Waiting. A shiver of purest delight, tinged with apprehension, rippled through her. I am escaping. I am about to see the real world and perhaps all the other worlds that exist . . .

As they slipped out, she said to Floy, 'Where are we going?' and waited, because although she knew, deep down, where they were going, she would like Floy to confirm it.

Floy looked down at her and smiled the reckless, we-can-do-anything smile that made her heart lift with joy.

'To the one place in Ireland where you can be safe,' he

said. 'To the Fire Rivers and your father.
'To the Palace of Wildfire.
'To Fael-Inis.'

Chapter Thirty-nine

As the immense Gateway of the Cruachan Cavern yawned wide, Nuadu and Fenella were instantly assailed by menacing darkness. Fenella supposed they had expected this, but she thought they had not expected the very air to have such clotted malevolence, or such a feeling of distortion. She stood at Nuadu's side, with the Cavern and the Soul Eaters and the Rodent Armies behind them, and looked out over the sinister world that they must enter, the Dark Underside, the Black Realm, the Other Ireland.

The mirror-image of all that was good and strong and filled with light . . .

The terrible domain of necromancers.

The skies were black and heavy, streaked in places with deep, angry crimson, as if the heavens had bled and they were skies that would be forever dark. They reminded Fenella of marshes and quicksands and black swamps and she knew it would be smothering and frightening to have to walk under those skies.

The sense of distortion was almost overpowering. There was the impression that everything was slightly warped and out of balance, rather like a house which has been built with every angle out of true and every chimney leaning and every window and door not quite square. Fenella began to feel dizzy, as if the landscape was tilting, or as if it was shifting surreptitiously, but in the wrong direction. It was a bit like standing in a very high place and looking down, feeling your senses spin and your ribs lurch with vertigo.

As they moved forward, the door behind them slowly closed and they both felt a swift wrenching, a dislocation, as if they had been torn out of the real world and flung forward.

Fenella thought: yes, we are shut out of the real world, the real Ireland now. There is no going back. But she still stood irresolute, waiting for Nuadu to move, trying to see what might be ahead, trying to hear what sort of creatures they might have to meet.

She was just framing the thought that for all its menace, for all the grim black mountain silhouettes and the crimson-streaked skies that you felt you could reach up to touch, the Dark Realm was silent, when she became aware of the sounds.

Voices, thought Fenella, transfixed. Murmurings. Just beneath the surface, or perhaps just on the other side of the menacing sky. It was as if hundreds upon hundreds of creatures were talking softly together.

At her side, Nuadu tilted his head, his eyes shadowed, and something flared in his expression, as if, for the briefest instant, he had recognised the sounds, or even as if he had been waiting for them. But he only looked about him and then, holding out the hand that was solid pure silver, he made a gesture encompassing the landscape.

'The Dark Ireland,' said the Wolfprince, softly. 'The Domain of the Necromancers. The fearsome mirror-image.' The lick of excitement was in his voice, stronger now, and Fenella could feel pulsating waves of anticipation from him.

'Can you feel it, Fenella?' he said, looking down at her. 'Can you feel the strangeness and the sense of being somewhere where there is no light and no truth or beauty or integrity? Only distortions and deformities and only stunted ugliness and lumpen malevolence?'

His voice was very nearly expressionless, but Fenella saw, in the strange, dark twilight, that his eyes were slanting more strongly than she had ever seen them slant before and that his lips had thinned, so that now there was a white gleam of teeth beneath.

Fenella stood very still and thought: I am about to walk forward into a terrible Dark World, peopled by evil creatures, and ruled by greedy malignant Lords. The air is fouled with dark enchantments and all about us are

501

eerie whisperings and murmurings. And I am here alone, thought Fenella; I am farther from Floy than I have ever been in my life, and I am farther from the world I knew, which is lost and dead anyway. I am alone but for a creature who is half a Wolf – and probably more than half – and I do not know whether I can trust him.

Nuadu said, 'This way, Lady,' and took her hand, leading her forward, deeper into the Dark Realm.

'You know the way?' said Fenella, looking about her at the dark desolation, seeing several different paths.

'We should go deep into those mountains, which are the Black Mountains of the necromancers,' said Nuadu. 'That is where they have their citadels and their towers. That is where we shall find CuRoi's Castle of Illusions. But before that, we must skirt the Fields of Blood.' He took the path that snaked away towards the mountains; Fenella could see, in the near distance, crimson fields with waving strands of things that looked like pieces of bloodied and torn Human skin.

'The Fields of Blood,' said Nuadu, softly. 'The harvest of the necromancers. The remains of their fleshly lusts.'

'I see,' said Fenella, carefully non-committal.

As they drew nearer, they could see that the Fields of Blood were as horrid as they had looked from afar.

'Must we actually go through them?' asked Fenella, staring at the Fields and feeling rather sick. The strips of skin were all the same length; about two feet in height, as if somebody had trimmed them to an exact size before embedding them in the ground and leaving them to dry and shrivel. In some sections of the Fields, this had already happened, and the skin-rags were tough and leathery-looking, but in others, the skin was still pale and fresh, streaked with new blood. Whoever had cut the skin so precisely had not troubled about trimming off pieces of bone or shreds of muscle and, the nearer they got, the more clearly they could see the white glint of splintered bone, or the glistening worms of intestine or dark red wetness of liver or kidney. Here and there were single eyes, attached to face skin, hanging downwards on thin stringy optic nerves.

Nuadu said, 'No, I think the path winds alongside, but we do not go through the Fields themselves.' Fenella was aware of strong relief, because it would have been inexpressibly dreadful to have to wade, waist-high, through the tattered, bloodied remnants. At the centre was even a ragged scarecrow, its sleeves flapping in the noisome wind that stirred the grisly surface of the fields.

'What are the Fields for?' asked Fenella.

'I believe,' said Nuadu, padding along at her side, 'that when a necromancer has used a Human in his work, he plants out what is left, so that it can be harvested in the future.'

Fenella said, in an expressionless voice, 'Pieces of Human skin and Human bone and Human eyes and muscle?'

'Yes. They would all be useful in the dark sorcery,' said Nuadu and, as he said this, the dark murmurings grew louder, and an eerie taunting chant filled the air.

Fillet the Humans, draw their fangs.
Strip their skins and pulp their hands.

Fenella and Nuadu both stopped and looked about them, and the dark murmurings swelled and chuckled.

Bones to jelly and blood to boil,
Eyes and hair and teeth and cauls.
Grist for the cauldrons and meat for the spells.

There was a greedy note to the murmurings, as if hidden, evil creatures might be watching and waiting and rubbing their hands.

From the corner of her eye, Fenella caught, fleetingly, the sight of reaching hands, long-fingered and greedy, and she drew in a sharp breath, because it was impossible to escape the impression of grisly blood-soaked beings, servants of the Dark Lords, hiding in the gore-spattered

503

undergrowth of the Fields, watching for victims for their masters.

Nuadu said, 'If we keep walking they will not harm us.'

'Can we be sure of that?'

'I think so.' In the lowering crimson light, the wolfmask was lying strongly across his features. Fenella, glancing at him, thought: the Wolf is waking again, and experienced a cold *frisson*.

Nuadu turned his head slowly to look at her and his eyes glittered.

'You are deep within the evil Dark Realm now, Fenella,' he said softly. 'You should be very wary indeed.'

Fenella said, 'Of you?' and met his eyes squarely.

'Of everything.' His eyes narrowed and red lights, reflections of the Bloodied Fields, shone deep within them. 'How do you know I have not brought you here to give you to CuRoi in exchange for the King?' said Nuadu.

'I don't know.'

He moved closer. 'How do you know I have not brought you here under the *order* of CuRoi?'

Fenella said, 'Have you?' and thought: I will *not* lower my gaze first! I won't! But a tiny thread of doubt trickled across the surface of her mind and she thought: after all, I don't know. He is quite right. But she stood very still, the light from the Fields casting its blood-laden shadows across them, and returned his stare, and saw that the Wolf was waking in truth now; it was in his eyes and it was in the curve of his hand and the thinning of his lips.

Nuadu said, 'Be wary of me, Lady.' He reached out and traced the line of her cheek lightly. 'Do not trust me,' he said, softly, and now there was no doubt about the wolfish note in his voice.

'I don't trust you,' said Fenella. 'Not entirely.'

'But still you came here with me.'

'To rescue the King.'

'Ah yes,' said Nuadu, very softly. 'The King.' His teeth gleamed whitely in a thin smile. 'Yes, we must not forget him,' he said. And then, abruptly, as if he was throwing off some unwished-for shadow, he said, 'The Black Realm

504

will wake all manner of darknesses, Fenella.' Something unexpectedly gentle twisted his mouth. 'Yet I think you have no darkness in you, Lady,' he said. 'I think you have never encountered any true darkness in your strange, lost world. But you may encounter it now.' The red glint showed again. 'Remember that I have a dark side. Remember that I am partly a Wolf.'

'I shan't forget,' said Fenella, and stared at him, and felt a shiver of something that was partly fear, but partly desire. *Because I have lain with this creature who is a half-Wolf, I have felt his strong surging passion and I have seen the vulnerable creature beneath . . .* I don't think I am afraid of the Wolf, she thought. But I think that so far I have only caught glimpses of it.

Nuadu led her forward, padding softly across the terrain, his head occasionally lifted to catch a sound. It was absurd to think that he seemed to know the way they should go, that he seemed to be choosing the paths unhesitatingly. But it was impossible to escape the thought that he might have been here before.

As they left the terrible Fields of Blood behind, the taunting chanting faded, and a charged, violent feeling stole over the air, rather like the heavy menace just before an exceptionally virulent storm. Fenella was conscious again of the feeling of standing at the edge of a precipice, looking down dizzily over a chasm, of dislocation. Perhaps this would pass. Perhaps she would become accustomed. Only – I don't think I could ever be accustomed, she thought. I don't think I could ever be accustomed to the tumbling vertigo and to the impression that everything here is distorted, askew, inequal.

They left the Fields of Blood with their gruesome harvests behind and turned in the direction of the Black Mountains, with their huge silhouettes, immense and towering and secretive, and tiny winking lights in their depths.

'The Citadels of the Necromancers,' said Nuadu, when Fenella pointed to them enquiringly. 'Where the Sorcerers retreat from the world to weave their enchantments and plot their evil wars against the true Ireland.'

'Fearsome,' said Fenella, shuddering, because there was an awesome, isolated look to the Mountains and she could not help wondering what it would be like to be up there, deep within those terrible mountains, knowing that every light you saw belonged not to a friend who would take you in out of the night, but to evil sorcerers.

To their left were lakes and rivers, dark and with an oily film on their surface, as if the miasma of evil was rising from them like the stench from a swamp. They toiled onwards, climbing as the path wound up, feeling the air change, become colder, filled with the reek of evil. Several times red, scaly creatures with glinting eyes and ragged-edged wings flew straight into their faces and reached for Fenella's hair with their claws and once a pair of screeching, ravaged-featured beings with the bodies of vultures and the faces of manic, grinning women flew overhead, and Fenella and Nuadu both ducked instinctively. But the creatures flew on quite purposefully, as if they had some destination and the strangers were of no interest to them. Fenella and Nuadu straightened up unscathed.

'What were they?' asked Fenella.

'Harpies,' said Nuadu. 'Servants of the Dark Lords.' He smiled. '*Minor* servants, Lady.'

'Then I hope,' said Fenella, firmly, 'that we do not meet any of the major servants.'

Nuadu shot her an amused look. 'I think you would somehow retain a sense of humour in any danger,' he said.

'I think it might be the last thing that would go,' said Fenella.

He regarded her, as if he might be learning her all over again, and Fenella, mindful of her decision to be friendly and cool and detached, smiled.

As they moved on they heard again, just under the surface of the landscape, the murmurings and the gloating whisperings they had heard from the Fields of Blood.

Yes, yes, these are two from the other Ireland, these are two who we can devour... Harvests for the Master, crops for the Black Reaper... Meat for the cauldrons that boil deep in the

black sorcery chambers, and grist for the looms of necromancy
that weave ceaselessly beneath the towers of the sorcerers . . .

Fenella found the whispering, mocking voices extremely sinister. She was rather glad when they seemed to fade as they neared the Black Mountains.

'Up here?'

'Yes. Will you mind, Lady?'

Fenella stood still, looking up at the towering shapes. 'Ever onwards,' she said, and grinned at Nuadu. 'That's something remembered and often quoted in my world. I suppose it has not yet been written as far as this one is concerned.'

Nuadu said, 'I wish I had known your world.'

'You wouldn't have cared for it.'

'No?'

'Boring,' said Fenella, shaking her head. 'No adventure.'

'Despite what you may be thinking,' said Nuadu, rather wryly, 'we do not always wage wars and challenge Soul Eaters here.'

Fenella said, 'Shall we defeat CuRoi?'

'We will try.' He took her hand. 'Absurd child,' he said, very gently, and Fenella found that she had to blink back tears very hard. 'Don't let me harm you,' said Nuadu.

'I shan't,' said Fenella, and he smiled.

They moved on, falling silent as the Mountains closed about them. Here and there were solitary buildings; lookout towers of some kind, rearing starkly against the lowering skies, straight columns of harsh dark stone with gaping windows like empty eye sockets or monstrous decaying teeth. The air was cold and thin now, and the red glint was beginning to fade from the sky.

'Nightfall,' said Nuadu, stopping and turning to look back down the path they had traversed. 'Or what passes for night here.'

Nightfall in the Black Realm of the Necromancers . . . And we are alone up here in the fearsome and desolate Black Mountains, thought Fenella.

They stopped to rest briefly, although Nuadu said they should not waste any time.

'We must remember that CuRoi seals the Castle of Illusions every night at sunset and that after that it will be impossible to get inside.' He sent her the slanting look. 'We should be alone out here,' he said. 'Should you be very frightened?'

'Yes,' said Fenella, consideringly. 'Yes, I should.'

'And yet, still you are here.' He studied her, as if he found her strange and intriguing.

Fenella said, 'Let's go on. Look, the path is quite easy now.'

She led the way and then, as they rounded a curve in the road, there directly ahead of them—

'Oh!' said Fenella softly.

It had been hidden by the fold of the Mountains, so well and so cunningly, that Fenella had not realised they were so close.

Directly ahead, surrounded by soft radiance, was a vast, turreted castle, spiralling up into the night sky, pinnacled and spinaretted, adorned with spires and slender, beautiful towers, glittering with pale iridescence, sending splinters of pure light into the dark landscape.

CuRoi's Castle of Illusions. The legendary fortress of the great sorcerer, the Master of the Dark Realm, the palace of myth where, according to the Soul Eaters, Ireland's King lay captive and helpless.

The Castle was limned sharply against the dark sky. It was a pure, sugar-spun edifice, crystalline and ivory and pearl, gleaming with its own inner radiance, sending out rays of light. Fenella tried to see the colours contained within it, but the Castle glistened with such prismatic brilliance that it was impossible. But she thought there was a pure, soft pink at the outer edges and that the pink was tinged with lilac and azure, deepening as it neared the heart, so that the very centre of the Castle was violet and deepest purple.

'The Castle of Illusions,' said Nuadu, softly. 'Referred to in every Book of Necromancy ever written, and in every dark legend ever told, and in every warning ever whispered round a night hearth.'

Fenella heard her voice say, 'And you knew the way to it.'

Nuadu looked down at her. 'Yes,' he said. 'Yes, I knew the way, Fenella. Are you thinking I should not have done?'

'You will admit,' said Fenella, 'that it was a little – unexpected.'

Nuadu said, 'I knew it had to be somewhere in the Black Mountains. Everyone in Ireland knows that. And there was only one mountain road we could take.' He looked at her. 'And it is wreathed in evil magic and steeped in sorcery,' he said. 'And if we can not get inside before the Dark Sun sinks, then every door and every means of access will be sealed and there will be no way of penetrating it until morning.'

As the darkness increased, so the Castle shone more brilliantly and sent out its glittering radiance. The pinks and lilacs deepened to crimson and violet and the Dark Sun described a fiery arc across the skies, much faster than either of them were accustomed to, sprinkling its baleful red light as it went. The portcullis was directly ahead of them, gold-tipped and glistening faintly.

'But it is becoming fainter,' said Fenella suddenly.

'I think it is the enchantment of the Master,' said Nuadu. 'I think the sealing is beginning, Fenella. CuRoi is drawing down power from the setting Sun.' And then, in a much more urgent voice, 'The turrets are vanishing,' he said. 'Dissolving. Do you see?'

'Yes. Yes, we'll have to hurry,' said Fenella.

There was no time to be lost. They began to run, heedless of where they trod, covering the ground in great leaping bounds, flying in the direction of the portcullis gate before the Dark Sun should sink altogether and the Castle seal itself with CuRoi's strong, sunset-linked sorcery.

The rock bridge curved downwards as it neared the portcullis, so that they found themselves half running and half slithering, dislodging tiny rocks and stones as they went. Fenella could see the gates straight ahead of them, wreathed in dark, swirling mists, dark and sinuous smoky spirals. Could they do it in time? And then: *do we want to do it in time?* she thought, because, after all, they had no idea of what would be waiting for them within the Castle.

The last ray of darkness touched the portcullis gates and, as they began to melt and blur, Nuadu took Fenella's arm and pulled her across the threshold and into CuRoi's Castle of Illusions.

Chapter Forty

The glittering light of the Castle was abruptly shut off.

Nuadu and Fenella stood very still, just inside the vast door, handlocked, and Fenella thought: I believe I can hear Nuadu's heart beating. Can I? Or is it my own? And then – and this was a terrible thought – or is it somebody else's heart altogether, she thought? Is someone, something, standing close beside us, listening and watching? But this was so eerie that she did not let herself think it for more than a breathspace.

It was very dark. It was so dark that they dared not move. Perhaps, in a very few minutes, their eyes would adjust to the light. People's eyes always did that. They would wait quite calmly and quite quietly, and presently they would begin to make out shapes, forms, things. Pieces of furniture, said Fenella to herself very firmly. Chairs and tables and cupboards. That would be all.

It was at that minute that the lights began to alter. Slowly, almost imperceptibly, slivers of radiance appeared on the outer edges of their vision, tiny sparks to begin with, and then increasing, growing, multiplying, until they splintered the darkness, silver and gold and scarlet. On and on they went, pouring and cascading and whirling, until Fenella and Nuadu were standing before a dizzying kaleidoscope, a blinding storm of light that hurt their eyes and which they thought would surely burn out their vision.

And then, quite suddenly, the quality of the light changed; it became softer, subtler, breathtakingly beautiful; it became tinged with pure, soft pink and lilac and the deep violet of twilight, and Fenella was just thinking that it was beginning to soften, and that they would be able to see properly at last, when there was a movement beneath their feet, as if the Castle's foundations had shifted and the floor tilted so that Fenella half fell forward and grabbed wildly at a stone pillar.

Little by little, so slowly that to begin with they could not believe it was happening, the Castle began to move; it began to spin and rotate, so that the walls became rushing, whirling shadows, and they could see the dark, crimson-streaked skies outside spinning past.

'This is the sealing!' cried Nuadu, pulling Fenella to him and holding her against him. 'The Castle is sealing! CuRoi is calling down the power of the dying sun and every door is dissolving! Look!' And without letting her go, he pointed to the great studded door through which they had fallen, and Fenella saw that it was melting into the stonework.

The spinning increased, until they had to struggle to remain upright and Fenella began to feel sick. Round and round it went, on and on, silently and effortlessly, as swiftly as a mill-stone, as smoothly as a child's top. The door had disappeared completely now and the windows also. Nuadu, his every sense stretched to the limit, heard beneath the whirling of the Castle a steady rhythmic chanting in an unknown tongue, a single, rather melodic voice that rose and fell in an intricate pattern. He had once heard, when a small child, the beautiful, sexless, sacred chanting of the Druids, the paeon of praise to light and the morning and the gods. This was the dark side of that ancient, sacred chant, and Nuadu knew it at once for the terrible Chant of the Necromancer. He knew that he had been right and that, from somewhere deep within the bowels of the Castle, CuRoi was indeed sealing every door and every entrance.

They were shut into the Castle of Illusions with the most powerful and the most malevolent necromancer Ireland had ever known. They were shut in until dawn, and there would be no possibility of escape.

The spinning ceased as gradually as it had begun and Nuadu and Fenella heard the strange Chant fade. Fenella put out a cautious foot, but the floor stayed where it was and the Castle was still.

The stone hall was quiet; the pouring brilliance had vanished. Fenella thought that, with the vanishing of the windows, there ought not to have been any light at all now, but from somewhere a gentle radiance burned, and they could see about them quite clearly.

They were standing in a vast, dome-ceilinged hall, with an immense stairway leading directly upwards in front of them to a great galleried landing. Deep velvet-blue light poured in from overhead and there were thick swathes and folds of cobwebs everywhere. Dust motes danced in and out of the light-beams and there was a faint drift of woodsmoke, which was unexpectedly pleasant. For some reason, the blue twilight and the woodsmoke and the dust made Fenella feel better, because there was something so normal about woodsmoke and dust, that CuRoi's Castle seemed to be not quite so ensorcelled.

Nuadu was prowling round the great hall and Fenella said, 'I think we must explore a little, don't you?' because it would be a good idea to appear unafraid and inquisitive. She was pleased to hear that her voice sounded quite ordinary.

'Certainly we should.' Nuadu's eyes went to a door deepset below an arch on the galleried landing and something glinted in his eyes. Fenella thought: I believe he knows what is inside there. Or if he does not know, then he suspects.

'It's *extremely* dirty in here,' she began severely, and then added in a practical tone, 'where ought we to begin?' At once a deep echoing chuckling reverberated all about them. Fenella started and turned back to scan the shadowy staircase, but Nuadu, who had been waiting for CuRoi to make some move, stayed where he was. The chuckling seemed to begin somewhere deep in the bowels of the Castle and end high above their heads. It was so gloating that they both flinched.

'Dissatisfied with my abode, Human Child and Wolfprince!' cried an echoing voice. 'Well, that is something that is easily cured!'

Before the voice had quite finished speaking, a flurry of movement had started up at the centre of the hall and, as they stood, transfixed, it whirled into a spinning cloud of activity. The grey and white column of smoke, shot here and there with red and gold sparks, slowed its gyrations so that they could see that it was a pillar of every cleaning implement ever seen; it was brooms and brushes and dusters and mops, all tumbling and falling into line, rather as if someone had rapped out a command.

'CuRoi,' said Nuadu softly. 'They say he has a certain sense of humour.'

The voice came again, on a note of command this time, but in a language Fenella could not recognise. But at the words, Nuadu stiffened and looked up, as if the words had meant something to him, and the voice chuckled again.

'So you know a little of the Ancient Tongue, Wolf-prince?' it said. 'Now, that I find *exceedingly* interesting. I wonder where you learnt *that*, Nuadu Airgetlam? But I think you do not know enough to match me. Certainly you did not know enough to free yourself from my friend the Robemaker. It was the Human Child who did that, Wolfprince, or have you forgotten?' The deep chuckling came again. 'But now a little entertainment for your Lady, who finds my Palace not to her liking,' said CuRoi. 'Watch now!' And again there was the odd-sounding five-syllabled word, and then there was a torrent of words, and before the words had finished, the brooms and the mops and dusters whirled about and, without the smallest warning, swept into a frenzy of activity, cleaning and polishing and sweeping and scrubbing. A great duststorm began to gather, and polish and soapsuds and beeswax and lavender flew in all directions, so that Fenella and Nuadu backed into a corner, coughing from the dust.

'But,' said Fenella in a whisper, 'they are actually rather amusing, don't you think?' and at once, as if they heard this, the brooms and the mops all arranged themselves in a straight row, and embarked on a kind of dance, with the feather dusters fluttering at each end, and the polish tubs

514

going off into a stately little march by themselves. The scrubbing brushes up-ended themselves and joined in with gusto and, at this, everyone seemed to jostle for pride of place and a mumbling, grumbling sort of quarrel seemed to take place between the mops and the brooms as to who ought to stand at the head; the feather dusters tripped up the scrubbing brushes, and the dusters tied themselves in decorative bows on the brooms, making them look as if they had large, floppy yellow feet.

Fenella started to laugh. 'It's an entertainment,' she said. 'A comic entertainment for children! How absurd!'

The brooms had finished sweeping by now, and there was the pleasant drift of lavender polish and beeswax. The great hall was gleaming and the floors were shining, and the copper pans hanging by the fire at the far end were bright. The mops tidied themselves away into their buckets and the dusters folded into neat squares and everything was quiet again.

'And *now*,' said the voice, 'perhaps my Castle is fit for you to occupy for a time, Human Child?' And Fenella forgot about being amused by the mops and the brooms and remembered where they were and what they had to do and about CuRoi being one of the great Lords of the Dark Realm.

At her side, Nuadu, said, 'Look. Over there. At the top of the stairs.' Fenella saw that at the head of the stairs, directly in front of the deepset shadow-wreathed door, a blurred outline was forming into the shape of a man.

CuRoi.

He was rather short of stature and dark and swarthy-complexioned. He wore a dark cloak with a scarlet silk lining, black boots of some shiny substance, and a starched collar with a cravat. In his left hand was a whip. He was just a little plump and there was an unexpectedly soft, pale look to him, as if he might, under certain circumstances, be very nearly effeminate.

Nuadu had not moved from Fenella's side but, as the necromancer stood regarding them, he felt a shiver of horror and he knew that they stood in the presence of extreme evil. He felt a brief puzzlement ruffle the surface of Fenella's mind and understood that she had been expecting to encounter someone sinister-looking and evil and cruel, another Robemaker. Nuadu had been aware, ever since they had entered the Castle, that Fenella had been tense and taut and wound up, ready to meet horror and power and leering menace. She had seen the Robemaker and she had seen what happened to his prisoners, and she had not been expecting this genially visaged, plump-faced gentleman who could whip up brooms and mops into an amusing display, and who looked as if he might wear scent and enjoy concocting dainty little dishes for his guests to partake of.

But Nuadu had absorbed the tales and the myths of the Dark Ireland and he had heard almost every snippet and tag-end of legend and lore ever encountered. CuRoi was called the Master of Illusions and Nuadu knew at once that they were being presented with a seamless, almost flawless illusion now. He is giving us the image of a good-humoured land-owner, thought Nuadu, studying CuRoi covertly. A genial gentleman, a soft-living dilettante, who dabbles in a little magic purely for the fun of it.

But with CuRoi's appearance, Nuadu had felt his skin prickle with fear. It was as if a cold, greasy hand had stroked the back of his neck and the finely honed instincts, inherited from his long-ago ancestors, the Wolves of Tara, were alert and alive, warning him to beware. He watched CuRoi descend the great curving stair and cross the hall towards them and he knew that here before them was one of the most powerful entities ever to dwell in the Dark Realm.

He summoned every ounce of resolve he possessed and braced his mental muscles to meet any attack that might come. There was Fenella to be thought of. Fenella, so straight and so completely without duplicity, would certainly be dreadfully vulnerable. Nuadu knew a great many stories about CuRoi, and he thought that he would tear out the necromancer's throat if he played any of his cruel cat-and-mouse games with Fenella.

But CuRoi was smiling and holding out a plump, well-kept hand to them. He said, 'You are well come indeed, my friends,' and it was the pleasant, happy tone of one who is delighted to discover unexpected guests on his doorstep.

Fenella smiled back, but Nuadu noticed that she somehow managed to ignore the outstretched hand and that she did so quite naturally and easily. So she is not so much dazzled by CuRoi's neat little illusion that she will trust him sufficiently far to touch him! thought Nuadu. And she is not so guileless that she cannot put up a pretence.

CuRoi looked at them both and chuckled. It was a roguish chuckle, the chuckle of someone who sees very well that there is a joke against him, and is more than prepared to join in that joke.

'Oh, dear me,' said CuRoi, 'dear, dear me, I can see that you have heard some *very* nasty stories about me. Well, they do love a gossip hereabouts, of course, but I promise you I am not really evil. It is only that I do enjoy a joke.' He regarded them, beaming, his head to one side. 'Did you enjoy my little bit of nonsense with the brooms and the mops?' he asked. 'Yes, I can see you did.'

He sketched a bow in Fenella's direction, and Fenella said, as if she found the subject rather interesting, 'It was a little like the puppets we had in a country I once lived in and the comic entertainments we arranged for the children, with music to heighten it all. Apparently quite simple, but actually extremely complex.' She regarded him thoughtfully. 'But amusing,' she said. 'Yes, I did enjoy it.'

CuRoi studied her rather intently for a moment, and then said, 'Oh, life is intended to be amusing.' He made as if to gather them in. 'Life is not to be taken seriously,' he said, and put his head on one side again and smiled and then said, 'but I am being most remiss. You have travelled far and perhaps fared ill, for the road through this land is not an easy one. You will perhaps take a bite of supper

517

with me and a glass of wine, yes? Oh, do say you will,' he added, 'because quite apart from anything else, I should be so interested to hear of your journey. There are many roads here and none of them especially pleasant. You would, perhaps, have to come past the Fields of Blood? Yes, I thought so. Very unpleasant. I hope you did not find it too offensive, my dear?'

'We assumed that it was necessary in the pursuit of necromancy,' said Nuadu, silkily.

CuRoi at once said, 'Oh, not necessary at all. You have been listening to some of the darker tales about us.' He made a quick, dismissive gesture with one hand. 'Blood and skin and Human hearts – no, no, that is very basic sorcery. Very crude work. As for the Fields – well, I am afraid that some of my fellow sorcerers are very unthinking in the storing of their raw materials. And that filthy, ragged effigy to frighten away the Harpies? Quite unnecessary. Rather tasteless. Do come this way.'

He led them through to a room on the right of the hall, richly panelled and hung with crimson silk and damask, with emblems and symbols carved into the panelling. A dying fire sulked in the hearth and a long oak table at the centre of the room was sketchily set for some kind of meal.

'Tsk,' said CuRoi, pausing in the doorway. '*Very* scanty, this. But I did not know I was to have guests tonight, and we can soon put matters to rights.' Lifting his hand, he murmured words in that strange cadence again and, at once, the fire spat and roared into life and chalices and plates spun about and, without warning, steaming bowls of soup appeared and platters of crusty bread and bowls of newly churned butter. At the centre of the table, a side of ham appeared, with a gleaming knife ready to carve it and, at the far end, silver bowls of glistening fruit materialised.

CuRoi stood benevolently watching, his plump little hands joined together over the modest swell of his stomach, the thumbs revolving. 'An easy enough trick,' he said to Fenella, 'but one which always impresses guests. Do sit down, both of you, and help yourselves. Sire, the wine is not poisoned, I promise, and you may drink your fill.'

Nuadu did not speak, but his head tilted just fractionally and his eyes narrowed. Fenella received the impression that his ears had pricked, which was patently absurd, but when he spoke, his voice held a silky, bitter note.

'I believe,' said Nuadu softly, 'that you mistake my standing, CuRoi. To address me as Sire, is surely to confuse me with my brother.' He regarded their host unblinkingly. 'And my world tells how you are never confused or mistaken,' he said, and smiled the mocking smile, which appeared to be saying: well? How will you handle that one?

CuRoi returned the stare and Fenella saw that his eyes had become hard and cold.

'A form of courtesy, no more,' he said, but some of the former joviality had gone from his voice and Fenella thought his features were suddenly leaner and sharper. It was rather ridiculous to think that the plump geniality had melted a little, but it was what she did think. And wasn't he known as the Master of Illusions? It was important to remember that. Anything that had happened here might be nothing more than illusion.

'But,' said CuRoi, turning to Fenella, 'you do not eat, my dear,' and when he said, 'my dear', there was such a lick of greed in his voice, that Fenella blinked.

But she smiled and slid into the nearest chair and accepted the bowl of soup that CuRoi handed her and took a slice of bread and some butter and ham and fruit.

CuRoi had seated himself opposite her and was watching her, his chin resting on his hand, to all appearances interested and benign.

The mask is back in place, thought Nuadu, who had seen, as Fenella had seen, the geniality slip, but who, unlike Fenella, had felt and seen what lay beneath.

Nuadu's every nerve-ending was stretched to its utmost, and he was again calling on the wolf-instincts of his strange mixed blood. He knew that CuRoi was not yet playing one of his subtle, evil games with Fenella, but he thought he might begin to do so quite soon.

He sipped the wine warily and saw that Fenella was apparently composed, that she was, in fact, listening with apparent absorption as CuRoi explained how the belief that the Black Ireland was always dark was erroneous; it had beautiful sunrises and exquisite afternoons and there was great tranquillity at times.

'And once,' said CuRoi, in a soft, lulling voice, 'once we had all the light and all the beauty in Ireland for the asking.'

'Who put the lights out?' asked Fenella in a down-to-earth voice and Nuadu felt CuRoi flinch and saw Fenella grin slightly.

But CuRoi only said, rather sadly, 'I fear there have been greedy rulers here, as there are always greedy rulers in all kingdoms.' He glanced at Nuadu, and said softly, 'But your world knows about greedy kings, Sire.'

'Undoubtedly,' said Nuadu, and lifted his wine chalice again. He had eaten but sparingly and had only sipped the wine briefly for refreshment. He was not afraid of poison, for it would not be CuRoi's way to dispose of unwanted guests so crudely. But he was stretching his mind to its utmost limits and he dared not blunt any of his awareness. When CuRoi said, quite amiably, 'Do tell me how life goes in the other Ireland,' Nuadu said at once, 'But are you not fully aware of that?' and regarded their host with a long, hard look.

'I have my small powers, it is true,' said CuRoi. 'Among them the simple ability to look across the barriers of Time.'

'That must be very useful,' said Fenella.

'It serves a purpose now and then, you know.' CuRoi smiled benignly at them again and, as he did so, Nuadu felt the white-hot knives of the *Stroicim Inchinn* slice through his mind and knew, quite surely, that the necromancer was playing with them. He knows exactly why we are here and who we are, thought Nuadu. But I suppose we must play his little game for the moment.

But all the same, he avoided meeting CuRoi's eyes, because he knew that for the *Stroicim Inchinn* to be completely effective, it must penetrate the mind through the eyes. And so he kept his glance averted and continued discussing Tara, and sipped the wine and ate sparingly. As CuRoi re-filled Fenella's wine chalice, Nuadu stole a covert look at the sorcerer and, as he did so, a log fell apart in the hearth and red sparks cascaded across the chimney breast, so that a red glow fell across the upper part of CuRoi's features.

The eyes of a devil, thought Nuadu. Yes, he has the eyes of a devil. I do not think that any of the stories lied. He recalled how CuRoi was believed to be steeped in what the Eastern Lands called *exquisite torture*, the torture of the mind . . . I wonder if he truly has my brother, thought Nuadu.

He looked at Fenella and knew a sudden strong wish to keep her safe from this evil, cruel creature. Was it because she was courageous and possessed of immense strength, and because she had an unquenchable sense of humour? I think that is all it is, he thought. For the moment, I must believe that is all it is. I dare not explore further.

But when CuRoi drew Nuadu back into the conversation, asking about their journey through the Cruachan Caves, Nuadu answered him with instant courtesy.

'I had always wished to penetrate the Gateway to Hell,' he said. 'Since I am popularly believed to have been born there, you understand?'

'You regard yourself as an outcast,' said CuRoi, and Nuadu knew at once that, despite his care, the necromancer had been reading his thoughts with supreme ease.

'It is how the world – my world – regards me,' said Nuadu.

'But you are a Wolfprince of the ancient lineage.'

'Bastard. Tainted stock.'

'Have you never – forgive me, but is an interesting question – have you never coveted Tara's Ebony Throne?'

CuRoi leaned forward, the red glint deep within his eyes again.

Nuadu stared at him, and thought: *the Ebony Throne of Tara . . . the ancient magical Throne created by the High King Erin for Ireland's true princes . . . How would it feel to ascend that Throne, knowing that Tara, glittering beautiful Tara was yours, and that Ireland, the blue and green misty Isle of Legend was yours to rule for good or evil . . .?*

Aloud he said, 'That would be a futile desire. My family wanted none of me, nor I of them.'

'And yet,' pursued CuRoi, thoughtfully, 'and yet you still attempt to restore your brother, the prince, to Tara.' He smiled at Nuadu. 'Come now, let us play this absurd game no more, Sire. You search for the captured prince. We both know it.'

'You are very direct,' said Nuadu.

Fenella, who had been listening carefully to the interchange, said, 'Directness is preferable on such an occasion.' She looked at CuRoi. 'We do indeed search for the prince, but we do so in the hope of arranging his release.' She regarded CuRoi thoughtfully.

Nuadu, not entirely following Fenella's thoughts, but trusting her instincts, said at once, 'And you will acknowledge that we are a small enough force to storm citadels or raid dungeons.'

'Greater wars have been won by little more than subtlety,' said CuRoi, non-committally.

'This is not a war,' said Nuadu. 'But rather a quest.'

'And in any world, nothing is obtained entirely free,' said Fenella. 'If we could find the prince, we might perhaps discuss terms for his release.'

'Really, my dear?' The lick of prurience was back, but there was no question but that CuRoi was intrigued. 'How might that be?'

Fenella said, 'Are there not bargains that can be struck? In the world I am descended from there is a history of such things. Of what was called state prisoners being exchanged, one side to another.'

'Indeed?' CuRoi sipped his wine, watching Fenella

over the chalice rim, the wine casting red shadows across his face. 'You would be prepared to bargain in that way?'

'My people frequently suffered what they referred to as *Cold* Wars,' said Fenella, and, for a moment, she was so rapt in the history of Earth that she almost forgot where they were and to whom they were talking. 'Wars where violence did not play very much part, but where a great deal of bargaining and pledging went on. Do you know the game of chess? I think it is extremely old?'

'I do.'

'The Cold Wars were a little like chess,' said Fenella. 'One side ceding a few pawns, the other side trying to gain more than a few. Interesting. Requiring great subtlety and cunning. Usually both sides won. And,' said Fenella, 'it is true, you know, that valuable assets can sometimes be given in reciprocation for valuable prisoners. Particularly where prisoners are held as hostages.'

'Assets? But surely there could be nothing more valuable than the hereditary High King of Ireland.' CuRoi regarded her rather indulgently. 'Any unscrupulous sorcerer who had in his power Tara's Wolfking would never give him up.'

'Not even if something better were to be offered in recompense? Because,' said Fenella, as if she was thinking aloud now, 'because there is not really anything that the King could *give* to that sorcerer, is there? It is not as if he would have particular powers. But as a pawn – yes,' said Fenella, still as if she was arguing it out with herself, 'as a pawn, I should think the sorcerer could regard the King as very valuable indeed.'

'I cannot think,' said CuRoi, his eyes never leaving Fenella's face, 'of anything in this Ireland or in the other one, that a sorcerer would consider to be of sufficient value to persuade him to give up such a valuable – pawn.'

'But in such a case,' said Nuadu, 'the pawn would, in the end, be valueless. Merely a body lying in a dungeon.'

CuRoi said, amusedly, 'Oh, were you thinking that the imprisoned King would be lying in a dungeon?'

He regarded Nuadu unblinkingly and Nuadu said,

silkily, 'Not in the least. Whoever has the prince will be far removed from such crude methods as dungeons and manacles.'

'And,' put in Fenella, 'would the King not have been taken for bargaining anyway?'

'I cannot imagine the kind of bargaining that would interest a High King's captor,' said CuRoi.

'Well,' said Fenella, half apologetically, 'I was really thinking of the Soul Eaters.'

Silence fell on the table and Nuadu, feeling the nuances that spun and shivered all about them, sat back and waited.

'You know of the Soul Eaters?' said CuRoi at last. And then, 'Yes, of course. You have traversed the Caverns of Cruachan.'

'Yes,' said Fenella. 'Horrid creatures. But they dwell in a place that is in the other Ireland.' She glanced from Nuadu to CuRoi. 'I have that right?'

'Perfectly,' said Nuadu, who had been so much enjoying listening to Fenella and picking up her thoughts, that for a few moments he had relaxed his guard. He thought that the rather unexpected, certainly unusual story she was telling about the exchange of prisoners was probably true; and although he could not visualise a war in which armies did not ride out and where people were not slain, he knew that in Fenella's strange, lost world, these things could well have happened.

'Soul Eaters,' said Fenella, buttering another piece of bread, 'would make a very good exchange for a High King. Always supposing we could discover who it is who actually holds the King, that is.' She smiled at CuRoi ingenuously.

'They are powerful beings, the Soul Eaters,' said CuRoi.

'Oh yes, but whoever has been able to capture and hold the Wolfking of Ireland would surely be able to control them,' said Fenella at once.

CuRoi said slowly, 'It is true that once the creatures had been overpowered, there are enchantments that would bind them and force them into servitude.' He looked at Fenella with renewed interest and Fenella smiled at him guilelessly. 'The Robemaker is in thrall to the Soul Eaters,' said CuRoi. 'But you would know that.'

'Ten thousand years of the Wolfkings' curse?' said Nuadu.

'He is something of a fool, the Robemaker,' said CuRoi. 'He fell victim to the High King Erin, who pronounced the Curse of Eternal Disease over him. But he has his uses, the Robemaker. I have occasionally trafficked with him.' He dabbed fastidiously at his lips with a damask napkin. 'Perhaps we may talk a little more of this on the morrow,' he said. And then, to Fenella, 'You have an interesting mind, my dear.'

'So I have been told,' said Fenella tranquilly.

'It is unusual to meet a Human – and even more unusual to meet a Lady who understands about bargaining for captives and about pledges and hostages.'

'Thank you.'

CuRoi stood up. 'And now I must remember my manners as host and escort you to your bedchambers,' he said. 'For you must be tired after your journey.'

'You are very hospitable,' said Nuadu.

'It is my great pleasure. You will know that my Castle is sealed until dawn, of course?'

'Of course,' said Nuadu.

'A strange custom,' said Fenella, and CuRoi smiled and said, quite equably, 'It is safer to seal one's home against the night creatures that prowl in the Dark Realm. You may hear some of them. But be assured that nothing can get inside my Castle after sunset.'

'Have you servants?' asked Fenella looking about her as they moved from the dining hall. 'Surely for such a vast place . . .?'

The red lights gleamed in CuRoi's eyes again. 'My servants are better unseen,' he said. 'But they are all around us.'

He took Fenella's arm lightly and led her from the firelit dining hall and across the stone-flagged hall.

As they ascended the curving shadowy stairway, CuRoi

said, 'Are you interested in my Castle, madame?'

'Old buildings are always interesting,' said Fenella.

'Yes.' The dark eyes regarded her. 'Perhaps on the morrow you will allow me to show you some of it.'

'Thank you.'

They moved down the corridor and up a flight of stone stairs that led to another floor and CuRoi showed them into two adjoining bedchambers and, uttering one of the strange, faintly musical commands, caused fires to burn up and copper jugs of hot water, wrapped in soft warm towels, to appear on the washstands.

'A useful skill,' he said, eyeing Fenella. 'And one that ensures my guests' comfort. But, for now, I shall leave you to your rest.' He looked at Fenella and again the mask slipped, and something red and glaring and incalculably greedy looked out. 'We shall meet in the morning,' said CuRoi, and left them.

Left alone, Nuadu prowled his room restlessly, waiting for the Castle to become quiet, hearing, on a level beyond consciousness, the little settling noises that all old buildings make, the creaking of timbers, the expanding of joints and joists. As he moved about the room, which was richly furnished with dark red hangings of silk, and which had a huge tester bed with a velvet counterpane, he was aware of something dark and vicious waking deep within his mind.

The Wolf stirring . . .

He had said to Fenella that this evil Realm would almost certainly call to the dark, hidden sides of their natures and now, in this warm, comfortable bedchamber, at the Castle's heart, with night closing all about, Nuadu was aware of an immense inner darkness. It was something he had felt now and again during his life, this deep, dark hunger, laced with golden strength, but also threaded with cruelty. There had been times during the years when it had woken without warning, when it had raked his senses into violent and voracious passion.

Nearly always, the taking of a woman had slaked the feeling and satisfied the hungers, but it had not always done so, and there had been nights when he had prowled the Wolfwood, stalking the tiny defenceless creatures who lived in the undergrowth . . . There had been nights when the only thing that could quench the ravening need was to see blood spilled and to feel soaring dominance and to scent the fear of the creature in his snare . . . *For I can hold my prey helpless simply by unveiling the wolflook, simply by staring at it with the slitted unblinking regard of my ancestors, the Wolves of Tara* . . . At such times, he had been more Wolf than Human and, although he had fought it, he had come to accept it as the consequence of his mixed ancestry.

He knew the stories, he knew that for many of Ireland's Kings, the wolfblood had been a warm golden current, a surging powerful strength. The High Queen Grainne, who was sometimes called Grainne the Gentle, had called it *the power and the light and the strength of the Wolves of Tara.* Her son, who had been the greatly loved Erin the Just, had known it as a source to be tapped and channelled in times of trouble. They had seen it as a golden thing, filled with light, a deep well of power and potency.

But there had been others in the Royal House who had misused the wolf-strength; renegades and wastrels and cheats who had consorted with the Dark Powers and created evil, selfish laws. For them the wolf-strength had been a dark tainted thing.

And I believe that I am one of the dark ones, thought Nuadu . . .

Now, inside CuRoi's Citadel, surrounded by the necromancer's evil forces, he was aware of the dark, sensual pull at his mind and his body. The dark side waking . . .

He wanted to bound out of the bedchamber and seek out the necromancer, sink his teeth into CuRoi's soft plump throat . . . *And I should fell him with a single leap, and then I should be at his throat . . . and the flesh would taste sweet and juicy, and the blood would trickle down over my lips, so that I could lick it* . . .

There was, as there always was, a strong sexual arousal,

and he found his mind re-creating Fenella's sweet innocence in the depths of the twilit Wolfwood, eager and warm and soft. The darkness was in the ascendant then, he thought, but he felt his lips curve into a smile because had it really been only that?

At the thought of Fenella, the warmth surged between his thighs at once and, despite the creeping danger of the necromancer's Castle, he began to plan how he would go quietly to the adjoining bedchamber. There was a violent and twisted arousal in the thought of making love to his Lady deep within the terrible Black Domain of the necromancers. When all is quiet, I shall do it, he thought. When the Castle is soundly asleep, I shall pad along the corridor and she will be there, Fenella, with the sweet, warm Human-scent that is composed of clean skin and long silky hair and that other, indefinable, Humanish fragrance . . .

And then he heard the door of Fenella's room open stealthily and soft, light footsteps go down the hall.

Fenella had not undressed, although the crisp, lavender-scented sheets had been alluring. It would have been a great luxury to slide between the sheets and fall into a deep satisfying sleep. And perhaps Nuadu would come, she thought . . . Would he?

But it would not do to even lie down, because clearly they would have to be out exploring the Castle for traces of the King's whereabouts. And so Fenella washed in the hot scented water and dried her face and hands on the thick fluffy towels and felt refreshed and very nearly ready for anything. She heard the Castle grow quieter and felt the dark night of the necromancer's Realm close about the great Castle.

She would not go to bed, of course, but she would just sit down in the rather comfortable chair that somebody had drawn up before the fire. There was something especially pleasant about sitting before a leaping fire, with no other lights, and looking deep into the flames.

Nuadu had at once understood her idea about offering

an exchange of some kind for the imprisoned King. He had joined in and added weight to her suggestions. Fenella did not suppose for a moment that CuRoi would let the King go, unless something extremely powerful and magical was offered in return, but it had bought them time, and it had enabled them to be fairly honest, which had been important because of CuRoi being able to see into their thoughts.

There had been a moment when Nuadu had eyed CuRoi with a sudden thin and hungry look, which Fenella had found unexpected, because she had begun to think that the thin trickle of wolfblood was very thin and that his feelings and emotions were entirely Human.

Now, curled into the deep, soft armchair, with firelight washing over the walls, she thought that perhaps, after all, he was not as Human as she had been thinking. It might be as well to keep this firmly in mind although there was surely no harm in remembering how his hands had felt caressing her body, thought Fenella, rather drowsily. There was probably no harm, either, in remembering how he had felt as he lay close to her, and how his eyes had darkened with passion, and how he had been suddenly and disconcertingly vulnerable . . . It was the memory of the vulnerability which had stayed with her. It was one of the things she would find it hard to forget when all of this was over.

She was not falling asleep. It was important to remain awake, which was why she was thinking about Nuadu; it was keeping her on the right side of sleep. She stared dreamily into the fire's depths and discovered, as many another had discovered before her, that if you half closed your eyes, you could see pictures in the flames, all kinds of pictures . . . There were deep-mouthed caves where goblins and demons might lurk . . . leaping fire creatures . . . Fael-Inis's salamanders . . . It would be nice to think they would meet Fael-Inis again . . . It would be better to think that they would find Floy and the brothers. Was Floy all right? But Fenella thought she would have sensed if he was not. She would have felt a sharp, deep loneliness and she would have known. Floy was all right. It was remarkable how she knew, but she did know.

The fire was burning lower now and there were slanting golden eyes peering out from it and a soft heady scent in the room. The fire was hissing very faintly – was it the fire? – and within the hissing was a soft beckoning voice . . .

Come into the fire, Fenella . . . Come deeper into the enchantment . . .

Fenella blinked and sat up a bit straighter and the fire burned steadily.

Come into the magic, Human Child . . . Surrender to the sweetest bewitchment of all . . .

Fenella stood up and walked softly out of the room into the dark waiting halls of CuRoi's Castle.

Chapter Forty-one

Fenella was vaguely aware that to go out into the dark, sealed Castle was to court danger of the most extreme kind, but there had been something so insistent about the fire-voice that it had not seemed possible to ignore it. The idea of an enchantment, some kind of luring, beckoning spell occurred to her only briefly. She was not very familiar with spells at all, but she thought that surely she would have known and guessed if CuRoi was sending out a subtle evil call to her.

In any case, it would be interesting to see more of the Castle. It might even be possible to find out about the King. She would have to be very quiet about it but there could surely not be any danger. The thought of Nuadu just touched her mind and, for an instant, her resolve wavered, because wouldn't Nuadu think it foolhardy of her to venture out alone? But as she stood, irresolute, the fire-voice enveloped her mind again, so subtle and delicate, that Fenella, unused to enchantments, unfamiliar with bewitchments, fell into its lure a little more strongly. All memory of Nuadu slid away.

She moved stealthily out into the wide gallery outside her bedchamber and stood listening intently, trying to decide whether it would be better to go off to the left or the right. Nothing moved, nothing stirred out there, and Fenella felt her doubts recede. She would have known if CuRoi was somewhere nearby waiting. She would have felt it.

And now it is the Master who calls to you, Fenella . . . Follow the beckoning, and all will be well . . .

I'll be very careful and I'll be very quiet, thought Fenella, beginning to move stealthily along the corridor. I'll keep all my wits about me and, if I see anything I don't like, I'll scream very loudly indeed. This made her feel considerably better and she fell to deciding which direction to take.

It would plainly be pointless to explore the rooms they had seen earlier; the great stone-flagged hall where the brooms and mops had performed their dance, or the long firelit dining hall. It would be much more sensible to penetrate to the Castle's heart, to explore the deep, dark, secret rooms. The dungeons.

Fenella had never seen a dungeon, but she knew about them, and she knew that they were always underground, dank, dark, airless. She moved warily along the shadowy halls, ready to scream and leap for cover at the slightest movement, seeing how the occasional tiny breath of wind stirred the hangings. She would quite have liked to stop and examine the hangings more closely, because they looked interesting and might be what the very early Earth-people had called *tapestries*: embroidered and sewn pictures depicting famous battles or heroic journeys or expeditions.

Ahead of her was a smaller gallery, stone-flagged again, and lit to shadowy life by flaring wall sconces. It had been quiet so far, but now Fenella was becoming aware of whisperings, horrid dark murmurings that swirled and ebbed all about her, rather like the murmurings they had heard when they had walked past the grisly crimson Fields of Blood.

Fillet the Humans, strip their skins . . .

Fenella whirled about, but the shadows were still and lying thickly in their corners. There was a low, throaty chuckling that seemed to begin in one corner and scuttle across in her path and then trickle away into the walls. But there was nothing to be seen; only the shadows, lying thickly on the ground. The wall sconces dimmed slightly, as if a giant hand might have reached out to snuff them, and then burned up again, as if a giant breath might have huffed on them. There was a rather rancid stench from whatever the torches were made of.

> *Dripping grease and boiling vat*
> *Melt the blubber, cool the fat.*

Hadn't there once been something written somewhere about evil necromancers who melted down Human fat for their spells? I shan't remember it, said Fenella very firmly.

Dead Men's grease and Dead Men's gut;
Bones to light and marrow to suck.

But CuRoi isn't that sort of necromancer, said Fenella, even more firmly. He told us he wasn't. The Fields of Blood are only used by sorcerers who employ crude methods – and whatever else CuRoi might be, he isn't crude. And so I'm not hearing those grisly murmurings at all. I'll just go along quietly and carefully and everything will be all right. I'll take this little stair here, because it winds downwards and probably it leads to the dungeons. Probably, that's where the King is. CuRoi pretended he never used dungeons but I don't suppose he was being truthful.

This was rather mixed thinking, but mingled with it was a strong, not-to-be-denied compulsion. Fenella did not quite feel the strong silvery threads that were pulling her firmly through the ancient dark Castle and down the stone steps, and she did not really hear the voice that still whispered to her. She did not know that the essence of a strong, subtle enchantment is that the victim should not realise an enchantment is being woven, and she certainly did not remember that CuRoi was the master weaver of illusions, the greatest necromancer ever to come out of the Dark Realm. She moved on, warily, and fell a little deeper into the dark spider's-web of the thrumming bewitchment . . .

The stone steps spiralled quite steeply down. They were worn away at the centre, so that Fenella had to try to walk on the inside of them, close to the wall, which was extremely difficult. The lower she went, the more decayed the stone walls became. There were spreading patches of discoloration and, in places, the stones had been partly eaten and partly nibbled by some kind of creeping mould.

This is very nasty indeed, thought Fenella, treading cautiously, one hand on the wall to steady her balance, trying not to touch the slimy, stained parts. This is very nasty, but it is not actually frightening. I'm not really frightened. Nothing has happened yet. I'll just go a bit farther on. I'll go to the bottom of these stairs and then probably I'll be in the dungeons.

So deeply caught in the glittering sticky mesh of CuRoi's subtle evil spell was she, that she did not pause to question the danger of it, but walked calmly and firmly forward.

Nuadu stood outside the door of his bedchamber and stretched his every sense to its utmost. Somewhere in the darkness of this fearsome evil Castle Fenella was walking, alone and unprotected. Nuadu did not stop to question why Fenella should have gone out like this without him; it was entirely possible – it was even probable – that CuRoi had in some way called to her, or perhaps tricked her out of her room. And if she was under a spell of CuRoi's weaving, then she would be in the most severe danger and she must be found and somehow rescued.

A sudden pain twisted Nuadu's vitals at the thought of Fenella in CuRoi's cruel plump hands, and he thought: so, my Lady, my love, you have slid under my skin and into my heart, have you? He supposed he ought to be wanting Fenella to be safe and warm and outside of the danger, but he did not. He wanted her here with him, sharing everything there was to share, even though some of it would be fearsome and most of it would be dangerous. They might both die here, tonight, at CuRoi's hands, but still he wanted her with him.

He moved softly forward, feeling the faint ruffle of awareness that was Fenella's presence near to the stone steps at the far end of the passage. Down there? Yes, I believe so.

He would have said that he had long since cast off the shackles of what his ancestors might have called chivalry, and he was certainly no gentle or perfect knight. But it suddenly seemed immensely right that he should be prowling through the dark, enchanted Castle, with the shadows shifting eerily about him, intent on rescuing his Lady.

The shadows were thicker as Fenella reached the foot of the stone stairs. From somewhere close by came the faint sound of trickling water, a steady drip-dripping that echoed bleakly and desolately. Fenella, staring about her, thought there was an underlying pain here as well, as if people had lived and perhaps suffered here, and probably died. What was down here? The dungeons? Prisoners? CuRoi's victims, held chained and manacled?

Standing very still in the dimly lit stone passage, Fenella felt the terrible weight of long-dead agonies and long-dead anguish and fear close about her. So intense was the feeling that the darkness lightened briefly and she glimpsed, for the first time, the silvery snail's-trail of necromancy which had lured her here. Alarm woke in her mind and with it fear. What am I doing down here! And, more worrying: How did I get here? She looked sharply behind her, but there was nothing to be seen.

But I think I am not alone, and I think that down here is something ancient and sinister and so powerful it is almost beyond Human understanding...

She was at the foot of the steps, standing in a narrow, low-ceilinged corridor. Ahead of her was another of the stone passages, lit by the smeary light of the wall sconces... *Human fat and Dead Men's marrow...*

To the left were tiny low doors with pointed arches above them, set deeply into the wall, so low that Fenella, who was not tall, would have had to stoop to enter. Seven doors, each one of them shrouded in shadow, and each of them with a great iron ring-handle. Each one, perhaps, holding the necromancer's secrets...

Fenella stayed where she was, because, although shreds of the spell still clung to her mind, she was becoming aware of the creeping evil everywhere, and the more she became aware of it, the more the spell dissolved. Surely, she thought, surely you did not, if you were sensible, pry into the dark dungeons in a necromancer's lair. If you were sensible, what you did was to go in search of someone to pry with you, someone you could trust . . . The half-memory of Nuadu ruffled the surface of her mind and a few more strands of the dark glistening enchantment fell away. Fenella thought: I am standing at the heart of a necromancer's ancient, spell-ridden Castle and it is dead of night and I am all alone . . . *Of course* he has woven an enchantment over me! How could I have thought he had not!

Fear surged up and she turned back to the stone steps, because she could be up the steps and back inside the warm, firelit room with the door bolted and Nuadu within reach.

But would it be safe and would it be warm and secure? Couldn't CuRoi simply call to her again, no matter how many bolted doors and no matter how much cosy warm firelight?

And now I'm actually here, thought Fenella, now that I'm confronting these rooms which I suppose are dungeons, I might as well look inside. I might as well see if there is any trace of the King, or if there is any trace of anything at all.

And it would be rather interesting just to see, whispered the silvery voice, it would be a great adventure to peer into the secrets of the sorcerers . . .

There's no one here, said Fenella firmly. It's perfectly quiet and it's perfectly safe – and if anyone had been prowling along after me, I should have heard.

I don't know whether this is one of CuRoi's horrid subtle spells, or whether it is my own curiosity, thought Fenella, and moved forward to the first of the doors.

The latch lifted easily and the iron ring-handle turned smoothly as if it was frequently used. Then this is no seldom-visited dungeon, thought Fenella. This is no forgotten underground prison – what did they used to call them? an *oubliette* – where victims rot to death in chains and gyves in the dark.

There was a twisted, rusting wall bracket directly opposite to the door and someone had thrust a flaring torch into it. It was burning strongly, and the thought touched Fenella's mind that it must have been only just lit and that this might mean that somebody had been down here very recently and that the somebody might still be here, hiding in the shadows, watching, waiting . . .

She turned the iron ring-handle and pushed wide the door.

Pain screeched inside her head at once. Loud, hurting, white-hot pain tore into her mind, as her sight and her senses were assaulted and lacerated and sent spinning by what lay within.

The room was small, perhaps ten feet square. It was hewn from the solid grey stone of the passage and there were no windows.

Of course not, my dear, for is not this the famous Castle of Illusions, where all the windows and all the doors vanish with the setting of the sun, and where every entrance and every means of egress is sealed . . .?

There was the same dank fetid stench she had been aware of earlier; a sweetish, rotting-meat, old-blood smell. A decaying tomb-like taint.

Great black iron hooks had been driven into the ceiling of the stone room, and from each of these hooks hung lumps of bloodied meat, Man-size, yes, *Man*-size, swinging to and fro slightly in the draught created by the opening of the door, moving, rotating gently on the terrible black hooks. The floor beneath each one was darkened and stained, and there was a steady dripping sound as the blood and the fluid and the juices of the carcases drained on to the cold stones.

Sides of meat. Carcases of red-streaked flesh and bone and gristle. Swathes of leathery skin and rattling bundles of whitening bone, and yawning, gaping trunks, with a stump at each corner, where the limbs had been hacked off.

Human carcases and Human meat. Truncated bodies, headless torsos, hanging in a butcher's dungeon. Fenella felt sickness rising in her throat and swallowed convulsively.

A slaughterhouse. A meat-house. A necromancer's spell-store.

Fenella was unable to move, but her mind was tumbling and her stomach churning.

CuRoi did not need to use the Fields of Blood, because he had his own storehouse here, he had his own private warehouse of Human flesh and bone and skin and hair.

Fenella backed away, her stomach lifting with nausea, and, as she did so, the whispering, murmuring voices echoed about the room.

The shadows moved and thickened, and Fenella, still half in and half out of CuRoi's spell, remembered his servants.

> *Better unseen, Human Lady,*
> *Or we shall rip you, Human Lady.*
> *Fair of skin and dark of eye,*
> *A Human to feed to spells, Lady.*

The unseen servants of CuRoi, peering from the shadows of the necromancer's slaughterhouse . . . Long, bony fingers reaching out, evil inward slanting red eyes peering . . . For a brief and terrible instant, Fenella saw them, grinning goblin faces, evil prancing shapes with long, scissor-like nails at the ends of their hands and jagged pointed teeth.

All the better to tear you apart, Human Lady . . .

Fenella gasped and choked down a scream and fell back into the stone passage. As she did so, a soft, light, footfall padded down the stone steps.

Nuadu was standing at the far end, watching her.

His head was tilted, and Fenella saw at once that there was something subtly different about him; something sleeker and leaner and something that you could very easily imagine bounding forward and felling you to the ground . . .

He regarded her silently, his eyes gleaming, and the shadows fell across the upper part of his face, so that his eyes showed red and slanting, and his mouth was thinner, a little cruel . . . Fenella stood very still and waited for him to speak. She felt the sticky spider's-web-spell fall from her, so that she no longer heard the silvery fire-voice and no longer felt the strong sweet beckoning.

The planes of Nuadu's face were altering, sharpening, becoming pointed and hungry . . . It might have been a trick of the light, but Fenella knew it was not. And wasn't there the faint – yes, more than faint – suggestion of a muzzle forming . . . a muzzle that would slaver and savour, and sharp gleaming teeth beneath that would tear and rip . . .?

Nuadu smiled and Fenella bit back a gasp, because it was not the gentle, ironic smile of the bastard Wolfprince, nor was it the sudden sweet intimate smile of the lover of the forest . . .

The smile of a Wolf stalking its prey . . . Alien and strong and possessed of such dark seduction that Fenella felt her senses somersault. A pang of longing sliced through her, followed at once by a wash of fear.

'Come here, Fenella,' said Nuadu in a soft voice.

He held out the hand that was flesh and blood and skin, and the thin smeary light from the wall sconce fell across it, so that his skin was no longer skin, pale and Human and ordinary, it was dark and silky and sable.

It was impossible not to be aware of the strong, dark allure of this strange creature who was certainly more Wolf than Human now. Into Fenella's dazed mind flickered the old legends of snakes fascinating their prey and holding them motionless, simply by the power of their eyes.

I believe he is holding me motionless and probably helpless simply by looking at me now . . . What ought I to do? If he springs upon me, what *could* I do? thought

Fenella, her eyes distended. I think I might be fascinated as well. I think I ought not to be, but I have to admit to it.

Nuadu was leaning back against the far wall, his eyes glittering, the shadows still twisting about his body, so that it was impossible to see where the Human ended and the Wolf began . . .

But when he spoke, his voice was the one she remembered, and when he said, 'Did I not tell you, Fenella? Did I not warn you?' Fenella heard the unmistakable note of anguish.

He stayed where he was, wreathed in shadow, and now Fenella could see the wolfmask lying across his face, and she could see that, although he still stood upright, there was an unfamiliar stance, as if he was unused to standing like this, as if he was uncomfortable . . . As if he was accustomed to going on all fours.

Nuadu said, very gently, 'I would not hide this from you, my love, but I would that you had never seen me thus. But I am what I am, Lady.' And waited again, with such a patient mien, that Fenella took a deep breath and fought to remain where she was, but felt her heart singing, because he had said 'my love'. He had called her 'my love', and surely this darkness would pass, wouldn't it? and he would be freed from whatever strange bewitchment walked these halls?

At last, she said, in a whisper, 'CuRoi. What has CuRoi done to you—?'

'I believe he has reached deep into my mind and found the darkness,' said Nuadu. 'Fenella, I felt it happen.' A brief smile. 'Did I not tell you what might happen?' he said. 'CuRoi has found the Wolf. He has uncovered the deeply buried hungers of my ancestors, the Wolves, and he has called to them.' He turned his head to look at her again and then, quite suddenly, he said, 'But CuRoi called to you, also.'

'Yes.' The strange fire-voice, the whispering grinning creatures . . . 'Yes, I believe he did,' said Fenella, slowly. 'Why?'

'To lure you down here.'

'Into the—' Fenella stopped and Nuadu at once said, 'You have found one of his storehouses? Human remains, perhaps?'

'How did you know?'

'No sorcerer who practises the dark art of necromancy can do so without using Human flesh and Human blood and bone and fat.' He regarded her, and Fenella found that she was able to look at him quite naturally and easily now, as if the thin, sharply angled wolfmask was not in the least sinister.

Not sinister and perhaps even exciting . . .

Nuadu smiled at her and moved towards her in one single effortless movement and Fenella felt his arms go about her and felt again the hard, masculine warmth, insistent, throbbing . . . *For CuRoi has woken the hungers . . .*

And then, putting her from him, Nuadu said, in a cool, practical voice, 'And now, my Lady, we have to explore further.'

Nuadu moved to the second door, and stood confronting it, legs slightly apart, the silver arm glinting dully. After a moment, he reached out a hand and pushed it open.

Sick greenish light poured out at once and, with it, the sour stench of decay. Fenella, at Nuadu's side, felt his arm come round her, and stood silently by his side, looking in.

The second room was smaller than the first, but it was the same dank windowless oblong as the first, shadowy and silent.

At first, Fenella thought it was empty and then, as her eyes adjusted to the light, she saw that thrown down into the farthest corner was a pitiful collection of tiny shrivelled bodies, blind and boneless-looking creatures, only just recognisable as Human babies. They lay as they must have been flung, huddled together, as if blindly seeking the warmth and the companionship their aborted lives had been denied. Their skins had the waxen quality of creatures who live underground and their tiny starfish hands reached out as if in supplication. Most horrifying of all, over each soft vulnerable little skull was a veil, a thin membrane, a pallid film, covering the head and in some cases reaching down over the blind closed eyes.

'Cauls,' said Nuadu, softly, a note of horror in his tone. 'The veils of unborn babies. Believed to hold immense power over death.'

Fenella thought she could not have spoken if her life had depended on it. She was unable to look away from the pitiful tumble of little soft bones, from the blind, barely formed faces, from the tiny reaching hands.

Ripped from the womb to serve a necromancer's lust for power . . . This is the worst thing I have ever seen in my life, thought Fenella, staring at the poor, mangled forms. Of all the terrible things, this is the worst yet.

The chuckling bony-fingered beings were somewhere close by, with their horrid grisly chanting.

> *Kill the babies, eat their eyes,*
> *Shred their skins and drink their slime.*
> *Rip the wombs, deny them life.*
> *Slit the birthsacs, wield the knife.*
>
> *Smear their fat and let it boil,*
> *Keep the caul, the caul is magic.*
> *The caul is strong, preserve the caul.*

'We can do nothing for them,' said Nuadu, very gently, closing the door. 'They are long since gone, Lady.'

'We can kill CuRoi,' said Fenella.

'Oh yes,' said Nuadu softly. 'Oh yes, we can do that.' He looked down at her and Fenella saw that the wolfmask was still lying across his features, but that it was gentler now, less pronounced. Or was it simply that she was growing accustomed to it? It ought to have been menacing and alien, but it was not. There was the feeling of vicious courage, as if he would be quite capable of springing forward on to an enemy and tearing the enemy's throat out with his teeth . . .

And enjoying it, Lady, and enjoying it . . .

Aloud he said, 'You are already hating the Dark Realm, Fenella. After so short a time, you are hating it.'

'Yes.' Fenella frowned. 'But you – your people – have lived with the threat of it for all their lives.' She looked at him, 'That is a terrible thing,' she said. 'We have to find a way to kill this creature.'

'I would kill him with my bare hands,' said Nuadu, his eyes gleaming again. 'But he would vanish before I could get to him. Teeth and claws and swords will not vanquish this one.'

'Probably he is listening to us now and chuckling to himself,' said Fenella, raising her voice challengingly.

'Almost certainly.' Nuadu looked towards the third of the doors.

'Can there be worse?' said Fenella. 'Can what is in there be worse than anything we have already seen?'

'Will you stay back this time, Lady?'

'No.'

They stared at one another and, unexpectedly, Nuadu's expression softened. 'Courageous but reckless,' he said, and shook his head. 'A dangerous combination.'

Fenella said, very deliberately, 'I am what I am', and Nuadu smiled.

'As you wish,' he said. 'But let it not be forgotten that I made some attempt at chivalry.'

'I'll remember,' said Fenella, who was actually beginning to feel rather sick.

The third door . . .

They heard the sounds before Nuadu reached out to the iron ring-handle and there was the sudden feeling that the room behind this door might well be larger and might well contain not pitiful Human shreds and fragments, but something else entirely.

There was a clanking, grinding sound, horridly reminiscent of the Robemaker's treadmills, as Nuadu turned the handle. There was the sudden feeling of huge power and great force and relentless machinery being harnessed for some terrible, grisly purpose.

Nuadu pushed open the door.

If the first two rooms had been small and closed in, this was neither. It opened on to a short round tunnel, a culvert, which was made of rounded brick, and which was so low that, although they did not have to crawl on all fours, they both had to bend quite low. The sound of the clanking machinery was louder and there was a vast, echoing sound to it, as if whatever was creating the sound was doing so in some kind of vault.

Nuadu took Fenella's hand in the now-familiar gesture and they moved into the mouth of the culvert and felt their way along its length. The floor was curved and there was a suffocating feeling, as if the smooth rounded walls might suddenly close in on them. There was not very much light, but there was enough to see that the sides were of rough black brick, pitted here and there as if something had scalded them or eaten into them or simply worn them away with the passing of time.

The floor was slippery in places and, as Fenella put out a hand for balance, the sides of the culvert felt cold and faintly slimy. She began to have the feeling that they were crawling through a drain, through which anything at all might have flooded and might still flood.

As they neared the sounds, they saw light directly ahead of them; a dull red, thick light. And then the mouth of the culvert widened and there was a brick archway and they were able to stand up and look about them.

They were standing on a small brick parapet, barely two feet across, and in front of them was a vast, echoing brick shaft, easily thirty feet across, stretching down into the bowels of the Castle. Nuadu, who knew only a little of Castles and ancient fortresses, had still absorbed a smattering of knowledge; he knew that Castles such as this one were sometimes built around a central hall or chimney which would extend from the turret tips down into the deepest part of the foundations and that these great, vault-like shafts could be used for a variety of things. They frequently held water containers near to the roof, which were designed to act as a reservoir for rainwater. Sometimes they were simply crude air shafts, with the Castle privies opening directly on to them. And although he had never seen the inside of Tara, the Bright Palace of his ancestors, he had listened to the stories of how it had been raised from the rock and how it had been used as a model for nearly every palace and castle built since. Tara's central chimney shaft was said to wind intricately upwards through the State bedchambers, so that each chamber could have a tiny separate garde robe where fur garments could be hung and kept fresh.

But the immense stone chimney shaft at the centre of CuRoi's Castle of Illusions had been used for none of these rather homely things. It contained a massive iron tank, a monstrous drum, smooth and cylindrical in shape and rather squat-looking. Nuadu, narrowing his eyes, thought it must be at least twenty feet in height and probably fifteen feet in circumference. Short, thick pipes ran in and out from it, as if it had to be fed, and then had to disgorge unwanted matter. The drum itself had the dull finish of steel or perhaps even tin; the sort of surface that would make your teeth wince agonisingly if you scraped your fingernails across it. There was the terrible charnel stench again, but there was a tin-like taint to it now, and Nuadu at once recognised it as the stench and the taste of a very great quantity of blood.

A reservoir of Human blood . . . A great smooth-sided iron cauldron, a cistern, twenty feet high and reinforced all around to withstand the immense pressures of the fluid inside . . .

The fluid inside . . .

At length, Nuadu said, very softly, 'This is CuRoi's Blood Reservoir.'

'Yes.' Fenella was staring up at the great squat cylinder, finding it horrifying and grisly, but finding as well that it had a dreadful *live* appearance, as if it might suddenly uproot its feet from their moorings deep within the

545

Castle's foundations and come waddling and lurching towards them, slopping its terrible burden over the sides as it came . . .

And then Nuadu's hand closed about hers and Nuadu's voice said, very calmly and very strongly, 'It is very nasty, Fenella, but it is simply a great cistern filled with liquid.'

'Yes.' Fenella bit down her repulsion, because it was quite absurd to be felled by this when she had managed to cope with everything else so far.

As they stood watching, there was the clanking, teeth-wincing steel-against-tin sound again and they saw that there was an inner drum, very slightly smaller than the outer one, and that it was being pushed upwards from beneath, quite slowly and quite naturally.

Nuadu said, his voice echoing against the cold brick shaft, 'The blood level is rising. It is being fed from somewhere.'

'We had—' Fenella stopped, and then managed to go on fairly normally. 'On Renascia, we had what we called water tanks – huge drums a bit like this, with mesh lids. There was a mechanism in them – fairly simple – which would measure the level and indicate when the tank was nearly empty, so that we knew to lever off the lid and catch the next rainfall. The tanks had an inner drum which rose when the level was high, and subsided when it was low. Not unlike this, I think.'

'Ingenious race,' said Nuadu. 'So, after all, there is nothing so very new,' and Fenella knew he was trying to force the conversation on to a simple, homely level, to reduce her revulsion.

At length, she said, 'There is nothing here that will tell us about the King. Ought we to—'

'Try the other rooms?'

'We'll have to,' said Fenella, firmly.

Creeping back through the culvert was nearly worse than creeping along it had been earlier. Fenella knew it was absurd to keep visualising the great Blood Tank suddenly lurching after them, reaching out its thick pipes like arms or tentacles to trap them, but she did think it.

546

She was grateful to reach the low door and be able to stand upright in the passage again.

'Onwards?' said Nuadu, looking down at her, and smiling to see that there was a smudge of dust across one cheekbone and that it did not make her any less beautiful. Her face was pale and her eyes were huge and dark, but he could feel, through her fear and revulsion, a strong, steady anger against CuRoi.

'Onwards,' said Fenella, at once, and from somewhere dredged up a grin, because if Nuadu had lived under the shadow of this evil, clever creature and this massive threat, then she could look upon whatever else they might find.

You do not need to try to match me, Lady . . .

'I know that,' said Fenella aloud. 'Mustn't we be nearing dawn now? Do necromancers lose a little of their power with the coming of the morning?'

'Truly I have no idea,' said Nuadu. 'But it is possible there is no dawn here as we know it. And CuRoi may be playing some kind of subtle game with us.'

'I know,' said Fenella, who had not stopped listening for soft footfalls, or looking for slanting peering eyes.

The fourth room held the heads of the necromancer's victims, but both Fenella and Nuadu found that their senses were still reeling from the tiny dead foetuses in the second room and from the terrible Blood Reservoir in the third. Fenella began to have the feeling that nothing could hold any terror for them any more.

The skulls were stacked against the wall, several dozen of them, each with its rags of neck skin streaming, each with its sightless eyes open and staring. Fenella shuddered,

The fifth room contained a jumble of golden, blood-crusted vessels; chalices and platters and bowls and etched into the floor were strange symbols and curious markings.

'The language of necromancy,' said Nuadu, studying it. 'Or at least, a few words of it. I wish there was time to study it more closely.' He glanced behind him. 'I wish we felt safe enough to study it more closely,' he said.

The sixth room was empty. 'But,' said Fenella, wrapping her arms about her body, to stop the sudden uncontrollable shivering, 'but there is *something* here.'

There was something in the sixth room that was cold and evil and merciless. They both recoiled and Nuadu closed the door tightly.

'Stored spells that we cannot see, perhaps?'

'Perhaps,' said Nuadu. 'CuRoi is called the Master and it may be that he can cover his real secrets with the Cloak of Invisibility. That is a fairly simple invocation, but it is extremely difficult to maintain for any length of time.'

He looked at her, and Fenella said, 'One room left.'

One room left . . .

'Yes. The seventh chamber, Lady. The seventh secret of the necromancer. All right?'

'All right,' said Fenella, and they moved to the room at the far end of the stone passage. Nuadu pushed the door wider and they entered the chamber.

The room was of a more normal size than any of the others; it was long and rather narrow, but it was about the same size as the hall where they had dined earlier. It was not as dark as the other rooms, but Fenella thought that the light was of a different quality, less evil. They stood very still, waiting for their eyes to adjust, beginning to make out bare floorboards, the shadowy shapes of furniture.

Dark blue light poured in from somewhere over their heads, showing up great swathes of cobwebs. They stirred as Nuadu moved, and touched Fenella's face eerily. She brushed them away impatiently and tried to search the shadows, because there was something here, something huge and incomprehensible and all-seeing.

Fenella followed Nuadu, treading cautiously, as if she was testing each step, and felt the shadows move with them.

At the far corner, standing by itself, was a massive carved chair, its back so high that it stretched above them, the arms and feet intricately carved and adorned with strange symbols. Light fell across the great chair, so that they could see the beautiful graining of the dark polished wood, and the gentle patina that only extreme age brings.

Nuadu stopped short, and an arrested look came over his face.

'What is it? Nuadu, what is it?'

'I am not sure,' said Nuadu, very softly, 'but I believe we are looking on one of the great symbolic treasures of Ireland.'

'A chair,' said Fenella, slowly, questioningly, her eyes still on the outline before them, seeing, now, that wolves were carved into the wood, and that here and there were other creatures . . . panthers, swans, deer . . .

'A throne, Lady,' said Nuadu, his eyes still on the dark glossy chair. 'And made of the black silky wood of the first Trees that grew in the Wolfwood at the beginning of Tara's history. Ebonywood.' He looked down at her, his eyes brilliant and alive, and Fenella saw that the wolflook had completely vanished now. 'There is a legend in Ireland,' said Nuadu, 'a long-held belief that—'

'That only Ireland's true King may sit in the chair and that all others who dare to do so will perish in extreme agony,' said a soft voice behind them.

Nuadu and Fenella turned at once to see, framed in the half-open door, CuRoi watching them. And at his side the sinister, cloaked form of the Robemaker.

Chapter Forty-two

Fenella was at once aware of a difference about CuRoi. She thought at first that it was simply that the light was casting odd shadows in here, and then she thought that perhaps it was just seeing him next to the thin, stooping figure of the Robemaker. And then she knew that neither of these had been right: it was that they were seeing CuRoi as he really was. The mask had been discarded, put aside, and this was the true evil creature, the legendary necromancer who ruled the Dark Ireland and who called down the force of the setting sun each evening and sealed the vast Castle of Illusions and had, at his beck, armies of Dark Servants . . .

He was taller and darker than he had been at supper; the swarthy look had gone from his skin and in its place was a pale, polished look, like ivory, like skinned bone. Translucent, the look of one who is not entirely Human . . . His eyes still had the faint slant to them, giving him a faintly exotic look, so that Nuadu, who had sometimes met and talked with travellers and pilgrims, remembered the stories and descriptions of Eastern princes.

As if to underline this, CuRoi was wearing a robe of scarlet silk, and his slender white hands were adorned with jewels. He moved, and at once the Robemaker moved with him, like a shadow.

Fenella felt Nuadu become very still and felt, as well, that he had tensed to spring.

'I really should not do so, Nuadu,' said CuRoi at once and, with the words, the Robemaker made a brief gesture with one hand, and the crimson rope-lights shot out and snaked about Nuadu's wrists, pinioning them.

Nuadu struggled, but the rope-lights held and Fenella could see that they bit deeply into his skin. The Robemaker glanced at CuRoi and, with a second quick movement of his hand, sent out a second shower of crimson, and Fenella found her own wrists as tightly bound.

'So,' said CuRoi, moving forward, and studying them both, 'so you have found your way to the Ebony Throne, have you, Wolfprince?'

'As you intended,' said Nuadu.

'Yes. Yes, that is perceptive of you. But do you know,' said CuRoi thoughtfully, 'I did not expect you to walk into my little trap quite so easily.'

'Let us say,' said Nuadu, 'that it suited me to appear to fall in with your little ploy.'

'Indeed? Well, the Wolves were never noted for their judgement,' said CuRoi, rather dismissively. 'But I confess that it pleases me to have succeeded. Did you enjoy my series of locked rooms, my dear?' he said to Fenella. 'A rather childish ploy, but one that pleases me. Each one worse than the last, until you see through the device and then, of course, the rooms become relatively harmless. Store-rooms for chalices and salvers and the occasional discarded enchantment.' He smiled and then turned back to Nuadu. 'But I admit that I wished you to confront the Ebony Throne, Nuadu Airgetlam.' He regarded Nuadu. 'That was the reason for luring your lady down here. Of course you would follow her.'

'Of course,' said Nuadu, equably. 'I see that you acknowledge the existence of chivalry, even though you do not practise it.'

CuRoi smiled and shook his head. 'Tsk, tsk,' he said. 'A bitter tongue. Do you know what happens to bitter tongues?' And he moved one hand in a curious, somehow inverted, gesture, and produced, from the long loose sleeve of his gown, a pink, wet Human tongue.

'You see?' said CuRoi, turning it this way and that. 'Unharmed until it utters displeasing sentiments. And then we simply—' Another of the quick, light gestures, 'We simply make it cloven,' he said and, as he spoke, the tongue parted and split and blood and saliva oozed out.

'A cloven tongue,' said CuRoi, showing them the two separate pieces, and then throwing them into the air and watching them vanish. 'A particularly unpleasant fate. But one I should enjoy inflicting on you, Wolfprince.' His eyes grew cold and hard suddenly. 'You know the legend of the Ebony Throne,' he said.

'The ancient Throne of ebonywood that will only accept Ireland's true King,' said Nuadu, rather off-handedly, as if the grotesque illusionist's trick had barely touched his mind. 'Yes, it is one of the earliest beliefs, that. Although I think that to most people it is simply a symbolic thing. And there are many such beliefs that surround all ancient Royal lines,' he said. 'There are many rituals attached to the crowning of kings. Stones that shriek aloud, swords that must be drawn from solid rock. It pleases the people to believe these things,' he said, as if the subject did not interest him very much, but Fenella saw that his eyes went to the immense, gleaming dark throne as he said this.

'It is not symbolic, Wolfprince,' said the Robemaker, and Fenella and Nuadu both repressed a shudder, because they had forgotten the whispery, diseased voice. 'It is very real and very powerful,' said the Robemaker. 'It was created from the first trees in the Wolfwood and the first sorcerers wove into it one of the most powerful enchantments ever known.'

Nuadu said softly, 'An enchantment so that it would accept Ireland's rightful King and no other.'

'So you do believe,' said CuRoi thoughtfully. 'I thought you did.'

'Not really.'

'You would care to try it, bastard prince?' said CuRoi, his eyes gleaming.

'I think not,' said Nuadu politely.

'I thought you would not wish to.' CuRoi smiled. 'It is a vastly unpleasant death, to call down the Ebony Throne's power. You have perhaps felt in the air the agonies of those who have been sufficiently arrogant to challenge me and whom I have flung to the Throne? They

552

linger on, of course, as do all strong emotions.'

'I have felt them,' said Nuadu in a level voice.

CuRoi laughed and Fenella saw the shower of silver and red amusement cascade through the air and fall to the floor at their feet. 'We are in no danger from your puny threats, Nuadu of the Silver Arm,' said CuRoi.

'We have never been in danger from you,' said the Robemaker.

Nuadu regarded them, his head on one side. 'But I have still teeth, CuRoi,' he said softly. 'I have still the ability to kill you.' He regarded the necromancer. 'I should take great pleasure in tearing your flesh, crunching your bones,' he said thoughtfully, and CuRoi laughed again and again the sparks of malicious amusement touched the air.

Nuadu regarded them both, his head on one side consideringly. 'Well, gentlemen,' he said, and Fenella caught the reckless note in his voice, and knew he might very well gamble on a sudden spring on either one of these two, 'what do you intend now? Are we to be given the chance to find my brother? Let us be open with one another, at least.'

'The Wolfkings are an accursed line,' said the Robemaker. 'Between us we have almost ended their reign.'

'Almost?'

'There is still you,' said CuRoi.

'But I am not a threat,' said Nuadu. 'Come now, we all know that I have no right to Ireland's Throne.'

'That is true.' CuRoi walked to where Nuadu still stood, and appeared to consider him. 'But supposing, Nuadu, that you were the last Wolfprince in Ireland, no matter your – ah – *irregular* birth. Might it not occur to some of your faithful Beastline creatures to propose you as a Monarch?'

'You have still the wolfblood,' said the Robemaker.

'And,' said CuRoi, 'to some, it might seem that any creature with a trickle of the ancient wolfblood could be enthroned at Tara.'

He waited, and Nuadu said at once, 'The creatures of the Beastline would take the Throne for themselves rather than see me on it,' and CuRoi nodded, as if this was the answer he had expected.

The Robemaker said, 'All creatures are venal, no matter their ancestry.'

'Also necromancers,' said Nuadu with extreme politeness, and CuRoi's dark features twisted in a frown.

'You see,' said CuRoi, moving back to stand behind the blackened silky-smooth chair, 'you see, Nuadu, we do not care to risk having you out in the world – either in this Ireland or the other one – where you might be the target for some kind of ridiculous act of what your world calls chivalry.' He studied Nuadu. 'We can permit no pretenders, no bastard princes,' he said.

'I understand.'

'And so we shall kill you.'

'As you have killed the King?'

'Oh, the King,' said CuRoi, and a cold smile touched his lips now. 'Perhaps he is dead and perhaps he is not.'

'Perhaps he is condemned to wander this Dark Realm, with the leaden Cloak of Ignorance about his shoulders,' hissed the Robemaker.

'A cruel torment which would be worthy of you,' said Nuadu, as if in agreement. 'Is that the fate you have reserved for me? The Lady can be let go, of course,' he said, rather off-handedly, as if Fenella's fate did not matter very much to him. 'She has served her purpose.' Fenella stared at the floor, because it was important not to let the two terrible beings before them guess at her thoughts, and she knew that Nuadu was trying to ensure her escape.

CuRoi said in a gloating voice, 'We shall find uses for the Lady,' and the Robemaker chuckled with a wet bubbling sound that made Fenella think of his eaten-away throat.

'She will be put into service in my Workshops,' he said, and lifted his head so that Fenella caught a glimpse of gleaming white bone and a great gaping cavern where the nose should have been, and caught, as well, the stench of ulcerous skin and leprous flesh. 'To replace the creatures she so *foolishly* set free,' said the Robemaker. 'A fitting fate, my dear.'

Nuadu pulled briefly against the crimson ropes and CuRoi laughed. 'You should know, wolf creature, that the Robemaker's ropes of light are not to be dissolved.'

Only to the Human's hand . . . The words touched Fenella's mind as lightly and as delicately as a batswing brush and at once something in her mind sprang to attention.

Open, locks, to the Human's hand . . . Schism, latches, and sever, turnkeys . . .

Of *course*, thought Fenella, still staring at the floor, because these two creatures would almost certainly listen to her thoughts if they wanted to. Of course. The spell from the Robemaker's own Workshops. The Robe of Human Hands and the chanted spell that freed Nuadu and the others. We have not the Robe, but we might have the chant. That's if I can remember it. Can I remember it? thought Fenella frantically. Oh dear heaven, can I? And then: but will it work without the Robe of Human Hands? What happened to that? Did we leave it in the Workshops. Yes, of course we did. Will the spell work without the Robe?

CuRoi was moving forward and the Robemaker with him. They stood on each side of Nuadu.

'We shall tie you to the chair,' said CuRoi, and he said it gently and reasonably.

'Why?'

A smile twisted the cruel lips again. 'Oh, let us say, that it will be a fitting end for you.' The dark eyes glittered. 'Let us perhaps rather say that we shall *feed* you to it,' he added.

'It is an unusual way to die,' said the Robemaker.

'But a fitting one for a bastard Wolfprince, I think? And you possess more than your share of arrogance, Nuadu Airgetlam.'

'He is an arrogant wolf creature,' said the Robemaker. 'He defied me and escaped me in the outside world. His concubine let loose my slaves. To see the Ebony Chair devour him will be a fitting recompense.' There was the suggestion of a terrible smile within the deep hood.

'But slowly,' said the Robemaker, and there was a lick of relish in his voice now. 'I shall draw him to it slowly, so that he has plenty of time to visualise what is in store for him.'

Nuadu said in a conversational tone, 'I see, Robemaker, that you still suffer the Curse of Eternal Disease, the *Draoicht Tinneas Siorai*. Do you still have to feed captured souls to the Soul Eaters?' He moved closer, his eyes reckless and shining. 'Have you not yet seen that they will take all you give and still not release you?' said Nuadu and the Robemaker drew back with a malevolent hiss and flung the crimson light again, so that it twisted about Nuadu's face and formed itself into the hateful mask once more.

'Accursed wolf-creature,' whispered the Robemaker. 'I do not have to listen to your poison! But you may be sure that your soul will go to the Lords of the Cruachan Cavern and be set on the Silver Scales, where it will weigh against my debt. And my debt is almost paid.' He raised his hand again, and began to draw Nuadu to the waiting chair.

'An interesting death, this one,' said CuRoi, and then, glancing at Fenella, 'and then, my dear, once your protector is gone, and his soul given to the Soul Eaters, we shall turn our attention to you.' He smiled, and moved to stand before her, inspecting her. 'Lovely,' he said at last, his voice thick and clotted with lust now. 'But then the Wolfprinces ever had good taste in women.'

Women . . . As if she was a concubine, a harlot. How dare this revolting creature treat them like this. Fenella put up her chin and regarded CuRoi haughtily and managed to keep her eyes from quite meeting his and sought furiously in her mind for the words to the enchantment that would dissolve the horrid crimson ropes.

Open, locks, to the Human's hand . . . If I cannot

remember, I shall have failed and Nuadu will die... *Open, locks, to the Human's hand... Schism, latches, and sever, turnkeys...*

CuRoi and the Robemaker had moved back to stand behind the throne and the Robemaker was lifting his hand again and Nuadu was snarling and struggling and, at any minute, the Robemaker would pull on the crimson ropes and Nuadu would be drawn forward...

Schism, latches, and sever, turnkeys... Fly open, bars, dissolve, untie, unchain, unfetter... Nothing was happening yet. The whole spell would have to be chanted, of course. And there was something farther on about cutting... That would be the salient part of the spell, surely... Fenella, her mind spinning, concentrating for all she was worth, reached deeper into her memory.

CuRoi was smiling now, his arms folded on his chest. 'The ancient Ebony Throne of Tara,' he said. 'The Seat of the High Kings of Ireland.' He paused, and looked deep into Nuadu's eyes. 'How you would have liked it,' he said. 'How you have coveted it, bastard Wolfprince, for all your cynicism and for all your rejection of your ancestry. Well, now you shall have it, you shall feel its cold embrace and you shall feel its burning maw. For it will only accept the True King of Ireland,' he said. 'It will burn and it will consume all those who have no claim to Tara. You will burn from within, Wolfprince, and you will burn *slowly*.' He smiled and turned to sign to the Robemaker to draw Nuadu forward to the throne.

Nuadu had stopped struggling and was standing very still and very straight. It seemed to Fenella that a different look had come into his eyes. Without warning, the words of the enchantment slid into her mind, whole and clear, and with them was an unexpected strength. She thought, and then was sure, that Nuadu was pouring the pure pale radiance into her mind and she experienced a feeling of such spiralling power that for a moment her mind was filled with nothing but the strong white light.

She stayed where she was, held by the crimson rope-lights, but she lifted her head slightly and repeated, in ringing tones, the words of the spell that had freed Nuadu and the other slaves from the Robemaker's treadmills.

Open, locks, to the Human's hand . . .
Schism, latches, and sever, turnkeys . . .
Fly open, bars, dissolve, untie, unchain, unfetter . . .
Slash and gash and carve and gnaw.
Pluck the splinters of iron and slice the thews of steel,
Scission and sunder, steal and plunder . . .

There was a moment, terrible, never to be forgotten, when the most profound silence blanketed them, as if the ancient castle was poised between two worlds. Fenella thought: it is in the balance. I believe that the spell is warring with CuRoi's evil. It is fighting it. I can *feel* that it is fighting it.

CuRoi had thrown back his head and stretched his hands out before him and Fenella heard the low, rhythmic chanting they had heard on their arrival. A dark, swirling vapour began to form on the air, fetid and suffocating.

There was time to think: CuRoi's dark servants! and to remember the grinning, bony-fingered creatures in the dungeons. There was a fleeting moment of sheer terror as the darkness, crimson-streaked and menacing, advanced towards them.

And then, at the centre of the room in front of the ancient magical Ebony Throne of the Wolfkings, Fenella and Nuadu saw the two enchantments collide and the white-hot sparks fly outwards.

The strong, incisive Robe of Human Hands glittered and sliced across the darkness, blue-grey and made of razor-sharp edges, cleaving the air with ease, scything through the dark turgid mass of CuRoi's terrible chant as it surged forward to where they stood. For a moment, the Human Hands faltered and at once the darkness reared up triumphantly, like heaving black waves. It will swallow us up, thought Fenella. It is like a muddy river, like a swamp that has boiled over. Like a slimy river bed, veined with crimson, palpating and threatening. It will smother us and suffocate us and we shall drown in it . . .

And then the blue-grey steel of the Robe of Human Hands scythed the darkness again and the seething black slime parted and seemed to hesitate and there was the flash of scissor-edges and sawteeth and of axe blades and knives and of every sharp thing ever known or dreamed or imagined.

Open, locks to the Human's hand . . .

The crimson rope-lights dissolved and fell to the floor, and Nuadu, freed, at once bounded to Fenella and grabbed her arm, pulling her from the dungeon, along the stone passage, past the six doors where CuRoi had laid his series of fearsome secrets.

They half ran, half fell up the narrow stone steps, gasping and struggling, and Nuadu pulled Fenella with him, through the firelit dining hall, and into the immense central stone hall.

Fenella, gasping for breath, holding tightly to Nuadu's hand, knew that the spell had not been exactly right; it had not been a spell to find hidden doors, only to unlock doors that had been locked. But it is all we had, cried her mind, it is all we had, and it has worked so far and if it does not release us from this Castle, then we are lost and Nuadu will surely die and Ireland will be lost and there will be nothing, anywhere, ever again . . .

The razor-sharp lights splintered the air all about their heads and CuRoi's Castle of Illusions began slowly to rotate.

'It is rescinding the sealing!' cried Nuadu. 'The Castle is opening! Fenella, be ready to get out!'

'Yes!' cried Fenella. 'Yes, as fast as ever we can!'

Great showers of angry crimson and purple sparks fell from the ceilings, starting up tiny vicious paths of fire all round them. The terrible chanting rose and heightened in intensity and, for a moment, the dark heavy clouds surged forward again. The Robemaker and CuRoi appeared at the far end of the stone hall and the Robemaker's crimson ropes snaked out. Nuadu dragged Fenella back until they were both standing with their backs pressed against the wall farthest from the two necromancers and they both flinched and dodged away from the whiplash of the rope-lights.

The scything blades and the mowing saws and the churning, snipping scissor-edges whirled again and flung clean sharp spears of blue-grey light against the wall. As Nuadu and Fenella put up their hands to shield their eyes from the brilliance, the outline of a door appeared in the wall.

'That's it!' cried Fenella. 'It's working! It's breaking the seals!'

'Yes, but quickly! Quickly!' cried Nuadu, and pulled Fenella forward.

As they moved, the door opened, and they could see the black wastes and the seething Dark Lakes and the terrible Fields of Blood beyond.

Hand in hand, they fell through, out of the necromancer's Castle.

Into the black night of the Dark Realm.

As they ran frantically down the hillside, they were aware, more strongly than ever, of the swirling eddying evil all about them. The skies churned and panted and great tongues of flame spat and curled out, so that several times they narrowly missed being consumed. Roaring winds whipped at them, snatching at Fenella's hair, and icy rain hurled itself into their faces, so that they had to turn their heads to avoid it as they ran.

They could hear CuRoi and the Ropemaker screaming imprecations after them, and there was not, surely, anywhere to hide.

As they neared the foot of the hill path, dozens of pairs of red eyes began to appear from the side of the path and the ground itself began to writhe and heave and throw them off balance.

Fenella said, 'I . . . cannot run . . . any farther.' And stopped, and bent over, helpless, doubling up over the stabbing agony in her left side. Nuadu, almost as exhausted, leaned against a tree.

'A few – minutes only—'

'Yes. All the time in the world, Lady.' Through the exhaustion and fear, the old grin slid out. 'Ahead are the Fields of Blood,' said Nuadu. 'If we can reach them, we may be within sight of the door created by the Soul Eaters!'

'But it vanished!' said Fenella. 'As soon as we were through it, it simply vanished!'

'But it's our only chance!' said Nuadu. 'Come now.'

'Yes. All right,' said Fenella, and gathered her strength, and they were running again, only now red-eyed creatures ran after them, bobbing and chuckling evilly, rubbing hands together, whispering and murmuring to one another as they ran.

Nearly there, nearly catching them . . . mustn't let these two go . . . Cut out their hearts and roast them for the trolls if we can . . . Throw them to the Lake people . . . Turn them into the Nightfields and hunt them down for sport . . .

Nuadu lifted the glinting silver arm and pointed. 'There!' he cried. 'The Crimson Fields!' Fenella stopped, shading her eyes against the livid scarlet of the skies.

'Are you sure? Nuadu, are you sure this is the right path?' The thought of being lost in this terrible evil Realm, pursued by CuRoi and the Robemaker, perhaps never emerging into the true Ireland, was so unbearable that Fenella found herself unable to focus properly.

'Yes!' cried Nuadu, pulling her with him. 'See the red glow rising against the darkness! And the figure of the scarecrow! Yes, come *on*, Fenella!'

Forked lightning was splitting the skies over them now and Nuadu, glancing behind, saw that CuRoi and the Robemaker were not pursuing them, but were standing together with the towering Castle of Illusions behind them. CuRoi had folded his arms across his chest, and he was suffused with light; the light was burgeoning and swelling, developing great elongated fingers which would reach out and down and scoop up the two creatures who had somehow outwitted the Master.

The Robemaker was standing in shadow, the deep hood of his cloak hiding his face. But Nuadu could see that the crimson rope-lights were spinning and whirling all about him and that they were forming a mesh cage which would imprison them both if they were not quick and if they could not find the doorway back to the Cruachan Cavern.

For a brief, scalding instant, his mind acknowledged the thought that, once in the Cruachan Cavern, they would again be at the mercy of the Soul Eaters and then he pushed it aside impatiently.

They were nearing the Fields of Blood – Fenella, whose lungs were hurting, but who was somehow managing to keep running at Nuadu's side, saw the deep red glow, like fire, like blood seeping into the skies. The faint charnel stench assaulted her nostrils once more and she shuddered, because the Fields had been so terrible, so pitiful and repulsive.

But this is the way we came, she thought doggedly; this is the road we took, and this is the only way we can take now.

The strong glowing clouds of light that CuRoi had spun exploded like a star bursting and, at once, brilliant fingers of light poured forth down the hillside after them, thin snakelike streams of reaching enchantment that would catch them up and sweep them aside. It was a little like trying to outrun a fast-flowing mountain river which has burst its banks, or the volcanic eruptions that Fenella remembered from Renascia. Crimson light sizzled through the air and rope-lashes whipped at them cruelly. Nuadu, caught by one of them, stumbled and half fell and Fenella at once dragged him upright.

As they drew level with the Fields, they could see the waving tatters of skin. The scarecrow's arms moved in the wind and its sleeves flapped sadly, as ravaged-faced Harpies screeched at it in derision, before flying off to attack another part of the Fields.

Fenella, drawing breath for a final sprint, was just thinking that CuRoi would certainly order the Harpies to attack them when Nuadu suddenly gripped her hand in a tight painful clasp.

'What—'

And then Fenella saw where Nuadu was pointing, the silver arm glinting redly in the eerie light.

The scarecrow had turned its head and was looking towards them.

It was alive.

It was one of the most remarkable moments Fenella had ever known. The scarecrow was alive; it was watching them from sad, dark eyes, and it was so clearly not a creature of this Realm, that there was no question but that it must be saved. Fenella and Nuadu both plunged at once into the terrible waving fields and, as they did so, the streams of CuRoi's molten lava poured harmlessly across the road behind them, leaving them unscathed.

Nuadu was ahead. He was waist-deep in the terrible waving fields, among the bloodied tatters of Human remains, the slithery fragments of Human innards. Fenella, trying desperately hard to close her mind against the reality of the Fields, followed him and, despite her resolve, felt the grisly harvests brush her thighs. The ground beneath the skin was wet and squelching; here and there it was slippery and slimed. Once, half-way across, she caught her foot in a root and half fell, and then looked down and saw that it was not a root at all, but a writhing length of white intestine, coiled deep beneath the necromancer's crop of flesh, snakelike and gruesome. Fenella thought that if she once gave way to the lurching, shuddering revulsion, she would sink down in the Fields and the bloodied tatters would close over her head and she would drown in the heaving sea of Human gore.

Nuadu was moving purposefully ahead, hacking his way through the Fields, using his silver arm mercilessly. Twice he looked back and Fenella felt his warmth and strength touch her mind.

All right, Lady . . .?

All right, whispered Fenella in her mind, and Nuadu

563

grinned as if to say: Courage, Fenella, we are almost there! and moved on.

The scarecrow had been somehow fastened to two strips of wood, roughly nailed together at the centre, forming a cruciform shape. The upright strut towered above them, casting a dense black shadow. Fenella thought it must have been ten feet in height, and the ragged, bloodied figure was fastened high on it, so that its bound feet were barely level with Fenella's eyes.

Its arms were extended the length of the cross-piece and even from the ground Fenella could see that the Robemaker's rope-lights bound its wrists and ankles firmly in place. There were more of the rope-lights about its waist, and they had cut deeply into the skin, so that the ragged garments it wore were darkened with blood. The pity of it slammed Fenella across the heart and she saw Nuadu reach up and then stand back frowning.

Fenella said, softly, 'We can't reach it.'

'No. And even if we could, it is bound with the rope-lights.'

'The Robe of the Human Hands?' said Fenella, a bit hesitantly. 'Would it dissolve the rope-lights once more?' At once the ravaged features of the prisoner – Fenella could see now that it was a young man, only a very little older than Nuadu – looked down at her with such trust and such blind faith that Fenella knew that they must find a way of ending his torments.

She did not stop to think if there was time to chant the Spell again before CuRoi redirected the molten lava, or whether the Spell would work. Nuadu, who had turned to watch their pursuers, saw that CuRoi had vanished – into the Castle? – but that the Robemaker was still screaming imprecations and hurling sizzling light-whips at them. He thought that both necromancers would hesitate to destroy the Fields of Blood and he thought it ironic that they should have found temporary sanctuary in the necromancers' storefields, a place which might so easily have been their own last resting place – indeed still might be so, he thought.

Fenella had not moved; she was looking up at the thin ravaged face of the dark-haired young man – it was a pale, rather unusual face – and the words of the Enchantment formed in her mind easily and smoothly. She stood very still and pronounced, for the third time, the ancient strong Enchantment stolen from the Robemaker's storehouse of spells.

Open, locks, to the Human's hand . . .
Schism, latches, and sever, turnkeys . . .
Fly open, bars, dissolve, untie, unchain, unfetter . . .
Slash and gash and carve and gnaw.
Pluck the splinters of iron and slice the thews of steel,
Scission and sunder, steal and plunder . . .

There was confidence in her voice, because although the Spell was still not complete without the robe, they had proved its efficacy inside the Castle and they had escaped and surely they would free this captive now? It worked for us and it will work for him, thought Fenella, fiercely. It will work, because it *must* work. I *believe* that it will work.

The rope-lights which had held the young man to the cross melted at once, dissolving and running into nothing, and the prisoner fell gasping from his terrible bondage into Nuadu's arms. For a moment, neither of them moved and Nuadu and the young man looked at one another very intensely.

And then the young man said, in a choking weak voice, rusty with disuse, 'How shall I thank you—'

'Do not thank me yet,' said Nuadu, straightening up and turning to look towards the Castle. 'Do not thank me until we have escaped.' And then he looked at the young man, and added, 'Your Majesty.'

Ireland's High King. Fenella stood transfixed, staring at the thin frail form, the exiled Wolfprince, Ireland's uncrowned King, who had been held in such terrible thralldom. She thought: he has been imprisoned out here, held by a necromancer's vicious cruelty, reduced to this poor wretched frail thing. There were scars on his arms and neck – talon scratches from the screeching Harpies who would have mocked him and flown at him and whom he would have been unable to drive off.

Nuadu had not spoken, but his face was white with bitter anger against CuRoi and the Robemaker. He said, 'There is much for us to say, Sire, but this is not the place. We must somehow get you out.'

'No ceremony,' croaked the young man. 'My name is Aed.'

'I know,' said Nuadu, and they looked at one another again.

Fenella had turned to look at the Castle again and, as she did so, the drawbridge lifted and framed in it were the figures of CuRoi and the Robemaker astride rearing black horses.

'The NightMares,' said Aed, who was also looking. 'Fearsome creatures who stalk the dreams of their victims.' A shiver went through his thin body and Fenella said, urgently, 'Sire – Your—' and at once the young man said, 'We will dispense with the formalities, Lady,' and Fenella heard the echo of Nuadu's voice, the same timbre, the same way of arranging words.

'I am in your hands,' said Aed. 'I have not the strength to do much other than follow you—' A sudden sweet smile touched his face. 'But I believe I have sufficient strength left to walk out of this place.'

'This way,' said Nuadu, who had straightened up and was scanning the landscape. 'This way, for we may still find the Gateway to the Caverns. Back on to the road and straight towards the swamplands!'

'The Black Marshes?' said Aed.

'Yes! That is where we came through the Gateway! That must be where the fabric between the two Irelands is at its thinnest!'

'Hurry!' said Fenella, grasping Aed's arm on Nuadu's other side. 'They are already out of the Castle!'

CuRoi and the Robemaker were riding hard down the

mountain slope, crouching over their steeds. Crimson fire surrounded them and, even from here, it was possible to hear the ringing out of the NightMares' hoofs on the ground. There was a grim, relentless, pounding about the sound. They would reach the Fields very soon.

Nuadu and Fenella, with Aed between them, began to push their way through the Fields again, moving as quickly as they could. Fenella, holding Aed's thin arm firmly, found it very nearly possible to ignore the horrid smeary skin shreds and the slinking trails of white intestines beneath her feet. It was more important to help Aed, who was so thin and so frail-looking that Fenella found her heart lurching anxiously every time he stumbled. He was so weak that it seemed impossible that he would survive the journey to the Cruachan Cavern. She glanced back. Could they outrun CuRoi and his creatures with such a burden to slow them? Then she remembered that their only way of escape was through the Cave of the Soul Eaters and that Nuadu had made that specious bargain to bring back the King of Ireland, so that the Soul Eaters could take his soul . . . And we cannot endanger him! cried Fenella in silent anguish. He has suffered so much already!

She glanced at Nuadu, but Nuadu's expression was unreadable; his eyes were deep unfathomable pits and his mouth was set in an uncompromising line.

It is the only way out, Lady . . .

They neared the road and Fenella began to scan the horizon for indications of where they might have come through the Gateway.

'But there is nothing,' she said to Nuadu, very nearly despairing. 'And CuRoi and the Robemaker are closing on us.'

They were, and with them were the Harpies, swooping through the night skies, forming a fearsome pattern, their ravaged-woman faces grotesque on their vulture-bodies and their claws vicious.

'Cruel things,' said Aed. 'But they cannot actually kill.'

Nuadu, who had been looking intently at the road ahead, stopped suddenly and looked first at Fenella and then at Aed. 'Listen,' he said, and there was a note of spiralling excitement in his voice.

Very distantly, as if it was a sound that must travel down a long echoing tunnel, or as if it was coming from behind a closed door, they heard the beating of leathery wings on the air.

The Gateway formed almost at once. There was a whirring, thrumming sound, the impression of an approaching dark force and the feeling of the huge shadowy wings of the Soul Eaters somewhere above them.

A string of glittering light stretched upwards in front of their eyes, splitting the crimson-streaked blackness in twain, and then a second string, exactly in line with it, appeared. As they stood together, watching, the third line appeared, joining the two at the top, and there before them was the immense Gateway through which Fenella and Nuadu had come earlier, and through which they must now go back.

Because it is the only way, Lady . . .

Into the Cruachan Cavern. Into the domain of the Soul Eaters who awaited the soul of the High King. Taking the frail weak Aed to the predators who would tear out his soul and fling his poor tormented body into the River of the Dead. And it was the only way back . . .

Fenella heard the leathery wings again and a great shadow fell over them. Nuadu, looking up, his hand shading his eyes, said, softly, 'The Soul Eaters. They are with us.'

'But why have they come now? They were to give us seven days! They promised!' Fenella cried, angrily.

Nuadu looked at Aed. 'They have sensed your presence, Sire. Perhaps they have scented it in the manner of all predatory beings. They know that we have rescued you and that we are fleeing to safety with you. Also,' said Nuadu, with a sudden wry smile, 'they do not trust me to fulfil my promise to them.'

'Promise?'

'I pledged that if the Soul Eaters would give us unchallenged passage into the Dark Realm, we would in return bring your soul to them.'

There was a sudden silence. Then Aed said, 'I see.'

'But of course they did not trust me,' said Nuadu. 'And so now they are coming for you and we must find a way of evading them.'

Fenella, who was watching the Gateway, said, 'CuRoi and the Robemaker will certainly fight them for the King.'

'Precisely,' said Nuadu, grinning suddenly.

'Of course,' said Fenella, staring at him in fearful hope. 'If they engage in battle, perhaps we might slip through the Gateway unnoticed.'

'It is what I had hoped,' said Nuadu. 'And it is our only chance of escape now.'

The Gateway was open to its fullest extent and the Soul Eaters were pouring through, a flight of great black predators, their huge wings spread, so that Fenella could see the scaly under-sides. They flew in a crouching fashion, their wizened bodies curled under their wings, talons poised to swoop on their prey.

There was no point in running now; to run would have made them more noticeable. The Soul Eaters and the necromancers would not lose sight of their three victims, but it might be possible to step lightly and stealthily back, a little at a time, until they were at the yawning Gate that would lead them into the true Ireland again.

At the sight of the Soul Eaters, CuRoi and the Robemaker had instantly reined in the NightMares, and the horses were rearing and prancing, their eyes glinting redly.

'But they have them in control,' said Aed, softly. 'The Master is able to control them.'

'Might they turn on him?' asked Fenella, thinking this would be a good opportunity to move closer to the Gateway.

'It is unlikely, Lady. The Master's ways with disobedient or rebellious servants is known to all his creatures.'

Nuadu said, 'Keep moving slowly towards the Gateway. If any of them look in our direction, stand absolutely still at once.'

The two necromancers were hurling light-shafts at the Soul Eaters, crimson and orange and flame spears that split the heavens and sent fire crackling across the dark terrain, lighting it to sharp and fearsome relief, and the Soul Eaters were swooping and diving to avoid the splintering fire. The Fields of Blood stood out starkly, so that the crimson-soaked, leathery harvest of the dark lords was blenched briefly to white.

The Robemaker was screeching curses at the Soul Eaters and his voice, rasping and ugly, came clearly to the three waiting below.

'They will take the King! The Soul Eaters will take the King! After them! We must keep the King at all costs!'

The NightMares reared, sparks flying from beneath their hoofs, and, to the three trying to escape, it seemed that the two immense powers would converge and clash.

The Soul Eaters were massing above CuRoi and the Robemaker, their monstrous wings blotting out the livid skies, and so strong and so imbued with pitiless soul-less determination were they, that Fenella thought they must surely vanquish the necromancers.

But already the screeching Harpies were flying straight at the Soul Eaters, their talons extended, reaching to lacerate the dry harsh wings. The grinning, prowling creatures Fenella had glimpsed in the dungeons were there as well now, assembled behind their Master, leaping and prancing, jabbing at the darkness with their scissor-edged fingers, chuckling evilly. They linked hands and began to circle directly beneath the Soul Eaters and, as one of the creatures suddenly fell from the air, torn and mutilated by the Harpies, they fell on it at once, ripping it to pieces, flinging the scaly fragments of its wings high into the air, chuckling with malevolent glee.

Through the half-open Gateway, Fenella could see

caves and flickering torchlight and surely, oh surely this was the moment to run, to flee for the cover of the caves and trust, to whatever gods could be trusted here, that they would somehow escape.

As if he had heard her thoughts, Nuadu said, softly, 'Not yet, Fenella,' and, in the same moment, Aed pointed to the Gateway.

The Rodent Armies were tumbling through in answer to the plight of the Soul Eaters. They were red-eyed and feral and they carried spears and barbed hooks and spiny-backed halberds and lances. They poured forth over the terrain, flinging the spears and the lances at the dungeon-creatures, whirling the great hooks on the ends of ropes so that the vicious hooks flew upwards at the Harpies. The Harpies screeched as several of the hooks embedded in their flesh and three of them fell to the earth.

The Weasels were brandishing great glinting axes, double-edged, and the Stoats carried thin, wicked javelins. They slunk close to the ground and swarmed upwards towards the Castle.

CuRoi reined in his rearing black steed and lifted his arm. At once an immense wall of fire reared up between himself and the Robemaker and the Rodent Armies.

The creatures flinched away at once and CuRoi's mocking laughter rang out clearly on the night.

'Puny creatures!' he cried. 'Is this all you can send against me in your fight to take Ireland's King! He is mine – and he will stay mine!'

As if in contempt, the Soul Eaters flew straight into the fiery wall, passing through it with apparent ease, and the Weasels and the Stoats burrowed deep into the ground, cutting themselves tunnels through which they would burrow, to emerge on the other side of the flames.

'Ours, necromancer! The King is ours. He was promised to us, and we have come to claim his soul . . .'

The Soul Eaters were circling CuRoi and the Robemaker, avoiding the fire, making their dry bone-against-skin sound.

Nuadu took Fenella's hand, and looked at Aed.

'They are intent on their battle,' he said very softly. 'This is our only chance. The Cruachan Cavern is empty for the moment. We must go through it and out into the passages.'

'Can we do it?'

'Let us see if we can,' said Nuadu. He glanced back to where the Soul Eaters were still hovering above CuRoi and the Robemaker, greed glinting in their tiny eyes. 'Ready?' he said, and slowly, stealthily, they moved towards the Gateway.

There was no time to look back at the battle; they were at the yawning Gateway and through it they could see the dark tunnels of the Cruachan Caverns.

Freedom! thought Fenella. Isn't it?

There was a moment when they paused in the immense, light-filled Gateway, seeing ahead of them the Cruachan Cavern and the dark winding tunnels, but seeing, as well, the glittering Castle of Illusions in the Realm they were leaving, seeing it beautiful and sinister, sharply limned against the dark, blood-veined skies.

CuRoi and the Robemaker were retreating, turning the great black NightMares about and riding hard towards the Castle. A great howl of triumph went up from the Rodent Armies as they surged forward in pursuit.

Fenella saw, through the pouring, feral Rodents and the swooping, angry Soul Eaters, the immense Castle begin slowly to rotate.

'The sealing,' said Nuadu at her side.

'And the Soul Eaters and their Armies will be shut out.'

'They will not breach the Master's magical defences, Lady,' said Aed.

'Then the Soul Eaters and their Armies will soon return,' said Nuadu, leading them into the Cavern and through into the tunnels that Fenella remembered. 'Therefore we have not much time.'

'What about sentries?' said Fenella, suddenly. 'The Rodent Armies might have left sentries behind?'

'Yes, that's true,' said Nuadu. 'But if we are stealthy

and quick we may evade them. We must melt into the shadows. There are only three of us.'

'And the sound and the lights of the battle out there will serve to quench any noise we make,' said Fenella, nodding. 'Yes.'

The Caves were silent and brooding and they could feel the miasma of evil all about them.

'But I think there are no sentries here,' said Aed, softly. 'You were right to think of it, Lady, but I think the Soul Eaters called upon every shred of their strength to defeat CuRoi.'

They were walking in single file now, Nuadu padding along ahead of them, and Fenella in the middle. Aed was keeping pace, but as they drew farther away from the raging battle, he stumbled and fell. Nuadu caught him. Fenella at once took Aed's hands, and saw that his face was white and strained, that he had the look of a creature driven beyond endurance. As if he had caught this, Aed opened his eyes and sent her a smile that was uncannily Nuadu's and said, gently, 'I shall hold together for a little longer, Lady. Although we are nearly at our journey's end.'

Journey's end . . . Fenella thought: but does he simply mean our journey back to the True Ireland, or does he mean something more?

Between them, they carried the barely conscious King, and Fenella saw that Nuadu's eyes were dark and shadowed. She thought: he cares very much that the King is weak and perhaps dying. He does not know him, but he cares. This is hurting him quite dreadfully.

As if in answer, Nuadu said, very gently, 'My mother's son,' and Fenella said, 'Yes. Of course.' And hoped that this did not sound insensitive or inept.

Ahead of them the tunnel was widening and becoming tinged with blue and violet shadows and they could see the familiar magical purple dusk.

'Closer with every step,' said Fenella. 'Shall we come out onto the Island?'

'Truly I have no idea,' said Nuadu. 'It is said that there

is only one entrance to the Cavern of the Soul Eaters, but that there are many exits.'

Many exits . . .

As the purple light poured into the cave mouth, heavy and heady, laden with the ancient magical Twilight Enchantments, they moved towards it and emerged into the pouring mystical Purple Hour.

Directly to the east, no more than a mile from them, were glinting spires and red-tipped gates and a soft radiance that lit the darkling skies.

The Palace of Wildfire.

Fael-Inis's country.

They laid Aed carefully on the ground and straightened up, the rainbow-tinged light streaming into the cave mouth, both of them breathing in the clean cool night air with delight. They felt the sweet scents of the Purple Hour and the gentle warm enchantments soaking into their skin.

'Safe,' said Fenella at length. 'Aren't we?'

'Yes, for we have only to cross to Fael-Inis's country.' Nuadu's eyes were blazing with sudden excitement as he looked across to the shining towers and the fiery walls. 'The Palace of Wildfire,' he said, half to himself. And then, as if pushing the delight away, bent to the still form of Aed.

Aed's eyes were filmed and his skin was cold to Fenella's touch. I believe he is dying, she thought. He used his last reserves of strength to come with us out of the Dark Realm. He did not falter until we were in sight of the True Ireland, she thought, with angry pain. He reached his journey's end.

Aed did not open his eyes, but he said, in a thread of a voice, 'You are right, Lady. It is unthinkable that a King of Tara should die in that place. I could not be content until I stood on the threshold of my own world and until I could look upon my own Realm once more.'

My own Realm . . . This Ireland, thought Fenella; this twilit land, this strange magic-laden world of enchanted forests and dark sorcery and half-Human creatures who prowl the woods and the mountains. It is this that was his journey's end.

She looked down again and saw that Aed was watching Nuadu and although his eyes were pain-filled, they were clear. He said, 'Nuadu – we should have known one another—'

'That we did not was neither your fault nor mine,' said Nuadu, and Fenella heard the bitterness in his voice and hoped he was not being cruel. But Aed seemed to understand. He reached for Nuadu's hand: 'My father was a good ruler but a hard man.'

'Yes.'

Aed moved weakly, and Nuadu slid his arm about his shoulders, propping him up. 'Nuadu – Ireland—' The dark gentle eyes rested on Nuadu and Fenella saw the two of them look at one another very steadily and very straightly and something seemed to pass between them.

Then Nuadu said, 'Ireland will be safe, Sire.'

'You promise it?'

'I promise it,' said Nuadu. And then, in a voice that was so low Fenella could never afterwards be sure she had heard it, 'On the memory of our mother, I promise you that Ireland will be safe,' he said.

'Then I am content,' said Aed, and his head fell back and the life and the light faded from his face.

Chapter Forty-three

The exiled Forest Court, under the direction of Tealtaoich and the eldest of the Oaks, had decided that the best thing to do was to march on Tara at dawn. Dawn, said Tealtaoich, his eyes glowing, wasn't that the time to be sweeping down on the unsuspecting Gruagach and catching them all by surprise? Wouldn't they all of them be still a-bed, lazy creatures, and now that they had woken the Beasts, wouldn't they be able to re-take Tara with the utmost ease?

They had been very nearly overwhelmed by their success with the Beastline Enchantment; even Feradach had shaken Miach's hand and admitted that Miach had succeeded in surprising them all, which, coming from Feradach, was quite a large compliment.

Dian Cecht had withdrawn from them all after the Ritual, seating herself apart at meals, staring soulfully into the forest depths.

'It's all a pose, of course,' said Feradach to Snizort. 'She would really like a silk-hung couch to recline on and slaves to kneel before her with food and wine. That's what she'd really like.'

Snizort thought this was very probably true. He had spent his time busily setting down the story of the Ritual. He had shown the results to Oisin, rather worriedly, because he had not wanted to get any of this very important matter wrong, but Oisin had thought it extremely well written and said Snizort had captured the spirit of the strange Beastline Enchantment exactly.

'When all this is over, we shall arrange for your writings to be bound in vellum and added to the great library in Tara,' Oisin said, and Snizort beamed, because he had not looked for such very gratifying recognition. He would have discussed this further, and he would certainly have tried to talk to Dian Cecht about the Swans and their history, but the Court had been thrown into further disarray by the unexpected arrival of Caspar and the freed slaves.

'Remarkable,' said Eogan, as the rather sorry little group came exhaustedly through the forest.

'I'll lay them some places at the table, shall I?' said Clumhach. 'They'll be glad of a bite to eat. Well, anyone would after being chained up by the Robemaker. Dear me, what a to-do.'

They had all been extremely heartened by the arrival of Caspar and the freed slaves of the Robemaker. Tealtaoich had made a speech of welcome, and Snizort had sharpened up his charcoal sticks again, because there would be a story to be told presently, when the poor young men had recovered. In the meantime, he was very glad to see Caspar who explained how Fenella and Floy and Snodgrass had escaped from the giants.

'Floy and Snodgrass will have a fine old time at the Fire Court and Fenella's with Nuadu,' said Caspar. 'I daresay they'll all turn up any time.' To which Snizort said, bless his soul, of course they would turn up, and felt happier than he had felt since the others had left him here, and went back to plotting how he could best record this latest set of events. One vellum-bound volume in Tara's library would be very nice, but two would be even better. He made a few notes while Clumhach went round with the mulled wine. Everyone was extremely pleased to see Caspar and the freed slaves, although Feradach was heard to remark in not-quite-a-whisper to Eogan that this handful of battered young men would not be of any great help to them in their march on Tara, but Eogan had said sharply that this was not the point. The point was that Caspar and Fenella had been able to outwit the Robemaker to the extent of setting free his slaves, which showed that the Robemaker was not as omnipotent as they had feared.

Caspar, appealed to about the attack on Tara, said that dawn would be a very good time.

'Although,' he said, 'it's entirely possible that the Gruagach are still all under the *Draoicht Suan*.'

'But if that's so,' said Oisin, 'then we could simply march into Tara unchallenged.'

'Well, yes,' said Caspar doubtfully, because it surely could not be as easy as all that. But he listened to the plans, and was made to feel at home, and began almost to think that for somebody who had not wanted to participate in a battle at all, he was doing really rather well.

He was just helping Oisin to unroll the map of Tara and the surrounding villages, when Eogan looked across the table, and said, 'Listen.'

'What is it?'

'There's something coming through the Forest.' He stopped, his head tilted to listen, and Feradach said, 'It's several someones.'

'My enchantments will catch any enemies,' said Miach, and stopped as well, because he could hear it now.

Marching feet.

And the sound of rather uncertain singing.

We're free of the giants, at last, boys,
We're free as we can be.
We climbed down the castle wall, boys,
And slipped out from their grasp, boys;
But they'll be chasing and running
And they'll be stamping and shouting,
So we'd better make for safety, bo - o - o - y - s,
We'd better hide from the giants, bo - o - o - y - s,
Or we'll be roasted for sure.
And we'll be eaten for keeps.
And we'll be never no more.

'And death to the *Fidchell*,' called a single, rather defiant voice, and at once the other voices said, 'And death to the *Fidchell*.'

As everyone rose and turned to stare in the direction of the rather unhappy singing, through the Trees, spades and satchels on their backs, hats determinedly jaunty, came the Gnomes of Gallan.

Tealtaoich moved at once to welcome them.

'Because,' said Oisin later, 'they were plainly seeking sanctuary of some kind and, anyway, the Gnomes have *always* fought for the High Kings.'

'Even when they have not understood the reason,' said Dian Cecht who had rejoined the others to hear about the freed slaves, and who had fixed her mournful dark eyes on the comeliest and least battered of the young men.

The Gnomes were extremely pleased to find themselves at the centre of the Forest Court and welcomed into it by no less a person than Tealtaoich of the Wild Panthers. They brightened up considerably and accepted large tankards of mead from Clumhach and sat themselves down by the fire to get warm. Culdub Oakapple spread out his neckerchief to dry, because hadn't it fallen into a puddle half-way here and a damp neckerchief gave anyone a terrible old attack of the rheumatics.

They bowed solemnly to each of the Beastline in turn, Bith lost his bog-hat when he bowed to Eogan, and then had to be presented to the Trees, because this was only polite.

The Gnomes were charmed to meet the Trees and Flaherty said he hoped the Trees hadn't been thinking them ill mannered at all for ignoring them earlier on, only that they hadn't precisely seen them until now, what with it being a touch dark in the forest, and what with it not being the sort of thing you'd be thinking to see anyway, and the others agreed that you wouldn't expect such a thing at all, and wasn't it the grandest thing ever to find themselves amidst a collection of such important people, and would their importantships be thinking of a bit of a battle at all?

'We'd be happy to help out if so,' said Bith of the Bog-hat. 'We're good fighters,' he added, and at once the others said they were, the grandest fighters to be found in all Ireland, leave aside the forging of a few swords which they would happily undertake, and maybe a plate or two of armour and a length of chain mail to round it all off.

'And,' said Pumlumon, 'haven't we the bit of spell-saying as well,' and the others joined in excitedly, saying they had, wasn't that the truth, and Pumlumon a great one in the spell-saying department, and him wholly responsible for sending the entire clan of the Gruagach into the deepest sleep ever known.

'And still in it!' shouted Flaherty, who had, truth to tell, taken a mite more of the mead than was strictly good for him. 'Aren't they still in it!' he repeated, and Bith of the Bog-hat told him to sit down and be quiet, it being the exiled Court they were talking to.

Tealtaoich, who remembered the Gnomes very well, and who had, in fact, consulted them on several occasions over the matter of some particularly special gems for one or two female acquaintances, asked to be told what had happened at Tara after Caspar and Fenella left, and Eogan seated himself at the head of the table, and said, 'Yes, good Gnomes, we should find it very useful to know all you can tell us,' and the Gnomes beamed and Bith rearranged his hat and Flaherty took another draught of mead to be sure not to run out of voice half-way through the tale, which would be a terrible thing to happen, and it the great Eogan of the Eagles and Tealtaoich of the Wild Panthers they were addressing, never mind all of the others.

And so Bith explained how they'd outwitted the Gruagach with the weaving of the *Draoicht Suan*, 'Although,' he added, 'I'd be bound to tell your dignityships that it was all Pumlumon's doing, and him knowing the spell as fast as the cat could lick its whiskers, not meaning any respect to your catship,' he said to Tealtaoich, and Tealtaoich grinned and said none in the world, and please to go on.

Bith scratched his head and said bother and blow him for a pair of giant's boots if that wasn't all there was to it.

'There we were,' he said, 'the entirety of us all fast asleep, because of the *Draoicht Suan* just catching us a bit unaware as you might say—'

Flaherty said that this was the sort of thing that might

happen to anyone, and the Gnomes said to be sure it was.

'But the spell wasn't directed at us,' explained Bith earnestly. 'Which is why we woke up without the counter-spell, although I'm bound to say it was as well we did wake up, what with none of us knowing the counter-spell very well.'

'And even if we had known it,' put in Culdub, 'weren't we all fast asleep and not able to chant it anyway.'

'So we were,' exclaimed the Gnomes, beaming because wasn't it like the Oakapple to spot such a thing.

Bith said, 'And there we were, with the giants still fast asleep, every last one, and all of us not knowing what was what, or whether we ought to go or stay. Although,' he added severely, 'I'd be bound to say that we weren't any of us happy about being up there in the first place, what with the *Fidchell* board ready and waiting, and Goibniu the Greediguts smacking his lips and reaching for the carving knife, and what with it being a well-known thing that giants are partial to a bit of roast Gnome now and then.'

'I never wanted to go in the first place,' said Culdub Oakapple, who was engaged in re-knotting his neckerchief.

'And the end was,' said Bith, turning round to frown at the Oakapple who could be a terrible old interruption, 'the end was that we all woke up when the *Draoicht Suan* wore off, and came creeping out of Tara as quiet as mouses—'

Several people said they had been quieter than that even, and Flaherty said he had been so quiet that everyone thought he had been left behind.

'And we came straight into the Forest,' said Bith, 'because there's no knowing when the giants might wake up and come chasing after us, what with Pumlumon having forgotten how long the *Draoicht Suan* lasts.'

Pumlumon said it was not a thing that you easily recalled, not when there was so much else to be thinking about, and most people turned to look at Miach, because you could surely expect the Court sorcerer to be knowing about things like this. Miach, who had taken longer to recover from Dian Cecht's ordeal than Dian Cecht, said that he could very easily look this particular piece of information up in the Sorcery Annals, always supposing anyone would ask him politely. He managed to make it sound as if he was very preoccupied with half a score or so of various enchantments, so that he could not for the moment bring to mind a very minor detail like how long the *Draoicht Suan* might be expected to last.

And while Clumhach was anxiously looking to see was there enough mead left to offer the Gnomes, Miach went off to discuss the *Draoicht Suan* and the counter-spell with Pumlumon and a couple of the younger Oaks who might be trusted to know such a thing. If they were to attack Tara and regain it for the Wolfking, wherever he might now be, they would have to rouse the giants before they could drive them out.

Chapter Forty-four

Reflection was in the worst temper she had ever been in. 'And,' she said to her assembled household, 'in the general way, I am the *mildest tempered* of souls,' and her household, most of whom were still bathing the wounds inflicted by the fire demons the previous night, all of whom could recount a good many tales about Madame's temper, nodded obediently, and said: to be sure, the temper of an angel.

'But,' said Reflection, striding up and down the Aurora Banqueting Hall, swishing her silk skirts angrily, and pausing to run a finger across an undusted chandelier as she went. 'But, when it is a question of my only child, my poor innocent babe, the comfort of my – of my retreat from the world,' said Reflection, and everyone looked sympathetic, and tried not to appear as if they all knew quite well that Madame had very nearly said, 'the comfort of my old age', which, as the chefs said, only went to show how very distrait Madame must be.

Reflection paused in her pacing and stopped at the foot of the stairs and then, remembering that to be higher than your audience gave you a good smatch of authority, ascended half a dozen stairs and turned to face them all.

'I am distraught,' she said, clasping her hands to her breast, and closing her eyes. 'When I think of my poor untried child at the hands of that – *seducer*. Ah me, she is succumbing to the very fate that was forced upon me at the *tenderest* of ages, for,' added Reflection, suddenly confiding, 'for I was the *merest* child when that villain Fael-Inis took my innocence.' She waited for a suitable response and her household, knowing their duty, nodded sympathetically all over again. And waited worriedly to see were they all about to be pressed into service for a bit of a battle, which was a thing which had happened once or twice before, and which could be remarkably nasty, what with Madame calling up a few enchantments to help out.

'She must be brought back,' said Reflection, glaring at the assembled Court. 'Whether or not she will be *unsullied* we cannot yet know, for I would not put anything past that vile, decadent Human. Also,' said Reflection, her eyes suddenly spitting fire at them, 'also, we must do so before Inchbad gets to hear what has happened. He will be quite demented,' said Reflection, limpidly, 'and I would not for *worlds* upset the dear creature when he has been so obliging – that is to say when he is so inflamed with passion for the poor child.

'And so Flame must be brought back *at once*,' said Reflection. 'We shall leave nothing to chance. I shall summon the help of my good friends to bring them back,' she added grandly, and the Court groaned inwardly, because this almost certainly meant they would have to welcome the Robemaker to the Fire Court.

'The Robemaker will lend his aid,' said Reflection and everyone nodded glumly, but said to be sure he would, and him the grandest ally ever known.

'And,' said Reflection, consideringly, 'I believe we should invite the Frost Giantess, for I hear she does not get out much these days, poor soul, and there is no knowing but that she may be of some help.

'Although I will *not*,' said Reflection, looking suddenly fierce, so that several people moved back a few steps, 'I will *not* have those Storm Wraiths in my house. They are nothing but trouble, and the Frost Giantess will have to be told we do not want them. We can be quite friendly about it,' said Reflection, which, as several people murmured, meant that it was a task that would be delegated.

Reflection then took herself off to her bedchamber, to look up the enchantment which would summon the Robemaker and also the *Geimhreadh*, and pondered as to whether CuRoi ought to be included in her party. He would probably accept for old times' sake – he and Reflection had been rather close once, round about the time of the last attempt but two to take Tara for the Dark Ireland – and it was rumoured that he still had something of a fondness for Reflection. This was only to be expected, of course, but the trouble with CuRoi was that he was a terrible old attention-seeker, and he would almost certainly want to grab the glory of the battle for himself. On balance it might be better not to invite CuRoi at all, because if there was any glory going, then it was going to be Reflection's.

She waited until the Purple Hour, which would give the incantation to call the Robemaker and the Frost Giantess a bit of a boost and issued orders to the household that she was not to be disturbed until they could report that the Robemaker and the Frost Giantess had turned up.

Snodgrass had listened to the reports about Madame's intentions with a worried frown.

'Dear me,' he said, shaking his head. 'I don't like the sound of this. The Robemaker *and* the Frost Giantess, you say?'

Snodgrass asked would the bailiffs be riding out in the expedition to catch up with Flame and Floy and the bailiffs, who had of late been a bit bored with their lot, looked thoughtful and said: very possibly.

'Then,' said Snodgrass, determinedly, 'I shall come with you.'

In the end they all went, although the furnace-room workers drew lots as to which of them would stay behind, because it would not do to be letting the fires die down and nobody wanted to risk Madame's wrath when she returned to a cold and fireless Court, and a few of the kitchen staff stayed behind as well, in case a victory banquet was needed later. You could not just drum up a ten-course banquet for a hundred people inside of half an hour.

Reflection had been regally welcoming to the Robemaker and the Frost Giantess, both of whom had materialised reasonably soon after the incantation. She had given them glasses of wine and had explained the nature of the task.

'I should be happy to place my powers at your disposal, my dear,' said the Robemaker, sitting in his chair with his back to the light. 'For I have had dealings with Humans lately that have roused my anger to a very high pitch against the creatures.'

'Indeed?'

'They disturbed the pact I have long since had with the Soul Eaters.'

'*Really*?' said Reflection, who knew all about the Robemaker's thralldom to the Soul Eaters and was charmed by this unlooked-for snippet of gossip. 'Oh, do tell us more.'

'A conflict of interest,' said the Robemaker. 'CuRoi had captured a *very* valuable hostage and was holding him in the Fields of Blood using the cruciform. You know of it, I daresay? It is an eastern method and one of the more *refined*.' The hooded head moved angrily. 'A vulgar quarrel arose between the Soul Eaters and the Master over the creature.'

'Who won?' asked the Frost Giantess and the Robemaker turned his hooded head to regard her. The bone-white smile showed briefly.

'The hostage escaped,' he said. 'For the moment. The Master was outwitted.' A malicious glint showed in the partly hidden eyes. 'For the moment, I am done with that one, with his posturing and his posing and his illusions,' said the Robemaker. 'But I have since sworn to the Soul Eaters that I shall find the creature and offer it to them.' The glint showed red. 'A very *valuable* soul,' he said.

Reflection thought, but did not say, that the Robemaker had clearly been up to his usual pastime of changing sides if it looked profitable to him. But she was rather pleased to think that CuRoi had for once been bested, and she was very pleased indeed to hear that he was engaged in some kind of tussle with the Soul Eaters.

She said, 'But you yourself – and also you, ma'am – are free to assist me?'

'I should relish it greatly,' said the Robemaker, and the Frost Giantess chuckled wetly, and writhed in the chair that Reflection had given her. 'Floy,' she said and her voice caressed the name. 'A *beautiful* young man.' The little dark eyes gleamed. 'I remember him. I shall enjoy helping our good friend Reflection to catch him.'

Reflection thought that you had to be charitable about your friends, but that, really, the Frost Giantess might be just a little less *obvious*. Also, she had already eyed several of Reflection's own courtiers, and had tried to bargain with Reflection over the question of some of the furnace workers.

'*Young*,' she had said. 'I like them young.'

Reflection liked them young as well, but did not go about saying so. She began to think that the Frost Giantess was abusing her hospitality, which, when you considered that Reflection had herself been thoughtful enough to tell the furnace workers to let the fires die down a bit, because the Frost Giantess could not be doing with too warm a room, was stretching friendship a bit far.

But she asked for their suggestions as to the enchantments they might best use to catch Flame and Floy, and agreed on the Robemaker's crimson rope-lights, which were always useful, and the Frost Giantess's tongues of ice and blizzard.

'Then,' said the Robemaker, 'they will burn and freeze at the same time, and that, as you know, my dear, is a *very* nasty fate.'

'But,' said Reflection, 'Flame must be spared, of course.'

'Ah?'

'For Inchbad,' said Reflection. 'Inchbad has made a most *generous* marriage proposal for the child.'

The Robemaker said in his hissing wet-lung voice, 'That is something to be taken into careful consideration, of course. If you wish it, then she can be spared.' There was a movement within the dark, enveloping cloak, and then he said, 'And the payment, Reflection? The payment for our services?'

'Well,' said Reflection and stopped, because this was always the tricky part, and these two both probably knew perfectly well that she was on the verge of ruin and a debtors' prison again. 'Well,' she said thoughtfully, and the Robemaker leaned forward, the deep hood slipping a little, so that Reflection caught a glimpse of the ravaged, noseless face, and shuddered, and thought that if you could not weave yourself an enchantment to make yourself a bit more appealing you were not much of an advertisement for your own wares.

'May I make a little suggestion?' said the Robemaker and then, without waiting for a reply, said, 'Payment could be the most amicable of arrangements.'

'Yes?'

The Robemaker sat back in his chair and the hood fell back into place, shadowing his face. He appeared to be perfectly composed, but his breathing had quickened and Reflection could hear the horrid slimy rasping sound more clearly now.

'Give Flame to me for a night,' said the Robemaker, and the breathing slurred and thickened into a bubbling croupy wheeze. 'That is all the payment I ask of you,' he said.

Reflection said, 'And you, ma'am?' and the Frost Giantess squirmed in lascivious anticipation and darted her thick neckless body in Reflection's direction.

'Our good friend has made an appealing suggestion,' she said. 'And since money and jewels hold little interest for me, then I will take my payment in Human flesh, also. If the Robemaker is to have the girl for a night, I will have the young man.'

Reflection looked at them both and remembered her mounting debts and Inchbad's growing impatience and his very lavish proposals. If Flame were to be lost, then it might be rather difficult to explain this to the Gruagach. It might be even more difficult to explain it to Reflection's growing number of creditors, all of whom had agreed to be patient until after the much-vaunted marriage had taken place.

'Very well.' She stood up. 'But we must leave at once.'

To those few members of Reflection's household who had remained behind, the setting out of Madame, together with her Court, made a remarkable sight.

If there were those who thought that Madame had assembled an extravagantly large number of people simply to bring back one errant daughter and one impudent lover, they were wise enough not to say so. In any case, Madame was ever extravagant in the settling of her quarrels.

Reflection rode at the head, astride a white horse with a golden flowing mane and tail; she wore a fire-coloured robe and about her head was the diadem of moonstones and rubies which the Gnomes of Gallan had made to Madame's own design and which incorporated the Amaranthine emblem. Her hair was loose and woven into it were tiny glinting rubies and opals. She carried the famous spear which legend said she had wrested from Fael-Inis on the night that Flame was conceived and which could hurl shafts of pure light at one's enemies.

The Robemaker rode at Reflection's left-hand side, dark and stooping and menacing. He carried the terrible night-black spear of necromancy and, wound about it, were the sizzling ropes of light which he would use to bind Flame and Floy.

The Frost Giantess did not ride on horseback. 'Too unwieldy,' said the watchers and told one another that it would have been hard indeed to have found a mount for the creature. But she had her own method of travel; a kind of canopied litter slung between silver poles, strewn with cold satin cushions, and with the poles embellished with twisting snake creatures and writhing worms and horrid bulgy-eyed fish-beings. 'An ancient line, of course,' said the watchers, trying to inject a note of respect into their voices.

She lay, half coiled on the litter, occasionally darting her head in one direction or another; the lidless eyes inspecting the young men who had been taken from the furnace rooms to carry the litter. She did not seem to be carrying any weapons of enchantment, but the watchers knew quite well that she was able to whip up a raging blizzard and call up the Storm Wraiths, never mind Madame had said she would not be seen within ten miles of a Storm Wraith.

The household rode or walked sedately behind these three, in careful order of precedence, garbed and accoutred as they thought fit.

Dusk had fallen and, although the moonlight was strong enough for them all to find their way, Reflection conjured up some half a dozen fire columns.

'I see you have not lost your skill, my dear,' said the Robemaker.

'The merest trifle,' said Reflection at once. And then, half turning to the *Geimhreadh*'s litter, 'I trust that they will not be too warm for you, ma'am?'

'Since you deemed them necessary, I shall not complain,' replied the Frost Giantess. And then, sharply, to the furnace workers, 'Do not tilt the litter so sharply, you!' The snake-head reared for a moment and the lightless eyes narrowed.

And then the Robemaker reined in his horse and lifted the dark spear and said, 'There they are.'

Flame had walked warily at Floy's side, liking the soft, cool night, liking, as well, the silence. She had known, in a vague way, that the Fire Court had been a place of unnatural blazing light, but she had not realised how dark and how tranquil the true night could be.

When Floy said, 'You have lived always at the centre of a maelstrom of noise,' Flame knew he had heard her thoughts and sensed her feelings and that he had left her to enjoy them and absorb the newness of everything.

There was a pale, silvery light from the moon, which was quite enough for them to see their way, and there were

Trees, growing wild, which was not anything Flame had ever seen, because Mother would not permit Trees in the Fire Court gardens, other than the stunted artificial shapes she created, half by sorcery and half by the skills of the sempstresses and the carpenters and the gardeners.

Once, after they had been walking for quite a time, she said, 'We are going to try to reach my – to reach Fael-Inis's Palace of Wildfire?'

'Yes,' said Floy.

'Can we do that?' asked Flame, meaning: do we know the way? and Floy said, 'I have no idea. But at Tara it was said that the Palace lies in the direction of the rising sun. Also, your father told me that if you follow the path of the moon and do not falter, all roads eventually lead to your heart's desire.'

He looked at her as he said this and Flame said thoughtfully, 'I see,' and fell silent.

'He is given to speaking like that,' said Floy.

'Yes?'

'Extravagant and colourful.'

'Yes.' Flame would not say what she was thinking, which was that the words had sounded a bit like someone trying not to give exact directions because he did not really want to receive visitors but was too polite actually to say so.

Floy said, quite seriously, 'I believe we are going towards the Palace, Flame.' He lifted a hand, pointing. 'Do you see there? Although it is night, there is an iridescence, a colour. Fael-Inis told us that for those who seek him, a path is always to be found.'

'Oh.'

Floy grinned. 'He will not be quite what you expect, Flame,' he said, but Flame had no idea of what she was expecting anyway.

They stopped to rest twice and the second time Floy unpacked the small store of food that Flame had managed to bring.

'Will your – will Reflection try to bring you back?' he asked, and Flame drew breath to say that it was very likely, because Mother would be so furious with them both, when Floy jumped to his feet and stared back down the path they had just travelled.

'What is—' And then Flame saw it as well.

Reflection riding at the head of her armies.

And with her the grotesque shapes of the Robemaker and the Frost Giantess.

As they waited, helplessly, the armies streamed towards them. There was nothing they could do, for there was nowhere to run and nowhere to hide. They were on open ground and, even if they had attempted to flee, Reflection would have overtaken them within minutes.

Floy scanned the horizon frantically. Was the glimmer of light they had seen earlier a little closer? He thought that it was, and, as he strained his eyes, he thought there was a glint of spires, gold-tipped and vibrant. Bitterness twisted within him, because it would be Fate's cruellest joke if they were to be caught so close to sanctuary. He was angry to think that he had not foreseen Reflection's vengeance when he had so heedlessly taken Flame away from the Fire Court.

Flame said, very softly, 'It was not heedless, Floy. You could not possibly have known what she would do. *I* did not know, even.'

'I ought to have known,' said Floy bitterly. And then, striving for a calm, practical note, 'Over there,' he said, 'is Fael-Inis's country. The Palace of Wildfire. I am sure of it now.'

'Yes, I see it,' said Flame. 'But I don't think we can reach it.'

'What about the Spell of Invisibility you used at the Court?'

'Impossible,' said Flame at once. 'Mother would rip it aside instantly and I could never withstand her.'

The armies were closing. They could see the outlines of Reflection herself now; her hair flowing out wildly in the night wind, the rubies catching the light of the fiery columns that road alongside her. The Robemaker was a little to her left, crouched low over his mount, but, as he rode, they saw him raise a hand and the crimson rope-lights spat and sizzled through the air. Floy and Flame threw themselves to the ground and the rope-lights went hissing harmlessly over their heads.

The Frost Giantess had reared up almost to her full height; Floy lifted his head cautiously and saw her, a massive ugly writhing thing, silhouetted against the sky, her little finlike hands whipping the young men who bore the litter on to greater speed, coiling and squirming in horrid, lustful excitement. Behind these three were the people of Reflection's Court, riding in what Floy thought of, even at such a moment, as rather a mechanical way. As if they were here only because they had been forced to it . . .

I do not believe there is any escape, thought Floy half sitting, half kneeling, his arms about Flame, searching the horizon for something that might help, something that might come to their aid.

From the east, out of the gold-tinged glow they had thought must be the radiance surrounding Fael-Inis's Palace, came the thin, sweet sound of a bugle call . . .

And hard on the heels of the sound, the rushing of chariot wheels.

Chapter Forty-five

Floy and Flame were at the exact centre, between the two rushing armies. Floy thought it was if they were at the heart of a small core of blackness, a miniature copy of the hole that had swallowed Renascia, and that it was entirely possible that the coming forces might not even be able to see them.

The armies bore down on them; Reflection riding her gold and white mount hard, shouting to her people to follow her. As she drew nearer, the air began to sizzle with the fiery columns and sting from the whiplash of the Robemaker's crimson lights that he was flinging ahead of him, so that the darkness was laced and latticed with the livid tendrils of light. Reflection stood up in the saddle and hurled shafts of light from the glinting spear and Floy and Flame huddled lower to avoid them.

The Frost Giantess was slower than the other two but, as Reflection's people slowed, they could see her ordering the slaves to lay the litter down and, as they did so, she coiled herself into a rearing, scaly creature ringed with glistening white slime, and made hideous by the distended fins in her neck. A cloud of white had formed immediately behind her and, from where they crouched, Floy could see the ghost forms of the sharp-nosed, pointed-fingered Wraiths. They both took all this in rapidly and then Floy turned his attention to the golden creatures approaching from the east.

To begin with there had been only a blur of shifting colour, luminous and iridescent, as if light had somehow leaked out into the night skies, and Floy had stood, shading his eyes, knowing how easy it would be to be deceived, knowing how desperately he had been hoping for some form of rescue. But then, quite suddenly, there was the outline of an immense rushing chariot pulled by swift creatures with flowing gold manes and tails of spun silk, and wise, ancient eyes . . .

Flame gasped and put both hands to her cheeks. She felt a sudden rushing hope that she dared not quite believe in yet. But surely, oh surely, it could only mean one thing . . .

And then he was there, standing at the prow of the fiery chariot, the wind whipped up behind him, his hair stirred to a storm about his head, his eyes molten gold, and such a look of reckless delight about him that Flame wanted to run from the safety of Floy's arms. There was a look and there was an aura about him which laughed at the absurd, ineffectual creatures that Reflection was leading, and which said, quite clearly: *we shall rout these ridiculous beings . . . we shall fight the world if we have to, and every creature in it, but for all that, we shall WIN, mortals, we shall WIN . . .*

Fael-Inis, the rebel angel, the being of fire and light and speed, riding to the rescue of the daughter he had never seen . . .

Flame heard Floy give a sudden shout of purest delight and saw that in the golden wake of the great chariot were two smaller chariots, glinting gold, laced with firegems, scything effortlessly through the curling waves of light pouring from Fael-Inis's chariot, harnessed to four more of the strange, spun silk creatures.

In the first of them was a dark-haired, slightly built young man, with slanting dark eyes, and very nearly the same reckless look as Fael-Inis. Flame blinked, and thought that here was someone else who might very well like to challenge the world and defy the gods, and ride straight at all kinds of danger and who might very well be the smallest bit dangerous himself. Standing in the third chariot was a girl with Floy's eyes, and his smile, guiding the beautiful salamanders, handling the thin, silken reins with such ease and such joy . . .

Floy shouted, 'Fenella!' and stood up and, at once, the girl turned the chariot aside, so that the two salamanders pulling it swerved and came sweeping across the ground, showering the golden light everywhere, directly towards Floy and Flame.

'Quickly!' cried Fenella, leaning down to help Flame into the chariot. 'Oh, quickly!'

Flame said, 'Floy—' and turned to see that the other chariot, the one being driven by the dark-haired young man, had been following and that Floy was already being pulled up into it.

'Sire,' said Floy, slightly out of breath, clinging to the sides of the speeding chariot, 'I believe I must thank you for—'

'Saving you from Reflection and the rest?' Nuadu was concentrating on keeping the salamanders in a straight line, but he half turned his head, and sent Floy the amused glance which Floy remembered. 'But Fenella would have been so upset. And since we managed to reach Fael-Inis's Palace unscathed and were taken in, it is perhaps only generous to give help to the rest of your party.' His eyes went to the slender form of Flame in the other chariot. 'You have been industrious, it seems,' he said politely, and Floy grinned.

'And of course,' said Nuadu, thoughtfully, 'it is almost obligatory to rescue a fair maiden from peril, these days.'

'Reflection's daughter,' said Floy.

'Really? And therefore Fael-Inis's. So you have stolen Inchbad's chosen bride, have you, Floy? But if she is his daughter, it would explain—'

'Yes?'

'It would explain why Fael-Inis suddenly stopped talking as we sat at supper recounting our adventures; why he stood up and summoned the salamanders,' said Nuadu.

'The *Samhailt*?'

'Well, I don't suppose it's *quite* that in his case,' said Nuadu, 'but he certainly had the salamanders harnessed and the Palace gates flung wide almost before any of us realised it.'

Fael-Inis had turned his chariot about and positioned it to face before Reflection and the Robemaker and the

596

Frost Giantess. He sprang to the ground, apparently unconcerned about the danger, and looked about him, as if he found his surroundings of interest. At once Reflection lifted her arm and, within a minute, the fire demons were forming, red eyes gleaming evilly, leaping and dancing. They circled Fael-Inis, grinning and pointing, hurling tiny wicked firethorns and Fael-Inis glanced down at them and brushed them aside as if they were no more than an irritation. But, as his hand moved, another of the cascading showers of golden light rippled from his fingertips and engulfed the demons, sweeping them aside. Flame, watching closely, saw fire tongues leap up, and engulf the demons and the terrible sound of demons screaming filled the night, and there was an acrid stench of burning.

Nuadu said, softly, 'He is burning them, as they have burned others. A fitting punishment,' and Floy, at his side, said, 'Yes. Yes, that is his creed.' And remembered, with sudden surprise, the ancient belief of the early Earth-people, that whatever evils you committed against others might one day be committed against you.

Fael-Inis was standing directly in front of Reflection now, studying her, his hands on his hips, his head tilted slightly as if in amusement. Fenella looked at Flame, and said, softly, 'There is still a score to be settled between these two, I think.' Flame, who was remembering all of the old stories about Mother and Fael-Inis, and who had not been able to take her eyes from Fael-Inis, her father, stared, and felt the deep delight begin all over again, because he had come riding out to her rescue and he was confronting Mother and the Robemaker and the *Geimhreadh* as coolly and as easily as if they were simple annoyances to be dealt with and forgotten. She thought it was impossible to imagine this remarkable being failing.

'I don't think he will fail,' said Fenella, who seemed to have Floy's way of hearing thoughts a little. But her eyes were on the slight figure of Fael-Inis and she was frowning, because she had not, until now, actually seen Reflection, and she had certainly not seen the Frost Giantess. She was thinking that the sight of these two, with the Robemaker at their side, was much more daunting than she had thought it would be. And then she remembered how, in the Palace of Wildfire, Fael-Inis had suddenly seemed to know – not exactly what was taking place, thought Fenella; only that *something* was. And then Fenella had felt it as well, a dark, massing danger very close by . . . something menacing and evil touching the Palace's pure warm light, threatening it . . . It had been like a suffocating cloak descending on her mind, shutting out the brightness of the Palace of Wildfire. And it is something to do with Floy, she had thought with sick horror. Floy is somewhere close by – I can *feel* that he is! she had thought – and something dark and evil is coming towards him . . .

Fael-Inis moved cautiously and slowly towards Reflection and the watchers fell back a little, because it seemed as if these two remarkable beings must first commune, agree terms about something. Snodgrass, who was at the very back with the bailiffs' contingent, and who had been trying to espy a chance to cross over to Floy and the others, stood on tiptoe to see better. Even while his heart was singing with delight at finding that Fenella and Floy were both safe, he could not help being interested in how Fael-Inis and Reflection were confronting one another, and thinking that it was exactly as if they were about to draw up rules of some kind for a battle of some sort.

Fael-Inis was looking at Reflection, and he was at his most catlike and graceful, entirely untroubled. After a moment, Reflection slid from her horse, and walked towards him, and it seemed to the watchers that, of the two, she was the more uncertain.

'She is very wary of him,' said Floy, watching them closely.

'She has cause to be,' said Nuadu softly.

Fael-Inis said, and everyone present heard the amused affection in his voice, 'Madame. We are destined to be on opposing sides of a battle once more, it seems.'

And looked at her and waited.

Reflection had wrapped her cloak tightly about her, but she still held the glittering spear that could send out the blinding white shafts of light. 'We always are on opposing sides, Fael-Inis,' she said crossly. 'And it is a remarkable thing that one does not clap eyes on you for positively decades, until the whim takes you to interfere in my affairs again.' She hunched a shoulder pettishly. 'I suppose,' said Reflection, 'that all of this *show* is purely to impress the child.'

'What else?' said Fael-Inis lightly, but Floy and the others sensed an awareness in him.

'Well, it is nothing but pure ostentation,' said Reflection. 'And I do not recall any battle that was ever won by a lot of pretentious dazzle.' She eyed him angrily. 'I suppose you want the child,' said Reflection.

'I do.'

'Well, I do not feel inclined to let you have her,' said Reflection, tossing her head. 'Even though she is nothing but trouble I am going to keep her.' She glared at Fael-Inis. 'And I must say, I think it is just like you to come sweeping in, all fire and empty pageantry, just to impress her,' said Reflection. 'I suppose you called the salamanders out especially, did you? Yes, I might have guessed it. Absurd creatures,' said Reflection, glaring at the salamanders. 'If sufficient people did not believe in them, they would not exist, did you know that, Fael-Inis!' She eyed him triumphantly, and Fael-Inis at once said, 'No, my dear, you are thinking of unicorns.' And seemed perfectly prepared to enter into a discussion with Reflection about mythological beasts and their transcendental existences.

'I have never seen a unicorn,' began Reflection.

'No, they will only reveal themselves to the very young and the completely innocent,' said Fael-Inis gravely, at which Reflection stamped her foot and flung two spears of light at him. He laughed and deflected them by holding up one hand carelessly; the light spears bounced harmlessly on to the ground.

'Your manners do not improve with the years,' said Reflection furiously. 'And if you have the impudence to suppose I should hand Flame over to you as if she was no more than a–a *chattel*—After all I have done for the child,' said Reflection, piqued. 'I have brought her up *quite* by myself, and I have never *once* grudged a penny piece on her education or her upbringing. She is *very* well tutored,' said Reflection, suddenly confidential.

'I am glad to hear it.'

'*Every* refinement. I have sacrificed a good deal for her, although I suppose that would not interest you. And as for her marriage, well! If I have arranged one advantageous marriage, I have arranged a dozen.'

'With giants and necromancers?' said Fael-Inis gently, and Reflection, who had been turning huffily away to remount her horse, instantly came back.

'Inchbad and the Gruagach will make a *very good* settlement for her,' shouted Reflection and her household, who had stayed mouse-quiet, exchanged nervous glances, because it was clear that Madame was boiling up for a fair old tantrum.

'And,' said Fael-Inis, softly, 'the very good settlement would have paid some of your debts, would it?'

Reflection drew herself up to her full height and brandished the glinting spear. 'How dare you imply that I would sell my only child, the comfort of my – that is the comfort of my exile, to settle a handful of miserable debts! I am *famous* for my debts, everyone knows it! I do not care a *fig* for creditors and bailiffs and prisons!' shrieked Reflection, and, whisking about again, she flung out an accusatory finger towards the section where the bailiffs, Snodgrass in their midst, were watching and listening, enthralled. '*That* is how I deal with bailiffs!' shouted Reflection. 'I *enslave* them!' The silken skirts of her cloak hissed angrily as she turned back to him. 'I thought the years might have mellowed you, Fael-Inis,' said Reflection, 'but I see now that you are a heartless adventurer, a gypsy, a time-travelling vagabond, and I should not *dream* of allowing my only child—'

'The comfort of your exile—'

'Into your hands!' finished Reflection triumphantly and, as she spoke, she swirled the dark cloak so that it billowed out behind her. A shrieking wind arose, howling and raging, dashing icy cold rain against the chariots and their occupants.

At once the Frost Giantess writhed upwards on her litter. 'Unfair!' she shouted. 'The ice-cold blizzard is *my* weapon! How dare that abandoned creature steal my weapons!' And uncoiling and hissing, she made a sudden darting movement. At once, the Storm Wraiths came swooping down, filling the night with their eldritch shrieking, diving for the salamanders, twining their cold, bony fingers about the flowing manes, crouching low on the salamanders' glossy coats and digging their icy talons deep into the silken skins, so that blood matted the golden pelts, and thin films of ice began to form, and the salamanders reared and tossed their heads, and tried to dislodge the clinging Wraiths.

'Cheat!' yelled Reflection. 'I told you – I expressly *forbade* you to bring those creatures with you!' Whisking about, she raised the glinting spear and flung several shafts of light in the direction of the *Geimhreadh*'s writhing form. 'Leave me to fight my own wars!' shouted Reflection at the top of her voice. 'Don't you know it is the height of bad manners to meddle in wars where you are only a *guest!*'

Fael-Inis made a sweeping movement and at once the Wraiths fell from the salamanders and rolled into tight, huddled little shapes, shrivelling and shrinking on the ground before them. The Frost Giantess let out a wail of distress and Reflection laughed.

Snodgrass, who had been waiting until a diversion was created, spied his chance and detached himself from the group of bailiffs, tiptoeing in the shadows in a wide circle until he was clambering up into the back of Fenella's chariot, and Fenella was hugging him, and it was grand to see her and Floy safe.

Fael-Inis walked to where Nuadu stood in the other chariot.

'The winning of this battle is in your hands, Sire,' he said, unexpectedly. 'If you called to the Wolves now, they would answer you. They have not been seen in Ireland since the days of the High King, Erin. But like the *sidh*, they have always been there, just beyond vision and just outside of hearing; ready to answer a cry for help from the Royal House of Tara.'

He regarded Nuadu, as if waiting for him to answer, and Nuadu said, bitterly, 'I am a bastard, a misbegotten son. It is not in my power. I can call the *sidh*, by the ancient enchantment of all of the Wolves but that is all.'

'It is not enough,' said Fael-Inis. 'The *sidh* would strengthen your fight, but to win you need the Wolves.' He regarded Nuadu, the golden eyes slanting and fiery. 'You possess the ancient wolfblood,' said Fael-Inis. 'And you are the son of one of Ireland's Royal Houses through your mother. The Wolves of Tara would almost certainly hear you if you called to them. Why will you not do it?'

Nuadu said, in a low voice, 'You know why.'

Yes, I know, but you cannot avoid your fealty for much longer, Wolfprince. You are what you are. You may not care for Tara, but you care for Ireland . . .

Nuadu said, angrily, 'You do not understand.'

'I understand it all, Wolfprince. I understand everything about the shelving of responsibilities and about the avoidance of duty. You are a rebel, a rogue prince, the odd one in the litter . . .

'But for all that, you are of the ancient royal House of Tara, and you made a vow to your dying brother.' The golden eyes were shining with hard brilliance now. 'Your half-brother's body lies in state in the Palace of Wildfire,' said Fael-Inis. 'You brought him out of the land of darkness, and out of the Fields of Blood and he trusted you. He bequeathed Ireland to you and, although you do not want it, I do not think you can avoid it. You are the heir,' said Fael-Inis. 'You are the natural successor, the Wolfprince who can call to the Wolves.'

'Supposing I cannot.'

'But supposing you can . . .' Fael-Inis's eyes were

unblinking like a cat's. 'Supposing you can send out the Summoning, the ancient mystical *Samhailt*, the Wolfsong. Supposing they answer. To harness the Wolves now would unleash a power that has been for so long trammelled, it would be unstoppable. It would sweep the Darkness away in a glorious torrent of light.' He looked at Nuadu very steadily for a long moment, and then, as Nuadu made no response, turned back to Reflection, and looked at her enquiringly, as if he might be saying: well, my dear? Is there anything else you would like to attempt? At once Reflection flung wide her arms, the palms turned upwards and crimson fire and blood and rain poured in torrents from the skies, splattering the occupants of the chariots, fouling the salamanders' glossy coats and clogging the chariot wheels.

Reflection turned back and stood with her arms crossed, a look of triumph on her face. 'Well, Fael-Inis!' she cried. 'That round is mine, I think! I have rendered your chariots useless and your *creatures* helpless. Let us see how you fight when your servants are rendered incapable! Let us see what *else* you can call up from your armoury! You have not done so very much yet, have you!' And then, as he stayed where he was, watching her, 'Well?' screamed Reflection.

Fael-Inis turned to look at Nuadu again. 'There is little more I can do for you,' he said. 'I have shown you the means. It is in your hands.' He began to move back, retreating into the shadows.

'Help me,' said Nuadu, and Fael-Inis shook his head.

'The help is there, Wolfprince,' he said. 'It is up to you.'

I have shown you the means, and now you must take the means, or let Ireland be overrun by the Dark Realm . . .

I cannot! cried Nuadu silently. *There must be another way!*

Then find it, Wolfprince . . . The words were not harsh or dismissive; if you can find another way, Fael-Inis was saying, then do so. But he had moved even farther back and Nuadu had the impression that although he had not quite gone from them yet, he was stepping back from them.

Reflection and the Robemaker had been conferring and, as Fael-Inis melted into the shadows, Reflection surged forward again, her eyes hard and shining with triumph.

'Well, creatures?' she said, and there was a taunting note to her voice now. 'So you have lost your champion, have you? Well, he was ever a fickle creature.' She regarded Flame. 'You see?' said Reflection triumphantly. 'You see how your father wants none of you? You see how he discards you and casts you off?' And then, looking to where the Robemaker was waiting, 'Do what you will, Master Robemaker!' she cried. 'Do what you will, and Flame is yours for a night before we sell her to the Gruagach!'

For a breathspace, the Robemaker did not move, and then he stepped forward and his terrible shadow fell across the blood-spattered chariots. He raised his left arm and the crimson rope-lights uncurled and snaked about the chariots' wheels. A second whiplash of sizzling ropes corkscrewed through the air and wound themselves into the salamanders' reins and about the occupants of the chariots. Behind him, dark clouds began to roll and gather and there was the sound of immense wings, dry and leathery, on the air. Reflection let out a peal of malicious laughter and the Frost Giantess began to writhe in excitement.

'The Soul Eaters! The Soul Eaters are approaching!'

Reflection regarded the captives with her eyes glittering, and the Robemaker stretched his hands upwards to the skies, his concealing sleeves falling back, so that the crumbling, discoloured wrist bones were plainly visible. The beating of wings grew stronger and, as they strained their eyes to see, they became aware of the terrible shapes of the ancient creatures from the Cruachan Caverns, filling the skies, their immense wings casting huge black shadows, their cruel talons already curved in anticipation.

Fenella stared at the ancient, wizened, evil things, and

knew at once that they were coming to claim payment for the bargain that had never been fulfilled.

We failed to keep our promise, she thought. We failed to bring to them Ireland's King, and now they have come to exact their revenge.

The creatures came to land at the centre of Reflection's people; folding their great wings across their scaly bodies, their horned heads tilted in anticipation, their dark inHuman eyes surveying the company. Flame, who was feeling rather sick and cold inside at Fael-Inis's apparent desertion of them, stared, and thought that surely there had never been anything so terrible and so utterly malevolent in all the world. She tried to count them because to do so might stop her remembering how Fael-Inis had walked away, but the Soul Eaters were moving, forming a circle. Their leathery wings opened occasionally and, in the shifting light, it was impossible to know their number. But Flame thought there were at least ten of them.

Fenella, at her side, saw that there were fewer than there had been in the Cruachan Caverns and remembered, shuddering, how the Harpies had flown at them, screeching and pecking, and how the red-eyed dungeon creatures had pounced on the ones who had fallen from the air, ripping and tearing . . . The Robemaker had stood at CuRoi's side and fought them for Aed, and yet they still answered his summons. Because he is still in thrall to them? wondered Fenella. Because they believe he can still render up to them the soul of Ireland's High King?

The Robemaker turned back to the chariots and lifted his hands again. At once, Floy and Nuadu, who were in the foremost chariot, felt the pull of the rope-lights drawing them towards the waiting Soul Eaters. The Robemaker gestured again and the second chariot, with Fenella and Flame and Snodgrass, began to follow.

Drawing them forward to where the Soul Eaters would tear them apart and eat their souls . . .

The wheels, still befouled and clogged with the shower of blood, stuck, and the salamanders dug their hoofs into the ground, but the Robemaker had advanced now and was standing directly before them, both hands raised, pulling on the crimson strands. Fenella saw Floy struggle and saw the rope-lights bite deeper into his arms, so that beads of blood sprang up. She reached into her mind for the spell of Human Hands which had freed them in CuRoi's Castle but, even as she sought for the words, the dreadful wheezing laugh of the Robemaker rose on the night.

'You do not think I should allow you to use that spell against me again, Human?' said the Robemaker, addressing Fenella directly. Fenella put up her chin and glared at him, and the Robemaker laughed again and flung out a second shower of crimson lights that twined about Fenella's face, into the dreadful mask. Fenella tried to cry out, and felt the mask tighten about her, hard and cramping and smothering.

'Speechless, my dear,' said the Robemaker, gloatingly. 'As all Humans should be.' He regarded them and malice gleamed deep within the hood. 'You are *caught*, Humans,' he said. 'You are caught, and you will be given to the Soul Eaters and your souls will be weighed on the Silver Scales. That is the vow I made to them when the Master's Harpies destroyed two of their number. A pact, Humans, just as you made a pact in the Cruachan Cavern, a pact that you did not fulfil.

'The Scales will tip in my favour at last and I shall be free of the Everlasting Disease pronounced over me by the accursed Erin.' He looked at Nuadu. 'Your Lady cannot pronounce the spell she stole from me, this time,' said the Robemaker. 'There is really no escape for you.' He chuckled and turned to Flame and said, with a dreadful lusting note in his voice, 'And as for you, my dear, you shall be in my embrace tonight.'

Flame, who knew in a vague way about the Robe of Human Hands, and who had been trying to remember whether the rope-lights could be dissolved by any other spell, and if so, what it was, looked at him, and said, very loudly, 'If you touch me, I shall kill you.'

The Robemaker laughed. 'Puny creature,' he said, and there was a note of indulgence in his voice now. 'But I shall teach you to obey me.'

The Soul Eaters had formed a circle, and Reflection and the Frost Giantess had moved to the outer edges, each one now holding aloft a glittering spear of light, crimson-tinged and malignant. The lights cast an eerie red glow across the circle and Floy, who was nearest, saw that the Soul Eaters were standing waiting. At the centre was an immense pair of silver scales, etched with curious symbols, gleaming with a cold inner light.

Nuadu made a convulsive movement and then was still, and the Robemaker, turning his head, smiled from deep within the dark hood, and said, 'Oh yes, Wolfprince, these are the Silver Scales, wrought by the Gallan Gnomes for Erin all those decades ago. They have been used to measure the years of my thralldom to Erin's sorcerers. But soon now, that will end, and I shall be whole again! I shall be a true Lord of the Dark Realm once more!' He pulled on the ropes and both chariots slid forward and the five prisoners were tipped on to the floor.

Chapter Forty-six

The five prisoners lay at the exact centre of the Soul Eaters' circle. Reflection and the Robemaker had lit flaring torches and stuck them into the ground and the fire was leaping upwards into the night sky, scarlet and orange, casting huge, fantastical shapes everywhere. The dark forms of the Soul Eaters stood out against the light, evil and sinister, their only colour the glinting ancient eyes set deep into the bony, horned skulls. As they moved, great black shadows moved with them, dancing and flickering grotesquely.

Reflection and the Frost Giantess stood on the outer rim of the circle between the flambeaux. The Frost Giantess was writhing and undulating and at her back were the hovering shapes of the Wraiths, frost-rimed and avid, their sharp fingers reaching out, occasionally touching the leaping torch-fires, causing them to spit and hiss. Reflection, on the Frost Giantess's left, was wrapped in the dark silken cloak, holding aloft the slender spear. Flame sent her a furious look and Reflection laughed, her eyes brilliant with malice.

'Begging for mercy, child!'

'No,' said Flame shortly.

'Soon,' said Reflection, 'you will wish you had not defied me.'

Flame said, 'You would let that evil creature feed me to the Soul Eaters?' And stared at Reflection and wondered whether she had ever really known her at all.

Reflection gave a shrug. 'After all, my dear, it was your choice to consort with a Human,' she said, and looked across to Floy. 'You could have had the Gruagach King. You could have had the great ritual of the Fire River at your wedding, with your father to lead you forward to bathe in the Eternal Flame. As it is . . .' She glanced to the waiting Soul Eaters and Flame thought a tinge of regret touched her face. 'As it is, you will end in the Robemaker's embrace and your soul will be taken and your body thrown to the River of the Dead,' said Reflection, and turned her head away as if the matter had ceased to interest her.

Nuadu lay where he had fallen, still and silent. The crimson mask bound the lower part of his face tightly and he could feel the rope-lights biting into his flesh. His mind was a tumble of anger and bitterness; he thought: we *cannot* all be given to the Soul Eaters! There *has* to be another way for us to outwit these creatures! But if I call to the Wolves, then I am taking up the mantle of my brother . . . No, cried Nuadu in silent anguish. No, I do not want it. I cannot do it! And I do not believe it is the only way. We shall outwit these creatures by some other means.

Floy had said little, but his mind was searching for a means to create a diversion. He thought that if one of them could somehow work the rope-lights loose, it would be possible to run from the circle, creating a diversion, and giving the others an opportunity to vanish into the night. Could they do that?

The Robemaker was standing before the Soul Eaters. Their massive wings were folded about their wizened scaly bodies like leather cloaks and their skulls tilted as if they were about to pronounce some kind of judgement. Before them stood the immense Silver Scales of Justice, sold, pure, silver, gleaming first silver and then red as the moonlight and then the leaping firelight caught them. They were larger than the prisoners had expected; they were almost the height of a man. Nuadu, who knew a very little of their history, knew he was seeing another of Tara's lost treasures. First the Ebony Throne, and now the Silver Scales of Justice . . .

He thought the Scales had been wrought by the Gnomes of Gallan for the High King Erin. They were imbued with magic, for the Gnomes had consulted with

Erin's sorcerers and a rather unusual enchantment had been woven into the silver. Nuadu thought that Erin had issued very specific instructions regarding the Scales, so that he might use them in the judging of miscreants at his Court. The legend said that Erin had believed in an unusually exact form of justice: *whoever brews the sour wine must needs drink it,* he had said, and the Scales had enabled him to actually weigh a sin, and pronounce a punishment precisely in accordance with it, no more and no less than the offence deserved. And I suppose, thought Nuadu, studying the Scales, there are worse methods of dealing with miscreants. He remembered that it had been Erin who had ordered the Court sorcerers to pronounce over the Robemaker the terrible Enchantment of Eternal Disease.

The two dishes of the Scales, one on each side of the central column, were easily visible; they were deep and their outer edges were embellished with strange symbols. Nuadu thought he could make out the Tree of Amaranth, which was one of the earliest known magical symbols, and the House from which all sorcerers must descend. But there were others, whose origin he could not guess at. In the red-tinged night, the Scales were unearthly and faintly sinister, and Nuadu thought that although Erin had used them for good, since then they had become imbued with the malevolence of the Soul Eaters and their grisly work.

The right-hand dish was much higher than the left; it swung high up in the frame of the machinery, light and floating, as if there was barely any substance in it at all. Nuadu thought: yes, of course, that is where they weigh the souls against the other side.

The other side . . .

The left-hand dish was weighted so heavily that it was almost touching the ground. The silver, so carefully wrought by the Gnomes in Gallan decades earlier, was nearly hidden by the contents of the pan; they foamed and writhed and spilled over the edges, alive and grotesque.

The *Draoicht Tinneas Siorai* . . . The Enchantment of

Eternal Disease. The spell which had held the Robemaker captive and helpless for centuries, creeping beneath his skin, eating away his flesh and his bones and his marrow.

It was a heaving nearly formless mass of tiny embryonic creatures; of half-formed foetuses, each of them covered with ulcerated leprous skin, bloodied and amorphous, most of the tiny inchoate creatures sightless, their clawed or webbed hands reaching out blindly. A thin film of membraneous skin covered them, as if the creatures had been flung indiscriminately into a sack and the sack's opening tightly sealed. Atop the sack was a discoloured skull, its bones befouled with putrescence, its eye sockets and nose cavity packed tight with wriggling maggot-creatures giving it the semblance of dreadful life.

At the sight of the squirming creatures, the Robemaker gave vent to a gasping cry and drew back. Nuadu heard him hiss, 'The *Draoicht Tinneas Siorai*!' and at once the heaving creatures on the Scales seemed to pulsate and reach their tiny incomplete hands out to him. Single eyes bulged out against the sack's surface and the Robemaker shuddered and threw up a hand to protect himself. Nuadu glanced to where Floy was watching and Floy looked at him. They shared a thought: *here, at last, is something the Robemaker fears!* And: *can we somehow use this?*

The Soul Eaters were moving closer; the ancient wizened one that Nuadu thought had spoken in the Cruachan Cave and who appeared to be their leader, said, 'You flinch, Master Robemaker. And yet you should not, for it may be that the hour of your deliverance is at hand. It may be that the curse ordered by Erin is about to be outweighed.' The old eyes slewed round to where Nuadu and the others lay. 'Nuadu of the Silver Arm.' He regarded Nuadu, and Nuadu stared back. 'You thought to cheat us, Wolfprince,' said the Soul Eater, softly.

'You thought to deceive us,' said another.

'To trick us into allowing you and your Lady into the Dark Realm, where no creature may go unless permitted by a Lord of that Domain,' said a third.

'And for that alone,' said the first, 'you will certainly die and render up your soul.' He turned to where the Robemaker was standing waiting, and Nuadu saw that there was an almost submissive droop to the Robemaker's head now, as if he was saying: I have done what I can and now I am in your hands. Nuadu saw Fenella's eyes widen in something that might have been pity and, nearby, Flame was almost certainly regarding the Robemaker with compassion.

And then the Robemaker straightened up, and began pulling at the rope-lights which held Fenella and Snodgrass. Floy felt Fenella's mind lurch with fear and pain as she was dragged forward, and saw, Nuadu's dark, slanting eyes show red.

Fenella felt the talons of the nearest Soul Eater reach out and pluck her from the ground. The shadows of the others fell across her and she saw them towering above her, their wizened faces suddenly avid and greedy, their talons opening and closing.

Our first victim . . . The leading Soul Eater was saying something about a young, unspoiled Human . . . They had unfurled their wings, so that the stark outlines threw great jagged shadows everywhere. They were baring their claws and there was something icily predatory about the movement. Fenella stared up at them, her mind tumbling with terror, and could see no way of escaping.

Nuadu had not moved, but the words uttered by Fael-Inis earlier had branded themselves onto his mind.

You cannot avoid your fealty for much longer, Wolfprince . . . You are what you are . . .

I *cannot* call to the Wolves! cried Nuadu, in silent anguish. There must be another way!

I have shown you the way, and now you must take the way, or let Ireland be overrun by the Dark Realm . . .

Cold clarity descended on Nuadu's mind. He thought: if I must, then I must. But perhaps there *is* another way.

Lifting his head, he pronounced, in ringing tones, the ancient enchantment which had come down to him, which had been a part of his blood for as long as he could remember and which must be answered by the most mystical, most inHuman beings in all Ireland. They had saved him from the Robemaker once before; they had answered the summons then, and they could not fail to do so now.

The magical faery *sidh*, the elven race who were rarely seen in Ireland, but who were bound, by the chains of an old, old enchantment, to aid the Royal House of Tara at times of extreme peril.

At once the darkness was splintered and the darting blue and green outlines of the *sidh* filled the skies, lighting the night to turquoise brilliance. Dozens upon dozens of pairs of iridescent wings beat the air angrily and Fenella, tumbling back from the Soul Eaters' circle, felt the brilliance sear her vision painfully.

'Look away!' cried Nuadu, on his feet at the centre of the cascading swooping *sidh*. 'If you value your sanity and your five senses, do not look directly at them!'

The Robemaker had fallen back, his hands flung to shield his ravaged, vulnerable face, and at once the rope-lights, no longer held by the force of his evil will, dissolved. As Floy pulled Fenella and Flame clear, the Soul Eaters let out a single rasping shriek of fury and moved together.

There was a singing on the air now, the eerie, enchanted singing of the *sidh* who were cold and soul-less and who were said to hunt Men for sport, but who had sworn allegiance to the Royal House of Tara at the beginning of her history. Nuadu, his arms about Fenella, knew the sound for a seldom-heard hunting song and, although his skin prickled with the cold allure and the icy seduction of the singing, he thought: they are hunting down the enemy of the true Ireland. I believe it will be enough. I believe they will vanquish the Robemaker and the Soul Eaters.

Great livid streaks of turquoise fire were splitting the skies as the *sidh* darted, arrow-straight, at the eyes of the Soul Eaters and Reflection's armies.

Floy and Nuadu bounded forward now, seeing their

chance: Fenella had just time to see that Nuadu was leaping straight on to the dark figure of the Robemaker and that Floy had knocked Reflection to the ground and was grappling with her.

The skies sizzled with the *sidh*'s angry brilliance and with the flying crimson shafts from Reflection's spear. The air was becoming thick and clotted with enchantments and with showers of blood and with the fire rising from the flambeaux.

The *sidh* flew straight at the Soul Eaters and Fenella, trying hard to shield her eyes, remembering all the warnings, glimpsed, on the outer rim of vision, creatures of gliding blue and green fire. At her side, Flame said, softly, 'They will take their eyes.' As she spoke, the Soul Eaters began to screech, terrible agonised sounds of rage and pain and fear. The strong, sweet humming swelled on the air again and the Soul Eaters began to fall from the skies like dried-out sticks, their wings flapping and broken. The *sidh* swarmed over them and their music flooded the night again, strange and inHuman, beautiful and un-earthly.

Floy, seeing that the Soul Eaters were vanquished, had wrested the spear from Reflection. He snapped it in two and then four across his leg. At once, Reflection slid away, darting into the night, a slender, silken shape. Fenella felt Flame's hand come down on hers and knew that Flame was thinking: should we go after her?

'We should never catch her,' said Fenella. 'But she has left the spear . . .' and then, suddenly, 'Flame – the spear!'

'It's broken,' said Flame. 'But its power won't be broken.'

'If we each take a piece of it,' said Fenella, pulling Flame forward, 'we can at least bring down the Storm Wraiths! Come on!'

They raced across the battlefield together. Fenella snatched up two pieces of Reflection's spear of light and Flame took two more, and they both hurled the pieces at the Storm Wraiths. The air spat with tiny, diamond-bright chippings of light and the Wraiths shrieked with pain and fury, darting away into the night sky.

Floy had snatched up a sword and gone straight to the Frost Giantess's litter. She reared up at once, the neck-fins distending, beating the air with her tiny hands. Floy leapt straight at her, lifting his sword high and bringing it down on the squirming undulating mass of cold flesh. Pale blood spurted and half covered him. He shuddered but lifted the sword and drove it home again. The *Geimhreadh* let out a terrible wailing and tried to crawl away, but the *sidh* swooped down, slicing at her with their ice-blue fire, and Floy, trying to avoid looking directly at them, saw the brilliant wings rise into the air again. He turned back and saw that the *Geimhreadh* was helpless on the ground, the thick, worm-like body flailing. He fell on her again and hacked at her until she lay still, her shapeless neck half severed.

Close by, Nuadu was facing the Robemaker; he thought he had inflicted some kind of sword wound already, but the Robemaker had whipped away, as slithery as a snake, and had stood facing Nuadu, a great spinning lattice of crimson lights surrounding him like armour. Nuadu was half blinded by the lights, but he advanced cautiously, a step at a time, the sword held out before him, his eyes narrowed. The Robemaker laughed and it was the terrible wet, bubbling laugh that Nuadu remembered. 'You can not get near to me, Wolfprince,' he cried. 'For all your precious *sidh*, you cannot penetrate my armour!' He gave another of his shrieking laughs and moved farther back and, as he did so, Nuadu saw forming, directly behind the cloaked shape, against the sky, the fiery outline of an immense door. The *sidh* flew at it at once but the outline held, and Nuadu could see that they were dashing themselves against it uselessly.

'You see!' shrieked the Robemaker triumphantly. 'You see, Wolfprince! I shall escape you. I shall escape into the Black Realm, where the Dark Lords will rise to my aid!' He turned about, the dark cloak swirling and, as he did so, slowly and menacingly, inch by terrible inch, the great Doorway began to open.

Floy was still standing by the mutilated body of the Frost Giantess, his eyes on the hooded figure of the Robemaker, outlined in the terrible glowing Doorway. He was holding the sword that had killed the Frost Giantess, but he thought that swords and knives would be of no avail against this one. Wasn't there something they could use? Wasn't there something that would defeat him, or, at the very least, disable him? With the thought came a stirring, a ruffle of memory, something tugging at the edges of his mind. What? Something that had happened earlier tonight, was it? Something that had made him think: so, after all, there is something that the Robemaker fears? After all there is something we could turn against him if we have the chance.

Of course! thought Floy, comprehension flooding his mind. Of course! The *Draoicht Tinneas Siorai*. The Enchantment of Eternal Disease.

He moved at once, swiftly and surely, crossing the stretch of ground to where the Silver Scales still stood, silent and sinister, gleaming dully in the moonlight. The Robemaker was silhouetted against the gaping Doorway and the opening was almost at its widest point now. At any minute the Robemaker would move back into the beckoning evil land and the Dark Ireland would swallow him. Once that had happened, there could surely be no following him. I have to stop him, thought Floy. Somehow I have to stop him, and I believe that this is the only way.

He moved until he was standing in the deep shadow cast by the legendary Silver Scales. He looked up at them and saw that although they had appeared to be man-sized, in fact they were much larger. Floy was fairly tall, but his head was barely level with the silver dishes. Standing beneath the immense and awesome Scales, he felt the waves of power and the insidious evil which had soaked into them during the years they had been in the Cruachan Caves. He felt the evil reach out and down to snake itself about his mind.

Come up to us, Human morsel, for we shall weigh you

616

against your sins and we shall pronounce judgement according-ly . . .

There was a ripple of evil mirth then. *And our punishments are such that you will wish you had never transgressed your puny laws, Human, and they are such that you will know yourself accursed and damned for this life and for all your lives to come . . .*

I can't hear you, said Floy silently. I can't hear you and I'm not afraid of you.

Come up to us, Human, climb the silver spine of the Scales, and feel the cold embrace of Justice . . .

I'm not listening, said Floy. You are simply cold, dead metal, and I'm not listening.

The left-hand dish was still weighed down with the gross and terrible Enchantment of Eternal Disease, its underside almost brushing the ground. Could he do it? Could he reach out and take the loathsome, wriggling sack of disease and filth and squirming matter in his hands? But I have to do it, he thought. I truly believe that it is the only way to defeat the Robemaker and I have to do it.

The writhing sliminess was still churning and seething in the pan; the *Draoicht Tinneas Siorai* thought Floy, staring, trying to harden his mind. But it is still all encased in the sacklike covering, it is unable properly to get out, he thought.

Are you so sure of that, Human creature . . .?

Yes! said Floy, silently. I do not believe that I am in any danger, and even if I am – he glanced to the menacing shape of the Robemaker – even if I am in danger, he thought, I believe there is more danger from that creature and his servants.

He reached up to the deep silver dish and, as he did so, tiny webbed clutching hands reached for him and bulging lidless eyes swivelled to stare at him. There was a wet sucking sound, as if fleshless, lipless mouths were already savouring him. *Here is sweet clean flesh for us to devour . . . here is untainted skin and firm muscle and strong white bone for us to burrow into and scourge and defile and poison . . .*

Dreadful. Don't think about it. Think that it is this that the Robemaker fears, that it is this which will surely overpower him.

Floy reached up to the left-hand dish, with the foaming amorphous things, and grasped the membraneous sack with his left hand and the grinning phosphorescent skull with the other.

There was a moment, terrible, sick-making, when the sack slithered and shifted beneath his grip, and when the misshapen hands seemed as if they would tear open the transparent outer covering, and Floy thought it would burst apart and spew its contents over his hands. And then the moment passed and the sack was quiescent and, although there was a horrid, cold, greasy feel to it, its contents did not move again. Moving carefully, Floy started to half carry, half drag the sack which held the grisly Enchantment of Eternal Disease across to where the Robemaker had already turned his back on them.

Nuadu and Fenella and Flame were standing motionless, watching. Behind them, the light of the *sidh* had dimmed, as if the *sidh* also were waiting. But Floy dared spare no energy for anything else. Every shred of concentration he possessed was focused on taking the bulging, disease-filled membrane to where the Robemaker was waiting to go through the Doorway into the Dark Domain beyond.

And then he was there, standing before the Doorway, and so strong was the evil emanating from beyond it, that he felt it engulf him in a thick, smothering mass, which for a moment made him fight for breath. The crimson glow fell across him, so that when he held out his hands, they were bathed in the hideous colour and the *Draoicht Tinneas Siorai* was instantly turned to blood-red.

Now! thought Floy. Now is the moment. When he is waiting for the Doorway to stand fully open, and when he is no longer aware of what is happening here.

'Robemaker!' cried Floy with all his strength. 'Robemaker! Turn about and face the one thing you fear!'

For the space of a heartbeat he thought the Robemaker

618

was not going to heed him. Am I too late? he thought. Has he already passed through the Doorway and is he beyond our reach? But he stayed where he was, still gripping the terrible Enchantment in both hands, his eyes never leaving the grim, black-cloaked shape of the Robemaker and at last, through what seemed like an ocean of time, the Robemaker turned slowly and looked straight at Floy and at the slithering, now-frantic, membrane.

Even on the outer edges of the watchers, the bolt of fear that went through the Robemaker was felt. Floy, who was directly in front of the necromancer, saw him flinch and put up a hand to shield himself. Confidence welled up within Floy, because he had been right, this *was* the only way to defeat this creature.

Deliberately, carefully, judging his distance, Floy flung the sack into the Robemaker's face.

A terrible cry rent the air and the Robemaker fell back, the dark hood slipping back so that his eaten-away face was revealed. The gaping eye sockets stared balefully and the white, crumbling bone was mercilessly exposed.

The bulging, dripping sack burst open, and the dread *Draoicht Tinneas Siorai* crawled forward. Everyone saw, in the angry light pouring from the Dark Realm, the living, breathing, corporeal diseases and illnesses and infections and poisons and plagues pour forward and smother the cowering figure of the Robemaker.

Flame was trying hard to remember the Robemaker had been evil beyond words; he had chained slaves and forced them to the treadmills; he had bargained to have Flame in his bed for a night. But she found herself flinching and putting up her hands to her face and had to tell herself, very sternly indeed, that she was not going to faint, and she was not going to be sick.

Fenella, standing at her side, was very white; she thought that perhaps, after all, the Silver Scales had meted out justice, for what could be more just, more precisely in accordance with any law, than to see the Robemaker at last defeated by the enchantment that he had rendered others soul-less to cheat? But, like Flame, she felt her own skin crawling with the horror and the pity of it.

The Robemaker was screaming now, dreadful gasping screams, nearly but not quite still-born out of lungs which were barely able to inflate any longer. As they watched, a swarm of bloated white maggot-creatures poured from the sack and descended on his face and Fenella, who was nearer than Flame, saw them burrow in through his eye sockets and knew they must be boring straight into his brain. With them came the snails' trail of leaking, oozing pus and matter. Decay and filth, thought Fenella, and, as the thought framed, she smelt the sweetish bad-fish stench of decaying flesh.

Floy had not moved. He had stood resolutely before the dying Robemaker, watching as the crawling, squirming, disease-ridden creatures of the *Draoicht Tinneas Siorai* overcame the necromancer. When, at last, the creature was still and silent and the creatures of the enchantment lay supine and bloated and satiated, he turned to Nuadu, his face pale, but his eyes steady.

Nuadu said, 'Well, Floy? The battle is not yet done. Shall we ride into the Dark Ireland and slay the Master?'

Chapter Forty-seven

As Nuadu's words died away, Fael-Inis, the salamanders at his side, moved forward out of the shadows and Flame looked up in delight. He touched the salamanders' glossy flanks, and at once the four who had taken Floy and Fenella and the brothers across the River of Souls came to stand before Nuadu, their heads bowed.

'We are yours to ride into the Dark Domain, Sire,' said the first one.

'If you will take us,' said another, and Nuadu reached his hands out and placed them on the salamanders' gleaming necks. He did not speak, but the others could see the delight and the acceptance in his eyes.

But he only said, 'We should be honoured,' and the salamanders tossed their manes and kneeled, bowing their wise, sleek heads, so that it was easy to slide on to their backs. Lovely! thought Fenella in delight, and remembered how they had ridden through the tunnels of Fael-Inis's Palace of Wildfire.

Nuadu looked across at her and sent the warm, sudden smile. 'Ready, Lady?' he said, and Fenella said, 'Ready,' and this time did not even stop to question anything. Of course they must go back into the Dark Realm, and of course they must seek out CuRoi and destroy him.

Snodgrass watched them, seeing them mount the gleaming sleek creatures, which were not like Snodgrass's idea of salamanders, and probably not like anyone else's either.

'But I'll stay with Fael-Inis,' he said. 'That's if that's acceptable, is it?'

'Assuredly,' said Fael-Inis, from his silent position on the edge of the light.

'It's a young man's battle, this,' said Snodgrass. 'Well,

and a young lady's, too, of course. As if Fenella isn't quite capable of giving a good account of herself, and Flame as well, I shouldn't be surprised.

'But I'd slow them down, you see,' he said, eyeing Fael-Inis. 'And if they're to deal with these matters properly, then the last thing they want is to be slowed down.'

Fael-Inis said, 'My hospitality is at your disposal, sir. Perhaps we may discuss a little of your world?' and Snodgrass, who found Fael-Inis alarming but intensely interesting, at once said he would be very pleased indeed to accept such a cordial invitation.

'We'll be watching for your return,' he said to Floy.

'And our thoughts will be with you and about you,' said Fael-Inis and, as Fenella said afterwards, it had sounded like some kind of ritual.

'Rather comforting.'

'Oh, yes.'

The four of them went through the immense Gateway in a single sweeping movement. There was time to realise that they were passing through what felt like thin, glinting light and time for Nuadu and Fenella to think: we are back in the Dark Realm again! And then they were streaming into the darkness and the salamanders were cutting a swathe of golden light through the Dark Ireland. The great Doorway opened up in the sky by the Robemaker was behind them and ahead of them was the glittering, sinisterly beautiful Castle of Illusions. And we have to enter it again, thought Fenella, remembering the dark radiance and the malevolent iridescence. We have to enter and we have to kill CuRoi.

The Dark Ireland was not nearly as dark as Fenella and Nuadu remembered. The skies were still black and low, so that you felt that you could reach up and touch them, but the strange distortion, the off-balance, out-of-kilter feeling was no longer so strong. To begin with, Fenella thought it was just that there were four of them and that it felt safer, or perhaps that it was the light from the salamanders. The *sidh* had melted away into their own strange world beneath the sea as soon as the Robemaker and the Frost Giantess had been slain and Reflection had vanished, but, once or twice, Fenella thought she glimpsed a smudge of blue-green against the skies.

But when Nuadu, riding the leading salamander hard across the ground, looked across and said, 'Do you see how the Darkness is already dying, Lady?' Fenella thought: of *course* it is dying! How could I have believed otherwise! And knew that it was nothing to do with there being four of them and nothing to do with the salamanders' gentle radiance or the hovering *sidh* light. In some incomprehensible manner, the evil and the darkness and the terrible clotted malignancy of the necromancers' Realm was weakening. Because the Robemaker was dead? Because something of Fael-Inis's radiance clung to the salamanders? Perhaps.

They rode hard past the black swamplands and the black boiling lakes and on to the fearsome Fields of Blood, where Aed had endured the agonies of his bondage to CuRoi, the salamanders pouring through the necromancers' realm in golden swathes of light, their manes streaming out against the darkness.

The sky was streaked with livid crimson and fingers of blood-red and, although there was a faint sound of beating wings and although they had the feeling several times that something dark and sinuous and boneless slithered across their path, there were no signs of the ravaged-faced Harpies or the prancing dungeon-creatures. Nothing came swooping down on them and nothing came scuttling across their path to bar their way.

The mountains reared ahead of them, stark black shapes, bathed in the evil of centuries, soaked in the terrible darkness of the fearsome Lords who dwelled within their depths. Fenella drew in a deep breath and glanced at the others, seeing that Floy was alert and intent and that Flame was at his side, riding hard, her hair streaming out as wildly as the salamanders'.

Fael-Inis's daughter, riding the fiery salamanders through the Dark Ireland, sprinkling her father's light...

And then there was no time to think about anything

other than what they must do, because CuRoi's immense Castle was in front of them, and spears of light were shooting outwards from it, as if CuRoi was already weaving the enchantment which would seal the Castle. The landscape was bathed in eerie light and Floy, looking up, caught sight of swooping, birdlike shapes above them.

'The sun is setting,' said Nuadu, suddenly. 'Quickly, now, or the Castle will start to rotate and it will be sealed against us!' He urged the salamanders on, but the salamanders needed no urging; they were pouring across the dark countryside, sparks flying from their hoofs, their eyes on the Castle of Illusions.

'Can we force an entry?' cried Floy and Nuadu half turned to look at him.

'We forced an exit,' said Nuadu, his eyes on the Castle. 'And we have the fire and the light of Fael-Inis's creatures. We have you, Flame,' he said, suddenly fixing her with his brilliant stare, and Flame started, because it was disconcerting to be looked at like this and it was disconcerting to be suddenly marked out.

The chanting of CuRoi's creatures was on the air all about them now; it ebbed and flowed on the darkness in a steady rhythmic pattern and, as it did so, Fenella felt the horrid distortion begin to creep back.

Flame, who knew a little more of the Dark Ireland than the others, and who had absorbed a smattering of sorcery in the Fire Court, recognised at once that this was the Chaunt of the Summoning, and that it meant that CuRoi was calling up every dark servant who dwelled here. Every creature of this terrible land would be flocking to the aid of the one they called the Master.

'He is calling up his armies!' she cried. 'Floy! Nuadu! At any minute they will appear.'

Nuadu spurred the salamanders on and, as he did so, the great Castle began to rotate slowly and the chanting swelled to a massive crescendo all about them, sending their senses dizzy and reeling, so that they were in a vast chamber of rushing, chanting sound.

The voices grew to a tremendous tumult of sound and,

as they did so, the four travellers saw the portcullis grow misty and faint. Dark heavy cloud swirled in, wreathing the great gates, and from deep within the Castle they heard the gloating chuckling of CuRoi.

Nuadu, who was a little ahead, shouted, 'The sealing! Quickly, or we shall be shut out! Onwards!'

'We can reach it!' shouted Floy, his eyes brilliant. 'Nuadu, if we use every ounce of speed, we can reach it before it seals!'

'Yes! But there is no time to lose!'

And then a dark wall of seething, grinning creatures reared up in their path: the Harpies with their wicked talons and their ravaged-women faces, beating the air with their powerful wings; the red-eyed dungeon-creatures, long-fingered and bony, prancing and leaping, whirling in a mad evil dance.

CuRoi's terrible servants, obeying their Master's summons, banding together to drive out the Wolf-prince . . .

There were other creatures in the boiling sea of evil beings, as well; fearsome, nightmare things.

Hydra-headed snake-creatures and grinning gargoyle-beings; thin grey Human-like shapes with sunken eyes and reaching claws . . .

Hags and ghouls and viragos and Furies . . .

Humans to catch and Humans to eat;
Bones to grind and flesh to strip.

'On!' cried Nuadu. 'Straight through them!' But the denizens of CuRoi were increasing with every minute; there were dozens of them, there were hundreds, thousands; the air was black with their filthy exudence and foul with their stench. Beyond them, the four friends could just make out the silhouette of the Castle of Illusions, rotating slowly still, its drawbridge still lowered, the portcullis still high. There was still time to get inside. If they could somehow rout these creatures, there was still time . . .

The chanting surged all about their ears and there was a note of triumph in it now.

See how powerful is the Master! See how easily he is able to defeat you!

There was a moment of the blackest, most vicious bitterness Nuadu had ever known. To come this far; to defeat the Frost Giantess and Reflection; to vanquish the Soul Eaters and see the Robemaker destroyed, and then to meet defeat like this. Nuadu stared at the Castle and thought: we were within minutes, we were within *seconds* of reaching the gateway. We could still reach it even now, before it seals, if we could but fling aside these dark servants of CuRoi.

He saw Floy brace his muscles as if for battle, but Floy would know, as they all knew, that they could not possibly overpower so many. Within minutes, the Harpies and the grinning prancing red-eyed devils and the hags and ghouls would be upon them to tear them apart and fling their remains into the Fields of Blood.

And then I shall truly have failed, thought Nuadu. I shall have failed and Ireland will be the poorer for it. CuRoi is stronger than I had bargained for and I have failed.

The others had reined in the salamanders and the salamanders were tossing their manes, pawing the ground and waiting, eyeing the Castle with unease.

I have failed, and CuRoi will spin his enchantments and he will reach out from here and take Ireland, and there is nothing any of us can do . . .

Deep within his mind, a tiny silver voice stirred, and Fael-Inis's words ruffled his thoughts.

The means are to hand, Wolfprince . . . Did I not show you the means? You must take the means, or let Ireland be overrun by the Dark Realm . . .

Ireland, thought Nuadu. Tara, the Shining Citadel, the Bright Palace . . . my family's stronghold, which I have never entered.

He did not want it. He had never wanted it. He had willingly embraced the strange half-life of the Wolfwood;

he had sought out the company of creatures whom he believed to be like himself: rebels, misfits, outcasts. And yet, he thought, and yet . . . were they not gratified at finding themselves in proximity to one who possesses a little of the enchanted Wolfblood? Did they not unthinkingly give me homage, and did I not accept that homage as unthinkingly? Have I ever really been free of Tara?

Staring at the grinning, gobbling creatures, seeing beyond them to the dark shape of the necromancer's stronghold, Nuadu felt the weight of Tara and the weight of all Ireland fall upon him.

After all, I am what I am . . .

And I promised Aed . . .

A great cascading wave of something strong and sweet and immensely powerful washed against his mind so that he all but fell.

But it is the power and the light and the strength of the Wolves of Tara, and already I am invoking it, already I am tapping the source of an old old ritual and of an ancient golden strength . . .

I have already set the magic working, thought Nuadu. There is no turning back now.

There was a blur of movement to the left and Nuadu turned his head and saw, limned on the distant horizon, silhouetted against the lowering skies, the shapes of dozens of lean, sleek creatures, sharp-eyed and pointed-muzzled, their outlines surrounded by nimbuses of fire, alive and glowing and slavering. On the scurrying night wind, came the unmistakable howling.

The Royal Wolves of Tara, waiting for the Wolfprince to summon them . . .

The golden strength was pouring through Nuadu, and he knew it was to be no longer denied.

And Tara, the Bright Palace, must be saved, and Ireland must be saved. I can no longer turn my back, thought Nuadu. I made a vow to Aed and I must keep that vow. Fael-Inis was right.

He lifted his hands and saw the power and the light and

the strength pour forth, and at once the Wolves gave a great howl and bounded forward across the dark domain towards him.

Livid streaks of lightning split the skies as the Wolves fell upon the dark servants of CuRoi. The Harpies screeched and rose at once, flapping their wings, but the Wolves leapt and clawed at them, bringing them down, and falling on them, tearing and lacerating, their white pointed teeth sinking into the Harpies' half-scale, half-Human hide.

Blood began to spatter the ground, and where there had once been a menacing army, now there was a raging maelstrom of fur and claws and teeth and talons.

The ghouls were shrieking, terrible mournful sounds, and leaping on to the Wolves' backs, sinking their teeth into the thick neck fur, but the Wolves simply rolled over and dislodged them on to the ground and then turned and savaged them.

Fenella saw two of the Wolves take one of the red-eyed devils between them and tear off its head, tossing the bleeding carcase into the Crimson Fields. The Harpies were hovering, out of the Wolves' reach now, but screeching their harsh, ugly cries, diving and swooping and then flying upwards again out of reach.

'But there is a way through now!' cried Floy, excitedly. 'See! Over to the left!'

'Yes!' Nuadu turned to look at Fenella and Flame and the reckless, brilliant light was in his eyes. 'Onwards now!' he cried. 'The Castle is still sealing! We may yet reach the evil one!'

'Hurry!' cried Fenella, gathering up the salamander. 'Will the Wolves follow?'

'If I wish it, they will follow me,' said Nuadu and, just for a fleeting second, there was something in his voice Fenella had never heard before. Imperiousness? She glanced at him, but he laughed, and reached the flesh and blood hand to her. 'For the moment they will remain here to deal with CuRoi's evil,' he said. And then he was turning the salamander's head about and riding straight at the gap in the battle.

The salamanders went effortlessly through the whirling creatures, heedless of the Wolves and the screeching Harpies and the ghouls and hags. They did not quite fly, but they leapt through the air with a smooth, soaring movement that was so clean and so lovely, that Fenella and Flame, both clinging on for dear life, thought they would never feel the ground again. But then they were no longer in the air; they were pounding up the mountain path, nearing the Castle, and it was still rotating, it was still spinning, with that strange incandescent whirling, and the gates, the great gates through which they must pass were becoming immersed in mist, and at any moment, at any moment . . .

There was another soaring, flying movement, and they were through the gates, and under the portcullis, and CuRoi's Castle of Illusions closed about them.

The four of them stood in the immense stone hall which Nuadu and Fenella remembered so well, the salamanders a little to their rear, spreading gentle radiance across the dark shadows.

The immense gates had vanished as they surged through – And we are shut in, thought Fenella. We are shut in with CuRoi and with whatever evil dark powers serve him. She stretched her mind to its utmost, trying to sense, trying to feel CuRoi's presence.

'He is here,' said Nuadu at her side, speaking softly. 'He is a dark muddied evil, at the Castle's heart.' As he spoke, Fenella thought: of *course* CuRoi is here! And felt, as Nuadu had felt, the waiting malevolence deep in the Castle . . .

They moved towards the stairway at the far end of the hall, wary and cautious, scanning the shadows as they went.

Floy said, 'The dungeons are down here?'

'Yes.'

As they reached the narrow stone stairway, the shadows

swirled and thickened and Fenella felt, tugging at the corners of consciousness, the silvery sticky threads of CuRoi's beckoning.

Come closer, my dear, for there are dreams here you have never imagined, and there are riches here that you have never envisaged . . .

I'm not listening, said Fenella inside her head. Begone, creature! I won't listen to you!

They walked cautiously in single file down the narrow worn stone steps, putting out a hand to the wall for balance, as Fenella had done, peering into the dark.

Nuadu was leading the way, with Floy bringing up the rear and the two girls inbetween. As they rounded a curve in the stair, and saw a thick, smeary light fall across the ancient stonework, Floy said very softly, 'They are not long lit, I think. Then, *someone* is here.'

Someone is here, Humans, someone is here, and someone is waiting and watching . . . Peering from the shadowy corners . . . watching from behind the wall hangings . . . Did that tapestry stir just then? Was it only the wind? Can you be sure it was only the wind . . .?

Fenella set her teeth and pushed the insidious whispering away but, as she did so, Nuadu said, in an ordinary, practical voice, 'I daresay we may have to fight back a lurking spell or two, you know.'

'If they are minor ones,' said Flame, 'they might not be too hard to get rid of.' She said this rather hesitantly, but Nuadu stared at her and said, 'The sorceress's daughter! Of course.' And then, very seriously, 'We need every bit of help we can get, Flame.'

'I have only a very little knowledge,' said Flame anxiously, because it would not do for them to be thinking she could hurl spears of light or call up fire demons. 'But perhaps there might be a protective chant which would help.' She thought it was not being vain to feel pleased that she could offer some small assistance in this very important and highly dangerous quest. She had contributed nothing at all so far. It would be a marvellous thing if she could just drive back the lurking dark creatures which they all knew were hovering, unseen.

Nuadu said, with sudden formal courtesy, 'Yes. If you would do that now, please,' and Flame gathered her thoughts.

It would have to be the strongest ritual she could remember, but it would not have to be a very long one. The Banishing Ritual of Mab might fit very well, because all its images were of shining light which would be a good thing to use down here, and there was mention of the ancient Amaranthine House, and the strong and pure magic of the first sorcerers of all. Yes, she would try that one.

She stood very still and summoned the words, calling up the images that went with them.

By the power of the heartwood *Croi Crua Adhmaid,*
By the light of the Bright Palace of Tara;
By the under-water world of the long-ago City of Tiarna,
By the glittering gates of the Palace beyond the Skies.

Light, thought Flame, her eyes half closed, concentrating. Shining glittering spires and brilliant iridescent seas . . . The setting sun plunging below the ocean and turning the seas to fire . . . Spears and shards of white moonlight sliding through the Wolfwood to *Croi Crua Adhmaid . . .*

By the ancient shining Amaranthine Tree
By the power of the Well of Segais.
By the Nine Hazels of Wisdom,
Darkness vanish, creeping evil begone.

She opened her eyes and saw at once that the creeping shadows had receded and she felt that the hovering menace had lifted. Floy grinned at her and Flame felt absurdly pleased with herself, even though it had been the simplest of rituals, one she had heard Mother chant if the Wraiths or the White Hags came to the Fire Court and Mother could not be bothered to receive them.

Fenella was fascinated, not only by the ritual, which she thought beautiful and strange, but even more fascinated by the way Flame seemed able to tap some inner source of power.

'Only a very little,' said Flame at once, and Fenella realised that Flame had sensed her thoughts.

'Sufficient to banish whatever was creeping after us, however,' Fenella said, and smiled Floy's smile.

Flame thought of saying that it was not actually a very difficult ritual, but decided not to, in case it might sound conceited. She was liking Fenella very much, but it was important to remember that customs and manners might be different outside of the Fire Court. She would try not to do or say anything that might offend anyone. But it had been marvellous that she had been able to pronounce the Ritual of Mab so successfully.

As they reached the foot of the steps, they saw the passage stretching ahead of them, empty and deserted.

'And the seven chambers,' said Nuadu softly.

'Each one more terrifying than the one before,' said Fenella.

They stood very still and looked at one another.

And then Nuadu said, 'The room with the Ebony Throne. That is where he is.'

Dark blue light flooded the small stone chamber and, as they stood in the open doorway, they saw that CuRoi was there, a smile just lifting his lips, his head on one side, regarding them. Behind him was the austerely beautiful Ebony Throne, the satiny black wood gleaming gently, the wolfshead carvings standing out.

'You are well come,' said CuRoi and, for an instant, so strong was the impression of a genial host, pleased to welcome guests, that they hesitated.

And then Nuadu moved, Floy at his side, and, as they did so, Fenella and Flame both cried out, for the rope-lights so often used by the Robemaker had snaked forward and whipped about Nuadu and CuRoi was drawing him forward.

'Dear me,' said CuRoi, chucking a little. 'Dear me, bastard Wolfprince, did you *really* expect to walk in unchallenged, and emerge unscathed? How trusting of you.' He lifted his hand again, almost imperceptibly, and the lights drew Nuadu farther in. Flame, her eyes huge with horror, began to chant the ritual of banishment again, but at once CuRoi flicked out a second rope-light, and Flame gasped and fell.

'And the mask, also, I believe,' said CuRoi. 'For I should not want any distractions.' Before he had finished speaking, the cruel crimson lights had formed into the mask about Flame's face. Floy made to move and CuRoi felled him with a third rope-light.

'And the Wolfprince's lady also, I think,' he said, and Fenella was caught and bound as well.

'Do you know,' said CuRoi, lifting his hand in a slight under-stated gesture that brought Nuadu even closer, 'do you know, I had been inclined to view the Robemaker's little array of spells with very nearly contempt. A minor sorcerer, I had always thought him. How it ill became me to do that! These are *very* useful.' Fenella thought he spoke in the slightly absent-minded fashion of someone choosing wares in a market place, or comparing one colour against another.

'And so now, Nuadu of the Silver Arm,' said CuRoi, turning back, 'so now, we are come full circle. You are again in my Castle and you and your friends are in my power. Did you really think to escape me? Did you really think your puny armies, your snarling Wolves and your absurd *sidh* could vanquish me?' He smiled at Nuadu again. 'It will be a fitting end for you to be fed to the Ebony Throne,' he said. 'It will be an *appropriate* death for a bastard prince to die in the terrible embrace of that ancient symbol of kingship. I do like neat endings,' he said, and again the rope-lights tightened. Nuadu was standing within a foot of the great, blackly gleaming Throne now and his eyes were on it, narrow and glinting.

'Are you ready to die horribly and slowly, Wolfprince?' said CuRoi, evil glittering redly in his eyes, the mask ripped from him so that they saw him for what he really was; a churning seething mass of undiluted evil . . .

'Well, Nuadu Airgetlam?' said CuRoi.

Of his own volition, Nuadu walked forward and sat in the chair.

Pure blue light poured on to the massive carved Throne, bathing Nuadu with radiance. The crimson rope-lights and the masks which had held them all spat and shrivelled and then dissolved of their own accord.

Nuadu was smiling, but there was a malicious amusement in his eyes as he regarded CuRoi and his hands were held out, palms upwards, the silver hand of his left arm gleaming gently.

Ireland's heir . . . Fenella, staring, thought: *of course!* Aed made him promise that Ireland would be safe. And in so doing, Aed *bequeathed* Ireland to Nuadu! thought Fenella, torn between awe and delight.

CuRoi had fallen back the instant Nuadu touched the Ebony Throne. His face was twisted in undiluted hatred, but there was a moment – Fenella had seen it quite clearly – when he had flung up his hands to shield himself from the pure light.

He rallied slightly, and hissed, 'Imposter! Bastard prince!'

'Am I?' said Nuadu softly. 'Are you sure of that, CuRoi?' As he spoke, the light fell all about him so that the Throne itself began to glow with an inner radiance. Fenella and the others were suddenly aware that the Castle was rotating.

But it is moving the other way round! thought Fenella confusedly. It is unsealing of its own accord! The evil is dissolving!

CuRoi was still staring at Nuadu. At length, he said, 'Your brother . . .' and Nuadu smiled.

'My brother is dead,' he said, gently. 'I think you know that. But perhaps you do not know that, before he died, he extracted from me a vow that Ireland would be safe.' He regarded the necromancer. 'He bequeathed Ireland to me with his dying breath,' said Nuadu, softly, and Fenella drew in a delighted gasp. 'And since he was the hereditary High King,' said Nuadu, speaking as one explaining something simple to a very stupid child, 'since he was the Crown Prince, by his bequest Ireland is now mine.'

CuRoi stared at Nuadu, black and bitter hatred in his eyes. 'Was it a deception after all, Wolfprince?' he said at last. 'Your repeated vows that you did not want Tara, that you cared nothing for the Bright Palace? Did they mask a deep and subtle plot?' He moved closer.

'I deceived no one,' said Nuadu. 'I never wanted Tara. I do not want it now.' His eyes narrowed. 'But I can not turn my back on it,' he said. 'I must take on the mantle of my dead half-brother. I must rout the dark evil of your kind, CuRoi.' Again the look, pitying yet merciless. 'I grew up in the Wolfwood,' said Nuadu. 'When the King repudiated his Queen's bastard, he did so violently. I was born in great secrecy in the ancient Grail Castle, sometimes called Scáthach the Castle of Shadow, but soon after my birth the King ensured that I should be taken into the Wolfwood and left to die.' He smiled. 'I did not die,' he said. 'I survived, because of my father's people.'

Floy, listening intently, said very softly, 'The Wolves.'

'The Wolves,' said Nuadu. A smile touched his lips. 'What else?' he said.

What else indeed . . .?

'And now, CuRoi,' said Nuadu, his eyes suddenly remote, 'you are finished.' He made a quick gesture, encompassing the slowly moving Castle. 'Your enchantments are dissolving and light is streaming in to your dark citadel.' He stood up and walked forward and, as he did so, Floy and the two girls moved to the door, barring the necromancer's path.

'I should like to kill you in the way of my father's people,' said Nuadu, his eyes on CuRoi. 'I should like to savage you and mutilate you and fling your bloodied remains to the Harpies that screech outside your castle.' Fear showed in the necromancer's face again, and Nuadu laughed.

'It is too swift an end,' he said. 'Instead, I shall follow the ways of the High King Erin who believed in exact forms of justice. The Silver Scales of Justice, which are accredited to him, were taken and corrupted by the Soul Eaters and can never be used for the punishment of evil again. But Erin's premise still holds. Whatever crop you have sown, you must reap its harvest.' He stood over CuRoi and, although he was not tall, he seemed to tower over the necromancer.

'You are about to reap your crop, CuRoi,' said Nuadu, and the others saw, fearfully and incredibly, the wolf-mask touch his face, the lips thin and the eyes slant and glow.

'If you were a true Lord of Sorcery, a real and strong scion of the ancient House of Amaranth,' said Nuadu, 'you would have withstood our attack.' He gestured to the other three. 'Four of us only, and the Wolves,' he said.

'But you are no true sorcerer, CuRoi, you are flawed goods, damaged stock. You are the imposter... And you know the fate reserved for imposters,' said Nuadu, very softly, and the planes of his face seemed to blur, so that for a brief moment the wolf looked out more strongly and more cruelly than the others had ever seen it.

And he is moving around CuRoi now, thought Fenella; he is circling him, driving him towards the Throne.

CuRoi was flinching now and the light that had poured from the great darkly beautiful Ebony Throne was sending its radiance towards him. Again he threw up his hands to shield his eyes from the light and in that moment Nuadu sprang on him, closing his hands about the necromancer's throat, the strong hard silver hand circling it like a vice.

And with a gesture that was very nearly off-hand, he threw CuRoi straight at the Ebony Throne.

At once the chamber was lit to white painful light. Sparks and splinters of pure radiance tore across the small oblong dungeon and sliced into the ancient stones, so that they shivered and fell apart. There was a terrible scream from the depths of the great Throne, the cry of a soul who sees Hell yawning and, for a brief, terrible moment, Fenella glimpsed a great fiery furnace, red-eyed demons reaching out. There was the acrid smell of burning and the thing that had been CuRoi sagged, lifeless, eyeless, burnt out from within, smoking and charred.

Nuadu did not falter. He grabbed Fenella's hand and bounded to the door.

'Quickly, now, for the Castle is about to sunder and we dare not be trapped!' He pulled Fenella with him, Floy and Flame at their heels, up the narrow stone stairway and into the great hall.

Deep blue light poured into the dark Castle of the necromancers; soft, purple-tinged dusklight, sweet and clean and untainted by the Dark Realm's foul malevolence. Fenella could hear wailing and screeching from beyond the Castle's walls; the scared running of creatures fleeing a great threat, the frantic beating of wings on the air of frightened beings who had served the dark powers, but who now saw those powers crumble before the might and the strength of the Wolfking.

The power and the light and the strength, Lady . . .

The Wolves were waiting. As the salamanders took them down the mountain path, they fell into line behind Nuadu, sleek and lean, their pelts dark and glossy, their eyes on Nuadu.

Fenella said, rather uncertainly, 'Will they follow us back into the real Ireland?'

'Yes,' said Nuadu. He looked across at her and smiled and at last it was the smile of the lover of the twilit Wolfwood, the warm, intimate smile that held the shared memory of what had been between them, and what would be between them in the future . . .

And then the Gateway was before them and the lights and the brightness of the true Ireland, the fabled land of blue and green mist which was fabled no longer for Fenella and Floy, but real and warm and loving, were rushing towards them.

The salamanders poured effortlessly through the

Gateway, the Wolves in their wake, and the Gateway closed behind them, leaving no trace.

Chapter Forty-eight

To Tealtaoich and the other Beastline creatures, who had all been accustomed to living at Tara and to being a part of its immense glittering Court, it was strange and quite dreadfully sad to have to approach it as aggressors.

'But we have to drive out the Gruagach,' said Tealtaoich.

'That's if they're awake from Pumlumon's *Draoicht Suan.*'

'Well, I meant that. That's what I meant,' said Tealtaoich.

Pumlumon and the other Gnomes had been very flattered to be included in the march on Tara. Culdub Oakapple had said, lugubriously, that wasn't it only that Tealtaoich and the rest needed Pumlumon's help with dissolving the *Draoicht Suan,* but the Gnomes had not paid this very much attention, because hadn't the Oakapple a terrible old way of squashing people's optimism and wasn't a bit of an optimism what was wanted now? Bith said it was very gratifying that Pumlumon was to go into Tara with Caspar, although wasn't it only what you'd expect, what with Pumlumon being the one who had pronounced the spell in the first place. A spell could only be lifted by the person (or Gnome) who had first chanted it, said Bith firmly. Anyone knew that.

Feradach muttered to Clumhach that it was to be hoped Pumlumon could be trusted to remember the awakening ritual, but Clumhach, who was so pleased to be returning to Tara that he would not believe ill of anyone, said that of course Pumlumon would remember it.

'He remembered the *Draoicht Suan,*' said Clumhach.

'I think that was a stroke of luck,' said Feradach.

Pumlumon had, in fact, consulted anxiously with

Miach about the exact wording of the ritual and a couple of the Oaks had helped. Pumlumon had repeated the ritual several times, just to be sure, and then Snizort had written it down for him, which was a grand useful thing to have done, and something Pumlumon would never have thought of doing. He would feel very important, he said, going on down to Tara alone with Caspar, and had asked couldn't he take along one or two friends. Flaherty was the one to be taking with you when you were on an important mission, he said, and wasn't Bith of the Bog-hat their leader, and ought, by rights, to be included as well. And the Oakapple never liked to be missing any bit of excitement that was going on.

But it had been explained to him that this first approach had to be very quiet and very stealthy, on account of not letting the giants know they were there until they had dissolved the *Draoicht Suan*. What they had to do, said Tealtaoich and Eogan, explaining it all to Pumlumon, was to wake the giants and then, just as the giants were blinking and feeling a bit sleepy from the spell, the armies would come roaring in and fell them before they had time to know what was happening. That was the way of it, said Tealtaoich, frowning at Pumlumon to be sure he understood.

And, of course, if it was stealth that was wanted, then Pumlumon was the one for the job, said Pumlumon, having seen the entire point of this plan. Hadn't his own grandfather been known as the stealthiest Gnome that ever wore a hat, and wasn't there a saying in Gallan to this very day, 'as stealthy as Pumlumon's grandfather'?

'I'll be there,' he said, beaming, and Tealtaoich said to Eogan that it was to be hoped that Pumlumon could remember the spell.

'Snizort's written it out for him.'

'He'll have lost it by the time they reach Tara,' said Tealtaoich.

'Snizort made a copy and gave it to Caspar.'

'Oh, I see.'

Snizort, who was walking with Caspar just behind the

Gnomes, thought that the procession out of the Wolfwood and on towards Tara was awesome and solemn and one of the most remarkable sights he ever thought to see. He had rather enjoyed the walk, which had been in the nature of an informal march, and which had gone along to the accompaniment of singing. This seemed to be a traditional thing, and Snizort had enjoyed it greatly. The Tree Spirits had unbent sufficiently to teach the Beastline creatures several songs from the time of Cormac which everybody had liked, and then the freed slaves had sung several rousing choruses of songs which had been sung in their villages before the days of the Robemaker, and Snizort himself had even managed to remember two ditties from Renascia, which had been received very well. It had made the march seem much shorter than it really was and, as Clumhach had said, it had brought about a grand spirit of comradeship.

'And of course,' he had said to Snizort, 'you won't be expected to be on foot for the actual charge.'

'Ah,' said Snizort, who had wondered about this, but had not quite liked to ask.

'Oisin will have a word with the deer, I expect, said Clumhach. 'They're very fleet and extremely nice. Unless you'd prefer a panther?' He posed this is a perfectly ordinary possibility and Snizort, who had taken several wary looks at the prowling sinuous panthers padding after Tealtaoich, said, hastily, that he was sure the deer would be entirely acceptable.

The Beastline Lords had walked at the head of the march with the creatures they had summoned in their wake and the Gnomes behind the creatures.

'If we had been strict about the precedence,' said Caspar, 'the Gnomes should have come last of all, after the Trees. But they've no sense of direction, Gnomes, and they might easily have taken a wrong turning. So Tealtaoich and Eogan thought they'd be safer in the middle.'

'If everyone had their rights,' said Dian Cecht, hearing this and turning round haughtily, '*Miach* would be spearheading the attack and going into Tara with the Gnome Pumlumon.'

'Why is that?' asked Caspar rather belligerently.

'If there is any sorcery to be done, Miach is Court Sorcerer,' said Dian Cecht.

'Well,' said Caspar, 'if you really want to know, Miach can have my place for the asking. The only reason I'm going is because if the giants *aren't* still asleep, they won't think it odd to see me. They'd think it very odd to see Miach walking back into their midst after they'd driven him out. It's simply a question of being practical,' said Caspar firmly, to which Dian Cecht said there was no longer any justice in the world but, in any case, she would not have given her support to Miach going into such a *sinister* situation, and it was extremely likely that the Gruagach were awake and lying in wait for anyone foolish enough to try to sneak past the sentries.

The freed slaves were walking with the Tree Spirits who brought up the rear. Snizort had managed to talk with some of the dryads and had found them extremely scholarly and rather formal.

'But I'm learning a very great deal,' he said to Caspar. 'My word, I wouldn't have believed the half of the things I've learnt here. Tell me, shall we take Tara fairly easily, do you suppose?'

'I don't see why not,' said Caspar, who felt he had acquitted himself firmly but courteously with Dian Cecht, and who was beginning to feel quite optimistic about this remarkable quest. 'I truly don't see why we shouldn't. If the giants are still under the *Draoicht Suan*, and if Pumlumon can wake them, they'll be too sleepy to put up much of a fight. As a matter of fact,' said Caspar, lowering his voice and glancing over his shoulder to make sure no one was listening, 'as a matter of fact, it isn't strictly honourable, attacking them like this. You're supposed to send all kinds of challenges and warnings before you attack people.'

'Ah yes. Chivalry,' murmured Snizort, entranced. 'The ancient code.'

'But,' said Caspar, 'I think they decided – that is, Tealtaoich and Oisin and the rest decided – that since the giants didn't observe the code when they took Tara, and since they're usurpers anyway, the usual practices could be shelved. Also,' he added, 'it probably means we'll be able to beat them.'

The armies approached Tara from the Western side and paused on the hillside behind the brilliant shining outline.

Oisin had told Snizort that this was the scene of many famous battles of the past.

'If you stand on that hillside and close your eyes,' he had said, quite seriously, 'you can almost feel the past flooding in on you. That was where the great Cormac of the Wolves led the final charge against the usurpers Eochaid Bres and Mab the Wanton and where he defeated the terrible sisterhood of the Morrigan. And then later, Cormac's great granddaughter, the High Queen Grainne, fought the necromancer Medoc there. It's steeped in history and soaked in blood,' said Oisin very solemnly, 'and it's a very good place indeed for us to assemble and begin the charge on the Gruagach.'

Below them, in the saucer-shaped valley, was Tara, the Bright Palace of legend, the Shining Citadel of Ireland's history, woven into the weft and the weave, threaded into the tapestry of every tale ever told or sung or written or dreamed.

As Caspar and Pumlumon approached the Western Gate, they looked about them cautiously, staring up at the blind, unlit windows, seeing the traces of neglect everywhere. Pumlumon, a cleanly soul, tutted and said didn't it make you feel a terrible old anger to see such shocking housekeeping.

'They aren't the tidiest of people, the Gruagach,' admitted Caspar, standing in the courtyard. 'But I think the neglect only strengthens our hope that they're still under the *Draoicht Suan*.'

Pumlumon said at once that wouldn't that be the way

of it and Caspar the quick-witted one for spotting it. Would they be taking a look inside now?

'Yes,' said Caspar, who was feeling better with every minute, and who was, by this time, almost certain that the Gruagach were still under the *Draoicht Suan*. The notion that it might all be a trap occurred to him, but he put it from his mind, because the concept of a trap was far too subtle for Inchbad's people.

And so he led Pumlumon through the echoing galleries and the vast chambers of Tara. Along the historic Wolf Gallery where, so said legend, Cormac had held the famous race with his court to see how many ladies they could each bed between sunset and sunrise. On down the great gilt stair with the curving, diamond-crusted balustrades, which was known as Mab's Stair, and which the ladies of the court always used to make grand entrances into the banqueting hall below when there was a particularly festive gathering.

Caspar, who knew the way without really thinking about it, hurried along, Pumlumon scurrying at his heels, holding his hat on, tutting all over again at the dust and the grime everywhere.

They walked rapidly through the rather sombre official rooms, among them the exquisitely beautiful Star of the Poets, where the King of the day met with his Councillors and his advisers to discuss matters of state; past the slightly eerie, spell-ridden Hall of Light and the Skyward Tower where once had lived the nine sorcerers of Dierdriu, and on until there ahead of them—

'The Sun Chamber,' said Caspar. '*Medchuarta*. Ready?' They moved forward, and Caspar pushed wide the great doors.

The first thing to assail their senses was the stale smell of unwashed giant and of onion-tainted, sleep-befouled breath. Caspar shuddered and Pumlumon shook his head, because wouldn't a few sprigs of lavender have been of some help here.

In the great Sun Chamber of the Wolfkings, the

immense glittering heart of the ancient Shining Citadel of all Ireland, the giants of Gruagach lay where they had fallen when Pumlumon spun the *Draoicht Suan* about them.

They were awkward and ugly; their jerkins were grease-spotted and their wide, stupid mouths had fallen open, showing blackened stumps of teeth. Most of them were snoring, and the Sun Chamber reverberated to the sounds.

The fire around which Caspar remembered them gathering that night had long since burned out and drifts of ash lay everywhere, sprinkling the silver floor so that it was tarnished and smeary. Inchbad's crown had slipped from his head and with it the elaborately curled and powdered wig he had been wearing. There were cobwebs that were beginning to thicken, and there were even mouse-droppings in a neat line across the floor.

Pumlumon said, in a whisper to Caspar, that wasn't this the most disgraceful thing you'd ever think to see.

'We should never have let them stay for so long,' said Caspar, staring at them, and looking fiercer than anyone had ever seen him. 'I am very glad indeed that they are to be soundly beaten.'

He looked at Pumlumon: 'If I go up to the Skyward Tower and give the signal to Tealtaoich, will you begin the spell to wake the giants?'

Pumlumon said he would, to be sure he would, and wasn't that why they were here and there'd best be no delay.

'Perhaps I'd better just run through it first to be sure I've remembered it, however,' he said, worried, and Caspar, who had foreseen this and asked Snizort to copy out the spell, said, 'Oh, *really*,' and rummaged in a pocket for the ritual and put it into Pumlumon's hands so there should be no further delay.

'And remember not to start the ritual until I've reached the Tower,' he said.

'How long—'

'Count to one hundred,' said Caspar and, as Pumlumon

looked even more worried, said hastily, 'Well, read the spell through *silently*, and *then* pronounce it,' and sped away, thinking that really, when it came down to it, he was doing a great deal towards winning this war.

To the waiting Beastline and the Trees, Caspar's signal came like a beacon of light, raying through the darkness.

'The Skyward Tower,' said Tealtaoich, softly. 'Then they are inside and the giants are still under the enchantment.' He turned to look at the others, and a mischievous, reckless grin lifted his lips suddenly, so that he was more catlike than Snizort ever remembered seeing him.

'Ready?' said Tealtaoich. 'Then onwards!'

They had agreed that there should be no call to arms, no blasts of trumpets, or shrieks of war.

'A swift, silent charge, it'll be,' said Oisin to Snizort, when he introduced the deer that Snizort would be riding. 'Not the way it ought to be done, of course.'

'Of course not,' Snizort had said, entranced.

'But practical.'

Pounding down the hillside towards the great, radiant Palace, the silence was unnerving. There was only the sound of the beasts' hoofs on the ground and the rushing of the wind in their ears, or the rustling susurration of the Tree Spirits as they streamed across the terrain. Overhead, the White Swans and the Eagles dived forward in a maelstrom of gold and white, beautiful and powerful.

And then they were nearing the great Western Gate, going along the straight wide avenue and Tara was ahead of them, beautiful, shining Tara that was in the greedy, greasy hands of the giants.

Inchbad did not know when he had been so flummoxed. He said so, very firmly indeed.

'I don't know when I've been so flummoxed,' he said.

The Gruagach were all flummoxed. It was difficult to know what to do. Goll the Gorm said, darkly, that they had all been the subject of a bit of a spell, mark his words, and everyone had agreed, because didn't they all know how sneaky and sly spells could be.

There they'd all been, sitting round the fire after supper, as friendly as could be, looking forward to a bit of a game with the *Fidchell* board. Goll the Gorm had actually looked out the board from last time, and seen that it needed a bit of a clean what with it still having all manner of unmentionable stains on it from the last lot of Humans, and it a lady they were to be roasting this time. Goll had not known what things were coming to.

They'd been sitting round the fire and the Girl-Human had been telling them a bit about her own world; they'd listened to it carefully, because you never knew when a thing like that mightn't come in useful. Fiachra Broadcrown had said to Arca Dubh that it almost seemed a shame to roast such a pretty little creature and was frowned at by Goibniu.

And then – no one quite knew how it had happened – they'd all dozed off, every last one of them, and when they came to wake up, not only had the Girl-Human and Caspar and the entire Gnome clan vanished, but Tara was actually in the hands of the Beastline again!

They'd all scratched their heads and been very puzzled indeed, but, of course, when you were confronted with such a display of force, there was only one course of action you could take.

Goibniu and Inchbad had gone off to the Star of the Poets (Goll the Gorm said they had been taken off, but this was untrue) to discuss something called *terms* with the six Beastline Lords and the rather odd person who appeared to take notes of everything.

Goll the Gorm said there was a powerful bad time ahead for them all, but in fact, when Goibniu and Inchbad emerged, it had all been quite reasonable.

They were to return to Gruagach, said Goibniu solemnly, adopting his old, truculent stance, legs planted apart, thumbs hooked in his belt. A *very* amicable arrangement, said Goibniu, and did not even look behind him at the four panthers and six bears, and at Clumhach and Tealtaoich and Eogan who stood sentinel.

They were to return to Gruagach and the Beastline would send with them a carefully chosen detachment of the beasts to help them drive out the Frost Giantess, explained Goibniu. They had signed a pact agreeing to this.

'I signed it,' said Inchbad, who felt it was time he made a contribution.

'So you did, Sire, and very nicely too,' said Goibniu, and Inchbad, who had not altogether followed the negotiations, and who had suspected Tealtaoich of making fun of him for most of the time, subsided. Goibniu would see to everything, of course. It might even be rather pleasant to be back at Gruagach. Providing, of course, that the *Geimhreadh* could be got rid of.

Goibniu was explaining, very smoothly, about how they had never really intended to stay at Tara for very long, and the giants were nodding and reminding one another of the Spring feastings just around the corner, and making a few plans for how they might celebrate it. Spring had always been very good at Gruagach.

Inchbad let Goibniu get on with it. They would none of them miss Tara, nasty draughty place. It would be grand to get back to a proper castle with decent-sized dungeons and the torture chambers and the *Fidchell* room with the heated squares properly built into the floor. Yes, it would be nice to be home.

He turned his attention to the really very interesting project of whether they might approach the nearly defunct Ogres of the Northern Isles, to see would Himself of the Ogres be interested in giving his daughter in marriage to the Gruagach.

On the whole, giants were better not tangling with Humans.

Except, of course, for the *Fidchell*.

Chapter Forty-nine

The immense gold-tipped Gates of the Palace of Wildfire soared high above them and the glow of the deep inner fires were turning the night sky to crimson and orange and amber for miles around, so that the strange, sleek lines of the Palace were sharply limned against the countryside. The will o' the wisp creatures came darting and circling about their heads delightedly, occasionally dancing in unexpected formation, so that elaborate and glittering patterns were formed briefly against the star-spattered, red-lit night sky.

Fael-Inis stood in front of Nuadu and Fenella, Flame and Floy, the Palace behind him framed in the fire-washed gates. The four salamanders who had ridden with them into the Dark Realm were at his side, sleek and glossy and somehow part of the pouring light, so that when he placed a hand on their silky necks, for a moment it seemed that his hand blurred into the fluid light.

Flame thought: I have truly never seen anyone like him. I truly believe there is nobody like him. What had Mother said? That he was arrogant and selfish and proud and imperious. But she had not said that he was wise and beautiful and that he had the reckless light in his eyes and the mischievous tilt to his mouth that would make you want to defy the world and tumble it about and turn it upside-down and challenge everything in it . . .

He is exactly what I thought he would be, and he is precisely what I hoped he would be, thought Flame, staring at him, and knowing that here was another who believed the world was there to be challenged . . . Was it too much to have found that with Floy – because Floy had certainly been brushed with this rebellious spirit – and then to find it here also?

Fael-Inis had beckoned to Nuadu, although it did not seem to Flame as if he had made any particular gesture. He had simply looked at Nuadu, and Nuadu, who had been standing with the Wolves at his heels, at once walked forward. He was still covered with the blood of the creatures he had slain in the battle against the Robemaker and the *Geimhreadh*; his clothes were blackened from that last desperate ride through CuRoi's fearsome enemies, and his dark hair was untidy and falling across his face. But Flame felt the silence from the other two and felt, as well, the sudden awareness of the Wolves and the obedience that radiated from them, and knew that there was something different about Nuadu now. He was no longer entirely the same creature who had ridden recklessly through the Gateway and led them to CuRoi's Castle of Illusions. He was Ireland's High King . . .

As Nuadu moved forward to stand before Fael-Inis, the firelight fell across his face and the wolfmask stood out clearly. As he moved, the Wolves followed him with their eyes.

Fael-Inis studied Nuadu. 'Sire,' he said, at last. 'Your Majesty.' And held out his left hand and touched Nuadu on the right breast, and Flame drew in a breath, because this was the ancient symbol of homage to Ireland's King, rarely seen, never commanded, but almost always present at a Coronation ceremony.

Nuadu regarded Fael-Inis, his head tilted, and then said, in his lightest, most casual voice, 'A reasonable battle, don't you think? The enemy slain and the Ebony Throne regained for Tara.'

Fael-Inis said, with unexpected gravity, 'Ireland will be proud of you, Nuadu Airgetlam,' and Nuadu stared at him and forgot about being light and mocking and felt the beginnings of something approaching humility because, after all, perhaps he could take his place in the line of Wolfkings.

Fael-Inis seemed to understand his thoughts; he said, 'You are not as unworthy as you think, Wolfprince,' and then grinned. And some of the gravity fell from him and the mischievous light shone.

'Did I not tell you,' said the rebel angel, 'that the means were to hand? And did I not say I could not help you unless you first helped yourself?' He tilted his head consideringly. 'Only when the odds against you are greater than you can match, am I constrained to help,' he said, and glanced down to the Wolves at Nuadu's heels. 'You called to them at last,' he said. 'And it is certain that they helped you to slay the necromancer, CuRoi and his dark servants. They will stay with you,' he said. 'They will obey you, as they have obeyed every High King of Ireland, for they are the Royal Wolves of Tara, and unless you had called to them and they had answered you could not rule. It is as much a part of your kingship as the acceptance by the Ebony Throne of Erin.'

'Yes,' said Nuadu. 'Yes, I see.'

Fael-Inis nodded, as if he had expected no more, and turned to Fenella and Floy, holding out his hands. They moved to stand before him.

'Mortals,' said Fael-Inis, and now the amused affection was strongly there. 'Always it is Mortals, Humans, who help to save Ireland from the Dark Realm.' He studied them, his head on one side. 'You will assuredly have your place in Ireland's long line of Mortals who have come here and found their destinies bound up with the Wolfkings,' he said. 'You will certainly miss your own world; that is natural and right. But it is sometimes necessary for worlds to die and for Humans to begin their history on a new page. The Dark Lodestar, the Angry Sun, has touched many worlds, and it will continue to do so. But always something survives. And you have been brave and resourceful; you have helped us to destroy some of the evil of the Dark Realm and for that Ireland will certainly salute you.'

Fael-Inis turned to Fenella and his eyes widened suddenly in a very *knowing* smile. 'Fenella,' he said, gently. 'Did you know, my dear, that in the history of Tara, it was always the Humans who were the King-Makers, and that it has frequently been a Human who

651

has helped restore an exiled King?' His eyes flickered to where Nuadu was standing with the Wolves. 'You will not find him easy to handle, my dear,' he said. 'You will wonder, at times, what kind of creature you have by the tail.

'But for all that, I think you must accept what he offers you, Fenella.' He paused, and then said, so softly that Flame barely heard the words, 'He will offer you Ireland, my child,' said Fael-Inis. 'He will offer you Tara. And if you accept, then Ireland will thank you.'

'Yes,' said Fenella. 'Yes, I see,' and Fael-Inis smiled again, as if he understood very well what Fenella was thinking and feeling.

To Floy, he said, 'So you will have my daughter, will you, Mortal?'

'Yes,' said Floy, returning the golden regard very straightly.

'You should remember that she is the daughter of mixed blood,' said Fael-Inis. 'And that blood is a very strange mixture indeed. It was not a mixture that was ever intended to happen.' A gleam of mischief showed. 'And it would not have happened,' said the rebel angel, 'if I had not, for one night, been – let us say a little more Mortal than usual.' The grin slid out, wickedly impudent.

'A good way of putting it,' said Floy, gravely.

'Well, she was very lovely, Reflection, although we never could agree about anything.' Again the grin. 'But Flame is therefore Amaranthine on her mother's side; fire-creature on her sire's. At times the two sides may war and it may not always be easy for either of you.'

'But,' said Floy, with a sudden grin, 'who said that life was intended to be easy?'

Fael-Inis looked at him very intently and then smiled. And Flame had the sudden feeling that her father had rather liked Floy for saying this.

Fael-Inis moved back and Flame thought: of course it was absurd to think he would even notice me, and it was ridiculous to imagine he would want to speak to me. I did nothing at all in the battle, thought Flame. I didn't help or think of a plan. I might have muttered the Banishing Ritual of Mab inside CuRoi's Castle, but it wasn't so very much. They would have managed without it anyway. All I did was run away with Floy and make the entire situation a hundred times worse. And anyway, probably he only came into the battle because of the pageantry and the brilliance, thought Flame. Mother had been right all along. It was important to remind herself that it did not matter in the least little bit, that she did not expect Fael-Inis to notice her. It was very important indeed to remind herself that she was not going to cry because there was nothing in the world to cry about.

Fael-Inis turned and looked straight at her, and something infinitely soft and gentle touched his face, and a smile of sudden, achingly sweet intimacy shone in his eyes. Light streamed outwards from him and surrounded Flame. He held out his arms wordlessly and Flame gave a sob and ran straight into them.

'So, child, you are free at last.'

'Yes,' replied Flame.

'And,' said the rebel angel, thoughtfully, 'is the Palace of Wildfire to your liking, after your mother's remarkable Court?'

'It is the most beautiful place I ever thought to see.'

'The Fire Court is dazzling, of course,' said Fael-Inis, and looked at her and appeared to wait.

'I think, now, that it was over-bright,' said Flame. 'I think it was tasteless,' she said firmly, and waited to see how this was received, because she was still strongly aware of being a little adrift in a very new, very unexpected world. It might not be very polite to be too disloyal about the place she had lived in all her life.

But Fael-Inis nodded, as if this was entirely acceptable. 'And now,' he said, 'you will brave the heat of the Eternal River with the Mortal, Floy?'

'Yes,' said Flame again.

Fael-Inis nodded, as if satisfied. 'He has a good deal of the buccaneer, that one,' he said. 'I should not have permitted you to go to one who was not, in part, a rebel, my dear. Would you have fought me if I had tried to dissuade you from marriage?'

Flame considered this and then said, 'Yes, I would have fought you. But I think it would not have been necessary, because I should not have wanted to be joined to one who was content with the world, and who never questioned its ways, or wanted to make it better.' She did not say: because I had grown up with the legend of the most dazzling rebel and the most remarkable buccaneer ever, and every man would be measured against that legend, but she thought that he heard her thoughts easily.

'Complacency leads to death, Flame, death of the mind and of the senses. And too much contentment has more than once killed civilisations and destroyed worlds.' He lifted the wine chalice to his lips again, so that the shadow from the deep golden wine cast a light over his face and Flame, listening, utterly entranced, thought: I do not quite know if he is an angel or a devil, and I do not quite know whether I believe him, or even whether I trust him.

At once, Fael-Inis said, 'You may believe me, and you may trust me, child, although whether I am quite angel or devil was never proven, you know.

'But do not look to find me with you always, for I shall not always be here.'

He walks by himself, Mother had said, contemptuously . . .

And then, without warning, his mood changed and the mischievous light poured out and he leaned forward and reached for her hand and said, 'But there will be times, Flame, when we shall harness the salamanders and ride the Fire Chariots of Time together . . . I shall show you the worlds, Flame, and I shall teach you to challenge the gods.'

Flame said, very softly, 'And between us we shall tumble the world about if the mood takes us and re-write history if we have to.' And looked at him, and sent him the grin that was so nearly his own.

And there is Floy, she thought, her heart warm with

sudden delight at the memory of Floy. I shall have Floy when my Father is gone.

The Honeycomb Tunnels were lit to warm, soft light as Floy and Flame, Fenella and Nuadu followed the slender radiant figure. Fael-Inis moved ahead of them, light and graceful, and although the tunnels were lit by the flambeaux, Fenella and Floy both thought that, as Fael-Inis walked, he sprinkled a soft radiance everywhere.

They could see, quite clearly, the ancient, rather beautiful wall carvings, and the pictures etched into the sides of the tunnels, and there was a swift, strange surge of memory, because this was where it had begun, this was where they had started, falling into the rebel angel's world which was neither quite outside Time, nor quite inside it.

As they emerged from the Tunnels, into the wide cavern with the golden waterlight, Flame thought it should have been stifling down here; it should have been smothering and suffocating to be here, below the earth, surrounded by leaping fire, close to the ancient immortal River of Time. But it was none of these things. It was beautiful and friendly and immensely comforting.

Fael-Inis had moved to stand before the arched, fire-washed doors and his eyes went to Flame. 'Do you hear it yet, child?' he said. 'Listen hard, and you should hear it beyond the singing of the fire.'

Flame stood very still, her eyes half closed, and at last she turned to him, her eyes shining.

'Yes! Yes, I hear it.' And then, frowning, struggling for expression, 'A kind of rushing, pouring sound. Cascading fire and what sounds like great torrents of water, only I do not think it is water at all. Beautiful. And also,' said Flame, seriously, 'also rather terrifying.'

Fael-Inis smiled as if this was the answer he had wanted. 'I am glad you can hear it,' he said softly. 'And I am glad that you recognise it for what it is. Beautiful and powerful, but to be a little feared. As one who possesses the fire-blood – even a little – it was unthinkable that you should not hear it and understand it.'

Flame returned the regard steadily. 'Was that a test?' she asked at last. 'Did you think that Mother had cheated you?'

'There was always the possibility. Reflection is not known for her fidelity,' said Fael-Inis lightly. 'Although I did not think it so very likely.

'Shall we go on? There is only a very little way to go.

'The River of Time flows nine times nine around the Palace of Wildfire,' said Fael-Inis, as they moved on. 'It is – you would perhaps say it is the converse of the River of Souls through which you journeyed on your arrival, when you encountered the soul-less creatures who are chained there. That River is the dark underside of this one, rather as the Dark Ireland is the underside of the true Ireland. The River of Time is endless and immortal, or so the legend tells.' He glanced back at them and, in the flickering torchlight, the mischievous three-cornered grin lit his face. 'But,' said the rebel angel, 'I hardly ever believe legends, and so I can not be sure about any of it.'

'Marvellous and terrifying,' said Flame. And then, 'I suppose it *is* safe, is it?' she said, suddenly. 'The River?'

'No,' said Fael-Inis, 'it is not entirely safe.' He glanced at Floy. 'Life is not intended to be entirely safe,' he said softly.

They moved on and, as they did so, Fenella and Nuadu and Floy heard the sounds of the River.

As they came out from the last tunnel, the fiery light from the Stables still casting red shadows and amber warmth everywhere, they fell silent.

They were in a massive domed cavern, with strange rock formations which bore curious carvings. There were none of the bronze wall sconces down here, for there was no need of light. The entire cavern was bathed in a strong, prismatic glow and there was a sudden solid heat, as if the door to an immense furnace had been opened, and they were standing directly in front of it.

Above them was the rock ceiling and all about them were the ancient cavern walls with their strange images of beasts and half-Humans and symbols that might have been magical and might have been powerful, or that might have been simply the recording of events of the Deep Past. Beneath their feet the floor was hard and, here and there, it was cracked as if the heat had slowly baked it over the centuries, causing it to contract and split.

Directly in front of them was the cascading fire of the legendary River of Time.

Fael-Inis moved forward and stood alone, a slender figure silhouetted against the rushing torrents of flame.

He does not fear it in the least, thought Flame. And then, Or does he?

If Fael-Inis feared it, he gave no sign. He stood, looking deep into the River for a while, as if he might be seeing things in it that the others could not see and, just for a moment, Flame thought she could see them as well . . .

Leaping unicorn shapes, rearing, prancing, winged beings who lived in the fires and who guarded Time and sometimes rescued lost travellers who had strayed or were pushed or fell into the echoing emptinesses that existed between the past and the present and the future . . . Slant-eyed faces and knowing three-cornered smiles, and beings who were so wholly magical and so completely lacking in Human blood that they would never be seen abroad in the world of Men . . .

And then Fael-Inis turned and held out his arms and smiled. And a deep and contented sigh went through the watchers, for now, at last, it was the warm smile of the companion and the guide and the creature who loved mankind and understood about its weaknesses and its frailties and who loved mankind not in spite of these failings, but because of them.

Fael-Inis, the rebel angel, the creature of fire and light and speed . . . Flame, unable to take her eyes from him, felt something harsh and painful close about her heart, because this was how she had always pictured him, exactly like this . . . The rebel angel, the wild, reckless being of fire and light, bathed in the leaping flames of the immortal River of Time, holding out his hands to the world . . .

And then Fael-Inis moved and the light changed and

he was no longer other worldly. He was very nearly mortal
– and he was holding out his hands.

Together, Flame and Floy moved forward.

Chapter Fifty

The ceremonial entry into Tara of Nuadu Airgetlam, Nuadu of the Silver Arm, the rebel Wolfprince who had been flung from the Royal House by the King, and lived in the Wolfwood, was a glittering and joyful event.

And although Nuadu had asked that there should be as little ceremony as possible, ceremony was there, nevertheless. It was in the crowds who flocked to Tara, and it was in the delight of the people who came from their villages and their farms and their towns, to cheer the procession and drink wine and dance in the streets. It was in the solemn procession of the Royal Wolves, who walked before the High King as he made the triumphal entry to Tara, the Bright Palace of his ancestors, the luminescent fortress of his predecessors.

He rode with the Lady who would take her place as his Queen, and everyone cheered, because wasn't it traditional, wasn't it historical, wasn't it *right* that the Wolfking should have a Human as consort? They cheered very loudly indeed for Fenella, who had already ridden down into the villages and the townships and had talked with them and wanted to know about them and hear how they worked and what they did, and about their families and their ways. A lovely, generous lady, they said, cheering for her all over again as she rode at Nuadu's side. A Lady for the people.

Behind Nuadu and Fenella came the ceremonial black-covered bier of the dead Aed, Nuadu's half-brother, and at this, the people instantly sank to their knees in silent homage to the young man who had suffered at the hands of CuRoi and his creatures, and who had died of his torments at last knowing himself to be free. The bier had been given the premier place in the procession which was only right, but the people told one another that wasn't it altogether grand to see that their new King was adhering to the proper formalities and the old traditions.

Behind the solitary horse with its sad carriage, was the beautiful fey creature who was Fael-Inis's daughter. Half sorceress, half fire-creature, said the watchers suddenly hushed, certainly delighted. A soft radiance was all about her, but she was smiling and at her side was the thin-faced dark-haired young man Floy, who had slain the Frost Giantess and the Robemaker and ridden at the King's side in the marvellous storming of the Castle of Illusions. It had been rumoured that the King was to confer some very high honour on Floy – the Noble WolfOrder of Cormac had been mentioned – which was no more than he deserved – and it had been announced, that very morning, that he was also to be given the command of the King's Fiana, the ancient honourable soldiery who had the guarding of the Royal Castles.

The Beastline creatures came next, each one wearing the insignia of his or her House, as was correct for such an historic occasion. With them, were the Tree Spirits, one representative for each Tree: Oak and Elm and Ash and Copper Beech and Holly and Poplar and Silver Birch. One for each, beautiful and wild and filled with the ancient woodland magic. You had to be wary of Trees, of course, but it was altogether grand that they were awake and very right and proper that they should be here.

Behind the Trees walked the two brothers, Snizort and Snodgrass, whom most people thought a bit odd but whom everyone had found to be surprisingly interesting to talk to. It was thought they had been appointed as the King's official *ollam*, and that chronicles were already being prepared about the newest chapter in Ireland's history. Caspar was with them and Miach, and everyone reminded each other of the important part in the battle these two had played. Wasn't it altogether grand to see an ordinary person such as Caspar helping to defeat the giants in the most casual way imaginable?

The Gnomes brought up the rear and as the ceremonial

line neared Tara's Western Gate the watching people suddenly stopped cheering and throwing flowers. Nuadu felt the silence and the anticipation fall upon the entire procession, because this was it, this was the moment they had all been waiting for. The Wolfking entering Tara...

As they passed under the pale, shining archway and into the embrace of the immense Palace, Nuadu looked up at the soaring turrets and the glistening spires, at the pale beautiful stonework, soaked with the magical prismatic colour that had been woven into Tara at the very beginning, and that could only be quenched by the forces of the Dark Realm.

Journey's end...

For a moment, he felt the weight of Tara fall about him and there was a terrible instant when he wanted to push it away and say: I am not worthy! Let me go, and let me not have to take up this burden, this weight, this responsibility! Let me go back to the forest shadows and to the ancient twilight magic of the Wolfwood.

But the call of his blood was too strong; he had summoned the Wolves and seen them answer; he had hurled the power and the light and the strength of the Royal Wolves at the malevolent dark forces, and he had taken his place on the enchanted Ebony Throne of Erin.

And the Throne had accepted him...

So this is it, thought Nuadu, moving ahead on his own, feeling the others fall back and stand silently watching. This is it, the moment when I take up the mantle, when I shoulder the weight of Tara's future and honour the vow to Aed. When I enter the place of my mother's noble house. The moment when all Ireland is mine.

All Ireland is mine...

It broke within him then, a soaring fountain of the purest delight he had ever known, almost overwhelming in its force, certainly painful in its intensity.

I am Ireland's rightful King and Ireland is mine by blood and by battle and by inheritance... I am a Prince of a Royal House and I have fought for Ireland, and Ireland is mine. I am coming home...

The darkness rolled back and finally and at last he saw Tara for what it was; not a place of stifling weight and heavy dragging responsibilities and fearsome bondage, but . . .

A place of light and space and radiance and joy. And Fenella would be with him . . .

The wolfsmile lifted his lips as he moved forward to where the Ebony Throne waited.

WOLFKING

A SPELLBINDING FANTASY OF THE NEAR FUTURE AND THE ANCIENT PAST

BRIDGET WOOD

WOLFKING

Remnants of the lives of the Letheans linger on in Tugaim, as do reminders of the Great Devastation: the Glowing Lands that border Flynn O'Connor's home - forbidden territory to all but the Keepers of the Secret; the House of Mutants - home of the unfortunate victims of the Apocalypse; stories of machines that flew or helped a man plough a field in less than a day...

WOLFKING

Flynn and his girl, Joanna, are united by their love for a time long before that of the Letheans - an Ancient Ireland of heroes and kings, adventure and glory. Only when Joanna is threatened with Conjoining to a repellent pig-farmer is the truth of the legends proven: the Glowing Lands conceal a Gateway to the Ireland of the High King of Tara, Cormac mac Airt, Cormac Starrog, The Wolfking...

WOLFKING

Bridget Wood's first fantasy is a compelling story of past and future, myth and magic, that is sure to live on in the reader's imagination long after the last page is turned.

FICTION/FANTASY   0 7472 3514 7

ROGER TAYLOR

DREAM FINDER

The epic new fantasy from the author of
The Chronicles of Hawklan

The City of Serenstad has never been stronger. Its ruler
Duke Ibris is a ruthless man when his office requires it, but
he is also a man of fine discernment; artists, craftsmen and
philosophers have flourished under his care, and
superstitions are waning in the light of reason and
civilization.

For the Guild of Dream Finders this has proved disastrous.
Since their leader Petran died, their craft has fallen into
disrepute, and Petran's son Antyr is unable to fill the
vacuum left by his father. Antyr finds himself growing
bitter, without the stomach to pander to the whims of the
wealthy, or the courage to offer them his skills honestly and
without fear. His nightly appointments at the alehouse have
lost him customers; and his quarrels with his strange
Companion and Earth Holder, Tarrian, have grown
increasingly unpleasant of late.

Then mysteriously one night, Antyr and Tarrian are taken to
Duke Ibris, who has been troubled by unsettling dreams. It
is the beginning of a journey that leads inexorably to a
terrible confrontation with a malevolent blind man,
possessed of a fearful otherworldly sight, and Ivaroth, a
warrior chief determined to conquer the Duke's land and
all beyond at any cost...

FICTION/FANTASY   0 7472 3726 3

A selection of bestsellers from Headline

THE PARASITE	Ramsey Campbell	£4.99 ☐
GAMEWORLD	J V Gallagher	£4.99 ☐
SCHEHERAZADE'S NIGHT OUT	Craig Shaw Gardner	£4.99 ☐
THE GIANT OF INISHKERRY	Sheila Gilluly	£4.99 ☐
THE HOODOO MAN	Steve Harris	£5.99 ☐
LIES AND FLAMES	Jenny Jones	£5.99 ☐
THE DOOR TO DECEMBER	Dean Koontz	£5.99 ☐
HIDEAWAY	Dean Koontz	£5.99 ☐
MIDNIGHT'S LAIR	Richard Laymon	£4.99 ☐
HEART-BEAST	Tanith Lee	£4.99 ☐
CHILDREN OF THE NIGHT	Dan Simmons	£4.99 ☐
FARNOR	Roger Taylor	£5.99 ☐

All Headline books are available at your local bookshop or newsagent, or can be ordered direct from the publisher. Just tick the titles you want and fill in the form below. Prices and availability subject to change without notice.

Headline Book Publishing PLC, Cash Sales Department, Bookpoint, 39 Milton Park, Abingdon, OXON, OX14 4TD, UK. If you have a credit card you may order by telephone — 0235 831700.

Please enclose a cheque or postal order made payable to Bookpoint Ltd to the value of the cover price and allow the following for postage and packing:
UK & BFPO: £1.00 for the first book, 50p for the second book and 30p for each additional book ordered up to a maximum charge of £3.00.
OVERSEAS & EIRE: £2.00 for the first book, £1.00 for the second book and 50p for each additional book.

Name ....

Address ....

....

....

If you would prefer to pay by credit card, please complete:
Please debit my Visa/Access/Diner's Card/American Express (delete as applicable) card no:

Signature ....Expiry Date ....